D0199708

WILDEST
DREAMS

ROSANNE
BITTNER

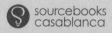

sourcebooks
casablanca

Copyright © 1994 by Rosanne Bittner
Cover and internal design © 2016 by Sourcebooks, Inc.
Cover art by Gregg Gulbronson

Published by Sourcebooks Casablanca, an imprint of Sourcebooks,
Inc.
P.O. Box 4410, Naperville, Illinois 60567-4410
(630) 961-3900
Fax: (630) 961-2168
www.sourcebooks.com

Originally published in 1994 by Bantam Books, a division of
Random House, New York.

Printed and bound in Canada
MBP 10 9 8 7 6 5 4 3 2 1

A special thank-you to my editor, Wendy McCurdy, for her patient attention to detail that has helped me grow and has taught me how to polish my writing. Behind every author there is that unseen person who contributes many long hours of careful reading, editing, checking details, and refining a manuscript in an effort to make it the best it can be. Every published novel is a combination of the joy of storytelling and the hard work of editing. Thank you, Wendy.

The wind…over the mountains, plains, and valleys
It blows…
Constant, persistent, haunting the heart
With its moans and whispers,
Telling of those who walked here,
Under Montana skies…
The Indian, the trapper, the miner, the farmer,
The ranchers…
They came with a dream,
And against the wind and the elements,
Against the lawless,
They fought for that dream.
Some died for it.
Some succeeded, but at a great price.
It took people of strength and courage
To settle the wild land,
To push against the wind,
To reach the dream…their wildest dreams.

PART ONE

One

LUKE TIGHTENED THE RAWHIDE STRAPS AROUND THE belly of one of the mules that carried his supplies. "Suck in that gut, you stubborn ass," he muttered. "I'm not going to hold up this wagon train because you spill my supplies all over the place."

The animal brayed loudly, and people turned to stare. "Shut up, damn it," he ordered the mule, yanking harder. It embarrassed him to have everyone witness his struggle with the obstinate animal.

He figured there were plenty of others amid this crowd headed west who were even less prepared for what lay ahead of them than he was. Including the children, there were about a hundred people camped here outside of Independence. He had counted eighteen wagons. He himself had decided against bothering with a wagon and oxen. His horse and four pack mules were enough. Some of his fellow travelers were herding cattle and extra horses as well, some had chickens with them, a few had pigs. Most of them were headed for California or Oregon, many fleeing the hideous War between the States and the ugly raiding that had been taking place between Kansas and Missouri. He had his own reasons for heading west, but they had nothing to do with the war.

He finished buckling the strap. He hated mules, much preferred horses. But he had taken the advice of experienced scouts back in St. Louis that mules were much better suited to carrying heavy loads for long distances, and it was a long way to Montana. As far as he was concerned, California and Oregon were already too heavily settled. He was going to a place where a man could still claim big pieces of land, where there was still hardly any law. That way a man could do whatever was necessary to keep his land without answering to anyone but himself. This wagon train would get him as far as Wyoming. From then on, he would be on his own. The prospect was exhilarating. He was determined to show his father and his brother that he didn't need the inheritance money that had been denied him. To hell with them both! His father could believe what he wanted. He knew in his heart he was not a bastard. He had every right to the Fontaine money, and he swore that someday he would be a hundred times richer than his father, and he would do it all on his own.

The crack of a gunshot startled him out of his thoughts. Horses whinnied, and a woman began railing at her husband for being careless with a handgun. When Luke looked up, a couple of horses had bolted at the noise of the gunshot and were running toward him.

Then everything seemed to happen at once. "Nathan!" a young woman shouted frantically. Luke turned to see a towheaded little boy running toward him from another direction, a stuffed animal in his arms, a big grin on his chubby face. The boy obviously thought his mother was playing a game by chasing him, but his path was taking him on a collision course with the runaway horses.

Luke ran to the boy, lifting him with one strong arm a split second before the horses would have trampled him. He ducked aside, landing on the ground and covering the child. He felt a blow on his right calf from a horse's hoof and grimaced with pain, wondering why it had to be that particular spot. He still suffered enough pain there from his war wound. He didn't need a horse's kick to awaken the agony. He heard the shouts of "whoa," felt people gather near him. Someone grabbed the little boy right out of his arms.

"Nathan! Nathan!"

A couple of men helped Luke to his feet, asked if he was all right. They held his arms as Luke limped over to a log to sit down. "I'll be fine," he insisted, rubbing at his leg. "Just got a little kick." He decided not to mention the war wound. In crowds like this there was usually a good mixture of Northerners and Southerners. Mentioning he'd fought for the Union army just might start a needless argument, and for the next four months or so, they all had to forget their differences and band together for the journey west.

"Sorry, mister," a man spoke up. "I accidentally spooked my horses."

"Don't worry about it," Luke answered. "I'm okay. All of you can get back to whatever you were doing."

The man who had misfired his gun apologized again, this time to a woman standing near Luke. "Thank God your boy wasn't hurt," he told her.

"It was partly my fault," the woman answered. "Nathan has just found his legs, and he is always running. He thinks it's a game. I think I shall have to put a rope on him and tie it to my own waist."

"Might be a good idea, ma'am." The man left to collect his horses, and Luke looked up at the woman who held the towheaded youngster he had just rescued. The boy still clung to his stuffed animal, which Luke could see was a homemade brown horse. Part of a feather from the stuffing stuck out of one of the seams. The child was still grinning, oblivious to the danger he'd been in. His mother chided him for running away from her.

"I don't know how to thank you, sir," she told Luke then. "Nathan could have been killed if not for your quick thinking. I do hope you're not badly hurt."

For the first time Luke truly noticed her and was

surprised at how pretty she was. That thought had barely registered before it was eclipsed by the pain in his leg and his irritation at how the whole morning had gone for him.

"I don't think so," he answered, "but you ought to keep a better eye on the boy there. On a trip like we'll be taking, you'll have to hold a tighter rein on him, or you'll be running into this kind of problem every day." Luke watched her stiffen at the words, and the concern in her pretty eyes gave way to consternation.

"It isn't easy to watch an active two-year-old every second, Mr.—"

"Fontaine. Luke Fontaine."

"Hossy." The little boy held out his stuffed horse to Luke.

"That's his word for horse," the woman told Luke. "As you can see, there isn't a bashful or fearful bone in Nathan's body."

Luke could see the deep hurt and anger in her eyes, figured she was holding her temper in check for the boy's sake. He ignored the child's gesture, at the moment more interested in how a woman with such deep red hair and luscious green eyes could have given birth to a blond-headed, blue-eyed child like the one she was holding, but then that wasn't his business. Her husband must be the one with the blond hair. Luke wondered where he was. "You might try tying a rope around the kid like you mentioned earlier." He rubbed at his leg a moment longer, then stood up.

"Well, thank you for the sage advice," she told him coolly.

Luke studied her full lips, the porcelain look to her skin, her slender waist. He could not help noticing how nicely she filled out the bodice of her flowered cotton dress, a dress, he took note, that was suited to the journey ahead, but still had a more elegant look than what the other women were wearing. Her hair was nicely done up, in such a pile of curls that he was sure it must hang to her waist when she let it down. "I'm sorry," he told her. "I haven't had the best morning."

The woman sighed. "No, neither have I." She struggled to hang on to her son, who was wiggling to get down again.

"Here, let me hold him for a minute," Luke said. "I'll walk you back to your own camp."

"That won't be necessary," she started to protest, but the husky boy was obviously more than she could handle when he had the desire to climb out of her arms. "Oh dear," she said, reluctantly handing him over.

Luke gathered the child into his arms, surprised at how easily he came to him when he had never met him before. "Well, Nathan, you've got to quit giving your mother such troubles."

"Hossy," Nathan said again, touching the horse's nose to Luke's. The gesture broke the strain between Luke and the boy's mother, and they both smiled.

"I am Lettie MacBride Dougan," she told Luke then.

Luke nodded, secretly touched when little Nathan put his head down on his shoulder. Over the last year he had given a lot of thought to what it might be like to have a son of his own. He'd certainly give him more love than he had ever known from his own father. "Glad to meet you, Mrs. Dougan."

She looked past him then at his mules. "You…you're traveling alone?"

"Yes, ma'am."

"Well, then, I insist, Mr. Fontaine, that you let me and my family thank you for saving Nathan by joining our campfire tonight for supper. This first day's journey is bound to be difficult. The least we can do is save you the trouble of having to fix your own supper tonight. That is our lead wagon over there," she said, pointing to a wagon with a pole, tied with a red cloth, sticking up above it. "We marked it that way so that if Nathan runs off, he could spot our lead wagon easily and find us again. Actually, we have three wagons. My father is both a farmer and a merchant. He is taking a load of supplies along to start his own store when we reach Denver."

"Denver? You aren't going all the way to California?"

"No. We and some of the others will stay with the train to the fork of the North and South Platte rivers. Then we'll follow the South Platte to Denver. Father feels there is a great deal of potential there for a business-man, much more than in California and Oregon, which are already so heavily settled."

"Could be," Luke answered. "And how does your husband feel?"

He noticed the woman's face redden as though for a moment she felt some kind of shame.

"Nathan's father is dead," she answered. "Killed in a border raid."

Luke watched her eyes, and what he saw there was not the look of a grieving widow. Something was amiss. "I'm sorry," he told her.

"Yes, well, that's part of the reason we're starting someplace new," she told him. "Father's store was burned, as was our home and farm. We're from up in the St. Joseph area."

Nathan reached out for his mother, and Luke handed him over. "I'm from St. Louis, headed for Montana," he told her.

"Montana! Oh, isn't it terribly wild and lawless there?"

Luke grinned. "A good place for a man to make his claim and set his own rules."

"Yes, I suppose." In spite of her initial irritation with the man for telling her how to handle her own son, Lettie could not help noticing how handsome he was. *Never have I seen such beautiful blue eyes on a man before*, she thought. Immediately she felt the crimson coming to her cheeks, along with another burst of shame. What right did she have to be attracted to any man, and what man would want her, if he knew the truth about her? "I had better get back to our wagons. My parents are in town getting more supplies, and my brother and sister are off wandering. When everyone is back I will explain what you did, and I know they will insist on cooking you a decent supper tonight. Please say you will come."

To be able to look at you again? Luke thought. "I'll be glad to join you."

"Good. Look for us when we make camp tonight, then, Mr. Fontaine."

Luke nodded, then reached out and gave little Nathan's chubby hand a squeeze. "See you tonight, then."

He turned and walked back to his mules, and Lettie noticed he limped badly. She thought again how handsome he was, but such thoughts only brought an ache to her heart, for in her situation, it was useless to allow special feelings for any man. There simply could never be another man in her life. She did not want one, and no decent man would ever want her.

She turned away. As she headed back to her own camp she kissed Nathan's cheek. Some people thought she should hate her son, but he was an innocent child, a child she had grown to love far more than she had thought possible in the beginning. No child should be blamed for a horror over which he had no control, a horror caused by a bloody, useless war. Nathan was never going to know the truth about his father, and leaving Missouri was the only way to make sure of it.

❧

"Fontaine. What kind of a name is that? French?"

Luke lit the thin cigar Henry MacBride had given him. Both men sat near the campfire, and all around them other campfires were lit and families settled in for supper and sleep. Lettie and her mother, Katie, and her fourteen-year-old sister, Louise, cleaned up dishes, pots, and pans. It was obvious to Luke that the family had money because of their dress and mannerism, and they had a Negro woman along with them to help with the work. She was a very large woman, her hair almost completely gray. She seemed to get along well with the family, hummed softly while she worked.

Beside Henry sat Lettie's nineteen-year-old brother, James. "My father is a descendant of some of the first French trappers who traded in furs," Luke answered MacBride. "His father and grandfather roamed the Rockies and places even farther west before most people ever gave a thought to settling out there. They became wealthy traders, then merchants. My father inherited all of it, owns a big mercantile emporium in St. Louis, even some warehouses and several riverboats for carrying supplies."

Henry arched his eyebrows, which were as red as his hair. It was obvious Lettie had inherited features from both parents. It was her father who had the green eyes that on her were so exotically beautiful, but she had her mother's lustrous, darker red hair and milky smooth skin. James was the image of his father in every way, but Louise was the opposite of her sister, with bright red hair and brown eyes. Henry spoke with a heavy accent. "Came over here because of the potato famine," he had already explained. "Didn't have much choice, seeing as how everybody was starving to death in Ireland. I miss my homeland, though. Me and Katie both."

"Well, it sounds like you've walked away from a pretty good thing," Henry was telling him now. The man took a couple of puffs on his own cigar. "Wouldn't you stand to inherit some of that wealth? What takes you to a place as wild and dangerous as Montana?"

Lettie kept her ears open as she dried a dish. She wanted to know the answer herself. She could not seem to shake off her attraction to Luke Fontaine, and for some reason, Nathan took to him as though he had known the man since birth. Even now he played near Luke, kept trying to give him his "hossy," which he normally never let anyone else hold.

There was a loneliness about Luke Fontaine that stirred something in her she had never felt before, certainly not for any man. She told herself she must be careful of those feelings, for they could lead nowhere.

"I decided I wanted to make it on my own," Luke answered her father.

Lettie detected a deep hurt, even anger, in the way he spoke the words.

"There are a few things my father and I don't see eye to eye on," he continued. "I figured I was better off getting out." He puffed his own cigar and glanced at her. Lettie quickly turned away, embarrassed he had caught her staring. "Besides, I guess I'm just not the kind to walk in someone else's footsteps and do the expected. That's for my older brother. He'll take everything over someday. Me, I enjoy the adventure."

Henry chuckled. "Sounds like a typical young man. You shouldn't turn your back on what's rightfully yours, though, Luke. There will come a time when you'll wish you had that inheritance. I'd think it could be a big help to you if you're going to be building something for yourself in Montana. Me, I wish I had had something to fall back on when we lost everything back in Ireland. Of course, that was before Lettie was born. We've been in this country a long time now. Trouble is, disaster came to greet us again."

Luke watched smoke curl up from the end of his cigar. "Your daughter said something about a raid earlier today. I gather you are victims of the border wars. Lettie said her husband was killed in a raid." He noticed the man exchange a warning look with his daughter.

Lettie suddenly put down her dishcloth. She came over to pick up little Nathan. "It's time for bed, Son." She glanced at Luke. "Thank you again for what you did today. If there is anything you need, please don't hesitate to tell us."

Luke looked her over, wishing she wasn't so damn pretty. He regretted barking at her earlier that day about not watching her son properly. It had to be difficult raising a son with no father. He warned himself not to care about her. Where he was headed was no place for a woman and a child.

"Fact is," he answered, "the wagon master has already asked me to do some of the hunting for the others, seeing as how I don't have anyone to look after. Maybe when I'm doing that your brother can take care of my mules. I'll see that the family gets some extra meat for it."

"Well, we'd sure appreciate it!" Henry told him.

"Yes. Thank you."

Luke nodded to Lettie, and for a moment their gaze lingered before she turned and quickly left. She climbed into the family's lead wagon. Luke looked after her, wondering about the change he had sensed as soon as he had mentioned the raid.

"We'll be glad to look after your mules when necessary," Henry told him then, interrupting his thoughts. "We'll have to tie them to one of the wagons, seeing as how me and James and my wife have our hands full with our own oxen." The man sighed. "I hate putting my family to this hard life, but it's only until we get where we're going. I gave them a damn good life in Missouri. I've become a wealthy man, Mr. Fontaine. Up in St. Joseph we had a fine big home and farm, as well as a couple of businesses in town. We even owned slaves, and I gave them all their freedom before we left. I figured the time is going to come when they'll all be free anyway. Be that as it may, I made a good life for my family back there, and I don't ever intend for any of them to suffer the way Katie and I suffered back in Ireland. I could see that was beginning to happen again, only for different reasons, so we left."

"I'm sorry about Lettie's husband. Did you lose everything?"

Henry stared at the fire thoughtfully. "They burned us out. That was all before Lettie even had her baby. We stuck it out because she was carrying. We tried to make it work for a couple more years. Finally, after a few more raids we decided to leave. I've got enough money to set us up good wherever we go."

Luke nodded. "That's good." So, Lettie's husband was killed before she even had the child. That meant he'd been dead for a good two and a half years. It also meant she must have been about fifteen when she married, practically a child. It seemed odd that the MacBrides had married off a daughter that young.

"Tell me something, Luke," Henry asked. "How old are you? Twenty-six, maybe?"

"Twenty-eight. Why?"

Henry studied him, then shrugged. "Just wondering how a big, strong young man like yourself managed to stay out of the war."

Luke braced himself. This might be the end of his short friendship with Henry MacBride and family. He rested his elbows on his knees. "I didn't," he answered. "That's why I was hurting pretty bad earlier when that horse kicked me. He got me on my right calf. I was shot and wounded in that same spot. I'd been in the war for about a year when it happened—almost lost the lower part of my leg. After that I got discharged and gladly left. There isn't anything uglier than what's going on in the South right now. Take your border raids and multiply that several hundred times, and you've got an idea what the war is like. It's bloody and senseless, and I have no desire to get involved in it again. I only joined up the first time to get away from my father. I had a lot of things to think about, wasn't sure what to do with my life."

Henry puffed on the cigar. "What side did you fight on?"

Luke gazed intently into the man's eyes for a moment. "Union," he answered. He waited for Henry MacBride to send him packing. MacBride obviously hated the Kansas jay-hawkers who had raided his farm and killed his son-in-law. He had even owned slaves. Surely he was proslavery and pro-South. It was well known that Irish immigrants had settled throughout the South.

Henry held his eyes. "You ever do any raiding on innocent people?"

"No, sir. I was in the regular army. The only people I raised a weapon against were Confederate soldiers in full battle."

Henry nodded. "Nothing wrong with that. I know it's an ugly war, and everybody has an opinion of who's right and who's wrong. It's when citizens appoint themselves as the law and decide to fight the battle their own way that it's wrong." He looked over at Sadie, who was singing as she scrubbed some pans. "I was good to my slaves, but I didn't really feel slavery was quite right. I felt better about all of it after I gave them their freedom. Sadie chose to stay with us. She's been with the family so long she'd be heartbroken if I made her go…and homeless. I pay her now." He looked Luke over. "Out here there is no room for feelings about the war, Luke. Out here we're all the same, and we all need each other. I don't hold it against you that you were a Union man. You're not wearing a uniform now. You're just someone who saved my grandson's life today, and I thank you for that. You're welcome to come back and join our campfire whenever you feel like it."

"Thank you," Luke answered. He rose. "I expect I'd better turn in. Tomorrow is going to be another long day."

"That it is, boy, that it is." Henry reached out and shook his hand. "We're glad to share our campfire with you anytime."

Luke glanced at the wagon where Lettie had so quickly disappeared, wondering why such a beautiful young woman had not found another husband by now. She'd turn any man's head, and her little boy would be easy to love. He bid another good night to Henry MacBride and left. Whatever Lettie's situation was, it wasn't his affair. His only concern was to get himself to Montana.

Inside her wagon, Lettie lay beside her son, stroking his white-blond hair, part of her longing to be a natural woman, another part of her terrified at the thought. Why had meeting Luke Fontaine stirred these surprising desires in her? It was foolish, wrong; more than that, it was hopeless. She studied Nathan by the light of a lantern that hung nearby, kept lit so the boy wouldn't be afraid of the dark. His big brown eyes blinked open, and he smiled softly at her before his eyelids fluttered closed again.

Lettie supposed she should have thanked Luke Fontaine again, but decided it was best not to encourage any man. It saved a lot of hurt later on. Weariness from the long, hard day finally overtook her, and her own eyes drifted closed. But as it so often did, the horror flashed into her mind…the raider's leering face…his white-blond hair…and the ugly eagerness in his brown eyes. She started awake, looked down at Nathan to make sure she had not disturbed him.

She gently pulled away from him, knowing that the only way to clear her head was to stand up for a few minutes. When she moved to the back of the wagon she saw her sister Louise climbing into the second wagon which she shared with her mother. Her father and brother slept in the third wagon. She wondered how Luke would sleep tonight. On the cold, hard ground, no doubt. Did he have a tent or anything for shelter?

After a time she lay back down. There was another twenty miles to cover tomorrow, most of it on foot. She would be carrying Nathan part of the way, trading the boy off with her brother and father. She closed her eyes again, this time turning her thoughts to Luke, how he had rescued Nathan, the way he had looked...how he had watched her tonight.

Two

Luke was glad to be hunting for the wagon train. It gave him plenty of the kind of experience he would need to settle in uncivilized country. He was getting used to being in the saddle most of the day, becoming adept at stalking his prey, getting a good feel for the new repeating rifle he had purchased back in St. Louis. He suspected that where he was going, a man had better be able to hit his target, or expect to die of starvation, or worse.

Thunder rumbled somewhere in the west as he sat on a rise watching the wagon train in the distance. All morning it had been miserably hot, but now a cool breeze met his face, carrying with it the scent of rain. He headed his horse away from the wooded ravine where he had shot a deer, the animal now tied over his horse's rump, along with three rabbits. It was easy to spot the MacBride wagons among the others because of the post showing the red flag. In the seven weeks they had been on the trail, he had eaten with Lettie and her family often, brought them meat, played with Nathan. He was sure he'd seen romantic interest in the way Lettie Dougan looked at him but she had not done or said a thing to betray that interest. Was it because they would soon go their separate ways? Or was she still mourning her husband, after two and a half years?

He halted his horse, took a thin cigar from his shirt pocket. And how did he feel about Lettie? At first he had not even considered the possibility of taking a woman

and child to Montana. But in just another week or so
they would reach the point where the North and South
Platte branched off in different directions. He would
continue on with the wagon train into Wyoming, then
go north into Montana from there. Lettie and her family
would head south into Colorado. He could hardly stand
the thought of leaving Lettie MacBride Dougan behind.
He was even becoming attached to Nathan. Sometimes
when he wasn't hunting, he had kept the boy with
him on his horse to relieve Lettie and the others from
having to carry him. They did not want the child inside
a wagon, for he was too active, and they were afraid he
might fall out.

Nathan was easy to love. The hell of it was…so was
the boy's mother. Yes, he loved her. And he thought
maybe she loved him too. But lately she had been more
distant; she seemed angry about something. And she'd
started refusing to let Nathan ride with him.

He lit the cigar, urged his horse, a strong, roan-
colored gelding, forward at a gentle walk. "What should
we do, Red?" he addressed the horse, patting its neck.
The animal shuddered and tossed its head. "I don't know
either, boy, but I think it's time Mrs. Lettie Dougan and
I had a good talk, whether she wants to or not."

He wondered just how bad the Indian situation was
up in Montana. He'd been warned that was where the
Sioux and Northern Cheyenne, the last of the truly rebel-
lious natives, roamed. Most others were on reservations
now, although there was still trouble with the Southern
Cheyenne. Even here, some Indians still roamed free,
but so far the only ones they had seen were the few who
hung around the forts and towns along the trail, begging
for handouts. He couldn't help feeling a little sorry for
them, imagining how proud they must have been at one
time, what fierce warriors they had been, riding free in
this big country. But things had a way of changing. It

had been like that since the beginning of time, and there was no stopping it.

At least now he understood them a little better. One of the scouts for the wagon train was a Pawnee Indian who spoke English. He'd had nothing good to say about the Cheyenne, but then the two tribes had always been enemies, according to Hank Preston, the wagon master. Still, Luke had asked a lot of questions and learned a lot from Standing Bull about how Indians think, how they fight, how to dicker with them. The Pawnee was even teaching him a little of the Sioux and Cheyenne tongue, and the most common form of communicating with any Indian—a universal sign language. He could only hope that what Indians he might come across in Montana would be *willing* to talk instead of wanting his scalp.

Other whites had settled in Montana and were surviving. He could do it too. He wasn't going to let Indians or the tales he'd heard of Montana's harsh winters stop him. And once he'd built the empire he dreamed of, maybe he would invite his father and brother for a little visit and let them see what he'd done all on his own, *without* Fontaine money.

"Big sky country," that's what Preston called Montana. Before resorting to leading wagon trains west, he had been a rugged scout who had lived out west most of his life, and he had taught Luke a lot about what to expect out here. As far as Luke was concerned, everything west of the Missouri River was big sky country. He'd never seen such wide-open land. Out here a man felt free; he could dream. He could be anything he wanted to be, and nobody gave a damn about his past.

A loud clap of thunder interrupted his thoughts, and he rode closer to the wagons, noticed they were passing several graves. Apparently this was an area where emigrants from other wagon trains had died. Some of the graves looked old, and it was obvious that in time they would be completely lost to the wind and the sand. This trail had been heavily traveled for a good fifteen years now, and everyone had read plenty of stories about the disasters others had encountered along the way. So far they had all been lucky, except for young David Nolan, who had died from a rattlesnake bite two days ago. As Luke got closer, he could hear the man's young widow, Hester, still weeping bitterly inside her wagon, which someone else had agreed to drive for her.

Even without many disasters, the trip was hard and sometimes miserable. They had encountered cold rains, mud, mosquitoes, and unbearable heat. Two weeks ago nearly everyone had come down with something that brought on a rash of vomiting, but luckily it had not been fatal. By now, many of them were irritable—women angry with their spouses for bringing them out here, some begging to go back. Through it all, Lettie did not complain. She and her family had apparently left a relatively comfortable life back in St. Joseph, but they were not soft and whining. They had the stubborn strength of the Irish. Henry MacBride had suffered famine and hardship back in Ireland so this was nothing new to him. His children seemed to have inherited his stamina. Lettie was strong, quiet, brave, uncomplaining…just the kind of woman he would need where he was going. The more he thought about it, the more he realized he didn't want to go to Montana alone after all. If he was going to build something of his own there, he needed a woman to share it with, children to inherit his land. Who better than someone young and strong like Lettie, and beautiful to boot?

Yes, by God, he was going to talk to Henry about asking for Lettie's hand in marriage. The man probably wouldn't want his daughter to leave the family and go to a place like Montana, but then it was really up to Lettie in the end. He'd do this the proper way and approach her father first. He stuck the cigar in his mouth and rode a little faster, relieved to have made the decision.

Dark clouds were moving in fast now from the west, and lightning was shattering the sky, followed by more cracking thunder. Luke noticed Hank Preston riding frantically up and down along the line of wagons.

"Get to the ravine up ahead!" he was shouting. "Hurry it up! Get yourselves to the lowest place possible! Could be a twister coming!"

The wind suddenly picked up to almost violent proportions, and it was icy cold, almost a shock compared to the oppressive heat they had felt all morning. Huge drops of rain mixed with hail began pelting Luke as he kicked Red into a fast run then, heading for the MacBride wagons.

~

The ground quickly turned white from hail. Luke barely had time to tie Red to the back of one of the MacBride wagons and grab his slicker before the hail became even larger. He grabbed Nathan from Lettie's arms, then pushed her under the wagon, which her brother had managed to get to the ravine. It was really more just a slight dip in the earth, but Preston had insisted they would be better protected there. Luke handed Nathan to his mother, then helped MacBride and his wife get the other two wagons to the low spot, praying none of the animals would go out of control because of the storm, dragging wagons with them, maybe hurting someone or wrecking a wagon.

The hailstones hurt as they pummeled him. Luke and the others scrambled under their wagons then, and women's screams were drowned out by the deafening wind, thunder, and torrential rain that was now mixed with the hail. Luke moved to lie over Lettie and Nathan, spreading his slicker over them. "Keep your heads under my body," he shouted. "If that wind blows the wagon apart, pieces of wood and iron will go flying everywhere!"

A few people did not make it to the low spot, but there was no time now to worry about that. Luke remained huddled over Lettie and the child, and it was impossible to know what was happening to the others. For the next several minutes there was nothing to do but lie there and wait for the worst of the storm to pass. Little Nathan turned on his back and looked up at Luke, showing not a bit of fear from the terrible thunder and roar of the wind. Lettie remained on her stomach, keeping an arm around the boy. She grabbed him a little closer when they heard a crashing sound. The rain came down so hard that the little gully in which they lay began to fill quickly with water and turn into a stream.

"I've heard how raging creeks can appear in minutes out here after a hard rain," Luke shouted to Lettie. "Be ready to climb out of here if we have to!"

The little trickle began turning into a bigger stream, until Lettie was forced to turn on her back to keep her face out of the water. She met Luke's eyes. Such a beautiful blue. She saw the love there, felt the trust. Did he feel the same about her as she did for him? She knew it would be better if he didn't. She would only have to turn him away. It was the only right thing to do, wasn't it? So why did she feel so safe here, with his strong shoulders hovering over her? Why wasn't she afraid? Why did she desire this man, when she had no right to desire any man?

She had tried so hard not to want Luke, not to care about him. She had even quit letting him take Nathan. It wasn't good for the boy to grow so fond of a man who would soon be leaving them.

All around them the storm raged, people screamed, horses whinnied, and mules brayed. The water deepened, soaking Lettie's hair and dress. But she felt no fear as long as she could look into Luke Fontaine's eyes. Don't feel this way, she told herself. Yet she remained immobile as he came closer then, and it felt like fire was surging through her veins when his mouth met her own in a savage kiss that both of them wanted, needed. He parted her lips, his tongue slaking into her mouth hungrily, his arms around both Nathan and her.

How could she let him do this? And why was she enjoying it? Never had she felt like this. Never since the night of the raid had she even dreamed she could feel this way for any man. But this man had dark hair, blue eyes. He looked nothing like Nathan's father, and there was something in his eyes that told her she could trust him, that he was not just using her, that he loved her.

But just as she was enjoying the feel of his powerful body against her own, the hardness against her thigh reminded her of what she had been so cruelly introduced to three years ago.

She tore her lips away. "Luke, we can't—"

"Why? I love you, Lettie. You've known it for weeks, and I know you love me. I've seen it in your eyes." He grasped her hair, made her face him. "What is it you're not telling me, Lettie? Your husband has been dead for a good three years. Don't tell me you're still mourning him, because I don't believe it! Nathan needs a father, and I already love him as if he were my own child. Is it Montana? Are you afraid to go there?"

"No." She was crying now. He let go of her hair and she looked away again. "It's no use, Luke. You wouldn't love me if you knew."

"Knew what? *Tell* me, Lettie! Give me a chance to decide for myself."

She met his eyes again. The wind roared, and thunder exploded all around them. "I never had a husband!" She had to yell so he could hear her. "Nathan's father raped me! It was during the raid! His friends held me down while—"

She couldn't go on. The roar of the wind became deafening, and they knew a tornado was ripping past them. Lettie screamed and buried her face in Luke's shoulder. He held tightly to both Nathan and her, praying the tornado would somehow miss them. It lasted only a few seconds, before the wind began to calm. Moments later the storm had turned to a steady downpour. Luke pulled Lettie out from under the wagon and out of the deepening stream.

"You'd better get in the wagon and get on some dry clothes," he told her. "You and Nathan both. You'll be sick if you don't."

Lettie took hold of Nathan and turned to climb into the wagon. She had not met Luke's eyes since her confession. He grasped her arm. "We'll talk."

"There is nothing to talk about," she answered.

"There's *plenty* to talk about, like why in hell you think you have to be ashamed of what happened! Did you really think it would keep me from loving you?"

Lettie looked up at him in surprise, her eyes brimming with tears. "No man back in St. Joseph would have me. I couldn't stand the looks any longer. That's part of the reason we left. We were just going to tell people Nathan's father was dead, but I love you too much to lie to you, Luke Fontaine." There! She had said it. She loved him. "Now let me go. And stop coming around and playing with Nathan. It isn't fair to him."

She turned and climbed into the wagon. Luke stood there for a moment, feeling numb, then angry. He wanted to kill the man who had raped her and left behind a shamed, shattered woman and a bastard son. How well he knew the feeling of being branded like that!

He realized then that Lettie's mother was standing nearby. She had heard their argument, and the look of tragedy in her eyes told him of the hell she and her husband had been through over what had happened to their daughter. There was no time now to talk about it, but a lot of things were clearer to him now. He realized that the married name of Dougan must be fake; he understood why Lettie had been afraid to show any love for him, why she seemed to cringe whenever a discussion of the border raids came up. He knew now why Nathan didn't look anything like the MacBrides, and why Lettie was afraid to let him get too close. She feared Luke would be repulsed by Nathan once he knew the truth, and she didn't want her son to be hurt.

He could not hate her or the boy. He could only love Nathan more, knowing firsthand how a son needed a father's love; and he admired the quality and stamina of the boy's mother. She had kept her baby, seemed to love the boy as much as any mother loved her child. She was a strong, brave young woman who had protected an innocent child from the ugliness of his conception. That took courage, and an immense capacity to love.

"She's a good girl, Luke," Mrs. MacBride told him. "She needs a man who can show her how to be a woman and not be afraid."

Luke stood there with rain pouring down his face, his hair soaked to his scalp. It was only then he realized he'd lost his hat somewhere. "I don't doubt that for a minute, ma'am. She thinks she's scared me away, but I don't scare that easy."

Lettie's mother smiled. "I didn't think you would, but it was up to her to tell you, not us."

Looking past Mrs. MacBride, Luke saw that one wagon had been destroyed. Someone began shouting, asking where Mrs. Nolan was, the young widow who had lost her husband to snakebite. She was nowhere near the wagons.

"I'd better go help with the cleanup," he told Mrs. MacBride, "but this isn't finished. Your daughter and I are going to have a good talk."

She smiled sadly and touched his arm. "I hope you do."

Luke glanced at the MacBride wagon once more, then left to help look for poor Hester Nolan.

༄

The rain turned to drizzle, a fitting accompaniment to the sad burial. Hester Nolan had run out into the storm and shot herself in the head. No one had seen her run away, and no one had heard the shot above the sound of the wind. Hank Preston said a few words over her grave, after which everyone went through the young woman's belongings, to decide whom to notify back east of her husband's and her deaths. Preston rather callously explained how everything would be done. Personal belongings would be left at Julesberg for relatives to claim. The wagon and oxen would be sold to anyone at Julesberg who might want them, or to a member of the wagon train, the money held with the personal belongings. A few other things would be divided up among the other travelers.

It seemed a cold and matter-of-fact way to dispose of everything, but Luke was fast learning that in this land there was little room for sentiment, little time for tears over what might have been. They had to keep moving or risk dying in the mountains. That was the way it was, and there was no getting around it.

While the others were still gathered over the Nolans' possessions, Luke pulled Henry MacBride aside. Lettie turned and gave him a discouraging look as though to warn him it was useless to say anything to her father; her answer would still be no. But Luke had already decided he would not take no for an answer, even if he had to forgo his plans to go to Montana for the time being and follow her all the way to Denver. He would keep after her until she gave in to what he knew were her true feelings.

"What is it, Luke?" MacBride asked him.

Luke drew in his breath, watched Lettie a moment longer before meeting Henry's gaze. "This seems like a strange time to tell you, but it won't be long before I'll be heading on north," he told the man. "I want to marry Lettie, Mr. MacBride, take her to Montana with me. Do I have your permission?"

The man's eyebrows moved into a frown. He looked as though he had expected the question. "I'd say that was up to Lettie, son. She's a woman with a child now. It's her decision. But there are things you need to know."

"I already know about the rape. She told me during the storm while I was holding her." He felt a little embarrassed then, ran a hand through his hair and turned away. "Damn it, Henry, I love her. I told her so, and she burst out and told me how Nathan came to be." He looked back at the older man. "I don't care, Henry. It doesn't change my feelings for her. In fact, I admire her for her courage, and for keeping the boy and loving him like she does. Any man who would blame a proper young woman for something like that is wrong. All I see when I look at your daughter is a beautiful woman, capable of a lot of love, a woman of strength and courage and stamina. She's the kind of woman a man needs where I'm going."

Henry rubbed at his neck. "My Lettie is used to a very comfortable life, Luke. I imagine it would be anything but that where you're going."

Luke leaned closer, towering over the much shorter Irishman. "You have my word that I'll give her everything she could want, just as fast as I can manage it. Yes, it will be rough at first, but I think Lettie has the strength for it. In time I intend to be a rich landowner, Henry. I'll build her a nice, big home. Someday she'll be one of the wealthiest women in Montana, I promise you that. We'll write as often as we can—maybe not at first, because I don't know where we'll settle, how easy it will be to get word to you. But we'll find a way, so you'll know she's all right. We'll write the general post office in Denver. You can check there until you get settled yourself and send us a proper address."

Henry sighed, putting his hands on his hips, his cotton shirt still soiled from the mud under his own wagon during the storm. Luke also still had not changed out of his damp denim pants, but he kept a canvas slicker around his shoulders.

"It isn't just the danger in Montana I'm thinking about, Luke. It's Lettie herself." Henry rubbed at his chin. "What happened… Well, she was a virgin. A thing like that is horrifying enough for any woman, but at fifteen, knowing nothing about men—"

"I don't intend to push her into anything, if that's what you're thinking. I'm not a fool, Henry. I've seen the fear in her eyes, but there's love there too. I kissed her under that wagon, and she *wanted* me to kiss her. I think it surprised and scared her. Once she learns she can trust me and realizes how much I love her…" He sighed. "I'd never hurt her or do anything to bring back that terror. Surely you know me well enough to trust my word by now."

The old man's eyes teared. "We love her so much, Luke. The thought of being parted from our Lettie hurts, but considering her circumstance, maybe you're the best thing for her now. The boy takes to you like a bear to honey, and he needs a father. He's got too much energy for this old man to keep up with." He grinned. "You don't need my permission, Luke. You just need to get Lettie to say yes. She thinks she's not good enough for any man now."

Luke shook his head in exasperation. "She's too good for most men as far as I'm concerned, probably too good for me."

Henry put a hand on his arm. "You talk to her, tell

her how you feel. And if you expect her to tell you all of it, then you've got to be straight with her too, Luke. Something tells me you haven't told us everything about your own past, the truth about the trouble with your father. She has a right to know all of it, just the same as you have the right to know everything about Lettie. You don't have to tell me if you don't want, but you tell Lettie. I want your promise on that."

Luke nodded. "I'll tell her."

Henry glanced at the lonely grave. "I don't want my Lettie to end up like that, Luke, buried up there in Montana in some nameless grave."

"That won't happen. I'll make sure of it."

Henry studied the sincerity in Luke's eyes. "I like you, Luke. I know you'll do your best, and I think you have what it takes to do everything you set out to do. I see a burning desire in those eyes, a hunger to be a man of wealth and importance someday. Whatever is driving you, and I think it's some kind of hurt your father has set on you, it will take you far. Just don't lose sight of what is really important along the way, like your wife and children. I've seen it happen."

Luke shook his hand. "I love her too much for that, the boy too. They'll always come first."

In the distance Lettie looked around from behind a wagon to see her father and Luke shaking hands. She grasped her stomach, anticipation and apprehension both fighting a war inside of her. She knew what that handshake meant. It would be up to her now, and somehow she would have to find a way to tell Luke Fontaine no. It didn't matter that she had enjoyed that kiss, that it still lingered on her lips. It didn't matter that she felt safe and protected when Luke Fontaine's arms were around her. It didn't matter that she had fallen in love with the strong, handsome, skilled descendant of a French trapper, whose touch sent fire through her blood.

She was not worthy of him, not worthy of any man. She could never belong just to him. She had been robbed of the most precious gift a woman could give her husband, and it had left her tainted. How could he say that what had happened could not keep him from loving her? It didn't seem possible. Maybe he wasn't even asking for her hand. Maybe he was explaining to her father why he had decided to go his own way soon. He had surely decided he could never marry her. Besides, the thought of marriage and what it meant frightened her, even though a part of her wanted to throw her arms around Luke and tell him she would follow him to the end of the earth; and God knew a place like Montana was as close to that as a man, or woman, could get. He might as well ask her to go to Australia or Africa. Montana seemed just as remote, and that was just one more reason to say no.

Three

LUKE DONNED HIS BEST SUIT OF BLACK SILK, WITH A white ruffled shirt and black bow tie. He glanced at himself in a mirror he had hung on a tree, smoothing back his dark hair by the light of a fast-setting sun, then rubbed at his clean-shaven face. For a moment he wondered, as he had so many times for the last fourteen years, if his features really had come from someone other than his own father. He didn't really look much like Jacques Fontaine, but he had the man's build. Maybe it was someone else's build he'd inherited. His coloring was completely different from his father's. He could hardly remember his mother, who had died when he was only four, and his father had refused to let him see any pictures of her.

He turned away from the mirror, shaking off the hurt such memories brought him. Maybe it didn't matter what Lettie had been through. Once she knew the truth about his own background, that would be reason enough to turn down his proposal. There had been another woman…back in St. Louis. Pretty Lynnanne Haley had loved him too, or at least she had claimed she did. She was the daughter of another prominent merchant, and he had loved her as much as a twenty-two-year-old man can love the woman he wants to marry. She would have been his wife already if her father had not put a stop to everything by telling Lynnanne that the man she was considering marrying was a bastard and was beneath her station. He had promptly sent her off to a finishing school, and the next thing Luke knew, she was married to a prominent New York lawyer.

He had received only one letter from Lynnanne, expressing her sorrow at having to break off their relationship, but also expressing anger that he had not told her the truth. Before Lynnanne, and ever since, there had been no one, just a string of loose women and tavern whores. He had no doubt his own father had instigated the heartbreaking mess. The man seemed bent on making sure his illegitimate son never knew an ounce of happiness. But Jacques Fontaine could not stop him now. He loved Lettie MacBride, and he would have her for his wife. Surely Lettie was nothing like Lynnanne and would not consider herself above him.

He brushed at the suit, grateful that one of the women among the travelers had offered to press it for him. It was the only dress suit he had brought with him on the trip, realizing that where he was going, there would be little need for fancy clothes. Most of the clothing he had brought along consisted of denim or heavy wool or buckskin pants, sturdy cotton and wool shirts, deerskin and heavy wolf-skin jackets and hats, boots lined with animal fur, as well as knee-high leather boots, the kind of clothes that would withstand riding and living in a rugged land with freezing winters. He would head into Montana with plenty of food, clothes, and other supplies, as well as an array of good weapons and the ammunition to use them.

He had everything he needed to get started...except the one thing he needed most. Lettie MacBride. He walked to the circle of wagons to see her standing in the distance with her brother and sister, her hair pulled up at the sides with combs, the rest of it hanging nearly to her waist in a rich, dark red braid. She wore a soft green dress dotted with yellow flowers, and it fit her figure fetchingly. He wanted to think she had worn the dress for him, but she had been so stubbornly evasive these last ten days, he couldn't be sure.

They were just outside of Julesberg now, and everyone had decided to do something to lift the pall of sorrow that had been hanging over them since burying Hester Nolan. A nearby farmer had welcomed them onto his land and was roasting a pig to share with all of them. The man's son played the fiddle with a flare, and now several of the emigrants, including Henry and Katie MacBride, clapped and danced to a fancy tune, skirts whirling around a roaring campfire over which hung the pig.

Dusk was growing toward darkness, reminding Luke there was not much time left. Tomorrow the MacBrides would keep heading south into Colorado. He had to convince Lettie tonight to stay with him and go on into Wyoming with the rest of the wagon train. She had been avoiding him, and he damn well knew why. She was trying to keep from having to answer a proposal of marriage. Ever since he'd talked to her father, she had found ways to keep from being near him, even staying in the wagon whenever he joined them for a meal. He was determined that tonight she would listen to what he had to say, even if he had to drag her off by force.

He drew in his breath for courage, headed across the clearing in the middle of the circle of wagons. Lettie MacBride had a stubborn, determined streak that made her a formidable challenge at times. It was the Irish in her. But, by God, he was not going to let her fend him off any longer. He ached for her. He dreamed about her. He loved Nathan, hated the thought of saying good-bye to the boy in the morning and never seeing him again. And he loved Lettie, more than he ever thought he could love a woman. He could not imagine any woman being better suited to help him realize his dream. She was not going to get away from him, nor was she going to let something she couldn't help keep her from enjoying the natural love between a man and a woman that she deserved to have for herself. Before this night was over, Lettie MacBride was going to agree to be his wife.

∽

Lettie saw Luke coming and considered hiding in the wagon again but she knew deep inside that this time she had to see him. After tonight she would never see Luke Fontaine again. He deserved at least a good-bye. Despite everything, she felt driven to look her prettiest. She was two women—one, full of shame, wanting nothing to do with any man; the other hoping that Luke Fontaine found her beautiful, wanting to dance with him, go to Montana with him, go anywhere with him. For Luke's sake, she was determined to hide that other side of her. He deserved better than soiled goods.

Her cheeks grew hot as he approached. Why did he have to look so handsome tonight? Something stirred deep within her at the sight of his snug-fitting black pants, his broad shoulders, his handsome face with its high cheekbones and full lips and provocative blue eyes. His thick, dark hair was slicked back. She felt an aura of power and masculinity as he came to stand before her. "Will you dance with me?" he asked.

Lettie looked down, and her brother gave her a nudge. "Go ahead, sis." He grinned at Luke. He liked the man, wished he wouldn't be leaving them tomorrow. Little Nathan toddled up to Luke and tugged at his pants. James leaned down and picked him up. "You leave Luke and your mommy alone," he ordered. "They're going to dance."

Lettie didn't know how to say no, nor did she get the chance. A big, strong hand was quickly folded around her own, and she was being led into the circle of dancers. Another strong hand was pressed against her back then, and in the next moment she was whirling around to the music.

"Lettie, look up at me."

She didn't dare, did she? If she looked into his eyes, so close to him as she was now, his strong hand squeezing her own, she wouldn't be able to think straight. She wouldn't be able to do what she knew was right.

"Lettie."

She raised her eyes to meet his gaze, and a wonderful warmth flooded through her.

"I love you, and if you try to say you don't love me, you're a liar."

She swallowed back tears. How could he possibly love her? "Sometimes love isn't enough."

"It's all a man and woman need."

"Luke, I've tried to do this the easy way."

"By avoiding the truth?"

"You know what I mean. The less we see of each other, the less hurt there will be. Tomorrow we'll go our separate ways. In time we'll both—"

She was unable to finish the sentence. He was suddenly whisking her away from the others into the dusky darkness, a firm arm around her waist. Not wanting to cause a scene, she didn't protest. She sensed that even if she kicked and screamed, he was going to take her off and have his say.

They were away from the light of the fire now, behind a wagon, a soft, evening breeze cool against her hot cheeks, just strong enough to keep the mosquitoes away. There was a warm, sweet smell to the air. The sun was fast setting, and a full moon was trying to make an appearance. Just as she was about to speak, Luke pulled her tight against him, lifted her off her feet, found her mouth in a warm, delicious kiss, a prolonged kiss that put a large crack in her stubborn will to deny him. Lettie found herself returning the kiss with unbridled passion, amazed that this second kiss was as wonderful and provocative as the first one had been; to know that again, this man had awakened something in her she was afraid had been lost forever; to know she really could want a man.

Then the alarm set in. There was much more to what a man wanted than kissing, and here was a man who deserved much better than Lettie MacBride. She turned her face away. He continued kissing her cheek, her neck. "Stop it, Luke!" she said with a small whimper.

"Why? Because you think you've been somehow tainted? Because you think this is wrong just because of what happened to you?"

"It *is* wrong! Tomorrow you'll go your way and we'll go ours, and everything will be much easier for both of us if we just let it go at that."

"Will it?" Luke slowly set her on her feet, enjoying the feel of her breasts against his chest as she slid down his body. "I don't think so, Lettie. I think both of us will suffer for a long time, missing each other, wondering if we did the right thing after all, for us and for Nathan. Marry me, Lettie. You know I've been wanting to ask you for the longest time. Come with me tomorrow. I'll be the proper gentleman all the way to Fort Laramie. I hear they have preachers and priests there. That's where we'll marry. If for some reason we're sure by then that it's wrong, I'll see you get full escort back into Colorado to find your parents in Denver. Otherwise, we'll go on into Montana from there. But even then, I swear I won't touch you until you want to be touched."

Lettie closed her eyes. She put a hand to her forehead, turning away. "How can you talk about being a proper gentleman around me? You obviously don't need to be."

"Don't say things like that. What happened to you was no more your fault than if you had been shot that night."

"I wish I had been." Her voice broke on the words,

and she took a step away from him. "Except for Nathan." She sniffed and drew in her breath to stay in control of herself. "Back in St. Joseph, our minister told me Nathan is a gift from God, in spite of how he was conceived. I've had to convince myself of that, or hate him. He's such a sweet, joyful little boy, and to him I'm just Mommy. How can I not love him?"

Luke watched her, his eyes full of compassion. "That's just one of the reasons I love you, Lettie. You're a woman of great courage, and with a tremendous capacity to love."

"I'm not all that courageous. Part of the reason we left St. Joseph is because I couldn't bear the stares and whispers any longer. No man wanted me as a wife. The couple of men who did try to court me soon showed their true colors. They figured since I kept the baby, I must not have minded the rape. Maybe I enjoyed it. Maybe I'd enjoy it again."

The words were spoken with deep bitterness, her fists and teeth clenched. "But it's just the opposite. I've hated the thought of being with a man, *any* man! You all think I enjoyed being raped. Well, I didn't, do you understand? I *hated* it! It was painful and ugly and humiliating. I vomited! I screamed and I fought and I vomited, and don't think that just because I kissed you, that I'm some kind of loose woman who—"

He grasped her arms, jerking her around. "You're the woman I love and want to marry. Would I feel this way if I thought that of you? I won't have anyone thinking that of you, nor do I think it! And I won't have *you* think of *yourself* that way, either! In your heart and soul, and in my eyes, you're as pure and untouched as before any of that happened."

Lettie stared at him, shivering. Then she crumbled, collapsing against his chest, savoring the feel of his strong arms around her, the luxury of being truly loved and respected, the way she would have wanted any man she would marry to feel about her, something she never thought she would find again.

Luke let her cry for a few minutes, rubbing her back. "Tell me how it happened, Lettie. Get it out in the open."

Lettie forced herself to have courage, deciding he might as well know. "I ran to the barn that night," she sobbed. "Father tried to stop me...but I had a horse that was...precious to me. I saw men going into the barn. I knew they were going to steal Dancer, and I...thought I could stop them. They were...carrying torches. One of them...a man with white-blond hair...had Dancer by the reins. I...tried to grab the horse away from him... but he just grabbed me, laughing. He pushed me into the hay...and the others...held me down."

She cringed, feeling ill at the ugly memory that was as vivid today as three years ago. "When I first went out there, I wasn't afraid...because I thought all they might do was hit me or something, and I didn't care. I wanted to save Dancer. I didn't know anything about men...and I never even thought of myself as a woman men would desire that way." She shivered in another sob. "When the blond one finished with me, he took Dancer anyway... but I lost much more than my horse that night."

Luke's arms enfolded her even more firmly, and she felt a great comfort, a serene feeling of safety and warmth nestled there against him. There came another torrent of tears as she clung to his ruffled shirt, and he let her cry for several minutes, stroking her hair, kissing it.

"He never really touched you, Lettie, don't you see? If a woman doesn't want to be touched that way, then she's not done one thing wrong, and nothing the man does can hurt her or change her. If he was here today, I'd kill him; but there's nothing that can be done about it now except to go on. Let me erase the memories, Lettie. I promise you I can do it."

He pulled away slightly, studied her face. It was nearly dark, but he could see her in the dim light of dusk, ached at the sight of the tears on her cheeks. He took a clean handkerchief from an inside pocket of his suit jacket and handed it to her. "Tell me you don't love me, Lettie. Tell me there isn't a part of you that wants me. Tell me you won't miss me and ache for me if we part ways tomorrow."

She wiped at her tears and nose, watching his eyes. Why should she fear this man who had shown himself to be everything any woman would want? Why should she not accept the love he offered? "I *would* miss you, Luke. I'm afraid to leave my family, afraid to go to a place like Montana; but I'm more afraid of going on without you. I was so determined I'd tell you I won't marry you, that we should part tomorrow, but I can't. I…I just want you to be sure that what happened to me doesn't bother you. You deserve the best, Luke."

He shook his head. "You're the one who deserves the best. Do you think I don't have my own reservations about being a good husband? Maybe you're the one who's not getting what she deserves. You've had a good life, Lettie. It's going to be rough for us at first, dangerous, lonely. There won't be any of the comforts you're used to. Besides that…" He sighed, pain in his eyes. "Don't be worrying about being worthy of me, Lettie. I guess it's only fair that you know the truth about what brought me out here. You might change your mind after all." He let go of her, a strange fear in his eyes.

"What is it, Luke? Is it something about your father?"

It was almost fully dark now, but the full moon was rising higher, looking huge and appearing to be sitting on the rim of the eastern horizon. "My father doesn't believe I'm his son. He says I'm a bastard."

Lettie blinked in surprise. "Luke, that's terrible! Why would he tell you a thing like that?"

He came closer again. "Because he believes it's true and never wanted me to share in any family inheritance. He told me when I was fourteen. I had broken something expensive in one of his supply stores, and in a fit of rage he told me." He swallowed, turning away again. "I felt as though somebody had shoved a knife into my gut. Later on he took me aside, told me he believed my mother had had an affair. She died when I was four, so I have no way of knowing the truth. I only remember her as a sweet, gentle, loving woman. I do know I don't look like my father the way my brother does." He rubbed at his eyes. "When he told me, I understood a lot of things, like why my father never kept pictures of my mother in the house, why he never showed me the love he showed my brother. Still, I stayed on, worked for him. I was young and confused, not sure what to do. He was the only father I knew. Then a year ago he told me he had cut me out of his will. He was getting older and figured I should know beforehand. He wanted to be sure I didn't give my brother, his *real* son, a court fight after he died. He gave me money—a payoff, I guess you'd call it," he continued bitterly. "He more or less told me to take the money and leave, that in good conscience and in fairness to my brother, he couldn't see letting me inherit any part of the family business and family fortune he had worked so hard to build."

Lettie could feel his pain. "Luke, I'm sorry. What a terrible thing for a father to do."

He breathed deeply, as though to stay in control of his emotions. "Maybe now you understand how I feel about Nathan," he said, his voice strained. "I know how it feels to be an outcast. And I know how it feels to be unloved, to be raised by a man, call him father, then find out he practically hates your guts." He turned to face her, and Lettie didn't need full light to know there were tears in his eyes. "I would never do that to Nathan, Lettie. We'll tell him his real father was killed in a raid. He'll know I'm his stepfather, but I'll love him just as much as if my own blood ran in his veins. He'll feel that love, be as close to me as he would to any real father. Whatever I build in Montana, however wealthy I might become, he will share in it equally with whatever children we have together. I promise you that."

Lettie smiled through tears. "I believe you, and I love you for it." She walked closer and touched his arm. "Luke, I think your father was wrong, terribly wrong. And any woman who could produce such a fine and handsome man as you couldn't have been bad. I'll bet she was very beautiful too."

Luke pulled her close. "My father didn't give me a lot, but it's enough to get started on. I intend to show him and my brother that I can do as well or better. I don't need his damn inheritance." He kissed her hair. "Lettie, it won't be easy at first, but I promise you that someday, you'll live like a queen. I'll make that happen, no matter what it takes. Whatever you have to suffer at first, I'll make up for it a hundred times. Someday we'll have lots more children, and you'll be living in a fine home, the wife of one of the biggest landowners in Montana!"

He let go of her then, taking hold of her hands instead. "They've already found gold up there, Lettie, but that's not what I'm after. It's the *land*—lots of it—for free if I homestead it. Some don't think that's worth anything right now, but I think they're wrong. Who knows what kind of minerals are under what I'll claim? And on top of the ground there's rich grass for grazing. Hell, they've already started building a railroad that's going to connect California with the East! Once that's done, more settlers will come, especially when the war is over. People who have lost everything will want to start over someplace new, build farms, ranches. I'm going to have a head start on them! Word is, once the railroad comes this way, there will be a big demand for beef, because it will be easier to ship it east. The railroad is coming through Colorado or Wyoming, so I wouldn't have to herd my beef near as far as the ranchers down in Texas will; and I'll have all that rich grass to fatten them up on. The *land* is the real gold mine, Lettie. There's an Indian problem, but the army will take care of that once the war is over. The Sioux will have to make way for settlement just like other Indians all over the plains have had to do. It's the way of progress, Lettie, and we'll be right there in the middle of it!"

She smiled through tears. "You really believe that, don't you?"

"I'm sure of it, as sure as I am that I love Lettie MacBride."

His own excitement began to move through her blood, and she took comfort in the strength of the hands that held her own. She nodded. "All right. I'll marry you. Just be patient with me, Luke."

He pulled her close again. "I'll never rush you or hurt you. I'll love you, protect you and Nathan, make a home for you." He kissed her forehead. "I should tell you there was another woman I was going to marry, back in St. Louis. Her name was Lynnanne Haley. That was six years ago. When she found out I was a bastard, she called it off...married someone her father considered more proper and respectable." He studied her lovingly. "I hoped you would be different, and I was right."

Lettie felt a sharp jealousy that he had ever loved anyone else. Now that she had made her decision, she wanted Luke Fontaine all to herself. "Do you love me more than you loved her?"

He smiled, tears in his eyes. "Oh yes, Lettie." He groaned. "Much, much more." He leaned closer, found her lips again in a gentle, grateful, possessive kiss that told her that from this moment on, she was Luke Fontaine's woman, come hell or high water. She wasn't afraid now,

not of Montana, and not of this man who embraced her
with gentle strength.

∽

Lettie clung to her mother, both of them crying. Never
in her eighteen years had she been apart from her family,
but she was promised to Luke now and she knew in her
heart she was doing the right thing, not just for herself,
but for Nathan. Still, she knew that it could be months,
maybe even years, before she saw her beloved mother
and father again, her cherished brother and sister. This
was her family, who had stuck by her through the awful
times after her rape, who had loved her, supported
her, loved their grandchild just as much as if he'd been
conceived in love.

Henry MacBride stepped up to Luke. "She's a good
girl, Luke. I'm trusting you to treat her with respect,
never to hurt her, to be a good father to the boy."

"You know I will," Luke answered, picking Nathan
up in his arms. "We'll write just as soon as we're settled
and can get a letter out to you. That might take some
time, so don't get worried."

MacBride took a smiling Nathan into his arms, while
Lettie finally managed to pull herself away from her mother
so she could hug her brother James, and her sister Louise.
Then Henry handed Nathan to his grandma and there
was another round of hugs. When Luke embraced Katie
MacBride and Nathan both, Katie wept against his chest.

"Do take good care of our little grandson," she
sobbed. "And my Lettie."

"You've got nothing to worry about, Katie. I love
them both more than my own life." Luke turned to
Henry, shook the man's hand firmly, their eyes holding
in trust. Then Lettie was in her father's arms, and Luke
wondered if all the tears and hugging would end in time
for them to leave with the rest of the wagon train. The

MacBrides were heading south into Denver with three other families, led by a new scout they had hired from Julesberg. Luke and Lettie would go on northwest into Wyoming with the rest of the wagon train. Luke had bought the Nolan wagon and oxen, and some of their supplies. They would marry when they reached Fort Laramie. They would be on their own then, heading into a wild country that held mystery and danger, but Luke was not afraid. He had never been happier in his life. He felt more love from Lettie and Nathan than he had ever known from his own father, and he was anxious now to get to Montana and prove his own worth.

"Let's get moving!" Hank Preston shouted as he rode past them. "Time's a wastin'."

"Oh dear!" Katie MacBride embraced her daughter once more. All of Lettie's belongings were already packed into the Nolan wagon, Luke's horse and mules tied to the back of it. The entire MacBride family hugged each other once more, cried even more, filled with the painful mixture of great happiness and sadness at the same time. Lettie turned to give Sadie a hug, and the big woman was sobbing, calling Lettie her "honey-child."

Finally Luke took Nathan from Mrs. MacBride, and lifted him up into the front seat of the wagon. He went to get Lettie.

"We have to go, Lettie," he told her, gently grasping her arm. "Nathan is already in the wagon."

Lettie wiped at tears with her handkerchief. "I'll write as soon as I can," she told them. "I love you. I'll always love you, and we'll be together in our hearts. Maybe someday we'll be able to visit somehow."

"And we'll always love you, child," Henry told his daughter. "No matter how far the miles, or how long the months apart, we'll be right beside you in spirit and prayer. You have a fine man, Lettie. You've made the right choice, and Nathan will have a good father."

Lettie squeezed his hands and nodded.

"Go with God, my precious," Katie told her daughter. "And always know you are surrounded with our love. If anything—" She glanced at Luke, then back to Lettie. "If anything goes wrong, you can always come to us. You know that."

"We'll be all right, Mama." Lettie kissed her mother once more, took one last look at her family, then turned and ran to the wagon.

Luke nodded to all of them. "Please don't worry about her. I love her very much, and I have big plans. She'll have a fine home someday and be living in luxury. That's a promise."

Henry shook his hand once more. "I believe you, son. God go with you."

Luke turned away and walked to the wagon, picking up a switch and giving one of the two lead oxen a little snap, with an order to get under way. Lettie sat in the seat clinging to Nathan, who in turn clung to his stuffed horse. She could not resist looking back once more. She waved and Nathan did the same, smiling, oblivious to what all the crying was about. In his little mind he was simply setting off on a great adventure with his mother and the nice man called Luke. He was telling Grandma and Grandpa good-bye, but it would only be for a day or two, wouldn't it?

"'Tana," the boy said, pointing to the wagons ahead of them.

"Yes, Nathan," Lettie answered. "We're going to Montana."

Four

LETTIE SHIVERED, PULLING THE BEARSKIN BLANKET Luke had bought her in Billings closer around herself. Nathan lay sleeping in her lap, bundled into a warm blanket. "It looks empty," Lettie told Luke, her eyes on a small cabin that sat nestled into the side of a foothill several yards away.

Luke turned up the collar of his own wolf-skin jacket against a stinging wind that hammered at them out of the nearby mountains. "Appears that way." He reached under the wagon seat and retrieved his Winchester, then climbed down. "Stay put."

Lettie watched anxiously as he approached the cabin. *Sure, there's plenty of free land yet just southwest of here*, the land agent in Billings had told them. *If you can wrestle it from the outlaws who use it to hide stolen cattle and horses.* The man's name was David Taylor, a short, stocky soul who had hinted that he would not be particular with facts and figures if Luke wanted to claim a little more than the one hundred and sixty acres he was allowed under the Homestead Act. Lettie didn't trust Taylor one bit, and she wondered how much money the man was making on the side by accepting money to "alter" deeds and land boundaries.

It mattered little at the moment. Right now, Luke had to decide on the land he wanted to claim in the first place, and as soon as they had come over the last rise and he saw the wide valley stretched out before them, he knew what he wanted. Although there was a dusting of snow over all of it, he could see acres and acres of winter grass. She prayed Taylor was right that the outlaws who roamed these parts usually didn't show up until spring. They needed a place to hole up for the winter without having to spend money on room and board. When Luke had spotted this little cabin across the valley, backed by splendid mountains that seemed to watch over it like sentinels, he was sure they were "home." He had driven the wagon up to the cabin, and now was inspecting it to see if anyone had lived there recently.

Lettie suspected the place was not livable. She watched Luke go inside, waited, weary from the weeks of hard travel it had taken to get here. They had managed to latch onto another wagon train heading out of Fort Laramie north to Billings in Montana Territory. From there the others went on west into the Rockies to look for gold, in spite of the danger of Indian attack. Luke was more interested in claiming land, and the first thing he had done was find the land agent. Taylor's office was nothing more than the corner of a sorry-looking saloon in a settlement that was hardly big enough to be called a town, but the citizens of Billings seemed proud of their accomplishments. Taylor himself was not so proud. He seemed to detest his job and detest the entire area, a government man doing only what he'd been ordered to do.

Lettie was grateful that they had had someone with whom to travel most of the way, since all anyone could talk about was the danger of Indians. So far, no Sioux had given them trouble, but now that she and Luke were alone, she was more frightened than she had been since leaving Fort Laramie to come here. She jumped with alarm then when she heard two gunshots. From the sound of them, they had come from the six-gun Luke wore on his hip, something he had started doing as an extra precaution since they had left Billings.

"Luke!" she called out in alarm. Nathan stirred on her lap, but he did not come fully awake. "What is it?"

She breathed a sigh of relief when he appeared at the doorway, the rifle in his left hand, his six-gun in his right. "Rats," he told her. "I got a couple of them." He turned back inside, reappeared with the dead rodents, and tossed them off to the side of the cabin.

Lettie struggled to hide her horror.

"The place looks as though it hasn't been lived in for quite a while," Luke continued, shoving the handgun back into its holster. He stepped off the sagging porch to come back to the wagon. "It's small, but there's a cast-iron heating stove inside, and a small, homemade bed. Nathan can sleep on that. It will keep him up off the floor away from drafts and varmints." He was beside the wagon now, his eyes apologetic. "Don't worry. We'll rig something up to keep *us* off the floor too. I'll gather some wood and we can get a fire going. It's getting dark. We'll bring in most of the supplies in the morning. I'll tend to the horses and maybe you can get some supper going as soon as we get the stove heated up." He leaned his rifle against the wagon wheel and reached up to take Nathan from her lap so she could climb down.

"Are you sure no one is around?" she asked.

Luke studied the surroundings while Lettie retied her hat against the cold. The only sound was the soft moan of the mountain wind. Lettie wondered if the wind ever stopped blowing in this land. They had not had a still day since before leaving Fort Laramie weeks ago, and sometimes she thought she might go crazy from the constant droning sound and the fact that everything had to be tied or weighted down to keep things from blowing away.

"No tracks anyplace, no food inside the cabin," Luke answered. "If we're lucky, whoever built this place isn't coming back, at least not until spring."

"And what if it's outlaws who want us out?"

Luke turned and handed Nathan back to her. The boy's eyes fluttered open, but he seemed to be too sleepy to realize where he was. He stuck his thumb in his mouth and kept a tight hold on his horse. "I like this area, Lettie. No outlaws are going to chase me out of it. Right now my biggest concern is to get you and Nathan settled inside and get some heat going. I've heard enough about Montana winters to know I have to get busy cutting wood. It's only the last of September, and if it's this cold already, you can imagine what it will be like by January." He saw the concern and fear in her eyes, gave her a light hug. "It's going to be all right, Lettie. I promised you that, didn't I? You have my word that, come spring, I'll build you something a lot better than this sorry shack, and I'll have laid claim to all of this and more." He turned from her and walked around to the back of the wagon to remove a couple of carpetbags of clothing and some blankets. "Come on," he told her, his arms full.

Lettie walked ahead of him into the shack, swallowing back an urge to vomit. Never had she been surrounded by so much danger and desolation. She didn't want to hurt Luke by showing her terror, or letting him know how crude and distasteful she found the cabin. She couldn't scream. She could only breathe deeply and make do with what was here. She heard the thud of the carpetbags, watched the blankets land on the small bed where Luke threw them. The bed was plenty long, but very narrow.

She gazed around the cabin, noticed a few cracks between the boards that were sure to let in cold drafts in the winter. Another rat scurried across the floor, and she stepped back. The room was very small, perhaps fifteen feet square, with a potbellied stove in one corner, a few shelves built against one wall, and a crudely built table in the middle of the room, with two crates to serve as chairs. The bed was made from pine, with ropes for springs and no mattress on top. She was glad her mother had given her two feather mattresses before they parted. Never had she longed more fervently to be with her family back at the spacious home they had left behind in St. Joseph, where people lived in reasonable numbers, and anything they needed was close at hand.

She was only vaguely aware when Luke left again. When he returned minutes later with an armload of food and other supplies they would need for the night, she was still standing in the middle of the room looking around in stunned disappointment at the shack. She said nothing when Luke took Nathan from her arms and laid him on a pile of blankets on the bed. Silently, she untied and removed the wool hat she'd been wearing. She was shaken by her sense of doubt, not only over her choice to come to this lonely, desolate place, but also over her decision to marry. She loved Luke, and he had been attentive and caring and protective throughout their dangerous, trying journey to get here; but being his wife meant fulfilling other needs he had not yet demanded of her. This was the first time they had been truly alone since marrying at Fort Laramie. When Luke had slept in the wagon with her, he had only held her. Was he waiting for her to make the first move; or had he patiently been waiting for this moment, when he had her alone? Between the realization that he would surely expect to consummate their marriage now, and the knowledge that she would spend the rest of the winter holed up in this tiny cabin, with rats running over her feet, she felt panic building.

"Lettie?"

She was startled by the touch of Luke's hand on her shoulder. She gasped and turned to look up at him, her eyes wide with fear and apprehension. "I...I don't know if I can stay here, Luke." Oh, why had she said that? She could see the hurt in his eyes. He should be angry. Maybe he would throw her down and have his way with her now, order her to submit to her husband, yell at her for being weak and selfish, tell her she would stay here whether she liked it or not.

He turned, looked around the tiny room, looked back at her with a smile of resignation on his face. "I can't blame you there. I don't know why I even considered this. I guess in all my excitement…" He sighed deeply. "I'll take you back to Billings in the morning. It's not much of a town, but maybe I can find a safe place for you and Nathan to stay while I make things more livable around here."

"But…you'd be out here all alone."

He shrugged, walking over to the stove and opening the door. "I knew before I ever came here there would be a lot of lonely living I'd have to put up with." He picked up some kindling from a small pile that lay near the stove and stacked it inside. "When you have a dream, you simply do what you have to do to realize it." He turned to face her. "I told you it won't be like this forever, Lettie, and it won't."

His eyes moved over her, and she knew what he wanted. He simply loved and respected her too much to ask for it. A wave of guilt rushed through her, and she felt like crying. "I'm sorry, Luke. I've disappointed you in so many ways already."

He frowned, coming closer. "I never said that. I don't blame you for not wanting to stay here. I'll take you back to town and you can come back here in the spring." He placed his hands on her shoulders. "I love you, Lettie. I never want you to be unhappy or wish you had never married me. I made you some promises, and I intend to keep them."

A lump seemed to rise in her throat. "You'd really take me to Billings? You wouldn't be angry about it?"

Luke studied her face. He wanted her so, but was not sure how to approach the situation because of what she had been through. He knew there was a part of her that wanted him that way, but he had not seen it in her eyes since leaving Fort Laramie. He had only seen doubt and fear. "I told you I'd take you. I wouldn't be angry."

She suddenly smiled, although there were tears in her eyes. "That's all I need to know. I...I thought you took it for granted, just because I was your wife...that you'd demand..."

She threw her arms around him, resting her face against his thick fur jacket. "Oh, Luke, forgive me. I haven't been much of a wife at all yet, except to cook your meals. I just...I need time to adjust to all of this. I know your intentions are good, and I trust your promises." She leaned back to look into his eyes, trusting more every day in the look of love she saw there. "You don't have to take me back. As long as I know I *can* go back, that's all I need to know. Does that make any sense?"

He grinned. "I think so." He moved his hands inside the bearskin blanket she still wore tied at her shoulders. "I'm not a man to demand anything, Lettie, except a woman's loyalty. There isn't anything you want that I won't try to give you, as long as you belong only to me."

She reached up around his neck. "I could never belong to anyone else." She reddened then, remembering the rape, and her smile faded.

Luke pressed her closer. "You remember what I told you. I'm going to be your first man, and your *only* man. There just hasn't been the right time or chance to show you. I'm sorry about all this, Lettie. I know it's hard for you."

Somewhere in the distance they heard the cry of a bobcat. Combined with the groaning mountain wind, the sounds only accentuated how alone they really were, a good five miles from the only town, and no sign of civilization for hundreds of miles beyond that. "I can't let you stay out here alone. You're my husband. I belong here with you," Lettie said, still clinging to him.

Luke kissed her hair, her cheek. She found herself turning to meet his lips, and he explored her mouth savagely then. She felt lost in his powerful hold, buried in the fur jacket, suddenly weak. How well he fit this land, so tall and strong and rugged and determined. She loved him all the more for it, loved him the most for not being angry that she might want to go back. She had that freedom, and knowing that only made her want to stay; just like knowing he would never demand his husbandly rights made her want to be a wife to him.

He left her mouth, kissed her neck. "I'd better get a fire going, bring in—"

"Luke." She felt her heart racing as all her fears began to melt away. She didn't know how to tell him, what to do. She could only look into those handsome blue eyes and say his name. She met his lips again, astonished at the sudden hunger in her soul. How could she have considered letting this poor man stay out here alone, when he had a wife and child who could help him, love him? And how could she keep denying him the one thing he had every right to take for himself? Most of all, how could she deny her own sudden desires, this surprising awakening of woman that ached to be set free?

He returned her kiss tenderly, searching more softly with his tongue now, groaning with the want of her. Little Nathan continued to sleep on the pile of blankets, oblivious to the awakening taking place between his mother and his new father. Lettie felt herself being lowered to the floor, the bearskin blanket providing a soft barrier at her back. Luke groaned her name, kissed and licked at her throat while he moved a strong hand along her leg, up under her dress and the several layers of petticoats she had worn for warmth.

"I should build a fire," he groaned. "We should use the bed."

"It doesn't matter," she whispered. "I want to be your

wife, Luke, in every way. I want to be one with you and know that it's all right. I don't want to be afraid anymore."

He looked down questioningly at her, his eyes glistening with love and desire. "Lettie, it's so cold and crude in here—"

She touched his lips. "Do it quickly, Luke, before Nathan wakes up…and before I lose my courage." A tear slipped down the side of her face. "We can make it nicer next time."

He met her mouth again, lingered there before moving to caress her throat. "Lettie…Lettie…" He moved his hand over her drawers, yanked at the waist. Lettie closed her eyes, her heart pounding wildly with fear and anticipation. Luke moved away from her for a moment, and she knew he was unbuttoning his pants. She could not look. In the next moment she felt her drawers being pulled away, down over her knees, her boots. Her skirts fell to hide secret places, but he pushed them back up as he moved between her legs then, kissing her eyes, her throat.

"There is so much more I want to do," he told her softly. "I can make it much better than this, Lettie."

She finally found the courage to open her eyes and meet his gaze. "I believe you, but for now, I just want to be Mrs. Luke Fontaine, in every way, not just on paper. I'll not deny you any longer." She reached up and moved her fingers into his thick, dark hair. "Just love me, Luke. Never leave me."

He licked at her lips. "Never."

Lettie drew in her breath when she felt his hardness then. He pressed against her thigh, while he met her mouth again, moving his tongue deep inside suggestively. For a moment the panic returned. She braced herself for the pain, but he did not enter her immediately. Supporting himself with one arm, he reached down with his other hand to guide that part of man she thought she hated, rubbing it softly against a magic spot between her legs and creating a new sensation she had never experienced. It made her want him more, made her open herself to him more willingly.

"Relax," he whispered between kisses that kept her breathless. Desire was building deep in her belly. It had not been like this before—the gentle kisses, the soft, teasing stroking against secret places. Suddenly she felt a rippling explosion deep inside that made her cry out his name, and to her own shock, she was begging him to enter her, pleading with him to fill her, to make her his own.

She gasped when she felt it then, the huge hardness invading her, pushing deep, branding her as Luke Fontaine's property. Flashes of her rape threatened to spoil the moment; but all the while he whispered her name, told her he loved her, how good she made him feel. In moments the ugly memories were erased by this man who had waited so patiently for this, who had told her she didn't have to stay here.

How could she leave him now? No, she would stay right here with Luke Fontaine and help him build his dream. She arched up to meet his thrusts, and in spite of the cold room, she was warm with passion, protected by his own broad body and the wolf-skin jacket he had not even removed yet. She knew they would do this again... soon...and the next time he would want to touch and taste her breasts and they would lie naked together. The thought no longer frightened her. He had awakened something wonderful in her, and she was overjoyed to know how good and sweet this could be. She felt a thrill at the way his strong hands grasped at her bottom while he thrust into her.

She truly belonged to him now, and he to her. She would make sure no other women shared his bed ever again, and she would never disappoint him the way Lynnanne Haley had hurt him.

To Luke's frustration, it was over quickly. He had been too long without a woman to be able to hold back. He figured maybe it was best this way the first time. As his seed spilled into her, he prayed it would take hold. Having a child together would put the past behind them once and for all. It would seal their love for each other, and help ease her longing for her family. He felt an ache inside at the realization that he had not minded leaving his own father and brother at all. He wished he had a family that missed him, like Lettie's.

This would be his family now. Nathan. Lettie. The children they would have together. This was all he needed, this and the land. He sighed deeply, kissed Lettie's eyes, studied them when she looked up at him. "You all right?" To his delight, she smiled.

"I feel wonderful."

Luke grinned. "It gets much better than this. I want to show you how much better."

She drew in her breath at the thought. "Then we'd better heat up this place and make it livable, and we'd better make up another bed so we can get up off this floor next time."

A rat skittered by several feet away, and Lettie cringed against him. Luke kissed her hair. "I've got poison for them. We'll be rid of them in no time. You'll see." He kissed her once more. "Thank you, Lettie, for marrying me, for staying here with me. It would be so lonely without you."

She traced a finger over one of his dark brows. "I'd have been lonely too, even with other people around." Her soft smile faded. "And thank *you*, for loving me, for taking away the ugliness. I really am just yours now, aren't I?"

He moved a big hand over her breast, on up to stroke at her temple. "Just mine. In your heart I've been your first man. The rest is forgotten."

The bobcat growled again, this time sounding closer. Outside Red whinnied, and a couple of mules began to bray. "I'd better get out there," Luke said. Reluctantly, he moved away from her, stood up, and buttoned his pants.

Lettie pulled her skirts down. "I'll get some wood and get that stove going so you can wash," Luke told her as she reached for her drawers. Now she felt a little embarrassed, glad when he turned away and went outside. She quickly cleaned herself as best she could for the moment with a handkerchief, throwing it in a corner and pulling on her drawers. Yes, she would be glad to wash. She wanted to clean up good before the next time they made love, wanted to be soft and powdered. She looked around the sorry little room, envisioning where to put another bed, where to hang blankets for privacy when she needed to bathe herself. There wasn't much room, but then as cold as the Montana winters got, maybe it was better this way. One little room was a lot easier to heat than a bigger house. Poor Luke would probably have little time for anything but cutting wood for the next month or so.

She tied her hat back on and went outside to help carry in supplies. Luke brought in some wood left stacked on the porch and got a fire going, then went back outside to unhitch the animals and see about putting them up in a lean-to several feet from the cabin. Lettie quickly washed herself as best she could. Amid all the bustle, Nathan finally awoke, rubbing his eyes in confusion. He scooted off the bed and stared around the room. Lettie turned from the sack of potatoes she was opening and picked him up. "It's about time, you little devil. You sleep as hard as you play when you're awake. I hope you'll sleep that well tonight."

"Pee, Mommy."

Lettie smiled and carried the boy to an outhouse behind the cabin, helping him undo himself. He was very proud of the fact that he'd learned to "pee" the way Luke had shown him. In the distance the bobcat squealed again, and Lettie felt a stab of anxiety. Luke had said he might have to hunt the thing down and get rid of it. What if he was attacked while he was out there working alone in the woods? There would be no one to help them.

As she and Nathan returned to the cabin, she gazed at the magnificent beauty of the surrounding country, the wide valley below the cabin, the purple mountains that rimmed the entire horizon. This was a treacherous beauty, a deceitful land, one that lured with its beauty and its promises of riches. She could only pray the land would not devour her husband, kill them all with its harsh climate and dangerous wildlife.

She spent the next few hours making the cabin as homey as possible for their first night. She hung a blanket in one corner of the room. Behind it she set a washstand and laid out one of the feather mattresses for her and Luke to sleep on. She put the other feather mattress on the small bed where Nathan would sleep and made up his bed properly. She cleaned up the rest of the cabin as best she could, stacking supplies wherever they would fit. Then she cooked supper, a difficult task on the small potbellied stove.

"I need a regular cookstove," she told Luke when he returned. He promised to see about it as soon as he could. He also promised to go to Billings and buy some tar paper to nail to the outside of the cabin to close off the cracks between the boards. But before he did any of that, he would have to spend the next several days cutting wood. Winter set into this land early, and any day could find them buried in a mountain snowstorm.

By the time Lettie got Nathan put down again for the night, both she and Luke were bone weary, yet both knew their work had just begun. Luke bolted the door and sat down on a crate quietly to smoke a thin cigar he'd taken from his gear. It was finally warm enough inside the cabin for them to take off their jackets. Luke even took off his shirt, under which he wore wool long johns. He watched Lettie take down her hair. "It's going to be hard, Lettie."

"I know. We can do it." She shook out her hair, turned to look at him. His long johns were unbuttoned, revealing the dark hairs on his chest. It was the first time she had seen him without a shirt on. Finally there was time to think about what had happened when they first arrived. She knew by the way his eyes moved over her that Luke was remembering it too. It had been beautiful. She wanted to feel that way again.

"Why don't you undress out here?" Luke asked, his voice soft.

The flames that flickered behind the open draft of the stove door cast ripples of light on her as she began removing her dress. She shivered, but she knew it was not from the cold. For the first time in her life a man would look upon her nakedness. The night of her attack, there had been only the rape. The men had not even removed all of her clothing. Luke would be the first man to set eyes on her breasts, to touch them, taste them. She was glad she had something left to give him that was still virgin, touched by no other man. She dropped her petticoats, removed her boots and stockings, unlaced her camisole.

Luke crushed out his smoke in a tin plate on the table, marveling that he had found someone so utterly beautiful on his way to Montana, that he had actually arrived here with a wife and a child to call his own. "Come here," he told her. He saw her nervousness as she approached and knelt in front of him. She closed her eyes when he moved his hands inside the camisole and pushed it away from her full breasts. They were firm, the nipples a lovely pink. He pulled the camisole down her arms and tossed it aside, gently grasped her breasts, caressing them, toying with her nipples, until he saw her breathing quicken. Her head was flung back, her hair hanging in a cascade of waves down her back. He kissed her eyes, her lips. "They never touched you here, did they?" he said.

Lettie grasped his wrists. "No," she whispered. She opened her eyes to meet his gaze. He leaned down, licking at the white swell of her breasts, then took a nipple into his mouth, gently sucking, pulling, creating a sharp need deep in her belly. She grasped his hair, offered herself gladly, enthralled at these wondrous new feelings he created in her. "Luke," she groaned, breathing deeply when he moved to her other breast to taste its sweet fruit.

"Lettie, you're so beautiful," he whispered. He picked her up in his arms, carried her behind the makeshift curtain, and laid her on the bed. Lettie had spread the bearskin blanket over the top of the feather mattress, then covered that with more blankets. She sank into the pile of softness. Luke bent to remove her bloomers. As she lay there naked she curled up her knees and watched him undress, allowing herself to look at that part of man that had held such terrors for her.

"Don't ever be afraid of it again, Lettie," he told her. He moved onto the bed, stretched out beside her. She ran a hand over his powerful arm, across his broad shoulders.

His lips met hers, and in spite of their weariness, their passion was too powerful to ignore. He moved between her legs, grasped one leg under the knee and pushed it farther to the side, and in the next instant he was surging inside of her for the second time in one day. He pulled a blanket over them. Again they were lost in each other, oblivious to anything around them, ignoring the dangers, sure their love would hold them together whatever the future held.

Outside the bobcat prowled, searching for wild

rabbits, perhaps some rats. It decided not to invade the realm of the humans who had moved into its territory... not yet. And in the foothills and distant mountains wolves began their nightly howling at the moon and to each other, making sure to remind any humans who came into this land who *really* belonged here.

Something else also prowled and watched, something human in form, but more animal in instinct and senses. A teenage Indian brave named Red Hawk sat on his spotted horse watching the cabin. A tiny bit of light created by a dimly lit lantern inside shone through one small window, the only sign of life in the dark night. Red Hawk turned to his father, a fierce-looking and honored warrior who sat beside his son on his own horse. The boy admired his father greatly, was proud of the deep scar on one side of the man's nose, where a Crow Indian had cut it partly off. That Crow man had died a slow, painful death at the hands of the mighty Sioux warrior. It was after that fierce raid that Red Hawk's father had taken the name Half Nose, a name feared by all white settlers and even some Indians in the region.

"Should we go and kill them, Father?" Red Hawk asked in the Sioux tongue.

Half Nose watched quietly for a few minutes. "No. He has a woman and child with him. He is one of those who has come to stay. He will still be here when the grass grows green again, when we come back to the mountains from the sacred winter grounds. Perhaps by then he will have more horses, something worth stealing. We have no use for oxen or mules."

"He has one good horse, that red one we watched him put in the shed when it was still light."

"Yes, and we will take it! He will never know we were here until he finds it gone in the morning. Then he will know how quietly a Sioux brave can take whatever he wants. He is new to this land. He has much to learn."

Half Nose grinned. "We shall teach him and have a good laugh over it. We will take his horse, then get back to our camp. Tomorrow we must head south and east. Winter is coming."

"Perhaps he and the woman and child will not last until the grass is green again. Perhaps they will die from the cold."

Half Nose laughed lightly. "Perhaps." He nodded. "They will learn that they cannot own this land. The land will own *them*. It will swallow them up and spit them out!" Half Nose dismounted, and his son followed suit. Both men crept down the hill with the stealth of the bobcat that prowled in the thick woods beyond the cabin. They sneaked into the shed where Luke kept his horse and mules, using their skill with animals to keep them quiet while they untied Red. They led the horse back up the hill and rode off into the night.

Inside the cabin, Luke and Lettie lay sleeping, naked body against naked body, dreaming of the empire they had come here to build together.

Five

"HELLO THERE!"

Lettie studied the man who had shouted the words, a bearded, burly-looking man named Will Doolan, whom Luke had already learned was thirty-five years old and once scouted for wagon trains headed to California and Oregon. The man stood on the porch of his sturdy-looking log home east of Billings, a piece of property Lettie thought was not nearly as pretty a setting as the one Luke had chosen, but then Luke had gone into country still prowled by outlaws and Indians alike, country beautiful because of its wildness.

"Hello, Will," Luke called back.

Doolan stepped off the porch, the fringes of his buckskin jacket moving with him. In the past two weeks the weather had remained stable, cold but bearable, not a lot of snow so far. Lettie wore a heavy wool shawl and a wool scarf wrapped around her head and neck. Nathan was wrapped in several blankets. Luke waved to the man as he steered the wagon in which they rode up close to Doolan's house. A huge dog chained to the corner of the cabin began barking wildly at their arrival. It was a beautiful animal, looked as though it had to be part wolf.

"Shut up, Bear!" Will ordered the animal.

The dog quieted, but it watched them warily. The front door of the cabin opened then, and a woman appeared, smiling. Lettie knew it must be Henrietta Doolan. Luke had met Will the first time they arrived at Billings, and the man had told him to come by for a visit anytime. All Lettie knew about these two was what Luke had been able to learn in town—that they had been here for about ten years, struggling against Indians and the elements to build a ranch, a man with the same dream Luke had. The couple was childless.

The woman Lettie saw in the doorway looked as though she had once been very pretty, but now her hair showed gray, and her face was beginning to wrinkle considerably. Lettie wondered if she was really a lot older than Will, or if the harsh living out here had just aged her well beyond her actual years. She was a little heavyset, but still had a nice shape.

"Henny, this here is the new couple I told you I met in town about three weeks ago—Luke and Lettie Fontaine. Luke went on west of Billings to see about claiming some land there."

"West!" Henrietta exclaimed in a rich voice. She looked surprised. "Well, what brave souls you are! Welcome! Do come in!" In spite of the cold, the woman rushed out to take Nathan from Lettie's arms so Lettie could climb down from the wagon.

Luke got down from his side and tied the lead mules, then shook Will's hand. "My wife could use a woman's company," he said with a grin. "This is the first time away from her mother and sister and the rest of her family."

"Well, I understand that feeling," Henrietta said in a friendly voice. Lettie smiled at the woman, and they exchanged a look of longing, both of them delighted to have another woman to talk to.

"I'm afraid I'm a bit of a city girl," she told Henrietta, taking Nathan back into her own arms. "I'm from St. Joseph, Missouri."

A distant loneliness shone in Henrietta's eyes. "Well, I was raised in a city myself. I came west from Chicago in '49 with my family. My father was on his way to California to look for gold. I took one look at our scout, who happened to be Will here, and I fell in love. I was only sixteen, Will was twenty-one. We got married at Fort Laramie, and I lived there for about five years while Will continued to lead wagon trains west—didn't get to see him much." She led Lettie toward the house. "We both finally got tired of being apart so much, and Will was always the type who hated too much civilization, so he chose to come up here to settle."

The woman rattled on nonstop, and Lettie sensed she needed to talk. She wondered if it would be that way for her in a few years, hungering for company, aging ahead of her years. If her figuring was right, the woman couldn't be more than thirty years old. She looked fifty.

"Luke and I had to come to town for more supplies," she explained as she walked inside the cabin. "Luke wants to get some tar paper for our cabin, and we need to stock up on more food."

"Well, out here it's a must that you get to know your neighbors, even if they're eight or ten miles away. You never know when you'll need them," Henrietta answered rather wistfully. "Please, take off your wrap and sit down. And let me see your little son! Will told me the boy's father was killed back in Kansas. I'm so sorry. I'm glad you found a good man who can be a father to him."

Lettie felt a flow of love for Luke at the words. In spite of the hardships and loneliness of the past three weeks, she couldn't be happier with the man she had chosen for a husband. The days were long and filled with back-breaking work that left them both exhausted at night, yet there had been few nights when they hadn't found the energy to explore the wonders of their passion. Luke was a good father to Nathan, always took time for the boy, even on the days when he worked so hard cutting and stacking wood and building fences for the animals that he could hardly walk straight when he came in at night.

"Yes, Luke is a good man," she said. "I met him

much the same way you met Will—on a wagon train west. My family was headed for Denver. I just couldn't bring my self to let Luke go on alone when we reached Julesberg. I had to make a decision, and I know it was the right one." She set Nathan down, and he toddled off to explore the cabin. "Luke wrote out a paper for me back at Fort Laramie, where we married. He put it in writing that he has legally adopted Nathan, giving him full rights to anything Luke owns. He even had it witnessed. He wanted it as legal as possible, considering there are no judges out here for such things. I told him it wasn't necessary to put it in writing, but he insisted, not just for me, but for Nathan's sake in future years. Nathan already looks to him like a father."

"And what a fine-looking little boy! Look at that blond hair! Oh, you're so lucky, Mrs. Fontaine." Lettie felt sorry for her, realized she must be longing for the child she'd never had. Henrietta watched Nathan a moment, then took a deep breath, as though to shake off bad memories of her own. "I don't know why these men can't choose to settle in civilized places," she said then, as though to change the subject deliberately. "They have their big dreams of getting rich by claiming all this land for themselves, but the price many of them pay makes me wonder if it's worth it." She turned to take some cups down from where they hung under a shelf of dishes.

The words worried Lettie, and this time it was she who changed the subject. "You have a wonderful home here," she spoke up, looking around the spacious main room. A huge stone fireplace graced one wall, and there were many shelves for pans and dishes built into another, as well as a countertop for the dishpan and water buckets. Braided rugs were scattered on the clean, hardwood floor and curtains hung at the windows. Although the pine table and chairs in the center of the room were hand-made, they were very well built and varnished to a shine.

She noticed a curtained doorway at the back wall, which she supposed led to a separate bedroom, something that would be a luxury for her right now. Lettie longed for just such a home.

"Well, thank you, but it wasn't always this way." Henrietta set the cups on the table, then took down some plates. "I do hope you intend to stay for supper. I'll have it ready soon." She set the plates on the table, then took a moment to admire Lettie's startling beauty as she removed her hat and coat. She ached at the thought of the hardships that lay ahead for the young woman. She could tell by Lettie's lovely green velvet dress that she was accustomed to a far different way of life. She wondered how long it would take the poor girl to start wondering if she had made a grave mistake. "In fact, you should stay the night."

"Oh, we couldn't do that. We're going back to Billings. We'll stay the night there and head home in the morning."

Henrietta self-consciously smoothed her own simple calico dress, then pushed a strand of hair behind her ear. It had fallen from the clumsy knot into which she had twisted her hair that morning. She walked over to the fireplace to stir a pot of stew that hung over the flames. "Nonsense. If you're going to stay in town, then you might as well stay here with us. You'll have company, and Luke can talk half the night to Will, learn a few things he'll need to know for the long winter ahead. My goodness, it isn't often we get company. It will be the same for you. Take advantage of the moment, Mrs. Fontaine. That's what you have to do in these parts." The woman picked up a hot pad and wrapped it around the handle of a big tin coffeepot. She carried the pot over to the table.

"Well, it's up to Luke," Lettie answered. "And please call me Lettie. My real name is Eletta, but Lettie is easier."

Henrietta smiled. "Well, most call me Henny, same reason. You can do the same." She poured coffee into two cups. "You do drink coffee, don't you? Would you rather have tea?"

"Coffee is fine."

Nathan let out a little scream, then a giggle, shoving his stuffed horse into his mother's lap as he ran past her, chasing a cat. Henrietta laughed. "That's Patch. The dog outside is called Bear. With no children, I have to have my pets for company, or go mad. Be glad you have your son, Lettie, and that you'll probably have more. That's good. Out here a woman needs children to keep her occupied and give her someone to talk to."

Before Lettie could reply, both men came inside, their big frames seeming to fill the room. Just then Nathan caught Patch's tail and the cat let out a screech. Frightened, Nathan ran to Luke, who picked him up with a laugh.

"You'd better stay away from that cat," he told the boy.

"Bad kee-kee." Nathan pouted.

"Well, it's also bad to chase the poor kitty all over the room, young man," Luke scolded gently. He patted Nathan's bottom before setting him down again so he could remove his own coat. Nathan went to his mother, climbing onto her lap and hugging his stuffed horse close.

"Looks like Indians already paid Luke here a visit," Will told his wife, pulling out a chair. "Have a seat, Luke. You two will stay for supper and spend the night here—no arguments."

Luke looked at Lettie questioningly.

She shrugged. "Henny already insisted. It's up to you."

"If you're going to stay in town, you might as well stay here," Will's wife put in, repeating what she had just told Lettie. "We won't take no for an answer, and it might be a long time before your poor wife gets to visit again. You never know when a snowstorm will hit and keep you buried for months."

Luke grinned. "All right. If you insist."

"What's this about Indians?" Henny asked Will.

"Luke got his horse stole the first night he settled in."

"My *only* horse," Luke added. "I came to Billings to see about getting a couple more. I need a horse when I go out hunting. Someone in town told me I could buy horses from Will."

"That you can," Henrietta answered. "We're in the horse trading business. Will is also a blacksmith, a scout, a gunsmith, and a farmer. You name it, Will can do it."

They all chuckled, but Lettie had not missed the worry in Henrietta's eyes when she'd asked about Indians. "Well, I hope it wasn't ol' Half Nose that visited you. He's a mean one," Henny said then, her smile fading.

"It could have been him," Will spoke up. "It would be just like him to steal one horse like that, just to tease you—let you know he's around but choosin' his own time to give you trouble. It's likely that whoever it was, they've headed south now to their winter camping grounds. You won't have any more trouble till spring." He frowned, leaning closer to Luke and resting his elbows on the table. "You start gathering many horses and cattle, you'd better get some help out there—hire you a couple of men to help watch over things. It's not safe you being out there alone with a wife and kid come spring. There's outlaws to worry about too."

Luke nodded. "I'll keep that in mind. I've gotten pretty damn good with my guns, if I must say so myself, and I'm teaching Lettie to shoot."

"Just the same, you get some help. I might mosey over that way myself come spring, see if there's anything I can do. You're determined to stay put then, are you?"

Luke glanced at Lettie. God, how he loved her, but even that love could not keep him from doing what he

knew he had to do to realize his dream. He knew deep
in his gut that someday this was all going to pay off big.
He looked back at Will. "I am. I've already given David
Taylor a general description of what I'm claiming. In the
spring, once all the snow is gone and I don't have to be
so concerned about getting in meat and wood, I'll ride
the perimeter, stake my boundaries, write down a better
description of landmarks and so forth."

"Well, technically, under the Homestead Act, you're
only supposed to claim a hundred and sixty acres," Will
told him in a rich, gruff voice. He winked then. "But
Taylor can be convinced to stretch that some. I'll be glad
to let you stake out another hundred and sixty in my
name, another section in Henny's name. You can even
claim more in your wife's maiden name." He grinned.
"There's ways of gettin' around the law out here, Luke.
You remember that. Me, I'm too old to worry about
gettin' really big. I'm happy with the five hundred acres
I've got. But from what you've told me about your plans
for raisin' cattle, you'll need a lot more than that. I'll
help you get it however I can. I'm just glad to see new
people come in. A man can build an empire up here, if
he's smart and willin' to work hard and put up with the
danger and hardships." The man glanced at Lettie. "It
can be real hard on a woman, though, sometimes harder
than on the man."

"I can already see that, Will," Lettie answered the
man. She looked at Luke, saw the apology in his eyes.
"Someday we'll be glad for what we put up with in
the beginning." She looked back at Will. "If Luke says
he'll be a rich man someday and I'll have a fine home, I
believe him."

Will grinned again, looking back at Luke. "You've
got one hell of a woman there, Luke, brave, and pretty
to boot. She's already given you one son, and if she can
give you more, that's just all the more free help you'll

have down the road. Have as many kids as you can. I guess I would have tried harder to build my place into somethin' bigger if I had kids to inherit it, but it's just me and Henny, so we don't need much more."

Lettie noticed the fallen look on Henrietta's face, and her heart went out to the woman. She was sure Will didn't mean for his remark to hurt, but how could it not? Nathan squirmed to get down, and he clung to the horse as he pointed to Patch with a scowl. He watched the cat carefully, staying close to his mother.

"I'll say one thing," the man continued, "a man couldn't ask for a better woman than my Henny, or a better cook. How's that stew comin', Henny?"

"It will be ready in a few minutes." The woman poured Luke and Will a cup of coffee.

Will leaned back in his chair, rubbing at his beard. "Now, as far as the Indians, you're better off lettin' them take a horse or two once in a while than to try to fight them," he warned Luke. "I know that sounds ridiculous, but for the trouble they can cause, it's worth losin' a few horses now and then. They're still pretty free up here, and until the war is over and the army can concentrate on helping people like us, we're on our own in land the Sioux figure is theirs by right. You rile somebody like Half Nose, and you've got big trouble."

"I'll keep that in mind," Luke answered. "But I'm not going to just sit and watch from the front porch while they pick and choose through my herds at will."

Lettie fought her horror at the thought of Indians. The morning they discovered Red was gone, the moccasin tracks in the snow had told them what had happened. That Indians had been so close by without their even knowing it had made Lettie sick with fear. She was sure Luke had felt the same fear, but he was determined not to show it, and his anger at being "taken" had far outweighed any fear he'd felt.

"Takes a special kind of dealin' to get along with the Sioux," Will was saying.

Lettie offered to help Henny serve the stew, but the woman refused. "I enjoy having the company," she insisted. "You've got your work cut out for you the next few weeks. When you get a chance to relax, enjoy it."

Lettie took heart from the visit. If she could have something at least as decent as this warm log house, she would be happy. Maybe someday she and Luke would have closer neighbors, women with whom she could visit, make quilts, talk about children.

For the rest of the evening the men talked about horses and cattle and the future of Montana; the women talked about dress styles back East, the fine china Henny had been given by her mother when she was left at Fort Laramie to marry Will. She had managed to preserve and protect the precious dishes. "Broke only one plate and one cup over all the years and all the traveling," she bragged. Her father had never found gold, but he and the rest of her family had settled in California. Henny had never seen them again, a thought that brought pain to Lettie's heart.

It was nearly dark when Will and Luke went out to look at some of Will's horses. Lettie helped Henny clean up. Nathan had taken to chasing the "kee-kee" again, and by dark, both boy and cat were worn out. In desperation the cat had taken refuge on top of the fireplace mantel. Nathan climbed back into Lettie's lap, where he fell asleep, clutching his horse.

Henny laid out a feather mattress near the fireplace. "You and Luke will have to share this mattress with the boy tonight. It's all we've got. I think you'll be comfortable enough."

Lettie smiled. "It can't be any worse than what we sleep on now," she answered. "Just a feather mattress covered with a bearskin rug and several blankets. The cabin is so cold. It's nothing more than a bunch of flat boards nailed to supports, with cracks in between. We have to keep the iron heating stove practically red-hot to stay warm. That's why Luke bought the tar paper. He's having a supplier in Billings bring out some bales of hay. He'll stack them around the outside of the cabin to help insulate it against the winter winds. Next spring we'll build a decent log house like this one." She got up from the rocker where she sat and laid Nathan on the feather bed. She covered him, then bent over to kiss his chubby cheek. "It's Nathan I worry about—either getting sick from a draft or burning himself on the iron stove."

Henny sat down in a rocker near the fire. "Just be glad you've got a young one to *be* worried about. The good Lord chose not to bless me with a child. I guess ours is not to question his decisions."

Lettie joined Henny before the fire. "I'm sorry, Henny."

The woman smiled sadly. "Don't be. It certainly isn't your fault. I hope you have many children, Lettie, and that you'll let me help you however I can when they come. In this land you need good friendships." She glanced at the doorway at the sound of her husband's bellowing laughter. He was just outside smoking with Luke. "And you need a good, strong man who loves you no matter what. That's what I have in Will. If I didn't love him so, I'd have gone crazy up here." She leaned forward, resting her elbows on her knees. "You've got to be very strong, Lettie. And if you really love your man, you'll let him live his dream and not try to stop him. Sometimes that means giving up some dreams of your own, but Luke is young and determined. I think someday he'll make a good life for you, if you can survive these first few years. And if you're real clever about it, you can finagle a man into doing anything you want him to do for you. Luke certainly loves you and the boy. Anyone can see that." Her kind brown eyes glittered with good wishes, but they also showed concern. "I hope the best for both of you. I can see you aren't used to this kind of life, but Luke has said it will get better, and it will. You just have to hang on. A man's success depends a lot on his woman, you know."

Lettie felt tears threatening. Sometimes she wanted to scream and weep, wondering how she was going to get through even one winter here, so far from family and the comforts of home. "Luke's love is the only thing that keeps me going. There is something he needs to prove to himself and to his father, and I want to help him do it. At the same time—" She stared into the flickering flames in the fireplace. "I'm grateful that he loves me, especially for how he loves Nathan. It isn't easy for a man to take so well to another man's son." *Especially when he's the product of rape.* No, she would not mention that. That was behind her now. Luke had come here to start a new life, and so had she. He had shown her how good it can be between a man and a woman. She had to forget the ugliness of the past, for Nathan's sake as well as her own.

"Oh, but the boy is so sweet and obedient."

"Not always." Lettie smiled. "We met when Nathan ran away from me and nearly got trampled by a couple of horses. Luke saved him. Nathan is so energetic, and since he learned to walk, he's taking full advantage."

Henny laughed. "Well, he's all boy, that's for sure. He'll be a big help to Luke someday."

"Yes, I suppose."

Henny leaned back in her rocker, and to Lettie's surprise she picked up a pipe, stuffed it, and lit it. Lettie had assumed the pipe on the stand beside the rocker was Will's. The woman puffed the pipe for a few seconds, then glanced at Lettie, noticing the shock in her eyes. She grinned. "Honey, don't be surprised at anything you see up here. A woman gets lonely, she looks for things to soothe her. Me, I like to smoke a pipe. I figured you might as well know it. Lord knows a woman can fast forget her femininity up here." She winked. "But you, you're too pretty for that. Maybe you'll bring some class to Billings and its surroundings. You buy yourself plenty of those fancy creams to keep that face from being ruined by the wind and sun. Wear a bonnet with a good wide brim on it in summer, and always be a woman. Did you go to school?"

Lettie finally managed to find her voice. "I…yes. I had ten years of schooling."

"Well, that's more than most folks in these parts." The woman pointed the stem of the pipe at her. "I predict that someday Mrs. Lettie Fontaine will be the first lady of Billings. We need more women like you here. We need schools and churches and all those things. Women like you will help see that we get them. Stick to your guns, Lettie. Be stronger than the land and the elements. Don't let them conquer you. *You* conquer *them*."

Lettie was still recovering from the sight of a woman smoking a pipe. "I'll try," she replied faintly.

The men came inside then, and all four of them talked well into the night. Bear was allowed inside, and the big dog curled up in front of the hearth. Will stoked up the fire before he retired with Henny. Then Luke and Lettie snuggled into the feather mattress without undressing, except for removing their boots. Lettie pulled Nathan close, and the cat he had chased all afternoon and evening quietly jumped into Henny's rocker and went to sleep on the padded seat.

Lettie pressed her back against Luke's chest, and he wrapped his arms around her.

"Can we have a cabin like this next spring?" she asked.

"It will be better than this."

"I think they'll be good friends, Luke. Did you know Henny smokes a pipe?" she whispered.

"I saw her when I came in." He kissed her hair. "You won't take to smoking pipes, will you? I'd rather you didn't."

Lettie laughed quietly. "I don't think you have to worry about that."

"This might be your last visit for quite a while, Lettie. I'm sorry."

Grasping his hand, Lettie said, "Henny says a man's success depends on his woman. I want to help you, Luke, and I hope I can give you lots of children to also help; but I also want to teach them to read and write. If a preacher ever comes to Billings and we have a church, I want the children to go. I want them to know about the finer things in life."

"Someday they'll *have* the finer things. We'll bring in a professional tutor. We'll have a ranch so big that I'll have help living right there, with their own families. We'll need our own school. Will thinks my idea of building a cattle ranch is a good one. He agrees there will be a big demand for beef after the war, and once the railroad is completed, it will be a bonanza for men who get a head start. God knows there's plenty of grass here for grazing big herds. Next spring I'm going to see about running down some wild horses, and it's possible I can get some beef at good prices out of Oregon. There is always a market for good horses, and the beef market is growing."

It was obvious Luke Fontaine was already deeply entrenched in the new land and new way of life. There was no going back now. The reality of that fact hit Lettie harder every day. She thought about St. Joseph, about her family, the friends left behind, the companionship of her mother and sister. That was all gone now. Her only friend since arriving here was a hardened, pipe-smoking woman who lived too far away to visit very often. Luke would have to be not only a provider, protector, and lover, he would also have to be her friend. There was no one else. Sometimes she felt so close to him, yet she realized they still hardly knew each other at all, in spite of their intimacy. "I love you, Luke."

He kissed her ear. "And I love you," he whispered.

Outside the wolves began their nightly calling, and Bear raised his head, whining softly, his tail wagging. Lettie watched his eyes, a bright orange in the glow of the firelight, and it seemed the wildness she saw there could also be found in Luke, a yearning to be master of their territory, to answer to no one. There had been a look in his eyes the morning he'd found Red missing. Already he was thinking of the little cabin and the surrounding valley and foothills as "his land." With no law out there, a man had to do his own defending and set his own rules, and that frightened her, but she was not going to let him know. Nor was she going to tell him yet that she suspected she was already pregnant.

"Don't let the land change you," she said softly.

She got no reply. His deep, steady breathing told her he was asleep.

Six

LETTIE TOOK THE IRON FROM WHERE IT SAT HEATING on the stove and began pressing a dress as best she could, using the table to iron on. Clothes hung all around her, pinned to ropes Luke had fastened from one wall to another, as there was no other way to hang a wash in the dead of winter. Even in the best of weather, wash day was difficult enough. Now it was even harder, carrying in bucket after bucket of snow to melt on top of the stove in order to have enough water to wash with, trying to find enough room in the little cabin to hang everything, helping Luke carry the washtub outside to dump it when she was through.

Having to make her way amid long johns and drawers, pants and shirts that seemed to fill the tiny cabin and hang nearly to the floor because of the low ceiling only added to Lettie's feelings of being trapped. She ironed almost frantically, wondering how much longer it would be before she lost her sanity entirely. Winter had come hard and fast, and for four months now, to her recollection, it had snowed every single day. Most of those days the wind blew in howling wails that made her want to plug her ears. She longed for total quiet, ached for warm sunshine and green grass. She wanted to be able to go outside without dressing like an Eskimo, to run through flowers.

Luke was gone most of every day, kept busy just shoveling snow in order to keep the wood supply and the animals from being buried. Now there was a tunnel going from the front of the cabin to the shed where the four mules and two horses were kept, as well as a pen for chickens so that they could have fresh eggs, although in such weather the hens did not do much laying. Another tunnel led from the cabin to the outhouse. Luke had made several more trips into Billings before the snows closed up the road completely, bringing back feed for the animals, which he kept covered in two wagon beds. The problem was, he had no building in which to store the hay and alfalfa and bags of grain, and the feed attracted other animals. Deer and elk managed to dig through the snow and have their share, and Luke feared he would run out of feed before spring melt allowed the animals to graze. Some nights he was up for hours, sitting out in the bitter cold guarding the feed. The only advantage to the problem was that they had plenty of fresh meat for themselves. At least Luke had not had to go out hunting for game. Animals after an easy meal made that job easy for him.

She folded the shirt she had been ironing and laid it aside. She glanced at the mantel clock her mother had given her, which sat on a shelf against the wall. Two a.m. She and Luke should both be asleep, but the wicked winter weather had totally upset their normal schedule. Lettie could not sleep because of the constant wind and the feeling of being buried alive. Sometimes she feared that if she went to sleep, perhaps she would never wake up again. She and Luke and Nathan would lie in this frozen wasteland, their bones found years later. If she stayed awake, she wouldn't die; she wouldn't be lost forever to civilization. Were there really other people out there somewhere? Were there really cities? Theaters? Railroads? Churches? Schools? Were her parents and family happily settled in Denver now, near supply stores and doctors, banks and eateries?

She set the iron back on the stove, checked on Nathan, who slept soundly on his bed. The boy didn't seem at all distressed by being buried up here. Thank

God he was a good boy. He took pleasure in the simplest things, like a tin cup and some little stones. He thrilled in going out with Luke into the winter wonderland just outside the door. He had no problem with cabin fever. Will and Henny had warned them about that before they parted, told them they'd have to guard against the loneliness that would hit them before winter was over.

She walked to the front door, leaned against it. It wasn't just the loneliness that made her want to scream, this aching need to have a nice visit with another woman, to go to town and see other people; what troubled her the most was this constant fear that something would happen to Luke, or that there would be an avalanche and they would all be buried alive, that they would all either freeze or starve to death before the snow ever melted enough for them to get back to town and restock their supplies. She reminded herself there was plenty of meat, but as the snow continued to fall and the loneliness and isolation set in even deeper, no supply of food seemed to be enough. If Luke were to get hurt…or die…she wasn't even sure how to get back to town, and here she was four months pregnant.

She looked down and touched her belly, which was just beginning to swell. What if the baby came early? Even if it didn't, there was no doctor in Billings, and they were so far from town and from Will and Henny. Who would help her? What if Luke was off hunting when the baby came?

She listened at the door, worried about Luke. He had gone out two hours ago with his rifle, determined to lie in wait for the cougar that had returned a few nights ago to raid the chickens and cause havoc among the other animals. Every night since then Luke had watched for the cat's return, and every time he went out, Lettie lived in terror. Maybe he would miss, be attacked himself.

There was no use looking out the one and only

window. Wood was stacked against it. She thought how hard Luke had worked cutting and storing that wood, from dawn to dark for weeks. Now it was piled on the little front porch and far beyond. The tar paper and hay piled around the cabin helped protect it against the fierce winds, but the snow had fallen so deep that it came nearly to the rooftop, creating a natural insulation that worked much better than the hay.

There was nothing to hear, nothing but the constant moaning wind and the swishing sound of new snow drifting and whispering against the door. She turned away, ducked through and around the maze of clothes, took down another shirt to iron. She had just folded it when she heard the distant screech of the cougar. A chill moved through her, and she set the iron back on the stove and hurried to the door. There it was—another shrieking growl, then a gunshot. A second gunshot!

"Luke!" she whispered. She grabbed a cloak from a hook near the door and ran out, putting it on as she ran through the tunnellike pathway toward the shed. "Luke!" This time she screamed his name. God, it felt good to scream. Yes, that was what she needed to do. Over and over she shouted his name, needing to hear her voice above the wind, needing to hear it just to know she was still alive and not lost to the rest of the world. It was dark. So dark! Where was he! Did the cougar have its fangs buried in her husband's throat? She put her hands against the wall of snow, feeling her way toward the little shelter Luke had built for the chickens.

Someone grabbed her then, and she gasped.

"Lettie, what the hell are you doing out here screaming like that?"

She collapsed against him, clinging to his fur jacket. How could she make him understand? Oh, how she loved him, was grateful that he loved Nathan and her. She wanted so to be a good wife, not to be a burden.

How could she tell him of her terror? How could she tell him that even though she loved him so, she felt she'd go insane if she couldn't talk to other human beings soon? How could she complain to him of this feeling of being buried alive, that it seemed summer would never come again, that she was deathly afraid of giving birth up here alone? She felt selfish and ungrateful, and yet it all flooded over her to the point where she could not control it.

"I thought you were dead! What would I do, Luke, if something happened to you? Nathan and I would die out here! I can't stand it, Luke. I can't stand any more snow, any more wind. I feel as though I'm going crazy! I want to go to town. I want to see other people! I want to feel the sun and smell flowers. And I miss my family so much!"

She broke into bitter sobbing, hating herself for what she was saying, yet unable to stop the words from coming. She waited for his own tirade, realizing he had to be having much the same feelings, with the added burden of knowing their survival depended a great deal on him, that they were buried alone here because of his decision to come to Montana.

To her surprise he picked her up in his arms and began carrying her to the house. "The cougar's dead," he said matter-of-factly. It seemed a strange statement in the middle of her fit of crying. "We both need to sleep. Will told me lack of sleep can affect the mind." He carried her inside the cabin, laid her on their makeshift bed.

"The ironing—" she started to protest.

"To hell with it. Lord knows you've got all day tomorrow to do it. Who cares, anyway, if our clothes are a little wrinkled? There's nobody to see but Nathan and the animals. You stay right there."

Lettie took a handkerchief from the pocket of her skirt, sat up to wipe at her tears and unlace her boots. For more warmth, they had removed the blanket they had originally hung to close off the corner where they slept, and she watched Luke stoke up the fire. He had rigged a snow shelter on the porch where milk, eggs, and meat could be kept cool but packed in enough snow that they would not freeze. He went out and brought in a covered bucket of milk, taking a ladle and dipping some into a tin cup. He set the cup on the stove and carried the milk back outside. When he returned, Lettie realized how tired he looked. He was also limping. She knew the cold weather made his injured leg ache, and she loved him for his silent, uncomplaining suffering, feeling guilty for her own whining.

"I'll warm this milk, and I want you to drink it," he told her. "It will help relax you. You're carrying. You've got to get more rest." He took off his jacket and walked over to hang it near the door. "Left my rifle out in the shed. I guess it'll be okay till morning. We sure don't have to worry about Indians or outlaws in this weather. Even the deer and elk have stopped coming around. They can't get through the snow."

It seemed to Lettie that he was just trying to make conversation to hear his own voice, and it struck her that he'd probably had visitations of insanity just the same as she.

"I'm sorry, Luke, for throwing such a fit."

For the first time since he'd brought her inside, he met her gaze. "It won't be like this next winter. You'll be in a nice cabin like Will and Henny have. You'll have that new baby to take care of, your own bedroom, some furniture. I'll get you a real cookstove. Will told me sometimes a salesman comes through Billings with books. We'll buy up the whole lot if we have to, so we'll have things to read come winter. We'll build our cabin farther down toward the valley where I'll build corrals for all the horses and cattle I'll be collecting. They might be able to find some of that good grass through the snow, and we won't go through so much extra feed. Eventually we'll have a big barn, hire some help. Hired help means company in winter. It won't always be like this, Lettie," he repeated.

She closed her eyes and looked at her lap. "I know. I guess…" She shook her head. "If only the wind would stop."

Luke brought her the cup of milk, holding a hot pad under it. "Here. Hold it with the pad. Drink it all."

Lettie took it gratefully, swallowing some of the warm milk.

"You're okay, aren't you?" he asked. "I mean, the baby and all?"

"I'm fine." She met his eyes and saw a fear there she had not read before.

"Don't think I don't worry about you, Lettie. I promise that when it comes close to time to deliver, I'll get you some help, and I won't do anything that takes me far from home. You won't be alone."

He stood up and removed his boots, walked over to bolt the door, then leaned down to kiss Nathan's cheek. "Must be nice to be a little kid and not worry about anything," he told her as he shoved aside shirts and underwear to get back to her.

Lettie finished the milk and set the cup aside. "Sometimes he's like a little ray of sunshine," she answered. She moved under the covers, too tired even to bother removing her clothes and put on a nightgown. Because there was no one to see her, she'd gotten in the habit of leaving off uncomfortable, stiff corsets and wore only a soft camisole and one petticoat under her dress, so she was perfectly comfortable going to bed this way. Luke removed his gun belt and pants, but left on his wool shirt. He got into bed beside her, pulled several blankets over them.

"At least we don't have to worry about whether or not we'll have eggs tomorrow," he told her. "I don't even know how big the cat was. I saw its eyes coming at me and I shot." He pulled her into his arms. "Don't think I don't get scared too, Lettie…and lonely." He rubbed a big hand over her stomach. "Any feeling of life yet?"

Lettie put her own hand over his. "Quite a bit of movement the last few days."

He held his hand there a moment, felt the flutter of life. He smiled. "Come spring, you'll see all kinds of new life, Lettie, green grass, wildflowers." He kissed her eyes. "Not long after that we'll have our first baby, yours and mine together."

She met his eyes in the soft light of the lamp they always kept burning in case Nathan woke up in the night. "Nathan won't like having to share you."

Luke grinned, and she realized she had not seen him smile in a long time. "He'll know he's loved."

And you need to know you're loved, don't you, Luke? "I really am sorry, Luke. You brought me here because you thought I was strong and brave and—"

"You are. Hell, a person has to let go of their feelings once in a while or lose their mind altogether. If you need to rant and rail at me, go ahead. It won't change anything, except to make you feel better. With all the snow out there, I couldn't take you out of here if I *wanted* to."

Lettie smiled, then began to laugh, realizing how right he was. "My mother told me once that sometimes it's better to laugh about things than cry about them. Maybe she was right."

Luke kissed her softly. "Maybe she was. I know I sure like the sound of it better."

He kept rubbing at her belly, and she saw the sudden want in his eyes. They had been so busy fighting the snow and wild animals and keeping warm that it had been days…no, weeks…since they had made love. She'd hardly realized it until this moment. "Luke," she whispered, touching his lips. "I need you."

He moved a hand to touch her breast, soft beneath her dress and camisole. "I've been afraid maybe I'd hurt the baby."

"I don't think you can hurt anything, not this early. Is that part of the reason you've worked so hard and kept yourself so busy?"

"Partly. Besides, I've seen you getting more and more lonely and depressed—figured it was all my fault and that you blamed me for it. I didn't think you'd want anything to do with me that way."

"Oh, Luke, that isn't true. All this time I've needed you more than ever, needed the closeness we shared when we first got here. I felt you pulling away, and it just made me even more lonely." She touched his hair. "Luke, we've got to tell each other how we're feeling, always. Here we've been needing each other so, and we've been pulling apart for all the wrong reasons. We should never let that happen, Luke. We're all we've got, just you and me and Nathan. We can't keep things inside and then blame the other for how we feel."

He sighed deeply, taking hold of her wrist and kissing the back of her hand. "I'm not used to letting loose of my feelings. After my father told me he didn't consider me his real son, I learned to shut off my feelings. It made everything easier, pretending nothing bothered me, ignoring the hurt."

"I don't want it to be that way between us."

Luke studied her green eyes, met her full lips. She responded almost desperately, and he knew that she needed to be touched, to feel alive, just as he did. Somehow it helped them shut out the howling wind and swirling snow and all the dangers that lurked just outside the door. He groaned when Lettie ran her hands over his chest, down to the hard bulge under his long johns. She massaged it gently, and he moved on top of her, strad- dling her as she sat up then to help him get her dress and camisole off. A little draft near the bed made her shiver, and her nipples hardened into ripe cherries. He leaned down and took one into his mouth.

It had been so long! Lettie gloried in the touch, grasped his hair and offered herself with the zest of a harlot. Tonight it seemed so necessary. She felt hungry for him. He pushed her back into the feather mattress, then grasped her drawers and pulled them off so that all she still wore were her knee-high hose. He pulled some blankets over them, and she spread her legs to let him settle between them as he came closer then to meet her mouth again in a deep, suggestive kiss. In the next moment he was inside of her, sliding himself over that secret place that made her forget all hardship, all loneliness, all danger. Now there was only the magic, this big, handsome man who was her husband invading her privacy in a most exciting, enjoyable way, warming her blood with a special kind of fire that made her arch against him, wanting more, more. Minutes later she felt the wonderful, gripping climax that made her gasp his name and work to pull him in as deeply as she could. He raised up to his knees, grasping her bottom and burying himself in rhythmic thrusts that reminded her why she had come to Montana…to be with this man who loved and needed her so, who loved Nathan like his own, who had a dream that must be her dream too. He had turned this act she once thought ugly into something beautiful.

His life spilled into her, and he breathed deeply for a few minutes before buttoning his long johns and relaxing beside her. He pulled the blankets over them again. "Let's not get up just yet." He groaned, kissing her neck. "I just want to hold you, Lettie. I want to stay just like this."

Lettie nestled into his shoulder, the sweet comfort of his strong arms bringing on a much-needed sleep. When she awoke, she was surprised to realize that Luke was gone from the bed. When she sat up she saw that Nathan too was gone. A pot of fresh coffee sat simmering on the stove, and although she couldn't see the light of day because of the barrier of wood and snow in front of the cabin's only window, she realized it must be morning.

She quickly rose and washed, surprised that she had slept through Luke's activity. She felt wonderful, relaxed, more at ease than she had in weeks. It was amazing what one night of spilling one's feelings and making love could do for a person. She combed her hair and twisted it into a bun, put on a clean dress. Today, finishing the ironing didn't seem like such a terrible chore. She took down most of the clothes. It occurred to her that something was different, but she couldn't figure out just what it was.

The door opened then, and Luke came inside carrying Nathan, who clung to his horse. "Well, Mommy is finally awake!" Luke exclaimed. He set Nathan down and the boy ran to her. Lettie picked him up and gave him a hug and a kiss.

"Mommy, shine!" he told her, pointing toward the door.

Lettie frowned. "Shine?"

"Come on outside. Nathan and I have something to show you," Luke answered.

"Don't you two want breakfast?"

"It will only take a few minutes." Luke threw her heavy shawl to her and took Nathan back into his own arms. When Lettie had put on the shawl, she followed them both outside. She realized when they got into the tunnel of snow that above it was a clear, blue sky. "Sunshine!" she exclaimed.

"That's what Nathan was trying to tell you," Luke answered. He climbed up a stairway of snow that he had dug from the tunnel so that a person could stand on top of it. He plunked Nathan on top, and the boy fell giggling into the snow. Luke took Lettie's hand and helped her up.

Lettie smiled in startled pleasure, realizing they were standing as high as the roof of the cabin. Glorious sunshine lit up the land for miles around, snowcapped mountains, sprinkled with the deep green of pine trees. Everything sparkled, and there was actually some warmth to the sunshine. "Oh, Luke, isn't it beautiful!"

"You see all that?" He waved his arm. "It's all going to be ours, Lettie. Someday I'll own this land for as far as you can see, and right down there in the valley is where our home will be, a big house, two, maybe three stories, lots of rooms for all the kids, lots of land for all the cattle. You've got to admit it's damn pretty."

"Oh, Luke." She turned in all directions. "Why didn't we think of climbing up here to see everything before? We've stayed buried in the cabin, making our way through tunnels like moles, when we could have been climbing up top and enjoying this wonderful freedom."

"This is the first nice day we've had since the snows started coming. And we've been so busy—" He put his arms around her from behind. "There's something else different. Do you realize what it is?"

She shook her head, puzzled, remembering that she had sensed something different as soon as she awakened.

"Listen, Lettie. Just listen."

She stood still, listening for a sound, then realized there *was* no sound. The air was utterly still, so quiet it almost hurt her ears. "No wind!" she said softly. "There's no wind!" She walked through soft snow that glittered like a fairyland, her feet sinking in some places, so that finally she just sat down in the snow and listened...to nothing... a glorious, wonderful quiet that brought tears to her eyes.

She looked back at Luke, her rock. He had remained calm through her fit of nerves last night, when he could have shouted right back at her. "Thank you, Luke." She threw her head back and breathed deeply. "For bringing me out here."

"Spring is just around the corner, Lettie."

She nodded. "Yes, it surely is."

Seven

Lettie took another blanket from the clothesline Luke had strung up for her outside. Spring had come just as suddenly as winter had, rapidly melting the snow through the month of April, at least in these lower elevations and in the valley even farther below, which at the moment was so full of water that part of it had turned into a small lake. Not too far from the cabin water rushed down from a mountain above, fresh, cold water. One simply needed to walk to the rocks where the waterfall was and hold the bucket under it. Luke was afraid the plentiful water would disappear or at least dwindle to a trickle in summer, but for now it was a godsend. All winter they had gotten their water by melting snow, or by bashing through the ice of a distant stream, a stream which now was more like a river.

It seemed Luke had spent most of his time through the winter hauling water and doing other chores to feed and protect the animals, as well as for his own family. Now the animals could be turned loose to graze, and they could drink all the water they wanted out of the stream. She could do her wash outside and hang her clothes in the fresh air; and they had stored more water in barrels left behind by whoever had lived here before them.

She had ached for the warm sunshine, and now it was here.

They had also been hit with two fierce and frightening thunderstorms. If their little shanty had been built a few yards to the left, it would have been completely washed away by the now-torrential creek; a few yards to the right, and it would have been enveloped and destroyed in an avalanche that had come roaring down from the mountains above only three weeks ago. The snow it had carried was mostly melted now, but from what they could tell when they inspected it, the swath of snow that had come down with it was several hundred feet wide. God had surely been with them, saving them from both flooding and from being buried alive.

She felt the life kicking inside of her. Six months pregnant, she was still not terribly big, but big enough for her condition to be obvious. It embarrassed her for Luke to see her naked, but he insisted she was more beautiful than ever because it was his baby she carried, another son for Luke Fontaine, or so they both hoped. Her condition had not interrupted their lovemaking, and when she thought about how gentle the man she had married could be, she loved him all the more. That love only increased when she remembered Luke's promise that no matter how many children they had, Nathan would be loved just as much, treated the same as the others. Luke was a good father to him, a devoted husband; and he was slaving away to keep every promise he had made to her.

She looked down the hill where he was working on the new cabin. He wanted it to be ready before the next winter. He was building it about two hundred yards below on a flat piece of land that was still higher than the valley. The spot would have a grand view of the foothills and mountains beyond the valley, and the area was big enough to build an even bigger home later. Luke had been careful to make sure it was an area unaffected by spring melt off, high enough that the floodwaters in the valley below could not reach it. It was a perfect site, and now Lettie was glad no one else had yet claimed this land.

As soon as he felt the road was passable, Luke intended to bring in some help to dig a well and build a windmill, finish the cabin, and build a barn. Lettie was worried he would work himself to death, as well as spend every last dime he had brought with him, but he was determined that by next winter life would be a little easier. As soon as he could get someone to stay there with her so he could leave for a few days, he intended to ride out and determine the boundaries of land he wanted to claim. Just how much he could claim legally, she wasn't sure, but he intended to get his hands on as much as possible, one way or another. She had decided she would not question the how of it. Owning it meant everything to him, and he was working so hard to make life better for her that she didn't have the heart to argue with him over how he would lay claim to all that he wanted when the Homestead Act allowed a man to settle on only one hundred and sixty acres. "No man can ranch on a little piece of land like that," he had complained. "Hell, there's more than one hundred sixty acres in the valley alone."

She folded the blanket and put it in a basket, then smiled when Nathan came running to her with some little blue flowers in his fist. He held them up to her with a proud smile. "For Mommy," he told her.

"Oh, thank you, Nathan," she told him, leaning down to take the flowers and kiss his cheek. She thanked God every day for his sweet nature. If he had not been such an easy child, she wasn't sure she could have survived the winter being cooped up in the tiny cabin, but the boy had seemed totally unaffected by the confinement. He was almost three now, his hair turning just a little bit darker blond, his eyes a pretty blue. She stuck the flowers into the bodice of her dress, between two buttons, then turned to take down a little more wash.

It was then she saw them coming, several riders and a herd of horses. Her smile faded as alarm set in. Could they be the outlaws Will and others had warned them about? Luke was leading one of the mules toward a pile of logs he was cutting and gathering for the new cabin. She was sure he didn't see the riders' approach, and she called his name as loudly as she could. Luckily the wind was behind her, and it carried her voice. When he looked up, she pointed across the valley. As soon as he saw what she was pointing at, he grabbed his rifle and headed up the hill toward the cabin.

"Get Nathan inside!" he yelled. She could barely make out the words. She picked up Nathan and ran into the cabin. Minutes later Luke got there, panting. He closed and bolted the door. "Get the other rifle down and make sure it's loaded!" he ordered. "Get the ammunition out here where it's handy, and get my handgun too."

Lettie obeyed without question, her heart pounding with fear. She ordered Nathan into a corner, telling him it was a game and it was very important that he stay there. "Do you think it's outlaws?" she asked Luke.

"Who else would be heading here with a herd of horses?" He cocked the rifle. "Let's just hope they'll deal with us. I'm glad now that wood and hay are still stacked around the cabin. They will make a good barrier and keep bullets from crashing through these thin cabin walls if those men out there decide to start shooting."

Lettie almost laughed at the remark. She had been after Luke to get rid of the hay because it was starting to smell, but now she was glad it was still there. She cocked the second rifle and knelt at the small window, which was hinged. She pushed it open and pointed a rifle through it. The wood that had been stacked outside the window had been used up to the point that it was below the window now, so she had a good view of the front of the cabin. No one could approach from behind because the little building was set against the side of a hill, and there were no other windows.

Luke strapped on his handgun, then checked to be sure his repeating rifle was fully loaded.

"Hey, somebody's buildin' a cabin down there!" someone shouted in the distance. "Looks like somebody's been livin' here, Cade!"

"Two riders are coming," Lettie told Luke. Her stomach tightened into a knot when Luke unbolted the door.

"Be ready to bolt this again if something happens to me," he warned her. He stepped outside and closed the door as two men arrived at the front of the house. They drew up their horses, looking surprised. Neither of them was clean-shaven, nor were their clothes clean. They looked well armed. Lettie shivered at the realization of how outnumbered Luke was. She felt suddenly naked, exposed to the lawlessness of this land, where the only code was survival of the fittest…or maybe the meanest.

"Well, well, what do we have here?" one of the men spoke up, a thin cigar between his teeth as he spoke. "Trespassers."

"You're the ones trespassing," she heard Luke answer. "This is Fontaine property now, all legal under the Homestead Act."

Lettie felt cold perspiration under her dress in spite of the warm afternoon. She gripped her own rifle tightly, watching both men carefully. She had never shot anyone in her life, never even imagined such a thing; but if they tried to hurt Luke, or Nathan…

"Who the hell do you think you are, mister, takin' over another man's cabin?" the one with the cigar asked.

"This place was deserted when we got here last fall, and I checked in Billings. Nobody had laid legal claim to this land, but now *I* have, so you boys can just ride on and take your stolen horses with you."

The man with the cigar just grinned. "Who says they're stolen?"

"I might be new out here, mister, but I'm no fool. Now get going, and I won't say anything about you having been here."

Now the apparent spokesman for the rest of them laughed. "Who would you tell, anyway? Ain't no law out here, mister, which means we can blow you to hell and nobody would ever know the difference. If I was you, I'd be a bit more friendly to your hosts. Hell, you been usin' our cabin all this time, squattin' on our land."

"I told you, it's not your land anymore; never was."

Two more riders came up behind the first two men. Lettie hoped she wouldn't faint from terror. They were just as unkempt and dangerous looking as the others. She tried to remember how many she had seen coming. Six? Eight? How would they ever get out of this?

"I mean business," Luke told the outlaw. "I'm giving you ten seconds to get off my property!"

The man just shook his head, glancing over at the clothesline. He rubbed at his stubby chin, turned to look back at the other three men. "We got us an irate home-steader here, boys." They all laughed then, as though none believed Luke was brave enough to shoot at them.

"I'm real scared, Cade," one of the others answered.

The one called Cade looked back at Luke as he spoke. "I think he's got a woman in there, boys. Could be we could have us a real good time at the end of our journey here once we get rid of this bothersome varmint."

Lettie felt sick at the remark. It was the first time in months that the memory of her rape was suddenly vivid. Never! She would never let that happen again, if she had to kill some of these men herself! Yes, she could do it, if it meant saving Luke and Nathan, and keeping these sorry examples of men from touching her!

Luke in turn felt rage at the remark. Lettie was not going to suffer more horror at the hands of these men, even if he had to die to keep it from happening. "Your ten seconds are up," he told them, his voice cold. He knew instinctively there was no room here for compassion, or for hesitation. It was just as Will and others had told him. Up here a man set his own laws, and his own punishment. He pulled the trigger of his repeater, and a hole opened up in Cade's chest. Before the other three could react, he fired again. A second man went down. At almost the same time he heard a gunshot from the window of the cabin. Lettie! A third man cried out and fell from his horse, wounded in the leg.

The fourth man stared at Luke with eyes wide in surprise. "What the hell—" He went for his handgun, and Luke fired again. A bloody hole appeared in the man's shoulder, and he screamed with pain and dropped his gun. As he turned his horse and rode off, the man Lettie had wounded fired at Luke then, but missed. Luke turned on him and shot him in the face. He charged inside the cabin then, closing and bolting the door. "You all right?" he asked Lettie, a frantic tone to his voice.

Their eyes held in mutual horror. "Yes," she said, the word coming out in a squeak.

"I think there are three or four more. They'll probably come up here. We've got to be ready." He looked at her pregnant condition, aching at having to put her through this. "Try to stay calm. Let's not lose that baby over this."

Lettie nodded, forcing herself not to collapse from fear, and from the knowledge that she had shot a man. She could hardly believe she had done it, but she'd had no choice. She heard the thundering hooves of several more horses then. "The rest are coming!" There was no time to wonder about the right and wrong of it now. There were loved ones to defend, and that was all there was to it.

"Mommy," Nathan whimpered from the corner, shaking from the loud gunfire. He clung to his little horse, tears running down his cheeks.

"It's okay, Nathan," Luke assured him. "You stay right there." He leveled his rifle at the window as five more men appeared at the front of the house, including the one with the wounded shoulder. All of them had guns drawn. "I think this is all of them," Luke said quietly to Lettie. "No more warnings. There's no time for it. It's got to be done before they get around the sides of the house."

Without a word, he shot down two more of them before they could put forth any more arguments or threats. Horses reared and whinnied, and the other three hurriedly dismounted and clamored for cover, one behind a large boulder, the other two behind a wagon.

For a brief moment there was nothing but silence. "What the hell is wrong with you, mister?" one of them shouted then. "We wouldn't have brought you no harm. Now come on out of there, or we'll just have to sit here till we *starve* you out!"

Luke took careful aim, glad he had done a lot of practicing over the winter with his repeater. He caught sight of the leg of one man through the spokes of the wagon. It wasn't an easy shot, but if he aimed real carefully… He squeezed off a shot, and the man grabbed his knee and cried out with pain.

"I'm gettin' the hell out of here!" another yelled. The one behind the rock held up his hands and slowly rose. It was the one with the wounded shoulder. "I'm leavin', mister. Let me go! I won't bring you no harm. Just let me go."

"Cleve, you goddamn coward!" one of those behind the wagon shouted. A shot rang out, and the one called Cleve stiffened, a bloody hole in the side of his head. He fell forward over the rock, then rolled off of it. The man who had shot him turned and fired several shots through the cabin window then, shattering the glass and spraying bullets everywhere. Lettie screamed, and Luke dove into her, pushing her against the wall away from the window and then to the floor, lying on top of her.

"Stay down," he said quietly. He crawled away from her, and Lettie could see blood on the back of his shirt.

"Luke!"

"I'm all right. It's just cuts from the glass. Crawl over to Nathan and keep him down."

"What are you going to do?"

"Just keep your rifle with you and stay low. If anybody comes through that door without me hollering out that it's me, you shoot first and ask questions later." He gripped his rifle and fired several shots through the window, then ducked away when the volley was answered with another spray of bullets that pinged around the cabin and put holes in the walls. Quickly Luke ran to a back corner of the cabin, setting his rifle aside and grasping at a loose board. "I just wanted them to know we're still alive and shooting in here so they stay behind that wagon for a few more minutes."

"What are you doing?" Lettie asked, holding a quietly crying Nathan in one arm while she gripped her rifle in the other.

"This damn board used to get me mad, but now I'm glad for it. From their position, they can't see me crawl out the side of the cabin."

"Luke, you can't go out there!" Lettie protested, keeping her voice to a near whisper.

"I've got no choice. I'll never get the last two, the position they're in now, and I'm not going to sit in here all day and worry about what they'll do once it's dark." He ripped the board completely away, then looked over at her. "Go fire a few more rounds through the window, but keep your head down. All they need is to hear the gunshots."

Lettie ordered Nathan to stay put and crawled back over to the window. She laid the rifle barrel on the sill, then ducked down and squeezed her eyes shut, firing the rifle aimlessly to draw the men's attention while Luke tore away some of the tar paper he'd nailed to the side of the cabin, then pushed at wood and hay, knocking it all away and crawling through the opening, taking his rifle with him.

"Daddy." Nathan started to follow his father through the opening, and Lettie put down her rifle and ran to grab him. "No, Nathan! You can't go with Daddy." She sat down against a wall with the boy, rubbing at her stomach and praying she would hang on to the baby through all this horror. "Luke," she whispered.

Outside Luke ducked behind a rock pile, then cautiously raised his head to spot the wagon in front of the house. Neither man noticed him as he crept along the side of the house then. He could see them moving behind the wagon, one of them cursing about the wound in his leg.

"I can't hold out much longer, Cy," he grumbled. "I think the bullet went clean through, but my knee is killin' me."

"We've got them now," the other man answered. "And there's a woman in there. Hell, if we can clean that bastard out of there, we've got the woman to ourselves and the profit from all them horses only has to be split between you and me. I was sick of Cade always callin' the shots anyway. That stupid sodbuster in there just conveniently got rid of him for us."

Luke figured his only chance was the element of surprise. He took a deep breath and ran, charging around the end of the wagon and firing point-blank before the startled outlaws had a chance to realize he had got out of the cabin.

Both men went down, but the one with the injured knee raised his six-gun to shoot. Luke quickly fired the rifle again, and the man fell dead.

"Luke! Luke, are you all right?" Lettie screamed from the house.

Luke stared at the dead bodies, startled at how easily he had killed them out of necessity. He knelt down and checked for pulses, felt none. He walked around the wagon to check the other bodies. None were alive. "I'm okay," he called out. "Keep Nathan inside until I can get these bodies out of his sight." He felt a cold sweat begin to envelop him then, as the reality of the fact that he had killed seven men began to sink in. He turned around and vomited on the spot, then wiped at his sweaty forehead with the sleeve of his shirt.

Lettie came running out to him then, ordering Nathan to stay inside. "Luke! Are you sure you're all right? You're not wounded?"

He shook his head, turning away from her. "Just the cut on my back."

Lettie could see that he was shaking. She touched his arm. "Luke, you did what you had to do."

He nodded. "I know, but I…I didn't think I'd kill every one of them. I thought a few would still be alive," he said quietly. He took a deep breath, turning to her with tear-filled eyes. "I killed men in the war, but they were distant, faceless. It was war." He looked around at the bodies again. "I've never killed point-blank like this." He forced a nervous smile, and Lettie knew he was trying to keep from outright crying. "It's a hell of a feeling. Maybe a man gets used to it. Maybe out here he *has* to get used to it." He sniffed and took another deep breath. "I guess I'd better get them buried. I'll go into town soon and ask what I should do about the horses they had with them."

Lettie gazed at the bloody bodies strewn about, feeling sick herself, but her own nausea came from the realization of how easily Luke could have been taken from her today, and in spite of the fact that he'd had to kill men, she felt safer in his bravery and skill. Yes, Luke Fontaine was made of the right stuff for this country. "They left you no choice, Luke. You heard the things they said. They would have killed you in the blink of an eye if you hadn't got them first, and you know what would have happened to me. It's all right."

He handed her his rifle. "Yeah. The only trouble is, I have a feeling this is just the beginning. These aren't the last men I'll have to kill defending this land and my family. Until there's some kind of law out here, this is the way it will have to be." He looked down at her. "Are you really all right?"

"Yes."

"I'm sorry you had to do any shooting at all." He gave her a sad smile. "You did all right."

She burst into tears then. "So did you," she whimpered.

Luke drew her into his arms, and they held each other, the air silent now, no wind, no more gunfire.

⌘

Lettie stood holding Nathan while Luke removed his hat and bowed his head. "Lord, if there was any good in any of these men, we hope you'll take them up there with you and forgive them for whatever bad thoughts and actions they were guilty of." He took a deep breath, scanning the eight graves he'd dug close together, seven of the dead laid out by his own bullets. "And forgive me for having to take their lives."

He swallowed and cleared his throat, then straightened, looking across the valley, a soft breeze blowing his dark hair away from his eyes. He had dug all the rest of the afternoon after the encounter with the horse thieves, continued digging into the night. He had not slept, but sat up smoking most of the night, finished digging the graves this morning. He had buried every last man, kept their identification, carved their names on wooden crosses. That morning Lettie thought he looked achingly tired. There were new lines about his eyes, a new set to his jawline, harder, the look of a man learning to bury his emotions because that was the only way to survive. She didn't know what to say to him.

"Riders coming," he said then. "Get inside till I find out who it is. Could be some men who were supposed to meet this bunch."

Lettie prayed they would not have to go through another encounter like yesterday's. She saw only three men, one of them in buckskins, as far as she could tell from this distance. They were making their way along the muddy rut of a road that led there from Billings. At least they were coming from a different direction, so maybe it was just someone from town. She hurried up the hill to the porch of the cabin and stood in the doorway, while Luke picked up his rifle, which he had left propped against a boulder. He had dug the graves in a spot that would always be relatively dry, even in spring, and well away from the rushing water supply of the creek on the other side of the house.

It took several minutes for the riders to come within calling distance. As soon as they did, one of them whistled, the one in buckskins. He was the biggest of the three, and when he called out, Lettie and Luke both realized it was Will Doolan, not just by his burly size, but because of the wolflike dog that ran beside his horse. "Helloooo, Luke Fontaine!" he hollered.

Luke raised his arm with the rifle in it. Lettie came back outside as the three men came closer. She did not recognize the other two, but she welcomed Will with a smile, wishing with all her heart that Henny were with him. Oh, how wonderful it was to see friendly faces, and how sad that the first human life they had seen after their long winter alone had to be vicious outlaws.

Will laughed. "By God, it's good to see you, Luke, you and the missus both. We was worried about how you'd make it through the winter." He rode closer and dismounted, shaking Luke's hand, his smile quickly fading at the gaunt, haunted look on Luke's face. It was then he noticed the graves. "Jesus, boy, what happened here?"

Luke removed his hat and wiped at his forehead and damp hair. "You were right. Horse thieves came here to hole up, decided they'd kill me and have a good time with my wife. I set them straight."

The other two men dismounted, and all three stared at the graves for a moment. "By God, I guess you did," Will finally spoke up. He looked over at Lettie. "You and the boy okay?" His eyes dropped to her abdomen. "You're carryin'!"

Lettie blushed at the remark. "I'm all right."

"She shot one of them herself," Luke put in. "Didn't kill him. I finished them all off."

Will stood back and looked him over. "Must have been quite a shoot-out. You didn't take any bullets?"

Luke shook his head and put his hat back on, while the other two men stared at him as though he were something to be idolized. "I gave them ten seconds to leave. They didn't believe me. I knew my only hope was the element of surprise, so I pulled the trigger before they had a chance to think twice about it, got three right off, four more after they came up behind the first ones. One of them wanted to light out and was shot by his own man...called him a coward and shot him in the head." Luke shook his head. "I'll give you more details later. Right now it's hard to talk about it."

"Well, I expect so." Will sighed deeply, a look of true concern on his face. He turned to the other two men. "Luke, this here is Perry Ward and Jim Calahan. I've known Perry for quite a few years. He's on his way to Oregon from down by Sheridan. Figures to find out about the rumor that there's lots of cattle to be had cheap out there. I thought you might be interested in him findin' out what you can get a good herd for."

Luke nodded. "I'd like that just fine." He shook hands with Ward, a tall, gangly man with dark hair and eyes. Although he was clean-shaven, he had an unkempt look about him. His pants and jacket hung loosely, and his wide-brimmed leather hat looked as though it had had a lot of use. His smile was friendly, but his teeth terribly crooked. "You got family back in Sheridan?" Luke asked.

"Oh no. Never been married." The man actually looked embarrassed at the remark, and he seemed very shy of women, reddened when he nodded quickly to Lettie in greeting, then looked away immediately. "I guarantee you, Mr. Fontaine, that I do know cattle," the man drawled, apparently anxious to change the subject. "Worked on cattle ranches in Texas for years, mostly with longhorns, of course. I hear there's a little bit different stock in Oregon. I'm lookin' to buy for several other ranchers—get a commission, if that's okay with you. I'll get you the lowest price possible, then you pay the cost of hirin' men to get them back here, plus ten cents a head extra to me for doin' all the footwork. 'Course, all I can do this year is see what kind of deal I can come up with, then let you know next spring and go back to get the beef."

"Sounds fine to me. I'll be too busy here this summer building a cabin and barn and fencing, getting in more wood for next winter and all. Takes a lot of time and work to get a place into shape, and I won't have my wife and a new baby living in that drafty shack next winter."

Ward looked past Luke at the valley beyond. "You picked a good spot, Mr. Fontaine. You can fatten beef up real good here, and I agree with what you told Will about how there's gonna be an even bigger demand for beef soon as the war is over, especially once they complete the transcontinental railroad."

"I think so," Luke answered. He put out his hand to the other man, who shook it vigorously.

"I'm Jim Calahan," the young man spoke up. His eyes

had not stopped shining with awe since he heard Luke had faced eight outlaws and survived the encounter. He removed his hat before nodding to Lettie. "Ma'am."

"Hello, Mr. Calahan," Lettie answered. He was a pleasant-looking man, with sandy hair and brown eyes. He only came to Luke's shoulder in height, but he was well built and looked clean.

"Will brought me out here because he thought you might need an extra hand," he was saying to Luke. "Both my folks died down in Colorado, and I came up here lookin' for gold, but didn't have any luck. I just kind of wandered into Billings last fall lookin' for work, been livin' with Will here most of the winter."

Will laughed. "Henny says we've got to quit takin' in strays." He put a hand on young Jim's shoulder. "He's proved to be a good kid, Luke, hardworking, willin' to do his share. For room and board, he'd be a big help to you. He needs the work."

Luke studied the young man. "As long as I can trust him. I need somebody who can keep a watch over Lettie and the stock when I have to be gone."

Jim glanced at the eight graves. "I don't think I'd care to cross you, Mr. Fontaine," he answered with a nervous smile.

Lettie caught the slight bitterness to Luke's smile. "Well, I don't want to get a reputation for killing a man for no reason." He held Jim's eyes with warning in his own. "Just don't give me reason." He grinned then, and Jim smiled in return. The two men shook hands again.

"Put on the coffee, honey," Luke said to Lettie. "You've finally got the company you've been longing for all winter."

"I'll bring Henny out sometime soon," Will promised.

"Oh, I'd like that so much," Lettie told him fervently. She felt uplifted by the unexpected visit. Will couldn't have chosen a better time to come. Luke needed the conversation and support more than ever right now. She headed inside to get more coffee going.

Luke turned and pointed to the valley, where a herd of roughly fifty horses grazed aimlessly. "What am I supposed to do about them?" he asked.

Will pushed his hat back a little and studied them. "Keep them."

"What? They're stolen!"

Will shook his head. "How in hell do you plan to find their owners? Some of them horses probably came from as far away as Utah, Colorado, maybe even Texas and New Mexico. Maybe this is God's way of helpin' you get started, Luke. Take advantage of it. You'll never find the owners now. Re-brand them and keep them. Hell, there's just as much a market for good horses as anything right now. I'll find you help in herdin' them down to a buyer in Wyoming. Don't feel guilty about it." He glanced at the graves. "You earned them horses fair and square. Now you've got a good start, good horses, help in buildin' your cabin, a man to buy cattle for you." He nodded toward the graves. "You survived your first Montana winter, and your first encounter with outlaws. You're gonna do okay."

Luke looked out at the herd. He hadn't even taken time to inspect the animals, but he figured if the outlaws were good at what they did, they probably stole only the best. Will was right. How was he supposed to find the owners of all those horses? It would be impossible. The best he could do was not sell any of them for at least a year, leave word at Billings that he had stolen horses on his land. If no one showed up with proof to claim any of them, they belonged to Luke Fontaine.

That meant they should be branded. All winter he had given thought to naming the ranch. He'd certainly had plenty of time to think about it, and he had come up with the Double L. It had to be something that represented Lettie too, for all she'd put up with coming here with him. Both their names started with *L*—Luke and Lettie—the Double L. He liked the sound of it, and now he had reason to name the ranch and use a brand. He hadn't told Lettie yet about the decision, but he was sure she would like the name.

First thing tomorrow he would carve a sign to hang at the east entrance to his ranch, where Will and the others had ridden in today. Later on he'd have a more professional sign done, but for now, when people came this way from town, they would know they were on Fontaine land, although he had not yet set his exact boundaries or finished up the legal end of it. Whether it was all in writing or not, he'd already fought and bled for this land. Lettie had suffered too. It was theirs by right, just as those horses were.

As soon as possible he would find a blacksmith to design a branding iron showing two *L*'s, the permanent brand for the Double L. That brand would go on all livestock belonging to Luke Fontaine, and on saddles, signs, almost everything he possessed. Any man who tried to take any of it away from him or hurt his family would end up beside the eight outlaws he had buried this morning!

Eight

LETTIE BREATHED DEEPLY, TRYING TO RELAX BEFORE another labor pain bore down to grip at her insides. She fought against memories of Nathan's birth. She'd been so afraid, so ignorant of conception and birth, let alone the horror of how he had come to be. She reminded herself that this was Luke's baby, conceived out of love. She wished her mother could be here, but there was only Henny, who had never even had a child of her own, and an old Crow Indian woman Henny had brought with her when Will brought them both out three days ago to stay till the baby came.

Henny had assured her that the Crow woman had overseen many births in her years on earth, had borne six children of her own. Her name was Willow, and her son and grandson were scouts for the army. They lived with a tribe of peaceful Crow Indians just south of the little settlement of Billings, one of the few groups of Indians who seldom caused trouble for the whites.

"Where is Luke? I want Luke," Lettie groaned as the old Indian woman massaged her temples and softly chanted something in the Crow tongue.

"This is not the place for a man," Henny assured her. "Luke is right outside the house with Nathan, waiting to see his new son or daughter."

"A son. It has to be a son. He'll need sons," Lettie answered, feeling another pain coming, hoping that talk would help ease it. Why couldn't Luke be here? What was so wrong about allowing the husband to be with his wife at a time like this? Following instructions from Willow, she breathed in quick gasps as another pain tore at her belly. She didn't want to scream, but it was impossible not to. She remembered the terror of thinking the first time this happened to her that she was going to die for being "bad," but her mother and a minister had helped her understand that nothing that had happened was her fault. The pain was just a sacrifice for the beautiful gift she had received from God, and now she would soon receive that gift again. She could bear the pain because this was all for Luke, to begin the family he so sorely needed and wanted, and to give little Nathan a brother or sister. The baby would help all of them get through the next long winter.

How she missed her mother and father, sister and brother. At least she knew they were all right. The last time she and Luke were in town before getting snowed in for the winter, she had sent a letter to Denver, telling them to write to her in care of Will Doolan in Billings, Montana. This last time Will and Henny came out to help them, Will had brought a reply from her family. To her great relief, they were all fine and doing well in Denver. They had even been spared in a terrible fire that had burned down most of the town the very same summer they settled there in '63; and they had come through a killer flood that had washed away most of the city just this past spring. God had been with them.

Now here it was August of '64. A whole year had passed since she parted from her family. As soon as she felt better she would write and tell them of her new home, her experiences over the winter, how big Nathan was getting…and she would be able to tell them they had another grandchild.

She relaxed again in a reprieve from pain. She looked around the spacious bedroom that was now hers and Luke's. The new cabin was barely finished enough to move into, but she wanted to have her baby here, not in the old shack up the hill. She had not even had a chance to put up curtains yet. Henny had promised to shop for material for her and help her make the curtains after the baby was born.

"You're all…so good to us," she told Henny.

Henny smiled. "Well, out here folks learn they've got to help each other. You never know when you'll *need* help in return. Besides, folks in town are always happy to help new people settle here."

Lettie managed a brief smile of her own. "The cabin is beautiful." She looked out her bedroom window at green grass and trees, wildflowers growing on the distant hill. Surely this baby would be born healthy. Their lives were getting better all the time. Will and Jim had brought in more men from town who had helped Luke finish the house. It was a sturdy log structure with three bedrooms. It even had a separate little room for washing that also contained a chamber pot so that she and the children could stay inside on the most bitterly cold days instead of having to visit the new privy behind the house. She had wood floors, fresh, varnished wood instead of the old, dried-up, cracked floors in the shanty. Luke had built plenty of shelves into all three walls of the kitchen end of the main room, and she had a real cookstove, a cast-iron contraption that had taken an extra-heavy wagon and a whole team of mules to haul out to the ranch from Billings's one-and-only supply store, where it had finally arrived in answer to a months-old order. It had then taken six men to get the stove into the house. It could be heated with either wood or coal, and for now it would have to be wood. There was no coal available in Billings, but Syd Martin, the owner of the store, had promised he would see about ordering some.

The part of the house she prized most was her stone fireplace, right in the center of the long back wall of the main room. The entire main living area was cozy yet roomy, with plenty of room for children to play when they were cooped up inside in winter, even room to hang clothes on one end without everyone having to duck under and around them to walk through the room. Besides Luke's and her bedroom, there were two more for the children. Luke wanted plenty of those, but at the moment she wasn't so sure she could keep going through this. She remembered her mother once saying some babies would come easy, others not so easy. Nathan had taken ten hours to be born. She had already been in labor for twelve hours with this one.

Another pain began to build, and she sat up straighter, Henny grasping her left hand, old Willow grasping her right. Again she breathed in deep gasps, but again, nothing she did helped much. Another scream filled the whole house and wandered across the foothills behind it.

❧

Luke lit yet another thin cigar, wondering if he would run out of the smokes completely before his son or daughter was born. He kept an eye on Nathan, who was running around chasing a butterfly. "If I hear one more scream I'm going to lose my mind," he said to Will Doolan. "Maybe we shouldn't have any more after this one."

Will smiled grimly. "How do you propose to stop it? You gonna keep your hands off your beautiful young wife the rest of your life?"

Luke felt sick inside at the sound of Lettie's screams. "Maybe." He walked a few feet away, then turned and caught Will's skeptical expression. He broke into a grin. "I said *maybe*." He took off his hat and hung it over a fence post. "Too bad there isn't some really good way of preventing these things without having to give up the one greatest pleasure a man has in life."

"Thought you wanted a big family."

"Not at this expense."

"It's what you have to go through, Luke. You and Lettie should both be glad as hell you're *able* to go through it. Henny would give anything to be sufferin' that kind of pain herself right now."

Luke's smile faded. "I'm sorry, Will. I sound pretty selfish, don't I?"

Will shrugged. "You're worried. It's natural." The man turned to study the nearly completed barn he and others from town were helping build. It too was made of logs, a big structure designed to hold a lot of animals. Luke had built several corrals to keep the horses in at night, but right now the animals grazed in the lush, green valley below.

"You were right, Luke. You've got yourself a gold mine here. That herd those outlaws so graciously gave you is a damn good start on horseflesh that will bring you some good money next summer. We'll take some down to Sheridan and you'll make your first big sale, I guarantee."

Luke looked around at the house, the barn, and corrals, another shed he'd built near the house for storing wood to keep it dry, a stone smokehouse nearby for curing meat. Now he was working on a small bunkhouse for Jim, something that could house at least four or five men, once he could afford to hire them. "I don't know what I would have done without all of you," he told Will. "I have a hell of a start, but there are still some hard years ahead, I can see that. I just wish the Indian problem would get settled. I lie awake half the night worrying about my horses getting stolen, or about something happening to Lettie and Nathan."

Will sighed in a kind of grunt. "That damn Red Cloud is really stirring up the Sioux. Ol' Half Nose is another troublemaker. They're all in a dither about so many whites going through their land in order to get to the goldfields up by Last Chance Gulch. If it makes you feel any better, I've heard the army is gonna send out more troops. Soon as the damn War between the States is over, we'll get even more help out here. The war surely can't last much longer."

Luke thought about the horrors of that war, the pain he still suffered at times from his own war wound. It had been roughly eighteen months since he was mustered out, and the realization that all that hell was still going on made him shiver. His own brother was still fighting somewhere. God only knew how many men had lost their lives or suffered horrible wounds by now. "Well, I'll be one happy man when they get more soldiers out here. They can build a fort right on my own land if they want to."

Will chuckled. "And how much land *is* that now, Luke?"

Luke glanced at the house when he heard another scream, this one more of a shuddering groan. He ran a hand through his hair nervously, called to Nathan not to go too far, looked out at the herd of horses grazing below, horses that now bore the Double L brand. "Right now about six hundred acres," he answered, "some under my name, some under yours, Jim's, even some under Lettie's maiden name. That's just a start. I'll own thousands of acres before I'm through."

Secretly he wondered if his father would be impressed. He had written the man a letter, telling him about his first year in Montana, his new wife, how beautiful and educated she was, his experience with the outlaws, how much land he already owned. He was not sure himself why he had bothered writing the man he hated so much. He supposed it was because deep inside he still loved him and would always think of him as his father…more than that, he hoped his absence had by some miracle made his father miss him, that his accomplishments here in Montana would impress the man and make him regret sending him away.

He scowled at his own thoughts. He had already proven his worth to Jacques Fontaine back in St. Louis, but that had not been enough. It was foolish to think the man would ever have an ounce of feeling for him, but he would continue sending the letters, just to show him he could make it on his own. Jacques wanted him to fail. That would never happen, and he would damn well make sure the man knew it!

"Ol' David Taylor likes to look good back in Washington," Will was saying. "Doesn't mind a few extra bucks either. You'll get your land, all you want, with no argument from him."

Luke shook off thoughts of his father. "I'd better sell some of those horses by next summer, or I won't have any money left to bribe Taylor with." He stuck the cigar in his mouth and talked with it resting between his teeth. "Anything he can't deed to me, I intend to take anyway. By next summer I'm going to start putting up a log fence, Will, however many miles long it will have to be to let outlaws, Indians, and other settlers know what belongs to Luke Fontaine. Anybody that wants to argue about it can answer to me."

Will faced him. "Like the outlaws buried out there by the old shack?"

Luke took the cigar from his mouth. "Maybe."

Will saw the pain in his eyes. "I know that took you some time to get over. Maybe you're not over it yet. But it was a necessary thing, Luke. Just make sure that if it happens again, it's *always* a necessary thing. You go ahead and claim what you want, because by God you deserve to. What the hell? Anybody that comes up here and puts up with the hardships and dangers has a right to call whatever part of this land he wants his own. Just be fair in your judgments, Luke." He walked a little closer. "And don't let the thing you told me about you and your pa turn you into somethin' you're not. I know how important it is for you to succeed here. Just don't lose sight of what's *really* important in life." It was then they heard the cry of a baby. Will grinned. "Like that new little life in there." He winked and grasped Luke's hand. "Congratulations, Papa."

Luke threw down his cigar and just stared at the house for a minute. Then he hurried up onto the wide front porch he'd added onto the house. He'd built it picturing Lettie sitting and rocking her baby with a view of the valley below.

Henny met him at the door, smiling. "You have a daughter, Luke."

"How's Lettie?"

"She's fine. You can go inside. Willow is bathing the baby. You can only stay a minute. We've got to work on getting the afterbirth."

Luke saw the tears in the woman's eyes, realized how hard this must be on her. He leaned down and kissed her cheek. "Thanks, Henny."

In the bedroom, Lettie lay looking pale, her hair damp against the pillow. She managed a smile.

"It's a little girl, Luke. I hope you're not disappointed."

God, how he loved her. "I'm just glad you're all right."

Willow held up the newborn baby, letting the blanket in which she had wrapped the baby fall away. The infant's tiny hands were curled into angry fists, and she was giving out a healthy wail. "I guess there's nothing wrong with her lungs," Luke said. He leaned down and kissed Lettie lightly. "I'm sorry about the pain."

She took his hand. "When I had Nathan, my mother told me it's the one kind of pain that is almost instantly forgotten, and she was right." She squeezed his hand. "There will be more, Luke. And there *will* be sons."

He thought about his decision that maybe they shouldn't have any more, and he already knew that was impossible. Of course there would be more. After all, he wanted sons; and besides, how was he going to stay out of this beautiful woman's bed? "I hate this part of it, Lettie. And I hate waiting outside while you're in so much pain in here. The next time I want to be here with you."

Lettie saw the fear in his eyes. "I wanted you here.

Henny said it wasn't proper, but I don't care. The next time I do want you with me."

"Thank you, Lettie, for our little girl." He gave her a wink then. "I guess instead of me getting a helping hand, you got yourself one."

She managed a light laugh. "Oh yes, I planned it that way." Her eyes teared then at the sudden thought of how she used to help her own mother with cooking and housework. "I want to name her after my mother, Luke. Katheryn Lynn. Katie. Is that all right?"

"Of course it's all right." He closed his eyes and squeezed her hand. "Thank God, you're fine and the baby is healthy."

Outside, Will soothed a weeping Henny, neither of them aware they were being watched from a vantage point high in the foothills.

෴

"You see, Red Hawk?" A fierce-looking Sioux warrior with a scarred nose turned to his fourteen-year-old son. "I told you these whites were here to stay, not just tend horses for the summer."

"It is just as you said, Father," Red Hawk answered. "He has collected many horses, built himself sturdy lodges."

Half Nose grinned. "Not sturdy enough, if we decide we do not want them here."

"Will we burn them down? Steal the horses?"

"Not yet. After another winter there will be even more horses. We will wait until we truly need them to keep fighting those who walk the road through our land to get the yellow metal. These here, they are not after the metal. It is the bluecoats, and the many men who come to dig the metal from the sacred Mother Earth, whom we will kill first. This man here, he will simply supply fresh horses for us…when the time is right."

"*I* will do it, Father. I will steal the horses from in front of his very face. The white settlers are cowards. They will shiver and hide in their log tepee when they see us."

Half Nose studied the several graves below, remembered that many bad white men often came to this place with many horses. He had stolen some of those horses from them a few times, but it had not been easy. Had they returned again this spring? Had the white man below fought with them and won? He was surely quite a warrior if he had.

"Do not be so sure this white man will run from you, like the other settlers, Red Hawk." He watched the little boy with white hair running about in the distance, and a soft wind carried the sound of the new baby's crying. "This one is here to stay. It will not be easy convincing him he does not belong here."

❧

The winter of '64 to '65 proved just as bitterly cold, burying the Fontaine family just as deeply as the previous winter, but this time Lettie did not suffer quite the awful loneliness as the year before. She was growing accustomed to her new life, the ache to see her parents and siblings not quite so painful now. She had Nathan, who would be four the coming May, and who loved to help her with housework and with the new baby, and she had little Katie, who kept her busy with feedings and scrubbing diapers.

It was obvious Katie was going to be a pretty thing, her hair dark like Luke's, her eyes a hazel color. She was a happy baby, plump and healthy and already crawling on fat knees. Lettie was wondering how she was going to keep up with Nathan and her after yet a third child was born. Being alone so much and having the privacy of a bedroom had led to another pregnancy. The baby was due in June, only two months away. Maybe this one would be another son.

She picked up a straw basket full of wet clothes to carry it outside. This year it had not warmed so quickly, and there was still snow on the ground; but today was the prettiest day they had had in months. She was sick of hanging clothes inside the house. She left Katie sleeping in a small pine bed Luke had built for her and carried the clothes basket outside, setting it under the clothesline Luke had strung between two cross posts buried solidly into the ground. She smelled deeply of the sweet spring air, left the basket a moment to walk farther away and watch Luke ride amid the herd of horses below to single out the pregnant mares. He intended to corral them separately so he could keep an eye on their progress.

She smiled, thinking how Luke bragged about the fact that out of his herd of thirty-eight horses, twelve were pregnant. "Those outlaws picked a couple of good stud horses," he had told her the night before at supper. "At least they knew what they were doing, picked good stock. I can thank them for that much." She knew the killings still ate at him a little, and he'd seemed harder in some ways since then; but she understood the necessity of the act. Sometimes she sensed he'd like to talk about it, but he had not brought it up again after burying the men.

Nathan ran past her then, grabbing the tail of a puppy Will had given him. "Bear's son," Will had told the boy. "Got it from a litter birthed by a big ol' collie that belongs to a neighbor of mine." Nathan simply called the dog Pup, and although it was obvious the animal was going to be as big as or bigger than Bear, Lettie had a feeling the unlikely name would stick.

"Be careful you don't hurt Pup," she warned Nathan.

Nathan petted the dog then, rubbing its soft fur. "My puppy," he said with a delighted grin.

Lettie watched the boy and dog, wanting to remember the sweet scene, but her attention was interrupted when she saw riders approaching from the other side of the valley. Even from this distance she could see that their horses as well as their half-naked bodies were painted, and that they wore feathers in their hair. Indians!

❧

Luke culled another pregnant mare from the herd, riding a sturdy gelded gray-and-white spotted Appaloosa he had favored since claiming the horses the outlaws had left behind. He called the horse Paint, because its gray coat was splattered and spotted with white, as though someone had spilled paint on it. He figured that whoever had originally owned the animal must surely have been bitterly angry over the loss when it was stolen, just as angry as he would be now if someone in turn tried to steal Paint or any other horses from him. He had grown as attached to the Appaloosa as he had been to Red, and he still mourned Red's loss to the thieving Indian who had stolen him.

He gave out a whistle and waved his hat, chasing the mare into the corral with eight others. He thought what a bountiful spring this was going to be, twelve foals, and another child of his own on the way. Life was good. He patted his own horse's neck and closed the gate to the corral.

It was then he heard the singing arrow. It whirred past him near his head and landed with a thud in the trunk of a nearby pine tree. He whirled Paint around to see eight or ten Indian warriors riding into the valley, shouting and whooping their war cries, out to claim some free horse-flesh for themselves, at his expense. More arrows narrowly missed him as he pulled his rifle from its boot and rode Paint hard up a small hill to a shed he had built to store feed. Quickly he dismounted and tied Paint, then took a position behind a few bales of hay. The Indians were still coming, and an arrow landed in one of the hay bales right in front of him. He glanced up the hill at the house to see

Lettie pick up Nathan and go running inside. He turned back and took aim then, realizing he had something much more precious than his horses to protect. Will had warned him that if Indians came to steal a few horses, he should let them have them rather than try to fight them, but he had two children and a pregnant wife to think about. He couldn't just sit here and let the oncoming savages get by him and possibly steal off with Lettie and the children. He leveled his rifle and took aim, waiting for them to get close enough that he was sure he could not miss.

All but one of them stopped then near the edge of the herd of horses. The one who kept coming looked as though he was built a little smaller than the others, maybe someone quite a bit younger. So be it. If he was old enough to steal horses, he was old enough to take the risks involved. If he let them get away with this the first time, they would keep coming back until he had nothing left. For all he knew this single warrior was some kind of decoy. They seemed to be playing a game, as though to tempt him, dare him. The lone warrior halted, daringly raised a bow, as though asking Luke to try to shoot him. He drew back the bow and let an arrow fly. It whirred through the air and stuck in the shed behind which Luke stood. The young man then maneuvered roughly ten of Luke's finest horses from the herd, laughing and whooping the whole time.

Luke kept his rifle level. He was one against many. Jim had gone into Billings to see about hiring more help. Had these Indians been watching him all along? Did they know he was here alone? Maybe they thought that because of that, he would behave like a coward. Maybe they thought he had run to the shed just to hide while they had their pick of his finest animals. He dared not allow any of them to get too confident or get too close. He kept the show-off warrior in his sight, then squeezed the trigger. The warrior jerked his pony to a stop, sat stiffly a moment, then crumpled and slid off his horse.

Luke felt his heart pounding as the rest of the warriors grew very silent.

"Luke!" Lettie screamed from the house.

"Stay inside!" he yelled back, keeping his eyes on the Indians. They seemed to be discussing something, and finally one of the biggest among them raised a lance with a white cloth tied to it, then rode toward the Indian man Luke had shot. He straddled a horse that looked familiar. "Red!" Luke muttered then. Was it the notorious Half Nose who rode his own stolen horse? He was too far away to get a good look at him. The man wore only a loincloth and a bone breastplate. He kept holding the lance in the air as though to signify he meant no harm, that Luke should not shoot.

Luke waited breathlessly. The warrior reached the fallen body, dismounted, and bent over it. After a moment he leaned back and let out a cry so heart wrenching that even Luke was touched. "Jesus," he whispered. Who the hell had he shot? Will had told him the one called Half Nose had a teenage son. The man picked up the body and laid it over the spotted pony that had carried it into the valley, then mounted Red. He picked up the pony's leather reins and sat staring up the hill at where Luke remained crouched behind the hay. He yelled something in the Sioux tongue, but Luke did not understand, except that the anguish in the man's voice told him he had killed someone very special. The man turned and rode off then with the other warriors.

Luke slowly rose, watching after them, glad Jim was due back tomorrow with extra men. They just might be needed in more ways than one. If the warrior who had just paid him a visit was the one called Half Nose, he would surely be back. "Damn," he muttered. His gut reaction had been to protect Lettie and the children, but now he worried he had just made things worse for all of them.

Nine

LETTIE TOOK ANOTHER LOAF OF BREAD FROM THE OVEN, weary from so much baking and cooking, yet glad to do it for the extra two men Jim had brought back with him as hired help. Not only would it be nice to have other human beings to talk to in the coming winter, but the extra men kept her busy…too busy to get upset over the fact that Luke should have been back two days ago from his hunting trip. Ever since he'd killed one of the Indians who had tried to steal the horses, she had been sick with worry that while he was out alone he would in turn be killed. He had left five days ago to hunt for meat that he would smoke and store for the winter. He had said he would be back in three days, and she decided that if he didn't show up by tonight, she would send all the help out to find him, even if it meant she had to stay here alone.

She set the bread on the table to cool. The pleasant smell of freshly baked bread in her cozy new house usually cheered her, but today she hardly noticed. Every Sunday she fed the help a fancy meal and baked extra bread and pies for them, but the rest of the week they had to feed themselves. They also scrubbed their own clothes, something which the two extra men, who had always lived as single men, seemed adept at doing, although not often enough as far as she was concerned. Zeb Crandal and Horace Little had worked as scouts, hunters, trappers, and ranch hands all their lives. Horace had never been married, but Zeb had. His wife was dead now, his full-grown son off to California. The two men were older than Jim, she guessed roughly forty, and although they were congenial and were respectful of Luke and her, they were rather crude in their ways, men who had never lived a genteel life.

Neither she nor Luke minded, as long as they earned their keep, which both men did to full satisfaction. The bunkhouse was completed, another storage shed built, and the windmill was finished. Now she could draw buckets of water from a well. The best part was that there was always someone to keep watch at night, although how much help that would be against an entire Indian war party was doubtful.

She was trying to be strong about this, stay busy, master this fear of reprisal from the one called Half Nose, if indeed he was the one who had paid them a visit two weeks ago. There had been no sign of Indians since, and she had told Luke and convinced herself too that they could not stop living or give up out of fear of what might happen. Life went on. Now there were extra men to help out in return for a roof over their heads and food from the family garden and her own ovens.

She was proud of what a fine garden she had grown last summer. Already she had another garden started, even bigger than last year's. She had never had a vegetable garden of her own before then, and she felt very accomplished that her root cellar still contained potatoes and carrots from last fall, as well as a basket of seed potatoes from last year that she would use to plant a new potato field this spring. Horace had already dug the trenches for her.

Two years they had been in Montana already. Two long, bitter winters. Nathan turned four just two days ago, little Katie was eight months. She thought she'd heard once that while a woman was nursing, she couldn't get pregnant again. How wrong that had proved to be!

Apparently, when it came to a woman's body, nothing was guaranteed. She had barely recuperated from Katie's birth before realizing she was pregnant again. At first she thought it was just taking time for her body to get regulated again, as she had not had a period for three months after Nathan was born. But then she felt the life in her belly and realized it was growing again. Now she wondered if she would always get pregnant so easily. Luke was thrilled to be having another child, but very worried about her health. He had sworn they would simply have to stay away from each other for several months after this one, to allow her time to regain her health fully. She had to smile at the thought. How could they possibly refrain from making love, when it was so enjoyable for them both, and when the winters were so long and dark and lonely?

She pinched the edges around the soft, raw crust of a pie, deciding that if and when God intended for her to have a child, she would have it, and that was that. Life with Luke, in spite of the dangers and hardships, had brought her more happiness than she ever dreamed she would have after the agony of her rape and the terrible loneliness that had followed; and she was glad that in turn, she and Nathan and all the other children she would have could help fill the emptiness Luke had known before meeting her.

She glanced over at Nathan who was piling up some blocks Luke had made for him. Katie crawled over to where he played and promptly knocked over the little tower. Nathan pouted and scolded her, then began showing her how to stack them up again. Lettie's attention was drawn from their play when Pup began barking and Jim knocked on the front door.

"I think he's comin', Mrs. Fontaine."

Lettie hurried over to the door and opened it. Jim pointed to the east, along the road that led to Billings.

Pup, who seemed to gain a pound a day, bounded from the porch, out toward the road, and back again, still barking excitedly. "Horace rode out to greet him," Jim told her. "Paint was comin' in slow, and it looks like Luke was kind of slumped over, like he's hurt."

"Oh dear God," Lettie muttered, stepping farther out onto the porch. She could barely make out horse and rider, but it did indeed look as though Luke might be hurt. She waited anxiously. It seemed to take forever for Horace to reach Luke, and she thought how in this land nothing was as close as it seemed. Whatever landmark a person picked, it took twice as long to reach it as one would estimate. Finally Horace reached him. He stopped for a moment, then dismounted and climbed up onto Paint behind Luke. "Jim, he *is* hurt. Horace is getting on Paint in order to hang on to Luke. Go out there and see if he needs more help!"

Her chest tightened as she waited and watched helplessly. Jim ran to the bunkhouse and mounted his own horse, yelling out to Zeb Crandal to get back to the house. Zeb was mending a fence several hundred yards down in the valley and was able to hear Jim only because the strong wind carried Jim's voice.

The wind. The constant wind. She remembered how it almost drove her crazy that first winter. Now she was so used to it that she hardly noticed it anymore, except on days like today, when the sight of her wounded husband reminded her how quickly one could get hurt and die out here. The land was so beautiful, and at the same time so cruel. A hundred things could happen to a man out hunting alone—flash floods in spring, drought in summer, ravaging cold in winter, wild animals…Indians. Had Luke been attacked by the Sioux? Was he dying? Was he dead already?

She reached down and petted Pup, who jumped up on her, tail wagging. He was already proving to be a good watchdog, guarded the children fiercely, slept on the front porch every night like a sentinel. "He'll be all right, Pup," she said absently, more to assure herself than the dog. She turned and went inside, ordering Nathan to take all his blocks into the bedroom he shared with Katie and to keep the baby in that room out from under people's feet.

"What's a matter, Mommy?" he asked.

"Daddy might be hurt. You be a big boy and help Mommy by staying out of the way."

The boy's lips puckered and his eyes teared as he hurriedly picked up a handful of the blocks and carried them into his room. Lettie did not have time to comfort him. She hurried into the bedroom and pulled back the bedclothes, then grabbed some clean towels from the washroom and set them on a table near the bed. She brought a wash pan from the bathing room and set it, too, near the bed, then checked to be sure the kettle of hot water sitting on the stove was full. She threw some more wood under the burner and said a quick prayer that whatever was wrong with Luke, it wasn't life threatening.

Zeb came riding up to the house then on his sturdy black mare. He was a short, hefty man who always wore buckskins and seldom shaved, a hard worker who spoke little. "What's wrong, ma'am?"

"It's Luke. It looks like he's hurt. Jim and Horace rode out to help him."

Zeb dismounted and tied his horse, then walked to the other side of the garden at the east side of the house. The three riders disappeared temporarily behind a stand of pine trees, then came into view again. Jim was leading Horace's horse while Horace remained on Paint hanging on to Luke. Finally after several minutes that seemed like hours to Lettie, the men made it to the gate at the east entrance to the drive leading to the main house. Lettie ran partway out to greet them, then struggled not to gasp when she saw Luke. The May weather was warm enough to go without a coat, but the wool jacket Luke had worn was still on him, although in shreds. Every stitch of clothing was soaked with blood, and more blood had crusted on the side of his face. He looked white as the snow that lingered on the surrounding mountaintops.

His eyelids drooped when he looked at Lettie. "I'm… all right," he muttered. "…grizzly." His eyes closed then, and he started to slide from Horace's hold.

"Oh my God," Lettie groaned, trying to help catch him.

"Don't you be strainin' yourself," Horace told her. The slim man was having trouble holding up the much bigger Luke, and Jim quickly dismounted to help. Zeb grabbed Luke about the waist and Horace dismounted then. The three men carried Luke up the hill and into the house, laying him on the bed as Lettie instructed them to do. She quickly poured hot water into a the dishpan beside the bed and asked Jim to keep an eye on the children, while Horace and Zeb helped get off Luke's gun belt, boots, pants, and shirt.

For a moment Lettie froze, just staring at the deep claw marks on her husband's body and one side of his face. He had lost a lot of blood, and her first thought was that if the wounds didn't kill him, infection might. There was still no doctor in Billings that they could send for. There was no one but herself and these two men to help, and they could only act on instinct and what little they knew about what to do for such wounds.

"You all right, ma'am?" Zeb asked. "We can tend to him if you want."

"No," she answered quickly. "I'll do it." She struggled against an urge to scream and weep. "I'll just need you to stay close by, help me turn him over after I get the front of him washed."

Both men saw the terror in her eyes. "In all my years, I've known the Indians to use moss to help against infection, ma'am," Horace spoke up. "It can work pretty good. Once we get him cleaned up, I'll ride up and down the streams, check out the north side of some of the pine trees and such, see if I can find some. We can use it to pack against the wounds."

Lettie swallowed, thinking how just minutes ago she had been so full of resolve, baking bread and pies, sure they could survive here after all. She had been worried about an Indian attack, but it was a grizzly that had nearly taken her husband from her. Luke had just written his father to tell him about the beautiful place where he had settled, that he had a wife and two children and another on the way. He was so happy and proud to be able to tell his father how well he was doing.

She wet a towel and laid it gently against the wounds on his chest to soften the dried blood so she could wash it away. His eyes fluttered open for a moment, and he smiled at her. "I still have…a lot to learn…about living out here… don't I?" he tried to joke. He grimaced with pain then.

"We'll learn together, and we'll make it, Luke," she assured him.

"Meat. I left…a nice buck…and a dead bear…up by Turtle Creek." He looked at Horace. "Take Zeb…try to salvage some…of the meat…before the wolves get it all. We'll need it…this winter."

Horace nodded. "We'll see if we can find it. Just don't you worry about it, Luke."

Luke closed his eyes again. "So much…to do. I can't…lay here too long."

"You'll lie here as long as it takes for you to be completely well," Lettie scolded, needing desperately to cry. She couldn't now. She had to be strong. She suspected Luke had no idea just how badly he was wounded. She gently washed away some of the blood, and already she could see signs of infection, a deep red in the skin along the line of the cuts.

Dear God, don't let him die, she prayed inwardly. She turned to rinse the towel, shivering at the sight of blood swirling in the water as she wrung it out…Luke's blood. He had shed blood in the confrontation with the outlaws. Now he was shedding blood again, all for this land he was bent on calling his own.

❧

Lettie lay listening to her husband's deep, steady breathing. Silent tears slipped down the sides of her face, tears of joy as she inwardly thanked God for giving Luke's life back to him. After eight days of terrible suffering, his fever was finally gone, and he seemed to be healing; but for the rest of his life he would carry scars from the grizzly attack.

It seemed that life out here was nothing but a succession of joy and sorrow. For the moment she was just glad she had hung on to her baby despite watching her husband's agony. Horace had planted the potatoes for her, as well as a few vegetable seeds. He and Zeb had retrieved a good share of the bear and deer meat and most of it had been smoked for preservation and was hanging inside the stone smokehouse.

Life went on. Spring wildflowers bloomed everywhere, the children were fine, and Luke was sleeping peacefully by her side. Just yesterday Luke had mentioned that Perry Ward should be back from Oregon anytime to let him know what kind of deal he could get on cattle from there. Next spring he would start building a herd, and the thought of it was helping him heal and get back on his feet. She hoped he would hear something from his father, prayed the man would show at least a little interest. That would make Luke so happy.

The thought made her realize she owed her own parents a letter. One thing was certain, her letters to them must be food for wonderful entertainment, describing what life was like here in Montana. Now she would be telling them about how Luke had been attacked by a grizzly. At least Paint had not been hurt or killed. Luke loved that horse.

She quietly rose, walking into the main room and getting some paper and ink from the drawer of a fine pine desk Jim had built for her. She thought how Will had done a good job of finding help for them. He was a good friend. She would tell her parents about Jim and Zeb and Horace…and the fact that a third grandchild was on the way.

She sat down at the desk and dipped a pen into an ink well. "Dear Mother and Father," she wrote. She paused, a strange feeling of alarm rippling through her. Something was wrong, but she wasn't quite sure what it was. Quiet. Yes, it was awfully quiet tonight. Almost too quiet. She strained to listen, heard a couple of horses whinny somewhere down by the barn. She decided not to worry about it. After all, Zeb was keeping watch tonight, and Horace and Jim were close by in the bunkhouse. She returned to her letter, but she could not concentrate. Her chest tightened in fear then when she thought she heard a man cry out. It was such a short, quick cry, and so distant, she couldn't be sure.

She got up from the desk, looked in on Luke. She hated to disturb him. It was midnight, and he'd been sleeping well since about eight o'clock. This was the best he'd slept since being hurt. There was no sense in waking him up without knowing there really was something wrong. She walked to where Luke's rifle hung in a rack above the door and took it down. She cocked it, went to look out a front window, pushing lace curtains aside.

At first she saw nothing. There was just a sliver of a moon tonight, not enough light to see much. She set the rifle aside and cupped her hands at the glass to get a better view, wondering why, if Pup was out there, he had not barked at the strange noises she had heard. She thought she saw shadowy figures darting silently about. She remembered Will saying how quiet and stealthy Indians could be, and instinct told her it was not white men moving about out there. "My God!" she whispered. Where were Zeb and Horace and Jim? What was going on?

She leaped to her feet and quickly closed the wooden shutters over the window, then ran to another window to do the same, but too late. A log came crashing through it, wielded by a painted warrior who quickly jumped inside, cutting his leg on the way in but paying no attention to the wound. Lettie screamed and ran for the rifle, but just as she reached it a tomahawk swished past her, narrowly missing her and landing in the wall beside the rifle. She gasped at the thud, whirled to see three more warriors had come inside, wielding an array of weapons ranging from rifles to knives. She decided that to fight them could only end in death, and with Luke helpless, what would happen to her children then?

She stared wide-eyed at the wild-looking intruders, petrified, not for herself but for the children and Luke. Were Zeb and Horace and Jim already all dead? "What...do you want?" she squeaked, feeling ridiculous asking the question. From the look in their wild eyes, they wanted blood. Maybe they were here to carry her off and do horrible things to her, or to kill Luke for killing one of their own. One of them stepped forward, his face disfigured, part of his nose gone.

Half Nose! This was the one Will had told them about, a warrior feared by all whites and even some of his own kind.

"Lettie? What's going on?"

Luke! She could not find her voice when he appeared in the bedroom doorway. Surely Half Nose wanted him dead!

Everything happened in a matter of seconds then. Luke lunged for the rifle, but quickly three warriors were on him, beating him. At the same time Nathan and Katie came out of their bedroom, awakened by Lettie's screams and Half Nose's loudly barked orders. Lettie started to run to the children, but by then three more braves had come inside, and two of them grabbed her and held her back. Nathan ran to her, grabbing the skirt of her dress and beginning to cry, keeping his stuffed horse, which he still slept with, enclosed tightly in one arm. Katie began crawling across the floor to her mother, also crying.

Half Nose shouted another command in the clipped Sioux tongue, and Luke's attackers let go of him and let him slump to the floor, still too weak from his injuries and now from the reopening of some of his wounds, to put up any real resistance. One of the warriors grabbed the rifle out of Lettie's hands and Half Nose stepped closer to Lettie, his dark eyes drilling into her. She waited in frozen terror, sure he was here to murder all four of them. He looked down at Luke then, knelt in front of him and grasped hold of his hair, jerking his head up to study his bloody face. He said something to him then in the Sioux tongue, the words spit out bitterly. Lettie waited for the man to take out a knife and lift Luke's scalp, but instead he let go of him. He said something to one of the other warriors, who came over and shoved a rifle against Luke's throat.

Half Nose looked at Lettie once more, then down at little Nathan, who stared back up at him with tear-filled blue eyes. By then Katie had reached her mother and was trying to pull herself up by hanging on to Lettie's dress, but Lettie could not reach down to lift her because two warriors continued to hold her arms. She kept her eyes on Half Nose, feeling sick at the way he was watching Nathan. She kicked at him, not knowing what else to do to make him get away from Nathan. The man only grinned wickedly, then grabbed Nathan, who wiggled and screamed as the fierce warrior carried him to the door.

"No! No!" Lettie screamed. "Take me! Take me, not my son!"

In an instant Half Nose had unbolted the door and walked out with Nathan under his arm. Luke tried to get to his feet to stop him. The warrior who stood over him with the rifle whacked him on the side of the head and he fell helplessly to the floor. Lettie struggled to get free of the two braves who still held her arms. Katie was screaming in terror, hanging on to her mother's dress.

When Lettie was finally released, she grabbed Katie and ran to the door, screaming Nathan's name. Outside, the rest of the Indians rushed past her, one of them shoving her out of the way. They mounted up and rode off. In the distance Lettie could hear war whoops and the sound of many horses—Luke's horses, being stolen. Half Nose had already ridden off with Nathan, and Lettie sank to the ground at the fading sound of her son's screaming as he disappeared into the night.

◆

A cold spring rain fell as Lettie drove the buckboard through the muddy main street of Billings, past people who stared curiously at the woman who drove the wagon with a blank stare on her face, letting the rain soak her wool jacket. Syd Martin, the owner of the general store, realized first that something was wrong. Luke had already been to town once this spring, and he'd mentioned his wife was carrying again, due in only a couple of months. He had left her home because he didn't think it would be good for her to be riding in a bouncing, jolting wagon at this stage of her pregnancy, yet here was Lettie Fontaine, driving the wagon herself.

"Mrs. Fontaine!" The man ran out to catch the mules, realizing the woman hardly seemed to know where she was. "Is something wrong?" He managed to slow the mules enough to climb up into the wagon while it was still rolling and take the reins from Lettie. "Mrs. Fontaine?"

"Syd." The man's name came in a groan from the back of the wagon. Syd looked back to see Luke lying in the wagon bed, also getting rain soaked. Little Katie sat beside her father, who was holding a rain slicker over the child to keep her dry. Syd could see Luke's face was bruised and swollen, and there were long, scabbed streaks down one side of his face.

"Luke! What the hell has happened?"

"Get us to Will Doolan's," Luke answered, grimacing as he struggled to sit up. "I've got...to get a posse together... go after...Half Nose. He took our son...Nathan."

Syd closed his eyes, hardly feeling the rain that began running off the brim of his hat and dripping into his lap. "Jesus," he whispered. He looked at Lettie, his heart aching at the look on her face. She seemed almost to be in a trance. He took the reins from her and slapped them against the rumps of the mules, heading them out of town to Will's place. "Indians!" he called out to several people who had gathered to stare. "They took Luke Fontaine's boy! Get some men together and come on out to Will Doolan's!"

Lettie almost vomited at the words. *They took Luke Fontaine's boy.* Where was her precious little Nathan? Would Half Nose kill him? Keep him to raise as his own? If he let him live, would he be allowed to keep his stuffed horse? She had made that horse for him with her own two hands. As long as he had it with him, he could have a little piece of her heart with him also, and he might be all right, be a little bit comforted. There was so much to grieve over, she couldn't bear to think about any of it. Zeb, Horace, Jim...all dead...butchered. Because of her condition and the need to get help for Luke and find someone who might be able to go after

Nathan, she couldn't stop to bury the three men whom she had grown to care for very much. Even poor Pup was dead. Most of the horses had been stolen. Luke's beating had surely set back his recovery, yet he was determined to join whatever posse could be gathered to go after Nathan. Would the beating and his insistence on joining a search party kill him? He was not well enough for this, but she knew how badly he was suffering on the inside, blaming himself.

Who *was* to blame? Luke, for coming here in the first place? The savage Indians? Half Nose had lost a son. He wanted revenge. At the moment she could understand the feeling. Maybe *she* was to blame, for not realizing what was going on outside last night...or maybe for a deeper reason. Maybe this was some kind of punishment from God. Maybe she was somehow responsible for her rape after all, and she was supposed to suffer for it.

She touched her swollen abdomen. Somehow, through finding Zeb and Horace and Jim's bodies, through stumbling over poor Pup, through struggling to hitch a team of mules to the wagon and helping Luke into it, then through the long, jolting, almost daylong ride into town, she had hung on to the new life in her womb. At the moment she didn't really want to live at all, but poor little terrified Katie needed her mother, as did the new baby growing inside her. The one called Half Nose well knew how to get his revenge. Killing all of them would have been the easy way. They would not really have suffered at all. He probably thought Nathan was Luke's son by blood, figured taking the boy was the best way of punishing Luke and her for what had happened to his own son. For all his savagery, he was a wise man, and he was probably hurting as much inside as she was right now.

What was the sense in all this bloodletting? If Half Nose and his people had come to her house hungry, she would have fed them. If they had needed blankets, she would have given them some. Luke would probably even have traded them some horses for some buffalo robes—anything to keep the peace. Instead, the Indians had tried to steal Luke's precious horses, the only thing he had to make money on last summer. That led to killing Half Nose's son, and now all this. It could all so easily have been avoided.

Nathan! She could hear his screams. The terror in his eyes as Half Nose carried him off would haunt her the rest of her life. How was she ever supposed to sleep again? Eat again? If Luke and the others could not find her son...

She was hardly aware of arriving at Will's, or of Will lifting her down from the wagon and carrying her inside the house and laying her on a bed. She said nothing, for if she opened her mouth, she would start screaming and never stop. Someone began removing her wet clothes then, and she heard Henny talking to her, but the words did not make any sense to her. Someone laid a sobbing Katie on the bed beside her. She could hear men talking in another room, loud voices, heard Luke cussing, groaning. Luke... He couldn't go riding off with a search party in that cold rain. It would kill him.

Anguish was evident in Luke's voice as he explained what had happened. Will exclaimed when he heard about Luke's grizzly attack, and she remembered that Will and Henny hadn't even known about that yet. Immediately talk turned to gathering men together to go out and find Nathan. Then someone mentioned sending men out to bury Zeb, Horace, and Jim. Good. That was good. She hoped they would bury Pup too so the wolves could not get to him. Wolves. Howling wolves. Constant wind. Fierce grizzlies. Screaming, bloodthirsty Indians. This was a cruel land in which Luke Fontaine had chosen to settle. She could bear all the hardships, anything the land and the elements wanted to throw at her. But she could not bear having her son taken from her. She could see his sweet smile, see the ever-present stuffed horse in his arms. His smile faded, and he began shrieking. "Mommy! Mommy!"

She should be with him. The horror of it made her gasp, and she looked up at Henny. "I...I didn't finish my letter," she told the woman, who looked at her with deep concern in her eyes.

"What letter, dear?"

"I was...writing a letter...to my parents in Denver. I was going to tell them how well things were going. I had my garden planted...another grandchild on the way... Luke's pregnant mares. Everything was so good. The letter and ink...are still sitting on my desk...at home. Jim made the desk for me. You really...should come and visit, Henny...see the desk." What was she jabbering about? Nothing but nonsense came out of her mouth. Nathan! No! She couldn't think about that. "What should I say, Henny...in the letter?"

Henny leaned over her, stroking some of her damp hair away from her face. Yes, Henny knew why she was talking about nothing. "They'll find him, Lettie," the woman told her gently. "God will help them find him."

Tears began to spill out of Lettie's eyes. She had to believe that, didn't she? If she didn't believe that, there would be little reason to go on living. Henny helped her put on a warm, dry flannel gown, and Katie curled up beside her. Luke came into the room then, looking like a wild man. His blue eyes blazed with determination, but he looked pale and bruised. One side of his face was still puffy from the grizzly scratches, and he had lost weight from being sick. He half stumbled to the bed, a mixture of horror and guilt and sorrow on his face.

"I'm so goddamn sorry, Lettie," he groaned, his own eyes tearing. "We'll find him. I'm not coming back without him. I don't care how long it takes."

"You can't...go out there, Luke. You'll die. I can't lose you too."

"If I can't find Nathan, I *deserve* to die! This is *my* fault, for bringing you here, for not understanding how in hell to deal with Indians. If I had known this was going to happen, I would have let Half Nose's son come at me and bury an arrow in my chest. Right now I feel like that's exactly what he did anyway!"

He turned and limped out of the room. Lettie heard men's voices again, someone telling Luke to get into some dry clothes, to get some rest. They would get organized and head out in the morning.

Ten

LUKE RODE TO THE CREST OF THE HILL WITH WILL, TWO Shoshone scouts, and the handful of soldiers he had been able to convince to help him. He had found them camped near Last Chance Gulch, where the last of the original posse who had ridden out with him from Billings two months ago finally had given up and gone home. They had families, businesses, farms to tend to. Luke couldn't blame them, wondered himself if he would ever be able to get back on his feet after this setback. Was anyone taking care of the ranch? Was there anything left to go home to?

There was only one thing that kept him going, and that was the realization that Lettie and Katie needed him...if Lettie even still loved him. And by now there was probably another child, maybe the son he'd wanted. He had promised Lettie he'd be with her the next time she gave birth. It was just one of many promises he'd had to break. He didn't mean to break any of them, especially his promise to Lettie and her parents that nothing would happen to her or Nathan.

He felt so guilty now for wishing for another son. Little Nathan was all the son he needed, and now he was gone. For sixty days he had ridden in a good hundred-mile radius of Billings, sometimes farther, searching, sleeping in a tent at night or under the stars, asking questions, chasing the wind. That was what finding Half Nose was like. This was his country, his and his father's and his grandfather's. The man knew every creek and mountain, every ravine and forest. He was as elusive as a puff of smoke. Several men had helped him those first few weeks, then had fallen away one by one. Only Will remained at his side now, and these two new Indian scouts and the few soldiers they had picked up.

It was June, and surprisingly hot for so early in the summer. The scouts had been sure Half Nose was probably camped deep in these mountains, and now, at last, they had come upon an encampment of tepees nestled below them at the dip of two rolling hills. A hundred times Luke had got his hopes up, but until now their search had turned up nothing. Yet all the while they had felt watched. Luke did not doubt that at any time an army of Sioux Indians could have come swooping down on them from out of nowhere to massacre them all. But no. Half Nose wanted him to live. He wanted him to suffer this agony of a lost child.

Only a few days after they had begun their search, they had found a few of Luke's horses, then Nathan's little fur slippers he'd been wearing the night he was taken. They were tossed beside a river. Farther downstream they had found the flannel nightshirt the boy had on when he was stolen away. It was soggy, caught on a stump along the other side of the river.

One man thought maybe the boy had drowned. Luke refused to believe that. He couldn't bear the thought of it, and he couldn't go back to Lettie and tell her Nathan was dead. He had to cling to the hope he would find their son, would be able to bargain with Half Nose to get him back. The scouts had told him it was very unlikely Half Nose would kill Nathan. Killing little children after stealing them away was just not something the Sioux usually did. If he was going to kill him, he would have done it immediately. Stealing him more likely meant that Half Nose intended to keep the boy in place of his own lost son. Steal the son of the man who had killed his own son, turn him from white to Indian—the ultimate revenge.

That was Luke's only hope. He had taken sick during part of the search, had been laid up for days, nearly died. Now he was leaner, harder, certainly more familiar with the lay of the land, more experienced at surviving in the wild. The weeks of searching had finally led Will and him here, a good two hundred miles from home. The scouts had studied the village below with a spyglass, and both were certain that one of the tepees below belonged to Half Nose. It was painted with red horses, the man's spiritual sign.

One of the soldiers spoke up. "We're all gonna be killed."

"We've come in peace," Lieutenant Jiggs responded. "We'll ride in with the scouts and a white flag of truce. The scouts speak their tongue. They can interpret for us." Jiggs was a veteran of the War between the States, a war he'd told Luke was just about over. He had been sent west to determine the best locations to build forts along the Bozeman Trail to protect Montana's miners and settlers. Luke was glad forts would be built, glad more protection was coming. It was just too bad that it might be too late for Nathan...for Lettie.

His heart raced. He prayed as he had never prayed before that finally he would have his son back. Poor Nathan. What must he think? That his parents had deserted him? Was he down there somewhere amid that circle of tepees? "I'm going down with you," he told the lieutenant.

"I'm not sure you should, Mr. Fontaine."

"I'm going. We've come this far. If my son is down there, I want to see for myself. If those Sioux wanted us dead, they would have killed us a long time ago."

"They still might," the lieutenant said. He took a white flag from his gear, unfurled it, and held it up in the air. "Let's go."

He headed down the hill. Almost immediately several warriors who had spotted them in the distance jumped on the bare backs of their mounts and rode out of the village toward them. Many more painted, half-naked braves rode up the sides of the hill. In moments they were surrounded. Obviously they had been watched all along. It irked Luke to know that these past two months Half Nose had probably been leading him on, watching him, laughing at him, teasing him. Now he had finally allowed himself to be found. Maybe that meant he was ready to give up the boy.

All of them could almost feel their scalps being lifted as they rode into the village, but Luke was too angry and too anxious to be afraid. Dogs barked, women and children gathered to stare at them. A couple of the braves who rode beside and behind them finally charged around in front of them, holding up their hands and ordering them to halt. One of them said something to one of the Shoshone scouts, and the scout answered him. By now Luke recognized the Sioux words for Half Nose. Their Indian hosts turned and led them to the tepee with the red horses painted on it.

"He is here," one of the Shoshone men told Luke.

Luke's heart pounded with anticipation. At last, after all the days of helpless searching, of great hope and terrible despair, he had found Half Nose, the one man who could tell him if Nathan was dead or alive, the one man who might be able to give his son back to him.

The proud, muscled warrior came out of his tepee as they approached it. Luke wondered if they would all get out of this alive.

"This is a well-armed, well-fed camp," Lieutenant Jiggs told him calmly. "Don't do anything stupid, Mr. Fontaine. One wrong move and we're all dead. I know how much you hate Half Nose and would like to kill him, but don't do it. The last thing your wife needs is to lose her son *and* you."

"It isn't easy looking right into the face of the man who stole away your own son," Luke answered through gritted teeth.

"He's holding all the cards. You remember that."

They halted their horses and dismounted. Luke stood before Half Nose, glaring at him. They would have been well matched if Luke had not suffered so in his quest that he was not up to full strength. Half Nose outweighed him, but Luke stood a little taller, and he had a hard edge to him now that would intimidate most men, except for this Indian brave who knew he had nothing to fear at the moment. The brave looked him over, said something to him in the Sioux tongue, the words bitter. They sounded familiar. Luke thought maybe they were the same words the man had spoken that night in the cabin when he grabbed him by the hair.

"He say you are child killer," Slow Deer, one of the Shoshone scouts, told him. "Bad white man."

"Tell him I was defending my family and my possessions, just like he would do," Luke answered. "Tell him I didn't know the brave who shot arrows at me was his son and so young. Tell him I am deeply sorry."

Luke hated having to apologize to this man, but he would do whatever he had to do to get Nathan back, and he truly was sorry about Red Hawk.

Half Nose sneered at him as he replied, speaking several sentences before waiting for Slow Deer to interpret.

"He say it is too late to be sorry. His son is dead. He say he has let you find him because it is time you give up searching. It is also too late for you. Your son is also dead."

Half Nose's look of defiance did not waver when he saw the terrible sorrow move into Luke's eyes. Luke studied the man's dark eyes. "Tell him I don't believe him. He wants me to stop looking for my boy because he wants to keep him."

Slow Deer told Half Nose what Luke said, and Half Nose stiffened at the accusation. He shook his head, then looked over at Slow Deer. He carried on in his own tongue, waving his hands, using sign language as he spoke. Luke recognized the sign for water. They'd found Nathan's slippers and nightshirt by a river, evidence that the boy had drowned. No! He would not believe it.

"He say the little boy run away while they are camped, fall in river, and drown. It is probably so. Sioux and Cheyenne do not like to swim in deep river water, afraid of spirits beneath the waters. If the boy fell into the river, they would not have saved him."

"Then ask him why we didn't find Nathan's body when we found his clothes by the river."

Slow Deer interpreted, and Half Nose carried on some more.

"He say body must have drifted farther down the river from where you look. They never find it. It probably washed up on shore, and by now wolves and buzzards have torn it to pieces and dragged it away. It will probably never be found."

The words were spoken matter-of-factly. Luke felt ill. He needed to hit something, to scream, to weep, to kill someone. Surely God wouldn't have let little Nathan's life end that way! He struggled to keep his composure. He had to protect Will and the other men who had so faithfully helped him. And the lieutenant had been right: he had to go back to Lettie. But if he returned without Nathan maybe she wouldn't want him anymore.

He had only one chance left to see if Half Nose was lying.

"Tell him I'm not the boy's real father. Tell him he hasn't hurt me as badly as he thinks, because Nathan was not my son by blood. He might as well give him back to me, because if he was looking to steal my son, he hasn't. I don't have a son of my own."

Slow Deer told Half Nose what Luke said. Half Nose studied Luke's blue eyes for several quiet seconds. He spoke more calmly then.

"He say now *you* lie. He say even if the boy was not yours, he can see by your eyes that the hurt is the same.

He say a child does not have to be a man's by blood for the man to love it."

Luke was taken aback by the mention of the word love. What did this man know of such feelings? Perhaps more than he'd been given credit for. "Tell him he is right. Tell him if he'll give me my boy back, I'll furnish horses to him for as long as he needs them…even guns, if that's what it will take."

The Shoshone scout repeated the message, but Half Nose shook his head, spoke, then waved them off as though he was finished with them. He turned away.

Luke grabbed his arm. "No!"

Hatred filled Half Nose's eyes, and he jerked his arm away, his lips curling into a sneer.

"Goddamn it, Luke, be careful!" the lieutenant told him. "You'll get us all killed."

"What did he say?" Luke asked Slow Deer.

"He say all the horses and guns in the world cannot bring back a dead boy. Even if the child was alive, he would not believe your promise, because no white man has ever kept a promise to an Indian; but it does not matter. The boy drowned. He is dead, and that is the end of it. We must leave now, or they will kill us."

Luke began to tremble at the awful truth of it. He had come to the end of the road. He had to go back to Lettie without Nathan. How in God's name was he going to face her? "Ask him what happened to the stuffed horse my son always carried with him."

In response to Slow Deer's words, Half Nose shrugged, then barked out a reply.

"He say the boy must have dropped the horse somewhere along the way. He remembers it, but suddenly it was gone. It could be anywhere. He say if you do not believe he does not have the boy, you may search every tepee, but you must do it quickly. He wants us out of here."

Luke glared at Half Nose. "Fine," he answered with his own sneer.

He proceeded to search every single dwelling in the camp, beginning with Half Nose's tepee. Some of the women and children shrank from the tall white man with the mean look in his eyes, but the men in the village watched him defiantly, showing no fear.

When Luke exited the last tepee, he thought he might pass out from a mixture of grief and weakness from the hard journey that had led to this moment of utter defeat.

He walked back to face Half Nose. "Tell him I think he is a coward for taking his revenge through a helpless little boy," he told Slow Deer, his blue eyes blazing with hatred. "His own son was bigger, already an experienced warrior. He came at me like a man, and I killed him with the thought that he was a brave warrior. Half Nose has taken revenge by stealing away an innocent little boy and then allowing him to die. I have no respect for Half Nose. Yes, he has hurt me, as deeply as any man can hurt another, but I would have respected him more if he had taken me and not my son, if he would have tortured me, let me suffer any way he chose. It would have been the more honorable revenge."

Slow Deer looked at the lieutenant, not sure he should interpret the words.

"*Tell* him!" Luke ordered, standing only inches away from Half Nose and glaring at him.

Slow Deer swallowed, then repeated the words. Half Nose stiffened, drawing in his breath. He folded his powerful arms, spoke briefly, then turned and went inside his tepee.

"He say you can take back eight of your horses and four of the foals. He say it is all he can do to make up for your son. We must get the horses quickly and leave, or we all die. I know these Sioux. We must do what he say."

"Let's go, Fontaine. There isn't one more thing we

can do here," Lieutenant Jiggs told Luke. The man mounted his own horse.

"I don't want my horses. I want my *son*!" Luke answered.

"Your son is dead, Mr. Fontaine. I'm damn sorry about that, but that's how it is. Let's go cull out some of your horses and get the hell out of here."

"Come on, Luke," Will told him. "There ain't nothin' more you can do. Go on home to Lettie and your new baby. You've got a wife and two other kids waitin' for you."

Luke looked at the man with tear-filled eyes. "I can't go home without Nathan."

"You've got no choice, friend." Will grasped his shoulder. "Luke, we've got to get out of here."

Luke turned away, wiping at tears with his shirtsleeve as he mounted Paint. "You know my brand. Go pick out a few of the better horses and four foals like he said. I need to be alone for a few minutes." He mounted up and turned his horse to ride out of the village.

Will gazed after him, his heart aching for the man. Something had happened to Luke Fontaine these last two months. There was a raw edge to him now, a man hardened by adversity and personal loss. This was not the same Luke Fontaine he had first met when he came to Billings. That Luke was gone forever.

❧

Lettie looked up from the rocker in which she sat on the porch of her own home. Every day she came out here to nurse her new son and watch the horizon for her husband and another son. She had wanted to come here to wait, so that Nathan could come back to his own house, his own room. The baby had been three weeks old when she asked Henny to find a man to bring her back. That was a week ago. Henny was still with her, and Lettie knew she was worried their husbands would never return, that they too had been killed by the Sioux.

It was July now, 1865. The garden had been overgrown with weeds and drying up when they returned, and Henny had kindly pulled some of the weeds and watered what plants had survived. She had brought Bear and Patch with her for company, knowing how much Nathan enjoyed playing with the animals. She had cooked and cleaned, helped with Katie. Lettie wasn't sure what she would have done without the woman's help and company over the nearly three months since Luke had left with Will and the others to find Nathan.

One by one the others had returned, each with the same reports. No Nathan, but Luke and Will had not given up. Meanwhile Lettie and Henny had hired two men to keep the ranch going, and to protect them, until Luke returned. There was irony in that, Lettie realized, since she no longer felt she needed protection from the Indians. Half Nose had already gotten what he wanted.

"Riders coming!" one of the new hired help shouted then. His horse thundered up to the front of the house. "Coming in from the northwest. I think it's your husband, ma'am."

Lettie's heart pounded with both hope and dread. "Did you see whether there is a little boy with them?"

"No, ma'am. Too far away, but they are bringing a few horses back with them. They must have made some kind of deal with the Sioux to get those horses."

Henny came out of the house to stand beside Lettie and wait. Minutes seemed like hours for the two women as they watched the distant figures approach. The two hired men rode out to greet them. Lettie could see them well enough now to know Nathan was not with them. She recognized Luke, knew how he sat in a saddle, recognized Paint. She wondered if she was going to faint. "Oh God, Henny; they didn't find him!"

Henny touched Lettie's shoulder reassuringly. "Wait and see what he tells you."

Lettie slowly rose as Luke came closer, and for a brief moment she forgot her own sorrow at the sight of him. He was somehow changed, leaner, harder, a terrible sorrow in those blue eyes, but also a new determination. And older. He looked older.

The men dismounted as they reached the house. Henny ran to Will, who embraced her and led her away to give Luke and Lettie a few moments alone.

They stared at each other for several long, silent, miserable seconds.

"I figured we'd ride through here first, check the damage," Luke told her then. "I didn't think you'd be here."

She swallowed back the lump in her throat. "I wanted to come home."

Luke glanced at the bundle in her arms. "I told you I'd be with you when this one was born," he said, his voice strained. "I'm sorry, Lettie, sorry about a whole lot of things." He dismounted wearily. "Where's Katie?"

"Sleeping inside."

He came up the steps, looked down at the baby again, his eyes questioning. She noticed that the scars the grizzly had left on the side of his face were beginning to fade a little.

"It's a boy," she told him. "I named him Tyler, after my grandfather. I hope that's all right."

Luke looked away, but Lettie caught sight of the tears that were beginning to trickle down his cheeks. "He's dead, Lettie," he said quietly. "He drowned. I'm not going to go into details about it right now. There's no sense in it." His body jerked oddly, and Lettie heard a choking sound. Suddenly he broke into bitter sobbing. Lettie hesitantly touched his shoulder, noticing his hair had grown past his shoulders while he'd been away. Part of her wanted to hate him, to blame him; but she knew better. This was no one's fault. It was a matter of circumstances, of savagery, of an age-old battle between two cultures. "I loved him...as though he were my own." Luke groaned. "God forgive me."

Somehow Lettie had known all along that he would come back without her son. She felt surprisingly calm as she rubbed his back. "There is nothing to forgive, Luke. You couldn't have stopped it, and you did all you could to find him. I was afraid I had lost you too."

He wept for several minutes before pulling away from her and taking a handkerchief from the back pocket of his denim pants. He turned away and wiped at his eyes. "I did everything I could."

"I know that."

He breathed deeply, walking a few feet away and grasping a support post. "We'll leave. You've never really liked it here. I'll take you to Denver if you want, so you can be with your family. I'll find a job there."

Lettie looked down at her little son, a strong, healthy boy whose birth had helped soothe her broken heart. "No. We're staying." Luke turned around in surprise, and she studied the terrible agony in his bloodshot eyes.

"How can you want to stay after what happened?" he asked.

Lettie held out the baby. "Take him, Luke."

Hesitantly he reached out and took his new son into his arms.

"Someday all of this will belong to him, and his brothers and sisters. We're not leaving, Luke, because God led you here, because your dreams are here. Our children were born here, and this is our home now. No wild animals or wild Indians or outlaws or the elements are going to make us leave." She turned and looked out at the valley below. "My son is not dead. I feel it in my bones. Whatever happened, whatever you learned from the Sioux, I know in my heart my son is not dead." She faced him again. "That is *my* reason for staying. Someday my son is going to come home. I intend to be here when that happens."

Luke shook his head. "Lettie—"

"No! I don't want to hear it. All we can do now is pray that if Half Nose or some other warrior has Nathan, they will treat him with love, take good care of him; and pray that he never forgets us, that somewhere in his memory when he's grown, there will be a place for us."

"Lettie, we found his clothes by the river. We actually found Half Nose, and he told us the boy drowned."

"Did you find his stuffed horse?"

The words ripped at his insides. "No. Half Nose said it was lost along the way."

"You know Nathan would never let go of that horse, especially if he was afraid. He is alive and he has that horse with him. I know it, and that's why I'm never leaving Montana."

Luke stepped a little closer. "What about us?"

Lettie frowned, confused by the question. "I don't know what you mean."

"Lettie, every bit of this is my fault. I'd understand if you didn't want me around."

She closed her eyes. "Oh, Luke, I need you now more than ever." She looked up at him then. "And you are the father of my other two children. I married you for better or for worse, Luke. I married you because I love you. We can't always control the things that happen, and we can't let fear of what *might* happen stop us from living. Just don't ever try to tell me again that Nathan is dead. I can't and won't believe it. He is alive, and someday he will come back to us."

Luke looked into her green eyes, ached at the deep sorrow there. If it helped for her to believe Nathan was alive, then so be it. He looked past her at the valley below, at the few horses that were left. The two new men were herding those he and Will had brought back into a corral. It was a beautiful day, warm, sunny, flowers blooming in the foothills, bees buzzing, birds singing. All his buildings were still intact, and he held a healthy new son in his arms. He looked back down at Lettie. "You really want to stay?"

She took the baby from him, kissing its forehead. "Yes."

Luke took a deep breath. "All right. We stay. I want you to know that from here on there will be no more broken promises. You'll have everything you ever wanted if I have to work myself into the grave to get it. No man, red or white, is ever again going to get the better of Luke Fontaine or try to steal anything from me. If a man has to set his own laws out here, then that's the way it will have to be—no room for pity, no hesitation. On Fontaine land men will live by Fontaine law. And *no* one will ever hurt my wife or any of my children again! *No* one!"

"No one but God himself can make such guarantees, Luke."

He pulled her and the baby into his arms. He wasn't sure anymore if he even believed in a God who would let a sweet child like Nathan be carried off by savages. Out here a man had only himself to depend on. Out here sometimes a man had to play God himself.

"I'll find some way to make up for all the hurt, Lettie."

She did not answer. There was an emptiness in her heart now that nothing could ever fill, no matter how many more children she had, no matter how wealthy they might become. The only way to bear that emptiness was to believe that someday, somehow, she would find her son, hold him again, bring him back into the fold of her arms and tell him he was always loved, never forgotten.

PART TWO

We hold that happenings which may even compel the heart to break, cannot break the human spirit...

—May Kendall, *The New Joy of Words*

Eleven

LETTIE RAN OUT OF THE HOUSE AFTER THE HIRED HAND told her who had come visiting, driven to the ranch in a buggy by Will Doolan. "Mama!" She reached up for the woman before Will could even bring the buggy to a halt, then ran alongside it until it stopped and Katie MacBride could climb down. "Oh, Mama, I don't believe it!"

The two women embraced, laughed, cried. Lettie's sister, Louise, also climbed out of the buggy, followed by a slender man of perhaps thirty, wearing eyeglasses and a neat suit. Louise joined in the hugging while Lettie's several children gathered around to stare at the visitor.

"It must be our grandma," eight-year-old Katie told her sister, Pearl, who was five. Two of their brothers also watched curiously, seven-year-old Tyler holding the littlest brother, Paul, only two, while four-year-old Robert ran off after one of several dogs that roamed the Fontaine ranch. For several minutes the MacBride women clung to each other. As they finally pulled apart, they were all wiping at tears. It had been nine years since they had last seen each other on the Oregon Trail.

"Well, this is quite a reunion," Will said with a grin. "Too bad Luke's not here."

Henny climbed down from the two-seater buggy Will had rented in town to bring Lettie's mother and sister to the ranch. She had come along just to see the joy on Lettie's face. A round of introductions followed, then laughter when Lettie realized her mother had of course already met Will and Henny.

"We never would have survived those first two or three years without Will and Henny," Lettie told her mother. "Out here, dependable friends are worth more than all the gold most people come to Montana to find." She hugged her mother again. "Oh, Mama, why didn't you tell me you were coming? After all the letters…you should have written. Luke would so much have wanted to be here. We would have told you to come earlier in the spring, or later in the fall. In the summer Luke is gone on the cattle drive to Cheyenne."

"I know, dear, but…" Her smile faded. "I had a special reason for coming now."

Lettie studied the woman, her hair so much grayer, her skin more wrinkled, but it was the same beautiful face, her lovely complexion as pretty as ever against the soft pink dress she wore. She saw the deep sorrow in the woman's dark eyes then, and she realized what her father's absence must mean. "It's Father, isn't it?"

Katie nodded, unable to speak.

"Daddy died about six weeks ago, Lettie," Louise told her quietly. "Mother thought, after all these years…well, we'd been meaning to visit anyway. She thought it might be easier just to come here in person and be together, rather than write you the news in a letter."

Lettie felt a terrible sorrow. It had been nine years since she had felt her father's embrace, and now she would never do so again. What hurt the most was that she could hardly remember what he'd looked like except for the red hair and the green eyes so like her own. A whirlwind of joy and sorrow, hellos and good-byes, that's all life was. "Oh, Mama." She fell into her mother's arms and the two wept again.

"James wanted so much to come too," Louise told Lettie, referring to their brother. "But he had to take over Father's stores, and he's so busy. His wife, Sara, just had a baby girl. That makes three children for them, two nephews, and one niece you've never seen, and of course my own two daughters. They're too small for such a rough trip so we left them with James and Sara." She turned to the man who had come with her. "Lettie, this is my husband, Kenneth Brown."

Keeping an arm around her mother, Lettie wiped tears from her eyes and studied her brother-in-law. A banker, Louise had explained in letters. It was difficult to think of her little sister as married, the mother of two daughters already. But Louise was twenty-three now, a grown-up woman, and their brother was twenty-eight. She was twenty-seven herself, and Luke thirty-seven! It seemed impossible. "Hello, Kenneth."

Louise's husband smiled and shook her hand. Lettie was surprised at how soft his hand was, how limp the handshake. Accustomed as she was to the burly, rough, rugged men on the ranch, Kenneth looked small and delicate to her and his suit and spectacles were a strange sight. It hit her then how much she had changed over the years, for there had been a time when most of the men she knew wore suits and drove fancy buggies. "I'm glad to meet you finally, Lettie," Kenneth was saying. "We've all tried to imagine what it's like here, tried to picture the ranch, the house. Your letters have taken us on some wonderful adventures!"

Lettie laughed through tears. "Yes, life certainly is that here. One adventure after another." Her smile faded as her thoughts turned to Nathan. He had not been found or heard from in seven years. Maybe he really was dead. "Some more exciting than others." She nodded toward the sad little shack that sat farther up the hill. "That's where we spent our first terrible winter. We use the shack now to store feed."

"Dear Lord," Louise whispered.

Lettie gave her mother a squeeze. "Mama, I want you to meet your grandchildren. Ty, run and get Robert and bring him back here."

After setting little Paul on his feet, Tyler ran down the hill past a wandering milk cow to chase after his brother. "Robbie, get over here. Our grandma's here," he shouted.

Lettie picked up Paul. "This is Paul Lucas, Mama. He's two. He's the only baby I had who was delivered by a real doctor. Billings finally got a doctor three years ago, and it's a good thing." Her smile faded. "It was a very difficult birth. I almost died, and probably would have if Dr. Manning hadn't been there. He ended up having to operate. I can't have any more children."

"Oh, I'm sorry, Lettie," Katie said sympathetically. "You should have told me in your letters."

"I didn't want to worry you. Luke feels it's probably for the best. This last birth gave him quite a scare."

Katie studied her handsome grandson. "He has his father's dark hair and your green eyes," she told Lettie. "Oh, let me hold him."

Paul went to her readily, as though he'd always known his grandmother. He rested his head on her shoulder while Lettie introduced the rest of the children.

"This is our oldest, Katheryn Lynn," Lettie told her mother. "She's named after you, of course. She's eight years old already."

"And tall for eight years old!" the elder Katie said with a smile.

"She takes after her father in build, has his dark hair too but her eyes aren't green or blue."

"I have hazel eyes," the girl spoke up, holding her chin proudly. She gave her grandmother a smile. "I'm glad you came, Grandma. Mother has told me all about you, and what it was like back in St. Joseph. Will you tell me all about Denver?"

"Oh, it's a big city and growing bigger every day. There are some buildings four and five stories high, hotels, theaters. They've even built a railroad from Denver to Cheyenne. That's how we got here. We took the train first, then a stagecoach from Cheyenne to Billings. It was quite an exciting trip, and it's all such beautiful country."

"Hi, Grandma!" A very pretty, fragile-looking little girl with braided red hair and green eyes interrupted the conversation then, offering her grandmother a kiss. "I'm Pearl Louise. I'm five years old!" she said proudly. She turned to Lettie's sister and kissed her too. "I'm named after you, Aunt Louise."

"Pearl is a bold little thing, and you should hear her sing!" Lettie told them, touching her daughter's hair. "Almost every night after supper she sings and dances and does anything she can to entertain us. I'd like to try getting a piano someday, find a way to give her lessons. I think she's very musically inclined."

"A piano! Can you get a piano clear out here?" her mother asked.

"Where there is a will, there is a way, Luke always says. He says if I want a piano, he'll get me one." Her heart ached at the words. Ever since Nathan was taken away, Luke had worked like a demon to build the ranch and give her anything she needed. She knew he had never stopped blaming himself for losing Nathan.

Tyler came running back to them then, dragging Robert with him.

"Oh, look at you two!" Lettie exclaimed. "All dirty and sweaty. What a way for your grandmother to see you for the first time!"

"Robbie kept running away from me," Tyler answered. "I got hot chasing him." He wiped at his sweaty face with his shirtsleeve.

"Oh, I don't mind how dirty they are, Lettie. I'm just so happy to see my grandchildren finally."

Lettie smiled and took Paul from her. "This is Tyler," she said, indicating the handsome boy who was already becoming a replica of his father in size and coloring. "He's seven, but anyone who doesn't know him thinks he's at least ten. He's going to be a big man someday, like Luke. And look at those blue, blue eyes. Just like his father's."

Tyler grinned. "Pa's going to take me with him on the cattle drives as soon as I get big enough," he told his grandmother. "Someday I'm going to help run this whole ranch."

Katie smiled indulgently. "I'm sure you'll do a good job, Tyler."

"His middle name is James, after his uncle James," Lettie reminded her. She set down little Paul and picked up the one remaining child, a boy with his mother's dark auburn hair, but his father's blue eyes. "This is Robert Henry. He's four already."

They were surrounded then by barking dogs, and Tyler scolded one of them for jumping up on Louise. "The big yellow one is called Pancake," he told his grandmother. He picked up the small black-and-white mongrel that had jumped on Louise. "This is Pepper. The beagle over there is Jiggles."

"This is Smoke," young Katie told her grandmother, petting a huge, shaggy black dog. "That over there is Wolf. His daddy is Bear, Uncle Will's dog."

"*Uncle* Will?" the elder Katie asked. She eyed the huge, wolflike dog that young Katie had pointed out. It hung back from the others, looking less receptive of strangers.

"All the children call Will and Henny aunt and uncle," Lettie explained.

"Well, they're like family to us," Will put in with a hearty laugh. He growled playfully and chased after Pearl and Robert, who screamed and ran from him.

As the children ran off to play, Henny joined Lettie and her family, putting an arm around her friend.

"Doesn't your daughter have beautiful children?" she asked Lettie's mother. "I helped deliver every single one of them, but thank goodness we had the doctor here for the last one. I can't have children of my own, so being a part of this family has been the next best thing. I was so happy when Lettie and Luke first came here. I had a woman I could share things with, visit with, someone who didn't wear red dresses and paint up her face, if you know what I mean. That's about the only kind of woman you ever saw around here before Lettie came. Now more families have come in. Lettie is thinking of forming a women's circle, some way we can all meet together at certain times."

"Except in winter," Lettie reminded her. "Most winters there are a couple of months when we can't get into town at all."

"Yes, I've read about that in your letters," Katie said, her gaze still on the children. "You have a handsome family, Lettie. Of course, with a father like Luke and a mother like you, how could you have anything but bright, handsome children?"

Lettie smiled. "Luke is such a good father, Mama. He's so proud of them. He wanted a big family. I'm glad I have as many children as I do, but I would have dearly loved two or three more." Her smile faded. She and her mother looked at each other, both of them remembering another child.

Katie grasped her daughter's hands. "You never hear anything?"

"No. Luke believes Nathan is dead, but I just can't get over the feeling he's alive, Mama." She turned to look out over the valley and to the mountains beyond. "He's out there somewhere. I just know it. He'd be eleven years old now. There isn't a day goes by that I don't think about him, pray for him. Time is supposed to heal all wounds, but this one will never heal."

Katie led her away from the others so that they could talk alone. "Is everything all right with Luke now, Lettie?"

Lettie's eyes misted. She nodded toward the playing, jabbering children. "See for yourself. A woman doesn't have that many babies without everything being all right with her husband."

Katie smiled softly, thinking how pretty her daughter still was, even with her hair piled into a plain roll on top of her head. She wore a light green calico dress. "You hinted in your letters that first year after Nathan was taken away that things were pretty strained. After that you didn't say much about it anymore."

Lettie breathed deeply to keep from breaking down. The pain of losing Nathan suddenly seemed as keen as it had just after it happened. "Things were strained for a long time, not because I blamed Luke for any of it, but because he blamed himself. He has never quite stopped suffering over it, Mama. He works so hard building this ranch, building our wealth so he can give me all the things he thinks I should have, building me a big house, giving me a life better than anything I had before. I know he thinks it can make up a little bit for losing Nathan, but nothing can take away the pain."

"Of course it can't. It's too bad Luke blames himself as he does. He's a good man, Lettie. I remember that about him. He loved you so much."

Lettie nodded. "I've never doubted that love. If anything, it's even stronger. For months after Nathan was taken, Luke didn't even sleep with me. He thought I wouldn't want him in my bed, and both of us were hurting so much on the inside that we had no desire for..." She blushed. "Things finally got better." She laughed nervously. "As you can see." She closed her eyes and took another deep breath. "Things are good now. We've both resigned ourselves to the fact that we'll probably never know what really happened to Nathan. We pray for him, pray that if he's dead, he didn't suffer; and if he's alive, God is watching over him, and that he's happy. We thank God we have each other and that we've been blessed with five more healthy children."

She waved her arm. "Look out there, Mama. As far as you can see, that's what Luke owns. I'm not sure about the legalities of all of it. Luke has learned that out here men set their own laws, their own boundaries. That's just the way it is. He needs the land, so he's laid claim to it, thousands of acres and thousands of head of cattle, most of the herd built up from cattle he brought here from Oregon. Every summer he drives cattle down to Cheyenne to be loaded onto the Union Pacific and shipped back East, mostly to slaughterhouses in Omaha and Chicago. He gets top dollar because his cattle are fattened up on some of the best grass in this country, right out there on his own land. He has ten men working for him year-round, hires more in the summer to help on the cattle drive so that some can stay here and watch the ranch. Those six cabins out there to the south belong to the families of some of the permanent men. It all seems so big to me already, but Luke says it will get much bigger—more land, more cattle and horses, a bigger house."

She sighed deeply. "With all this success, I feel sorry for Luke, because I know he still hurts inside, not just over Nathan, but also over the situation with his own father. I told you in my letters the story behind why Luke came out here. He has written to his father several times, but the man never replies, nor does Luke's brother. I know it hurts him deeply, but he refuses to show it."

Katie took her daughter's hands. "And what about you? You went through so much hell those first couple of years."

"Life goes on, Mama. Actually it was Luke who thought about giving up, right after Nathan was taken.

He said we could move to Denver so I could be with you, that he'd find a job there. I know he didn't really want that. He just made the offer for my sake, but I couldn't take his dream away, Mama; and I couldn't leave this place, not when I know in my bones Nathan is still alive. I've always thought that if he ever comes back, he'll come here looking for us. I want to be here when that day comes. At the same time, we've both grown to love this land. This is home now, Mama." She squeezed the woman's hands. "Except for the ever-present longing to find Nathan, we're fine. Our love is strong, and we have the other children. Life is still often very hard. It will be a long time yet before Montana is as civilized as most of the rest of the country; but we're getting there."

Katie smiled sadly. "I'm glad you're doing so well." She sighed deeply. "We saw the graves on the way in. Will reminded us about the outlaws buried there. I remember you telling us about it in one of your letters. I just couldn't imagine Luke shooting down seven men."

Lettie looked up the hill toward the graves, their mounds now sunken and weathered by time. "That was not an easy time for him, but out here men have to take the law into their own hands. In some ways Luke is a much harder man than the one you knew when we first parted on the trail. He's actually feared by some, respected by all. He has taken to this land and to ranching like a fish to water. Not all men can come here and settle. It takes a special breed." She looked back at her mother. "But when it comes to me, and to the children, he's always good and gentle," she added.

She put an arm around her mother then. "No more talk of this. We're happy and everyone is healthy, and it's been nine years since I've seen my mother. I can't believe you're really here. You'll stay till Luke gets back, won't you? Surely you didn't come all this way just to stay a couple of days. We have a brand-new bunkhouse that the men haven't moved into yet. It would be a very nice place for the three of you to stay. With five children and three bedrooms, there isn't room in the house, but you'd be quite comfortable in the bunkhouse; and of course, during the day you'll spend every minute with me, every meal. I'll introduce you to the wives of some of the help. We can have a big picnic when Luke gets back! That would be fun. He should be back within a week or two. You *can* stay that long, can't you?"

"We were figuring on a nice, long visit, unless we wear out our welcome!" The woman laughed lightly. "Louise's husband owns two banks. He's his own boss, so he can do what he wants. Their little girls will be fine with James and Sara. We had already agreed that we would stay as long as necessary. After all, I'm getting on in years myself. This might be the last time we see each other, Lettie."

"Oh, Mama, don't say that."

"Well, it's just a fact of life; but we won't think about things like that. Let's enjoy the visit. I want to see your house, Lettie."

They returned to Louise and Henny, and all four women strolled into the house, chattering and laughing.

"There's nothin' that can gaggle more than a bunch of women," Will commented to Kenneth.

"I fully agree!" Kenneth answered, rather intimidated by the much bigger, buckskin-clad Will Doolan. Will was friendly enough, and as soon as he'd got word that Lettie Fontaine's mother was in town and looking for someone to bring her to the ranch, the man had readily obliged, renting a comfortable carriage for them, introducing them to his wife.

As Kenneth looked around the sprawling ranch, it was obvious what a different life people led out here. "She must be a very strong woman," he murmured.

"What?"

"Lettie. She must be very strong, for all the things she's been through."

Will nodded. "That she is, Mr. Brown. She's a good match for Luke."

One of the hired help rode past them then, dressed in dirty denim pants, his shirt stained with sweat. His horse kicked up a cloud of dust, and Kenneth looked down to brush at his suit.

"You'd better be wearin' some sturdier clothes than that if you intend to stay here awhile," Will told him with a laugh.

Kenneth took out a handkerchief and wiped dirt and sweat from his eyes. "Yes, I can see that." How did these people put up with being so far from town and civilization, with no schools, no bricked streets, no law? "I am looking forward to meeting Luke," he told Will. "He sounds like someone a person never forgets once they've met him."

Will laughed. "Oh, he leaves an impression, all right. You mark my words, Mr. Brown. Luke Fontaine is a name a lot of people will know someday, even down in Denver."

❧

"You do good this time, boss?"

Luke looked over at Runner, a half-breed Crow Indian who worked at the ranch and had gone on the cattle drive to Cheyenne. "Good enough to pay you enough to buy some *good* whiskey," he answered, "instead of that rotgut junk you bought from those whiskey runners last spring. I don't want you dealing with them anymore, Runner. Next time I see them on my land, I'll bury all of them."

Runner grinned, remembering how Luke had chased off the whiskey traders he'd found camped on Fontaine land a few months ago. He hated them because they sold whiskey to the Sioux, and he hated the Sioux for stealing his son from him. Runner didn't mind that. All Crow Indians hated the Sioux also. They had been warring with each other for generations, but that was over now. The Crow were at peace, most living on reservations. They no longer roamed wild, competing with the Sioux for land and game. The Sioux were one of the last of the American Indian tribes to continue resisting white settlement. Red Cloud and a new warrior called Crazy Horse were causing a lot of problems, had even chased out the army and burned forts. They were aided by another warrior whose name no one dared mention in front of Luke Fontaine. He was called Half Nose.

"I don't like you drinking at all, Runner," Luke warned. "But as long as you don't cause trouble and as long as you don't drink when you're supposed to be working, I'll put up with it."

"Runner not do you wrong, boss. Double L a good place to live. Better than reservation."

"What's the matter, Runner? Don't you like farmin' and livin' that quiet life on the reservation?" Ben Garvey, a bearded, grizzly old man who Luke suspected was as strong and hardy as a twenty-five-year-old, looked over at the half-breed from where he rode on the other side of Luke.

"Reservation life no good," Runner answered. "Nothing to do. Just sit and drink and die. No good. I like working for Luke Fontaine."

Luke laughed as he removed his wide-brimmed hat and wiped at sweat on his brow. "You're just soft-soaping me, Runner, so I'll let you have your whiskey."

"Soft soap? What is this, soft soap?"

Luke put his hat back on. "Never mind. You're a good worker, Runner. That's all that matters. We had a good drive, didn't we, boys? For once we didn't have trouble with renegade Sioux stealing some of our beef, and we only had one stampede. If it wasn't for that damn thunderstorm, even that wouldn't have happened. I have a feeling that from now on our biggest problem will be rustlers and squatters. According to men I talked to in Cheyenne, rustling is getting to be a big problem down in Colorado and Wyoming. It won't be long before they come our way."

"We can handle them," Ben answered, patting the six-gun on his hip.

"Maybe so, but I'm going to hire even more men next year for the drive. Shelby Preston wants me to bring an extra five hundred head next summer, twenty-five hundred total."

"Ah, those city people back East, they're getting a taste for good beef, huh?"

The question came from Sven Hansen, a Swede Luke had hired after the man had given up in the goldfields around Helena, the new name for Last Chance Gulch. It was one of the few gold towns that had survived and was still thriving. Most of the men who worked for Luke were men who had given up their dream of getting rich by finding gold. Some miners had found the precious metal but could not afford to mine it properly. Others had died at the hands of angry Sioux Indians who wanted the white men off their land.

Ben Garvey was one of those ex-miners. He was Luke's top hand now, and a close second was a quiet but rough-looking dark-haired man simply called Tex, who rode out ahead of the rest of them now, taking turns with Runner in scouting for any trouble that might lie waiting for them. Tex appeared to have some Mexican blood, but he never talked about his heritage, family, or where he had come from. He had arrived at the ranch one day looking for work. At first Luke had not trusted him. He suspected the man was wanted for some crime back East. But Tex had proved to be extremely talented in breaking horses, as well as in using a rifle. He was hard but dependable, a man who did not hesitate to pull a trigger when necessary. Out here, especially on cattle drives, that was the kind of man Luke needed.

He had also brought young Billy Sacks on the drive, wanting him to learn the ropes. Billy, twenty-three, had come to Montana with his then-seventeen-year-old wife, Anne, just last year. Both were orphans from the Civil War and had come west to forget the horrors of that war and start a new life. Billy thought that by working for Luke, he could learn the things he needed to know about settling in this country, and Luke had promised him that if he did a good job, he'd let him have a prime piece of property on his own land eventually, so that Anne could continue to live near Lettie. He well understood the strain of loneliness for a woman in this country. Maybe Anne wouldn't have to suffer that pain as intensely as Lettie had those first couple of years.

Billy was the only married man he had brought on the drive. He had left the rest of the married ones at the ranch, hired another six extras, all single men, for the cattle drive. Single men had fewer mental distractions to keep them from concentrating on the cattle, and they were more willing to put their lives on the line in times of danger. Most of the extras had stayed on at Cheyenne once the cattle were sold and were someone else's responsibility; but two, Cade Willis and Bob Dolan, were returning with him to the Double L.

They were all good wranglers, dependable men he could trust. He looked down at his saddlebags, stuffed with money paid by Shelby Preston, a buyer from Omaha. He'd got four dollars a head for his two thousand steer; eight thousand dollars. He'd heard in Cheyenne the army sometimes paid up to six dollars a head. With new forts being built in Montana and northern Wyoming because of a new campaign against the Sioux, he figured he'd see about getting a government contract to sell beef to the army, which would in turn help ensure that he could continue to use government land for grazing.

It wouldn't be long now before he could build Lettie the biggest, finest home in Montana. He smiled at the thought of it, but those thoughts were interrupted when Tex came riding back to them at a gallop.

"Some men camped on the other side of the hill," he told Luke. "They've got a good-size campfire going, and it looks like they're roasting something over it."

Luke and the rest of the men followed him to the crest of the hill, where they halted their horses and studied the camp below. "Who do you think that is, Runner?" Luke asked.

Runner watched them for a few seconds. "Got a wagon down there. Looks like it's piled with robes. Buffalo hunters, I think. There be more and more of them lately. They skin the buffalo and leave all the meat. I no like these buffalo hunters."

Luke squinted against a setting sun. In his years of riding the perimeter of his property, rooting out squatters, outlaws, and Indians, he had become as adept at scouting as Tex and Runner. He sniffed the air. "Smell that?" he asked.

"Smells damn good," Tex spoke up, "like roastin' meat."

"Like beef," Luke answered.

"A man gets tired of buffalo meat," Tex kidded.

"I suppose he does," Luke answered, "but he doesn't come onto Fontaine land and take whatever beef he wants for free. Let's go."

All eight men rode down the hill toward the strangers camped around the fire. As they came closer, Luke could see they were a rough-looking bunch, although after weeks on the trail and some hard riding to get back home, he and his men didn't look much better. The intruders rose, and Luke counted six men. The wind carried their smell, which overpowered even that of the roasting hindquarter of beef that hung over their fire. It was an offensive smell, the scent of old blood, buffalo robes not yet fully dried and cured. A few of the hunters still had bloodstains on their clothing and hands, which they had not bothered to clean.

"Enjoying your meal, boys?" Luke asked.

The apparent leader of the bunch stepped away from the others, putting on a smile. "You fellas want to join us? They's plenty of meat for all."

Luke looked past him at a dead steer lying in the distance, its body covered with thousands of flies. The carcass was hacked up but not even gutted. They had apparently killed the valuable animal just for the meat they needed at the moment. "Do you know who that steer belongs to?"

The man he was facing eyed all eight of them carefully, stepped back a little. The others with him all straightened, one man resting his hand on a six-gun at his side. "I don't reckon it matters," the leader answered. "It's just one little ol' cow, wanderin' around where it don't belong."

"That 'cow,' as you put it, belongs to *me*, mister. Luke Fontaine! You're on Fontaine land, *my* land, and you've killed one of my best steers. I suggest you get the hell off my land, right now!"

"Or what?" One of the others spoke up then, leaning on a rifle with the longest and biggest barrel Luke had ever seen. "You know what this is, mister?" The man, so tall and skinny he hardly looked strong enough to hold the big gun, slowly picked up the rifle. "This here's a buffalo gun, made special for huntin' the big beasts. It shoots farther and makes a bigger hole than any other rifle there is. I hate to tell you what it can do to a man. It would—"

Before he could even finish the sentence, Luke's six-gun was drawn and fired. The man screamed out when the bullet ripped through his right wrist, and the buffalo gun fell to the ground.

"You son of a bitch!" one of the others spoke up.

Luke waved the six-gun. "All of you, get the hell off my property!"

"You gonna let him do this, Cully?" one of the others asked their leader.

"You bastard." The one called Cully sneered. "We didn't see no fences! If your goddamn beef stray beyond where they're supposed to be, that ain't our problem! Keep your damn beef on your own land!"

Luke rode closer, suddenly kicking out at Cully and landing a foot in the man's chest, knocking him onto his rump. "Mister, as far as you can see from here is Fontaine land! I just haven't fenced it all yet. And even if it wasn't, Fontaine beef is Fontaine beef, whether it's on my land or *off* it, and theft is theft! Now you take your stinking bodies and your stinking buffalo robes and get the hell out of here, and don't let me catch you anyplace around here again!"

Out of the corner of his eye Luke saw the man with the six-gun start to draw. He whirled and shot, opening a hole in the man's chest. Only a fraction of a second after his own gunshot, he heard another gun fired. Another buffalo hunter went down, and he turned to see Tex's gun smoking.

Cully had got to his feet by then. He stepped away, glaring at Luke. "You shot my brother, you bastard!"

Luke aimed his six-gun at the man, and the rest of Luke's men had rifles and handguns ready. "A man pulls a gun on another man, he takes the chance of getting shot," Luke growled. "It's just a fact of life out here. Now you take those two dead bodies and your gear and get going! *Now!* And leave the buffalo guns behind! I don't intend for you to turn around and use them on us after you get a couple of hundred yards away!"

"We need those guns for our livelihood!"

Luke nodded to Tex and the others. "Take their rifles."

His men surrounded the buffalo hunters and picked up all the buffalo guns they could find. The skinny man with the wounded wrist and Cully both let off a string of curses then as Luke's men forced them to pick up their things and get on their horses. Two of them picked up the dead bodies and threw them onto the wagon full of robes.

Cully rode up to Luke then, bitter hatred in his eyes. "You'll regret this, Fontaine! You can't be everyplace at once, and I expect you're gone a lot, runnin' such a big ranch, ain't you? You got a wife, Fontaine? Kids? You'd best keep a good eye on them."

Luke charged off his horse and landed into him, both men plunging to the ground and rolling in the gravel and sage. Luke's men backed away and watched guardedly, keeping an eye on the rest of the buffalo hunters. Cully rolled on top of Luke and pulled a huge knife. He was a big man, shorter than Luke, but strong and burly. Luke grasped his wrist, straining to keep the knife away from him. Tex and the others kept their six-guns ready, afraid to fire for fear of hitting Luke as the two men tumbled and rolled.

Finally Luke was the one on top, still grasping Cully's wrist. Cully reached up and grasped at Luke's face, trying to gouge his eyes, while Luke slammed the man's knife hand against a rock, over and over until finally Cully dropped the knife. He grabbed Cully's other wrist then, pulled it away from his face and managed to jerk the big, burly man to his feet. Cully kicked at his legs, but Luke landed a big fist into the man's belly, making him grunt and knocking the air out of him. Several more hard blows to his gut, ribs, and face sent the man sprawling, his face bloody, no fight left in him.

Luke knelt down then and pulled him to his knees, his own eyes bloodshot and bruised from Cully's attempt at blinding him. He jerked the man close, teeth gritted, his face smeared with sweat and dirt. "*Nobody* threatens my wife and my kids, you stinking bastard! You be glad you're leaving here still breathing! If I ever see your face anyplace near here again, I'll shoot you on sight, whether you're armed or not!" He shoved the man back to the ground, where Cully lay groaning. Luke looked at the other hunters. "Get him the hell out of here, before I decide to drag all of you to the nearest tree and hang you!"

The rest of them were sullen but appeared humbled. "We're goin', mister," one of them spoke up. The tall, skinny man dismounted and asked one of the others to help him pick up Cully. They helped the man walk to the wagon and climb into it, where he moaned as he fell into the robes beside his dead brother. The other two mounted up, and one of them picked up the reins to Cully's horse. Another climbed into the wagon. Then they all rode off.

"Keep an eye on them till they're completely out of sight," Luke told his men. If they rode hard they could get home by nightfall, and he missed Lettie and the kids. He didn't want to be gone one more day, and he knew Billy was anxious to get home to Anne.

"You okay, boss?" Runner asked.

Luke rubbed at his eyes with his shirtsleeve. "I'm all right." He picked up Cully's knife, and saw that it was very well made. "Looks like Lettie's got a new butcher knife," he commented.

The others laughed, beginning to feel the relief of a successful confrontation.

"Pick up those buffalo guns. They're damn good weapons. You men divide them up among yourselves." Luke grunted when he bent down then to pick up his hat. He mounted his horse, a big roan gelding he'd chosen to replace Paint, who was getting too old to hold up on a cattle drive. "Billy, get yourself a clean blanket and wrap it around that quarter of beef. You take it home to Anne and you can have a royal meal. Have her cut some off for the rest of the men." He rubbed at his right calf. The old wound still hurt him whenever he did anything strenuous. "It's too bad they let the rest of the carcass go like that. If it had been gutted and wasn't covered with flies, I'd take it back and get some use out of the meat. What a damn waste!"

"Now you know how the Indians feel when they see the same thing happen to the buffalo," Runner commented.

Luke nodded, the pain of Nathan's capture still hitting him hard at times. He wanted to hate the Sioux, and most of the time he did. But there was a part of him that could understand how they felt. There ought to be a way the Indians and whites could share the land, but drastically different cultures prevented that. Though he didn't believe Nathan was alive, if he was, he might be out there living with those Indians who still refused to go to a reservation. He might be dependent on the buffalo for survival.

He turned his horse, telling himself it was a foolish thought. After all these years, none of the Crow or Shoshone scouts he had checked with from time to time had heard anything about a white captive with the Sioux, or a "white Indian," who rode with them. He had never quite given up his search, but he knew it was hopeless. It was Lettie who wouldn't give up believing Nathan was still alive, and he didn't have the heart to try to discourage the thought. It helped her to believe it.

Billy wrapped the cooked meat and tied it onto his horse. "Let's get the hell home, boys," Luke told them. He kicked his horse into a gentle lope, heading north across Double L country.

This far out he considered the land his simply because his cattle and horses sometimes grazed here. It really belonged to the government, but who the hell cared?

They weren't doing anything with it, and he intended to fence it off eventually, adding to his empire. A lot of ranchers did that now—used the land beyond their own borders for grazing. It was necessary in order to feed herds that got bigger every year. In a couple of weeks cattle agents would be bringing him more sturdy stock from Oregon and California. He needed a good half-million acres for enough grassland to feed his growing herds, which numbered close to eight thousand now. Soon there would be more, meaning he would need even more land. He would get it, one way or another; but the powers that be in Washington were reluctant to give up too much land, wanting to save it for the railroad, wary that there might be valuable minerals under a lot of it. What he and the other ranchers in Montana needed was to gather together and force their hand to get what they needed. He had formed the Cattlemen's Association, an organization still young. They would be holding their second meeting in only three weeks. Similar groups were forming in Colorado, Utah, Wyoming. It was time for Montana ranchers to band together and protect their land and their rights, encourage the government to send more soldiers out here to alleviate the continued danger from renegade Indians, allow the ranchers to claim more land.

He removed his hat and ran an arm over his face and hair to wipe away more dirt and sweat. He hated to go home to Lettie this way. But after all these weeks away, she wouldn't much care how he looked when he got there. She in turn would look damn good to him…and feel damn good in bed tonight.

Twelve

KATIE MACBRIDE LOOKED UP FROM HER PLATE OF BEEF and potatoes to study the son-in-law she had not seen in nine years. His reunion with Lettie and the children when he'd arrived home this evening had been warm, full of excitement and questions. It was obvious he was a good husband and father, but she had seen the fear and concern in Lettie's eyes at the sight of him. How many nights did her daughter lie awake wondering if her husband would come home at night alive and uninjured? He had bathed and shaved before sitting down to supper, which Lettie served on a big pine table Luke had built himself; but cleaning up could not hide the scratches and bruises about his eyes, nor could he cover up the limp awakened by the scuffle with the buffalo hunters. She noticed that between bites he rubbed at his ribs.

Yes, there was a lot about Luke Fontaine that was different from the Luke she had known. Thank God he was the same loving man toward his family she remembered, but she suspected that beyond their sight and hearing, he had learned to be ruthless. He had been very evasive about what had happened. A little problem with some buffalo hunters who decided to dine on Fontaine beef, was all he had told Lettie. She had asked no further questions, had sought no details. A little problem? He and his men had come back with the beef the hunters had been roasting, as well as several long rifles they had taken from them. How had they managed that?

She decided it was useless to worry about it, as long as

he was good to Lettie and the children, who all seemed to adore their father. It was obvious Luke was a man who could take care of himself, and from the looks of some of the men who worked for him, he had plenty of help enforcing whatever laws he set for his land. In her visit of several weeks, she had concluded that out here men set their own laws, and they enforced them however they had to. There were no sheriffs, no judges. If a man wanted to survive, he simply had to be more skilled with fists and guns, a better scout and hunter than the next man, and yes…ruthless when necessary. This was indeed a very different world her daughter lived in, and she surmised that by now, Luke and even Lettie would not be happy in a place like Denver. This was their little empire, and even Lettie had the land in her blood; but she at least had not lost the softness and genteel manners she'd been taught as a child.

"Did the buffalo hunters shoot at you, Pa?" Tyler asked Luke.

Katie noticed Lettie look at her husband, the same question in her eyes. Luke turned to Tyler. "No, Ty," he answered. "We just chased them off, that's all."

Tyler grinned. "I bet they ran scared. You must have been real mad seeing them eating our beef."

Katie suspected Luke was lying about no shooting going on.

"Yeah, I was pretty mad," he answered. Luke could feel Louise and her husband Kenneth watching him. All evening Kenneth had gawked at him as though he were the most unusual creature he'd ever seen.

Lettie looked down at her plate, no longer hungry. She knew without asking that there *had* been a shoot-out. Over the years Luke had had to kill more than once in defense of his property and family. Had he killed again today? She hated to see him have to resort to such measures, worried what it would do to him; and she hated knowing that every time he rode away he could himself be killed.

"I'm glad you came, Katie," Luke was telling her mother, obviously trying to change the subject. "At least Lettie had some good company while she was waiting for me to get back. I'm just sorry to hear about Henry's death."

"Well, it has certainly been an adventure up here," Kenneth spoke up.

Luke glanced at the man, thinking how easy it would be to pick him up and throw him several feet. He had not seen such clean hands on a man in a long time, nor met anyone who wore a suit every day. He was friendly, and Luke supposed smart as hell, being a banker and all, but he probably wouldn't last long out here on his own.

"Life tends to get pretty exciting around here at times," he answered. He finished his last piece of meat and leaned back in his chair, looking from Louise to Katie. "I know you both worry about Lettie. I want you to know I take damn good care of her. I have plenty of men working for me now. There's no danger to her as long as she's on this ranch, and I take her into town as often as I can. Within another couple of years I'm going to build her as wonderful a house as she could have in Denver or anyplace else, and I'm going to have a piano shipped out here. She'll have fine furniture, all the trimmings. She's forming a ladies' circle, and between that and the kids, she doesn't suffer the kind of loneliness she did when we first got here. I promised you I'd make a good life for her, and I'm doing everything I can to make that happen. The ranch is getting bigger all the time. This last trip I made good money on the beef I took to Cheyenne. The buyer already told me he wants five hundred more steers next year. We're doing okay."

Katie smiled. "I don't doubt that, Luke. We didn't come here to question how you take care of Lettie. I just wanted to see my daughter and my grandchildren."

She reached out and put a hand over his. "Just don't let
the things you have to do to defend this place and your
family make you too hard. Don't lose sight of compassion and fairness, Luke."

He squeezed her hand in return. "That won't happen.
You just have to understand that out here, with some
men, you have to make the first move or you won't be
alive to make the second. If a man wants to protect his
own, he has to shut off his feelings and do what must be
done. That's just the way it is, Katie."

Kenneth smiled nervously. "You're quite something,
Luke." He studied the faint scars left on Luke's face
by the grizzly attack. "Listen, if you ever need a loan
to expand, you let me know. I'll gladly lend you the
money from my own bank. Just wire me in Denver. I
think you're going to be quite a wealthy man someday.
You've done a heck of a job, considering what little you
had to start with."

"Thanks, Kenneth. I'll remember the offer." Luke
glanced at Lettie, knew she was as anxious as he was to
get this meal over with and be alone. He was grateful
for her family's visit, overjoyed to see them himself. He
knew how much it meant to Lettie. Still, he and Lettie
had been away from each other for nearly three months.
He longed to be alone with her.

"How about dessert?" Lettie asked. "I have apple pie
that's still warm."

Luke watched her lovingly. It felt so good to be home,
to be surrounded by softness and love again. What a contrast this was to a trail drive and buffalo hunters. Kenneth
peppered him with more questions about ranching
as they ate their dessert, and after supper the women
cleaned up while Luke and Kenneth sat smoking and
talking. All five Fontaine children clamored to sit in their
father's lap, giving him hugs and kisses, asking a thousand
questions. It seemed forever before Lettie's family finally

returned to their own quarters and the children were all tucked into bed. Because of the extra visiting, it was nearly midnight before the house was finally quiet and Luke and Lettie were alone in their bedroom.

"My God, it's been a long day," Luke muttered, yawning and removing his shirt.

Lettie's heart tightened at the sight of bruises on his ribs. "You killed someone today, didn't you, Luke?"

He hesitated as he unbuttoned his pants, then sighed deeply. "He pulled a gun on me. They were a bad bunch, Lettie. One of them threatened to get back at me through my family. Nobody threatens me that way, especially when they're standing there roasting a hindquarter of my own beef over their fire and squatting on my land."

She walked closer to him. "I wonder if the day will ever come when I can stop worrying about you every time you ride out of here." She ran her hand over the scars on his chest.

"That day *will* come," he promised. He pulled her into his arms, then took the combs from her lustrous hair and let the deep auburn locks fall down her back. "I'm sorry, Lettie, about the things I've had to do. The Luke you know and love is right here with his arms around you, and right now all he cares about is being home with his woman. I miss you more every time I leave."

Luke Fontaine had changed, she thought. No longer did he agonize over killing another man, as he had over the outlaws. She could not blame him for it. This land did that to a man, the sheer struggle to survive. She knew that behind those still-provocative blue eyes and that still-handsome, suntanned face the feelings were there, buried deep. He didn't dare dig them up. It hurt too much, just as it hurt too much to talk about Nathan.

"I love you, Luke," she whispered.

He met her mouth in a savage, hungry kiss. She knew

what this first time would be like...just like all the other first times when they had been apart for a long time. She didn't mind. It was exciting to be so wanted by a man like Luke, to know that after six children, she could still please him. The new lines on his face from years of outdoor life did little to affect his handsome features, and knowing he could have been killed himself today only made her want him more.

The bedroom door was closed, but she feared that would not be enough to hide the sounds of their love-making from the children. They both tried to be quiet about it, but it was difficult when a man and woman needed each other so desperately. It was so good to feel his strong arms around her, to feel his hard body against her as he laid her back on the fine brass bed he had bought her two years ago. His kisses left her breathless while his big hands felt at her breasts. He touched and tasted as he removed her clothes, and she was hardly aware of him removing his own. She grasped his hair as he moved over her, and she loved him for not caring that she was a little fuller, a little rounder, a little softer than the eighteen-year-old woman he had brought here. She still pleased him, and Luke Fontaine most certainly still pleased her. This first time had to be quick, no prelimi-naries necessary. He surged inside of her, filling her hard and deep, groaning with the intense want of her. She dug her fingers into his broad shoulders and arched up to him in naked glory, and it was only moments before she felt the delicious climax that made her insides pull at him in spastic desire. Luke raised up on his knees and grasped her hips, pushing hard and deep, his dark skin already bathed in perspiration. His own release was quick and pounding, making him shudder.

He breathed deeply, came down on top of her, and took her in his arms, kissing and licking at her face, her neck. "I love you, Lettie." He relaxed beside her then.

"I'm glad your mother came, but I hope it didn't make you want to go to Denver. I'm sure they're full of stories about how nice life is there." He sank his head into the pillow they shared.

"Luke, you don't really think I could ever leave here now, do you? Or that I would even consider it?" She touched his face, kissed him lightly. "This is home. If we can't go to civilization, we'll bring civilization to Montana. You and men like you will set the laws, and I'll gather with other women to bring in education and the gentleness this land needs. Besides, I could never take the children from here. This is all they've ever known. Ty already shows signs of following in your footsteps, and Katie is a strong girl, so helpful already with chores and things. She already talks about someday marrying a rancher and being just like me." She smiled. "Not that I expect all of them to stay right here and do what we do. Little Pearl has such a talent for music, and Robbie— who knows? Ever since that horse kicked him last year, he's been deathly afraid of them. I don't know how a son is going to help on his father's ranch if he won't get on a horse."

Luke laughed lightly. "He'll get over it." His smile faded and he sighed deeply. "Do you think I'll go to hell, Lettie, for taking the law into my own hands?"

She kissed his muscular chest. "I think God knows exactly what a good man you are." She moved her face to be close to his, kissing his lips again. "And so do I."

Their lips met in a tenderer kiss, and this time they moved more slowly. Lettie relaxed to deep, suggestive kisses, allowing him to explore her mouth while he massaged at her breasts, her belly, her bottom, and that secret place that belonged only to Luke Fontaine now. She had long ago learned to bury the horror of her rape. In this man's hands sex had never been anything but beautiful and necessary and achingly satisfying. She returned his

kisses with increased vigor, feeling on fire for him. It had
been so long since she'd had her man in her bed.

"Make love to me all night, Luke," she whispered.

"That's asking a lot from a man who's been in the
saddle most of the day," he teased.

She ran her hands over his muscular arms. "It's a lot
of man I'm asking it from."

He moved between her legs again. "I missed the hell
out of you, just as I always do."

"I missed you too," she whispered.

He moved inside of her again, deep, rhythmic thrusts
that made her groan with pleasure. There would be
no more talk about God or outlaws or the children or
anything else. There would only be this for the rest of
the night… Luke lying naked beside her, claiming her,
taking his pleasure while he gave her so much pleasure
in return.

Yes, her mother had suggested she'd be safer and
probably happier in Denver, but she could not imagine
leaving the Double L, leaving this land Luke loved so
much. It had become a part of him, and Luke was a part
of the land. She was married to Montana just as surely as
she was married to Luke Fontaine.

&

On a high mesa that overlooked Fontaine land, Lettie
guided her horse beside Luke's.

"I know how much you miss your mother since she
went back," Luke told her.

"It would almost have been easier if she'd never
come at all," Lettie answered. "I'll probably never see
Mama again." She patted the neck of her gray-and-white
Appaloosa mare, glad Luke had suggested that they do
something alone after her mother and sister left for Denver.
She missed her family dearly, but it felt good to have this
time alone with her husband, away from the children. At

home he was always busy with chores, often gone from before dawn until suppertime; and for at least ten days out of every month he was gone on a trip around the Double L, riding the fence line to check on men posted as guards at various line shacks, watching for Indians, squatters, and rustlers. Each man also had the duty of mending fences and watching for stray cattle and horses.

Luke watched the few head of cattle that had wandered to this area to graze. "I'm sorry you can't see your mother more often."

Lettie adjusted her sunbonnet. "There is nothing to be sorry for. I wouldn't change anything now. I could never be happy anyplace else."

Luke's shiny black gelding shuddered and tossed his mane as he shifted restlessly. "Take it easy, boy," Luke said softly, pulling on the reins. He grinned. "This one likes to run. I ought to race him."

Lettie smiled, watching the beautiful animal. Ever since losing Red to the Indians and recently losing Paint to death, Luke had given up allowing himself to get attached to one particular horse. Among his herd, there were four horses he kept for himself and Lettie, refusing to sell any of them. One was the Appaloosa she rode, a gentle mare he trusted with the children and her; the black gelding he rode now strictly for pleasure; a huge roan-colored gelding sturdy enough for all ranch work; and a buckskin-colored gelding with black tail and mane that was his best cutting horse, used on cattle drives and at spring roundup. "He's so beautiful," she said to him about the horse he rode now, "but a little too nervous and fidgety for me."

"Whoa! Whoa!" Luke commanded then, as his horse turned in a circle. "You're right about that," he answered with a grin, finally calming the animal again. "Tex had more trouble breaking this one than any he's worked with yet." He took a thin cigar from his pocket, looking several yards back to make sure Ben Garvey was still with them. He had asked the man to come along in case of trouble, wanting an extra guard on Lettie. Ben stayed far behind them so he and Lettie could have some privacy. The man gave him a signal that everything was all right, and Luke turned back to Lettie. He lit the cigar.

"Luke." Lettie spoke his name softly.

He puffed on the cigar a moment. "What is it?"

"Don't let yourself change completely. I wouldn't want you to become as coarse and unfeeling as Tex."

Luke shrugged. "Tex isn't all bad. He told me he grew up an orphan in the streets of Chicago, learned to steal at the tender age of five just to stay alive, killed his first man at eleven. He never has told me who it was or why he killed him, has never said what his real name is or any other details about his life, but I know there's a side to him that knows right from wrong, appreciates honesty in a man. He as much as saved my life the day we faced off those buffalo hunters. The same time I shot one of them, another had his gun out. Tex got that one. Otherwise I might have taken a bullet."

He met her gaze, and Lettie thought how very handsome he looked today. Was it just because his being home was still new and such a sweet pleasure, or was it that the weathered, rugged look about him had only added to the masculine features she already loved? His eyes were bluer today than the vivid blue sky above them.

"Don't worry," he was saying. "Men like Tex are necessary out here, and part of me has to be just like him. That doesn't mean I'm not the same man you married." He looked away again. "I do have to say that part of that man died when Nathan was taken. I'll never quite forgive myself for not being able to get him back for you, Lettie."

Lettie gazed at a sea of green grass spread out before them as far as she could see. It had been a good summer, just enough rain to keep the plains green with good feed for the cattle. She worried what would happen if they ever had a drought and had to buy feed for so much stock. Surely it would ruin them financially. "You did all that you could. There is no sense going back over it again."

They both sat there quietly for several minutes, a gentle breeze blowing the smoke from Luke's cigar off into nothingness. "You see that fence line way out there?" he finally asked.

Lettie strained to see the dim, dark line of fence made of logs notched into fence posts. "I see it."

"I'm going to claim another hundred thousand acres beyond it. That will give us a total of close to a million acres, all Fontaine land. I'm buying more beef out of Oregon and California. The market is growing every day, and I intend to be ready to meet the demand. That's all good grassland out there. With the buffalo being killed off the way they are, there's just that much more of it for my cattle."

Lettie tried to fathom so much land. She had never even ridden the full perimeter of the land they owned. She'd been too busy with raising the children to get fully involved in everything Luke was doing with the ranch, and sometimes she worried about what she would do if something happened to him. "Isn't that government land?"

Luke shrugged. "Some of it, but they'll never do anything with it. Lots of other ranchers use government land to graze their beef. It's mine for as long as it sits there not being used, and I intend to fence it in so others understand that. Some of it I'll try to buy from other homesteaders, and some of it I can claim legally."

Lettie sighed with worry. "Through David Taylor?"

Luke turned to look at her again. "Everybody does it, Lettie. The government doesn't understand how much land it takes to graze one steer."

"And the richest man out here is David Taylor. Henny said on her last visit he's building a huge house north of Billings."

Luke chuckled. "Who cares? A little bribery money up front means a lot more money down the road through the sale of prime beef. It's all legal, once it's on paper, with deeds, titles, all of that. Don't worry about it, Lettie. We've formed our own cattlemen's association to help protect ourselves, sent out invitations to the next meeting, which will be in a couple of weeks. We even invited that Englishman who bought all that land from the homesteaders southwest of Billings who lit out because of so much Indian trouble. I've never met him yet. Sounds like quite an interesting fellow."

He squinted to watch an eagle flying low over a distant butte. It suddenly dived and came up with something small dangling in its talons. "I'm not too crazy about foreigners coming here to buy land," he continued, "but what the hell? Civilization is civilization. We need people who will stay put, and he can afford to hire men to guard his land. He won't run like some of the smaller farmers have done, and if he intends to get into raising cattle, he might as well belong to our group. There's strength in numbers. We figure if we all join together, set some laws on how to deal with Indians, rustlers, and the like, figure how we'll deal with the government if they ever come knocking on our door, we'll be protected. No sense in all of us fighting against each other and trying to outdo each other. We'll all be better off if we get organized. We're even going to register our brands, have lists printed of ranch names, locations, and brands so everybody knows whose land is where, knows who stray cattle belong to by the brand they see on them. Keeps us from mixing someone else's cattle into our own herds."

"Sounds as if it could turn into quite a powerful organization."

"That's the whole idea. The more power, the more freedom we'll have to deal with rustlers and the like in our own way, the more clout we'll have with Congress, and the more strength we'll have in affecting territorial land laws. Someday Montana will be a state, and when it is, we intend to have laws in place that will protect men like me from being taxed out of business, protect my boundaries." He turned his horse. "Come on. We'd better get moving, or we won't reach that line shack by nightfall. You don't want to sleep out in the open tonight, do you?"

Lettie smiled. "Oh, I don't know. That might not be so bad."

Luke rode in front as they made their way along a narrow trail through scraggly rock formations. He drew up his horse when he reached a clearing just big enough for the two of them, then reached over and grasped the back of her neck. "What I have in mind, we wouldn't want to be out in the open where Ben could see and hear us," he told her with a wink. He leaned over and kissed her lips.

Lettie blushed, realizing Ben most certainly had to have seen the kiss. "Luke Fontaine! If that's the case, then you'd better save *everything* for inside the shack. Don't be kissing me in public!"

He laughed lightly. "Public? All there is to see us are rocks and pine trees, birds, and a few cattle. Ben is back there around the corner someplace."

He studied her with hunger in his blue eyes, and Lettie felt a tingle of desire. It had been years since they had done something like this, where they could be truly alone again. She loved her trips into Billings to visit and shop, and that was what he had suggested this time; but she had decided she wanted to do something different, go someplace where there were no people at all. It seemed strange to want that, after those first lonely years when she longed to see other faces. "What is the line shack like? Is it as bad as that first place we lived when we came here?"

Luke grinned. "Not quite that bad. I chose this one because I haven't had a man up in this area for several weeks, so I can check things out myself, and we can still have the cabin to ourselves when we get there. I might leave Ben there to keep guard for a few days. We've had trouble with wolves in this area."

Lettie shivered, remembering how the wolves had frightened her in the early years. They were still a danger to men out riding alone, and a menace to the cattle. "It's too bad we can't settle this land without disturbing the wild things," she said, gazing at distant mountains then. "Even the Indians."

Luke knew her thoughts had again turned to Nathan. "How about that women's group you told me about?" he asked, deciding to change the subject. "You got that sewing circle started yet?"

She smiled. "Yes. In fact, several of us are meeting in Billings in just two weeks, when you men get together for the cattlemen's meeting, so you'll have to get us a room at that new rooming house in town, or we could stay at Will and Henny's. I'll leave the children here with Anne and Billy, and please warn the men not to cuss in front of the children. We'll have to stay the night in town. By the time you finish with your meeting, it will probably be too late to get home from there before dark." She sighed longingly. "The next thing we need is a church. I do wish a preacher would come to Billings. I miss real church services, the singing, praying together. If there were as many churches in this territory as there are saloons, there wouldn't be such a dire need for organized law."

Luke chuckled, heading his horse even higher on the narrow path. "Why is it women think of churches and men think of guns and ropes?"

"Because women have more common sense and more compassion," Lettie answered teasingly. She breathed deeply of fresh air as they rode on for several minutes, each of them enjoying the peaceful afternoon. One thing she had to admit, Luke had chosen some of the prettiest country in America to call home. Never had she seen bluer skies, greener grass, more colorful rocks. The air smelled of sweet pine and wildflowers, clover and... She frowned, a little warning deep inside telling her something was wrong, but she couldn't quite place it. "I hope the children are all right."

"Why do you say that?"

Lettie looked around. "I don't know. I just have this funny feeling."

Luke led them to a shelflike clearing, then turned his horse, looking back along the pathway. Lettie saw the concern in his eyes then. "You too?"

Lettie kept a tight hold of the reins of her horse. "What is it, Luke?"

Luke took his rifle from its boot and carefully scanned their surroundings, taking on the look of a suspicious wild animal. He seemed to be literally sniffing the air. "I don't know. I just realized Ben never caught up to us when we stopped that last time. We'd better go back and—"

The sentence was interrupted by a booming shot from somewhere above them, and in the same instant a bloody hole opened in Luke's right thigh, accompanied by a sickening cracking sound. Lettie screamed at the hideous sight and sound. Luke cried out with awful pain, and his horse jerked and whinnied, then fell. Luke rolled off and tumbled down the steep embankment to the left of the path they had been following. His horse lay still. Whatever had hit Luke had gone right through his leg and into the horse. Before Lettie could decide what to do about the horror she had just witnessed, another shot thundered from above, thudding into her horse's neck. Lettie gasped as the animal trembled and fell, whinnying in agony.

"Oh my God!" Lettie cried, quickly getting her feet out of the stirrups. She ducked down against the rocky wall of the pathway they had been following. "Luke!" she screamed. She couldn't see where he had fallen, and there was no reply. "Luke!"

Thirteen

LETTIE REALIZED THAT SOMEHOW SHE HAD TO GET TO the other side of the pathway and down the embankment. Luke was down there somewhere—maybe dead. She would be a target for whoever had shot at them, but she had no choice. She took a deep breath, telling herself she must stay calm for Luke's sake. She charged across the pathway then, clambering over the edge of the bank down which Luke had fallen. More shots rang out, but quickly she was out of sight as she slid and tumbled down the rocky ledge, thorny, dry plants tearing at her buckskin riding pants and her cotton blouse, cutting into her hands as she tried to grab something, anything, to slow her fall. Finally she landed on firm ground, breathless, filthy, and bleeding. She took a moment to get her bearings, looked up, and saw no one. Desperately she looked for Luke, jumped when a small rock spit past her to her left. She looked in the direction from which it must have been thrown and saw Luke, sitting behind a large boulder. He waved her over but did not call out to her.

Lettie looked up again, still saw no one. She ran to Luke's side then, felt sick at the sight of his leg, the pants and his thigh ripped open, blood everywhere. His eyes showed the incredible pain he was suffering, and he already looked pale. "Tie it off." He groaned. "Hurry! And don't talk." He dropped his voice to a near whisper. "I want them to think I'm dead. Stay behind the boulder so they can't see us."

Lettie struggled against a need to scream. Luke

grimaced as he helped her get his shirt off to use as a tourniquet to slow the bleeding. "You hurt?" he asked.

"No," she whispered. "They killed my horse."

Luke closed his eyes for a moment, and when he opened them, she saw the Luke she did not know. Now he was like Tex, like the outlaws who had first attacked the ranch. "Two of my best goddamn horses!" he seethed through clenched teeth. "I wonder if Ben is dead."

"We never heard a gunshot."

He put his fingers to her lips and drew her closer. "They could have done it some other way," he whispered. "Right now they're after you, and if my guess is right, they won't kill you right away."

Lettie cringed against him, her rape becoming vivid again in her mind. "What will we do?" she whispered. "Who is it, Luke?"

He looked down at his leg. "From the size of this wound...I'd say it was done by a buffalo gun. They shoot long distances and make big holes." He trembled, clenched his teeth, his whole body already covered with sweat. "My guess is it's those buffalo hunters...we ran into on the way back from the cattle drive...out for revenge." He swallowed against an urge to vomit from the pain. "I can't go charging up after them, Lettie. My leg's broken. Our only chance is to get them close enough for me to shoot. That means you're going to have to be very brave—step out and let them see you— start crying. Tell them I'm dead. Beg them not to kill you too."

"Luke, if I lure them down here, they'll kill you for sure!"

"Not if I can surprise them. There's no other way, Lettie." He closed his eyes and took a deep, shivering breath. "We've got to do something quick, before I pass out." He grasped her arm. "If I think I can't take them, I'll shoot you instead."

Her eyes widened in surprise.

"There's no other way, Lettie. I know what they'll do to you if they catch you…and they'd kill you afterward anyway. I'll…never let that happen to you again." He took his six-gun from its holster on his hip and put it in her hand. "Hide the gun behind you until they get close. However they come in, take the one to your farthest right," he whispered. "That way I'll know which ones to aim for myself. If they're…close enough…you should be able to hit one of them."

Lettie nodded, not sure she could do any of the things he asked. Knowing what they probably had in mind for her brought on black memories she thought she had buried. And Luke! Was he dying? Why hadn't she agreed just to go to Billings for their little trip together as Luke had suggested? And where was poor Ben?

"Hey, down there! Your stupid old partner up the road is dead, your horses are dead, and you ain't got no way out!" someone called then from above. "Might as well come on out of there."

"Hey, little lady, we done killed your main cock," came another voice. "Come on out and we'll show you what it's like to be with *real* men!"

There came the sound of laughter, and Lettie carefully peeked around the boulder and looked up to see three men making their way down the embankment. The biggest one smiled, and even from this distance she could see his front teeth were missing.

"That your husband we shot, lady?" the third man asked. He was a big, burly, bearded man who looked filthy. All three men held back when they saw Lettie look around from behind the rock. "Sorry, lady, but I told Luke Fontaine that I'd have his ass one of these days," the biggest one told her. "He killed my brother a couple of weeks back, and I've been waitin' for this chance ever since."

Luke seethed at the voice. Cully! The man had threatened revenge, and now he was getting it!

"We been watchin' you for quite a while, waitin' for your husband to get himself in a situation where he wasn't surrounded by his little army of men," Cully was telling Lettie. Luke could hear that the man was getting closer. "He ain't so big and important without his pack of wolves along, is he?"

"How many are there?" Luke whispered gruffly.

Lettie reached out her hand behind the rock where the men couldn't see and held up three fingers. "Please don't kill me," she called out, breaking into tears. It was an easy thing to do, for she was afraid her husband was dying. "Please! You've gotten your revenge. My husband is dead. Please let me go home to my children."

She moved away from the rock, trembling with fear, praying she could get them close enough not to miss with her own gun. The condition Luke was in, he'd be lucky to shoot even one or two of them, let alone all three. If she missed, the third man might put another one of those huge buffalo slugs into her husband, this time in his chest. What a cruel, ugly weapon the guns were. They looked huge and menacing in the hands of the buffalo hunters, in spite of the size of the men themselves.

"You want to go home, do you?" the toothless man spoke up. He stood to the right of the other two men. *My left*, Lettie thought. That one was for Luke. The one to her right was tall and skinny, his face bearded and his clothes stained from sweat and buffalo blood.

"We'll see you get there, little lady, after we're through with you," the skinny one spoke up.

"Please don't hurt me," she begged, tears streaming down her face. "You've already killed my husband."

The one in the middle chewed on a weed. "And the old man who was supposed to be lookin' out for your fancy little ass," he spoke up. "Ain't it amazin' how quiet a knife can be?" He rubbed at himself, and Lettie remembered all the horror of her rape. "We ain't gonna hurt you, lady," he added. "We're just gonna make you feel real good. *Then* we'll take you home…or maybe not. Maybe we'll just keep you with us for a while and slit your tits off later. Jugs like yours make good tobaccy pouches."

The others laughed, and Lettie stepped farther away from the rock. "Why are you doing this?" She wept, shivering, all the while watching them step a little closer. "I've never done anything to you!"

The toothless one stepped even closer. "Let's just say it's part of your husband's payment for takin' my brother from me and knockin' out my teeth."

Lettie backed away even more, gripping the six-gun behind her. She moved to her right, closer to the tall, skinny one, who had moved around in that direction. She waited, not daring to glance at Luke for fear the men would realize he was alive. She could only pray he had not already passed out. All three men came even closer, and she quickly whipped out the gun, aiming and firing at the skinny one to her right. His body jerked backward. He stared at her in surprise before collapsing with a bloody wound in his gut. Lettie did not even have a chance to look toward Luke before she heard the two shots that thundered from his own repeater, catching both the other men. The toothless one had run for cover, but screamed out, falling to his knees when Luke's bullet slammed into his back. He crouched there a moment before sprawling onto his face.

Lettie stared dumbfounded. The man she had shot was writhing on the ground, his knees drawn up, horrible gurgling sounds coming from his throat. Before she even realized Luke had crawled near her, he was grasping her hand. She sucked in her breath in surprise and fear until realizing it was Luke.

"Give me the gun!" he demanded.

"Luke! You shouldn't be——"

"Give me the goddamn gun!"

He was horribly pale. She knew his pain must be excruciating. She handed him the gun, and he dragged himself over to the one man who was still alive. "Turn around!" he growled at her.

Lettie blinked, then realized what he was going to do. She turned away. In the next second she heard the gunshot. The skinny man no longer moved or made any sound when she looked back. Luke was laid flat out beside him, and she ran to him, forcing herself to ignore the hole in the skinny man's head when she went to her knees beside her husband. "Luke!"

"You've got...to get help," he said. "I can't last much longer."

Lettie looked around, realized she was a good four or five miles from the homestead, with no one to help her. She was not even sure how to get back. Luke grasped her hand.

"Follow the path...the way we came...maybe find Ben's horse. Horses...have a nose for finding home. The horse...can take you." He squeezed her arm. "Take... my rifle...the six-gun."

"No! Not both! You'll need something," she answered. "Keep the rifle." She unbuckled his gun belt. "I'll take this with me. I'll get your ammunition pouch off your horse and bring it to you. You might need the rifle to keep wolves away tonight; and I'll bring you water and some blankets."

She hurried off before he could answer, her mind reeling with the horror of what life would be like without Luke. She had no idea if she could find Ben's horse or find her way back. The longer Luke lay out here with no help, the worse it would be for him. She scrambled and crawled up the embankment, got the ammunition pouch, a canteen of water, and a blanket from Luke's horse. She unstrapped his saddlebags, which contained some food, and threw them over her shoulder. The black gelding whinnied and groaned as she started to rise, and she realized the poor animal was still alive. She knew what Luke would do in such a situation. She cocked the six-gun and held it close to the top of the animal's head, then pulled the trigger. There was no time to weep over what she'd had to do, or over the loss of such a beautiful animal.

She grasped the supplies then and slid back down the embankment on her rump. She laid the supplies next to Luke. "I'll get my own canteen and a blanket when I go back up," she told him, not even sure he was comprehending what she was saying. She covered him with two blankets. "Luke?"

His only reply was to moan, and his eyes drifted shut. "Luke, don't you die on me! Don't you leave me alone with five babies and no father!" She leaned down and kissed his cheek. "I love you, Luke," she said gently near his ear. "Hang on for me. Please don't die, Luke."

She wiped at her tears, and breathed deeply to stay in control. This was no time to fall to pieces. Somehow she had to find her way back to the house and get help, and if she couldn't find Ben's horse, she'd have to walk the whole way. That part wasn't so bad, if only she was certain just which way to go…and if only there was more daylight left. With the night would come more difficulty finding her way, and it would be harder to see rocks and holes in her way. Worse than that, with the night came the wolves. Would the men return to find Luke torn apart by them? Maybe she would die the same way and they'd both be found with buzzards floating above them, picking over what the wolves left for them.

❦

Lettie crouched under a huge pine, taking a moment to get her breath and her bearings. She vowed to herself that if she and Luke lived through this, she was going to learn more about this vast piece of land her husband owned, become more familiar with its boundaries and landmarks, ride out with Luke at least twice a year when he checked the line shacks, so that she would never get lost like this again on her own land. She struggled not to think about poor Luke lying out there somewhere in terrible pain, maybe dead.

Every bone and muscle in her body ached from walking, climbing, running, falling. Her clothes were ripped and her hands and arms covered with cuts and scratches. The darkness had distorted things and confused her as to which way to go, and the constant howling of wolves made her feel crazy. She thought after all these years she had grown used to the sound, but to be out here in the darkness alone, vulnerable to the animals, made their howling seem more threatening again.

Wolves were not her only concern. Why was it that most wild animals did their prowling at night? She reminded herself of what Luke had told her many times, that most wild animals were much more afraid of humans than the other way around. Right now she wasn't so sure. It made little difference. She had no choice but to keep going, or Luke was going to die. No one would be looking for them. The men would think they were at the line shack by now, and that Ben was keeping guard.

Poor Ben! She had found him on the return pathway, stabbed to death. His horse was nowhere in sight. Apparently it had been run off by the buffalo hunters, and probably all the gunfire had spooked the buffalo hunters' horses. Maybe they had just tied them farther away so they could sneak up on Luke and her on foot. Whatever the answer, she had found no horses. She had walked for what seemed miles, unsure which way to go once the pathway along the ridge had ended. She followed what she thought were their own tracks, but by dusk nothing looked the same, and now in the darkness it was impossible to see any tracks at all.

She uncorked her canteen and took a swallow of water, then got to her feet, which were badly blistered. She slung the canteen around her neck, wishing it and Luke's gun belt were not so heavy around her shoulders, but both were necessary to her survival. She rubbed at her neck and shoulders for a moment, then started out again, forcing herself to ignore her own pain, reminding herself that she had five children waiting for their mother to come back to them. She wrapped the blanket she had brought with her around her shoulders, worrying that Luke might not be warm enough lying on the cold ground. She prayed he was alert enough to keep the blankets she had left him pulled up around himself.

She shivered at the thought of him lying out there alone and hurt. He was depending on her to get help, and she didn't even know where she was. She realized she had come up against some kind of steep bank. When she looked away from it, she saw nothing but total darkness. The moon was just a sliver tonight. She couldn't even see the shadows of any mountains in the distance, nothing to give her some idea where she was. She started up the bank then, feeling her way, not sure how steep it was. She thought that if she could just get to the top, maybe she would see something on the other side.

She grasped rocks, tree trunks, anything she could find to help her climb, as the bank grew so steep that her feet kept slipping on pine needles and grass. Her hands were so sore she wanted to cry, and she chastised herself for leaving a perfectly good pair of leather gloves behind. How could she have been so foolish? How could she have lived out here this long and still be so inept? It infuriated her to realize how she had neglected to familiarize herself with the Double L and with survival in this kind of situation.

"Never again," she muttered, teeth gritted. "This will never happen—" Before she could finish, her hand slipped on a moss-covered rock, and she went sliding and crashing back down the embankment, screaming all the way. She landed hard against the trunk of a pine tree, felt its sap sticking to her shirt as she pulled away from it. She cried out with the pain of what she was sure must be a cracked rib, maybe several cracked ribs, and she realized that on the way down she had lost her blanket. She felt for her gun and canteen, thanking God they were still draped around her shoulders.

She sat there a moment to get her breath, and she could not help breaking into tears, which only angered her more. She took several deep breaths and wiped at her tears with hands sticky with dirt and sap. She looked up into darkness. Somehow she had to get up that ridge. She started up again, thought she heard something growl not far away. Everything turned cold inside, and her heart pounded wildly. She took the six-gun from its holster. She waited a moment, listening to the snarling and barking somewhere below. In a moment of terror she fired the weapon three times, the shots roaring in her ears, the gun kicking in her hand. She heard a yelp, heard what sounded like animals running, then nothing. She hoped the noise had frightened away whatever was there, probably wolves.

"Dear God, help me," she muttered. She wasn't sure she could even reload the gun in the dark, and she shoved it back into its holster, reminding herself there were only three bullets left. After that she would have to try to reload it. "There's another thing you should have learned, Lettie Fontaine," she scolded herself. If she lived through this, she was going to get back to practicing with a rifle and learn how to load and shoot a six-gun. Ever since Luke had hired more help, she had never bothered to practice with her rifle again, and she had never shot a six-gun until tonight.

She stopped climbing for a moment, realizing she *had* shot the gun, earlier today! She'd shot that tall, skinny buffalo hunter, but she hadn't killed him. Luke had taken the gun and shot him dead. Later she had used the gun to shoot Luke's horse. That made three more shots! She pulled the six-gun from its holster, realizing that it must be empty now after all. She held it in the air and pulled the trigger, and it only clicked. "Damn," she muttered. Why hadn't she loaded in the other three bullets before she left Luke? She felt along the gun belt and pulled out more bullets one by one, shoving them into the gun's chambers by feeling for the holes. She prayed she was loading the weapon correctly as she locked the cartridge chamber and put it back into the holster. She started climbing again, whimpering with the pain in her ribs. Her hands were so cut and sore that they were almost numb, and she suspected her feet were bleeding inside her leather boots.

She fought and struggled and crawled and grunted her way close to the top of the ridge, then heard something that was music to her ears.

"Hello out there!" someone called.

She clambered to the top. Far off in the distance she saw a dim light. The house! It must be the house! The children! Home! "Help!" she screamed. "Help me!" She drew the six-gun and fired it twice more, realizing the shots she had fired at the wolves must have drawn someone's attention. "It's Lettie! Luke's hurt. Somebody! I'm up here!" She fired again.

"Stay there!" someone yelled. It sounded like Tex. She waited, breaking into tears and thanking God she had made it this far. She couldn't tell what was happening, couldn't even hear a horse at first. Finally she saw a small light. Someone was lighting a match. "Can you see me? Tell me which way to go," came the shouted voice again.

"Here! To your left," she yelled back. "I'm at the top of the ridge, a couple of hundred yards up."

"Stay put and keep talking," the voice answered. "It's me, Tex!"

Lettie kept yelling, explaining what had happened with the buffalo hunters, that Ben was dead, the horses killed, and Luke was badly hurt somewhere along the road to the northern line shack. Finally, when Tex lit yet another match, she realized he was only about fifty feet away. These men knew the land almost as well as Luke, could find their way in the dark. Oh, how she hated this helpless feeling. She was not going to let this happen again. "Up here," she shouted. "Watch for the flash from my gun." She fired the six-gun into the air again, and moments later Tex was there.

"Mrs. Fontaine! Are you hurt?"

"Mostly bruises and cuts." She grimaced with pain. "I think I might have cracked a rib. I fell down the other side of the ridge."

Tex helped her up. "My horse is a few feet below. Be careful. This last stretch is pretty steep." He helped her down to his horse, and she gasped with the pain in her ribs when he lifted her up and put her in the saddle. He climbed up behind her. "I was out riding guard when I heard three gunshots, kind of muffled," he explained.

"I thought I heard wolves. I fired into the darkness to scare them away," she told him.

"Well, it's a good thing, or I never would have known anybody was out there. Hang on. I'll get you to the house and gather some men to go find Luke."

Lettie grasped at her middle as the man rode at a gentle gallop toward the house. As they got closer, she realized more men had come alert at the sound of all the gunfire in the distance. Already, Fontaine men had formed a small posse ready to head out.

"Tex! What's happened?" Billy asked.

"Those goddamn buffalo hunters came back. Killed Ben and shot down Luke and Mrs. Fontaine's horses. Luke's wounded bad. Mrs. Fontaine had to leave him along the trail to the north line shack. Somebody's going to have to ride into Billings and get the doc for Luke."

"I'll go!" Sven Hansen volunteered. He turned and rode off into the night, and Anne Sacks came running out of Lettie's house, awakened by all the shouting outside.

"Lettie! What happened?"

"Try not to wake the children," Lettie answered as Tex helped her down from his horse. He climbed on again and rode out with the others, all of them determined to find Luke as soon as possible, in spite of the danger of darkness. "Please don't let Luke die," Lettie whispered in prayer.

Anne, herself with child, helped Lettie into the house, leading her to the bedroom. She left to heat some water, and Lettie removed the canteen and gun belt from around her shoulders and sat down wearily on the bed. She looked down at her hands, so bloody and scratched she hardly recognized them as her own. Pain jabbed at her ribs, and she closed her eyes for a moment, then turned to look at the bed she had shared with Luke Fontaine for so many years now. They had talked about making love tonight, just the two of them alone at the line shack. Their little trip to be alone had turned to disaster, and again the land and the lawless had risen up like beasts to try to devour them. She had survived many things, but she was not so sure she could survive anything happening to Luke. If he died, she would finally have to give up. The land would win after all.

❧

Luke felt the ground vibrate. Horses were coming. He could not move to see who it was. Hard as he tried, he could not even raise his head. Had help come? Would they find him down here? He was well off the pathway. Maybe Lettie had not given a good enough description of where to find him. Maybe she had never even reached help and was dead herself. What he heard could be nothing more than a herd of buffalo somewhere.

Then again, maybe he had died already. He was in so much pain he felt as though he were in a trance. When he opened his eyes, he saw everything as though looking through a haze. He realized it was light, and he could hear a bird singing somewhere nearby. Dawn. He had lain here all night. How much longer could he hold on to the bit of life left in him? How much longer could he bear this sickening pain? He couldn't even move his arm to drink something from the canteen he remembered Lettie saying she'd left for him, yet he was so thirsty he felt as if he might choke.

He moved his head just slightly to see the body of the man he'd shot in the head still lying close by. The other two bodies couldn't be far away. He looked past the foot of the closest one and saw them coming, horses, painted horses. They came closer, and he blinked to see better. The sun was behind them, making it difficult to see their faces, but it was obvious the riders he'd heard coming were painted warriors, not the help he had expected. They slowed their ponies, stared at him a moment. Then a couple of them dismounted, and from what he could tell, they were young—a group of fresh young warriors out hunting, probably, out to prove their worth to the elders. Would they try to take his scalp as a trophy? He wouldn't be able to do a damn thing to stop them.

The two who had dismounted stooped down and leaned closer. Luke blinked, trying to focus. He was sure one of them had light hair and blue eyes. Damn the sun, and damn his pain! It was so hard to see. They said something in the Sioux tongue, looked him over. The one with the light hair pointed to the other dead bodies. Luke licked his lips, trying to speak.

"Nathan," he whispered, but the one with the light hair either did not hear him or simply did not respond to the name. He tried to speak it again, but the word stuck in his throat because of his miserably dry mouth. He started to cough, and the light-haired one knelt near him again. Luke wasn't sure what he was doing until he saw the canteen. The young man poured some water over his face and into his mouth, then corked the canteen and left it.

Luke blinked more, struggling to see better, to talk. From what he could determine, the warriors were wary of what they had found, probably didn't want to get mixed up in what was apparently white man's business. Another came riding in, shouting something at the others, and quickly they all remounted and rode off at a gallop. Minutes later Luke heard more horses.

"There he is!" someone shouted. He recognized Runner's voice.

"Jesus, I hope he's still alive."

That one was Tex.

Someone knelt over him, another Indian. This time it was Runner. "He's still alive."

"Mrs. Fontaine will be glad to hear that," Tex said.

So, Lettie was all right, thank God. Everything became a blur then. He wanted to ask them about the Indians. Hadn't they seen them riding away? Had it all been a dream or some kind of hallucination after all? No one said anything about them. Someone picked him up to place him on a makeshift travois, and it was then the pain hit him full force. Who was that screaming? It sounded like someone far away.

"Watch his leg," Tex was saying. "Jesus, I never saw something that looked that bad. We'd better wrap it some more. I can't believe he's still alive."

Billy Sacks spoke up. "Takes a lot to kill somebody like Luke. What about these other bodies, Tex?"

"You and Runner go back and bury Ben first, and get the gear off the dead horses and bury them too. Leave the goddamn buffalo hunters for last. If the buzzards pick at them, so be it. I'll start back with Luke and send you some help in burying them soon as I get back."

Luke felt someone wrapping his leg, then felt himself being tied to something. Someone else put a blanket over him. He wanted to thank them, and he wanted to ask them about the Indians. Surely if one of them had light hair, the men would notice. He tried to ask, but every time he opened his mouth, he could do nothing but groan. He felt the travois begin to move then, and he cried out with pain at every jolt and bounce. The way home was going to be a miserable trip, but there was no other way to get him there.

Thank God Lettie was okay. He'd be home soon. He could hang on now, for Lettie and the kids. His leg would mend in no time, and everything would be back to normal, except that every time he closed his eyes he remembered being carried another time, on a stretcher, to a medical tent. He remembered the smell of blood, the blood on the doctor's apron. He remembered the ugly saw and how it felt when he realized the doctor was thinking about cutting off his leg. He thought about the Indians, and suddenly the vision of them was blurred by another vision, soldiers bending over him, blue uniforms, the hideous saw.

"Don't let them…take off my leg," he finally managed to mutter, but no one heard.

In the distance, from a thick clump of trees where they hid, the band of young Indian boys watched the white men pick up the wounded one. The one called White Bear had considered taking the wounded one's scalp, but something had stopped him. When the man had looked at him, his eyes were the bluest he had ever seen, blue like his own. That fascinated him, and there was something familiar about the man, but he wasn't quite sure what it was that stirred this wonder in his soul. He would tell his father, Half Nose, about what had happened today, about finding the white man badly wounded, other dead white men around him. The dead ones were the evil buffalo hunters they had seen other times. It was good that they were dead. But something told him that the wounded one was different. He was not evil like the buffalo hunters, and the way the man had looked at him…it gave him a strange feeling.

❧

For ten days Lettie suffered the worst nightmare she had known since settling in Montana, worse even than when she nursed Luke after the bear attack. Then, infection had certainly been dangerous, but it had not run deep into Luke's body the way this one had; and there had not been the awful pain of a badly broken thigh bone, an operation to try to mend it, the threat that he might never regain full use of his right leg…if he lived at all.

In spite of her own cuts and bruises and what the doctor believed were two bruised ribs, Lettie refused to take to a bed herself. Never would she forget the sight of Luke's leg once she and Dr. Manning had cut away his denim pants and his long johns. Lettie thought she had seen the worst, but she had nearly passed out. By now she had grown accustomed to looking at the terrible wound, for every day, several times a day, she had to clean and rewrap it. Every day she watched her husband lie semiconscious, racked with pain, hovering on the brink of death from infection. Never would she forget how he looked when the men first brought him back, and at first she had thought he was already dead. Tex had complained about having to send men to "bury the sons of bitches" who had hurt Luke and had killed two of the Double L's best horses. "I broke that beautiful black myself," he lamented. "If it wasn't for their dead bodies attracting wolves that might later go after the cattle, I'd have left them there for buzzard feed."

In this case, Lettie had to agree. They had shot Luke down in cold blood, no warning, as though he were a coyote. She knew what they would have done to her if Luke had not used his last bit of strength and willpower to shoot those who came after her.

The last two days had been better for Luke. The infection finally seemed to be abating. She tied off a clean bandage, then noticed he was watching her quietly, his blue eyes sunken in a thinner face. She gave him a smile and moved around to the other side of the bed to sit down on the edge of it. She took his hand. "Is the pain any better today?"

"A little." Such a weak voice for such a big man. "I'm sorry, Lettie."

"For what?"

He closed his eyes. "I don't know. Everything you've had to go through since we moved here, I guess. That night…when you walked off to get help…I thought maybe I'd never see you again. Either I'd die…or you would. Now here I am laid up for what the doc says could be months, and there's this big ranch to run—"

"You have plenty of men who know how to run it and who care about you enough to do it right. You can help me learn how to do the paperwork. I intend to take a bigger part in running the Double L, Luke. I think it's important. If anything ever *did* happen to you, I don't intend to be left helpless and in the dark. I realized that when I was trying to find my way home that night. I want to ride out once in a while with the men, get more familiar with the landmarks and just how big this place is. I want to get involved in the book work. That's something I can always help with, even after you're well. You're too busy to have to spend hours with a ledger. I want to learn more about horses and cattle, the different kinds, the diseases they can get, the proper feed. I want to see all the grazing land, which fields you reserve for hard times, which ones have the best water. I want to learn all of it, Luke."

"A woman belongs at home with her children."

"I'll find a way to do both. Once you're well, I *will* be home with them. All I'll have to worry about is the book work." She raised her chin. "Besides, you don't think I'd let the Double L go to waste just because you're sick, or died, do you?"

He squeezed her hand. "If I die, you should go to Denver."

She leaned over and stroked his thick, dark hair away from his forehead. "Never. This place was your dream in the beginning, Luke; but after all I've been through to stay here, it's my dream now too. And because I love you so much, I would never let go of what you've built here. I don't want you to worry about any of it. I just want you to get well."

He moved his hand to rub it over her lap. God, how he hated being laid up like this. Who was going to take care of things? His biggest fear was that the Double L would go to hell while he was incapacitated. He had worked so hard to get this far. Wouldn't his father just love it if he failed now, after coming this far? "Lettie, there's so much to do to get ready for winter. And there's that Cattlemen's Association meeting in Billings in just a couple more days—"

"The Double L will be represented, by me. *I'm* going to the meeting. I'll take the children and let them stay at Henny's. It will be an adventure for them. While I'm in town, I intend to see about getting more books for teaching the children to read, and I'll look into the price of feed for you, so we can determine how much it will cost to stock up in case of an extra hard winter. You just make a list for me—all the things you want me to bring up at the meeting, as well as a list of supplies you want me to bring back from Billings."

Luke grinned sadly. "You'll miss your sewing club meeting."

"That will have to wait. The other wives will understand."

Luke studied her lovingly. "They won't like having a woman at the cattlemen's meeting."

She straightened and sniffed. "That's just too bad. There are two L's in the Double L. One of them stands for Lettie Fontaine, which gives me every right to be there."

Luke squeezed her thigh. "You sure you're well enough yourself to go?"

"My ribs were just bruised, not broken. I'm not in much pain anymore. I'll be well enough to go." She leaned down to kiss the back of his hand. "There's no reason why I can't stand in for you, make some of the decisions, do the book work, all of that. I promise I would keep the Double L alive if something ever did happen to you." Tears formed in her eyes. "But nothing in this life would ever be the same without you. I just thank God you lived and the fever finally broke." She took a deep breath. "Dr. Manning will be out tomorrow to put a splint and permanent wrapping on your leg. He had to wait until the swelling went down and the infection was gone. He said in another week or so you'll have to start flexing it, using it little by little, or the muscles will draw up and begin to die. For a while there, he thought you might lose your leg altogether."

Luke pulled his hand away. "I'd rather be dead. I went through that threat in the war. Don't you ever let him take my leg off, Lettie, you hear? If you love me, you won't let him do that."

She leaned over him, bending down to kiss his cheek. "I won't let him."

Luke closed his eyes, sighing deeply. "I feel like a failure."

"Don't be ridiculous. The Double L is the biggest ranch around here, and doing well. Besides that, you've fathered five beautiful children. You're a successful rancher, a good father, and a good husband, Luke Fontaine. Don't ever call yourself a failure."

He studied her, so pretty today, her hair pulled into a

pile of twists and curls, her green eyes as fetching as ever. She could have died so easily that day, been raped, shot down. "I should have known they were there. If I had been more alert, Ben wouldn't be dead, and I wouldn't be lying in this bed, my two best horses killed, my wife going through a night of hell and then having to tend to me this way."

"Luke, no one could have known those men were there. For heaven's sake, look at the things you've been through and survived—those outlaws, Indian attack, bear attack, all the hell you've been through on the cattle drives, the terrible winters you've suffered having to work out-of-doors. As badly hurt as you were, you managed to shoot down those buffalo hunters. You're a brave, skilled man. I don't want you to worry now about being in this bed. You stay here for as long as it takes for your leg to heal right. Better to be laid up a little longer than to be a cripple. You have to be able to walk and to get back up on a horse under your own power if you're going to get back to running the Double L. In the meantime, I'll do it. A wife isn't just for giving a man babies and cooking his meals, at least not this wife."

He grinned, wanting her; but it would be a long time before he could be a husband to her again in every way. He was proud of how well she had taken all of this, of the way she had managed to find help that night, her bravery and determination. He wondered if he should tell her about what he had seen while lying out there waiting for help.

No. Why give her false hope after all these years? He had been in such terrible agony that morning, lying there close to death, that what he saw could very well have been some kind of dream due to his pain and loss of blood. Maybe it was just something his mind had conjured up, wishful thinking that had taken the form of realistic visions. Even if he *had* seen Nathan, the boy was a wild thing now and could probably never be found if a person tried; nor would he want to live like a white man now. What he had seen was an Indian, in spite of the light hair and blue eyes, as wild and untamed as the worst of the Sioux renegades. Why should he reawaken all that old pain for Lettie, make her suffer the thought of her son growing up among the Sioux, never seeing his mother again?

As long as he had been so lost in pain and not even fully conscious, how could he claim he had truly seen the boy? Hadn't he heard that even the one called Crazy Horse had light-colored hair? Maybe that was who he had seen, except this one seemed much younger than Crazy Horse would be. Even if it was Nathan, the young man he had seen was a far cry from the innocent little four-year-old who had been stolen away seven years ago.

"Get some paper and a pen," he told her aloud. "You might as well start writing down the things I want discussed at that meeting." He grinned. "Those men are going to get the starch...jerked out of their shirts when they see you walk in. I have a feeling you'll be able to stand right up to the best of them." He took her hand again. "Come to think of it, they'll be so struck by how pretty you are...they'll probably just sit there with their mouths open and let you talk all you want."

Lettie stood up and straightened his blankets. "They'll listen to me and respect me because I am Luke Fontaine's wife. You don't think any of them would dare insult you by ignoring your wife or by trying to say she can't attend that meeting, do you? I don't think you realize your own importance, Luke." She looked down at him, her hands on her hips. "I promise to do a good job of representing the Double L."

She walked out of the room to get the paper, and Luke watched her, still smiling. "I'll just bet you will, Mrs. Fontaine," he said softly.

Fourteen

LETTIE FELT ALL EYES ON HER AS SHE WALKED INTO THE
town hall, which was really nothing more than a good-
size barnlike structure of logs the citizens of Billings had
constructed for socials. She had worn her best fall dress,
a burgundy-colored velvet that accented a waistline she
was proud of after bearing six children. The bodice was
trimmed in white lace along the several buttons that
made their way to a high neckline, also lace trimmed,
as were the cuffs of the dress's long sleeves. Her velvet
feathered hat matched the dress, and her several petticoats
rustled around new brown leather high-top shoes as she
walked forward to take her place at the Cattlemen's
Association meeting. Every man there rose in respect
for her gender, but she did not miss the irritation and
downright animosity in the eyes of some.

She walked in on Will Doolan's arm, and he showed her
to one of the wooden chairs that were arranged in a circle
so everyone could see each other. "Gentlemen, I know
you might be upset by a woman's presence," Will said,
"but this one has a good reason for bein' here. She's—"

"I can speak for myself, thank you, Will," Lettie interrupted. She still had not sat down. She turned to scan all
the faces, a few she knew, many she did not. "I am Lettie
Fontaine, Luke Fontaine's wife." Already she could see a
few of them relaxing. "Luke was badly wounded a little
over two weeks ago by buffalo hunters who ambushed
us while we were out riding. Between the two of us, we
shot them down, but not before Luke took a slug from a

buffalo gun in his right thigh that broke the bone. He'll be laid up most of the winter."

Those who did not already know what had happened to Luke looked surprised and concerned. "We're sorry to hear that, ma'am," one of the men told her.

Lettie recognized Calvin Briggs, who had a ranch northwest of hers and Luke's. He and his wife, Leanna, had visited the Double L once. "Thank you, Mr. Briggs."

"*You* shot one of the buffalo hunters?" one of the others asked.

Lettie could feel the growing respect among them. "I had no choice. I do hope, gentlemen, that the day will come when we have law and order in Montana, and men like that can no longer attack innocent people. In the meantime, I understand that we have to set our own laws, and that is part of the reason I am here. Luke knew you would talk about that and more at this meeting, and since he could not come, I told him I would take his place and represent the Double L so I can tell him everything that was discussed here today. I am sure none of you is excited about having a woman present, but half of the Double L is mine. I have just as much interest in what happens to our land and anything that is decided in these meetings as any of you."

Another rancher Lettie was slightly acquainted with took a cigar from his mouth and nodded to her. "Luke's a good man. You two were among the first to come out here and settle in Indian country. We know what you've been through over the years, Mrs. Fontaine. I see no reason why you shouldn't be here in Luke's place."

"I think we shall all have to be careful of our language, gentlemen," another said.

Lettie was struck by the man's British accent, an unusual sound in a place like Billings. She turned her attention to the man, who had risen when she entered the hall. He was tall, and quite handsome. She guessed his age at perhaps forty, as his dark hair showed a little gray at the temples. His dark brown eyes sparkled with kindness and, it seemed, admiration, as they quickly moved over her appreciatively.

"Nial Bentley," he told her, bowing slightly. "I am the Englishman who has started a ranch southwest of Billings. In fact, my land borders the Double L. I have been meaning to pay your husband a visit but have been too busy. Please give him my regrets over his misfortune."

The man seemed gracious and well-mannered, and he dressed immaculately, a wondrous sight in Montana. "Thank you, Mr. Bentley."

"We might as well all introduce ourselves," Will said then. "Most of us know each other, but this is the Englishman's first cattlemen's meeting, and I see a couple of other new faces. I'm Will Doolan—own a small ranch east of Billings—been good friends with Luke and Lettie Fontaine ever since they first settled here. I expect me and my wife Henny have been here longer than just about anybody, but we ain't had near the bad luck the Fontaines had when they first arrived. Ol' Luke, he shot down seven outlaws who tried to run him off his place the first spring after he got here. Mrs. Fontaine here, she shot one of them herself, but it was Luke who finished him off."

Lettie reddened slightly at the man's contribution of family history. She would rather not have brought up so many details, but with every word she could see the men's respect and acceptance growing.

He went on to relate how they had lost Nathan. "If I told you everything else they've been through to hang on to the Double L, we'd be here all day. I will add that the day Luke was shot down by the buffalo hunters, Mrs. Fontaine here had to walk almost five miles to get help, most of it in the dark. She—"

"Will, please." Lettie shook her head, her embarrassment growing deeper.

Will grinned. "All I'm sayin' is, you men should accept Mrs. Fontaine as a temporary member with no objections, at least till Luke's better and he can come himself. She came here out of love and respect for her husband, even though she's still healin' from a couple of badly bruised ribs herself."

"No objection on my part," the Englishman spoke up, looking at her with such admiration that Lettie felt downright uncomfortable.

"We agree Luke Fontaine's wife has every right to be here," another added.

One by one each man introduced himself, not just for Lettie, but for each other. "James Woodward. Got a ranch northwest of here. Wife's name is Ellen. We've got four kids, three girls and a boy. My brand is *JW*."

"Calvin Briggs. My place is northwest of the Double L. Wife's name is Leanna. We've got one boy, eight years old. My brand is just the letter *B*."

"Nial Bentley," the Englishman repeated. "I am a widower, come to your beautiful country for an adventure and to make investments for my family. My brand is crossed swords, my family's crest." He gave everyone a gracious smile, and Lettie could tell that some of the men were ready to laugh. "I have a suggestion for all of you regarding the best beef cattle in the world," Bentley added. The remark wiped the smiles off the others' faces and brought a curiosity to their eyes. "But please, finish the introductions first," Bentley added.

The next man straightened, nervously fingering his soiled hat. "Carl Rose. My place is south of Billings. It's not as big as what I hear the Double L is, but I don't think anybody here has that much land, except maybe the Englishman." They all laughed lightly. "Anybody sees a stray steer with a rose on his rump, he's mine."

They all laughed again before Will spoke up. "You already know who I am. I ain't never picked a brand for my beef, but now that we're formin' this group and figurin' on registerin' our stock, I reckon' I'll have to be thinkin' about that." He looked past Lettie at the next man.

"Joseph Parker," the man spoke up. "Everybody calls me Park. My place is to the southeast. My wife died last year in childbirth, so I ain't got a family. My brand is *JP*."

"Henry Kline. North of Billings," the last man spoke up. "Wife's Lucy. We've got two grown sons who was both killed in the war. We came out here to forget, if that's possible, me and my wife Lucy. My ranch is called the Lazy K, and my brand is a *K* restin' on its back." Kline was older than the rest of them, a big, heavy man, with a full, graying beard that came nearly to his belly.

Lettie spoke up. "I'm sorry about your sons, Mr. Kline. And about your wife's death, Mr. Parker. I'm sure everyone here has suffered losses of one kind or another. Friendship and support of one another is so important."

Kline and Parker thanked her for her concern.

"Well, let's get started," James Woodward said. "We'll pick a president, see if anyone knows of other ranchers who aren't here but should be. We have a lot of things to discuss, how we'll go about registering our brands, what to do about rustlers. And, of course, Mr. Bentley apparently has something to tell us about beef, although I can't imagine what an Englishman would know about such things. As far as I'm concerned, Montana already grows the best and hardiest beef in this country."

They all laughed and nodded. "Before long we'll be outselling Texas, and we've got the Union Pacific to ship it without having to herd our cattle so far like the Texans have to do," Carl Rose spoke up.

"Won't be long before the Northern Pacific starts building into Montana, I hear," Will said.

Lettie watched all of them, a variety of sizes and ages, some cleaner and better dressed than others, all rugged men willing to sit down and try to organize themselves and ultimately organize Montana. She was glad to be a part of the meeting, wished Luke could be here. If anyone should be president, it should be Luke, as far as she was concerned. After all, this organization had been his idea to start with. They were starting small, but as more men came into Montana to settle, the Cattlemen's Association was bound to grow in size and importance. She reached into her handbag and took out some paper she had brought with her, and a pen, setting a bottle of ink on the floor beside her. She did not want to forget anything important and had promised Luke she would take notes.

"I've got something here that's got to be discussed right off," Briggs said. "It's something that's going to cause a lot of trouble between ranchers and farmers if its use isn't stopped." The man held up a piece of wire. "It's barbed, and believe me, it can maim and kill. Some damn squatters north of my place put this stuff up to keep my cattle out of their cornfields, and several of my beef got tore up by it, and so did one of my men when he rode his horse right into it before he even saw it was there." The man passed the wire around. "I hear more and more farmers are startin' to use this stuff to keep cattle and other animals out of their fields. I say we all agree that wherever we find this stuff, we cut it down."

Lettie took the wire when Joseph Parker passed it on to her. She gasped when she accidentally poked her finger with one of the barbs.

"Are you all right, Mrs. Fontaine?" the Englishman spoke up.

Lettie stared at the hideous wire. "Yes." She rubbed at her finger, which had already begun to bleed. "I just need a handkerchief or something."

Almost instantly several men offered her their hankies. She took one from Parker and held it against her finger, passing the wire to Will. "Luke would be totally against this," she told the rest of them.

"As far as I'm concerned, the stuff ought to be out-lawed," Carl Rose grumbled.

"Wherever we find it, it gets cut down," Henry Kline suggested. "If some farmer wants to make trouble over it, let him deal with all of us."

Everyone nodded in agreement, and Lettie watched the wire as it was passed around, thinking something like that could cause a good deal of trouble. She would take that piece of wire home and show it to Luke. She had never even considered that farmers would put up something so dangerous, not just to domestic animals, but wild ones too.

There was more discussion over the wire, after which talk turned to writing a letter to the Northern Pacific, requesting the route chosen by the railroad pass near Billings, an advantage to Montana ranchers who now had to herd their cattle south to Cheyenne, Wyoming. Cattle drives were expensive and dangerous, and there were always losses to Indians, wild animals, and the elements, as well as weight loss in the cattle. The fact that Billings had a sheriff now, Bill Tracy, was also discussed; but it was determined that the man could do little more than keep order in town. Any law outside of Billings would still be set and enforced by the ranchers.

"I hear there's a big-time mine owner from Denver here wantin' to talk to some of us about lookin' for minerals on our land," Will said. "His name's Jeremy Shane—stayin' at the new boardinghouse the widow Anderson opened up. He was fixin' to visit some of us. I told him about this meetin', told him it was closed to outsiders, but I said I'd go get him if any of you wants to talk to him."

"There's no gold this far east," Parker stated.

"Well, there's other minerals besides gold that can be worth somethin'," Will replied.

"I don't want any business with miners coming in and tearing up my land," Carl Rose objected.

Most of them grumbled, but Lettie thought it a wonderful idea. She made a note of it. She would go and see this Mr. Shane. She had been after Luke for years to consider options that would keep them afloat in case of a bad year. Finding valuable minerals on their property could be the answer.

"I have wired a buyer from Omaha," Nial Bentley spoke up. "He will come to Billings next spring. His name is Bradley Mills, works for Patterson's Meat Supply, one of the biggest butcher markets in the country. I checked on all these things before coming here to invest in land and cattle. I believe we should allow him into the meeting. We might all be able to contract with him for our beef. That way we have a definite buyer for years ahead instead of wondering from one year to the next. I have already had dealings with Mills for the cattle on another ranch I own in Wisconsin. He's an honest man."

Lettie kept writing. Yes. A solid contract would certainly make Luke rest easier. Shelby Preston's promise to buy cattle was only word of mouth. He could always change his mind and tell Luke he didn't want all twenty-five hundred head next summer after Luke had taken the time and spent the money to herd them to Cheyenne.

She made a note that Nial Bentley also owned a ranch in Wisconsin. Apparently the Englishman knew more about cattle and running a ranch than any of them had thought at first.

"With all her note taking, perhaps Mrs. Fontaine can write up a summary for us of everything we discuss here today," Bentley added.

Lettie glanced his way and saw him smiling at her. She was flattered that the man seemed to be quite attracted to her, but it also upset her. No man should look at a married woman the way Nial Bentley was looking at her. She turned her gaze to the others. "I'd be glad to, if that is what everyone wants."

Briggs nodded. "We'd appreciate it, Mrs. Fontaine. Next meeting, you can read back your notes. In the meantime, I want everybody to bring a piece of rawhide to the next meeting with your brand burned into it. We're corresponding with a printer from Cheyenne, trying to talk him into coming to Billings and opening a newspaper here. With his equipment, he could print up some registration sheets, showing everybody's brand. By this time next year I'd like to be organized enough that we have files on all these things, records of what we discuss. Cattlemen are getting organized in other territories and states. We want to keep up. We could eventually have a lot of power in setting laws for our benefit when we become a state ourselves someday."

"Well, I vote we don't go electin' no president until Luke can start comin' to the meetin's," Will said. "He's the biggest landowner around here and should have the most say anyway."

They all took a round of votes and agreed to wait for Luke.

"I appreciate that," Lettie told them. "Luke will too." She looked at Nial Bentley then. "Now, I would like to hear what Mr. Bentley has to say about a new kind of cattle."

"Ain't no fancy new breed gonna survive Montana winters," Will claimed.

"These will," Bentley answered. "And if you sell your beef by the pound, they'll make you a fortune."

"I say we take a little break first and stretch our legs a bit, go outside and have a smoke so it doesn't bother Mrs. Fontaine," Carl Rose suggested. "Twenty minutes. That's enough time to walk across the street to the Lonesome Tree Saloon and have a swallow of whiskey."

They all readily agreed to the suggestion, up and out of their chairs in the next breath and heading out the door. Will went with them, and Lettie leaned down to put a cork in her ink bottle. When she straightened, she realized that Nial Bentley had stayed behind. "Aren't you anxious to puff on a cigar and gulp some whiskey like the rest of them?" she asked with a hint of sarcasm.

"Oh, I like my tobacco and good whiskey as well as any man," he answered. He got up and walked closer. "I just couldn't pass up the opportunity to tell you I think you're one of the most beautiful women I have ever met, Mrs. Fontaine, and surprisingly refined and gracious for these parts. I didn't know such a woman existed out here."

Lettie looked up at him, not sure how to take the remark. "Mr. Bentley, I appreciate the compliment, but I would also appreciate it if you would stop looking at me the way you have been all through this meeting. It is annoying and embarrassing. I am, after all, a married woman, and you are a widower. I will remind you that most of these men are good friends of Luke's. I don't care to have them wondering at the way you look at me. Being the only woman here is difficult enough. I hate to appear rude, but from now on, please keep your compliments and your stares to yourself."

The man bowed, grinning. "My humblest apologies. I didn't mean anything disrespectful, I assure you. It is just refreshing to find someone like you out here. I do hope your husband appreciates what he has."

Lettie drew in her breath in irritation. "Luke Fontaine is a good man, and one, I daresay, you would not want to tangle with. And whether or not he appreciates his wife is really none of your business, is it, Mr. Bentley?"

The man reddened a little. "No. It really isn't. Please forgive me, Mrs. Fontaine. I hope I haven't offended you to the point that I would not be welcome if I should come visiting the Double L. I would like to meet your husband, and I would like to tell him in person about the new breed of cattle I intend to bring to Montana. I truly do believe he will be interested."

"You're welcome to come to the Double L anytime."

The man put on his hat, admiration still shining in his eyes. "Thank you. I believe I'll join the others now, so you won't be embarrassed that I lagged behind." He hesitated. "I was simply fascinated, Mrs. Fontaine, not just by your beauty, but by the things Mr. Doolan said about you. Not many women would endure and survive out here, suffering the things you have surely suffered. I deeply admire your strength and bravery. Did you really shoot one of those buffalo hunters yourself?"

Lettie folded her arms and looked up at him. "Yes. And years ago I shot one of the horse thieves that tried to claim our land when we first settled here. I'm beginning to think maybe I should shoot *you*, Mr. Bentley."

The man laughed with delight, holding up his hands. "All right, I'm leaving." He laughed again as he turned and walked out the door, and Lettie looked after him, not sure if she liked the man, or despised him. She decided she would let Luke be the judge. She was not going to tell him how she felt about the Englishman, because if he thought she disliked him, he might not even discuss the new breed of cattle Bentley was suggesting. It could be good for the Double L, and she didn't want anything to interfere with improving profits. A good businessman would put facts and figures before personal feelings, and as long as she was representing the Double L, she had to do the same.

❧

Luke watched from where he sat on the front porch as the rider approached, accompanied by Tex. Per Luke's instructions, no stranger ever came up to the Fontaine home without being met at the gate and accompanied by one of his men. He adjusted the homemade wheelchair the men had constructed for him, moving it a little closer to the steps and being careful to avoid bumping his right leg on the porch railing. The leg stuck straight out, supported by a wooden brace and trough-like structure the men had built onto the chair to support the leg, which Luke still could not bend or put any weight on.

He breathed deeply of the fresh air, glad to be out of the bedroom, aching to get back on a horse and back to his duties as owner of the Double L, but he had resigned himself to the doctor's prediction. It would be weeks, maybe months, before that would happen. He hated this helplessness, hated having to send poor Lettie on errands that should be his own.

Little Pearl came out of the house wearing a shawl because of the crisp September air. She brought one of Luke's buckskin jackets with her. "Mommy said you should put this on."

Luke winked at her, proud of how beautiful the tiny girl was, her red hair a mass of curls, her green eyes sparkling. "I don't need it just yet." He took the jacket and laid it across his lap, keeping his eyes on the approaching rider, who sat on a fine, sleek black horse and was dressed in a gray suit and ruffled shirt. He sported a black felt hat, and Luke knew without asking that it was the fancy Englishman Will and Lettie had told him was at the cattlemen's meeting a week ago. Will had brought Lettie and the children home, carrying on about all that had been discussed at the meeting, showing Luke the despicable barbed wire. Lettie had more calmly informed him of everything that had happened, asking for his opinion, telling him about the new breed of cattle called Herefords that Nial Bentley had talked about.

She had not mentioned that Bentley had seemed infatuated with her. Will had told him that when they were alone. "The others call him the fancy man," Will had joked. "He's sure that, but he seems to know cattle. Trouble is, he knows women too. You should've seen how he looked at Lettie, like she was some kind of angel. All the men, they showed her nothin' but respect, Luke; and Lettie, she did a right fine job representin' the

Double L. You would have been proud, but I'll bet that fancy Englishman wouldn't have looked at her like he did if you was there."

"You've got a visitor, boss," Tex said, grinning. Luke could tell the man was about to laugh at the way the Englishman was dressed. Luke controlled his own urge to chuckle, and he could already guess Nial Bentley was backed by old money, probably came from some English family of wealth. Maybe he was a lord or had some other damn fancy title. Whatever the case, he was certainly a handsome man. Luke guessed him to be a little older than himself.

"Go get Mommy," he told Pearl.

The girl ran inside, and Luke nodded to Bentley. "Afternoon."

"Good day, sir!" the man answered, dismounting. He tied his horse at a hitching post and climbed the steps, putting out his hand. "I already know from your man here that you are Luke Fontaine," Nial said with his strong British accent. "I am Nial Bentley, as you have probably already guessed. I thought it was time we met, Mr. Fontaine, since my land borders yours to the south. Your wife invited me to come and tell you about the beef I plan to raise there. She thought you might be interested in buying a few head yourself."

Luke reached up and shook the man's hand, squeezing just enough to let Bentley know he'd better not underestimate him just because he was in a wheelchair. "I'm willing to listen," Luke answered. "But like most of the other ranchers around here, I doubt anything but the shorthorns we've been breeding around here for years can survive."

"Ah! And where did the shorthorn first come from? England!" Nial removed his hat and laid it on a nearby table. "They were bred with the sturdy Texas longhorns, and you ended up with some of the finest beef in the world. I'll wager you bought your first cattle out of Oregon?"

Luke shifted in his chair, wincing with pain. "I did. The last few years I've mostly been breeding my own."

"Yes, well, you started out with good stock. The shorthorns managed to survive being herded clear across the country when Oregon was first settled. They've proved their worth. You had great foresight to buy up all that you could back when there was a surplus in Oregon." He winked. "Little did those people know just how valuable that beef was going to be someday. Am I right?"

Luke nodded, wanting to like the man. He was amiable enough, and he certainly knew his cattle, and American history. Too bad he had an eye for Lettie. Maybe Will had just exaggerated. "You're right. You seem to know an awful lot about the subject, for a foreigner."

Bentley laughed. "Well, I don't feel like a foreigner. My family has owned property and businesses in America for years. I myself studied at Harvard, and I own quite a large cattle ranch in Wisconsin. My father is the one who could see there would be a demand for beef after your Civil War ended. He invested in this new breed, raises them in England. He had several hundred shipped to America a few years ago. I've been raising them in Wisconsin. I brought a few hundred into Montana this summer, but I've kept them close to the main house, so you probably didn't notice them when you herded your cattle over my land on the way to Cheyenne this past spring. At any rate, these cattle are worth much more on the hoof than shorthorns because of their weight. I already have a contract with Patterson's Meat Supply in Omaha. Perhaps your wife told you a buyer from Patterson's is coming here next spring to talk to you and the other cattlemen?"

Luke watched him carefully. "She told me."

Lettie came out then, and Luke noticed her stiffen slightly at the sight of Nial Bentley, who quickly rose in respect, his eyes lighting up with delight. Luke felt an irritating jealousy at the way the man looked at her. No man had looked at his wife that way since they'd been here in Montana. He knew the other ranchers and his own men couldn't help but see she was beautiful, but they showed her complete respect, as the woman who belonged to Luke Fontaine.

"Well, hello, Mr. Bentley. So, you accepted my invitation to pay Luke a visit. You should have warned us. I could have prepared a fancier supper than what I have already planned." Lettie walked to stand behind Luke, putting her hands on his shoulders.

Nial bowed slightly, wishing this flutter Lettie Fontaine created in his soul would go away. He was hoping that when he saw her again, dressed more plainly as she was today, caught off guard with her hair drawn back into a simple bun, perhaps she would be less beautiful. Perhaps he would feel completely different from the first time he met her, but nothing had changed. He struggled not to let his feelings show in front of Luke, who he could tell, even sitting in a wheelchair, was a formidable man, obviously tall, looking strong and rugged. He'd heard stories about men like Luke, and about Luke himself. He belonged to a breed of men who guarded their land and possessions to the death, and that surely included their women.

"I am delighted to see you again, Mrs. Fontaine." He looked down at Luke. "Your wife did a fine job the other day at the cattlemen's meeting."

"So I'm told."

Nial swallowed at the look in Luke's eyes. He knew! The man already knew what he was thinking! He made a point of not looking back at Lettie. "Well, you are a lucky man, Mr. Fontaine. And might I add, I am very sorry for your injury. I heard the story of the buffalo hunters."

"Probably from Will Doolan," Luke answered, reaching up and touching one of Lettie's hands. He grinned. "Will loves to tell tall tales."

Nial cleared his throat and sat back down. "Yes, well, I have a feeling it was not such a tall story. A person could write a book about the experiences you and your family have had since coming here."

Little Pearl came back out to stand beside her mother and stare at the oddly dressed visitor, and Paul toddled out after her, grasping his mother's skirts and wanting to be picked up. Lettie reached down and lifted him, introducing Pearl and him, then Katie, who also came out to have a look. Robbie and Ty ran by then, screaming and playing Indian. "Our other two sons," Lettie explained. "Tyler is the oldest boy. He's seven and Robert is four."

Nial caught the pride in her voice, saw it in Luke's eyes. "You have a fine family, Mr. Fontaine."

Their eyes held for a moment, and Luke nodded. "I think so."

Nial could see that having any feelings for Lettie Fontaine was hopeless. He put on a grin. "Well, about my cattle. They're called Herefords, and believe me, they carry more pounds of beef on the hoof than any shorthorn. They have very broad heads and big necks, huge chests and short legs. An eight-month-old steer can weigh well over six hundred pounds, maybe a thousand. I've known mature steers to reach close to two thousand pounds. They're a sturdy animal, I assure you, and resistant to disease."

"Can they survive a Montana winter?"

"The ones I brought with me did just fine last winter."

"We've had winters that were a lot worse than last year's."

Nial leaned forward, resting his elbows on his knees. "I'll make a deal with you. Buy five hundred head from me, and if they don't make the next winter or don't breed well, I will refund your money. I'll sell you three bulls and several cows so you'll have some breeding stock. The rest will be young steers, money in the bank for you when they're grown and fattened. I have a lot more cows, but

I need them for my own breeding purposes. I'll let you have all five hundred for eighty cents a head. That is very cheap compared to what you'll get for the steers later on, probably at least six to eight dollars a head."

Luke took a thin cigar from his shirt pocket, along with a match. He lit the smoke, looking out at some of his own cattle grazing below as he took a few puffs before replying. "Why are you so anxious to help the rest of us? We're your competition."

"We're all part of the Cattlemen's Association now, all here to help each other, are we not? Besides, I don't really own the cattle on any of my ranches, Mr. Fontaine. I only own the land itself. My father and several others formed a company back in England that invests in American cattle. They foresaw the profit that could be made in this industry. I came here to manage those investments and find a market for the Herefords. My father's company strongly believes in the breed and I am here to promote them and find new buyers."

"All right, Bentley. Lettie and Will both already told me a lot about this new breed. I'll give them a try, but I'll pay you half their worth. I'll give you the rest after they've proven themselves." He looked back at the Englishman. "For all I know, you could hightail it back to England and I'd never see you or my money again. The damn cattle could die off on me over the next winter, and I'd be out four hundred dollars."

Bentley smiled. "Agreed. Half up front. But I assure you, I am here to stay, Mr. Fontaine. I promised my father I'd find a big market out here for him, and I do love this land. It's so beautiful. Everything is so big and spectacular! I'm not sure I could ever go back to England!"

"We love it here too, Mr. Bentley," Lettie put in. "That's why we've never left, in spite of the bad times. There have also been a lot of good times."

Nial glanced at her again, wishing she hadn't spoken

so he wouldn't have to look her way. How could a woman who had lived out here for so long and borne six children look like she did? Did she often think of her firstborn? He'd heard the woman actually thought the boy might still be alive. He supposed any mother would have to think that or go crazy.

"Would you like something to drink, Mr. Bentley?" she was asking. "Coffee? A little whiskey, perhaps?"

"Actually, I would love some tea. Would you have any?"

Lettie smiled. "Of course. I'll go heat the water." She went back inside, wondering if Luke noticed how Bentley looked at her. Bentley seemed to be on better behavior today, thank God. She was glad Luke was trying out the new breed of cattle, but she would be glad when Nial Bentley was gone. She hoped he didn't intend to visit too often. It made her much too uncomfortable.

Luke and Nial talked for another hour. Lettie served the tea, bringing a shot of whiskey to Luke, then stayed inside the house, away from Nial Bentley's roving eyes. She noticed Luke seemed wary of the man, gave him a few helpful hints on ranching in Montana but not offering a lot of details. She noticed he did not mention his plans to contract with the army. That was one deal he wanted for himself.

Finally Bentley rose and shook Luke's hand. "I'd better be off. Some of my men have made camp a few miles from here. We'll sleep under the stars tonight—too long a ride from here to my place to make it before dark."

"Aren't you a little uncomfortable in those clothes?" Lettie heard Luke ask him. She stifled a laugh as she came to the door to bid Nial Bentley good-bye.

"Oh, not at all, I assure you. I do have clothes more fitting to this kind of living. I only dress this way when I am visiting or going to an important meeting."

"Well, you don't need to dress fancy to come visiting here," Luke told him, shaking his hand.

Lettie came out then, carrying Paul, who was always begging to be picked up. "Good-bye, Mr. Bentley."

"Please, both of you call me Nial," the man answered, his eyes quickly moving over her before he bowed again. "It was so pleasant meeting you again, Mrs. Fontaine."

"Lettie," she answered. "Just Luke and Lettie."

Lettie, Nial thought. *My beautiful Lettie. Such a strong, handsome, loving husband you have. If only I could woo you away from him.* He donned his hat then, nodding to Luke again. "Well, then, Luke, I'll have my men bring over a couple of my best Herefords for you to see, and I'll send word to the overseer of my ranch in Wisconsin that you are willing to try them out. Next summer he'll ship five hundred of our best to the Double L, and you can start building from there. You won't regret it, Luke. Wait until you see how big the steers get after castration."

"Well, I always have my own shorthorns to fall back on if it doesn't work out. I might even try breeding the shorthorns with the Herefords."

Bentley brushed at his suit. "Sir, I guarantee that in a few years you'll be breeding nothing but Herefords." He nodded once more. "I'm off. I do pray that leg will heal much more quickly than the doctor thinks. When you can ride again, do come and pay a visit to Essex Manor. Feel free to bring the missus. She is quite a wonderful woman. You must be very proud to have a wife who is so intelligent and supportive to stand up for the Double L as she did at the cattlemen's meeting." He turned and walked off the porch, mounted up on his fine black horse, and gave another wave before finally riding off.

Lettie set Paul down. He toddled to the steps, then sat to scoot down them, then grabbed fistfuls of dirt from the driveway and threw them into the air, letting it blow back into his hair. Lettie pulled up the chair Bentley had used beside Luke and sat down. "Quite a character, isn't he?"

Luke smoked quietly, watching Nial Bentley ride

through the gate. "Who? Paul? Or were you referring to Nial Bentley?"

Lettie caught the irritation in his voice. "Are you all right, Luke? You never put your jacket on. It's getting chilly."

Luke met her eyes then, a teasing smile on his face. "You *are* a hell of a woman, you know."

Lettie reddened, looking at her lap. "I can't help how the silly man looks at me, Luke. In fact, when I got the chance, I set him straight at the cattlemen's meeting. I told him that being a married woman, I did not appreciate him staring at me. He was quite apologetic and quite the gentleman after that. I don't think he means any harm."

Luke reached over and grasped her hand. "Why didn't you say something when you came home from the meeting?"

She shrugged. "I don't know. I guess because I wanted so much for you to see about those Herefords. I was afraid if I made you dislike the man before you even met him, you wouldn't consider trying the new breed. What's good for the ranch comes above everything else."

"Lettie."

He squeezed her hand. When she met his eyes, she saw the love there, but also the stern look of a man who sets his own rules.

"Not when it comes to you and me and the kids. All of that *always* comes first. We said once that we'd tell each other everything, remember?"

She leaned forward and kissed him lightly. "I love you, Luke."

He closed his eyes and groaned. "Then don't kiss me. It's too hard on me, wanting you and being laid up like this. We're going to have to figure something out pretty soon, or I'll go crazy."

Lettie smiled. "Then think about other things, like breeding a new strain of cattle, and letting me send for that mine owner from Denver."

"I don't want any damn mining company coming in here and tearing up my land."

"He promises not to disturb the land any more than necessary. Luke, we've had enough hard times to know we can't just count on the cattle. We have to have something to fall back on in case of disease or drought. It can't hurt to let him see what's out there."

Luke sighed deeply. "You drive a hard bargain, woman." He gave her a wink. "Go ahead and send for him. I'm only doing it because if he finds anything valuable out there, I can build you that house that much quicker."

"I don't need the house, Luke—"

"Yes, you do, and a lot more. I promised you a big house and a tutor and maids and fine furniture—the works. You'll have it. This family has outgrown this place anyway. The girls should each have their own room, and Ty and Robbie shouldn't have to share a room with Paul. He is constantly getting into their things."

Lettie laughed. "He *is* a wild little thing. Sometimes he reminds me so much of—" Her smile faded. She turned then and ran to pick Paul up when he started toddling off toward some horses tied near the barn.

Luke watched her, still wrestling with whether he should tell her what he thought he had seen that morning he was found. Even if Nathan was alive, the little four-year-old boy who had been torn from his mother's arms was gone forever. Luke would never get over the guilt he felt for being partly responsible. Maybe that was what had stirred this fierce possessiveness he felt when he saw how Nial Bentley looked at her, his own fear of someday losing her she might blame him, deep inside, for losing Nathan. That was why he had to keep all the rest of his promises, build her that big house, cater to her whims. He'd let the miner from Denver come out because it was what Lettie wanted, and he'd vowed a long time ago that whatever Lettie wanted, Lettie would get.

Fifteen

As soon as Luke walked into the spring dance, a crowd of well-wishers surrounded him and Lettie. They made such a fuss over the fact that Luke was on his feet again that he was embarrassed suddenly to be the center of attention. Even though he had to use crutches and still felt pain, it was good to stand tall again, to be among his friends, to get out of the house. He shook a sea of hands, and the wives of ranchers and townspeople hugged Lettie at the same time, the women exclaiming over Lettie's wardrobe. She had worn a muslin dress printed in a paisley pattern of yellow and white, the bodice made of handkerchief linen, the long sleeves bearing ruffles at the cuffs in the yellow paisley design. The same design ran through the ruffles at her waist, down the front of the bodice, and in the four tiers of ruffles that graced the full skirt. The straw bonnet she wore was decorated with yellow ribbon and flowers. The bright color only accented her dark auburn hair and green eyes.

"You look like spring yourself!" Henny told her. "How do you always manage to look so beautiful, Lettie?"

"It's because her handsome husband is alive and back on his feet," Henry Kline's wife, Lucy, said. "She's glowing with love, that's what."

The women all laughed, and Lettie glanced at Luke. Yes, he certainly did look handsome this evening. He had worn a black suit, with a blue shirt and black tie. The shirt accented the color of his eyes. The clothes were just some of those made for them over the winter by an

Italian tailor who had come to town last summer. Luke had insisted on paying for a whole new wardrobe for her, but getting him to let Gino Galardo measure him for a suit of his own had been like pulling teeth. She had had Tex bring Gino to the ranch, literally ordering Luke to allow the man to measure him, reminding Luke he dearly needed a new suit.

The heavy wrapping and brace were off Luke's leg now, and he only wore a firm wrap of gauze for support. Over the winter she'd had to cut the right leg out of several pair of his pants, and she had already talked with the owner of the town's only general store, Syd Martin, about ordering new denim pants for him to replace the ruined ones.

"Next thing we know, you'll be on a horse joinin' spring roundup," Will was saying. He slapped Luke on the shoulder, and Lettie felt uneasy at the words. She worried Luke was too anxious now to get back to work. It was important to be sure the leg was completely healed.

"That's exactly what I intend to do," Luke answered. "It's time to get back to business. My poor wife has been handling things too long. The kids hardly know their mother."

"Well, she's done a hell of a job," James Woodward put in.

Lettie did feel rather proud of her accomplishments over the winter. She'd had to make some important decisions herself, had talked with Luke about familiar landmarks she should learn, valleys, ridges, mountains, the best rangeland, where there was water all year round and where there was water only in winter and spring. Luke had drawn a crude map for her to study, and they had long talks about cattle breeding, and other matters pertinent to running a ranch. She had kept the books for Luke, staying up late at night after the children were asleep to balance the budget. She knew about the cost of feed, what Luke paid the men, how to judge what they might make this year after the summer drive to Cheyenne. Bradley Mills had visited the ranch, and Luke had signed a contract with the man in which Patterson's Meat Supply agreed to take all the beef Luke could send for the next five years at fair market value, with a stipulation that no beef would be expected this summer if Luke's original buyer, Shelby Preston, who represented a rival packinghouse, came through with his promise to take twenty-five hundred head.

Things looked very good for the Double L, in spite of Luke's being laid up most of the winter. Jeremy Shane had come calling last fall, and Luke had agreed to allow the man to send geologists to the ranch this summer to test for any valuable minerals that might lie under the rich grassland.

This was the happiest Lettie had been since the awful day the buffalo hunters shot Luke down. She would never forget the sound of their thundering guns, or the chilling crack of Luke's leg being broken by the powerful slug that had smashed all the way through it and into his horse. She was still haunted by the memory of how it had felt when she was sure he would die. Now here he stood, getting back his old strength, as handsome as ever at the age of thirty-eight. If only he would get a letter or a visit from his father. That was a heartbreak she knew still ate at his soul.

The Fontaine children filed in behind their parents, Katie, almost nine, carrying Paul, who had just turned three. Tyler was nearly eight, and Lettie watched him stretch himself as tall as he could. She smiled, suspecting he wanted everyone to notice how much he looked like his father. Nearly every day he said he wanted to be just like Luke when he grew up, and he was already excited about when he would be big enough to start riding with his father on roundups. The boy puffed out his chest as he shook hands with a few of the men, who laughed about him being a "chip off the old block," something Lettie knew made him proud.

The town hall was packed so full there was little room left for dancing, but that did not deter the happy throng, all ready to celebrate the end of another hard, cold Montana winter. Lettie noticed several couples were already stomping about on the wooden floor planks. Will had come up with the idea of a spring celebration two years ago, a chance to "shake out the cobwebs and get the blood runnin'," as he put it, before men got to work with spring roundup and then left on cattle drives. A makeshift orchestra that consisted of two men on fiddles, one on a banjo, and another pounding the keys of a beat-up piano borrowed from the Lonesome Tree, played a snappy tune that made skirts whirl and men yelp in celebration.

Lettie noticed a few men from town had women of questionable character on their arms. She had seen those same women hanging around in front of the Lonesome Tree, some lounging in front of the many other saloons in Billings, but she supposed they deserved to celebrate spring as much as anyone else. She often wondered which ones might have flirted with Luke on his many trips to Billings. She had no doubt he enjoyed a few drinks at the taverns when he came to town. There wasn't a man here who didn't, and considering Luke's handsome physique, and his growing wealth and importance, any woman would be attracted to him. She was surprised at a sudden fit of jealousy, and she knew the reason. Luke was better, but still not free enough of pain to make love. She needed him that way, and she knew it was the same for him.

Men offered Luke glasses of whiskey, and Lettie carried a pie to the food table, followed by all the children, who began loading their plates. Anne Sacks also came along, carrying her newborn son. "Billy and Luke are already drinking," she said with a laugh.

"I'm not surprised," Lettie answered. "We'd better give them some food, or they'll be falling down before ten o'clock. A drunken man and crutches just don't go together."

They both turned to watch the dancing. As Lettie started back through the crowd toward Luke someone grasped her arm. She turned to see it was Nial Bentley, who was dressed in a dark suit, his black hair slicked back, his white shirt collar starched stiff and proper.

"Lettie! How good to see you again after a long, lonely winter!" His eyes moved over her almost hungrily. "You look wonderful! Such lovely taste you have in clothes. Perhaps you would allow me a dance later?"

Lettie gently pulled her arm away. "I don't think a dance would be proper, Nial, but thank you anyway. I am sure there must be some single young women or widows here who would be thrilled to dance with a wealthy Englishman." She smiled, hoping to turn him away without insulting him. She watched his smile fade a little.

"Yes, perhaps. What a pity that none of them is as beautiful as Lettie Fontaine. How wonderful it must be to have such a lovely wife and family to get one through the dead of winter. I was just on my way to greet your husband. I see he is up on his feet at last."

As always, Lettie wasn't sure how to take the man's compliments. "Yes, Luke is almost back to normal."

Almost? Nial followed her to where Luke stood. Was the man well enough to make love to his wife again? Oh, how he would love to have that pleasure himself. He greeted Luke with a smile and a handshake. "You'll have your cattle by July, Luke," he told the man. "I just received correspondence from my Wisconsin ranch two days ago. They'll be shipped out by rail in May, then herded to Billings, where your men can take over. It's costing me a fortune for the twenty rail cars it will take to carry them all, and I'll make no profit, but it's worth it to get someone to try the breed. If it's a success, I'm sure I'll get the other ranchers to buy in."

Luke glanced at Lettie, then set one crutch against a table and used his free arm to put around her shoulders. "Maybe we can let the other ranchers know when they'll arrive so they can be there to see the stock."

Nial noticed Luke's possessive gesture. "Yes, I'll see about that. There are others interested, but the heavy snows this winter kept them from coming to my ranch to see for themselves. The men you sent last fall to have a look seemed very impressed. I'm sure you were relieved when you heard their opinion."

"I take it your Herefords made it through the winter with no problems?" Luke was asking.

Nial kept his smile. He liked Luke Fontaine, yet part of him hated the man for being married to the only woman he had truly wanted since his own wife died six years ago. "No problems," he answered. "I do hope you and your wife will come visiting this summer. I have a building crew there that I hired back in Wisconsin, who started constructing my new home last fall. It will be made completely of stone, which they are bringing in from the mountains by the wagonful. It is quite a project. You really must see it. I am fashioning it after my family home in England—bringing a bit of my country to Montana, you might say, although this lonely man certainly does not need such a big home. Still, it helps relieve my homesickness." He realized perhaps he could impress Lettie Fontaine with his money and the castle of a home he was building. Her husband was rich enough in his own right, but not a man who could dip into the almost endless old money that he could. What did he have left to impress her with besides his wealth? "Fifteen rooms and a ballroom," he added. "When it is finished, I intend to hold some sort of gala event there every summer, perhaps a big cookout and a dance for everyone for miles around who wishes to come."

His eyes rested on Lettie on the last words.

"Do you miss England, Nial?" Lettie asked.

"Oh yes, but as I told you last fall, this country is as beautiful as anything I have ever seen, and so big! I could never be completely happy in England again after this. I have decided to make this my permanent home, which is why I'm building my 'stone castle,' as some of the men call it."

The little band struck up a waltz, and the wife of one of Billings's new arrivals, Sidney Greene, a lawyer, came up and grabbed Nial's arm. Mrs. Greene introduced him to her sixteen-year-old daughter, Chloris, a modestly pretty girl who looked very embarrassed when her mother insisted that she dance with Nial, who kindly obliged.

Luke pulled Lettie closer then. "Every mother with a marriageable daughter within two hundred miles of here will be trying to hitch them up with the wealthy Lord Bentley," he said with a hint of sarcasm.

Lettie smiled, turning to face him. "He never said he was a lord."

Luke scowled, setting his other crutch aside and leaning on her for support, putting both arms on her shoulders and bending closer. "Whatever he is, he's still infatuated with you. You sure you wouldn't like to go and live in that fancy castle and be the wife of an Englishman?"

Lettie laughed, grasping hold of his powerful forearms. "If I did, I would be a terribly unfaithful wife." She studied his blue eyes, a surge of desire rushing through her with such intensity that she had to draw in her breath. Her smile faded. "I'd be constantly running off to sleep with another man, a big, strong, handsome man with blue eyes, who doesn't have to build me a stone castle to keep me in his bed. If being with the man meant I had to go back to living in that shack we use to store feed now, I'd do it."

Luke studied her lovingly. "I believe you would." He

kissed her forehead. "How about if I ask Will and Henny to keep the kids tonight and we go back alone to that room I rented at the hotel?"

Lettie blushed. "Will and Henny would know why we asked, and I would be embarrassed to death."

He grinned. "They'd understand. They'd tease us unmercifully, but we're used to them." His smile faded. "It's been a long time, Lettie. I've never seen you look more beautiful than you do this evening."

"What about your leg? Maybe you still aren't well enough—"

"Oh, I'm well enough," he said with a wink. "Watching that damn Englishman put his hand on you gave me a little boost."

"Hear! Hear!" Will's voice interrupted their conversation as he handed Luke another glass of whiskey. "Henny says to tell you you're needed over at the food table," he told Lettie. "Sorry to interrupt!"

Luke kept his eyes on Lettie for a moment. "No more whiskey for me," he told Will. "Just bring me some punch or whatever they've got over there."

"No whiskey? Why, Luke, you—" He hesitated, then burst into laughter. "I get it! There's times when a man's better off not takin' down too much alcohol!" He gulped the whiskey himself. "I've got a feelin' me and Henny should watch the little ones tonight."

Lettie blushed even more, handing Luke his crutches. "I'm going to join Henny." She left him standing there, shivering with desire as she headed back to the food table. She could hardly concentrate on watching the children and serving food after that, and every time she glanced at Luke, he was watching her, which only brought more color to her cheeks. People danced and ate and celebrated until dark, and to Lettie's delight, Chloris Greene kept Nial Bentley occupied most of that time. Whenever he was alone, a couple of women of questionable reputation insisted on dancing and conversation, flirting outrageously with the rich Englishman. Still, neither diversion could keep him from coming to her after several hours of imbibing and asking her again to dance, this time grabbing her hands and half pulling her onto the dance floor to join him in a square dance. Lettie obliged only to keep from making a scene. Nial's face was flushed with too much liquor and too much desire, and whenever the man who called the dance asked the men to put a hand to their partner's waist, he pulled her much closer than necessary.

"How sad that you are taken, Lettie," he told her. "I would be so proud to present you to my family in England as my wife and tell them what a magnificent, brave woman you are. They would be fascinated by your beauty and the adventures you have known out here!"

Lettie pulled away. She noticed Luke was up on his crutches again and talking to the two prostitutes who had been flirting with Nial earlier. A rage of jealousy moved through her when they laughed and flirted with him, but when the dance ended, she realized why he had been talking to them. They both came over and grabbed Nial, giggling and flirting and both insisting on having the next dance. "You are ours for the rest of the night," one of them told him seductively.

Lettie sighed with relief, saw Luke watching her. She knew he had deliberately sent the two women to get Nial away from her. For the first time since hours earlier, he held another glass of whiskey in his hand. She quickly and gladly left the dance floor, walking close to Luke. "I thought you weren't going to drink any more tonight."

Luke glanced over at Bentley, who was prancing around the floor again with both prostitutes. "It helps the pain in my leg," he answered. "Besides, some things call for a little whiskey, like when one man tries to move in on another man's property." He met her eyes.

"Luke, the man dragged me out there. I didn't want to make a scene." She stood close so that others could not hear their conversation. "And please don't *you* make a scene. The man is drunk."

Luke finished his own whiskey. "Nothing like alcohol to force a man to reveal his true feelings."

Lettie could see the burning anger in his eyes. He nodded to Will and Billy, who walked over to Nial and started a conversation with him, suggesting they go outside for some fresh air and talk about Herefords. When they got him to the door, she saw that Tex stood quietly at the entrance. He followed the other three men out.

"Luke, what is going on?"

Luke braced himself on his crutches. "I'm just going to have a little conversation with Lord Bentley."

"You aren't going to hurt him, are you? Don't get in a scuffle, Luke. Your leg!"

"Don't worry. Everything will be just fine."

"Don't let the men gang up on him. That would be so unfair."

He scowled. "Jesus, woman, don't you know me better than that? Nobody is going to hurt him, and nobody fights Luke Fontaine's battles for him. I'll take care of this in my own way. I intend to set Bentley straight very calmly, that's all." More people had joined the celebrating over the course of the evening and in all the commotion no one noticed what was going on. "You get the kids together. Will and Henny are going to take them home with them in a few minutes. I'll be right back."

Lettie knew there was no use arguing. She left to gather up the children, and Luke headed outside, taking a moment to adjust to the darkness. There were others outside smoking and drinking, and Luke made his way through the small groups of men, stopping to talk casually to a few of them. He searched for his own men, heard a woman laughing somewhere in nearby bushes.

Some young girl had apparently come out here to have some fun out of sight of her parents. Luke moved around to the side of the barn where Tex, Will, and Billy had lured Nial Bentley per his instructions. He did not want this confrontation witnessed by someone who might take it wrong and spread dirty rumors about Lettie. She bore no fault here, and he would not have her talked about. His men had Nial completely at ease, Will handing the man a bottle of whiskey. Nial took a swallow, then noticed Luke approaching.

"Well, Luke!" he greeted. "Join us!" He raised the bottle, then sobered at the look in Luke's eyes.

"Did you enjoy the dance with my wife?" Luke asked.

Nial moved his gaze from Luke to the other three men, smiling nervously. "I was just being friendly." He looked back at Luke. "I thought that since you were on crutches and couldn't dance, maybe she'd like to dance at least once."

Luke raised one of his crutches, and Nial grunted when the end of it was poked against his chest and shoved hard, slamming Nial against the outside wall of the town hall. Nial dropped the bottle. "Maybe you should have asked her husband first if he minded, or asked *her* if *she* minded!" Luke growled.

Nial held up his hands and looked down at the crutch, barely able to breathe from it being pressed so tightly against his breastbone. "I, uh, I apparently took a little too much for granted, probably because of too much whiskey," he answered. "My apologies, Luke."

Luke released the pressure on the crutch but kept it against the man's chest. "Don't think that a bad leg would keep me from stepping in when I see it's necessary, Bentley! You stop bothering Lettie, you hear? It upsets and embarrasses her when you make it obvious to everyone around you that you've got an eye for her." He lowered the crutch and stepped closer. "I didn't ask my men to come out here to fight my battle for me. I fight my own battles. I just wanted you lured out here so we could settle this without others seeing. For reasons you wouldn't even know about, I don't ever want my Lettie gossiped about, you understand? It would devastate her! From here on you won't give her more than a first look when you're in public. You'll stop ogling her and stop drooling your compliments in front of others; and you'll keep your goddamn lily-white hands to yourself! God knows I appreciate her beauty and her worth, and I'm not stupid enough to think other men don't notice; but they know better than to show it in front of me or to try moving in on Luke Fontaine's wife! That's a lesson you'd better learn, *Lord* Bentley! There's a lot more substance to Lettie than you'll ever know, and your fancy suits and your stone castle don't impress a woman like that! Just leave her alone! Understood?"

Nial swallowed. "Understood."

"Good. We're still in business as far as those cattle are concerned, but you remember that your land borders mine, and out here a man can get away with a lot of things in the name of honor and vengeance."

Nial looked him over. "I am aware of that, Luke. Let me tell you, I have only the greatest respect for you and your wife. It's true I…I have allowed myself to become somewhat infatuated, but I would never think of…well, I do apologize for the misunderstanding."

"I don't think there was any misunderstanding at all. I think I understand your feelings and motives *perfectly*! From now on, keep it all to yourself."

Nial nodded. "I lost my own wife six years ago. I've been a very lonely man, especially after leaving England. I have apparently let that loneliness cause me to behave unwisely. Please, I do want to remain friendly neighbors, and continue to do business together."

Luke nodded. "Fine with me, as long as you leave Lettie out of the picture. From now on *I'll* be at the cattlemen's meetings, and *I'm* the one you'll talk to when you come to the Double L. And at occasions like this one, you'll not pay any particular attention to Lettie. I won't warn you a second time. I'll just light into you, and we'll see how far your money and fancy ways get you in a flat-out brawl—no swords, no guns, just fists. I don't really think you want that."

Nial stood nearly as tall as Luke, but he knew he was no match for the man's brawn and ruggedness, let alone the fact that Luke would be defending the woman he loved, the mother of his children. That was enough fuel to fire any man into a bloody match he'd be determined to win. "No. I don't think I do."

Luke nodded. "I'm sorry about your own loss, Bentley, but that doesn't give a man a right to move in on another man's wife." He turned and left, and Tex, Will, and Billy all eyed Nial a moment longer before following.

Nial breathed deeply, brushed at the spot of dirt Luke's crutch had left on the front of his shirt. He suspected he had got off lightly, and he sighed in frustration. So be it. It didn't do a man any good to go up against someone like Luke Fontaine, not even the son of an English earl. Out here that meant nothing. Out here it was the man with the most experience, the most brawn, and the most land who got all the respect. Before he could get back inside, the two prostitutes who had been flirting suggestively with him all evening came out to meet him, hanging on him and suggesting he go with them to the Lonesome Tree.

"Why not?" he answered, walking off with them. Maybe spending a night with both voluptuous ladies would help get Lettie Fontaine out of his system, but he knew deep inside that the only woman who could satisfy him was Lettie herself.

❦

"I have to tell you, Lettie, this summer we're cutting down any barbed wire we come across." Luke led her inside the hotel and to their room. "We're starting to see more and more of it, mostly put up by farmers."

"There will be trouble, Luke. I don't want to see you get hurt again, nor do I want to see any innocent farmers get hurt."

"Don't worry. I'm thinking of ways to compromise without bloodshed."

They went inside, and Lettie closed and locked the door. "I'd like to go out on roundup with you this year, watch the branding, help count the new calves," she told him.

Luke removed his hat. "It's dirty work. You've already done enough while I've been laid up. It's time you got back to being the woman of the Double L, spending more time with the children."

"I will, right after spring roundup. We can take Tyler with us. He would be thrilled. He's so anxious to start learning." Lettie took the pins from her hat. "It's one thing I haven't done yet, Luke. In all the years we've been here, I've never ridden out to help with roundup, watched the branding, how you determine which cattle will be shipped to market and which will remain to build the herd. I want to know everything about it. I've told you that before. And, by the way, I don't think you should go on the cattle drive this summer. You have men who can handle it for you."

"I'll manage. I'm not sending twenty-five hundred of my best steers off without being along to make sure they get where they're going. Problems with rustlers are getting worse, and lately there's been more trouble with other landowners allowing cattle to cross their land. Now we've got barbed wire to worry about." He walked closer to her and set one crutch aside.

"Luke, I worry—"

He pulled her close. "You won't have time to miss me or worry about me this summer. I'm starting that house for you. That's your summer project while I'm gone."

She frowned. "We can't afford it yet."

"We can afford at least to get it framed in. I'm going to see about hiring good builders out of Denver. I talked to Jeremy Shane at the dance, and he said he'd talk to some contractors when he goes back to Denver and wire me some information."

"Luke, don't do this just because Nial Bentley is building his ridiculous castle of a home. And by the way, you didn't hurt him, did you?"

He shook his head. "I just very firmly warned him to stop bothering and embarrassing you." He kissed her hair. "As far as the house, I'm not doing it because of Nial Bentley. I'm doing it because I promised this to you years ago. It's time we built a home fitting for the Double L, and fitting for the most beautiful woman in Montana. I'll have the builders show you some blueprints and you pick out whatever one suits you best. I don't care about size or cost."

"Luke, I don't need or want—"

He kissed her lightly. "No more objections." He sighed, rubbing her back. "I haven't been much of a man to you this winter."

"You couldn't help that." Their eyes held, both of them aching to be one again.

"Tell me you don't find Nial Bentley attractive."

"Of course I find him attractive. Any woman would." Lettie watched the jealousy and disappointment come into his blue eyes. She smiled teasingly. "But he's no Luke Fontaine. He doesn't have your rugged strength and good looks, and he didn't father my five children. He hasn't sacrificed for me, and he isn't nearly as handsome." She ended the words in a whisper, reaching up and running her fingers into his hair. "And while we're on the subject, you seemed to be quite familiar with those two women of questionable reputation you sent after Nial tonight. Just what do you do in the times you come to town without me, Luke Fontaine?"

He pulled the combs from her hair. "They only know me because I've had a few drinks in the Lonesome Tree. I don't need women like that to keep me satisfied, and you know it."

"Do I?" She gave him a seductive look. "Come to bed, Luke." She helped him to the bed, where he sat down. "I'll make it easy for you," she told him with a sly grin. For tonight she wanted to be as wanton and fetching as those saloon girls, imagined what they might do for a man. She began undressing for him, watched his eyes begin to glaze with desire. She felt both excited and embarrassed as she pulled her clothes off layer by layer, down to her shoes, stockings and garters. She smiled bashfully then, folding her arms over her full breasts.

Luke reached out and grasped her hips. "God, you're beautiful," he groaned. He leaned forward and kissed her stomach, moved his lips to the fold where her thighs met the soft hairs of that private place that had belonged to Luke Fontaine for nearly ten years now. "I want you to have everything, Lettie."

"I already have everything I could ever want." She shivered, wrapping her fingers in his dark hair as she reveled in touches she had not enjoyed for months. He licked at her stomach again, and she sank to her knees and let him taste her breasts. "Let me undress you," she said softly then, pulling away for a moment. She helped him remove his suit coat, untied his tie and tossed it aside. She unbuttoned and removed his shirt, then the top half of his long johns. She kissed his chest. Through the winter he had lifted heavy rocks to keep up his strength, determined not to wither away because he was forced to be immobile. He was returning to his old strength, and she caressed the solid muscle of his chest and arms.

She removed his boots, then helped him stand up so she could take off his pants and long johns. She kissed the wrapping on his thigh, drew in her breath at the

sight of his manliness, swollen hard, ready to fulfill a
need for both of them that had been long neglected. For
months she had bathed him, had been forced to look on
his nakedness without emotion. At last she could allow
herself to enjoy this man she loved and desired.

Luke reached over and pulled back the covers, managing to scoot himself farther onto the bed. He held open
the covers, and Lettie moved in beside him, their mouths
meeting in a savage, hungry kiss as Luke hovered over
her then, pressing his eager hardness against her belly,
his tongue exploring her mouth as he ached to explore
her depths and be one with this woman he loved so,
this woman another man wanted but would by God
never have. He groaned with the want of her, started
to maneuver himself between her legs but stiffened then
with the pain of trying to support himself on his knees.

He gritted his teeth and moved away. "Damn! I'm
sorry, Lettie."

Lettie leaned over him, her auburn locks tumbling
over her shoulders and brushing against his broad chest.
"I'll do it," she whispered, feeling wanton and daring in
her aching need to feel her man inside her again. She had
no idea where she got the courage, but until his leg was
better, there was only one way it could be done. He had
hinted at times he would like to make love this way, but
she had always resisted, thinking it seemed terribly bold,
maybe even sinful, even if it was with her own husband.

She moved on top of him, straddling him. He reached
up and fondled her breasts, his blue eyes full of love,
desire, gratefulness.

"Lettie, you're so beautiful."

She reached down and guided him into herself, gasp-
ing at the pleasure his manliness always brought her,
the thrill of feeling this wondrous ecstasy again. She
never dreamed such boldness could be this fulfilling, this
gloriously beautiful. His strong hands moved down to

grasp her thighs, moved to that part of her only Luke had touched lovingly, almost worshipfully. He toyed with that secret place that had been so long neglected, and in moments she felt the thrilling climax she had not enjoyed for months. She threw back her head and moved rhythmically then, grasping his strong arms to support herself, feeling wild and free, as though she were out on the range riding a wild stallion.

It had been a long time. Luke's life quickly spilled into her, and he grasped her breasts and groaned with the sweet release. Lettie leaned down, and they kissed hungrily. "Thank you, Lettie," he groaned. "I never thought you'd do that. It was beautiful."

"I want to do it again," she whispered.

Luke grinned, thinking how she had been worried he might be attracted to the town whores. What she had just done was just as daring and delicious as anything any of those women could do, let alone the fact that she was so beautiful...his wife...his Lettie. He stroked her damp hair back from her face. "As soon as this leg is completely well, I'll make love to you the way a man should." He kissed her several times over, relishing the feel of her nakedness against his own.

Lettie smiled and got up to wash, thinking how Luke Fontaine had taught her to enjoy being with a man, so much so that she could do something so bold as to ride him like a wild thing. She cleaned herself and came back to bed, snuggling beside him. "I just want to feel your arms around me for a little while. It does feel good to be able to turn everything back to you, Luke. I need your strength. I never realized how much until this winter."

He kissed her hair. "I'm proud of the way you took over. I guess if you want to go out on roundup and bring Tyler, you've earned the right."

Lettie traced her fingers over his full lips. "It's just made me love the Double L even more, Luke. I understand your dreams better. They're my dreams too. If anything ever happens to you, I'll stay on, keep the Double L alive for your sons."

He took one of her fingers into his mouth, licked it, moved to her lips. Lettie laughed wickedly as he rolled her back on top of him. He grasped her thighs from behind and gently pulled them apart, then guided himself into her again. He did not doubt that Nial Bentley was not the only man who fantasized about loving her; but she belonged to Luke Fontaine.

Sixteen

LETTIE PARTED THE LACE CURTAINS OF LUKE'S AND HER bedroom window to look across nearly an acre of green lawn to the branding corral beyond. From her second-story vantage point, she could see the men working to the right of the new barn Luke had built last fall. The only request Luke had made for the design of their new home was that he be able to look out his own bedroom window and see the barn and corrals in case of trouble.

In the distance she could hear the men whistling and yelling, some of them, including Luke, riding their cutting broncs and whirling their ropes. One by one, young cows and bulls were being roped and branded, and most of the bulls would be castrated to make them easier to handle on a cattle drive and in the grazing fields. Only the best would be singled out to use for breeding. Lettie breathed deeply with the satisfaction that she had been right about trying the Herefords. The herd Luke had ordered from Nial Bentley nearly three years ago had bred well and multiplied in numbers enough that this year Luke could include several hundred head in the drive to Cheyenne.

Good, solid, huge steers they were, and hardy too, just as Nial had promised. She had never seen the Englishman again after that spring dance in '73. His dealings had been strictly with Luke, and last year the man had decided to go back to Wisconsin to check on his holdings there, then, according to what he had told Luke, he was going back to England for a visit. He had good men to watch his land and cattle, and might be gone two or three years, so he said. She understood deep inside why he had left, and she couldn't help feeling a little sad that the great stone mansion at Essex Manor now sat empty except for a skeleton maintenance crew. She hoped perhaps Nial would come back from England with a wife.

She sat down on the wide bench just beneath the window to watch the branding. She could recognize ten-year-old Tyler even from here. He sat on a fence rail observing the work, wanting to learn all he could. The boy already rode nearly as well as the grown men. The boy burst with pride and excitement during roundup time, and she knew it would be difficult to get him to settle down to reading lessons once Luke left on the summer drive. He was proud to call himself a "cowboy," which they had learned through the *Billings Extra* was what men like Luke and the others were called by people back East. There were even little books called dime novels being written about such men, and she couldn't help smiling to herself at the fine adventures she and Luke could write about themselves.

Life was good—so good that Lettie was almost afraid to relax and enjoy it. After three years of construction by one of the finest builders out of Denver, the home Luke had promised her was almost completed. The second-story bedrooms were each large and roomy, with big paned windows for light, windows that could be unlatched and swung open to let in the sweet mountain air as soon as it was warm enough. Each child had his or her own room, but Luke's and hers was the biggest, stretching across one whole end of the second floor so that there were windows at the front, the side, and the back. The hardwood floors were waxed and shiny, decorated with Oriental rugs. Luke had wanted her to order a four-poster bed, but she preferred to keep the brass bed he had bought her, just as she had kept the old pine table he had built for her, now in her spacious kitchen.

She liked little reminders of the past, never wanted to forget what it had taken to come this far. That first little shack they had lived in could fit in one corner of their bedroom, and now it couldn't snow deep enough that they couldn't see out their windows. The house sat even higher than the larger log home they had lived in for the past ten years. All the bedrooms were on the second floor, servants' quarters on the third. There lived Mae Diggs, a middle-aged woman who had lost her farmer husband last summer when he was struck by lightning. Their two grown sons had given up on the hard farming life long before that and lived in Denver. With eleven-year-old Katie and eight-year-old Pearl getting big enough to help her with the housework, Lettie didn't need an extra maid. But Mrs. Diggs had been left destitute, and Lettie had given the woman the job just so she would have a place to live. It had all worked out well. Mae had turned out to be a wonderful cook, and she loved the children.

The children's tutor also lived on the third floor. Lettie had written to a school in Boston to inquire about having someone sent out, and the result had been Elsie Bansen, a lovely, blond twenty-year-old, who came from an orphanage. Elsie could not only teach reading and writing, but also knew how to play the piano. She was giving lessons to Pearl, who sat downstairs in the parlor right now plunking away at a lesson. Lettie loved the sound of the grand piano they had ordered out of Chicago. It filled the whole house with music, and sometimes she felt like crying at the sound of it, remembering when the constant wind was all there was to listen to.

Elsie had seemed uncertain at first that she wanted to live in such a remote area. But then she had fallen head over heels in love with one of Luke's new hired hands, Peter Yost, a handsome young cowboy who had come to the Double L because he "wanted to work for the biggest rancher in Montana Territory." It seemed that out here, if a man couldn't be a big-time rancher himself, the next best thing was to work for one, and at least if Elsie and Peter got married, they were almost sure to stay on at the ranch. With all the hired help, some with wives, the Double L was becoming its own little settlement, and there were no more horribly lonely winters.

Lettie rose and walked over to smooth the colorful quilt on the bed, a quilt she had made herself. She moved to the separate washroom then, just off the bedroom for Luke's and her private use. She cleaned up Luke's shaving table, poured water from a porcelain pitcher into a marble sink to wash it out. Luke had rigged the sink and a porcelain bathtub so that water ran outside through pipes. Old wash water would never again have to be carried out and dumped. Supplies of fresh water were kept in holding tanks built into a special room on the third floor, so that the rest of the house had running water through simple gravity, and a coal-fired boiler in the basement heated the whole house, as well as providing hot water for bathing.

She felt like the most modern woman who ever lived, although she knew there were even more advanced plumbing systems for people in places like Denver. For now, and for this part of the country, this was the height of elegance. Everything was still so new that she had not tired yet of looking at her grand home. The rooms were big and airy, cool in summers because of the wonderful cross-ventilation of the home's many windows. A veranda ran the entire circumference of the house, supported by white pillars that stood out beautifully against the red brick of the outside walls. The porch had not been part of the original design, but Lettie had insisted on having one, so the builder had obliged, and every window was graced with white shutters. Green grass surrounded the house, watered by ranch hands who sprinkled it by means of a hydraulic system from a creek higher in the mountains.

Fine mahogany and walnut furniture decorated the home throughout, from the elegant highboy in Luke's and her room to the magnificent buffet and the huge dining table and chairs that matched it in the dining room downstairs. The library was fast filling with books, works by great writers of the time, books for teaching the children, even books on banking and investments for Luke.

She walked downstairs, running her hand along the rich mahogany stair rail, stopping at a wide landing to rearrange a few knickknacks in a corner cupboard before descending the carpeted stairs to the lower level. The stairs ended at the back of the grand front entry hall, its walls, ceiling, and arched entry into the rest of the house made entirely of the same rich mahogany that graced the rest of the house, the woodwork beautifully detailed along the edges with a scroll design. She made her way down a hallway then, past the library and a drawing room, through the large dining room and into the kitchen, where beside her old coal-burning cookstove sat a newer stove heated with kerosene. Above a working island in the center of the kitchen hung several copper cooking pots and pans, made especially for Luke by Shane Copper Mills in Denver with copper taken from the Double L.

She had been right to suggest to Luke that they allow Jeremy Shane to send his geologists to the Double L. There had indeed been a valuable mineral on their land, copper, not as rich as gold, but certainly rich enough to continue a very comfortable life in case some disaster should wipe out their beef market. For now, beef remained their primary source of income, a new army contract bringing them seven dollars a head this summer, another contract with Patterson's Meat Supply in Omaha ensuring that they would take any excess beef the army couldn't use, at the same price.

She reached the kitchen, where Katie and Pearl were helping Mae knead bread dough. The girls were giggling at the feel of the dough between their fingers and occasionally flicking flour into each other's faces. Five-year-old Paul sat on the floor playing with wooden blocks.

"Where is Robbie?" Lettie asked the girls.

"He's in the garden shed out back, sitting with Pancake," Katie answered. "Ever since Pancake got bit by that rattler, the dog just lays there. Pa says he'll live, but you know how Robbie hates to see anything hurting. He still thinks Pancake will die if he doesn't stay right by him and talk to him."

Lettie sighed, feeling sorry for Robbie. Big, old, yellow Pancake was his favorite of all the dogs. Robbie would not go near horses ever since being kicked by one when he was little, but he loved dogs. He had a penchant for nursing things, from birds with broken wings to his own brothers and sisters whenever they took sick. Now it was Pancake who needed his tender, loving care. He was such a good boy. She wished Luke would be a little more patient with him. Luke expected the boy to be just like Ty, eager to learn about the ranch and learn to ride. It had upset Luke that Robbie would no longer come out to watch the branding. He had cried every time he watched, and this year he had refused to go out at all. It was a source of great frustration to Luke.

"Mommy, read to me," Paul asked, abandoning his blocks and reaching up for her. She picked him up, knowing that of all the children she had spoiled little Paul the most. After all, he was the baby of the family, her last "little one." She didn't want him to be five already. Somehow she had thought perhaps he would always stay a baby. She still ached to give birth again, but that would never be. She gave Paul a hug. There was so much about his personality that reminded her of the way Nathan was when he was small, full of energy and mischief, yet often wanting to be coddled.

She stood there torn between obliging Paul's request to read to him, and going out to the shed to poor, sad Robbie. "Let's go see how Pancake is doing first," she told Paul. She carried him out to the back porch, smiling when she heard Mae chiding Pearl for poking her finger into the rising bread dough.

Lettie walked down a path lined with roses just beginning to show some buds. Soon they would bloom in a splendor of red, white, and yellow. They led to a lovely flower garden of which she was very proud. Green grass, bright flowers, all things she thought she'd never have during that first awful winter spent here. She wished her mother could see all of this, but Katie MacBride had died only one year after her visit. Lettie still had not quite gotten over the fact that her mother was gone from this earth and she would never see her again.

Before she could reach the shed, Robbie came running out of it, smacking into her before he realized she was there. "Mom! Come and see! Pancake got up. I rubbed his head all morning with cool water, and he's better! Ain't I a good doctor, Mom? Ain't I?"

Lettie laughed. "'Aren't' is the word, Robbie, not 'ain't,'" she reminded him, following him into the garden shed, where Pancake had lain on an old blanket being nursed by "Dr." Fontaine. The big dog stood panting, his eyes brighter than they had been since his run-in with a rattler out by the barn three days ago. "Well, look, Paul! Old Pancake *is* better!"

After Lettie set Paul down, he hugged Pancake around the neck, and the dog licked his face. "Come on, Pancake!" Robbie called. "Come outside and go for a walk with us!"

Paul followed after them forgetting he had wanted his mother to read to him. Lettie, relieved Pancake had gotten better, returned to the house and walked around the veranda to the front steps. She had just decided to walk to the corral and ask Luke when he would come in for lunch when she noticed someone riding hard up the long drive from the gate below the hill. She recognized Will Doolan, and Runner was with him. They both charged past her to the corral to find Luke.

Lettie shaded her eyes, her heartbeat quickening at the apparent urgency of Will's visit. Had something happened in town? She watched him speak excitedly to Luke without dismounting. She couldn't hear what was being said. Then every man working in the corral, as well as Tyler and all the men sitting on the corral fence, turned to look her way. What on earth was going on? She watched Luke, who seemed to be arguing with Will. Luke also looked her way. He brushed himself off and mounted his horse, shouting some kind of order to Tyler and the rest of the men. He had apparently told them to stay put, as they all remained behind, even Will, while Luke rode up to the house. When he reached her, Lettie noticed his face was ashen, his eyes full of sorrow, the eyes of someone about to give a person terrible news.

"Luke, what is it?"

He slowly dismounted, sighing heavily. He tied the horse, then limped up the steps. His leg never had healed quite right, but he refused to allow the pain to keep him from his work, and he could rope and wrestle a steer as well as any of his men. He was covered with dust and perspiration from a long morning of hard work. He took her arm and led her around the side of the house where the men could not see them.

"Some Sioux attacked James Woodward's place day before yesterday," he told her, "stole some of his beef, all of his horses. Killed Jim, his wife, and his son."

Lettie closed her eyes. "Dear God. What about his daughters?"

"They survived—hid in a root cellar. A few of Jim's men were killed too, but they managed to down some of the Indians. Those who were just wounded, they shot dead…all but one. They saved him, brought him to town. People are talking about hanging him, but Sheriff Tracy talked them into waiting."

Lettie frowned. "Waiting for what? If they left him alive, why not turn him over to the army at Fort Ellis or Fort Robinson?"

Luke took off his hat and wiped at the sweat on his face with the sleeve of his red shirt. He turned away for a moment, threw his head back as though weighing what he had to say. "Because he's white," he finally answered, "with light hair and blue eyes. Will says he looks about the age Nathan would be…if he would happen to be still alive."

Suddenly, for Lettie, the sun was not shining, the roses were not budding, the birds were not singing. For a moment she could not find her voice. She turned away, not sure she could even breathe. She grasped a wicker rocker, telling herself to stay calm. In the next moment a big hand was squeezing her shoulder.

"It might not even be him, Lettie, and if it is, you've got to realize he's not the innocent little Nathan who was stolen away ten years ago. Will says he's a painted warrior, wild, can't even speak English. He could even be the one who killed Jim and his wife."

"No!"

"You've got to face this, Lettie. It's your decision what we should do about this. Will talked the townspeople into not harming him until you get a chance to go into town and see if you think it's Nathan. You know where he might have had scars or birthmarks. If anybody can tell it's him, you're the one; but I'm afraid of what it will do to you to see him that way—maybe to have to let him go again. You can't just go there and expect him to greet us with open arms and come home with us. He might not even remember you. I know what that will do to you."

She turned to face him, and the agony in her eyes tore at Luke's heart. Should he have told her he'd seen that same boy three years ago after he'd been wounded? What good would it have done then? What good did it do now, even though he'd been captured? His own piercing guilt for being responsible for all of this returned full force. He'd give his life to erase the look in her eyes right now.

"We have to go and see, Luke. We have no choice."

He sighed deeply and pulled her close. "I know." Seeing Nathan like this would be harder on her than if he'd been found dead. "I'll loan Will a fresh horse so he can ride back with us."

Lettie shivered, pressing against him for strength, wanting to scream. It all came back just that quickly, as though her little Nathan had been stolen away only yesterday.

❦

"There they are!" A man standing in front of the jail shouted the words, pointing at Luke and Lettie as they rode into town at a near gallop. Will and three of Luke's men accompanied them.

Lettie paid no heed to anyone in the crowd as she guided her buckskin mare in front of the jail. She had chosen to change into a riding skirt and go by horse because it would be much quicker than a wagon or carriage. It was already nearly dusk, and their horses were lathered from the hard ride. People backed away as she and Luke dismounted and tied their horses.

"What are you going to do, Fontaine? That boy in there is a killer, white or not!" one man shouted.

"You don't know he's the one who actually killed Woodward and his family," Luke shot back. "It could have been some of those who got away!"

"He was with them. That's all we *need* to know!" another man put in.

The crowd agreed, holding up fists, one man holding

up a rope. Lettie had already rushed past everyone to go inside. Luke yanked his rifle from its boot and stepped up to the jailhouse door. He cocked the rifle, leveled it at the crowd. "The first person who touches that boy in there before my wife decides what to do, *dies*! I don't give a damn if you hang *me* for it!"

The crowd quieted. Will took out his own rifle, riding around behind the crowd. "Same goes for me," he spoke up. People turned to look. "You folks agreed with Sheriff Tracy to wait till Mrs. Fontaine could come in and have a look at the boy. She'll know if it's her son, and if it is, it's up to her what we do next! You women in the crowd—men too—how would you feel if one of *your* sons had been ripped out of your arms by wild Indians when he was hardly more than a baby! Wouldn't you want to find him again? And wouldn't you want to try to bring him back into the fold?"

Luke motioned to Tex and Sven. The two men dismounted and came to stand guard at the door while Luke called to Runner to follow him inside. Sheriff Tracy stood at the door to the jail cells, nodded to Luke. "She's already in there."

Luke set his rifle against the sheriff's desk. "Thanks for keeping those people out there at bay." He rushed past the man and into the back room, followed by Runner, who knew the Sioux tongue and had come along to act as an interpreter. Lettie stood staring at the "white Indian" in one of the jail cells. If it was Nathan, he would be fourteen. In the eyes of the Sioux, that was old enough to go on the warpath, and this boy was painted like the wildest of warriors. Luke stepped cautiously up beside Lettie, and the boy stared back at them…light hair…blue eyes. Luke inhaled sharply, recognizing the boy he'd seen the morning after he'd been shot, the one who had given him water.

"Nathan," he said.

The boy showed no signs of recognition. He breathed heavily from a bullet wound in his side, which he had not let Dr. Manning remove. His wrists and feet were tied to the side rails of the cot on which he lay, so that he could not escape.

"We had a time getting him calmed down," Tracy told them. He unlocked the cell door. "He's wild as a bobcat, amazingly strong for his age and condition. Is he your son, Mrs. Fontaine?"

Lettie could hardly move or speak. He was older. All the baby fat was gone; but she would know her Nathan anyplace. "Yes," she finally answered. "He got that little scar under his left eye one day when he fell. He was only about a year and a half old. He cut his left knee badly in that same fall." She stepped inside the cell, moved a little closer, wondering how she was going to keep her knees from collapsing. The boy lay there panting, dirty, bloody, his eyes wide with fear and hatred. He watched her carefully as she leaned to look closer. He lay there wearing only a breechcloth, apron, and breastplate, his legs and arms bare. "There it is," Lettie told Luke. "The scar on his left knee." She closed her eyes. "My God," she moaned. Luke could see her begin to sink. He grabbed hold of her as she broke into tears.

The boy, who only knew himself as White Bear, watched them both in surprise and confusion. Why was the woman crying? There was something about her that was faintly familiar, but he was not sure what it was. Did these white people know him from when he was a small boy? Half Nose had told him he had found him abandoned along the white man's trail to the goldfields. The tall man with the very blue eyes also looked familiar. Wasn't he the one he'd seen badly wounded a few winters ago, lying among the dead buffalo hunters? Nathan. The man had spoken that same word that morning, when he had given him water. What did Nathan mean?

Was it a name? Here and there he had understood a word or two of what people were saying, and he supposed it was because somewhere deep in his mind he remembered those words from when he was very little, before his white parents had either died or deserted him. He wished he could remember more.

Luke kept an arm around Lettie, who wiped at her eyes with a handkerchief and turned to look at her son. "So grown up!" she said through a shivering sob. "Oh, Luke, it's Nathan. I know it's him. Why did Half Nose lie to you? Why couldn't he have just bargained with you, given our son back to us?"

Luke blinked back tears of his own. "A son for a son. He wanted us to feel the pain of his loss, but at the same time he wanted us to stop hounding him, stop searching for Nathan. Jesus, Lettie, I'm so sorry. If there had been more of an army out here then, I could have attacked, forced his hand—"

"No." She squeezed his arm. "He probably would have just killed Nathan for spite. At least he's alive." She left him to move closer and kneel beside the cot.

"Be careful, Lettie. He's as wild and full of hate as any full-blood. You can see it in his eyes."

Lettie sniffed. "He's my son...my boy. He wouldn't—" She touched his arm, and the minute she did so Nathan's whole body jerked. He gritted his teeth and spit words at her. Lettie pulled her hand away. "Oh, Nathan, my precious Nathan!"

The boy wondered at the look the white woman was giving him. It was so loving, so agonizingly sad. Why did she care about him? He looked at the other man who had come into the cell behind the white man. He was a Crow Indian! He could tell by the way the man wore the feathers in his hair, and by the way he was dressed mostly like a white man. The Crow people had given up long ago, had turned to the white man's ways, many of them even accepting the white man's religion. Some Crow even scouted now for the bluecoat soldiers, helped them find the Sioux who did not want to live on the reservation. He spit at him, furious when the man only smiled and said something to the tall white man with the blue eyes.

"Whoa! He is a wild one!" Runner told Luke. "What do you wish me to tell him, Mrs. Fontaine?"

Lettie breathed deeply to compose herself. "I want you to tell him I am his mother. Please explain why we're here, that we've saved his life by coming. Tell him I want him to let our white doctor help him, and that I want him to come home with us."

Runner, who wore his own long black hair in a tail at his neck, kept his distance. White or not, this boy had been taught to hate the Crow. He carefully explained who Lettie was, what she had told him.

White Bear listened in disbelief. He shook his head, told Runner his real parents were dead. His adoptive Indian father, Half Nose, had told him so. And his name was not Nathan. It was White Bear. He had already suffered the Sun Dance sacrifice, had seen the vision that made him a man. He was Sioux. He could not go with these white people.

He watched Runner explain, watched the woman shake her head. Her reply was firm.

"She says Half Nose lied to you. She is your mother. Half Nose stole you away from her when you were four years old." Runner spoke to him in the Sioux tongue. "His own son had been shot by the tall white man here because he attacked him. Half Nose wanted revenge and wanted to replace his son, so he took you. The tall white man is called Luke, Luke Fontaine. The woman is called Lettie. Your real father was killed in a white man's war many years ago, and your mother took Luke for a husband. He adopted you and loved you. After you were taken, he searched for you for many months. Finally Half Nose told him you were dead. He and your mother were deeply grieved."

White Bear could hardly believe the story, but the way the woman looked at him… "How does she know? I am grown now," he told Runner. "Perhaps she is mistaken."

He waited. The woman spoke, and Runner translated that she knew where his scars were and what caused them.

"It is easy to talk of scars. She can easily see them," White Bear answered. "Other whites have been captured over the years. Perhaps I came from some other white family."

As Runner translated, a lump rose in Lettie's throat. Though she had just saved his life, her son was looking at him now as if he might kill her as easily as a rabbit or a deer. "Tell him I know his horse and belongings were taken by the Indians who got away," she told Runner. "Tell him I think that among those belongings is something I am betting he has kept all these years. Perhaps he thinks it is an omen, some kind of charm that brings him luck." She looked at Nathan. "Ask him if he carries a small brown stuffed horse with him. It had one eye made from a button. The other eye was missing."

When Runner had interpreted her words, White Bear was astonished. He had had the horse ever since he could remember, and even now it was inside a parfleche that was tied to the neck of his horse.

"Your mother made the horse for you. She sewed it with her own hands," Runner told him, "many years ago, when you were only one summer."

White Bear stared at the woman with the fascinating green eyes. There was a look there that told him not to be afraid. "Yes," he answered. "I have a stuffed horse. Now both eyes are missing."

When Runner translated his words, the white woman covered her face and wept. The white man with her put his arms around her. She said something to him through her tears, and the white man in turn spoke to the Crow Indian.

"The white man wants you to let a doctor fix your wound. He is a good doctor. You can trust him. I would not lie to you, even though I know you hate me because I am Crow," Runner told Nathan. "Your mother wants to take you from here so that you will not be harmed. She wishes to take you to her home, where those people outside will not bother you. You have brothers and sisters there, people who would take care of you. Your mother would like you to stay there with them forever, but she says that when you are well, you will be free to choose, to stay with them, or go back to Half Nose and the Sioux."

White Bear watched the woman cry. Considering what she knew about him, she must be his white mother. If this was true, she surely would not lie to him. He moved his gaze to the man holding her, studied his blue eyes, saw honesty there, and something else. The man looked at him lovingly, as a man would look at his son. Something told him he could trust these people. He did not like the idea of staying with a whole family of whites, but for the moment he had no choice. The bullet in his side burned fiercely. He knew he needed help. He told Runner he would go with them…for now. As soon as he was well, he was returning to his people, and to Half Nose, the only man he knew as father. He saw pain in Luke Fontaine's eyes when the Crow interpreted his words.

Luke turned to the sheriff. "Go get Doc Manning."

Tracy nodded and left. Luke gave Lettie a hug. "You keep your distance until the doc gets him sedated," he told her. "Keep in mind that in his mind and heart he's still Sioux. I'm going to take care of that crowd outside."

He left her then, and Lettie could hear him arguing with the people outside the jail. If anyone could straighten them out and make them leave, it was Luke and his men. How sad that now she had to defend her precious son against those who accused him of killing innocent whites. She felt so sorry for Jim Woodward's orphaned daughters. Could her Nathan have done such a horrible thing? She refused to believe it.

She ached to hold him, embrace him. What did he think of her? That she had abandoned him? That she had given up on him? Where had her bright, smiling little Nathan gone, the little boy who clung to that bear so tightly when Half Nose tore him away from her? He lay there painted and half-naked, his hair grown long. There was so much she wanted to know and learn, and so much he needed to learn in return. She closed her eyes and thanked God for bringing her son back to her. Surely he didn't mean it when he said he would go back to his people when he was well. The Sioux were not his people. She and Luke, Katie, Ty, Pearl, Robbie, and Paul—*they* were his people.

"I love you, Nathan. I never stopped loving, or hoping, or praying. We're taking you home, Son."

She knew he didn't understand, but the words sounded good, words she had begun to think she would never be able to say. She stepped closer to the cot, knelt beside it. Again she touched his arm, and this time he did not try to jerk it away. He just watched her in wonder. She rested her head against his arm and wept.

Seventeen

LUKE CARRIED NATHAN OUT OF THE JAIL IN HIS ARMS, to a waiting wagon Henny had brought to take him home in. Dr. Manning had sedated him with laudanum before removing the bullet from his side, and he was still groggy enough not to put up a fight or to notice the crowd of onlookers. Will helped Luke get the boy into the wagon, laying him on a bed of straw covered with blankets.

Luke worried that none of this would end the way Lettie hoped it would. She herself had helped Doc Manning operate on the boy, and while he was being stitched up and bandaged, Lettie took advantage of his sedated condition, stroking his hair, kissing his cheek, talking to him as though he were four years old again. The doctor had said Nathan would be all right, but what about Lettie? Her wounds ran much deeper. What if she lost him again? What would it do to their marriage, and how was he going to handle his own guilt?

He helped Lettie climb into the wagon so she could sit beside her son. He was irritated at the gawking, whispering onlookers, some of the men still bent on hanging the boy. His men surrounded the wagon, keeping people at bay. He put a blanket over Nathan, then stood up in the wagon bed and looked out at the townspeople.

"This young man is our son, and we're taking him home," he told them. "He was only four when he was stolen from us, back when Billings could hardly even be called a town, and when most of you hadn't even come here yet! The boy can't be blamed for the way he is, and no one can prove he killed *any*body. I'm damn sorry for what happened to Jim Woodward. He was a good friend of mine, but I'm not going to let you hang my son, not just for his sake, but for my *wife's*. I'll kill any man who tries to hurt him!"

As he climbed down from the wagon, people stepped back.

"You're askin' for trouble, Luke," one man warned. "His people will come after him, maybe kill all of you."

"I have too much help at the Double L to worry about Indians. And any of *you* thinking of coming and getting my boy will have to go through my men first!"

"Once you breed wild ways into a man, he can't be changed," another called out. "You keep that boy on the Double L, Fontaine. We can't guarantee what will happen to him if he shows up in town."

Luke turned to see who had spoken. It was Clarence Goodman, a farmer who two years ago had decided to squat on government land rather than file a legal claim. He had put barbed wire around his place, causing injury to several of Luke's steers. Goodman had vacated his farm after Luke and his men tore down the fence and had deliberately allowed Fontaine cattle to graze on Goodman's corn. Luke hated the man for his cockiness, and for not trying to build his farm the right way. He had little use for farmers in general, but he tried to be fair with the ones who were respectful of other peoples' property.

Luke approached Goodman, towering over him. "I *can* guarantee what will happen to *you* if you lay a hand on my son!" he growled.

Goodman swallowed, and tried to stand his ground.

"It ain't right—"

"Shut up, Goodman!" Joe Parker spoke the words. "The boy can't be totally blamed, and if it was any of *our* kids, we'd want to try to help them, just like Luke's doing. Any mother would want to have her son back.

Give them a chance, and let poor Mrs. Fontaine enjoy the fact that she has found her son."

"I'm with Luke," Carl Rose spoke up.

"So am I," Sheriff Tracy put in.

Will and several others voiced their support.

"Which one of you is gonna string up a fourteen-year-old boy in front of his own ma after she's been prayin' to find him for ten years?" Will asked them.

They all looked sheepish, and a couple of women quietly dabbed at their eyes.

"You all remember one thing," Will said then. "That there boy is *white*! No matter how he looks now or what he's done or how he's been raised, he was born white. He's one of *us*! He's a victim of our trouble with the Sioux just the same as those who've lost their lives. Luke and Lettie, they came here before most of you, been through hell to help settle this land. Let them take their son home in peace."

The crowd began to disperse. Luke climbed back into the wagon to be with Lettie. Luke's men took hold of the reins to Will's, Luke's, and Lettie's horses to bring them along, and Will perched himself beside Henny in the wagon seat and snapped the reins over the rumps of the mules pulling the wagon. As the wagon lurched forward, Henny looked back in wonder at Nathan, remembering a beautiful, blond little boy who had been playful and loving, always smiling. She remembered how he'd loved to chase her cat, Patch, who had died several years ago.

Lettie was remembering too…a smiling, gentle child who had once brought her a bouquet of little purple flowers, smiling proudly because he'd made his mommy smile.

⁂

White Bear opened his eyes, lying still for a moment to gather his thoughts. As his vision focused, he turned his head to see a little redheaded girl staring at him from the doorway. She immediately turned and ran.

"Mommy! Mommy! He's awake!"

White Bear had no idea what the words meant. He only knew he was in a very strange place, lying on a bed so soft it was almost uncomfortable. For years he had slept on robes on the ground. He did not like this bed, nor did he like this strange dwelling, hard walls all around, odd structures of wood sitting about. He could see light through openings in the walls, but when he looked up, there was no sky! There was not even a hole, like in the top of a tepee.

Panic began to build inside him. He felt closed in. How could he commune with the Great Spirit in a place like this? The Great Spirit would never find him in here! He had to get out. He started to rise, but pain pierced his side, and he realized only then that his hands and feet were tied to the posts of the soft bed.

He heard some kind of commotion somewhere below him, then pounding footsteps, rising, coming closer. "Hurry!" he heard a woman saying. "He's in the guest room."

A herd of white people entered his room then. He strained at his ropes for a moment. Then he saw her... that woman with the dark red hair and green eyes...the one who said she was his mother. She was the first one through the door, followed by the Crow Indian who knew the Sioux tongue. Then came the tall white man with the blue eyes, followed by a string of young ones. They circled his bed and gawked at him as though he were a ghost.

The woman smiled, touched his arm. She said something to the Crow man.

"She says to tell you she is sorry about the ropes. If you would promise not to run away, she will untie them. She wishes to know how you are feeling."

White Bear looked around at all the staring eyes. Surrounded by whites, and by walls! He hated this place! "Well enough to get away from here," he answered Runner. "I do not like these walls. I want to see the sky. The Great Spirit cannot find me in this place." He was surprised at the understanding look in the Crow man's eyes. Yes, even though he was his enemy, this man was still Indian. He said something to the woman, then looked back at him.

"I am called Runner, in case you do not remember. The woman who is your white mother is called Lettie, and her husband's name is Luke. Do you remember they told you they are your mother and father?"

White Bear studied them, noticing the white man watched him with a look of love and terrible sadness in his blue eyes. "I remember," he answered.

"Lettie says that as soon as you are strong enough, she will take you out where you can see the sky. The openings where you see the light are called windows. She says she will take away the coverings over them, and she will open the windows themselves, so that you can smell the air and see the sun and sky through them. The Great Spirit will be able to come through the openings and find you."

The woman rattled on about something else, all the while rubbing at his arm and watching him with such love in her eyes that much of his initial fear of being in this place left him. Following her instructions, Runner introduced the children as his brothers and sisters. The one called Katie was tall for being almost eleven summers. He wondered how soon she might marry. In the eyes of the Sioux, she was almost old enough. She was already developing breasts. The oldest boy was Tyler. He too was tall and looked older than ten years. The pretty little girl who had gone running out of the room was Pearl, Runner told him. White Bear had never seen such bright red hair. She had the same unusual green eyes as her mother.

These white people certainly had hair and eyes of many colors. Half Nose had kept him away from white people, and he had imagined they were all the same as himself, with light hair and pale blue eyes, but all around him were different-colored eyes and different-colored hair. Some had skin as pale as the clouds, others, like the tall one called Luke, were dark from the sun.

Next came a boy called Robert. "He will be seven when the leaves turn to gold," Runner told him. "The youngest is Paul. He was five only two moons ago. Lettie says to tell you they are all your brothers and sisters, and that you are welcome to stay here with them, learn the white man's ways. You have a home here, and will be loved and cared for. You are her natural son, a white man. It is right that you stay. These are your people, Nathan. That is your real name. Nathan Lee Fontaine."

White Bear looked around at all of them. "I have not said I would stay," he told Runner. "And I do not wish to be called Nathan. I am White Bear. And the woman should not look upon me as though I am a small boy. I am a man! I am fourteen summers, and one summer ago I sacrificed blood at the Sun Dance. She can see the scars on my breasts."

Runner translated, and the woman called Lettie looked ready to weep when her eyes fell on the scars.

"I told her earlier about the Sun Dance and how sacred it is, what an honor it is to make the sacrifice," Runner told him. "It made her proud, but also sad that her son suffered this way. She wishes for you to stay long enough to learn enough words that she can talk to you. She wants to teach you about her God, who is not so different from the Great Spirit. Perhaps they are the same. She wants you to give yourself time to learn the white man's ways. It is only right, for you *are* white. You are not Sioux."

White Bear looked up at the Indian. "You keep saying this, as though you have to keep reminding me. But in my heart I am *Sioux*! I know you understand how I am feeling. You tell her the Indian way is a good way. Half Nose is a good father to me. He has taught me well, taught me to be a man. He showed me love, and his wife was like a mother to me. His children are my brothers and sisters, the same as these white children around me. But I do not know these white children. I do not care for them the way I care for my Sioux brothers and sisters. I must go back to them. Half Nose will worry. He will think I am dead and he will be very sad. I must go back. My people are hungry and dying. Most of the buffalo are gone. That is why we steal the white man's cows. We are starving. The land that was supposed to be left to us and to the buffalo has been stolen away by the white man. We have no place to go and nothing to eat! The young ones like myself must hunt and steal to live."

"You could go to the reservation. There you get blankets, food—"

White Bear cursed with such venom that Lettie drew in her breath and pulled her hand away. Runner explained all that he had said, then spoke to Nathan again.

"She says if you hate the reservation so, then you can live right here. You are white. You don't need to live on a reservation, nor do you need to live with the renegade Sioux, who will surely die in the end."

White Bear suddenly wanted to cry. He looked into his mother's eyes, not sure how to feel about her. "Tell her that if they must die, then I shall die with them. No man of pride lives on the reservation, begging for his food and blankets, sitting there useless, unable to hunt or make war, nothing to do but sit and wait for death. We refuse to die like cowards. We will ride free and hunt and live where we choose, as we have always done. Tell the woman she must understand that in my heart I am not white, and I cannot stay."

"She saved your life, Nathan," Runner reminded him.

White Bear kept his eyes on his mother. "For this I am grateful, and for this, I can promise that my people will never attack her or her husband or her children or anyone on her husband's land. Nor will we kill and eat any of his beef. We only wish permission to ride across his land without being harmed. I will tell this to Half Nose, and he will agree."

Runner sighed and related his words to Lettie. Lettie closed her eyes, covered her face for a moment before speaking again.

"Your mother asks if you will stay one month, one full moon. After that you are free to choose."

White Bear thought for several quiet seconds, sorry for the sorrow in the woman's eyes. "I will stay," he answered. "But if she tells the truth that I will be free to leave if I choose, then she must prove it by releasing the ropes around my wrists and feet now."

When Runner had interpreted, Lettie looked at Luke. He took something from the pocket of his pants then, unfolding a blade to make it turn into a small knife. White Bear was amazed at the sight of it, a knife that opened and closed! He watched warily as the man called Luke came closer and used the knife to cut the ropes. So, he thought, the white woman is true to her word. He reached up, pointed at the knife, told Runner to tell Luke he wanted to look at it more closely. Luke knelt beside him, closed it, opened it again. He handed it to White Bear, who studied it carefully, then closed it again. Luke said something to Runner, who told Nathan that Luke wanted to give him the knife, a gift from his white father. "He says you must promise never to harm anyone in his family with the knife."

White Bear worked the knife a little more. It was a grand thing indeed! It made him smile. "I promise," he answered. "My Sioux brothers and sisters will envy such a gift."

"Ask him if he will let me embrace him," Lettie told Runner.

In response to Runner's words, Nathan frowned. "A Sioux warrior does not embrace his mother in front of so many."

Immediately the woman spoke to the others, and all the gawking children left the room.

"Your father says to tell you that whatever you decide, you are his son. That will never change. He loves you the same as all the other children who were here. All that is his can be yours if you should decide to stay. If you leave and choose to come back later in life, you will always be welcome. He asks that you never forget this, that you trust his word."

White Bear looked up at the man who had given him the wonderful knife. "I will not forget."

Luke glanced at Lettie lovingly, then turned and left the room. Runner followed.

White Bear watched Lettie. This mother of his wanted to embrace her son. He supposed he could oblige her that much. She leaned down and took him into her arms. She smelled good, and he felt a wonderful warmth, but he did not move his arms to embrace her in return. Mother or not, she was still white, and a stranger to him.

❧

Pearl giggled as Nathan picked up mashed potatoes with his fingers. He looked at her questioningly, then angrily flicked the potatoes off his fingers and picked up a piece of meat instead.

"That was very rude, Pearl," Lettie reminded her. "It's been hard enough to get him to sit in a chair at the table and accept his food on a plate. In time he will learn to use table utensils properly." She looked around at the rest of the children. "I might remind all of you that there are probably things Nathan could teach *you*, like how to survive off the land, how to make do with only the things nature gives us. He could teach you how to use a bow and arrow, and all the things that are made from one buffalo. Now, I want all of you to help him learn, and through Runner, you can also learn from Nathan. I want you to make him as welcome and comfortable here as possible, so that he will want to always stay with us. I do not intend to lose my son a second time."

Luke glanced her way, irritation evident in his eyes. "Lettie, I've told you not to get your hopes up. You can't erase ten years of upbringing in two weeks."

"I don't want to hear it," she snapped. "God won't take him away again."

Nathan, disgusted with the strange, mushy food and the way everything was cut up, suddenly rose. It was obvious he was being discussed, and he did not like it, not when he couldn't understand everything that was being said. He glared at all of them, then reached over and picked up a large, uncut piece of roast from its platter and bit into it. He smiled proudly, nodding his head, as though to tell them that this was the best way for a man to eat. Blood and juice dripped from the roast as he proceeded through the dining room and kitchen to go outside and eat it there.

"Bless my soul!" They all heard Mae exclaim the words from the kitchen, and all the children began to laugh, all but Tyler, who sat sulking. He watched his mother blink back tears, saw the look of concern on Luke's face. "Pa?" he asked.

Luke let out a long sigh. "What is it, Ty?"

"Do you and Mother like Nathan better than the rest of us? Will he get to run the ranch someday instead of me?"

"Oh, Tyler, why do you ask such a foolish question?" Lettie asked, dabbing at tears.

"It's not a foolish question," Luke told her, a ring of anger in his voice. "I know the feeling of wondering if one brother is favored over another."

Lettie could not look at him, knowing what she would see in his eyes. Ever since bringing Nathan home, they had disagreed over what to do about him. Luke loved him as much as ever, but he was not so sure as she was that the boy would or even should stay, that he could be changed. She knew he was only trying to buffer the pain she would feel if he left again, but at the same time she refused to take such a hopeless attitude.

"Tyler, my own father favored my brother over me, for reasons I will explain when you're older," Luke was telling his eldest son. "I will never forget how that felt. I can only tell you that when I married Lettie, I accepted Nathan as my son, with all the rights to my love and my possessions as any children we might have together. I will never go back on that promise, and I could never stop loving him as my own. But that has nothing to do with how I feel about the rest of my children. When you have sons of your own, you'll understand that no one child is loved more than the next, but each child is loved in a different way, for different reasons. Every child here is loved equally and will be treated equally, including Nathan, but you will get your just rewards, Ty. You've worked hard to show me you want to run the Double L someday. Such things don't go unnoticed." He looked around at all the children. "Nathan is your brother, just as surely as if I had fathered him. You should treat him with the same respect as you do each other, as a Fontaine."

They all mumbled "Yes, Father," but deep inside, Tyler resented Nathan's coming home. He hoped he would run away again. Until now he had enjoyed what seemed a favored position with his father, whom he worshipped. He did not like all the attention Nathan was getting. The boy didn't even want to be here, so why didn't they just let him go?

Robbie in turn felt less favored than Ty. He knew

his father was disappointed that he was not interested in riding and roping and branding, that he had never asked to go on roundup or on the cattle drive. He wished he cared more about those things, but it just wasn't in him. He supposed maybe when he was older those feelings would change. For now, he stayed away from his father.

"Pearl, when we're through with supper, I want you to play the piano for Nathan," Lettie was saying. "He likes to hear you play. It seems to calm him."

"Yes, Mother."

Outside, Nathan finished the piece of roast, licked his fingers, then wiped them on the front of the shirt Luke had given him. It belonged to the man called Billy, who was built small, but it was still a little big on him. He did not like these white man clothes, especially the britches, which chafed his legs because he was not accustomed to such harsh cloth rubbing against his skin. He longed for soft buckskins. He had refused to wear the white man's hard boots, preferring his own moccasins.

He stood up and gazed at the mountains in the distance, longing to ride free, to sleep on the ground in a tepee again. He missed his Sioux family and friends. He wanted to see them again, to eat meat roasted over an open fire, to hunt buffalo and deer, to watch the stars at night and know that he was close to the Great Spirit. He needed to go into the hills and pray. The longer he stayed here, the weaker he felt he was becoming. If it wasn't for the pathetic love and hope he saw in his white mother's eyes, he would already have left.

⁂

Luke climbed into bed, wearing nothing because of the hot night. He watched Lettie brush her hair. She wore a sleeveless cotton gown, and he thought how beautiful she still was for a woman of thirty years who had borne six children—beautiful but untouchable lately. For the last three weeks her whole world had been wrapped around Nathan, teaching him, watching him, afraid to let him out of her sight for one second.

"Lettie, the other children are starting to feel neglected."

She put down her brush and faced him. "They just have to understand. As soon as Nathan begins to feel that he belongs here, I won't have to give him so much time and attention."

Luke sighed, lying back into his pillow. "Do you know how it makes me feel to know what it will do to you if you lose him again? I've carried the guilt for ten years, Lettie. It will just be worse if this doesn't work out the way you think it will."

Lettie came over to the bed and got in beside him. "I've told you a hundred times I never blamed you, Luke. Now I just want you to believe Nathan is back to stay. He's learning more every day, and he—"

"Stop it, Lettie!" He turned on his side, resting on one elbow and reaching an arm around her. "You know damn well he's only biding his time. I can see it in his eyes!"

"You're wrong."

"I'm *not* wrong! I wish to hell he'd never been found in the first place. It would have been easier on you than this!"

Her eyes widened, misting with tears. "How can you say such a thing?"

"Because it's true! You know damn well how much I love that boy. If I thought for one minute he was really happy here and wanted to stay, I would myself be the happiest man alive. But his heart is out there on the plains and in the mountains now, Lettie, with a people he calls his own. The Indian spirit is very powerful. It will call him back."

A tear slipped down the side of her face. "More powerful than a mother's love?"

God, how the words hurt. How could he look into those green eyes and tell her the truth? "Maybe," he answered. "I've talked to Runner a lot about it. He doesn't think you should get your hopes up."

She jerked in a sob. "He's my little boy. My son. How dare you tell me not to hope and believe?"

"My God, Lettie, I love you more than my own life. Do you think I like any of this? You've got to remember you have other children who need you, a *husband* who needs you! We're all here and we love you. If Nathan goes off again—"

"I won't listen to it!" She turned her face away.

Luke put a big hand to her face and made her look back at him. "I need you, Lettie. I need you to be a wife to me, to look at me as though you realize I still exist. The kids need that too." He leaned down to kiss her lightly, but she lay there unresponsive. Luke angrily jerked off her drawers and moved between her legs, forcing them apart with his knees. He pushed himself inside her out of sheer need, moving rhythmically until he felt the necessary release of pent-up emotion and desire, but through the entire intercourse he got no response from her. He relaxed then, pulling away and resting beside her.

"You're so far away, Lettie. I feel as though I've lost you."

"Then you shouldn't keep telling me I might lose my son again. How can I respond to a man who says he wishes my son had never been found?"

Luke angrily threw back the covers and got up, pulling on his long johns. "For Christ's sake, you know I only meant that for what it would do to *you*! Do you think *I* didn't pray every day for years that we'd find him? You know goddamn well the hell I went through searching for him, the hell I've been through thinking you blamed me. It's pretty damn obvious now that you *do* blame me, or you wouldn't be acting this way!" He pulled on his pants.

"Where are you going?"

"Outside to have a smoke." He pulled on a shirt and headed for the door. "We'll have Nathan's decision within a week or two. By then it will be time for me to leave on the cattle drive. We have to get some things straightened out between us before I go, Lettie, no matter what Nathan decides to do. I feel so far away from you that it's as if you aren't here at all." He turned and walked out.

Lettie wanted to go after him, but she couldn't move. She knew he was right that ever since Nathan had come to live with them, he had become her whole world. She also knew he was right that the boy might leave again. That was why part of her had begun to hate her own husband, just for being so damn right. She felt as though if she lost Nathan again, it *would* be his fault this time, just for suggesting that could happen.

She got up and quietly washed, then walked to the guest room where Nathan slept. She opened the door. In the moonlight she could see he was not in bed, but was sitting staring out a window. He quickly turned, like an animal on the defense. "It's me. Lettie." She walked toward him. He rose, already standing as tall as she. Lettie quietly put her arms around him, and this time his own came around her in return, an embrace that was more wonderful than anything she had ever experienced. She wept, for she knew in her heart Luke was probably right; but at least God had let her see him and hold him one more time.

❧

Nathan sat up in his bed at the sound, a trilling call, like a night bird. He recognized that call, one used by his Sioux uncle, Stalking Wolf. He was out there somewhere! He quickly but very quietly leaped out of bed, pulling on his moccasins. At night he wore his breechcloth and nothing more, always glad to shed the white man's clothes. He walked on padded feet to the chair where his bone breastplate lay. He tied it on, then picked up the precious folding knife Luke had given him. He walked to a window then. It was a warm night, and the window was open. He leaned out to listen.

There it was again, a soft call that only another Sioux would recognize. It came from a thick stand of trees far off to the east, beyond the gate that led to Luke Fontaine's ranch. He smiled, realizing that if anyone could sneak this close to Fontaine land without being caught, his uncle could. Somehow he had to get out to the man and find out why he had come, how he even knew he was here. He moved his legs over the window ledge and crept along the roof of the first-floor veranda to a side of the house where he knew there were no guards posted. He put the knife between his teeth, and, making no more sound than a rush of air, he grasped the edge of the roof and lowered himself, dropping to the ground. He moved like a shadow, darting from bush to tree to wagon, waiting at each stop to be sure he had not been noticed. He made his way through the night, climbing over the fence far from the entrance, rather than drawing attention by opening the creaky wooden gate. He headed for the stand of trees, taught well how to keep from making any sound as he made his way over fallen twigs and pinecones.

He stopped then, shoved the folding knife into the waist of his breechcloth, and gave his own call. The trilling sound was returned, and he moved toward its source. Several times over he heard it until he was close. "Stalking Wolf," he said in a loud whisper.

"Here!"

Now he could see the man in a shaft of moonlight that came through the trees. With a glad heart he came closer and greeted the man. "How did you know I was here?"

"Half Nose said that you might be. When we told him the white men had caught you, he said that if they let you live, they would bring you here."

Nathan's heart fell a little. So, Half Nose *did* know who his white parents were and that they were alive. Luke and Lettie had not lied to him.

"Your Sioux father is very sick," Stalking Wolf told him. "He wishes to see his son before he dies. He fears you have chosen to stay here with your white family and he will never see you again. I have brought your horse."

Nathan turned to look at the ranch house in the distance. He had promised his white mother he would stay a full month. That meant he had another seven days to go, but what if he stayed and Half Nose died before he could go back to him?

He had little choice. Whatever the reason Half Nose had lied to him, it mattered little. He was the only father he could remember, and he loved him. Luke Fontaine was a good man, but he had not raised him, and he was not happy in that big house in that soft bed. "I go with you," he told Stalking Wolf.

He started to mount up, then hesitated. Part of him felt sorry for the white woman, who he knew would mourn greatly when she found out he was gone. He considered going back and trying to explain, but feared she would ask Luke to tie him and force him to stay. He still could not completely trust the white man. After all, they were known to break nearly every promise they ever made to the Sioux. No. He dared not tell anyone he was leaving.

Still, he had to leave something that might soothe his mother, let her know he would not forget her. He took the folding knife from his breechcloth and shoved it into the leather bag of supplies his uncle had tied to his horse, and from the same bag he retrieved the faded, tattered stuffed horse he had carried with him for so many years. "Wait!" he told his uncle. He disappeared for several minutes. Stalking Wolf waited anxiously until White Bear finally returned.

"We go!" the boy said then, leaping onto his horse without the benefit of a stirrup. They turned their ponies, moving stealthily through the trees until they crested a ridge to a place where the land was open. They made off then, guided by the bright moonlight.

❧

Lettie rose from the chair on the porch when at last she saw Luke and Runner returning. Nathan was not with them. Her stomach ached at the realization that her son was gone again, this time probably forever. Everything Luke had warned her about had come true. She wanted, needed, to blame someone. Could Luke or the children have done more to make Nathan stay? Could she have done more herself? What had compelled Nathan just to sneak off in the night like that, with no explanation and no good-bye? He had promised to stay!

This was almost worse than the first time he'd disappeared, just as Luke had predicted. She watched as they rode closer, saw the devastation on Luke's face, knew he was hurting the same as she, yet she could not make herself go to him, hold him, allow him to hold her in return. He dismounted and took something from his saddlebag. She could see it was the stuffed horse! He came closer and handed it to her, his eyes misty.

"We found it on a fence post near the gate," he told her. "Moccasin tracks from there led to that stand of trees beyond the gate. We found horse tracks leading north from there, horses with no shoes. Runner has no doubt they were Sioux ponies."

Lettie took the horse with a shaking hand, pressed it close to her breast.

"You know there is no use in gathering any men to try to find him this time, Lettie. If he wanted to be here, he would have stayed. I think he left that horse to let you know he won't forget you. He has given you something of him to keep, something that was very dear to him. He thinks maybe it will comfort you if he never returns."

"No," she answered, so softly that Luke could barely hear her. "He left the horse as a sign that he *will* come back."

"Lettie, don't—"

"He'll come back!" she said sternly, her voice firmer this time.

With that she turned away and walked into the house, past the staring children, up the stairs and to her room, closing the door. Luke went after her, but he found the door to their room locked. He could hear her wrenching sobs.

He turned and walked away. It was nearly time to leave out on the cattle drive. He decided he might as well speed it up and go tomorrow. Maybe she was better off not seeing him at all for a few weeks.

PART THREE

Just as a seed can sprout new life
After being tossed aside,
Forgotten and left to die;
So can love buried by pride and guilt
Come to bloom again…
Stronger, healthier, even more beautiful.

Eighteen

LETTIE SHIVERED AS WINDOWS RATTLED FROM WICKED winds, winds that once nearly drove her insane, but to which she thought she had grown accustomed. Now she hated the sound again, for the howling monster outside brought with it a blizzard that kept everyone buried in their homes. These past winters had become more bearable, with the additional company of Elsie and Mae and all the children, but now winter brought something much more dreadful than the loneliness she'd once felt. Now the wind and snow meant they could not get help for little Paul. Her baby was suffering with a terrible fever, and what she and Mae were certain was pneumonia. She bent over Paul's small bed to bathe his face again with a cool rag, aching at his groans and whimpers of pain.

Straining to lift another pitcher of water, seven-year-old Robbie poured it into a washbowl on the stand near his mother. "What else can I do, Mama?" he asked. "Should I see if Mae has the hot tea ready yet?"

Lettie turned to meet Robbie's blue eyes, blue like his father's. Luke. She needed him, but something kept her from telling him so. He needed her in return, yet she could not bring herself to go to him. What was this barrier between them? And poor Robbie. All her children needed her, but first there had been the agony over losing Nathan again, now this. Little Paul seemed to be dying, and the winter storm outside was not going to allow any Double L man to get into town and back with the doctor quickly enough to help. Robbie tended his little brother almost as faithfully as she did herself, always the little doctor, always wanting to help, just like with Pancake.

"I don't think he can swallow anything," she told Robbie, struggling to keep control of herself in front of the boy. The cloth she'd been holding to Paul's head was already hot, and she turned to rinse it in the water again to cool it off. She wrung it out and handed it over to Robbie. "Would you like do it this time?"

"Okay."

She fought tears at the sight of Robbie gently laying the cloth on his brother's forehead. Her two youngest sons had always been close, always playing together. Robbie watched his five-year-old brother more like a father would. He was so different from Ty, who cared only about learning how to ride and rope and handle cattle; Ty, who was his father's image and worshipped the man like a god. Ty and Robbie had nothing in common, except that they shared the same blood.

She took a moment to stretch and rub her neck and shoulders. Everything ached. She had been sitting by Paul's bedside for two days straight, afraid to go to sleep, hardly eating. She walked to a window, but the snow blew so badly she could barely see the barn beyond the front lawn. Adding to her worry and agony over Paul was her additional concern for Nathan. Where was he? How did he and the Indians survive in this kind of weather? Was he starving? Freezing? She looked down at the ragged old stuffed horse that sat on the window ledge. She had put it in Paul's room, telling him always to take care of it, telling him that someday Nathan might come back for it...come home to stay...but now she knew that was only a fantasy. She surely would never see her firstborn again, and for no truly logical reason, she blamed Luke; just as part of her blamed him now for Paul's being sick and unable to get help. If they were not so isolated here, so far from civilization...

A tear slipped down her cheek when she noticed something else, a shiny little black stone lying on the ledge beside the horse. She remembered the day she had taken a walk with Paul, before Nathan was found. Little Paul had always demanded so much of her attention, and she had not minded, for he was her precious baby, her last child. When they went for that walk, Paul had found the stone and was fascinated by its color and gloss. He had handed it out to her, telling her he wanted her to have it as a gift. She told him to take care of it for her, that it was very special because it was a present sent from God.

She picked up the stone and rubbed it between her fingers, realizing Paul had put it beside the horse because both were dear not just to him, but to his mommy. It hit her then how she had neglected her baby after Nathan ran off. She had gone into such a depression that she had been lost in it and had not given any of the children the attention she should. That neglect only made Paul's sickness even more devastating now, her agony over his pain made worse by her guilt for not spending enough time with him.

She could not even take comfort in Luke. She loved him so, yet sometimes she hated him. She had taken to sleeping in the guest room since Nathan left, aching to be held, yet needing to be alone. Luke had not demanded that she come to his bed. He had been quiet and withdrawn himself since getting back from the summer's cattle drive. He had dived headlong into claiming more land, involved himself intensely in the Cattlemen's Association, even made a trip to Denver to talk to cattlemen there about ways to deal with farmers and with sheep men who were beginning to filter into Montana. He had invested in the Northern Pacific Railroad and had gone to Helena to talk to the railroad's representatives about the best route to be considered through Montana. The trips had kept him away several more weeks after the cattle drive, and between his absence and the inability on both sides to share their feelings, he was becoming like a stranger to her.

She put her head back and looked around the lovely little room, with its flowered wallpaper. Luke had built this beautiful, elegant home for her. She could live no better, even in more civilized parts, yet in spite of their comfort, the dangers of the land continued to threaten them. She turned to look at Paul lying there, so miserable. Robbie wet the cloth again and put it to his brother's fevered brow. Yesterday her baby had coughed so hard he had spit up blood. Now the coughing had stopped, but his breathing was labored, nearly every breath bringing a gurgling sound. Her once-lively, loving little boy just lay there with his eyes closed, while outside the wind battered everything in its path.

She heard heavy footsteps coming down the hallway then, heard the familiar jangle of spurs. She recognized her husband's gait, slightly off rhythm because of the broken leg that had never healed quite right. His big frame loomed in the doorway, and he glanced from her to Paul, then walked over to the bed to lean down and touch the boy's hot cheek.

"Do you think Tex and Runner will get through the snow to town, Pa?" Robbie asked his father.

Luke straightened, breathing in a deep sigh. "I don't know, Son. They should have been back by now. They might be buried someplace themselves by now, maybe had to take shelter."

"Will the cows all die?"

Luke ran a hand through his hair. "Not if this wind keeps up. There will be big drifts in some places, but in other places the wind will blow the snow away and leave bare spots. If the cattle can get to those places, they'll be all right. The biggest danger is when the snow gets deep without any wind, so there's no place to find grass. Cattle won't dig for grass like horses and deer will. They just stand in the deep snow and—" He stopped short, not even wanting to mention the word "die."

He closed his eyes, realizing he had been babbling like a fool. Did Lettie know what Paul's sickness was doing to him? His precious little son was so sick, and there wasn't a damn thing he could do about it. Did his mother really think she was the only one aching over little Paul's sickness and suffering over Nathan? If he could take the pain into his own body, he would do it in an instant. He would rather die himself if it meant little Paul would live.

He turned to Lettie, knew what it would do to her if she lost Paul. She would in turn be forever lost to him in love and spirit. "We just have to pray Tex and Runner get through to Doc Manning," he told her aloud.

Luke, I feel so guilty, she wanted to tell him. Little Paul had needed her more than any of the other children, always a mama's boy, always wanting to be held or read to. In these last few months he had grown closer to Robbie because he'd lost his mother's attention.

"Yes," she answered Luke, turning back to look out the window. Piano music floated into the room from the parlor downstairs, where Pearl sat playing some of Paul's favorite songs. Katie was in the kitchen helping Mae fix supper, but no one had much of an appetite. She felt a big hand on her shoulder then. Why couldn't she turn around and let Luke put his arms around her?

"He'll get here, Lettie. Paul will be all right." When she did not answer, Luke went to Paul. "I love you, Paul," she heard him saying softly. "Daddy's here."

"He's a lot cooler now, Pa," Robbie spoke up. "Touch his hands. They're not hot anymore. See what a good doctor I am?"

"Well, I guess you must be, Robbie. He *is*—" There came a moment of silence, and then Luke let out a strange, guttural sound. Lettie felt a knot come into her stomach. "Oh my God! My God!" Luke groaned. "Not my son!"

Lettie managed to turn around. Luke sat on the edge of the bed holding Paul close to his chest, bent over the boy, his shoulders shaking with the deep sobs of grief. She did not have to ask why. Her son was dead. She should have been holding him when it happened, not standing at the window. All these hours she had kept such a close watch, and the moment she got up and moved away, her baby's spirit had left them.

Robbie stood staring in disbelief, his eyes wide and full of terror and sorrow. He ran out of the room then, screaming Paul's name.

◆◆

"More nesters!" Luke was almost glad to find them. His search to find ways to vent his anger had become almost an obsession. "Cut those goddamn barbed-wire fences and ride through their crops!" He pulled his six-gun and began firing into the air, charging forward ahead of his men, the first to cut down enough barbed wire to ride into a cornfield and begin trampling it. The eleven men with him followed, cutting more fence, stomping their horses over vegetable gardens and through more corn, all of them firing their guns to bring terror to the hearts of the family that had unwisely chosen to settle on government land Luke considered his own for grazing cattle.

Luke charged his horse to the sod house, and a woman came running out of it, hoisting a baby on her hip, screaming obscenities. Her straight hair hung limp and unwashed, and her face was that of a young woman aging too soon, dry and drawn, her lips parched. A worn calico dress hung on her too-thin body. "What do you think you're doing?" she screamed. "You men get out of here!"

Luke recognized her as Betty Walker, the wife of Johnny Walker. The young man and his brother, Jeeter, and his father, Zack Walker, had been warned several months ago to get off Fontaine land. They were squatting there in hopes of farming the land without legally paying for any of it. Luke suspected when he first found them that they had stolen some of his cattle for their own meals. They were a sorry lot, better at making trouble than at farming.

"Where's your husband?" Luke demanded.

The woman looked around frantically. "He's in town! They're *all* in town! I'm here alone." She backed away. "You get out of here, Luke Fontaine! How dare you do this?"

Luke rode closer to her. "And how dare you Walkers come back here to settle on someone else's land! When Johnny Walker and his pa and brother get back here, you tell them to get their things together and find someplace else to settle! I warned you last spring! This is Fontaine land, and I won't put up with grazing land being plowed under, or with barbed-wire fencing. You understand that? If you stay here, we'll keep destroying the fences *and* the crops! We don't want any nesters around here! Next time somebody is going to get hurt!" He turned his horse and rode off, the woman's curses filling the air around him.

"Damn you, Luke Fontaine! You're a bastard! A bastard!"

"Maybe so," Luke muttered. His father had said so, hadn't he? Maybe the real Luke was now emerging, the one who hated his father, hated everything, hated himself; the bastard child who was doomed to fail. Yes, he was achieving his dream of building his own wealth, of proving he could succeed on his own; but he had failed as a father, failed as a husband, even failed as a son. He had never received one reply to the letters he'd written to his father. His dream had cost him two sons...and a wife. As much as he loved Lettie, he had never realized just how important she was to him until he had lost her. They still shared the same house, but it was as though she was not there at all; and he had withdrawn his own presence as much as possible. He could not bear the way she looked at him, could not bear sleeping alone in their bed at night.

Ever since Paul's death nine months earlier, the barrier that had already formed between them had grown even higher and wider. Things got worse when they got the news about the slaughter of George Custer and more than two hundred of the Seventh Cavalry at the Little Big Horn. They couldn't help wondering if Nathan had been a part of the awful massacre, if he was even still alive. The Sioux were being hunted relentlessly now by the army. Life must be hell for them, and many Sioux had fled to Canada.

Luke couldn't face his guilt, and the only way to avoid it was to stay away. He used roundup and branding time as an excuse, then the summer's cattle drive. Now this, a tour of his own land and surrounding government land he considered his own, routing out nesters, sheepherders, searching for rustlers. He wasn't sure how he would get through the winter. He hoped it would not be a bad one, so that he could make it into town to the saloons and play cards and drink away his loneliness and sorrow. The trouble was, he still loved and needed Lettie. She was the only woman he wanted, but neglected needs made him wonder how much longer he could go on without a woman.

In the distance Betty Walker continued screaming her curses. He wondered just when it had all changed for him, when he had gotten so cold and hard. It wasn't just Paul's death, or even when Nathan ran off. It had begun long before that, slowly building in his soul. It had begun the day his father kicked him out, had festered even more when Nathan was first taken and he had been unable to get the boy back. Those two things had given him the determination to prove he could make it in life, and do it here in Montana. Nothing was going to stop him, and nothing had. He remembered Lettie asking him once never to let himself become like Tex was, ruthless and cold-blooded, but that was exactly how he felt. This was much easier than loving, much easier than caring.

He rode to a hill overlooking the pitiful homestead and watched his men finish trampling the crops. Tex rode up beside him, taking off his hat and raising it while he let out a war whoop. "That ought to convince them to move on," he told Luke with a grin. "Them Walkers ain't nothin' but trouble."

Luke nodded, taking one of his favorite thin cigars from a shirt pocket and lighting it. "The big problem is going to be those Mormons who are bringing in sheep. Hank Kline up at the Lazy K says he's had a hell of a time with them." He puffed on the cigar a moment. "The Cattlemen's Association has made the unanimous decision that each rancher can get rid of them any way they choose." He looked over at Tex. "If we have to kill all the sheep, that's what we'll do. We're heading on northwest, Tex. Runner said that's where he spotted some of them. I'll give them an ultimatum, a few days to get the hell out of Montana. If they don't go, the buzzards are going to have themselves a feast on lamb chops."

Tex grinned even more. "I'm with you, boss."

Luke turned to watch his men set fire to a small shed below. A little boy came running out of the sod house to cling to his mother's skirts...a boy about Paul's age. Paul. His precious little Paul who had his father's dark hair and his mother's pretty green eyes. Little Paul, bright, lively, always running and laughing...now lying under the ground, forever silent. The thought of it still made him so sick inside he wanted to vomit. Sometimes he thought his heart would literally burst from the ache of it. He couldn't face his son's death. He could hardly bear seeing that little grave behind the house. Somehow, someone had to pay for letting Paul die. He couldn't vent his wrath on God himself, so he would vent it on these people who dared to try to destroy what he had built. The ranch was all he had left.

Tex rode back down the hill to gather the men. He wondered at the change in Luke Fontaine. Everybody knew that since Nathan had run back to the Indians, there had been a strain on the Fontaine marriage. Things had gotten worse since their littlest boy died. Luke probably had the prettiest wife in all of Montana, but the man looked for all kinds of ways to stay away from home. It was too bad. He could remember when Luke and Lettie were about the happiest couple he'd ever come across. He'd never been in love like that, never had kids; and now that he saw what loving and losing a son could do to a man…and a woman…he didn't want any. Caring that much was not for him. Some of the men said Lettie Fontaine had lost her mind with grief, and for some reason, she blamed her husband for the boy's death. That was too bad. Luke was a good man. The things he was doing now were simply not the kind of things the Luke he had always known would do, but then frustration over the love of a woman, combined with the kind of grief everyone knew he was suffering, could change a man; and Luke Fontaine had definitely changed.

❦

Lettie walked into the parlor, surprised at the visit from someone she thought she'd never see again. "Nial!" Much as she had resented the man for being so forward the first time she had known him, it was good to have company. For months she had not had the desire to go into town and attend the women's gatherings, had not had the desire to do anything but stay home and visit Paul's grave almost daily. Women friends had stopped coming out, and she knew it was because they didn't know how to comfort her; and they probably knew her marriage had been crumbling ever since Paul's death. They didn't know what to say to her anymore. Poor Henny had had a stroke and couldn't get out. She should go see her again. It had been months. But she just couldn't seem to leave home. Nothing seemed to matter anymore except the house and the children she had left to her.

Nial smiled, removing his hat. "How good to see you again, Lettie. My God, it's been four years since I left for England."

"No one was sure if you would ever come back. What has happened? What brought you back to Montana?"

You did, my beautiful Lettie, he wanted to answer. She had not changed, except that she was too thin. He could see the sorrow in her eyes. Why wasn't Luke here, instead of carousing in town? "Well, you know how I always felt about this land. It's too beautiful for a man to stay away from forever. And the man who was managing the ranch for my father quit to buy a ranch of his own in Colorado. I was getting bored in England, so I decided to come back and take over Essex Manor again. After all, the cattle industry is booming now, better than ever!" He reached out and took hold of her hand, squeezing it in an effort to show how glad he was to see her again, but he longed to take her into his arms. He had thought that four years away would change these feelings, but the moment he set eyes on her again...

"Sit down, Nial!" Lettie pulled her hand away and offered him a love seat. "Would you like some tea? I'll go have Mae make some for us."

"I would enjoy that." He shivered. "The March winds are mean this year."

Pain moved into Lettie's eyes. "The wind is always mean out here." She left the room for a moment, then returned to sit down beside him. "A lot has happened since you left, Nial." Her smile faded.

Nial frowned, turning to set his top hat on another chair. "So I have heard. First your missing son was found, then ran off again. And then…" He took her hand again. "I heard about your little Paul, Lettie. I came here to express my sympathy, to you *and* to Luke. Alas, I am told it is difficult to catch your husband at home. Perhaps I'll see him at the next cattlemen's meeting in Billings. I understand he has been spending a lot of time in town this winter."

He could see the pain in her eyes. He hated to see her suffer, but if her son's death could open the door to getting her away from Luke, he would take advantage of the situation. A woman in grief was easier to manipulate, wasn't she? The news of Paul Fontaine's death over a year ago had reached him all the way in England, by letter from the manager of Essex Manor. A child's death could either bring the parents closer together, or tear them apart. Apparently, in this case, it had separated Luke and Lettie—perhaps enough that he could at last find a way to have this woman for himself. The right words, giving her the comfort her husband was apparently failing to give her, could pull her right into his waiting arms, and that hope was really what had brought him back to Montana. He let go of her hand, not wanting to seem too forward right away.

"Yes, he has," Lettie answered, looking at her lap. "Paul died over a year ago, and it hasn't been the same between us." She sighed deeply. "I think Luke blames himself because we live so far from town. The doctor couldn't get here in time. There had been a terrible blizzard, and…" She rose. "It's a long story. Luke has a lot of ghosts that haunt him. He thinks I blame him too. I want to tell him that I don't, but he's turned so cold and silent, I can't find the right words; and I don't think he'd believe me anyway, because at first I *did* blame him. Now he's like a crazy man, burning out nesters, chasing out the sheep ranchers." She blinked back tears and turned to face him, her face crimson from spilling her feelings. "I'm so sorry. I don't know what made me say all of that."

Nial smiled gently. "You just needed someone to say it to, that's all. I don't mind, Lettie; but it should be Luke you talk to, not me. He's probably in town right now spilling his own emotions into a glass of beer, or perhaps crying them out on the shoulder of Annie Gates or one of the other—" He hesitated when he saw the devastation in her eyes. Yes, he had hit the right nerve! It was only a rumor that Luke Fontaine had been sleeping with the town's prettiest and highest-paid whore when he was in Billings, but it was enough to suggest to Lettie that her husband had not only abandoned her emotionally, but was probably cheating on her besides.

"Annie Gates?" she asked.

Mae brought in a tray of tea, and neither of them spoke for a moment. Lettie came over to sit back down, but Nial noticed her hand shake as she poured his tea.

"I'm sorry I let that slip, Lettie. It's entirely none of my business, and it might not even be true. I didn't come here for any of this. I only meant to express my sympathy and let you know that I am back." He touched her arm. "If I can be of any help, in any way, please let me know." He turned to squeeze lemon into his tea while Lettie poured her own cup and added sugar to it. He had to force himself not to smile, for he had apparently shaken her to the bones with his remark about Annie Gates.

"Yes, I'll do that," she answered. She sipped some of her tea and closed her eyes for a moment, as though to compose herself. "How did you know so much about what's been happening here?" she asked.

"My ranch manager kept me updated. I suppose you fear your son, Nathan, might have had a part in the Custer massacre?"

She sighed deeply. "I can only hope he didn't, and that he's all right. He could be in Canada now, for all we know. Or he…could be dead." She took another deep breath, needing to change the subject. "How was England, Nial?" Was that true concern she saw in his eyes? It felt good to know someone cared. "I don't suppose you found yourself a wife?"

"No wife," he answered. "Oh, I did my share of courting, but none of them had the stamina it would take to come out here and live in such desolation, away from London's paved streets and lovely theaters. There aren't many women like you, Lettie, with strength and courage. I'm just sorry for what you have gone through since I was here last."

Lettie saw the admiration and sorrow in his eyes, and she realized the man's feelings for her had not changed. She turned to pour a little more tea. "Well, maybe you'll find a wife right here in Billings," she said, hoping he would take the hint that he should look elsewhere. Strangely, his attention did not annoy her this time. It only confused her. So many things confused her since Paul had died and Nathan disappeared again. She felt removed from herself, as though she were watching life from outside of her body.

"Chloris Greene has never married. She seemed to be quite taken with you. Have you seen her since returning?"

"No. I may pay her a visit, but she's so young."

"Not anymore. She must be at least twenty by now. Maybe she has been waiting for you to come back."

He smiled. "You flatter me." *I wish you had been waiting for me, Lettie.*

"How do you like our new home?" Lettie asked then, turning and looking around the parlor.

Nial wondered if she had read his thoughts and was trying to change the subject.

"We finished it after you left. It's no stone mansion," she continued, "but it's big and airy and has plenty of rooms. Luke insisted I design it however I wanted."

"It's absolutely lovely, elegant," he answered. *Just like you, Lettie.* "I saw Pearl for just a moment before you came in. She is such a beautiful child! How old is she now?"

Lettie set her cup on the coffee table. "She'll be ten this year. My children are all growing up much too fast!"

Nial laughed. "Pearl told me she is doing very well with the piano. I don't suppose you could get her to play for me?"

Lettie smiled. She loved talking about the children. Those she still had were her whole world now. "She loves showing off. I'm sure she'd be very happy to play for you. And before you leave Robbie will probably want to show you Punkin's new puppies. Punkin is the daughter of our big yellow mutt, Pancake. Robbie prides himself in taking care of all the dogs and cats. He dreams about being a doctor one day, but not for animals. He wants to doctor people." Her smile faded. "I'm afraid the poor child was deeply affected by his little brother's death. He was right there at Paul's side when it happened." *It should have been me. I should have been holding him. If only I could have him back for that one last moment, just long enough to tell him again that I love him.*

"And what about Katie and Ty? What are they up to?"

Lettie rose. "Ty spends almost every day practicing roping. He is going to go with Luke this year on the spring roundup and branding. He's so excited about it he hardly eats. He's becoming a handsome young man. He looks more like fifteen than twelve." *Tall and handsome, like his father. Luke! Please don't sleep with that whore! Please be patient with me.* "Katie is the little homemaker, always helping Mae in the kitchen." She walked out into the wide hallway and called upstairs to Pearl. "Come and play the piano for Mr. Bentley," she told the girl.

Pearl hurried out of her room, red pigtails flying, green eyes on fire with delight. Her fair-skinned face showed a few freckles, and it was obvious she was going to be a beautiful woman someday. Lettie smiled and gave her a hug. "You have an audience, love." Lettie nodded toward Nial, and Pearl grinned and curtsied.

"I'm not real good yet, but I'm getting better," she told the Englishman.

"Oh, I hear you play beautifully."

"Really? Who told you that?"

"Oh, Will Doolan brags all over town about your playing!"

Pearl laughed. "Uncle Will tells such big stories." She hurried to the piano and opened it, positioning herself on the bench. She began playing some hymns, and Nial agreed that, for her age, the child was a wonder at the keyboard.

"She could go far with this," he told Lettie after several minutes of playing.

Lettie felt the pain of wishing Luke were here to listen. Because of the death of one son and the desertion of another, he was missing out on these special times with the rest of his children.

"You might consider letting her study music when she is older," Nial was saying. "I know of a very good music school in Chicago. I have contacts there, people who would take excellent care of her."

Lettie met his eyes, gratitude in her own. "Music is all she talks about. Thank you for the offer." Here was a man who cared about the finer things in life, who seemed to care more about her children's futures than their own father did right now. Had she misjudged Nial Bentley? Was it wrong to appreciate his friendship and attention in this dark time? Anne Sacks had little time for visiting. She was busy with two young sons, as well as helping Billy build his own small ranch on land Luke had given the young couple. Mae was constantly cleaning and cooking, and in her free time she had begun seeing one of Luke's hired hands, Bob Franks. The children's tutor, Elsie, had married Peter Yost, and when she was not teaching, she was at her own modest home Peter had built for them about a half mile from the main house. Now she was expecting a baby.

It seemed everyone had abandoned her, or was it just her imagination? Maybe it was she who had abandoned all her friends. She had to be careful of her feelings. Depression, guilt, and grief had distorted her ability to reason. Maybe they had also distorted her view of Luke. She wanted everything to be the way it used to be between them.

Pearl played for nearly an hour, reveling in the attention of the newcomer. She did not remember Nial Bentley from the one other time he had visited here, but she liked his fascinating accent and the way he doted on her talent. Her own father used to listen to her often, until Paul died. It seemed as though a lot of things had changed since then. Her father was almost never home, and her mother seldom smiled. Nial Bentley had made Lettie smile again, and she was glad when her mother asked him to stay for lunch. He told them all stories about London, and about cities like Chicago and Omaha. She tried to imagine what such places must be like, and she dreamed about going there someday, began to daydream about being a famous pianist. Mr. Bentley seemed to know everything about everything, even about a university in the state of Michigan that he suggested Robbie might want to attend someday to study to be a doctor. All he had to do was pass the necessary entrance exams.

The only thing she didn't like about the Englishman was the way he grasped her mother's hands before he finally left. There was an intimacy about the way he held them that struck her as something that should be reserved only for her father. But her father wasn't here. He so seldom sat at the family dinner table now, and she knew something was terribly wrong between her parents. She didn't understand it completely, but it worried her, especially when her mother told the other children and her that perhaps they had better not be too enthusiastic around Luke about Nial's visit.

"Your father and Mr. Bentley have had their differences in the past," she told them, without explaining what those differences were. "And lately your father gets angry so easily. It might be best not to make too much of Mr. Bentley's visit. He was just trying to be friendly."

"I don't like him," Ty grumbled. "He's soft, and I don't like the way he looks at you."

Lettie met her son's eyes and saw Luke there—protective, jealous, possessive. It seemed those emotions and more had left Luke, all except hate, with no purpose left in life but killing or ousting every stranger on his land and continuing to build his little empire, with or without her at his side.

Nineteen

LETTIE DISEMBARKED FROM THE FAMILY'S THREE-SEATER buggy and walked up to Will and Henny's log home, grabbing hold of her straw hat to keep it from blowing off in a stiff, hot wind. She could see Henny was sitting in a rocker on the porch. She forced herself to smile, though she was shocked at how white the woman's hair had become. She lifted the hem of her yellow cotton dress as she went up the steps, then leaned over Henny to give her a hug.

"Oh, it's good to see you again, Henny! I miss you being able to come out to the ranch."

"Lettie! I didn't know you were coming. I'm so glad, dear." The words were slightly slurred. Since her stroke, Henny could barely walk, and Will had hired a woman to come and do the cleaning and cooking. One of Henny's several cats sat on her lap, and the woman petted it lightly with her right hand, which was weak but usable. She could hardly move her left hand and arm, and the left side of her face drooped slightly.

"It's been so long, Lettie. I was so worried about you. The other women say you almost never leave the house. I'm so glad to see you're getting out."

Lettie noticed the woman's eyes were more sunken, and she appeared to be even weaker than the last time she had seen her. Was her good friend dying? Oh, how she hated death. She couldn't bear losing Henny too. Not now!

She pulled up a chair and sat down beside the woman, while Bob Franks, who had brought her to visit, headed the family buggy back to Billings. "For reasons even I don't understand, I find it hard to leave home anymore, Henny. I'm so sorry I've neglected visiting as often as I should. Somehow I feel as if I'm deserting Paul when I go away. I know that sounds ridiculous, but I can't help it."

Henny reached over and touched her arm. "No one knows how they will react to losing a loved one until it happens, Lettie. Each of us works out our grief differently."

Lettie sighed deeply. "I suppose. At any rate, the girls needed some things that they wanted to come to town to pick out themselves, and Luke and Ty are on the cattle drive to Cheyenne. Bob Franks was bringing Mae into town, so we all came together. He left Mae and the girls at Syd Martin's store. Mae and Bob are married now, you know. Mae is staying on to help me, though. She and Bob share a room on the third floor, and Bob will stay on as a ranch hand."

"Will told me they got married. How nice for Mae!" Henny managed to turn her head to meet Lettie's green eyes, her own dark eyes all-knowing. "What about *your* marriage, Lettie? It's all the other women gossip about when they visit, you know."

Lettie paled. "They do?"

Henny squeezed her arm, an understanding smile making her face break into its many premature wrinkles. "Lettie, everyone knows Luke spends more time over at the Lonesome Tree or out on the range than he does at home. Ever since Paul died—"

"I don't want to talk about it," Lettie interrupted, pulling her arm away. "I didn't come here for that."

"Didn't you?"

Lettie put a hand to her forehead. "That stroke certainly didn't affect your mind or your insight, did it? You get right to the point."

Henny smiled. "We've always been close, Lettie. I've been so worried about you, not visiting, keeping yourself away from people, not attending the women's meetings. You've always been the one to bring people together, a leader, so strong and elegant and sure. I hear the rumors and I hurt for you. As far as getting to the point, I have to, Lettie. You're my friend, and I love you; and God knows we might not get another chance to talk, my health the way it is."

"Oh, don't say that, Henny! I don't know what I'd do if I couldn't talk to you sometimes. Even when I don't visit, just knowing you're here is somehow a comfort. What does Doc Manning say?"

Henny began stroking the cat on her lap again. "There isn't much he can do. I try to do things to build my strength, but every day I feel a little weaker. I don't really mind for me, you know. I just hate being this way for Will. He's been so patient and good." She sighed. "Enough of me. You're trying to change the subject, Lettie Fontaine, and I won't let you do it. You're hurting. Luke is hurting. But you aren't sharing that hurt and helping each other. Why not?"

Lettie shook her head. "I give up." She smiled sadly. "There is so much I want to say to him, Henny, but the words just won't come."

"You had a good marriage, Lettie. Everyone could see how strong it was, how much you loved each other. Love like that doesn't die without a good fight. Maybe that's what you need—a good fight—scream, yell, get it all out."

"Maybe. I just don't quite know how to get the conversation started, and Luke is gone so much now." Lettie grasped at her hat again as a gust of wind tugged at it. "It's so hot today."

"Ah, ah! You're changing the subject again."

Lettie sat quietly thinking for a moment before

continuing. "At first I blamed him for everything, and I guess he sensed that. He grew so cold and hard. Now I don't know how to get him back. I'm not even sure how I feel about him anymore. Since Nathan ran off and Paul died... I don't know. I just don't have those feelings anymore. It's as though all the love and passion have gone out of me. I don't even do the books anymore. I used to love doing that for Luke. Now everything is changed. It's as though we're on different pathways. We don't even—" She looked down at the handbag in her lap. "We don't even share the same bedroom anymore."

"Oh, Lettie! Surely you know how much that man loves you."

Lettie met her eyes. "So much that he spends his nights with Annie Gates?"

Henny frowned. "Do you know that for a fact?"

"No," Lettie answered, rising. "But it wouldn't surprise me." She walked over to grasp one of the porch posts. "Has Will ever said anything about it?"

"No. But you know how men are. They stick together. He knows if he ever mentioned it to me, I would tell you. But maybe there is nothing to tell, Lettie."

Lettie smiled bitterly. "Part of me doesn't even care and doesn't blame him. And part of me wants to run to him, beg him never to go near that woman."

"So what is stopping you? Nial Bentley?"

Lettie turned in surprise. "What?"

Henny shook her head. "I *told* you you're the most talked-about woman in Billings. Luke's men see Nial coming to visit every couple of weeks while Luke's gone on the cattle drive; they tell other men; word gets around."

Lettie sighed and came to sit back down. "Nial is just being a friend. He has a wonderful, gentle nature, now that I've gotten to know him better. He has visited several times, listened to Pearl play the piano, brought some books about medicine to Robbie. He is entertaining, easy to talk to, and his concern for the children and my own losses over the past year and a half have made me appreciate his visits. I didn't much like him when he first gave me attention four years ago, but I see him through different eyes now."

"Nial Bentley wants to be more than just a friend, Lettie. You must know that. You'd better be careful. You know how Luke feels about him, and Luke has never been an easy man to tangle with."

Lettie leaned back in the chair. "I know. I worry for Nial, but he insists on coming around. He has a way of making me talk, Lettie. I've shared things with him that I once would only have shared with Luke; and he's so attentive to the children, teaching them about life in England and in big cities, telling them about universities and schools. He has Pearl dreaming of studying music, and Robbie determined to be a doctor. They're starved for that attention. God knows Luke hasn't been much of a father to any of them these past months, except to Ty. They're still very close." She looked at Henny. "Ty doesn't like Nial, but the other three children do, very much. When Nial comes over, it's like we're a family again; but when Luke is there, the children grow quiet. They're almost afraid of him, and now I don't know how to reach him myself."

"Lettie, Luke couldn't help any of the things that have happened."

Tears formed in Lettie's eyes. "I know that."

"Then tell him, and get rid of Nial Bentley before he destroys your marriage."

Lettie watched three cats run by, all chasing a chipmunk. "If our marriage is destroyed, it won't be because of Nial Bentley or Annie Gates."

Henny sniffed. "They're both biting at the bit. Don't you fool yourself. Annie's probably been telling Luke you're not the right woman for him, that you're too refined and too educated to be married to a rancher; she's probably filled his head with hints about what might be going on with Nial. And Nial is probably doing the same with you, hinting that you're meant for better men than Luke Fontaine. But they don't *come* any better as far as I'm concerned, and he's still damn handsome for all his forty-two years."

Lettie thought about the first time she'd set eyes on Luke, when he saved Nathan from being trampled. There were moments when she could vividly remember the passion Luke stirred in her, and all the reasons she had married the man. "You're right about everything you're saying, Henny. There's just this terrible rift between us now. With my baby buried, it just doesn't seem right that I should ever enjoy life and love again."

"That's ridiculous! Do you think denying yourself happiness for the rest of your life is going to bring back Paul? It's time you straightened things out with Luke, Lettie, before all of this goes too far. You love each other too much to let this keep happening. Nial Bentley is like a vulture, waiting for something to die, picking at it little by little even though it's still alive." The woman took Lettie's hand again. "Paul is dead, Lettie. You have to face that fact and get on with life, give your attention to your other children, your husband, yourself. There is no bringing Paul back, no matter what kinds of sacrifices or penance you try to make. It's nobody's fault. *Nobody's!* Not yours, not Luke's, nobody's."

Lettie swallowed at the eternal lump in her throat. "Poor Robbie thinks it's something he did. He was bathing Paul with a cool rag when it happened. It was a terrible thing for him. He needs to talk to his father about it, but Luke isn't there. Nial has talked to him, has encouraged him in being a doctor. He needs that right now. I can't help but be grateful for how he has helped Robbie emotionally. Me too. I've suffered so, knowing that I neglected

Paul when Nathan was home…and the moment he died, I should have been holding him in my arms. He should have been in my—" She could not finish. As the sickening grief revisited her, she broke into sobs.

"My God, Lettie, have you given Luke the chance to help you through this? Does he even know how you or Robbie or anyone is feeling?"

"I don't know."

"You don't know because you haven't *told* him. Talk to Luke instead of that damned Englishman. Let him back into your life. Don't let Nial Bentley take advantage of your problems. You and Luke have something Will and I were never blessed with. Children. Yes, you've lost two sons, but there is hope one will come back to you; and you have four other children who need their mother and father. Those children are something you and Luke share that you can never share with Nial Bentley. You also share a past, memories, lots of them good ones. Don't you see how much you have to be thankful for, Lettie?"

Lettie quickly wiped at her tears and turned to take both of Henny's hands. "I know one thing I am thankful for, and that's my very best friend, Henny Doolan. You *are* going to be all right, aren't you, Henny? I need you."

Henny smiled lovingly. "You need Luke, Lettie, not me. You remember that. You remember who loves you more than anybody on earth could love you, even though he might be afraid to show it right now."

Lettie leaned over and kissed her cheek. "Always ready with sage advice, aren't you, Henny?"

She shrugged. "A woman has to be good for something."

Lettie smiled then herself. "You're good for me, and for Will. Where is Will, anyway?"

"Haven't you heard? There has been a lot of trouble with rustlers lately. Will and several other ranchers formed a posse. All but Luke are back from Cheyenne. They got word some of the outlaws might be camped down by Pine Creek, hiding cattle in that canyon area where hardly anybody ever goes, probably figure on sneaking them out of there and on up into Canada. At any rate, Will and the others hope to catch Luke on his way back from the drive so he can join in on the hunt. Your men at the Double L probably don't know about it yet because they all just rode out yesterday. They had enough men that they weren't even going to stop at your ranch. They probably didn't want you getting all upset."

Lettie's smile vanished. She rose. "No, I didn't know. I've been so wrapped up in my personal problems. Nial never said anything about rustlers and men forming a posse. He must know about it."

"Of course he knows. Some of his own men are with the posse. Nial probably doesn't want you worrying, not for your sake, but because it would make you start thinking about Luke, and he doesn't want that. If the man had any sand in him, he'd be riding with the posse himself; but he's not one to get in there and handle things himself like Luke. He lets his men do his work for him, while he goes off trying to steal another man's wife."

Lettie felt a heat come into her cheeks. Was that how it really was? Had she let her emotions over Paul blind her womanly instincts? She had most certainly let her loneliness and need draw her to another man. Did everyone else think there was something intimate going on? And what if something happened to Luke, before they had the chance to find each other again? If she lost Luke now...and Ty! She hadn't spent much time with him these last months while he was learning to run the ranch. She had never even asked her son how he felt about little Paul's death. Ty was with Luke. If he went along on the search for the rustlers, he could be hurt!

She turned to look up the road from town. Bob Franks wasn't back yet. She was suddenly impatient to get back home in case Luke came back before going after those rustlers. There was so much to tell him. And she hadn't hugged Ty in the longest time. Henny was right. She had been so involved in mourning the children she had lost, that she had failed to give enough love and attention to the children still with her.

～

Luke and his men watched from the high plateau where they had made camp the night before. A cloud of dust on the open plains below signified several riders.

"Who do you think it is, Pa?" Tyler asked his father. The boy sat straight and proud in his saddle, feeling every bit a man for being allowed to go with his father on the cattle drive this summer. Even though he was only twelve, he was big and strong enough in body to handle Stomper, a big, roan-colored gelding often ridden by Tex.

"I'm not sure," Luke answered. He looked over at the faithful scout who had been with him for several years now. "What do you think, Runner?"

"Can't tell. Maybe a posse. They are white men, and they ride all together like they are very determined."

"They're headed southwest," Tex put in. "Looks like they're real intent on gettin' where they're goin'."

"I don't think they're outlaws or rustlers," Billy Sacks added. "I've always heard they usually travel with extra horses, and this time of year, coming out of the best range like that, they'd already have stolen cattle and horses along."

"I agree," Luke spoke up. "Let's ride down there and meet them, see what's going on." He kicked his horse into a hard ride, his riding agility tested when the animal slipped and slid down a steep hillside that was a mixture of clay and gravel. He glanced back to be sure Ty was doing all right in the dangerous descent, proud of how well his son had handled his first cattle drive, taking night watch at times just like the other men, sometimes helping the cook, taking his turn at tending the remuda, never complaining. He was a ranchman, born and bred. Maybe someday Robbie would come around and want to be as much a part of the ranch as his brother. There was a time when he'd dreamed of all three of his sons taking over someday, but Robbie was lost in his dream of being a doctor; and Paul…

He couldn't think about Paul. Couldn't talk about him. He wished he could. Maybe then he and Lettie could find each other again. The pain was just too great, of remembering holding his littlest boy in his arms, already dead; of knowing he might have lived if he hadn't been so far from help; of recalling the look in Lettie's eyes when she realized the last child she would ever have had been taken from her. It was so much easier to be out here under big skies, or to drink himself into a stupor in town, than to face the reality of his son's death and the loss of his wife's companionship. How had he managed to be such a success in matters outside the home, and such a failure at his personal life?

He and the eight men with him, plus Ty, reached the bottom of the plateau and broke into a hard gallop, the cook, simply called Oatmeal, lagging behind with the chuck wagon, and three more men herding the remuda even farther back. He could see that the riders they were trying to reach before they got too far past had finally noticed them and were pulling up. Luke glanced over at Ty, who was riding hard right alongside him, his dark hair flying away from his face, his wide-brimmed hat caught by its cord around his neck and bouncing at his shoulders. He grinned as he realized Ty was turning this into a race, and he let up a little on his own gray-and-white speckled Appaloosa, letting the boy nose ahead of him. "All right, you win!" he shouted as they neared the waiting riders.

Ty let out a war whoop and laughed. "You *let* me win, didn't you?"

"No. I swear," Luke answered with a grin. Yes. Out here he could feel good. Out here he could laugh. He wanted to share laughter again with Lettie and the other children.

"Luke! We was hopin' to run into you!"

Luke recognized his good friend Will's voice. It reminded him of poor Henny, partly crippled now. He knew how hard it was for Will to see her that way, but at least the woman wasn't crippled emotionally, as Lettie seemed to be. "What's going on?" he shouted in reply, slowing his horse to a trot as he rode closer. He recognized several of the others now, Carl Rose, Calvin Briggs, Joe Parker, Hank Kline, and several other men, some of them small ranchers, some businessmen from Billings who had joined them, men sworn to help uphold the law in Montana the only way it could be done in these parts—through vigilante committees. "You boys look like you're hot on somebody's trail." Luke's men formed a line beside him.

"We're headed for Pine Creek, Luke," Calvin Briggs answered. "We would have waited for you, but we couldn't wait on this one. Annie Gates had a customer the other night who got so drunk he bragged about how he was going to meet up with some buddies of his at Pine Creek Canyon and help herd some cattle north, said he'd be making a lot of money for helping because they'd get a good price for the cattle up in Canada. Told Annie he'd bring her a diamond necklace when he came back. There's no ranchers we know of around Pine Creek, and nobody we know takes their cattle to Canada except rustlers. Annie told Sheriff Tracy about it, and he sent messengers out to the rest of the ranchers. Figured it was a job for us instead of him. We had us a little talk with the one who bragged about helpin' herd the cattle. By the time we finished with him, he told us the truth. It's rustlers, all right, and part of their gang is the Walkers, them two boys and their pa that you chased off the Double L last year."

"I thought they were far away from here by now. Don't they realize we all know they're the ones who raided Matt Duncan's place and killed Duncan? They raped the poor man's wife besides, then made off with all his livestock. How can they be stupid enough to come back here?"

"Well, it's a good thing that hired hand of Duncan's managed to get to town to tell us he seen it was the Walker boys. Now we've got no doubt what to do with them if we find them."

"Bastards," Luke fumed. "I've lost at least three hundred head myself over the past couple of years. It was probably the Walkers who took them."

"It's just too bad it took so long for Duncan's man to get to town to tell us about what happened," Will put in. "Otherwise we could have followed their tracks if they were fresh. I'd have chased the bastards all the way into Canada if necessary, but by the time we got out there, it was too late. Rain had washed away the tracks. Now we've got a chance to get our hands on those sons of bitches."

"We'll get them this time," Hank spoke up. He scratched at his gray beard. "If we do, I guess that means Annie is good for more than a roll in bed."

They all laughed, and Luke felt an ache for a woman. He wanted that woman to be Lettie, but she hadn't come to his bed in months, and because of Paul's death, he couldn't bring himself to force his wife into submitting, but his estrangement from Lettie had led him into Annie Gates's bed. He knew some of these men were aware he'd been with Annie, probably thought he had done so more than once. He was not about to bother trying to explain it to any one of them. Men like these understood such things were private, and they made no judgments. "I'll send my cook and a couple more men home with Ty. The rest of us will join you," he told Will and the others.

"No, Pa! I want to go with you!" Ty protested.

"Not on your life. You might be old enough for the drive, but not for rustlers. There will probably be a lot of shooting."

"But, Pa—"

"Ty, you'll go home!" Luke said sternly. "The last thing your mother and I need is to lose another son."

The other men lost their smiles and signaled to one another to ride on ahead a ways and let Luke talk to the boy alone. Will stayed behind.

"Pa, it sounds exciting."

"And in two or three more years, I'll let you take part in these things, but not yet, Ty." Luke moved his horse closer, removing his hat and wiping at his brow with the sleeve of his blue shirt. "Ty, you know what a strain this past year and a half has been. This could be dangerous, and it would be *more* dangerous for me if I have to worry about where you are and if you're all right. You go on home with Oatmeal and the remuda. Explain to your mother where I've gone and that I'll be back as soon as it's over. A good ranch hand obeys orders, Ty. You know that."

Tyler nodded, pouting. "You be careful, Pa. Ma needs you. She might not say so, or act like it, but she does."

Luke felt the growing pain in his heart, wishing, hoping the boy was right. He and Ty had had a lot of time to talk on the trail, and Ty had told him about Nial Bentley's visit last spring. In some ways Luke thought maybe a man like Nial was better for Lettie after all; but his own possessive jealousy refused to allow it. Nial had stayed away from the cattlemen's meetings, and Luke had not had a chance to talk to the man before he left on the cattle drive. He hoped Bentley had sense enough to stay away from the Double L while he'd been gone. "Things will work out, Ty," he said now. "I promised

you I'd stay home more this fall and winter, and I will."
He reached out, and father and son hugged briefly. "You
did a damn good job, Ty. You go back and take care of
your mother and brother and sisters until I get back."

"Be careful, Pa."

Luke nodded, turning to his men and ordering three
of them to go on to the ranch with Oatmeal and Ty and
take the remuda with them. They all headed out, and
Luke waved when Ty turned for a last look at his father.
He waved back, then rode around the remuda to help
herd the horses.

"The boy did good, did he?" Will asked, riding closer
to Luke.

"Real well. When I'm gone, the Double L will be in
good hands," Luke answered. "I just hope Robbie will
be a part of it too."

"You can't order your kids' lives, Luke. You know
how much Paul's death affected poor Robbie. If bein'
a doctor makes it all better for him, you've gotta let the
boy try."

Luke sighed, turning his horse. "I don't know, Will.
It seems that my family is going in six different directions. Maybe it would all be easier for me to cope with
if I could feel close to Lettie again, but it's as if she's in
another world, as though she hardly knows I'm around
when I *am* home."

"Well, you'd best *stay* for a while this time and get
things straightened out before that damned Englishman
steals your woman right from under your nose. You
might as well know Bentley has been over to the ranch
quite a few times over the summer, accordin' to what
your men tell me. He dotes on Pearl and Robbie mostly,
but Katie too. I think the man is tryin' to get to Lettie
through the kids. Lord knows their own father hasn't
been around enough to know what's goin' on in their
lives. If you don't want to lose them all, Luke, you'd

better tend to the family. If Lettie won't talk, then find a way to *make* her talk, but first, get rid of Nial Bentley. And don't tell me it don't bother you to know the man is after your wife again. A woman in her state needs a man's strength, and don't think Nial don't know that. He's movin' in for the kill, and you're lettin' him do it."

Luke drew his horse to a halt, and when Will looked over at him, he shivered at how dark the man's eyes looked, their blue color seeming to change to smoke. "I'm not *letting* the man do *any*thing! I had no idea Bentley was damn fool enough to keep coming around. I let that first visit go by as an expression of friendship and sympathy. I didn't know there were others."

"Everybody in town talks about you and Annie and Lettie and Nial. I just thought you should know. I don't doubt Nial has put ideas into Lettie's head about you and Annie Gates. If she thinks you're sleepin' with the woman, it ain't gonna help anything." He paused, studying Luke intently. "*Have* you slept with Annie?"

Luke looked away. "Only once." He heard Will sigh, and he met the man's eyes again. "Jesus, Will, Lettie hasn't slept with me since before Paul died. A man can only take so much." He turned away again. "But I'm not taking it anymore. Something is going to get straightened out when I get home, and it's going to start with Nial Bentley!" The last words were spoken with bitter venom. "Let's bag ourselves some rustlers!" He kicked his horse and headed toward the posse, which was well ahead of them now. Will charged out after him, glad to see a new spark of life in Luke's eyes. Henny was right to suggest that he tell Luke about Nial Bentley. Jealousy could do a lot of things to a man.

Twenty

LETTIE KNOCKED ON THE BACK DOOR TO THE LONESOME Tree, hoping no one had seen her duck into the alley after leaving the hat shop. She had asked Bob Franks to take the children back to the ranch and had stayed two nights with Henny. Because of Henny's illness, she wasn't sure how much time there was left to be with her friend, and she knew Henny was lonely with Will gone, so she had decided to keep her company for a couple of extra days.

The visit had done her heart good. She had come to town to comfort Henny, but Henny had comforted her instead. Her good friend had a way of making her think, and she realized how wrong she had been to withdraw from the rest of her family because of Paul. She should be grateful for what she had left, a beautiful home, four other strong, healthy children, a husband who had practically killed himself to give her the life he thought she deserved. The women of Billings and the surrounding area had finally brought in a minister this summer, and a church had been built. Yesterday Reverend Gooding had come to visit Henny, but it was Lettie who had ended up having a heart-to-heart talk with the man. He had prayed with her, and she had come to accept that the reverend was probably right that God had had a purpose in taking little Paul. Maybe the whole experience would make Robbie a more dedicated doctor, a man who would someday save many lives. She had to believe there was a reason for her baby's death, or she could never go on with her own life. Now there was one more thing to be dealt with before she went home and waited for Luke. She had to know the truth about Annie Gates. She didn't really hate or blame Luke if he had been with the woman. He had literally had no wife for almost two years now. She just wanted to understand, wanted to hear from the horse's mouth if it meant anything, how many times he had been with the woman, or if perhaps there was no truth to it at all.

She almost jumped back when the door opened, and a mustached man wearing an apron scowled at her. She recognized Ben Pritchert, the owner of the Lonesome Tree. "What the hell do you want this time of morning?" He squinted his eyes. "Jesus! Ain't you Luke Fontaine's wife?"

Lettie held her chin high. "I am."

The man looked her over in surprise, and she wanted to die at realizing he probably knew why she had come. "I would like to see Miss Annie Gates, alone. Right here in your back room will suffice."

The man smoothed back what little hair he had, suddenly looking self-conscious. "Well, uh, Mrs. Fontaine, women like Annie, they don't exactly get up early in the mornin' like this. Why don't you come back after twelve?"

"I want to see her *now*! Go and get her, please." Lettie looked past him into the dark, stuffy storeroom. "I know Annie lives above your saloon with the other town prostitutes." She looked at Pritchert again. "Who, I might add, will someday be banished from Billings, if the women's group has their way."

Pritchert's face reddened a little. "That would hurt my business. Look, lady, don't go runnin' me out of business just because you've got it in for Annie on account of your husband. That's your problem, not mine."

Lettie had to contain herself to keep from hitting the man, but she could not control the crimson color that

came to her cheeks. How could she have been such a
fool! The whole town knew, and they probably blamed
her for not being a good wife! "Please go and get her,
Mr. Pritchert. I won't leave until you do. And believe
me, *that* would hurt your business."

The man rubbed at sleepy eyes. "Shit," he muttered.
He stepped back. "Come on in and close the door. I
can't stand all that sunshine." He turned and left, and
Lettie waited with a pounding heart. She had worn a
new dress, a soft green summer cotton that fit her still-
trim figure and full breasts perfectly. The high neck and
the ruffles at the end of the three-quarter-length sleeves
were trimmed with white lace, and the waistline was set
off by a sash that tied into a wide bow at the back. The
front of the skirt was fitted, then gathered into the back
in a cascade of ruffles that fell into a short train.

She carried a parasol that matched the dress, wore her
auburn hair swept up into curls and topped with a little
straw hat with a band of the same material as the dress.
Her ears sported tiny diamond earrings. She wanted to
look her best, to show Annie Gates that Luke Fontaine's
wife was still pretty and slender. She didn't need paint
on her face, didn't need to deck herself out in low-cut
satin dresses and dangling earrings. She had been here a
lot longer than Annie Gates, had done much more to
contribute to the growth and taming of Montana and
Billings than the whores who came here after the fact to
bring their corruption.

She winced at the room's musty smell, glanced at barrels of beer and bottles of whiskey stacked everywhere.
This was a world only men understood…and women
like Annie. She could not imagine a woman going to
bed with just any man, many men. For her it would be
like rape, and she well remembered what that had been
like. It made no sense to her that a woman could do such
a thing, but if she did have such uncontrollable urges, it

was easy to understand why she would be attracted to a man like Luke. Any woman would be attracted to him, not just because of his wealth and power, but because of the man himself, his build, his looks…the gentle side of him she had not seen for such a long time. Was he gentle with Annie?

She hated the very picture of it. Luke! She had caused him to turn to another woman. The only thing she could be grateful for was that it was someone who could not possibly mean anything to him. What if it had been some young, decent, single woman he had taken an interest in? She might have no chance at all of fixing the damage and getting her husband back. Did he think she had been doing such things with Nial Bentley? If Luke came across the other ranchers who had gone after those rustlers, what would they tell him about Nial's visits to the Double L? She was grateful for Nial's attention these past months, valued his friendship, and had even been somewhat attracted to him. But no man could take Luke's place in her heart. Surely he knew that.

Now she wasn't sure what to think of Nial's attention. When she needed genuine sympathy and understanding, he had been there, but was Henny right in thinking he was just playing on her emotions? She realized that the only time he came calling was when Luke was gone. How sad that his attention to the children might not have been because he really cared about them but only to win her over. It made her sick to realize how blind she had been since Paul's death, how vulnerable. Over the years out here she had learned to be strong, to fight back; but Paul's death and Nathan's desertion had taken the fight out of her. Now she felt that old will returning. Seeing Henny failing so fast had made her realize how little time anyone had on this earth.

She drew a deep breath for courage when she heard a woman yelling then. So, Annie Gates did not appreciate being rousted out of bed so early. Maybe she still had a customer with her! The thought made her ill. She wasn't sure what to expect. She had seen Annie a few times in town, but the woman had not attended any social or family events since the fall dance nearly five years ago. After that, the women of Billings had made it very clear they would not condone prostitutes being around their young sons and daughters and flaunting themselves in front of good, Christian people.

Suddenly the door to the back room was flung open, and both women just stared at each other for a moment. Lettie felt sick at what she saw, a woman more beautiful than she wanted to admit. What a waste of such a lovely creature. In spite of the mussed blond hair and the bloodshot eyes she was still pretty. Rouge and lip color had been rubbed away through the night, probably by some man. She wore a flimsy gown and a robe with feathered sleeves, thin enough to make it obvious that the body underneath was perfectly curved. "If you're looking for Luke, he's not here," the woman spoke up.

Lettie tried to determine how old she might be, but it was impossible. Was she young but looked older because of her hard life? Or was she older than it appeared, seeming younger because of all that pretty hair and her nice shape? Lettie remembered the night of the dance someone had said something about how sad it was that someone only twenty had already fallen so deeply into sin. Were they talking about Annie? That would make her twenty-five now. "I'm not looking for Luke," she answered, forcing herself to remain calm. "I'm looking for you."

Annie sniffed, running her fingers through her hair and suddenly appearing self-conscious. "Ben, bring me a shot of whiskey!" she hollered through the door. Lettie heard the man's muffled answer, then felt almost naked as Annie stood there looking her over. "You sure are a pretty woman for your age," she said with a sly grin. "Is that what you want to know? If Luke still thinks you're pretty?"

Lettie wanted to crumble at the familiar way she spoke about her husband. "Does he?"

The door opened, and Ben handed Annie the drink. He glanced at Lettie with a worried look on his face, then closed the door again. Annie slugged down the whiskey as readily as any man would. "You're a fool, Mrs. Fontaine. I know your boy died and all, and I'm sorry about that. I just don't think you know what his death did to Luke. And I don't think you have any idea how much that man loves you."

Lettie blinked back tears, never dreaming she'd be grateful to hear those words coming from someone like Annie Gates. Annie folded her arms, shaking her head. "Of course he thinks you're pretty. He thinks you're the most beautiful woman who ever set foot in Montana, or anyplace else for that matter. He worships the ground you walk on, and he thinks he's disappointed you, failed you. He can't handle that because he was already rejected by his own father, who *expects* him to fail, *wants* him to fail. He could handle rejection by his father, but not from you. You mean too much to him."

Lettie frowned, amazed that this woman seemed to understand so much, that she seemed to care about Luke, the person. "He told you about his father?"

Annie let out a snicker, looking almost sorrowful. "Sure." She dropped her arms, stepped a little closer. "We talk, Mrs. Fontaine—something he hasn't been able to do with you for a long time. And believe it or not, talking is just about *all* we do. He's only slept with me once, and I don't think he got much out of it because it wasn't you. He's not a man who easily cheats on his wife, Mrs. Fontaine. He had a need and I filled it. It's that simple. That's my job."

Lettie turned away, jealousy raging through her. Until

now it was just a rumor, and she had made herself believe it couldn't be true. Never had she burned so deeply to have her husband back sexually. It hit her so hard it almost hurt.

"Don't you go blaming him, lady," Annie told her. "He's a man, and he fought his needs for a long time."

Lettie swallowed, struggling to find her voice. "When...did it happen?"

Annie rolled her eyes. "Does it really matter? I told you it was only once. The point is, there is only one woman for Luke Fontaine, and you're it. The minute you set things straight with that man, I'll be lucky he even gives me the time of day. You don't think it *meant* anything, do you?" She chuckled. "Honey, I'm not that stupid, and don't you be. I like Luke. I helped him through a bad time, that's all. It's not his nature to have anybody in his bed but his wife, but the way I understand it, his wife hasn't *been* in his bed for close to two years now."

Lettie turned to face her. "I see you know just about everything there is to know."

Annie looked her over again. "I know you suffered a terrible loss, and that it is something the two of you should have shared instead of letting it come between you." Her eyes suddenly teared. "And I know I would give anything, *any*thing, to be in your shoes. No man will ever love me like that, Mrs. Fontaine. I know that for a fact. God knows I'd give my right arm for a man like Luke. I could love him so easily. Fact is, maybe I *do* love him. Women like me, we do have feelings, in case you don't realize it. But it wouldn't do me any good to allow them to surface, especially for Luke Fontaine. Compared to you, I'm nothing in his eyes but someone he can have a drink with and spill his guts to and use for his manly needs when he gets to the point where he can't ignore them anymore." She wiped at a tear and took a deep breath. "You have something wonderful, Mrs. Fontaine—a good man who's handsome to boot, four beautiful children; you live in a mansion on the biggest ranch in Montana. My God, woman, don't throw it all away!"

Lettie wanted to hate her, scream at her; but she knew the woman was right. "I don't intend to. I just… I wanted to know if the rumors were true. Thank you for being honest with me and for…for apparently caring. I didn't think—"

"That I had any feelings?" She laughed lightly. "Honey, when you're raised like I was, by a stepfather who beats you and starts coming to your bed when you're only eight, you learn how to shut off your feelings. But they're still there when necessary."

Lettie shivered at the realization of what had led the young woman to such a hideous life. Surely she felt unloved, dirty, unworthy of a decent life. "Annie, it's never too late for anyone, you know. If you wanted to get out of here, do something else with your life, you still could."

The woman waved her off. "You wouldn't understand."

Lettie thought about her own rape, how she had felt about herself afterward…until Luke came along. "Maybe I understand better than you know."

Annie frowned in confusion, and Lettie realized Luke had probably never told her about her own rape. He knew she never wanted anyone else to know. Even in his hour of deepest need and outpouring of heart to someone else, he had not said anything about his wife's rape, the illegitimacy of her first child. "Annie, I mean it. If you show you are trying to change your life, you can have friends besides men like Ben Pritchert, who you know doesn't give a damn about you; friends besides men who only want to use you; *better* friends than the other prostitutes that you know. Those women only like you because you're just like them."

For a brief moment Lettie could see that the words

had cut deep. Annie looked almost as if she were going to start crying, but then she forced another laugh and tossed her head.

"Don't preach to me. There's been enough preaching here and I've done it. Don't ask me why. I've surprised even myself. Just take my advice, Mrs. Fontaine, and straighten things out with your husband. And stay away from that damned Englishman. He can't hold a candle to Luke Fontaine, in spite of all his money and his title."

Lettie's eyebrows arched in surprise. "What have you heard about me and Nial Bentley?"

Annie yelled out for more whiskey, then turned back to Lettie. "Nothing bad about you, honey. Everybody in this town respects you, knows you've been a woman in deep mourning over the loss of two children. It's Bentley everybody talks about, how he's just trying to take advantage of the situation, using your emotions to win you over. It's obvious the man was infatuated with you the first time he came around a few years ago."

The door opened again, and Ben handed Annie a whole bottle and another shot glass, then left again. Annie poured herself another shot and drank it down. "Nial is a smooth, clever man, Lettie. He's visited me a few times. You're a lucky woman. The two richest men in the territory are in love with you, but only one of them fathered your children and would die for you without question. Only one of them has guts, and only one of them got his wealth by getting his hands dirty and building it on his own. It wasn't handed to him. He had a woman to help him, a woman with as much guts as he has. They belong together. You don't match up with somebody like Nial. You belong with a man like Luke, helping to civilize this territory and make it grow. My kind—" She shrugged. "We'll move on to places where there isn't so much law yet, if there are any places like that left."

Lettie was dumbfounded at the entire conversation.

She had expected a cat fight, shouting, eye scratching. "You're an unusual woman, Annie."

Annie laughed loudly. "I've never had it put that way before."

Lettie remained sober. "I mean it. And I meant what I said about getting out of this. I would openly call you my friend."

Annie's laugh faded to a soft chuckle. "You just go on and take care of your own life. I'll take care of mine."

Lettie turned to the door, then hesitated. "Please don't tell Luke I was ever here."

"Of course not. Something tells me I won't see much of him from here on anyway."

Lettie met her eyes once more. "I hope not." She swallowed back an urge to cry. "Thank you, Annie."

As Lettie left, Annie watched after her, tears slipping out of her eyes. "Anytime," she muttered. She poured herself another drink.

❧

Luke and the vigilantes with him numbered seventeen men all together. They made their way quietly below the rim of red rock that was the last barrier to the rustlers they knew were on the other side, grazing stolen horses and cattle along Pine Creek. Runner had stealthily sneaked close to their camp last night. The sly Indian was the only one of them who could get that close without being noticed or heard in the still night air. He had verified their suspicions. It was the Walkers, and he had recognized Luke's own brand on one of the stolen horses. They had talked about hitting another ranch before heading for Canada, and Zack Walker would pick up his son Johnny's wife on the way. Where she was living was unknown, but that didn't matter to the vigilantes. There was no doubt the men they had caught up with were the rustlers they had been after for months, the men who had murdered Matt Duncan and raped his wife. Runner reported there were at least ten outlaws that he could see in camp, but there could be more.

Luke suggested they split up, half the men riding in from one end of the canyon, the others cutting off the outlaws' flight from the other. It was just barely dawn, and thin clouds filtered the rising sun's light into shades of purple and peach. Runner had gone back on foot to find a place to hide, ready to cut loose the rustlers' remuda of riding horses as soon as he heard Luke and the other men coming in for them.

Luke petted his horse's nose to soothe the animal and keep it quiet, and no one spoke. They stayed to soft ground as much as possible and led their mounts rather than riding them, hoping to keep the rustlers from hearing the sound of squeaking saddles. The attack had to be a surprise, or they would fail.

Luke pulled out a pocket watch, checking the time. Six a.m. He knew it would take the other men another twenty minutes to get around their side of the rock formation, and he put up his hand for everyone to stop, as they were nearly in position to attack. He pulled his Colt revolver from its holster and checked to be sure every chamber was loaded, then put it back and mounted his horse, a buckskin gelding that was his favorite. The animal was fast, and quick to obey. He pulled his Lightning repeating rifle from its boot and rested it across his knees, waiting.

The dead quiet was almost deafening, the only sound the squeak of leather and an occasional cough. While he waited, Luke took time to think, all the things he could and should say to Lettie parading through his mind. Should he be angry with her for letting Nial Bentley come visiting while he was gone? No. Nial was the one who should receive the brunt of his anger. The man had been warned once. Their next encounter would involve more than a warning. The thought of some man thinking he could move in on Luke Fontaine's wife…the bastard! Then again, what would Lettie think of his turning to Annie Gates? Did she know? Maybe she didn't even care. Maybe she and Nial had… No. Lettie wouldn't do that, even if she knew about him and Annie.

"Luke, you with us?"

Luke turned to look back at Will.

"Get your thoughts on matters at hand," Will told him quietly. "It's time we rode in."

Luke nodded, raising his rifle as a signal. He kept the rifle in hand and kicked his horse's flanks, breaking the animal into a gallop and heading around the south end of the canyon wall. From there on the ride had to be hard and fast. They could not attack by riding down from above, or the rustlers would have the chance to flee the canyon with their pursuers behind them. Attacking from both ends of the canyon was the only way. A climb out would be very difficult if the outlaws wanted to escape that way, but there was always that possibility, at least for a few of them. Reaching them as quickly as they could, guns ready, was the only answer.

Dust and gravel flew as Luke and Will and the others charged forward, some of them splashing through the shallow creek. Horses and cattle began to stir restlessly, and some of the men shot off their guns to scatter the herds and confuse the rustlers. As they got closer, Luke could see men running everywhere, some heading for where they probably thought their remuda waited. They would find nothing there, if Runner had done his job. He heard the whir of a bullet, felt the rushing sound near his ear, and he knew the rustlers were shooting at them now. "Take cover!" he shouted, pulling his own horse to a sliding halt and dismounting to take a position behind a large boulder. He pulled the horse around with him, and Will joined him.

Luke positioned his rifle, took aim, and fired. One of the men screamed and went down. He shot at others who were running in every direction, trying to get to their horses. Bullets spit back at them, pinging at the rock, biting off bits of the boulder. A piece of the rock shattered against Luke's face, cutting into it in several places. Instantly he squeezed his eyes shut and turned away for a moment. He put a hand to his face and saw considerable blood on his palm. "Damn!" he swore. "Watch yourself, Will."

He got no answer but there was no time to turn to see how his friend was doing. He could see the rest of the vigilantes riding in now from the other end of the canyon. He heard the rustlers screaming obscenities over being trapped. A second man went down from Luke's own gun. A third. He saw four others down from bullets from other guns. One of the outlaws was writhing in pain. Two men were trying to sneak up the canyon wall, and Luke took careful aim with his rifle and fired. One of them cried out and tumbled back down the hill, his body bouncing against boulders. The second man made it to the top and disappeared over the edge.

The remaining rustlers threw down their guns and put their hands in the air, and the vigilantes who had ridden in from the north end of the canyon surrounded them. "We got them, Will!" Luke grinned, wiping more blood from his face as he turned to share the moment, only to see Will lying flat on his back, a bloody hole in his face. "Will!"

Luke bent down to feel for a pulse. Will's eyes were still open, and horror moved through Luke at the realization that his good friend was dead. He thought for a moment that his heart would stop beating, and a painful lump formed in his throat. "Will!" He groaned. Tears formed in his eyes, and he gently reached over and closed Will's eyelids. He leaned across the man to pick up his hat and he placed it over Will's face. Anger and grief filled him in overwhelming proportions, and he stood up. "Is everybody all right?" he shouted.

"All okay, Luke," Tex shouted in reply. "We've got three of them over here. I think just one got away!" He let out a war whoop. "All the rustlers, and we got our horses and cattle back to boot!"

Luke looked back down at Will. What would he have done in those early years without this man? He would never find a more faithful friend again. This man was one of Montana's original settlers. And Henny—she had suffered the worst loneliness, for not only were there no neighbors in the beginning, but she never even was able to have children. She'd be so alone now, half crippled, so sick. How in hell could he go home and tell her Will was dead? The man was her whole world. "Bastards!" He sobbed.

He quickly wiped at tears, smearing them with the blood that continued to stream down his face from the superficial wounds. He turned then and stormed toward the others. "Will's dead!" he shouted. "The sons of bitches killed him!"

Tex reached out and grasped his arm. "Your face, boss. It's covered with blood."

"I'm all right. Just got hit with pieces of rock." He wiped at it again with his shirtsleeve, walking up closer to glare at the rustlers, whose faces showed their terror. Two were young, perhaps in their twenties. The third man was older and bearded. "The best man who ever set foot in Montana is *dead*!" he growled at them. "So is another good man. Matt Duncan! His wife raped! Those cattle and horses out there carry all our brands. We don't need any more reason than that to hang the lot of you!"

A fourth survivor lay groaning on the ground. Tex turned around and shot him in the head without hesitation.

The older of the three captives gasped, looked around

at the vigilantes. "Look, I...I don't know anything about killin' a man or rapin' his wife," he told them, shaking. "I just met up with the Walkers here a few days ago."

Luke looked them over carefully, his steely blue eyes resting on the younger boys. "Walkers! By God, you *are* the sneaking thieves I chased off my land over a year ago! Zack Walker's boys! We heard you were behind this, but I thought you were smart enough to stay the hell out of Montana! How in hell did you end up with a whole gang of rustlers?"

"To show rich bastards like you, Luke Fontaine, that you can't have it all," Johnny Walker answered with a sneer.

"Johnny, shut up!" the other warned. "Don't rile him more."

Luke shoved his rifle barrel against Johnny's throat. The young man smelled as though he hadn't bathed in months. His dull blond hair was pasted to his head from too much oil and dirt, and his thin face was set off with narrow dark eyes that reminded Luke of a small animal rather than a human. As far as Luke was concerned, he *was* an animal. "My best friend is dead," he told Johnny through clenched teeth. His jaw flexed in his rage. "I'd rather lose my entire herd than lose Will Doolan's companionship!" He looked at the other brother, who he remembered was called Jeeter. "I'm already as riled as I've ever been in my life!" he growled. He stepped back and looked over at the older man. "Who are you?"

The man blinked and swallowed, visibly shaking. "B-Baker. Clyde Baker. It's like I said. I...I just joined up with this bunch. I don't know nothin' about killin' no Matt Duncan, and...and I never fired a gun just now. I ain't even wearin' one."

Tex spoke up. "You had a hand in stealin' horses and cattle. Out here, that's enough to hang a man."

The others joined in agreement. "I vote for hanging too," Calvin Briggs put in. "We've got the right. All the cattlemen agreed on it, and Sheriff Tracy doesn't have any say out here."

"Hang them, Luke, or they'll just come back with more men and make more trouble," another one of Luke's men said. "Matt Duncan's dead, and you and the other ranchers have had too much stock stolen the past couple of years. This probably won't stop it completely, but we can slow it up. Don't forget Duncan's wife was raped, and one of Duncan's men lived to tell us he for sure knows these Walker boys and their pa were part of the gang that did it. These bastards don't *deserve* a trial!"

"Hey, look!" Baker spoke up, nearly ready to cry. "I told you, I never killed anybody, and I sure never raped no woman! Maybe these other two were there, but I wasn't!"

"You stinkin' coward!" Johnny turned his head and spit on Baker, who just cringed. He turned to glare at Luke then, realizing Luke was looked to as a leader by the other vigilantes. "If you hang us, Pa will get you, one way or another!" he told Luke calmly. "He got away, and he's probably up there someplace watchin' you right now. You'd better let us go, Luke Fontaine, or he'll get you. *You're* the one he'll come after, 'cause *you're* the one he hates. He'll get you, your wife, and your kids! Two of your kids for two of his!"

"Damn it, Johnny, shut your damn mouth!" Jeeter warned.

The rage in Luke's eyes made Baker break into tears. Luke stepped up closer to Johnny. "Just *threatening* my family is a hanging offense in my book." He sneered. "And if your pa has any sense at all, he'll be wise to get as far away from the Double L as possible. Fact is, he'd better get the hell out of Montana completely, or he'll end up in a noose too!" He turned to the men who had ridden with him. "My vote is to hang the Walker boys and let the older man go. I believe him about not being part of the bunch that killed Matt Duncan."

Baker sank to his knees and cried even more, this time with relief.

"Bastard!" Johnny cursed. "You rich goddamn bastard! Your wife's gonna die, Fontaine! To hell with *all* you Fontaines, your wife, your sons, and your daughters!"

"Jesus, Johnny, you're only makin' it worse," Jeeter pleaded, himself breaking into tears.

"Baker here stole cattle," Tex reminded Luke. "He ought to hang too."

Luke glanced at Baker. "I think he's smart enough to get the hell out of here and never come back...maybe smart enough to think twice before joining a bunch of rustlers again. Let him go." He walked over to Baker and poked him with his rifle. "Get up. You're going to help us bury all these men when this is over with, and then I want you to rustle up one of your own horses and get your ass out of Montana."

Baker stood up, wiping at his eyes with dirty hands. "Thanks, mister. You won't never see me around here again." He hurried away, and Luke turned to the rest of the men.

"You know what my vote is. The rest of you vote and I'll abide by what you decide. I'm going to ride back to where we left the packhorses and take care of Will. I don't give a damn about the rest of this shit." He walked away and mounted his horse, wondering how he was going to break this to Henny.

Twenty-one

LETTIE STUDIED HERSELF IN THE MIRROR. SHE WORE A plain pink cotton dress today, and her hair was pulled back at the sides with combs. She supposed that for thirty-two years old, she was still attractive. Everyone else was always telling her so, and she knew women her age who looked sixty. Luke had always insisted she keep creams on her skin and wear wide-brimmed hats to keep the sun off her face—Luke, who was himself becoming tanned and leathered from that same sun; but on him it looked good.

Lately the thought of him made her heart flutter again. She had been in better spirits since her visit with Henny, and her talk with Annie Gates. She wasn't sure what she was going to do or say to Luke when he got back. She only knew that she missed her husband.

Seeing Ty again had awakened an ache for her husband she had not felt in a long time. Ty had come home with Oatmeal and a couple of other men, and she could swear her son had grown even taller over the summer. Her first glance at him when he came through the door, still dusty from the trail, had stirred memories of Luke coming home that way.

She walked over to straighten the bed, remembering what she and Luke had once shared in it. What if something happened to him before they could work out their problems? What if she never got the chance to hold him again, tell him again that she loved him? She walked to the window, looking out at familiar sights, the ranch

Luke loved so much, even more barns and outbuildings, a lovely lawn and gardens around the house now, new men being hired every year, cabins scattered throughout the valley to house them.

Her pleasant thoughts were interrupted when she spotted a buggy coming up the drive. She recognized it as Nial Bentley's, and this time his appearance stirred the old irritation she had once felt for the man. She hurried downstairs, realizing she did not look her best today and not caring. Her thinking had not been this clear and sure since Nathan ran off, and she knew what she had to do. She had to set things straight with Nial before she saw Luke again.

She opened the double front doors just as Nial was tying the horse that pulled his buggy, and she thought how unlike a true rancher he was. There he stood, in a dapper suit, all neat and manicured. His men did all his work for him, while he sat directing things from his stone mansion, or went visiting another man's wife. Why hadn't she noticed all these things before? She was glad Ty was out helping with the hay harvest, and the other three children were upstairs taking lessons from Elsie, who had her six-week-old daughter with her. The birth of Elsie and Peter's baby had been one of the few bright moments at the Double L since Luke had left on the cattle drive.

Nial's eyes lit up at seeing she was already at the door, as though he supposed she was eager to see him.

Lettie did not smile. "Come in, Nial. I want to talk to you."

He frowned then, coming inside. Lettie closed the door and whisked him into the parlor, sliding closed the parlor doors.

"What is it, Lettie, dear?"

Lettie closed her eyes and took a deep breath before turning around. "Don't call me dear, Nial. It isn't right."

He laughed lightly. "Well, we've grown so close—"

"That was my mistake, Nial. I think it would be best if you stopped coming here. You always pick a time when you know Luke is gone."

Nial stiffened, alarmed. What had happened? She was changed. He had been so sure his plan for winning her over was working. "Well, that—that isn't so. I thought he would be back from the cattle drive by now."

"No, you didn't. You know a posse has gone out after cattle rustlers. You know they hoped to intercept Luke so he could go with them. You knew it the day you visited me before I went into town to visit Henny. Some of your own men went with them. Why didn't you tell me, Nial?"

The man reddened slightly. "Well, I—I didn't want you to worry. You have had so much worry and sorrow over these past months—"

"You didn't want me to start fretting over Luke. You didn't want me to think about him at all." She shook her head and walked past him. "I've been a fool, Nial. I don't blame you for what you've been trying to do. I blame myself for letting it happen."

"Lettie, I—"

"Nial, I love Luke." She turned to face him. "Can you possibly understand what we share? Did you really think you could take his place?"

A deep sorrow came into his eyes. "Lettie, I admit that I love you. I can give you so much more—"

"No. You could never give me more in life than Luke can. It's something more than money and title and education, Nial; something you and I could never share." She stepped closer to him. "I never had any romantic intentions about this friendship. You were here when I needed someone to talk to, and you helped the children when they needed it; but I wanted to think it was all out of the goodness of your heart. Now I know everyone in town is talking about us, and I intend to put a stop to the gossip, because it isn't true. And someone…someone who knows men well told me everything you've done has just been a ploy to try to win my heart. Is that true, Nial? Is that the only reason you've been coming here, bringing books about medicine to Robbie, and music for Pearl? Did you truly care that my son had died, or were you just *using* my sorrow to get closer to me?"

Nial shook his head. "Who has told you all of this?"

"It doesn't matter. I only know it all makes sense, considering your behavior the first time you came to Montana." She sighed deeply, rubbing at her eyes. "My God," she muttered.

Nial grasped her arms. "Lettie, listen to me. Please don't hate me. I love you. I've never loved anyone as I love you, not even my first wife. You're everything a man could ever want. I've wanted to say all of this from the moment I laid eyes on you again when I came back from England. Yes, I did try to use your sorrow, but I truly cared that you had lost a son, because I can't stand to see you hurting. Luke is hurting you too. Why do you let him do it?"

Lettie jerked away. "I've done a lot of hurting myself, and this is part of it. I don't want you to come back here alone anymore, or to come when you know I'm alone. Do you understand? In fact, you would be wise to stay away altogether when Luke gets back, because by then he'll probably know you've been coming here all summer, and I don't think he'll be too happy about it. Your friendship and your interest in the children has not been genuine, Nial, and *that* hurts as much as anything Luke or anyone else has done. I couldn't see it, but a good talk with Henny and with Reverend Gooding, and knowing the rumors spreading about us, has opened my eyes to the truth."

"*Henny* put all these ideas in your head?"

"Some. It was Annie Gates who opened my eyes the rest of the way."

"Annie Gates! My God, you went and talked to that whore? She's sleeping with your *husband*, for God's sake! How can you overlook that? How can you forgive such a thing?"

Lettie blinked back tears. "It isn't what you think, and I could never explain in a million years how I could forgive it. One thing I do remember is that *you* were the first one to tell me about Annie and Luke. Now I know why you did it. You were hoping to plant doubt in my heart, trying to confuse me even more about how I felt about Luke. That's why you came that first time, isn't it? You had heard about Luke and Annie, and you had heard I was in a sorry state because of Paul's death. It's just like Henny said. You're like a vulture, circling around, waiting for something to die."

Nial seemed to wither at the words. "Please don't put it that horribly, Lettie. Can you blame a man for trying to capture the woman he loves?"

"Yes, I can, when he uses devious ways to do it; when he plays on that woman's grief; and most certainly when that woman is married to someone else. I'm sorry, Nial, that I cannot return your love; but you always knew that I could not. I'm sorry if my accepting your friendship led you to believe there could be more; but that is partly your fault. You instigated all of this, and you are the one who kept coming back. I never went to you."

He moved closer to her, his eyes moving over her. "No. You never came to me. Every morning I prayed you *would* come. I'd wait until I couldn't stand it any longer, and then I'd come here because I had to see you again." Without warning he grabbed her close, pinning her tight against himself. "Oh, Lettie, just one kiss, just one more chance to make you see you belong with me." He captured her mouth so quickly that at first she could not react. He forced her lips apart, but she managed to turn her face away. He continued kissing her cheek, her neck.

"Stop it, Nial! Stop it, and please just go! Go away from here and never come back!" She pushed at him, but he kept pleading with her, kept his tight hold on her. Suddenly one of the parlor doors was shoved open with a loud thud, and there came the sound of a rifle being cocked.

"Get away from my mother, or I'll kill you!"

Nial stiffened, and Lettie gasped at the sight of Tyler standing at the parlor doors, holding a rifle on Nial. Except for his size, it could have been Luke standing there, blue eyes on fire, a sureness to his stance. "I haven't killed a man yet, but Pa taught me how to shoot real good," the boy told Nial. "My mother asked you to leave this house and not come back. You better do it. There's not one man on this ranch or any in town who would blame me if I shot you. I'm Luke Fontaine's son, and I caught you forcing yourself on my mother."

Nial swallowed. "Well, I do believe you mean it."

"I sure do. Now get going!"

Nial smoothed back his hair and picked up his hat from where he had thrown it on a chair. He looked back at Lettie, who was shaking and rubbing at her lips. "You'll never know how much I love you, Lettie. I'll never forgive myself for this moment. I hope that you can. The last thing I want is for you to hate me. I'm sorry." His voice broke on the last words, and he turned and left.

Lettie stood frozen, listening to the door close, listening through an open window to the clatter of the buggy as Nial drove it away. She wilted into a chair then and wept, not for Nial, but for the fact that Tyler had seen the man trying to kiss her. "None of it is what you think, Ty. I love your father."

Tyler set the rifle aside and came closer, kneeling

beside her. "I know that, Ma. Pa loves you too. He talked about you all the time out on the trail, how he wanted to patch things up, hoped maybe you could talk when he got back. I knew Nial was just taking advantage. I've never liked that man. When I saw him come up the drive, I came into the house, scared I'd hear you telling him you love him. But I heard you say how you feel about Pa, and that all you ever cared about was being friends. When I saw through the crack in the doors— him trying to kiss you—I got mad and went to get the rifle out of Pa's study."

Lettie smiled through tears, reaching out and hugging her son. "Oh, Ty, I've neglected all of you so since Paul died. I'm so very sorry! It's all going to be different once Luke gets back. I promise!"

Ty pulled away, old enough to be embarrassed at the embrace. "We miss Paul too, Ma. You always acted like you were the only one hurting because he died, but it hurt Pa real deep; we all were hurt, especially Robbie."

"I know, Ty."

The boy rose when he heard a horse gallop up to the front of the house. "Maybe that's Pa now." He hurried out, and Lettie got up, quickly taking a handkerchief from her dress pocket and wiping at her tears. The outer door opened and closed, and to her surprise, Ty led Reverend Gooding into the parlor. Her first thought was that he had heard something had happened to Luke. "Reverend! What's wrong?"

The reverend's face showed his sorrow. "I'm afraid it's Henny Doolan," he told her gently. "I know she was your best friend, Mrs. Fontaine. I'm afraid…she passed away this morning. I thought you should know right away."

Henrietta! Her faithful friend! Lettie's whole body suddenly ached with sorrow.

"She died in her sleep, as far as we can tell. I don't think she suffered. I thought, with her husband off with that posse, well, maybe you'd like to handle the funeral arrangements."

Lettie forced herself to stay calm. "Yes. Thank you for thinking of me."

"Poor Will," Ty muttered.

"Yes. Poor Will," Lettie repeated softly. "This will just about kill him." She closed her eyes and prayed for strength. "Hitch the buggy, Ty. We're going into town."

⁓

People stared and followed as Luke and the rest of the posse rode into town, heading for the new hall the ranchers had built for local cattlemen's meetings. They were peppered with questions, most of them from Herbert Grass, a new reporter for the *Billings Extra*. Someone sent for the sheriff, and Luke announced that no questions would be answered until he and the others had a private meeting with Sheriff Tracy. Grass was welcome to come inside, but no one from outside the vigilante group would be allowed. They could read about what happened in the paper tomorrow.

Luke was anxious to get the meeting over with and find Lettie, who he knew would be at Will and Henny's place. On his way back with the rest of the posse, he had stopped at home first, only to discover Henny Doolan had died. Ty told him he and Bob Franks had taken Lettie and Robbie and the girls into town for the funeral, but that they had all come back home afterward without Lettie because she wanted to stay behind and get the house in order for Will.

Poor Lettie didn't even know yet that Will was dead too. He ached at the thought that Lettie had had to bury her best friend alone. How ironic that he in turn had buried Will alone, yet how fitting that Will and Henny had each died without knowing what had happened to the other. Now they were surely together again, and

Henny was free of pain. But what about Lettie's pain? What had her best friend's death done to her? He feared she would slip even farther away from him now.

He rode up to the cattlemen's hall and dismounted, then noticed Nial Bentley had been running with the rest of the crowd and had hurried inside the building. Good! So Nial was in town. He probably thought he was safe as long as he was in a crowd or in the meeting with all the other cattlemen. He'd find out differently! Once this meeting was over, he was going to have more than a talk with the Englishman! He was still hurting over Will's death, and seeing Nial only added to his wrath. Before he left the ranch to ride into town, Ty had told him about the incident in the parlor with Nial and Lettie. The bastard had no right trying to sneak into Lettie's life, no right coming around every time Luke was away. He was proud of what Ty had done, but there was still unfinished business between himself and Nial Bentley.

He tied his horse, and he and the rest of the vigilantes filed into the building along with Sheriff Tracy and the reporter. Joe Parker closed and latched the door behind them to keep out the general public. They all sat down, facing the sheriff, and Herbert Grass hastily turned to a clean sheet on his tablet and began scribbling as Tracy asked for a full report.

Luke rose, glancing over at Nial Bentley with an icy glare. He reveled in the way Bentley looked away from him, his face reddening. The bastard! He'd probably try to hurry out with the others once the meeting was over, but he wasn't going to get away with it! He turned to face the sheriff and spoke up. "We found them, shot it out with them." He removed his hat and wiped sweat from his brow. He hadn't even stopped to clean up at the ranch before coming on into town. When he'd heard about Henny, he'd just wanted to get there quickly and get this over with so he could go to Lettie.

"No prisoners?" Tracy asked, eyebrows arched warily.

"They're all dead," Luke answered, "except one that got away. There were three left alive." They had all agreed not to tell about the fourth man that Tex had shot in the head. "We hanged two of them."

The reporter looked up, mouth open, then began scribbling again, obviously excited that he could write about a vigilante lynching.

"We let one man go," Luke continued. "Name of Clyde Baker. He said he didn't have anything to do with Duncan's death or Mrs. Duncan's rape. Said he'd just joined up with the rest of them. I believed him and we let him go. I think the whole matter scared him bad enough that he'll stay out of Montana. The other two were the Walker boys, who we know were in on the Duncan killing. We hanged them on the spot. Most of the cattlemen got back a good share of the horses and cattle that have been stolen over the summer, but we'll probably never get back anything that was stolen before that. It's probably all in Canada."

"Who got away?" Tracy asked.

"Zack Walker, maybe one other man. We're not sure," Luke answered.

"And it was his sons you hanged?"

Luke nodded.

"Didn't you already have some trouble with them squatting on the Double L?"

"I chased them off last year," Luke answered. "I thought I'd seen the last of them."

Tracy shifted and cleared his throat. "You'd better watch yourself, Luke. All of you should. You've hanged the man's sons. From what I know about Walker, he's from the deep South, one of those clanny types of men who believes in an eye for an eye. There has been enough bloodshed. Let's hope there isn't any more. No casualties on your side?"

Luke felt the pain pierce at his heart again. "Will Doolan. He's dead."

Tracy closed his eyes. "Damn," he muttered. "This town will sorely miss him." He shook his head. "Now at least the man doesn't have to come home to find his wife dead."

"We heard about that," Luke answered. "My son told us when we stopped at the Double L." He glanced at Nial again. "He filled me in on everything," he added, hinting that he knew about Nial's visit.

"What about your face?" Tracy asked. "What happened?"

"I just got pelted with pieces of broken rock," he answered. "It looks worse than it is."

"Someone should thank Annie Gates for the tip-off," Joe Parker spoke up.

They all laughed lightly, wanting to erase the hurt of Will's death.

"Maybe Luke should do the honors," Nial said snidely. "He seems to be close to her."

The laughter died, none of them appreciating the remark about a man they all respected. The reporter was still writing, and Luke glanced his way. "You write anything about that remark, and you'll never do another story for the *Extra* again," he warned.

Grass reddened. "Oh no, Mr. Fontaine. I don't report rumors. Only facts."

"What I said is a fact," Nial spoke up, now looking braver. "Everybody knows it."

Luke turned to glare at Nial, realizing he was just trying to come up with something he thought he could threaten him with so that Luke wouldn't harm him over what had happened between Lettie and him. "You just opened your mouth one too many times," he told the Englishman, his voice calm but cold.

"Uh, I have a list of names," Calvin Briggs interrupted, trying to change the subject. "We took identification off those that had any before we buried them. There were three men we couldn't identify at all, but we wrote down what they looked like in case anybody ever inquires."

Tracy asked the reporter to write down all the information, and the rest of the men broke into conversation. Bentley rose, walking over to converse with those standing farthest away from Luke, but Luke followed him, planting a powerful grip on the man's arm. "I want to see you, out behind the building."

Nial paled. "Yes, well, can't we talk right here? I mean, if it's about my own missing cattle, I'll send some of my men over to pick them up. Are they at the Double L?"

"What's wrong, Bentley?" Luke sneered. "You don't want to come get them yourself, now that *I'm* home?" Luke kept his voice low, but those standing near could hear.

Nial smiled nervously, casting a desperate look to the others, but he knew by their eyes where their loyalty lay. Luke Fontaine had a score to settle, and they were not about to stop him. There wasn't a man there who didn't respect Luke and Lettie both, and Nial realized that whatever gossip had been circulating, not one of them was going to blame Lettie Fontaine. Suddenly he wished he had not been in town when the posse returned, wished curiosity had not compelled him to come to the meeting; but, after all, he belonged to this group. He had as much right to be here as any of them. "There really is nothing to talk about, Luke," he said, facing the man squarely.

Luke gripped his arm so tightly that the man winced. "Get your ass outside, or I'll make a scene right here and give the reporter something to write about our resident Englishman who likes to move in on other men's wives," he said in a near whisper. "Is that how you want it, Bentley? You want this whole town to ostracize you? And do you want to do that to Lettie?"

Nial swallowed, jerking his arm away and

straightening his jacket. He picked up his hat and headed for the back door.

"Keep the rest of the men inside," Luke ordered Joe Parker, "especially that reporter."

"Sure, Luke."

Luke hurried after Nial, suspecting the man might try to run off the minute he got outside. He reached the door just as Nial was going through it, and before Nial could turn around, Luke wrapped a strong arm around his throat and dragged him a few feet, then slammed him against the outside wall. "It's time to get something straight, Bentley! I gave you fair warning a long time ago, but you apparently decided not to heed it!" He pressed the man against the wall and clamped a strong hand around his throat so that his eyes began to bulge. "If I ever hear you've come anywhere near my wife again when I'm gone, you're a *dead* man! I don't care if I hang for it! You got that straight?"

Nial managed a nod, and Luke released his grip slightly. "Did you plant ideas in Lettie's head about Annie Gates?"

Nial began to tremble. "I...I only told her what anyone might have. Everyone in town knows you were sleeping with the woman! How could you do that to your wife? She's a wonderful woman who deserves better."

"You don't know anything about my private thoughts and the reasons for anything I do." Luke sneered. "I don't need the likes of you telling me what a good woman Lettie is. She's the mother of my *children*, for God's sake! I'm not going to dignify any of this with explanations about Annie or my marriage or anything else. Lettie and I will straighten out our problems, and *you* will stay *out* of it from here on. Lettie Fontaine is my woman, and don't you ever forget it!"

He released his hold. Nial swallowed, rubbing at his throat and taking deep breaths. He faced Luke, panting.

"If you think anything went on between me and Lettie, it didn't. I was simply there to help her, because I happen to love her, and I don't care that you know it. She needed friendship, someone to talk to. God knows *you* weren't around."

Luke's face darkened with rage. "So you thought you'd move right in and take over." He looked the man over with contempt. "You fool! Do you think I'd believe Lettie would ever cheat on her husband? There was nothing like that between you because Lettie Fontaine isn't that kind of woman, no matter how lonely or desperate she might get. It's no thanks to you, though, is it? I heard from Ty how you tried to keep things from getting too serious. You tried so hard, you forced a kiss from her! You forced it because you knew it was the only way you would ever get to touch my wife that way!"

"It wasn't that way—"

"My son doesn't lie!" Luke cut in. He slammed a big fist into Nial's gut, and the Englishman grunted and bent over. Luke grasped hold of the man's collar and raised a booted foot to his privates, then slammed his fist into Nial's left jaw, sending the man sprawling into a pile of empty crates. He walked to stand over the man. "That was my last warning, Bentley! Next time I have to light into you, you'll never get up again!"

Luke turned away and headed back inside, rubbing at a sore right hand, and flexing it. He wiped his bloody knuckles on his pants, then took a deep breath and reentered the cattlemen's hall to get his hat.

"Everything all right, Luke?" Joe Parker asked him.

Luke's blue eyes glittered with satisfaction. "Everything is just fine. Just keep that reporter away from the back alley."

Joe grinned. "There ain't nobody dead back there, is there?"

Luke donned his hat. "No. But he's probably wishing

he was." He walked outside and mounted his horse, heading for Will and Henny's place.

❧

Lettie bent down to lay some daisies over Henny's grave. A bird sang in a nearby bush, as though to thank her. She remembered how Henny had loved to sit and watch the birds, how she laughed when her cats would chase them. Three of those cats lay about the grave site now, following their mistress from the familiar log cabin to the graveyard in town, still wanting to crawl into her lap.

Forty-four. The woman had only been forty-four, but had looked like a shriveled little woman of seventy when she was laid out for visitors. *In this land you need solid friendships.* She remembered Henny telling her those words when they first met. How true they were. *And you need a good, strong man who loves you, no matter what...and if you really love your man, you'll let him live his dream and not try to stop him.*

She rose, a soft wind blowing her gray dress. Her sadness was not just for the loss of a friend, but the knowledge that years from now, there would be no one left to mourn this woman's passing. Henny had lost track of her family, who had never bothered to come back and try to find her, visit her. There were no children to carry on the name and the memory. How sad that a person could be so treasured one day, and forgotten the next. Someday Montana would be a state, she had no doubt. How many of its future citizens would ever know or care about Henrietta Doolan, one of the true pioneers?

She swallowed against more tears, her throat hurting fiercely. She vowed then and there that she would begin keeping a record of people like Will and Henrietta, that she would form some kind of historical society that would preserve Montana's precious past, in books, perhaps even museums. Little Paul would be part of those records, one of the children who lost his life because of living so remote from help. And there was Ben Garvey, who had lost his life against outlaw buffalo hunters; and Nathan, the "white Indian" who was like a ghost to her now.

She felt older today, the reality of death visiting her again. But the nearby birdsong reminded her that life went on, and the thought of Katie, Tyler, Pearl, and Robbie were examples of that. The incident with Nial had brought Ty and her closer. Now there was one last fence to be mended. Henny's death brought home that she had no one to turn to now but Luke. The woman's last words to her had been that she should be a wife again.

Tears trickled down her face. She brushed gently at the still-fresh earth mounded over the grave. The service two days ago had been touching, the reverend speaking just the right words for a woman like Henny. Half the town had been there, for half the town owed Henny something in one way or another. Lettie had insisted that the woman's pipe be buried with her, and one of Will's buckskin jackets, so she would have something of his to keep her warm, something that carried her husband's scent. It seemed only right.

"Lettie?"

The voice startled her. She turned and rose, her heart suddenly pounding, and everything she had planned to say and do when she saw her husband again left her. She just stood there, not sure what was right and what was wrong, until he held out his arms. "Luke!" She ran to him, and in the next moment she was lost in his embrace, relishing the feel of his powerful arms, weeping his name as she rested her head on the shoulder that had always been strong for her. Her feet were off the ground as he held her close, and he whispered her name several times over.

"I knew I'd find you here," he said, finally setting her on her feet. "I heard about Henny back at the ranch, came straight to town. I never even stopped to clean up. I'm dirty and—"

"It doesn't matter," she answered, still clinging to him. "Nothing matters but that you're here. I was afraid something would happen to you, and we'd never get the chance to see each other again. Oh, Luke, we have so much to talk about."

Luke held her away from him so that he could look at her face. Something had changed. This was not the Lettie he had left behind. He had figured that telling her the things he needed to tell her might be impossible, that she would still be the silent, withdrawn woman he'd been unable to reach for so long. It was just too bad they had to face this first, the loss of their best friends. He had feared Henny's death would plunge his wife deeper into despair and silence, but the way she touched him, the way she looked at him...

"Luke, what happened? Your face!" She reached up to touch the several red scabs left from being sprayed with rock.

"I'm all right. A bullet broke some rock I was standing behind and the pieces hit me in the face."

A bullet! She could have lost him! Being here in his arms made her feel like a young girl again, the girl who had followed her new husband to Montana. "Did you get the rustlers?"

He closed his eyes. "I'll tell you about it later. It wasn't very pretty." He squeezed her arms. "Lettie, Will is dead too."

Her eyes widened in dismay. "No!"

Luke nodded. "Shot by one of the rustlers. He's the only one who got hit." He glanced at Henny's grave. "It's almost like God knew he wouldn't want to go on without Henny, and she couldn't have gone on without Will, so he took them both."

Thunder rolled in the distance, and dark clouds

loomed on the horizon. "They should be buried beside each other," Lettie said sadly, resting her head against his chest.

"I wanted to bring him back, but we were too far out, and in this heat it would have been impossible. They're together now, though. It doesn't matter where they're buried, Lettie. Neither one of them is in their grave."

She wept quietly. "Thank God you're back. I have so much to tell you, Luke."

He sighed deeply. "I have a lot to tell you also. I want to take you away alone, Lettie, maybe out to the northern line camp. It will be safer this time. I'm taking several men along to repair a windmill at one of the watering holes. They'll camp in the valley below the cabin, so they'll be close by, and we won't have to worry about something happening like the last time we went off alone."

"That was five years ago," she said softly. "We never did go off to be alone after that."

"That's where we went wrong. From now on, once a year, no matter what is happening, we're going to find time for us, just us. I won't let work at the ranch or the children get in the way. I have to take care of some things here in town that I know Will would have wanted me to do for him, and I want to spend some time with Katie and Pearl and Robbie. Then we'll leave."

She looked up at him, the thought of him being with Annie Gates stirring her desire to be a wife to him again. She would never again give him reason to go to a woman like that. "I have so much to tell you."

He closed his eyes and leaned down to kiss her hair. "And I have a lot to tell you. For now just believe that I love you, Lettie, and I'm sorry I allowed us to drift so far apart."

"It was mostly my fault. I never should have blamed—"

He put his fingers to her lips. "Not now." A sharp clap of thunder shattered the heavens. "We'd better get to

Will's place. He probably has some papers of some kind that shows what he wants done with his ranch. I'm not sure. I just figured I'd look into it for him, talk to that lawyer, Syd Greene, make sure things are done properly."

"Yes, Will would want that." She studied the blue eyes that were not so cold now. "I love you, Luke." The tears came again. "I never stopped."

He leaned down and met her lips lightly, and she relished the taste of his mouth on hers again, a warm, sweet kiss that told of something much more wonderful to come. "I love you too," he whispered. He put an arm around her and led her away from the grave, and rain began to sprinkle the fresh earth. The cats at the grave curled up against the stone, seemingly unaffected by the weather. It was warm there, near their mistress.

Twenty-two

"WHAT ARE YOU GOING TO DO WITH WILL'S PROPERTY?" Lettie pulled on her flannel nightgown in the darkness away from the light of the campfire, so that the Double L men who had accompanied them could not see her. She moved into the firelight then and settled into her bedroll.

"I don't know yet," Luke answered after taking a moment to consider her question. "Will told me a long time ago he wanted to leave it to me if anything happened to him, but I never thought much about what I would do with it. I figured he'd be around a good long time yet."

Lettie pulled the blankets around her neck and looked up at the stars, feeling safe because her very able husband was near her, just on the other side of their campfire. Four more Double L men were camped nearby, close enough to come if there was trouble, far enough that they could not hear Luke's and her conversation.

Luke wanted this trip to the northern line camp to be as private for them as possible, but he also wanted to be sure that nothing would ever again happen like the first time they had ridden off together to be alone. He was a little worried about Zack Walker looking for revenge, and he had left instructions for plenty of men to keep an eye on Mae and the children while they were gone.

"You miss Will terribly, don't you?" Lettie asked.

Luke moved his arms behind his head. "Just like you miss Henny. The hard part was, one minute he was there talking to me, and the next he was gone."

It was two days ago that Luke had come to Billings to fetch her. They had stayed one night at Will and Henny's, had found Will's handwritten will saying he wanted Luke to have everything. It was really more of a letter, not very well done, written by a man who had never had much schooling. "I don't want nobody but my best friend, Luke Fontaine, to have my *proppity*," it had read. "*Ain't* no better man around. He'll do what's best with it, and he'll take care of my Henny for as long as she needs taken care of." Lettie smiled at the words, written just the way Will would have spoken them; but there was no Henny to be taken care of. It still didn't seem possible they were both gone. The loss had affected both Luke and her deeply, and combined with being apart for over three months and the problems they had had for almost two years now, had made them continue to feel a little like strangers. They kept busy sorting through things and closing up the Doolan house until Luke could decide what to do with it. There had been little talk about their own personal problems, and the night before they had slept in separate rooms at home, as they had been doing for months now. They both silently understood that there were too many things to talk about before they could sleep together again, make love again. They had left early in the morning for the northern line camp, but it would be another day before they reached it.

Lettie studied the sky, feeling more at peace than she had since Nathan ran off and little Paul... Was he up there somewhere, laughing, playing?

"Have I told you how beautiful you looked today in that riding outfit?"

Luke's words interrupted her thoughts, and she smiled. "You haven't told me I was beautiful for quite a long time."

He turned to look at her, aching to have her beside him. Not tonight. With four of his men nearby, this was not the time or place to make love to his woman for the first time in almost two years. But he vowed that by tomorrow night their differences would be settled and Lettie Fontaine would be reminded of the pleasures of making love. "You've *always* looked beautiful to me. I just…" He picked up a stick and poked at the fire, causing little sparks to scatter into the air. "I just wasn't sure you wanted to hear me say that or much of anything else these last few months."

Lettie thought how he hadn't changed himself, except to look more tanned and brawny and rugged than when she'd first married him. He had taken off his shirt, and in the firelight his arms and shoulders were as hard-muscled as fourteen years ago when they first married. "I'm sorry, Luke. So much of that was my fault."

He sighed and lay back. "I could have done more to help what you were going through. We could have helped each other. We broke our promise, Lettie, to tell each other everything we were feeling." He turned his head to look at her again. "What happened while I was gone? You seemed different when I got back, more like the Lettie I used to know."

A wolf howled in the distant hills, and others began to join in. Lettie thought how the sound used to frighten her, but now she realized she probably couldn't go to sleep without it. "I had a long talk with Henny." *And with Annie Gates.* "I saw her sitting there all crippled up, childless, looking so much older than she really was; and I knew it was wrong to pine over my own losses, when I still had so much left to me. I had already been thinking that way; Henny just helped clarify things for me. It's so sad to realize that was our last conversation. Her very last deed on earth was to help me save my marriage." She looked over at him. "I guess I never stopped to think until lately that it could really end."

Luke rose up to rest on one elbow. "No, Lettie, it could

never end; not on my part, anyway." He read the question in her eyes. "You're wondering about Annie Gates."

Lettie looked away then, feeling the crimson of anger and jealousy come into her cheeks.

"Annie is a good woman in some ways, Lettie, but she never did and never could mean a damn thing to me," Luke continued. "I might as well tell you so you can digest it for a while before we reach the cabin tomorrow. I slept with Annie, but only once, and only because I thought I'd go crazy with the want of you. I'm sorry, because I know it hurts you. It meant absolutely nothing."

Lettie could not control the tears that came then. She quickly wiped at her eyes, swallowing and breathing deeply to find her voice. Luke flopped back down, putting a hand to his head. "I shouldn't have said anything," he apologized. "I just figured someone had told you about Annie and me, so I thought I'd better clear it all up."

"Nial Bentley told me about you and Annie," she said with a sob. "I was too blind to realize what he was trying to do." She reached over to her supply pack that lay nearby and fished for a handkerchief. "I know you're wondering the same thing about Nial that I was wondering about you and Annie." She sniffed in another sob. "Oh, Luke, I would never, never—"

"You don't even have to say it. Nial Bentley is a closed chapter in both our lives."

Lettie glanced at his right hand, which rested on his chest. It was still stiff and swollen. "You told me you hurt your hand fighting one of the rustlers, but that was several days ago. That looks like a more recent injury to me. You saw Nial, didn't you? You saw him and you hit him."

Luke lay there quietly for a moment. "I had a right to."

"Where? When?"

"Don't worry. Nobody saw us, and I didn't do any permanent damage. The bastard actually admitted to me, your own husband, that he loves you." He rubbed at his eyes. "Damned if I can blame him. I don't doubt there are other men I know who secretly admire you. They'd be crazy not to, but they're not stupid enough to go sneaking around actually trying to win you over behind my back. If he wants to try to get my land or my cattle, that's one thing; but my woman is another. That's what got to me, especially when Ty told me about him trying to kiss you. The son of a bitch thinks his money and title can win him anything."

My woman. The words sounded good, stirred something deep inside Lettie. Suddenly she wished they were already at the cabin, so she could show him she could love him in a special way that Annie Gates never could. She found the handkerchief and used it to wipe at more tears. "Ty reminded me so much of you that day, standing there protecting me, looking so sure. Nial was truly afraid of him. Ty is exactly like you, in looks and temperament. He and I drew a lot closer that day, and when I realized how Nial had used my grief and my children to try to get to me, I began to see a lot of things more clearly." She felt better then, wiped at her eyes again, keeping the handkerchief in her fist. "It looks like Ty is the only son who will walk in your shoes, Luke."

"Robbie will come around."

"Robbie wants to be a doctor."

"He's only twelve."

"He'll never get over Paul dying while he was helping take care of him. Being a doctor means everything to him, Luke. You've got to let your children do what's in them to do. Katie already wants to teach, Pearl has her music, and Robbie wants to go to the University of Michigan when he's old enough, if he can qualify. He's been reading books on medicine, devours them."

"Books Nial Bentley gave him. He innocently showed

some of them to me last night, little realizing how I felt knowing that bastard has been trying to take my place. I don't like another man planting ideas in my children's heads. I need Robbie on the ranch. I want all my..." He hesitated, realizing there were only two sons left. He wondered if the ache of losing little Paul would ever go away. "Both my sons to be a part of the Double L."

"A man's heart has to be in his work, Luke. You know that better than anyone. You had a dream, and Ty's is the same. Robbie has a different dream."

Luke scowled. "And a mother always sticks up for her children, whether they're right or wrong."

"Is it so wrong to want to be a doctor? To help people? Save lives?"

He sighed deeply. "You *are* back to your old self." He turned on his side again. "We didn't come out here to talk about the children."

"We have to, Luke. The only one you're really close to is Ty. The other three love and miss their father. When we get back home, you need to spend some time with them. Your idea of sharing time with them is to have them all come out and help with the work, but they aren't all cut out for herding cattle and roping and branding. You've got to face that, Luke, do other things with them, listen to Pearl's piano playing, listen to Katie and Robbie tell you what they want in life, share their dreams. We can't talk about us without bringing them into it, because they *are* us. That's why it was so hard to bury Paul. Burying a child is like burying a part of your own body. Reverend Gooding told me—"

"Lettie, I don't want to talk about Paul. I can't."

She turned to face him. "We *have* to talk about him! That's what this is all about. Paul's death is what drove us apart."

Luke lay back down and turned his back to her, and for several minutes there was only the sound of the crackling fire and the wolves howling to each other in the soft moonlight.

"Luke, the misunderstandings that come from silence can bring more pain than shouted words. It's silence that has kept us apart, and I'm just as much at fault as you."

He finally turned to lie on his back again, but he looked at the sky, not at Lettie. "I feel like such a failure, Lettie, as a father, a husband, a protector. If I hadn't chosen to settle where I did, we'd probably still have both Nathan and Paul. Do you think I don't realize you blame me for that? Do you think that if I could give up everything I have built here just to have them both back, that I wouldn't do it?"

Her eyes teared again. "Oh, Luke, I know I made you feel to blame, but I was so wrong. I was looking for someone to blame, so I wouldn't have to face my own guilt."

He finally met her eyes. "*Your* guilt? For what?"

"Luke, I made the choice to come here with you, knowing how difficult and dangerous it would be for all of us, especially Nathan. I was young and madly in love, and I couldn't believe anything bad could ever happen to my son. And after Nathan disappeared, you offered to give up the ranch and move closer to town. I'm the one who wanted to stay right where we were, in case Nathan ever returned. I'm the reason we lived so far from town when Paul got sick." She sighed deeply. "I'm not so sure any doctor could have done much more for him than we did. It isn't only the fact that we couldn't get help that I feel terrible about. My guilt over Paul is…" She hesitated, always finding it difficult to talk about her baby. "I will always regret not giving Paul the time and attention he so craved those last few weeks before he got sick."

The memory overwhelmed her again, and she lay quietly crying. She never heard Luke get up. She only knew that in the next moment he was there beside her, pulling her into his arms. He pulled one of her blankets around her shoulders and kissed her hair. "Lettie, I think it's natural to blame ourselves for all the things we might have done differently. I know now that it's all just a reaction to losing someone precious to us. We want to make it better by blaming someone else; and then we turn the blame on ourselves, thinking that by doing some kind of penance, we can bring them back."

"I was so wrong to blame you at first. I know what that must have done to you. Until these last few months when you stayed away so much, you were a good father, Luke. I just want that man back. I want my husband back."

"He's right here, Lettie. Come sleep beside me tonight. I just want to hold you." His voice broke on the last words. "I miss little Paul so much, Lettie." He wept. "We should share that grief."

She wrapped her arms around his neck, and her own tears came harder then. "He's up there, Luke," she whispered. "He's up there, playing among the stars."

༺❦༻

"I want you to come back with me, Irv. You and your boys. You're my brother, and them nephews of mine is like my own sons, sons I've lost." Zack Walker downed another shot of whiskey. "Luke Fontaine and that bunch with him had no right hangin' Johnny and Jeeter. Killin' Matt Duncan was self-defense, and the boys was just havin' a little fun with the man's wife. They didn't hurt her none. She probably enjoyed it."

He did not notice Irv's wife cast him a look of disdain. The woman had long ago learned to keep her mouth shut when it came to having her own opinion about anything. She had suffered enough beatings to know when to keep quiet. She pushed back a piece of stringy hair and turned to stir a pot of stew. Sweat stained her plain, long-sleeved dress, which was too warm for such a hot day; but her husband refused to allow her to show any part of her body but her hands and face, except to his own groping hands at night. That had resulted in ten children, the three oldest, Ben, Larry, and Jim, already twenty-two, twenty, and nineteen, respectively. Her youngest was five. In spite of how they had been conceived, she still loved her children, and she did not like the idea that her brother-in-law was proposing now—that her husband and three oldest sons go with him on a journey of revenge; but no one was going to ask her opinion, and she dared not offer it.

"Think about it, Irv. How would you feel if it was *your* boys you seen strung up like pigs?"

Irv scratched at a graying beard, his dark, beady eyes studying his brother's own aging face. "Back home in Tennessee, we wouldn't have let somethin' like this go," he drawled.

"And not here either! Come back up to Montana with me, Irv. We'll gather some more men so's we have plenty. We'll find a way to pay Fontaine back for my sons, and we'll ride on up into Canada with some of the finest cattle and horses anywhere around; or we can bring them back down here to Wyoming, take 'em on down the Outlaw Trail. There's plenty of outlaws and rustlers there who'd pay us in gold for the stolen beef. I can see you ain't makin' it on this here ranch."

"Some big rancher north of here cut off my water supply. My grass dried up, and I had to sell my beef."

"There, you see what I mean? You've had the same problems I've had with Fontaine, the big landowners comin' down on us poor folks who are strugglin' to make ends meet. It ain't fair, Irv. In this family we believe in an eye for an eye, and it's time to get even. On our way back into Montana we can rustle some beef away from that rancher north of here who has given you so much trouble. We'll be helpin' each other, Irv. You must know how important this is to me. I've rode day and night just to get here as fast as I could."

Irv sighed deeply, glancing at his wife. "Ought to be enough food stored up that the woman will get by till I get back, and Billy and Drew are old enough to stay here and take care of their ma."

"But we want to go with you, Pa!" Billy spoke up.

"Shut up, boy! I told all of you to sit quiet and let me talk to your uncle!"

All ten Walker children sat in a circle around the big wooden table, faces dirty, hair oily, clothes soiled, faces stony. They too had learned from an early age to be silent unless given permission to speak.

"Liz, Marybeth, come help me dish up the stew," their mother ordered.

The two older girls immediately obeyed. Thirteen-year-old Dennis sat pouting. He too wanted to go with his father and uncle to steal cattle and see how exciting it might be to ride into Montana and take revenge against a rich, powerful rancher like Luke Fontaine.

"What do you think, boys?" Irv directed the question at his three oldest sons. "You willin' to take the risk to defend the Walker family honor?"

"Yes, sir," Benny answered immediately.

"I'll be glad to go," Jim said. *Glad to get the hell away from this boring place*, he thought.

"Sure, I'll go, Pa," Larry added. "I can shoot real straight."

Zack Walker grinned. "Hey, boys, Luke Fontaine's got a daughter just about old enough to be findin' out about men. I seen her in town once. Her name's Katie, and she's right pretty. I'd guess she's about thirteen or fourteen by now."

All three boys grinned, and Zack directed his gaze to his brother. "I can't think of no better way to get revenge than to soil that man's own daughter. Let the Walker boys stick her good. We'll take the man's cattle *and* his daughter; and maybe we'll get one of his sons too."

"How are we gonna get in there to do it?"

"I'll have to think on it. We'll find a way. He figures I'm long gone, that I'd be too afraid to come back. But that son of a bitch don't scare me none. I've got a little surprise for him."

"You sure we ain't bitin' off more than we can chew?"

"Not if we plan it right and bring in some more men to help us." Zack put out his hand. "After it's over, we'll go get Johnny's wife and the grandkids. They're all still in northern Montana, where we've been livin' in a deserted cabin. You with me, Brother?"

Irv grinned, displaying yellowed teeth, one of them missing in front. He grasped his brother's hand firmly. "I'm with you."

⌘

"I'm thinking of forming a society for preserving the memories of people like Will and Henny," Lettie told Luke. She picked up his plate, smiling at the fact that he had eaten two huge bowls of beef stew and nearly half a loaf of bread. The beef, of course, came from Double L cattle, a smoked roast she had brought along with potatoes and vegetables so she could cook her husband a real meal once they arrived at the cabin. She had even baked an apple pie, and she carried it over to the table to slice it. "I want to be sure people like that are remembered. We could save some of Will's buckskin clothes, some of Henny's dresses, things like that. I think you should also start saving certain tools and equipment as they become outdated. Years from now those things could be of value. I remember visiting a museum in St. Louis when I was little, and the courthouse where people used to gather before heading out on the Oregon Trail. With the railroad being built, things like that are becoming a part of history. I want to preserve Montana's history, Luke." She sat down again. "Men like Will...and like you...should be remembered."

He put a hand over hers. "It's the women who make it all possible. You mark my word. Someday the women will be remembered with a lot more enthusiasm and melancholy than the men."

She smiled softly. "Maybe." She studied his dark, strong hand, feeling almost like a newlywed again, even more nervous because they had let themselves become such strangers. An approaching storm had turned dusk to an early darkness, and she knew that tonight… "Do you want some pie?"

Luke noticed her avoiding his eyes. "Lettie, let's save the pie for later."

Thunder rumbled in the mountains that surrounded them, and Lettie remembered his first kiss…on the wagon train west. It had been storming then too. She finally met his eyes. "Tell me that being with Annie wasn't as pleasurable as being with your wife."

His handsome blue eyes showed the anguish he felt for having turned to another woman. "Do you really need to ask?"

She looked down at the table again. "Sometimes I hated you, Luke, but it was only because I loved you so much. Does that make any sense?"

He squeezed her hand. "Yes. I've felt the same way about you at times, mainly because I hated *myself*, for failing you. I hated the fact that you came from a life that I couldn't give you for a long time. I figured you were beginning to resent the fact that I've made you live in a place where there are no theaters, no paved streets, no formal schools. I wanted to hate you because it was easier than loving you and having you reject me for someone who could truly give you the finer life, travel with you to Europe, take you to the theaters of New York—"

"Oh, Luke, surely you know those things mean nothing to me! How could I enjoy those things without the man I love at my side?"

"A bastard, who has had to struggle for every bit of what we have and who has made you struggle right along with him and has put you through hell. Nial Bentley comes from a highly respected English family. He's a man whose parentage is legitimate, a man for whom the money will never run out. If his ranch went under tomorrow, he'd still be well set."

Lettie shook her head. "I would rather have nothing material and have you at my side, than to have all of England's wealth and have to share it with a man whose touch does nothing for me, a man whose love can never be anything but shallow, who wants me only as a decoration on his arm. He did not build what he has with his own two hands. He didn't risk his life for it. And he did not father my children." She felt her cheeks warm at the last words, and she looked down again. "I feel so strange," she whispered. "Being here in this cabin reminds me of the early years."

Luke got up, came around and took her arm, gently pulling her out of the chair. The thunder came closer, but it could not rumble any louder than the thundering of their hearts as Luke pulled her close and embraced her warmly, kissing her hair, her forehead, her eyes. She kept those eyes closed, turned her face up more so that his lips could caress her cheeks, her nose, finally her mouth, in a sweet, warm, provocative kiss that awakened buried desires.

There was no ignoring the desperate need they both felt from that moment on. He picked her up in his arms and carried her through a curtained door into a little room that held only a bed and chest of drawers. Their kisses became heated and hungry, and the feel of his hands moving over her hips, her breasts, only made her want him more. She wanted to prove to him that he did not need someone like Annie Gates to pleasure him; and Luke in turn wanted to prove that this woman belonged only to Luke Fontaine, that no man could love her with as much passion, no man could please her more.

In the deep passion of renewed love their clothes came off with eagerness, until naked skin touched, pressed, rubbed. Nothing needed to be said, and no preliminaries were necessary. All the intimacies, the tasting and exploring, would come later. They had all night to do this a hundred ways, all night to go more slowly, to savor every inch of each other's bodies again. For the moment, there was only the need to brand and be branded, to share that one special thing that was special only for them, to express long-buried love in the most intimate way, the ultimate joy of the union of two bodies, two people who had shared great joy and great sorrow.

Outside the cabin the summer storm raged full force, just as their own physical needs raged to be released. Lettie gasped when he entered her with the full force of his need. It had been so long for her that it was almost painful, for he was greatly swollen with pent-up desire. His shaft was hot and hungry, and he moved in wild rhythm, groaning her name, his heated body sliding against her skin, his broad shoulders hovering over her possessively, protectively.

She had never wanted him with such aching passion, not even in those first years of marriage. The troubles they had seen had come full circle and now seemed to bond them more closely, sealing vows made long ago. He grasped her hips and shoved himself deep, shuddering when his life spilled into her, and they both knew, in that moment, that nothing, no sorrow, no hardship, no other human being, could ever again come between them.

Twenty-three

"I swear, Luke, it's just not fair." Joe Parker laughed and finished a cup of punch. "You've got the prettiest wife and prettiest two daughters of anybody around."

Luke gave Katie and Pearl each a light hug, his arms around both of them. He was proud to bring his family to the spring dance being held at Billings's new, larger town hall. It felt good to rejoin society after a long, cold winter, good to be out in public as a family again. The past winter had been one of discovery. He had made a point of staying home more, sharing wintry nights with Lettie and the four children around the fireplace. There had been a lot of talking, and more than a few tears. They had read together, played games together, and Pearl had entertained them nearly every night with her piano playing. The family had never been closer.

Behind the refreshment table, Lettie dipped more punch into Joe's cup. "These pretty girls get their looks totally from their mother," Luke answered Joe with a grin.

"Oh, Luke, Katie looks just like you," Lettie answered, handing the cup back to Joe.

Joe nodded. "Pearl there, now she gets her looks from her ma; but Lettie's right about Katie. She's tall like her pa and has your dark hair, Luke. I guess she's just a real pretty mixture of the both of you. How old are you now, Katie?"

Katie blushed, always shy. Tonight she worried that the elegant, mint green dress her mother had had specially made for her fit her too perfectly. The darts in the bodice drew the dress over her developing breasts in a way that made them look too big for her thin build, and she felt that she should hide them, wear something looser. Lettie had insisted she looked beautiful and not at all out of proportion. Part of her enjoyed the fact that she was becoming a woman in many ways, but the child in her was embarrassed by her blossoming body. "I'm almost fourteen," she answered Joe.

"Fourteen! Girl, you look closer to sixteen."

Katie wondered why he said that. Because of her breasts? She folded her arms over them self-consciously.

"You see that line of boys over there?" Joe pointed to four young men who stood across the way, watching other couples dance. "They're all wanting to ask you to dance, Katie, but they're afraid because you're so pretty, and because you're Luke Fontaine's daughter. They're not sure your pa wants you dancin' with young men yet."

Katie reddened more. "I don't really want to dance anyway," she said shyly.

"Katie, it's all right if one of them asks you," Luke told her, giving her another squeeze.

"I don't think so, Pa." Katie wasn't sure how she felt about boys. Only lately had she begun to look at them differently, with a new curiosity.

"I'll dance with them," Pearl spoke up with a dimpled grin. "I'm only ten, but I can dance."

"Pearl! Ten-year-old girls don't dance with anyone but their brothers or father," Lettie scolded, a teasing smile on her face.

Katie wished she could be more like Pearl, who didn't have a bashful bone in her body. It was easy to see that Pearl was going to be the most beautiful sister, at least in Katie's eyes; and Pearl was the most talented child in the family. She could picture her sister attending a fancy school far away and making a great splash with her piano playing. She didn't fear anything, and she loved attention. Katie, on the other hand, wanted only to stay close to home and maybe teach school and read quietly in her spare time. She hated attention as much as Pearl loved it, and sometimes she even wished she were not a Fontaine. Then people wouldn't stare at her as the oldest daughter of the richest rancher in Montana Territory.

"Right now I think it's Lettie and I who will dance," Luke told his daughters. He let go of Pearl and put his hand out to Lettie, already aching for her again just from the sight of her this evening. He had spent less time on the roundup and branding this spring, had let the Double L men do most of the work. For the first time since they married, he gave more of his attention to his wife that spring than he did to the ranch and cattle. He had come to realize how important his family was, and all winter he had felt like a newlywed. It was good to have his wife back in their bed.

Lettie asked Pearl to come around the table and serve punch for a while. The girl gladly obeyed, and Katie told her parents she was going to find Robbie. Luke whisked his wife onto the dance floor, fully agreeing with Joe Parker. He did have the prettiest wife in Montana. Tonight she wore her deep red hair twisted into a pile of curls on the top of her head, and her sea-green silk dress matched her provocative eyes. It fit her slender waist perfectly, accented all the right curves, curves he intended to trace with his fingers later tonight.

Because the ranch was so far from town, they would stay the night in Billings. Outlaws and wild animals still made travel at night dangerous, but that was not the reason for Luke's decision. He simply still had not gotten over the worry that the vengeful Zack Walker might try to harm his family. He had taken rooms at the Billings Inn, a new hotel built by William Richards, who had come to Billings six months ago to open a bank, then had built the hotel.

Richards was himself the son of a wealthy banker from Illinois. He had come to Montana with his wife, Betty, and their daughter, Alice, to branch out on his own in a growing community. Alice was twelve, too young to be in love; but it was obvious that the girl was infatuated with thirteen-year-old Tyler. She had met him when Luke and Lettie had invited the Richardses to the ranch for dinner as a welcome to the area. Ever since then, Alice made a point of finding a way to be near Ty whenever they were at the same social event.

"I see Alice and some of her friends are over there giggling and having a good time with Ty and a few other boys," Lettie told Luke as they danced.

Luke looked in their direction. "Young love," he said with a grin.

Lettie watched them a moment longer. "Maybe. I have seen Ty and Alice just talking sometimes, like good friends. I suppose being good friends is the best way to start, if you *are* going to fall in love."

Their eyes held. "I suppose," Luke answered. "We didn't have time for such preliminaries. The friendship just sort of developed right along with the rest of it."

"Thank goodness," Lettie said with a smile. She sighed deeply, looking him over. "Luke, you look so handsome tonight in your suit. I haven't seen you dressed this way in so long."

He made a face. "I hate it. I can't wait to get back into my work clothes." He pulled her a little closer, making her blush at his boldness in front of others. "You, on the other hand—" His eyes dropped to drink in the tantalizing fullness of her breasts, which showed teasingly above the white lace of the scooped neckline of her dress. "I doubt any man here is noticing my suit. You look good enough to eat."

The suggestive remark sent a ripple of passion through her as she held her husband's gaze. Since their physical and emotional reunion, the sex between them had never been better. They had gone beyond anything they had ever shared before, rekindled hot coals into raging flames. She felt like a whole woman again, beautiful, alive, glad to have her husband back, grateful for her remaining four beautiful children. "I'll be glad to get to our room tonight," she said softly.

"We'll gather the kids after a few more dances and do just that," Luke answered, hunger in his eyes. He whirled her around the dance floor, thinking how far they had come over the fifteen years they had been in Montana, and how he couldn't have made it through those early years without this woman at his side. It was Lettie's wisdom that had brought in Jeremy Shane's men, who ran the Fontaine copper mines; her forward thinking that had compelled him to try raising Herefords; her faithful strength that had gotten him this far.

It was just too bad that the Herefords had to be Nial Bentley's idea. The thought of the man trying to steal his way into Lettie's bed still brought on anger, jealousy, and possessiveness that would probably never leave him, even though Nial had married Chloris Greene. The newlyweds were in Europe, and Luke was glad. Married or not, he still did not like Nial being near Lettie. At least Nial's marriage had helped quell any rumors about Lettie and him, and gossip about himself and Annie had settled. He was glad to be able to show others tonight that the Fontaine family was just as strong as ever. He just wished Will and Henny were still with them.

"I've been thinking about investing more in Billings," he told Lettie. "What do you think about another hotel, bigger than the Billings Inn?"

"A hotel!"

"Sure, why not? Something really elegant. Martin Stowe, the man who bought Will's place for a boardinghouse, could manage it for me. I've already talked to him about it, and even though he's enlarging the board-inghouse, his wife can do a fine job of running it during the day by herself. Stowe knows the hotel business. He seems very willing to run the Hotel Fontaine."

"Oh, so you've already named it?"

"Sounds pretty good, don't you think?"

"Maybe you think Billings should change *its* name to Fontaine."

"Not a bad idea." Luke grinned. "At any rate, if we built our own hotel, there would always be a guaranteed place to stay whenever we have to spend the night in town. One suite could be held at all times just for us. And we wouldn't be hurting Bill Richards's business, *or* Marty Stowe's. Billings needs another hotel, at the rate it's growing."

"I suppose that might be a good idea at that."

Luke turned her to the music, wanting to kiss her but knowing how embarrassed she would be. "I think it would be a good investment, bring in good money."

"Don't we have enough money?"

His eyes dropped to drink in the sight of her full cleavage. "Not for my Lettie."

"All I need is you, Luke. That's all I have ever needed. It's never been a question of money."

He sobered. "I love you, Lettie."

"And I love you." She smiled again. "And if you want to build a hotel, then build it. Just so the project doesn't keep you away from home too much."

The waltz ended. Luke led her back to the refresh-ment table, where two of the other ranchers' wives gathered around Lettie to talk about the next women's club meeting. "I'll go round up the kids," Luke told her. "It's getting late."

Just as he started toward the door Robbie came run-ning inside. He looked a little pale, and his eyes were watery with tears that planted a sick fear in Luke's gut.

"Pa! I think somebody took Katie! I was…she was with me one minute…and then I heard horses, and a man gave me this note!"

Luke grasped his arm. "Calm down, Robbie, and tell me slowly!"

Lettie turned away from the other women as several men gathered around Luke. He yelled for the musicians to stop their playing. People whispered and stared as Luke took a tattered and soiled piece of plain paper from Robbie. Tyler pushed his way through the crowd to go to his father and brother, and Pearl hurried to her mother's side. Luke read the note silently. Terror slinked through Lettie's blood as she watched a gray color come into Luke's face.

"Jesus," he muttered in a near whisper. He grabbed Robbie's arm tighter and shook the boy slightly. "Where is she? What the hell happened?" he nearly shouted.

Tears began to trickle down Robbie's cheeks. His lips puckered.

"Luke! You're scaring your own son!" Lettie moved behind Robbie to put her hands on his shoulders consolingly. She kept a steady gaze on Luke, seeing devastation in his eyes. "What does the note say?"

The blue eyes that had looked at her so lovingly only a moment before began to change to ice. "It's from Zack Walker!"

"My God," Joe Parker exclaimed. Some of the other men muttered among themselves. "What does it say, Luke?" Joe asked.

Luke handed the note to Joe. There was anger and murder in his eyes, but also a terrible fear. Lettie knew what that fear was—that he would lose another child, that maybe Lettie would blame him for this one too. After all, he had been the one who first chased Zack Walker off his land.

"'Got your girl,'" Joe read aloud, "'the tall one that's

nearly a woman now. If you want her back, bring ten thousand dollars to Pine Creek, where you hanged my sons. Come alone, day after tomorrow. If you ain't alone—'" Joe stopped to look at the others. "He puts 'ain't' right in the letter—spelled most of these words wrong too, the ignorant bastard!" He sighed with concern for Luke, then finished the letter. "'If you ain't alone, we'll hang your girl. Makes no difference to us that she's female.'" He shook his head. "It's signed Zack W."

Lettie closed her eyes and breathed deeply for strength. She pressed a sobbing Robbie's shoulders tightly. "What happened out there, Robbie?"

The boy shuddered and wiped at his eyes and nose with his shirtsleeve. "Katie…came out to find me. I was looking at that…that horse we saw earlier outside…the one that looked like something was wrong with its leg. I was going to see if I could find out whose it was… tell them they shouldn't ride it home because it was hurt." He shivered before continuing. "I told Katie I'd be right in, and she left. I thought…I thought I heard some man say something like…like…'Can you help me a minute, little girl?' When I turned to look, it was too dark to see anything. I heard…horses riding off…and some man came up and gave me the note…like he was in a big hurry. I didn't even see him good. He just said 'Give this to your pa, and tell him he better do what it says…or he won't see his girl again.' Then he rode off real fast. I…looked for Katie…called for her…but she didn't answer."

Luke's jaw flexed in rage. He looked down at Robbie. "If you had come right in with your sister instead of worrying about that lame horse—"

"Luke!" Lettie interrupted. "Don't you dare say it! This is not Robbie's fault. And if he *had* come back with her, Zack Walker might have taken Katie *and* Robbie!" Did he realize how much harder this was on her, thinking what such ignorant, evil men might do to her daughter? The emotional scars of her own rape had never quite left her. The thought of such a horror happening to Katie…and she was so young! For a moment she thought she might pass out, but she knew she had to be strong now, not just for Luke and the family, but so that she could be there for Katie when they got her back…and they *would* get her back! Luke Fontaine would make sure of it, maybe even die in the effort.

"What do you want us to do, Luke?" An aging Sheriff Tracy stepped closer. "I can get a posse together."

Luke took the note back from Joe, read it again, while the room hung silent. "No," he answered. "He said to come alone, and that's what I'll do."

"How are you going to get your hands on that much money that quick?" Henry Kline asked him.

"I know how," Lucy Kline answered, moving to put an arm around Lettie. "We can everybody in this town temporarily withdraw our savings from the bank. It won't create a run, because Bill Richards over at the bank knows Luke is good for it. Right, Bill?"

Richards stepped out of the crowd and nodded. "Luke and Lettie and my own family have become close. I've got no worries Luke would pay it back."

Alice Richards was glad her father could help. She felt like crying, imagining what it would be like to be stolen away by bad men. Poor Ty! Awful things could happen to his sister!

Luke crumpled the note in his hand. "You, uh, you all know I'm worth a hell of a lot more than ten thousand dollars, but what a man is worth and getting that much in cash within a few hours are two different things. I've got money in a bank in Denver, but it would take too long to get it, and withdrawing that much from the local bank without taking it from all of your savings would be impossible." He felt like weeping over the generous offer, and he looked around at all of them. "If I can find a way, Zack Walker will never even get his hands on *any* of your money," he told them, rage emanating from him.

Lettie felt an aching fear at the words. How was he going to keep from giving over the money, and would he really go out there alone? Zack Walker probably wanted Luke Fontaine dead worse than he wanted ten thousand dollars.

"However I handle this, you have my word you'll get your money back, with interest," Luke told the rest of them. "If something happens to me, Lettie will see that you get it."

"We don't want no interest," Joe Parker told him.

Luke quickly rubbed at his eyes, as though to hide tears. "I, uh, I can get my hands on a thousand or so at home. I just hope there's enough cash in the bank to make up the difference."

"If there isn't, we'll come up with it somehow," Henry assured him.

"I'll take you over to the bank right now," Richards told him. He looked around the room. "All of you willing to withdraw your savings come with me and sign for your money."

The crowd grumbled and shouted, some of the men cursing Zack Walker, as the room nearly emptied because of people heading over to the bank, ready to hand their money to Luke in total trust. The daughter of one of Montana's own was in trouble, and they would do what they could to help her.

Luke looked down at a still-sobbing Robbie, knew the boy still had nightmares about Paul dying while he was trying to help him. "I'm sorry, Robbie. Remember our talks about none of us blaming another for anything that happens from here on?"

Robbie just nodded, wiping at his eyes again.

Luke touched the top of the boy's head. "I meant

that." He looked at Lettie, and she knew that at the moment he could not quite apply that opinion to himself.

"Luke, the man was determined. If not this way, he would have found some other."

"Pa, I want to go with you!" Tyler spoke up. "They've got Katie, Pa, and you know I'm a good shot. I can help you."

Alice felt alarm at the words. Ty could get hurt! How she loved the handsome Tyler Fontaine, but she was too young to speak of such things. Right now she just wanted to cry, and to hug Tyler for his bravery and his love for his sister.

"I don't know just what I'll do yet, Son. I've got to talk to the men when we get back to the ranch. You heard what Walker said. He wants me to come alone."

"He'll kill you!" Tyler protested. "That's all he *really* wants! He's probably got a whole new gang of men."

Luke ran a hand through his hair and walked over to where he had hung his hat. "Maybe," he answered. "Get everybody else into the buggy and take them to the hotel. Lettie and I will walk over to the bank. Before we can do anything else, we've got to get the money together. Walker probably doesn't even intend to keep his promise, but if he does, he won't be giving Katie back over until he actually sees the money."

"Come on, Robbie." Tyler took hold of Robbie's and Pearl's hands. "We'll go to the hotel and start packing, Pa." He led his sister and brother outside to the family buggy and drove off. Some of the people still at the hall whispered among themselves, a couple of women crying.

"What a terrible way for such a lovely time to end," one woman grieved.

Luke turned to Lettie, who wrapped a shawl around her shoulders. He touched her, and she turned, embracing him. "Oh, Luke, we can't lose another child," she said softly.

"We aren't going to," he answered, a determined, steely edge to the words. "Not this time, Lettie. Zack Walker just made the biggest mistake of his miserable, stinking life!"

Lettie thought how only moments ago they had all been so happy. "You can't take that money to him alone, Luke."

"I have no choice."

"Then I am going with you."

He grasped her arms and pushed her away. "What in God's name makes you think I would let you go?"

She turned away and walked outside so others could not hear. Luke followed her out, grabbed hold of her arm again. "Answer me, Lettie."

"If you don't take me with you, I truly *won't* ever forgive you this time! We both know what could happen to Katie. When and if you get her back, she is going to need a woman, preferably her own mother—and God knows I understand rape better than anyone! I can help her."

Luke closed his eyes and turned away, his hands forming into fists. "Not my little girl. Not Katie! I have to kill them, Lettie! I have to find a way!"

"Wait until you can talk to Tex and Runner. Whatever you do, I'm going with you. They won't question why you'd want to bring Katie's mother."

Luke turned to face her. "They could rape and kill you too, if I'm unable to get you out of there."

"I'll take the risk. I know what Katie is going through. Besides, *I* can shoot pretty well myself, you know. Please let me go with you, Luke!"

Luke threw back his head and took a deep breath. "I could lose both of you. I'd kill myself if I lost you, let alone another child."

"You probably wouldn't have to. If Zack Walker kills Katie and me, he'll probably kill you too. We're *all* taking a chance. Maybe after you talk to the men at the ranch, you can come up with a way out of this."

Luke studied her by the light of an outdoor oil lamp, surprised at how well she was holding up. "You've grown a lot stronger, Lettie."

She put a hand against his chest. "Because of you, and the love this family has found these past few months. We've come too far to let the likes of Zack Walker defeat us now, Luke. We'll find a way to help Katie. At least we know where Walker is holding her. That's a start, isn't it?"

Luke's eyes began to glitter with hope. "You're right. He told us more than he should have. He ought to realize how well I know my own land. I know every inch of Pine Creek Canyon."

"He's meeting you on your own territory. A stupid move by a stupid man."

He smiled through tears, touching her face. "I'll be damned. What would I do without you, woman?"

Lettie could hardly see the front of the bank for the tears in her own eyes. In spite of what they had suffered settling here, they had been blessed with one very important gift, the gift of true friendship, love, and support from people who pulled together when times were rough. What they were seeing now, people lined up to withdraw their life savings and hand it over to another in a time of need, this was Montana…the people, not the land. She took great hope in what they were doing. Surely God would not let this come to a terrible end. *Please comfort and protect our Katie*, she prayed silently, *and let us get her back*.

"We'd better get over there," Luke said. They walked together to the bank, and as soon as they entered, an old widowed woman named Tilly Gray handed Lettie some money. "Here's fifty dollars," she told Lettie. "I hope it helps."

Lettie embraced the woman. "Thank you, Tilly," she said softly.

Lettie had never felt so alone and exposed. She rode beside Luke across the wide, flat grassland that led to Pine Creek Canyon, now only about a half mile distant. Already she could see someone standing on top of the eastern canyon wall, watching them. She had never even been this far west on Fontaine land. Luke had owned this piece only four years, and since it was so far from the main ranch, and in the opposite direction than she would take to go to Billings, she simply had never had reason to come here. Here was where Luke and the vigilantes had hanged the Walker brothers nearly a year ago, where poor Will was buried. And here, they hoped, their daughter waited, alive and well.

The carpetbag full of money hung over Luke's saddle horn. Her own heart pounded with fear, not for herself, but for Luke and Katie…and Runner, Tex…and Ty. Ty had demanded to be allowed to be a part of Luke's plan to capture these men, although they had no idea just how many men they were talking about. Luke and Ty had argued, but Ty was so upset about his sister that Luke had not had the heart to forbid the boy a chance to help. He had allowed Ty to be a part of his plan to save Katie *and* the money, and to kill Zack Walker; but that rescue and capture would never take place if Runner had been unable to accomplish his part of the plan last night. Today they could all die, and for all they knew, Runner was already dead.

The man at the top of the canyon wall raised his rifle. "Stop right there, Fontaine!" he shouted.

"Zack Walker," Luke muttered, the name spoken with seething hatred.

"I told you to come alone!" Walker shouted.

"It's just my wife!" Luke yelled in reply. "She has a right to be here. Our daughter might need her!"

Lettie cringed at the way Walker laughed. "What for? To talk to her little girl about what it's like to get poked for the first time?"

As though sensing his master's burning rage, Luke's Appaloosa snorted and bolted slightly. Luke yanked on the reins. "Where's my daughter, Walker?"

"Where's my money?"

Luke held up the carpetbag.

"Bring it on into the canyon and we'll make an exchange! You ride easy now, Fontaine, and you'd better be unarmed. I'll be watchin' your every move, you murderin' son of a bitch!"

Luke glanced at Lettie. "You know the plan. You wait here," he said quietly. He handed her his rifle and six-gun.

She took the weapons, her heart sinking at the thought of how defenseless he would be now. "I love you, Luke. God be with you." She watched him ride toward the canyon, making sure she did not glance back to the high boulders surrounded by a thick stand of pine behind them that hid Tex and Ty. She dared not do anything that would make Zack Walker suspect they were not alone, but she smiled inwardly at the knowledge that she had been right. Zack Walker was stupid to pick Luke's own land for the meeting. Luke knew every inch of what he owned, and he knew a man could get to that rock formation and stand of trees behind her without being seen from the distant canyon wall. On the other side of that wall was Pine Creek, and beyond that another canyon wall with a sheer drop of several hundred feet. The only escape from the canyon was out both ends and into the clearing where she sat now. If they could close off the north end, Walker and his men would have to come out the south end, where Luke was riding in. Once they did that, they would be close enough for Tex and Ty to shoot them down as they came out. Luke had not dared to bring any more men than he had, afraid too many men would create too much dust and noise and somehow give away his plan. She was afraid for poor

Ty, worried he could be hurt, just as worried that her son, barely thirteen, would be shooting at men for the first time. He was a very mature young man in many ways, but neither she nor Luke liked the thought of him possibly having to kill another human being.

Zack Walker apparently believed that she and Luke had come alone. At least that much of their plan had worked. Now they had to depend on Runner, who had snuck in after dark last night with dynamite. He could move with a silence only an Indian was capable of, and he too knew this area. Under cover of darkness last night he was to make his way to the northern end of the canyon and set sticks of dynamite in strategic places that would, they hoped, close that end of the canyon, or at least scare the outlaws' horses enough to force them to flee out the other end, to the waiting guns of Tex and Ty and herself. It had been a long time since she'd had to fire a gun in self-defense. She had hoped those days were over, but as long as men like Zack Walker existed, and there were not enough lawmen to handle the problems, citizens would have to keep doing the job for themselves. Runner should be hidden right now somewhere up in the canyon wall, waiting for just the right moment to begin lighting dynamite fuses. She prayed he would not be seen or hurt.

She watched Luke disappear around the southern end of the wall, and Zack Walker left his guard post and disappeared down the other side. From here on, Lettie would have no idea what was going on. Luke intended to grab Katie if he could and simply ride like hell for the south end, leading Walker and his men on a chase that would, they hoped, take them right into a death trap. Then again, Luke might never come out of that canyon, especially if Runner had been unable to accomplish his end of the plan.

The sun shone down hot on her shoulders, but she only felt a shivering cold.

Twenty-four

LUKE WANTED TO LASH OUT IN RAGE AS HE APPROACHED Zack Walker and his men, but he forced himself to stay calm. His only chance at getting Katie and himself out of this mess alive was to make no wrong moves. He prayed Runner was somewhere in place and unhurt, ready to blow the dynamite. He saw no sign that the Indian had been caught and found last night, but it was always possible Walker had chosen not to say anything about it, so that the man could lure him closer before killing him.

It was difficult to concentrate on anything but Katie now. She sat on a horse in front of a grisly-looking young man who obviously did not know the meaning of soap and water. Her head hung limply, as though she had lost some terrible battle. The sight of his pretty, proud daughter sitting there looking so forlorn and defeated tore at his heart.

Katie! Sweet, young Katie, so shy and quiet and smart. He had imagined saving such treasure for a respectable, honorable man who would know how to treat her; but by the sight of her, he already knew the worst had happened. She still wore the pretty mint green dress she'd had on at the dance, but it was torn and tattered, and she had to hold up the front of it with one hand to keep it from falling open.

"Let's see the money," Walker demanded, riding closer to Luke.

Luke met the man's gaze squarely, studied the stubble on his dirty face, the tobacco stain at the corner of his mouth. "You didn't keep your end of the bargain."

"In what way?" Walker looked back at Katie. "She's alive, ain't she?"

"You scum." Luke seethed. "Why should I pay off a man who has obviously violated my daughter?"

Walker shrugged. "Weren't me. It was my nephews there." He nodded to the one holding Katie. "That there is Benny. The ones each side of him is his brothers, Larry and Jim." The man spit some tobacco juice onto the leg of Luke's horse. "You know how young boys are. They git hard easy, seein' a purty thing like little Katie there. So what if she got stuck some? It was bound to happen sooner or later anyway. Now she's all broke in for her weddin' night." He leaned closer, reeking of stale perspiration. "I believe one of my boys told you that us Walkers git our revenge. An eye for an eye, Fontaine. You're lucky we didn't just shoot down that boy of yours the night of the dance. We could have, you know." He grinned again. "Far as that girl over there, the boys say she's a nice, tight piece. We're thinkin' on takin' her with us when we leave here. Ain't a whole lot you could do about it, 'specially if you're dead."

Luke had to concentrate to keep the sound of Katie's quiet sobbing from making him do something foolish. *Wait it out*, he told himself. "You won't kill me," he told Walker, never flinching. "You don't want to bring murder into this because then you know every lawman from here to Mexico would be looking for you."

"There's places to go to git away, and I expect we're gonna be hunted either way."

"There aren't so many places to hide out anymore, Walker. You'll never live to enjoy this money."

Walker held his chin higher in defiance. "We know the right places to go, and if we have your girl along, anybody that comes after us is gonna have to be awful careful if they don't want nothin' to happen to her. Hell, we could even take your wife along for extra protection from the law. They ain't gonna want nothin' to happen to her, and I expect she's still fit enough to please an old man like me."

Luke felt like vomiting. "You go ahead and try, Walker. I guarantee that whatever happens, one thing is certain. *You* will *die!* Make no mistake about it. Your only chance to live is to take this money and hand over my daughter right now and let me ride out of here."

Walker held his gaze, then showed a hint of the coward Luke knew he was. He swallowed, and Luke knew he had shaken him. He removed the carpetbag from his saddle horn and tossed it over with a force that startled Walker. "Look inside, you stinking coward, and be proud of how you earned your precious little fortune! You were a fool to ask for only ten thousand. You're so goddamn ignorant you probably think that's a lot of money for me, probably because you've never earned an honest dollar in your life, you lazy bastard!"

Walker's smile faded. "You shut your mouth, Fontaine, or you'll be hangin' from a noose, just like you did to my boys. I expect that's how you'll end up anyway." He opened the bag and looked inside, then began laughing as he fingered the money. "It's here, boys!"

Several of them let out war whoops and rebel yells, while Katie still sat whimpering. Luke moved his horse a little closer to her, taking advantage of the fact that for the moment Zack and some of the others were lost in an eager celebration, grabbing stacks of bills from the bag to count through them.

"Katie, look at me," Luke told her.

Benny chuckled. "Oh, the poor little thing is ashamed," he cooed. He kissed at her neck, and Katie flinched.

"Katie, you don't have a damn thing to be ashamed of," Luke told her calmly. "Raise your head up, god-damn it! You're a Fontaine, and these people are nothing more than animals! Don't you dare let them make you hang your head!"

The girl slowly raised her face to look at her father, a face that was battered and bruised, her eyes swollen from crying. "Daddy," she sobbed, using the term she had only used when she was a tiny girl. For years it had just been Pa, but now she was like a little girl wanting her father's protective arms around her.

"It's going to be all right."

"They said…they were going to…hang both of us… after they get the money."

Benny chuckled again, nodding to Luke. "You didn't really think we'd let you live after what you did to my cousins, did you, Fontaine? You must really be stupid to think we'd just take that money and leave."

Luke kept his eyes on Katie. "We're going to be all right, Katie." He looked around, taking a quick inventory. Nine men total. Could he get himself and Katie out of here without dying? All he needed to do was get her onto his own horse and Runner would set the dynamite that would create enough chaos and commotion to allow him an escape…he hoped.

"A couple of you boys go and get the woman," he heard Walker saying.

Luke knew it was now or never. Bringing Lettie into the middle of it all would just complicate things even more. Two men started toward the south end of the canyon to get Lettie, and Walker ordered a third man to throw a rope over a limb on the very tree where Luke had hanged Walker's sons. There was no more time to waste in deciding what to do.

"Just ride easy back over here," Walker ordered Luke. "You willin' to give up your life for your wife and daughter?" The man grinned, hooking the bag of money over his own saddle horn. "You're gonna hang, Luke Fontaine. The easier you make it for us, the easier we'll go on the girl and your woman after you're dead. You make trouble, and all three of you will be swingin' from that there tree. Which will it be?"

Luke glanced at the two men headed out of the canyon. If they got outside, and Tex and Ty started shooting at them too soon, he and Katie were doomed. "Give me a few seconds to hold my girl," he answered. "Let me at least have a good-bye."

Walker rubbed his chin for a moment, then nodded. "Put her on his horse," he told Benny.

Luke almost laughed aloud at the man's stupidity. He reached out and pulled Katie onto his own horse, and she sat sideways in front of him, cringing against his chest. Luke held her tightly with one arm and pretended to be whispering a good-bye. "Keep right on crying," he told her, "but you be ready to hang on tight, Katie girl. I'm not leaving you here, understand?"

The girl clung to his shirt and nodded, purposely weeping harder. It was easy, for she wept with relief that her father was not going to submit to a hanging and let her mother and her suffer at the hands of these miserable wretches who had already done such horrible things to her.

Come on, Runner, Luke thought. At almost the same instant, two explosions only a second apart blew out huge boulders at the north end of the canyon. Walker and the others turned in surprise to look, a couple of their horses whinnying and rearing. Luke took advantage of the diversion and kicked his own horse in the flanks. Clinging to Katie, he charged toward the south end of the canyon, bending over slightly to keep his body between his daughter and any bullets that might get fired at them.

"Swing around and hang on!" he ordered Katie, scooting farther back in his saddle. Like Ty, Katie loved riding, and her skill and ease with horses became a valuable asset as she leaned back and managed to swing one

leg over the neck of Luke's horse so that she straddled the
animal. She leaned down then and grabbed hold of the
horse's mane, hanging on for dear life as Luke rode like
a demon. Above the pounding hooves and the noise of
the air rushing past her face, she could hear more explosions in the distance, as well as gunfire. She cringed when
something whizzed near them, knew instinctively it was
a bullet. Then she felt a jolt behind her. Luke grunted
and slammed into her, his chin bumping against the back
of her head.

"Daddy!" she screamed.

"Just hang on no matter what happens!" he yelled,
amid more thundering explosions. "'I'm getting you out
of here!"

Luke could feel horses behind him, knew the Walkers
and their hired men were right on their heels. He headed
his horse toward the stand of rocks across the flat valley,
relieved that Lettie was nowhere in sight. Apparently
she had done what she was told and had headed for the
rocks herself as soon as Runner began setting off the
explosions. He could only pray now that Runner would
be all right, and that he would himself reach the safety of
the rocks and his own men before taking a more deadly
bullet in the back. He knew he'd already been hit in the
upper right shoulder, but there was no time to think
about the pain or worry about how badly he'd been
injured. He had to hang on, for Katie's sake.

In the distance he could see a horse running off
without its rider, then spotted the body several yards to
his left. Apparently Tex or Ty had gotten one of those
who had ridden out ahead of him to try to capture
Lettie. He had no idea where the second man was and
no chance to look. He kept his eyes on the cluster of
trees and rocks ahead, which, though only about a half
mile away, seemed to take forever to reach. Katie's dark
hair blew into his face as he stretched his gelding to its

maximum effort, charging the horse across the flower-filled meadow toward the rocks.

Now he could see the spit of guns from the rocks. Tex and Ty and probably Lettie were shooting at the outlaws. He did not fear being accidentally hit by any of them. All three of them were skilled with firearms, and at the moment he could not be more proud of his brave wife and son, but he never would have let them come without Tex and Runner along. Even at that, he'd had his doubts he was doing the right thing, but he knew how important it was for both of them. His heart leaped with joy as he got closer and realized he just might make it. He guided his horse around the south side of the rocks, relieved to see Lettie waiting there. She reached up for Katie as Luke brought his horse to a sliding halt. With his left arm he helped Katie down from the horse, but he was beginning to feel excruciating pain in his right shoulder and all the way down his right arm.

"Luke! You've been shot!" Lettie yelled.

"Just take care of Katie," he ordered, dismounting and hurrying over to grab his rifle from her gear. He ran over to where Tex and Ty were still shooting at the outlaws. "How many did you get?"

"Not sure," Tex answered. "About six are down, I think, probably some of them just wounded. Your wife got a couple of them herself."

Luke looked back at Lettie, who was holding a weeping Katie. He was glad he had let her come, for Katie's sake. So, he thought, Lettie had shot at the outlaws right alongside Tex and Tyler. She was truly strong again, but what would Katie's awful experience do to her?

"There's the money bag!" Tyler shouted. He fired, then cussed. "I got the damn horse instead of the rider!"

"I think that's the last one," Tex answered. "I can see Runner farther out. Looks like he's rounded up a couple of them himself."

"The one on that horse I just shot is getting up, Pa, running off with the money."

"Leave that one to me!" Luke barked. "It's Zack Walker!" Almost before he finished speaking, he was back up on his own horse and riding out into the clearing.

"Jesus," Tex cussed, jumping up and heading for his own horse. "Your pa is wounded and gonna get himself killed. Stay here with your ma and sister," he told Ty. He rode out after Luke, who charged toward Walker. Walker turned and shot at Luke but missed, and in the next moment Luke rode his horse directly into the man, knocking him to the ground and deliberately riding over him. Walker screamed out in horrible pain, but Luke only gloried in the sound. He turned his horse and headed back, purposely riding over the man again. He halted his horse then and jumped off, running over to grab Walker around the throat. He began strangling the man, and by the time Tex reached them, Walker's face was purple, his tongue bulging out in an effort to open his throat and find some air.

"Luke, don't kill him here! Let him hang!" Tex tried to reason.

"They raped her," Luke growled. "They raped my Katie!"

Tex grasped Luke's powerful wrists, knowing full well that if not for Luke's own injury, he would never have managed to pull him off of Walker. By then Tyler reached them, disobeying Tex's order to stay put.

"Pa, you need help!" he urged. "The man is hurt bad. He isn't going anyplace."

Tex fell back with his arms still around Luke from behind, still holding his wrists. "Damn it, Luke, you know there ain't nobody who finds killin' a man easier than me," he said. "But you're always preachin' about law and order in this goddamn territory. You promised Sheriff Tracy there wouldn't be no revenge killin'. You said we'd bring in the survivors for a proper hangin'."

"He's got to die, and I've got to do it!" Luke fumed, lurching backward and pulling out of Tex's grip. He headed for Walker again, but Tyler stepped in front of him, pushing his rifle against his father crosswise.

"Pa, Tex is right! Think about it! A public hanging will get written about all over. After that men like Zack Walker will think twice about coming to Montana and making trouble! We can show everybody we've got laws here now."

Luke calmed down some, and Tex took hold of his arm. "Luke, do this one the right way. We all helped lynch the Walker boys, but some think that's no better than what outlaws do. You're always talkin' about bringin' good people to this territory. A proper trial and hangin' will show folks we've got things under control here, that we take care of these things the proper way. And after what these men did, *everybody* deserves the pleasure of watchin' them hang!"

Luke breathed deeply to stay in control, but his eyes brimmed with tears. "I won't have Katie sitting through any public trial and having to tell people what happened to her!"

"Then you can make sure no public gets in," Tex answered. "You've got the pull to do this however you want. Only the jury needs to hear Katie's story. Then let everybody in Billings and for miles around watch these bastards hang!"

"Oh, God, I'm hurt bad!" Walker groaned. "Everything's broke!"

Luke looked down at the man, then walked over and kicked him in the ribs. The man screamed out in agony. "Go ahead and hurt, you stinking piece of filth! You're going to hurt a lot worse when I'm through with you! You're going back to Billings over the back of a horse, and you're going to feel the pain of every broken bone all the way back! If you're lucky, you'll die on the way!"

Runner rode closer then, herding two men ahead of him, his six-gun leveled at them. "I think we got them all, Luke," he spoke up.

"I got a couple myself," Tyler told Runner. He looked down at Zack Walker. "I shot this one's horse from under him. I just wish I would have got him instead of the horse."

"You did good today, Ty," Tex told him. "After today I won't call you boy anymore."

Ty wanted to feel good about the remark, but he was too sick over what had happened to his sister. If it wasn't for Katie, he would have celebrated being allowed to come after outlaws with men like Tex and Runner... and Luke Fontaine. "Pa, you'd better let Runner look at your shoulder. Your shirt's all soaked with blood."

Luke looked down at himself, only just beginning to realize how badly he'd been hurt. He looked up at the men Runner had brought in. One of them was Walker's nephew, Jim. Luke remembered Zack Walker telling him Jim was one of those who had raped Katie. "You're going to feel a hot rope around your neck in a few days, boy!" he spit out. "You'll regret what you did to my Katie! You and any of the rest who are still alive!" He grimaced and grasped his right arm then as the pain in his arm and shoulder grew more intense. "Tie them up, Runner, then I think you're going to have to throw some whiskey on this wound and wrap it up." He looked at Ty. "You okay, Son?"

"Sure, Pa, I'm fine."

Luke nodded, and their eyes held in understanding. Tyler knew his father was proud of the good job he'd done, but that this was not time to celebrate anything. "Help Tex round up the bodies," Luke told the boy. "We'll send men back to bury the dead, and we'll take the wounded back to Billings for a trial and hanging." He looked over at Runner, who was already tying Jim

Walker's wrists behind him and bringing the rope under the man's horse to truss his ankles together under the horse's belly. "I'll be over by Lettie and Katie." He hated the thought of having to face his wife and daughter, hated this feeling that he was partly responsible for all of this. He sighed with grief. "Pick up the money," he said dejectedly to Tex. "I'd gladly give up every last dime of it if it would mean they had never touched Katie." His voice nearly broke on the words, and he closed his eyes for a moment. "Maybe it isn't right to kill them right here," he added, "but by God when the day comes that they get hanged, I'd like to be the one to pull the lever!" He left them then, and Tyler watched after his father, struggling against his own urge to cry.

❧

"I can't go, Mama. I can't even face Pa or my brothers or Tex and the other men, my own family and friends. How am I going to tell all those ugly things to strangers?"

Lettie walked to the window where Katie sat in her room bundled in a flannel gown and robe in spite of the heat. It was only her second day home, and already she had bathed six times. Lettie well knew the feeling of wanting to wash away the filth, hoping the memories would be washed away with it; but that was impossible. She touched her daughter's lustrous dark hair; this young girl who had been cruelly introduced to sex in the worst way. In so many ways she had still been such a child, but now the child in her was gone.

"You will go and tell your story, Katie, because you are a Fontaine, and you're strong and proud. You did absolutely nothing wrong and have nothing to be ashamed of, and there isn't one person in this family, or on this ranch, or in all of Montana who would think less of you. You will go because the right thing to do is to get those men hanged, because it will show any other outlaws who think about coming here what happens to men who steal and kill and rape. You'll do it to help bring law and order to Montana, and because if you don't get them hanged, your father will find a way to kill those men himself, and then *he* might be the one to go to prison."

Katie closed her eyes, and more tears spilled down her cheeks. Her stomach ached so badly that she felt constantly nauseated and could not eat. Everything hurt, and she couldn't sleep because of the haunting, ugly attacks that kept revisiting her every time she lay back on her bed. "All those people—"

"Katie, Sheriff Tracy said he would talk to the federal judge when he gets into town, and he is sure the man will allow only the jury in the room with you, if that's the way you want it. The men on trial don't even have to be there. You don't ever have to look at them again."

"But you don't know," Katie sobbed. "You don't know how it feels."

Lettie closed her own eyes and took a deep breath for courage. There was only one way to help her daughter, and that was to face her own experience, something she had buried deep in her soul long ago. Oh, how it hurt to dredge it up again! "I do know, Katie. I know better than you think."

Katie sniffed and turned to look up at her mother. "What do you mean?"

Lettie felt her heart beating faster. What would her daughter think of her if she knew the truth? She pulled a chair over near the girl and sat down across from her, reaching out and taking her hands. "Katie, the same thing happened to me. I was a couple of years older than you, but I had also never been with a man before. I had the same cruel awakening that you have had, but I would suffer it all over again if I could just take it away from you. I wish those men had taken me instead."

Katie's eyes widened in shock. "*Mama!* You were...raped?"

Lettie held her gaze. She had been preaching to Katie about not feeling shame; how could she turn around and show any of her own? "It was back when we lived in Missouri, and there was a lot of raiding just before the Civil War. Our place got raided by Southern sympathizers because we were for the Union. I ran out to the barn to try to save my favorite horse from being stolen, and that's when I was attacked."

Katie looked her over as though she were someone she didn't even know. "Why didn't you ever tell us? Does Pa know?"

Lettie nodded, love beginning to shine in her eyes. "He was the one who helped me see it wasn't my fault and that I shouldn't feel ashamed. Pa made me see I had every right to go on with my life, to love and be loved. He taught me the gentle side of man, and it was through your father that I learned that being in love and making love can be a beautiful thing, Katie. It can and will happen for you. What those men did...it isn't like that when you truly love a man. Someday you will learn to give yourself out of true joy and desire; but I still remember how I felt back then. I know exactly how you are thinking and feeling right now. It was almost worse for me because...because I was left in a family way."

Katie drew in her breath, and her eyes teared anew. "Oh, Mama, will that happen to me?"

Lettie squeezed her hands reassuringly. "No. I remembered that the day before the dance you had just finished your time of month. It's very unlikely." She sighed deeply. "Oh, Katie, I had intended to talk to you about men and marriage and such, but I never expected to have to do it so soon. We'll wait and talk more about the magic between a man and a woman when you're more ready to listen. I didn't tell you about what happened to me to frighten you. I just thought…as long as I felt compelled to tell you what happened to me, you should know that Nathan was the result."

Katie's mouth dropped open, and Lettie thought that in spite of the difficulty of having to tell the girl all these things, maybe the shocking news would help get her mind off of her own problems, at least for a time. "You mean…you were never married to Nathan's father? You weren't really widowed from the war?"

Lettie's eyes teared. "Katie, there was a baby inside of me, a human life, and it was not my place to judge why God blessed me with that life. I learned to look at my baby that way—as a blessing, a gift with some purpose. That purpose might have been nothing more than to show that something precious and beautiful can come from something terrible. I only know that when Nathan was born, and that little baby clung to me and looked to me for love and survival, I couldn't help but love him in return. I think that's partly why I took his disappearance so hard, Katie. I suffer from the guilt of thinking maybe I should be punished for the times I hated that baby inside of me and wished it would be born dead." She saw the disbelief in her daughter's eyes. "Yes, Katie, I couldn't help feeling that way at first. But as I told you, I grew to love my little boy, and when he was taken from me, I felt such a terrible sorrow for the times when I hadn't wanted him because of how he was conceived. I came to realize it wasn't that baby's fault. He was just a little human life that needed his mother."

She let go of Katie's hands and stood up, walking over to look out the window at Luke and Tex, who were in a corral trying to break and train a stubborn but beautiful stallion. Since taking Zack Walker and the other four surviving men to town to sit in jail and wait for the traveling judge, Luke had kept himself busy again, trying to channel his anger, refusing to get any bed rest because of his wound. Instead, he kept his arm in a sling and worked, from dawn until after dark. Lettie knew he was in physical pain, but his emotional pain was much greater.

"This has to be our secret, Katie. I don't know if or when I will tell the rest of the children. I might never tell them. I wouldn't have told you if not for what happened. You need to know that someone else understands, and you need to know that you can go on with your life, just as I did; and that you'll find a good man who will look beyond what happened to you and just love you for who you are…the way Luke did with me. He took us both, loved Nathan as if he were his own. If Nathan came back today and wanted to be a part of this family, Luke would welcome him as eagerly as he would welcome Ty or Robbie. There are evil, ugly men in this world, Katie, but there are a lot of good men too, like your father. I promise you that time will heal your wounds, and a man will come along who will erase the ugly memories and turn something vicious and painful into a beautiful experience for you."

Katie rose. "I'm sorry, Mama, for what happened to you. It must have been hard for you to tell me, but I'm glad you did." She put out her arms, and Lettie walked over and embraced her tightly.

"Please dress and come to the supper table tonight, Katie. It would make your father so happy to see you trying to rise above this." She kissed the girl's hair. "Don't you see, Katie? If you let this destroy you, if you allow yourself to be ashamed and go around looking like a fallen woman, then even if they are hanged, those horrible men will have won. They will have defeated not just you, but your father, also. They will have achieved what they set out to do—to hurt him in the worst way. If you go talk to the judge and the jury, hold your head proudly and tell the truth and refuse to be ashamed, you'll be proving what the Fontaines are made of. We can't let people like the Walkers defeat us, Katie, just as your father taught me not to let my rapist destroy me; and as he has refused to let other men defeat him in any way while building all that we have here."

Katie sniffed and hugged her mother tighter. "You and Pa are happy now, aren't you? I mean, you're over the bad time you had when Paul died?"

Lettie stroked her hair. "Yes, my darling, we're all right now. I think our love is stronger than ever."

Katie pulled away, wiping at her eyes. "I'll go down to supper tonight. Will you help me pick out something to wear, and fix my hair?"

Lettie smiled through tears. "Of course I will."

Katie left her and walked to the window herself, watching her father work the stallion. "Pa risked his life for me, shielded me with his own body. I felt the punch when that bullet hit him, and I remember his groans when Runner dug the bullet out of his shoulder. I also remember how he looked at me when he first saw me with that horrible man. I know how much Pa wants to see those men die, and I do too." She turned and faced her mother. "I'll go tell my story to the judge and the jury, as long as I only have to look at those men long enough to identify them to the jury."

Lettie nodded. "Your father will be proud. We'll all be with you, Katie, every step of the way." She walked closer and grasped the girl's arms. "Remember, what I told you is our secret."

Katie studied her mother's gentle green eyes, seeing the woman in a whole new light, understanding her own suffering. "I won't tell." She blinked back tears. "I'm glad you found somebody like Pa."

Lettie smiled, looking out the window along with Katie, noticing Luke was standing outside the corral then talking to Robbie. She knew how miserable Robbie had been over what happened to Katie, blaming himself for

not watching out for her, sure his father hated him and
would never forgive him. Her heart swelled with love
then when she saw Luke embrace the boy. Oh, how
Robbie needed that. "I'm glad too," she told Katie.
"Your father and I have had our differences, but nothing
could ever get in the way of how much I love him."

"When will the judge get to Billings?" Katie asked.

Lettie watched Luke and Robbie walk toward the
house, arm in arm. "Sheriff Tracy says he should be
here by Saturday." Oh, how she hated the thought of
what poor Katie would have to go through, but it had
to be done. There would be law and order in Montana,
and men like Luke would make sure of it. Talk about a
hanging was already rampant, and word was, people were
already filtering into Billings from all over Montana and
even from Wyoming to see the event. How sad that all
that excitement had to be from her daughter's personal
horror. *God be with us all*, she prayed.

Twenty-five

LETTIE COULD SEE TYLER AND ROBBIE IN THE STREET below. They had been permitted to join the crowds that swarmed into Billings for the hanging, but were ordered to stay together. Because of the delicate reason for the hanging that would take place today, Katie had chosen to stay away from the staring eyes of others and watch the hanging from a room Luke had taken on the second floor of the Billings Inn.

Lettie thought how almost none of the people milling about outside were originally from Montana. Nearly all were from other parts of the country and from all walks of life, some with past lives no one else would ever know about, come to Montana for a hundred different reasons. The Stowes, the middle-aged couple who had bought Will and Henny's place, had lost a son in the Civil War. They had owned and managed a hotel back in Ohio, then lost it all to a fire. They had moved west with their daughter to try farming, and when that failed, they had come to Montana because they had heard it was growing fast and figured they would get back into the business they knew best. Nial Bentley was from England, now married to Sydney Greene's daughter, the Greene family from Pennsylvania. The tailor, Gino Galardo, was born in New York, and his parents had come to America from Italy. Reverend Gooding was from Illinois; Herbert Grass, the reporter for the *Billings Extra*, was from Wyoming and from places back east before that. Bill and Betty Richards were from Illinois.

The Double L was itself like a little village in its own right, with whole families living there now. Gone was the terrible loneliness of winter, but such a price they and others had paid for settling this untamed land. James Woodward was dead, and Matt Duncan. Little Paul was gone, and Nathan was out there…somewhere. Maybe he was dead too. Will was gone, Henny dead, simply from a hard life. Now living here had cost poor Katie dearly.

The atmosphere outside was like a circus, people having come in from miles around. The boardinghouse and the hotel were packed to overflowing. Luke was indeed right that Billings needed another hotel, but what a hideous way to find out more room was needed. Some citizens had even rented out storage rooms, or rooms in their own homes, deciding to make a fast dollar off the hanging. Those who could not get rooms had set up wagons and tents outside of town, and vendors in the street were making money selling everything from food and drinks to little signs that read, I Saw the Hanging in Billings, Montana Territory, May 25, 1878. Programs had been printed up and handed out, giving the names of those to be hanged: Ben Walker, Jim Walker, and their uncle, Zack Walker. Because the kidnapping and blackmail scheme was Zack Walker's idea, and because he did nothing to keep his nephews from raping Katie, he was sentenced to be hanged right along with the two young Walkers. Two other men who had been brought in, a Terry Brubaker and Matt Peters, did not take part in the rape. They were given five-year prison sentences and had been sent to Montana's territorial prison at Deer Lodge, nearly two hundred miles to the west. A U.S. Marshal had already come to take them away, although the prison was not even finished yet. Only the north wing was completed, and they heard it was already filling fast with horse thieves and murderers, as Montana continued to struggle to bring law and order to its citizens, who had demanded an end to vigilante justice in their territory.

Lettie hoped such justice would end, that men like Luke could stop risking their own lives keeping the lawless out of Montana. He had brushed against death too many times over the years. If the bullet he'd taken rescuing Katie had hit him just a few inches to the left, it would most certainly have killed or crippled him. He still could not fully use his right arm, and to this day he limped from the bullet wound that had shattered his right thigh the day the buffalo hunters had shot him down.

Today justice would be served legally. A hangman would pull the lever that would open the trapdoors beneath the three Walker men and send them to their reward, whatever that might be. Lettie hoped they would burn in hell forever for what they had done to her daughter, and she had no regrets over killing one of those men herself. By the time bodies were collected and identified after Luke's rescue of Katie, Tex told her that one she had shot was dead. It was learned he was Irv Walker, father of the two Walker boys to be hanged today, brother to Zack Walker, and just as no-good. Katie had told her that the one called Irv had urged his "boys" to have themselves a good time with their captive. Also killed were another nephew, Larry, who was one of those involved in the rape; and a man called Coolie, both shot down by Tex. They had picked Coolie up along the way on their journey of vengeance, and the man had never told them his full name. Tyler had wounded another man named Ken Justice, and the man had died on the trip back to Billings. It was Ty's first killing, and Luke and Lettie both hoped their son would never have to kill again. It had gone hard on him, and his only consolation had been that the man had been a part of the terrible gang that had hurt his sister. Ty had also wounded Brubaker, but the man had lived. Runner had

captured Matt Peters, as well as the fleeing Brubaker, and
it was those two who were headed for prison.

Nine men, Lettie thought, *four killed, two going to prison,
three to hang*. Even that did not seem like justice enough
for poor Katie. It would take more than ending their
lives for her daughter to recover from her ordeal. She
well knew the kind of nightmares that would haunt the
girl for a long time to come. The family had surrounded
her with love. They were all doing everything they could
to encourage her, and she was glad she had shared her
own tragedy with her daughter. That had seemed to help
more than anything.

Pearl came to stand beside her mother at the window.
"Katie, you should see the crowd down there!" she told
her sister. "I never saw so many people!"

Katie sat in a corner of the room knitting. "I don't
want to look," she answered quietly. "Just tell me when
it's over."

Lettie's heart ached at the evident pain in Katie's voice.
The trial had been held inside the cattlemen's hall, and the
poor girl had had to live her rape all over again when she
testified to the jury about what had happened. Although
the general public and the outlaws involved were not
allowed in the room during her testimony, it had still
been a humiliating experience for her, and she still had
had to face the Walkers once more, just long enough to
point out the culprits who had actually raped her.

It seemed almost ludicrous that the crowd in the street
below was laughing and celebrating as though they were
attending some grand picnic; but then deep inside she
celebrated herself that this would be the end of men like
the Walkers. It was too bad that two of them were so
young. Perhaps if they had been brought up differently,
they might have been decent young men. They had
complained that they were worried about their mother
and seven siblings left behind in Wyoming, and a wire

had been sent to Cheyenne for the U.S. Marshal there to deliver a message to the woman that her husband and one of her sons had been killed, and that her brother-in-law and two more of her sons would be hanged. Lettie wondered what the woman would do, where she would go. It was a sad situation, but the Walkers had chosen their path in life, and a man's sins had to be accounted for.

Piano music filtered through the window, as well as laughter, people in saloons having a jolly time…all these people in a gay mood, making money, enjoying the gossip, visiting and picnicking…all looking forward to the hanging as though it was the event of the decade. Perhaps it was. She wondered how many of those below cared about poor Katie. Most of the citizens of Billings did. They had contributed their life savings to help get her back, and Lettie was glad the money had been recovered and returned. The others, the strangers who had come into town, probably didn't care one whit what Katie had suffered. They were just here to see the results. Whole families had come, determined that their children should watch and be "taught a good lesson." This is what happens to a man who chooses the wrong path in life.

She caught sight of Luke then. He walked to the hanging scaffold that he and his men had helped build. It was right in the middle of the main street of Billings, not far from the hotel. Lettie turned and looked at a clock on the wall. It was 1:40 p.m. In just twenty minutes the hanging would take place. The crowd grew more excited and louder when Sheriff Tracy, accompanied by two deputies, came out of the jail farther up the street then, herding the three Walker men in front of them. "They're bringing them out," she told Katie, who did not reply.

Lettie noticed Luke look up at the hotel window. He saw her standing there, and their eyes held for a moment. Even though she was not right beside him, she knew he felt her with him. Both of them wanted this, yet they knew that the death of the Walker men could never erase what had happened. People began to shout curses at the three men as they were brought to the gallows, but a few gathered nearby and started singing hymns. Young Jim Walker walked just fine on his own, but Benny limped from a bullet Tex had planted in his right leg as he was trying to escape. Zack Walker had to be aided by two men, one on each arm. His injuries from Luke riding his horse over the man were extensive, and he was obviously in great pain, unable to walk on his left leg at all. Lettie wished she could feel sorry for him, but she felt nothing but contempt, glad for his pain, glad that soon he would feel nothing at all. The man was shouting terrible curses, and a few women either covered their children's ears or hurried them away. The two younger men said nothing, but Jim looked as though he were crying. Lettie was not touched by his tears, and she knew Luke was not either. Lettie could only imagine how the young man had probably laughed at Katie's tears while he was raping her.

Jim and Benny made it up the steps of the scaffold with no protest, neither of them even looking at Luke; but Zack Walker noticed him, and he let off another string of curses. "The devil will have his day with you, Luke Fontaine!" he shouted. "Piss on you, you rich, greedy bastard! Piss on your whole family! I wish I'd have kilt them all! All your pampered sons and that bitch of a wife and your prissy, ugly daughters!"

Lettie put a hand to her chest, glancing back at Katie, who had surely heard the words through the open window. She continued knitting feverishly, never looking up.

"Mama, Father just punched that awful Walker man!" Pearl spoke up. "And Ty is in there too!"

Lettie looked back to see a tumble of men around Zack Walker, who was yelling with pain. A few women screamed and moved farther away, and finally several men managed to pull Luke away from Walker. Tex had hold of Ty, and Robbie stood nearby looking ready to cry. Luke was holding his arm, and Lettie knew he had lost his temper over Walker's cruel, ugly words. Luke bent over for a moment, holding his shoulder, and Ty and Robbie went to stand next to him while the sheriff and his deputies managed to get the still-cursing Walker up the platform and into position under his noose. The crowd was in an uproar of gossip now because of the scuffle, and some began shouting, "Hang them! Hang them high!" in a kind of chant.

Reverend Gooding climbed onto the platform then to talk to each man. Jim cried harder, but Ben just stood silent. Zack continued his curses, screaming so loudly that Lettie could hear some of the words above the crowd. He shouted to the reverend that the devil would get him someday too, just like he'd get Luke Fontaine. The reverend ignored the man's swearing and turned to raise his arms, finally managing to quiet the crowd. Then he began reading from the Bible. When he finished, those who had been singing hymns began another song, "In the Sweet Bye and Bye." The rest of the crowd quieted as black hoods were placed over each man's head, then each noose put in place and tightened. The singers finished their hymn, and Reverend Gooding said a prayer for the souls of those about to die. He led the entire crowd then in singing "Shall We Gather at the River," after which Sheriff Tracy read each man's name and the charges for which he was being hanged, "murder, kidnapping, extortion, rape, and cattle rustling." He pulled a watch from his vest and announced that in just two minutes the hanging would take place.

The crowd was nearly silent then. A few of them began singing "Shall We Gather by the River" again, and Reverend Gooding and Sheriff Tracy stepped down from the platform. The two minutes seemed to take forever.

Sheriff Tracy walked behind the scaffold with the hangman the town had hired, and people stared silently.

"I hope you all burn in hell!" Zack Walker suddenly shouted from under his black hood, just before the trapdoor beneath his two nephews and him was sprung, silencing all three of them.

Lettie gasped, as did just about every person in the crowd below. The sound moved through the street almost in unison so that the "Ohs!" went up almost in a roar. Pearl and Lettie stared; both the young Walker men seemed to have died right away, their necks snapping and their heads hanging oddly to the side. Zack Walker continued to kick for several seconds before finally hanging still. Everyone waited breathlessly as each body was dropped under the scaffold, where Dr. Manning waited to check each one. After several minutes Sheriff Tracy came out to climb up onto the scaffold.

"Ben Walker, Jim Walker, and their uncle, Zack Walker, are officially dead," he announced. A cheer went up from the crowd, which began mingling and celebrating again. Luke looked up at Lettie once more, then she turned away from the window, putting her arm around Pearl, who was holding her stomach.

"I'm glad they're dead," the girl told her mother, "but I don't think I want to see something like that again."

"Nor do I," Lettie answered. She left Pearl for a moment to walk over to Katie, who had dropped the knitting in her lap and was just staring at it. "They're dead, Katie. Are you all right?"

The girl shook her head and began sobbing. "They took…part of me with them," she wept.

Lettie knelt beside her and put an arm around her. "Katie, no man can take what a woman doesn't want to give."

Pearl touched her sister's hair. She did not totally understand what had happened to Katie, but she knew it was something horrible and humiliating. "I love you, Katie," she told her.

Minutes later Ty, Robbie, and Luke came back to the room, Ty strutting inside with a manly air. "They're dead, sis," he told Katie.

Robbie timidly walked up to Katie, tears in his eyes. "I'm sorry, Katie. If I had watched you better that night—"

"We'll have none of that," Lettie interrupted. "Nothing that happened was anyone's fault," she reminded him again. She had had several talks with the boy since Katie was taken, assuring him that he was not to blame for what happened, any more than he should blame himself for Paul's death. Both things would have happened whether he was there or not. "The Walkers were out to get us, one way or another," she told the boy. "We're lucky they didn't take you too, maybe kill you."

Katie reached out and hugged Robbie. "Don't ever blame yourself, Robbie." She sobbed.

Lettie looked up at Luke, saw the agony in his eyes. She rose and walked over to him. "You shouldn't have gotten into that scuffle. How is your arm and shoulder?"

He sighed deeply. "Feels like fire is raging inside my shoulder and down my arm," he answered. He reached out with his good arm and embraced her. "Let's go home, Lettie."

Outside men covered the bodies of the three Walker men and carried them off for burial.

❧

It was four months after the hanging before Lettie could get Katie to come to town again. The only reason the girl had obliged her mother was because Pearl was to play during a special Saturday church service that was to take place just before a church social being held to celebrate harvest time. Luke grumbled that he had no desire to celebrate a farmer's holiday, as he had no use for farmers in general; but he came to attend a cattlemen's meeting, and because he wanted to hear Pearl in her first public piano recital.

Lettie's heart glowed with pride, and she could see that same pride in Luke's eyes as the entire congregation sat spellbound by Pearl Fontaine. She turned simple hymns into something glorious, her fingers flowing over the keys in rich melody that brought goose bumps, the music made more touching and thrilling by the simple fact that the girl playing the hymns was only a child. How much better would she play by the time she was an adult?

Lettie grasped Luke's hand, turning to look at him. He smiled, and she knew she would eventually win the argument she and Elsie Yost had been giving him—that Pearl should study music when she was older. It was obvious each child was going in a different direction, Robbie still talking about wanting to be a doctor, Pearl adamant that she wanted to go to the music school in Chicago that Nial Bentley had told her about. Lettie knew part of the reason Luke had fought the idea was simply because Nial had suggested it; but Nial was no longer a threat to their marriage, and there was no doubt in their minds now that to deny the girl her heart's desire would be a shame.

When Pearl finished playing several hymns in a row, the congregation cheered and clapped and whistled, in spite of the fact that they were sitting in church. Such a performance simply could not be met with silence afterward, and Pearl stood up and curtsied. The sight tugged at Lettie's heart. Pearl had always behaved like someone older than her real age. She had an elegance about her that no one had had to teach her, and she seemed to welcome an audience eagerly. She was a natural-born performer, with no fear of playing in front of others. Her beautiful young face was lit up with a smile and personal pride, and her red hair was twisted into a tumble of curls that made her look older.

Katie stood up and clapped right along with everyone

else, and Lettie was glad Pearl's playing had brought Katie to town. For the moment she seemed to have forgotten her ordeal, and Lettie decided to bring the girl to town more often from now on. The best way to get over the worry of what others thought was to face people and show them she was not ashamed, that she was the same generous, loving Katie she had been before the Walkers tried to destroy her.

The crowd pleaded for more, and Pearl gladly obliged, playing requests for several more minutes before Reverend Gooding reminded everyone there was food waiting outside and laughingly hinted that a lot of the men were getting hungry. The congregation clapped once more for Pearl and began breaking up, and Lettie spotted Nial Bentley talking to Pearl. He embraced her and was obviously congratulating her. He had young Chloris on his arm, and Lettie almost laughed at the proud look on the rather plain girl's face. She had been after Nial for a long time, and had finally snared him.

She had not seen Nial herself since she had sent him away after he had tried to kiss her. He had invited Luke and her to his wedding at Essex Manor, but Luke had made up an excuse for declining. Now Lettie could feel Luke's irritation by the way he held her arm as they approached Pearl. Not only did he not like Nial talking to his wife, he didn't even like the man talking to his children. They made their way to the front of the little church, greeting Nial coolly. Nial reddened a little, nodding to Lettie, putting his hand out to Luke, who shook it reluctantly.

"I was just congratulating Pearl," Nial said, looking at Lettie again. "I have missed hearing her play, and I see she has only gotten better. Have you decided whether to send her to Chicago?"

"Yes, I believe we will," Lettie answered cordially. "It's rather obvious we would be doing our daughter an injustice if we did not allow her to study music."

Nial did not miss the accent on *our* daughter. He looked at Luke. "Yes, well, you must be a very proud man today, Luke. And, by the way, I am sorry about what happened a few months ago. I was in Europe at the time. Chloris and I have been traveling even more since then, just got back only a month ago after visiting my ranch in Wisconsin. I apparently missed quite a spectacle with the hanging and all. I'm just sorry for the reason. I truly mean that. If I had been here and more money had been needed, I would have given it to you without ever expecting it back."

Luke was surprised by the sincerity in the man's eyes, but he knew the main reason for the gesture was Lettie and Katie. "I appreciate what you're saying," he answered, putting an arm around Katie, who was looking down. "Katie's going to be all right." He gave her a squeeze. Katie raised her eyes to look at Nial, knowing Luke hated it when she acted bashful or ashamed. Her parents had helped instill a new pride in herself, had smothered her with love and attention, had prayed with her and preached to her, to the point that coming to town today and facing people had not been nearly as unbearable as she had thought it might be. "In fact, Katie baked several of the pies out there waiting to be eaten," Luke added. "She's one hell of a pie maker, and damn smart to boot. Elsie Yost is expecting again and having a hard time of it, so Katie has taken over tutoring Pearl and Robbie in their lessons, as well as several of the other children living at the ranch."

"Well, I'm glad for you, Katie," Nial said with a smile. He put an arm around Chloris. "And I want all of you to know that Chloris and I are very happy. We appreciate your wedding gifts."

Chloris blushed as Luke and Lettie congratulated her, but when Lettie met Nial's eyes, she knew who was still first in his heart. He had only married Chloris because he wanted a woman in his bed, so he had probably figured

he might as well pick someone young, who could give
him children. Luke shook the man's hand again, and
Nial and Chloris left, as did all the Fontaine children.
Luke and Lettie lagged behind, Luke watching Nial from
the church steps. The grounds around the church were
alive with picnickers, tables full of food brought in by
the congregation, people laughing. Katie walked to the
table that held her pies and began slicing them, and Lettie
noticed Ty sitting under a tree with Alice Richards. Alice
was such a pretty girl, with blond hair and blue eyes, eyes
that always watched Ty with adoration.

Robbie ran up to his brother then and seemed excited
about something. Ty jumped up and ran off with him,
and Alice stood up and watched after him with a forlorn
look on her face. Then she hurried over to where a girl-
friend was standing and grabbed her arm, both of them
running after Ty. Lettie grinned. The girl's affection for
Tyler was so apparent that she almost felt sorry for her,
since Ty still was not old enough to realize how the girl
truly felt about him.

"I guess the little 'talk' I had with Nial in the alley
behind the cattlemen's hall last year taught him something," Luke said, his mind on Nial rather than the
puppy love between Ty and Alice. "But I saw the way he
looked at you just now. If you were available, it wouldn't
be Chloris on his arm."

"Oh, Luke, don't be silly. Walk me back to the hotel.
I want to change into a cooler dress before we eat. I had
no idea it would end up this hot today." She walked over
to tell Katie where they were going, and Pearl joined
Katie in helping serve pie, accepting more praise and
congratulations from people who came to the table.

Luke watched, proud of his family. In the distance he
could see Ty and Robbie had already discarded their hats
and jackets and were preparing to join a sack race, which
was not going to be easy, since Ty's legs were so much

longer than Robbie's. He watched them practice and fall down laughing, and he thought how this gathering was good for the family, good for Katie. He took Lettie's arm when she returned and headed across the church lawn to the street to walk her back to the hotel.

"Maybe things will go right from now on," he told Lettie. "All we have to deal with are some lingering problems with rustlers, and there has been a new influx of sheepherders this summer. We'll be meeting later today to talk about how to keep them out."

"Luke, you can't keep out every single person who wants to do something other than raise cattle. Montana is a big territory."

"Not big enough for sheep and cattle together. We've got enough problems putting up with more and more farmers coming in and losing federal land to them. If we let the sheep come too, there won't be any grazing land left for the cattle."

"Why don't you just try talking to the sheep men first? Maybe there is a way to work things out. From what I hear, they get kicked out of everyplace they go. We've both read about the awful range wars in Colorado and Wyoming. I don't want to see that happen here too, Luke." She grasped his arm tighter. "And I don't want to have to go through the hell again of worrying about you out there maybe getting hurt or killed. I'm so tired of it all. I want some peace."

"We'll find a peaceful way to stop them, if that's possible. I'm not out to slaughter the sheep or kill innocent men like some cattlemen have done, but we'll do whatever we have to do to get the message across, Lettie. We own a lot of land, but we still need the federal land for extra grass. We'd have to cut way back if we lost it, and I didn't build the Double L to the size it is just to have to turn around and take a step backward. No sheep man is going to make me do that."

They walked past the Lonesome Tree, and Lettie could not help glancing toward the swinging doors at the sound of piano music and laughter that came from inside. Luke led her across the street and down toward the hotel. "She's gone, Lettie."

"Who?"

"Annie Gates. I went into the Lonesome Tree for a drink a couple of weeks ago when I was in town, and she told me she was leaving the next day. She decided to go to Denver to try to start a new life."

They walked quietly to the hotel, each lost in their own thoughts of Nial Bentley and Annie Gates. Luke led her up to the room and unlocked the door. They went inside, and Luke closed and locked the door again. "Why didn't you tell me you had been to see Annie?" he asked. "She told me it was you who convinced her she could change her life if she wanted."

Lettie removed her hat. "I don't know why I didn't tell you. I guess it just didn't seem to matter. It was before you came back from going after those rustlers last year, back when Henny had just died. I guess I needed to hear from the horse's mouth what was going on between you and Annie." She began unbuttoning the front of her dress, turning to face Luke. "Actually, it was because of some things that Annie told me that I decided I wanted to make things right between us."

His eyes moved over her lovingly. "I guess we've both had reminders today of big mistakes we made." He walked closer, grasping the back of her neck and pulling her closer. "I don't ever want anything to come between us again, Lettie. This thing with Katie was a big test, but thank God it didn't keep you out of my bed. We can't let that happen again."

Lettie arched an eyebrow teasingly. "And did you give Annie Gates a kiss good-bye?"

Luke grinned the handsome grin that had always

stirred her deeply. "Maybe I should let you wonder about that."

"Luke Fontaine—"

He met her lips before she could finish, his tongue searching suggestively. He left her mouth and moved to kiss and lick at her neck. "Only on the cheek," he answered. "A quick peck on the cheek for good luck." He sighed deeply, pulling some combs from her hair. "Annie Gates is gone for good, and Nial Bentley is married. We're getting our lives back to normal, and Katie seems to be getting stronger every day." He kissed her eyes. "And right now the kids are all over at the church having a good time. How about you and I have our own good time right here before we go back?"

"Luke!" She pulled away. "In the middle of the day? While everyone else is at a church social? That is absolutely wicked."

He just kept grinning and began removing his shirt. "You have to undress anyway."

Lettie drank in the sight of his still-solid chest and arms. At forty-three, and after all he had been through, Luke Fontaine had only grown more masculine and handsome. Age and hard work had been good to him, and the sight of his many scars from the grizzly attack and bullet wounds brought back aching memories, and awakened her heart to how it had felt every time she thought she might lose this man to death. Still, through it all, he had somehow remained invincible, and now he had accomplished every dream for which he had come to this land. The only thing that she knew still troubled him deeply was that he had never heard from his father and brother back in St. Louis, in spite of all the times he had written them.

She finished unbuttoning her dress as Luke sat down to remove his boots. They had come through the loss of Nathan, had survived little Paul's death and Katie's rape. They had risen above trouble with the land and the weather, rustlers and outlaws, the loss of their two best friends. She knew Luke still missed Will, and she sorely missed Henny; but their deaths had brought them closer, both realizing that all they had was each other.

Luke stood up and removed his pants and underwear, and Lettie finished undressing, blushing, hoping she still looked as good to her husband in broad daylight as he still looked to her. "This is ridiculous," she protested.

"Then why did you strip naked?" he asked with a grin, walking closer. "You could have just changed your dress."

"You forced me," she replied. "I have to do what my husband commands."

He chuckled, pulling her close and rubbing his chest against her breasts. "You don't seem to be fighting me, and I don't hear you arguing." He hoisted her up so that she wrapped her legs around his waist and her breasts were near his face. He kissed eagerly at them as he carried her to the bed.

"This is absolutely outrageous," Lettie told him, grasping his hair and closing her eyes in sweet ecstasy.

"Mmm-hmmm," he answered. He knelt down and set her on the bed, laid her back. He licked at her breasts, then gently tasted a nipple before moving his lips to her throat while massaging a breast teasingly. "Do you realize you're just as beautiful as that first night I took you in that awful little cabin we use now for a storage shed?"

Lettie ran her hands over his solid shoulders, feeling a familiar fire make its way through her body. "Your eyes are getting old, Luke Fontaine. You must not see so well anymore. My waist is a little thicker, my breasts have fed six babies and—"

He cut off her words with another kiss, this one deeper, hungrier, hotter. She said nothing more, returning his kiss with equal hunger, parting her legs in welcome. He quickly moved downward, tasting her breasts again, trailing his tongue over her belly and finally to that most intimate part of her that only Luke Fontaine had tasted.

"Luke," she whispered.

His only reply was a groan. He licked his way back up to meet her mouth again, then pushed himself inside her, his shaft hard and hot, filling her to surprising pleasure, considering the fact that she had borne six children. She had worried over the years that she would not please him as she once had, but the ecstasy of this splendid coupling never seemed to change. In moments they were moving in perfect rhythm, each trying to give as much as they could, glorying in this act that represented the deep love and affection they had shared over the fifteen years since they had settled here.

The thought of Luke doing this with Annie made Lettie grasp at him desperately. She dug her fingers into his arms, arching up to him in an effort to please, to erase any memory he might have of being with someone else. All the while Luke was reminded of how close he had come to losing this woman to another man. How he hated the thought of someone else touching his Lettie. He raised up to drink in her nakedness, grasping her hips and pushing deep, wanting to show her that in spite of all the babies, he was still man enough to please her.

Lettie threw her head back and cried out his name as a sweet climax engulfed her. Luke came down closer again, moving more gently now, teasing, moving in slow circles, licking at her cheeks, her mouth. "Luke, please," she cried. He grinned, kissing her savagely then, moving in hard, quick thrusts and burying his head in the pillow near hers to muffle his groans as his life spilled into her in blessed release.

"Stay there," he whispered. "Just once more before we join the others."

Lettie's only reply was to meet his mouth in another hungry kiss.

Twenty-six

KATIE WALKED UP THE STEPS OF THE NEW LOG BUILDING that sported a sign reading Billings Library. At Lettie's urging that she start socializing more, she had begun several months ago to join her mother at the women's club meetings, and it was at one of those meetings that she had proposed the idea of a library for Billings. All the women had raved that it was a wonderful thought. A library was another step forward in civilizing Billings, and through the library Katie planned to begin keeping records of local pioneers, those who had settled here first, where they were from, when they had first arrived and what businesses they ran or ranches or farms they had settled. It was part of Katie's plan to help her mother keep records that could be used to build a museum one day in honor of people like Will and Henny.

She felt good now about how receptive the women had been to the idea, and to her. All were kind and friendly, and she realized why her mother had wanted her to begin joining the meetings. Gradually over the past two years she had managed to come out of the shell into which she had withdrawn after her ordeal with the Walkers, and she loved her mother even more for the constant support she and her women friends had given her.

She carried a stack of new books inside, glowing from the fact that her father had also been proud of her desire to found a library. Luke had given the money necessary to put up the building, as well as making a generous contribution, along with other businessmen in town, toward buying books from New York and Chicago. Her parents, along with others, had also contributed books from their own libraries at home.

It was a dream project for Katie, who loved books more than jewels or pretty clothes or anything else she could think of. For five days out of every week she lived at the Stowes' boardinghouse on Will and Henny's old property, sharing a room with a new female teacher from Chicago, a widow named Yolanda Brown. Mrs. Brown had been hired to assist the town's only other teacher, Howard Task, who had been hired out of Kansas through an ad the Billings citizens had placed because of a great need for a school for the ever-growing community. Her father and other businessmen had built a large, two-room school last summer, and already two teachers were needed. Sometimes Katie also helped teach, but most of her time was spent organizing the hundreds of books that now lined the shelves of the library.

She had spent hours setting up a method of keeping records of all the books that came in, as well as a way to keep track of books by title, author, and subject, and records of books checked out. She knew her mother supported her new "job" because it kept her busy, and being busy meant less time to dwell on ugly memories. People treated her as though nothing had ever happened, and she felt important and needed. It felt good to hear people tell her how clever and industrious she was for coming up with the idea for a library and being willing to stay in town to run it. Many had already visited her, some of the older ones unable to read but wanting books for their children. They also brought with them or dictated to her information about their families and backgrounds so she could incorporate the information into the ledger she kept for the future museum. Everyone had been eager about both ideas, making it easy to raise the necessary money to maintain the building and buy more books. All the shelves inside had been built by Phillip Crane, a fairly new resident of Billings. Crane was a carpenter and furniture maker, and to show his support of the town, he had donated the material and his own labor to build the shelves. His contribution had immediately put him in a favorable light, and already the man's carpentry and furniture-making business was rapidly growing, as many of the female citizens of Billings and the surrounding area were anxious for new furniture in their homes or to have old furniture refinished. Now his biggest project was to put the finishing touches on the new four-story Hotel Fontaine, which her father had had built over the past winter. Already Luke Fontaine's latest business venture was doing well, and soon a plaque would be placed on the front of the library reading Billings Library, Est. 1880 by Luke and Eletta Fontaine.

She breathed deeply of the smell of fresh pine as she laid the newly arrived books on a desk, thinking what an important role her mother and father had played in settling the area. She went outside to get more books from the freight wagon that had been parked in front of the library by a man from Hendrixon's Freighting and Supply, through whom the books had been ordered. It would take a while to unload all of them, but she didn't mind. She opened another box, having to take a few books in at a time because a full box was too heavy to carry.

She stopped for a moment to open one of the books and sniff it, enjoying the wonderful smell of new pages; yet she also loved the smell of older books. It was reading that had gotten her through the past two years and had helped take her away to places of the mind, where she could forget about what had happened to her. It was books that had helped her heal, as well as spending this time in town organizing the library. Her parents had not wanted her to leave home, but they understood that for now, maybe this was best. She had a good roommate in Mrs. Brown, who was a childless, middle-aged woman who enjoyed the same things Katie enjoyed, reading, learning, and teaching. She was proud to be living partly on her own at sixteen, and she felt comfortable at the boardinghouse because she used to go there to see Will and Henny when she was little. The house had been enlarged several times so that now the original cabin was nothing more than a large dining room where boarders gathered for daily meals, but Katie remembered playing in that very room when she was small, chasing Henny's several cats, some of which still hung around the property. Martin Stowe and his wife had added on ten rooms, and with the three extra rooms that had already been a part of the main house, there were twelve rooms that could be rented in addition to the room in which the Stowes slept.

Because of the way Billings was growing, the boardinghouse was nearly always full, and the Stowes were already talking about adding on again. The barn and shed out back that were once used by Will for his stock now served as shelter for the horses of those who rented rooms. Mrs. Stowe ran the boardinghouse while her husband managed the Hotel Fontaine for Luke.

Katie took another armload of books out of the box, thinking how happy Will and Henny would be to know that their property was being used to help new settlers, people who contributed to the growth of the once-tiny town they had helped found. She headed back up the steps with the books, which were heavier and harder to balance than she thought. She realized she had taken too many, but decided to hurry and get them inside before she dropped them. In her haste, she walked right into someone. She heard a yelp as the books went tumbling against whoever it was, some of them landing on his foot. She managed to cling to three of the books, then stepped back to see a young man bending over to pick up those she had dropped.

"Oh, I'm so sorry!" she told him. "I didn't see you. I guess I just took too many at once."

"It's okay, ma'am." The man straightened with the rest of the books in his arms, and for a moment he stared at her.

Katie blushed at the obvious pleasure in the man's eyes as he quickly looked her over. Those eyes were a soft green, the strands of hair that stuck out from under his leather hat a sandy color. In spite of the fact that she had never had any particularly romantic feelings for any young man, something about this one stirred an odd feeling deep inside that almost frightened her. She was sure that after what she had been through she should and could never have feelings for anyone of the opposite sex, but this young man impressed her in a special way. She was surprised to realize she was wondering how she looked. Until this very moment, she had never cared how she appeared to anyone else, certainly not to a man. This one was handsome, with a sure look in his eyes, his smile bright and kind. He stood only a couple of inches taller than she, but he had a husky, brawny build. She was nearly five foot eight herself, something else that had always made her feel awkward around young men, since the ones who were her age were usually shorter than she.

"You want me to take these inside for you?" the stranger asked.

Katie realized she had been staring, and she wished she could hide the crimson she was sure showed in her cheeks. "Yes, that would be very nice. I truly am sorry I walked right into you like that."

His gaze moved over her again, and strangely, she did not feel insulted or offended by the way he seemed to be gauging her every curve. She wondered if he thought her pretty or ugly, maybe too tall and gangly. Her mother was always telling her how pretty she was, but all mothers thought that way. Maybe to men she

wasn't pretty at all, and any who knew the truth about
her probably wanted nothing to do with her. She had
only socialized with women since the ugly attack, had
not gone to any dances or other events that might put her
into contact with men on a social level. Because of that,
she had no way of knowing what the other young men
in town thought of her, except that none had formally
called on her. She knew that could be because she was
Luke Fontaine's daughter and they were afraid of Luke;
or because she was simply still too young. Then again,
she was sure the primary reason was that they surely felt
awkward, knowing what had happened to her.

She went inside, followed by the young man, who
carried the rest of the books. "Just lay them on this desk,"
she told him.

He obeyed, then looked around the little log structure. "I've heard about libraries, but I've never seen
one before."

Katie folded her arms self-consciously. "Well, I have
never seen one either, but my tutor back home taught
me about them, how they are set up and all. I would love
to see a really big one, like in Chicago."

The young man shrugged. "You must read real good.
I can read some, but not enough that I would sit with a
book for hours." He met her eyes. "You run this place?"

Katie felt herself blushing again. "It was my idea. I also
teach at the new school down at the west end of town.
Billings is growing so much that we already have two
school teachers, and they still need my help."

"Sounds like the town is growing real fast."

"Oh, it is! When my parents settled near here seventeen years ago, they tell me there were just a few log
buildings here, mostly saloons. Now we have a school and
all kinds of businesses, two hotels and a boardinghouse,
now a library. I'm even organizing records of founding
families that will be used in the future for a museum.

We have a sheriff and a jail, a church and preacher, and the town citizens have gotten rid of a lot of the saloons. Only a couple of those left still have permission to allow gambling. We have completely outlawed pros—" She hesitated, felt the heat come into her cheeks. She was amazed at how she was babbling like an idiot.

The young man grinned. "In other words, Billings has become very respectable," he finished for her.

"Yes." Katie looked away.

"I know about the boardinghouse," the man told her. "I just took a room there."

She met his eyes again, her curiosity aroused. "You did? I live there too, during the week, with one of the schoolteachers, Mrs. Brown. I stay in town so that I can manage this library, and, of course, because of the need for a teaching assistant. The property the boardinghouse is on used to belong to my parents' best friends. They both died over a year ago, and my father inherited the property. He sold it to the Stowes. Mr. Stowe also manages the Hotel Fontaine. My father owns it."

"The Hotel Fontaine? Is that your name then?"

"Yes. I'm Katie Fontaine." She waited for a reaction. Had he heard anything about her? She saw nothing in his eyes that told her so.

"Excuse me, ma'am, for not introducing myself. Bradley Tillis. I'm from Colorado. I'm up here looking for land."

Katie put down the books she had carried in. "Oh? Are you going to farm, or ranch?" She noticed a wary look come into his eyes at the question, and he seemed hesitant at first to answer.

"Ranch."

"Oh, then, you must meet my father. He's one of the biggest cattle ranchers in Montana. He can get you into the Cattlemen's Association, introduce you around town."

Bradley suddenly appeared nervous. "Well, I guess

your pa must be a pretty big man around here, owning the hotel and all."

Katie shrugged. "He has a hand in a lot of businesses, even owns some copper mines. But cattle are his first love and that is what he has built everything around. He and my mother were among the first to settle in this area." Katie wondered why she found him so easy to talk to. She felt as though she had known this stranger forever, and she felt a flutter at the way he smiled, a warm smile, with clean, even teeth and dimples in his cheeks. He seemed to be a grand mixture of man and boy, handsome and well built, with a sure look about him, but a boyish charm to his grin. She caught herself staring again and quickly looked away. "Well, I had better get busy unloading the rest of those books. Mr. Hendrixon will be back soon to pick up his wagon."

Bradley set his hat on one of the bookshelves. "Let me help you."

"Oh, you must be busy. You really don't have to—"

"I'd like to. I've finished what I intended to do today—got a map from the land office showing where the other ranches are. Come to think of it, your father's was the biggest area on the map. Does he use a lot of federal land for grazing?"

"All the ranchers do. They couldn't get by without it. That's why they try to keep out the sheep ranchers."

Katie's back was turned to him as she answered on her way out the door. She did not see the look of concern in Bradley Tillis's eyes. "Is that so? Is there a lot of trouble around here over sheep?"

Katie reached into the wagon again. "Oh, not like the things we heard happened in Colorado and Wyoming—no killings or anything like that, at least not yet. My father and the other cattlemen can give a man a lot of trouble if they set their minds to it, but so far they've managed to keep things fairly peaceful. Some

Mormons tried to settle in with sheep last summer, but the cattlemen convinced them to leave. So far threats are all that have been necessary."

Damn, Bradley thought. *I meet a pretty girl, and she's the daughter of the biggest cattle rancher in the area.* Maybe this was some kind of omen that he should give up right now on the reason he had come here. Then again, maybe it was a different kind of omen. If a sheep man married a cattleman's daughter...

He finished helping her with the books, all the while studying the way Katie Fontaine carried herself. She seemed proud and sure, and she filled out her blue calico dress in all the right places. She was the prettiest thing he had seen in his entire life, and she was smart and independent too, considering that she could surely be living at home doing nothing. The girl had class, was probably pampered, her father's ranch house most likely a castle. Instead, she was here in town on her own, teaching school and running a library. Her parents were pioneers here, so she came from strong stock. What a fine wife she would make, just the kind of woman he was looking for; but first he had to find a way to continue to earn his own way at what he knew best—raising sheep. A terrible drought in Colorado had nearly wiped out the family ranch. He wanted to go off on his own and start his own ranch, but he needed someplace new to start. He had been told he would find less trouble in Montana as far as not having to face the ugly range wars he and his father had suffered the last few years. They had been forced out of Nebraska, Wyoming, and Colorado, and things were even worse in Arizona and New Mexico; so he had come north to find peace, and enough good grassland to start anew.

Now he wasn't so sure he could bring sheep up here without more problems. He had told no one yet why he was here. Like Katie Fontaine, the land agent had taken it for granted he had come here to raise cattle. Already he could see he was not going to have an easy time of it, but he was determined to find a way. Sheep ranching was all he or his father or his grandfather had ever known.

He finished helping Katie carry in the books, then picked up his hat. "Well, I, uh, I guess I'll see you at suppertime at the boardinghouse, then?"

Katie felt her heart beat a little faster, amazed to find herself attracted to anyone of the opposite sex. She actually noticed how strong he looked, the way he filled out his checkered flannel shirt. His denim pants fit his slender hips nicely, and there was that charming smile again. Was it wrong to be aware of such things in a man, after what she had been through? What was happening to her? Was her mother right when she had told her someone would come along who could erase all the ugly memories?

"Yes, I'll see you at supper," she answered. "Mrs. Stowe makes wonderful biscuits. I often help her. I love cooking and baking, but I don't always have a lot of time for either one."

So, she cooks too, Brad thought. He chastised himself for thinking the daughter of a wealthy cattle baron, especially one as pretty as this one, would even give him the time of day. Once she found out his real reason for being here, his chances of courting this pretty girl would go down to zero.

"Well, we can talk more tonight, then."

Katie smiled bashfully and nodded. "How long will you be in Billings?"

"I'm not sure yet. Depends on whether I can find some decent land. Men like your pa probably already own the best pieces. I might have to go on west of here, or maybe farther north." Was that disappointment he saw in her eyes, or did he just *want* it to be there?

"Well, I hope you find what you need somewhere close to Billings." Katie immediately wondered why she had said that. Would he take it the wrong way? "Thank you so much for helping carry in the books. You didn't have to do that."

Bradley tipped his hat. "It was my pleasure, Miss Fontaine." He turned to leave, and Katie watched him, tiptoeing to the doorway so he would not know she had gone there to watch him walk away. He was a fine-looking young man, interesting because he was a stranger in town. She guessed him to be about twenty-five. Part of her was terribly attracted to him, for reasons she could not even explain; but when she thought about any young man touching her...

She shivered and turned away, chastising herself for allowing romantic thoughts for any man. No matter how she felt about Bradley Tillis or anyone else who might come along, she didn't think she could ever be intimate with any of them. She might as well give up thinking about marriage and children and ever living like a normal woman. Despite how it had worked out for her mother, she didn't see how any man would want her for a wife once he knew the awful truth.

❧

Bradley Tillis took a job at the livery in Billings, and Katie knew why. Both were aware of the attraction between them, and although Bradley had said he should go on west to find land, since all the land for a hundred miles or more around Billings was claimed, he stayed in Billings...for Katie. She looked forward to every meal they shared, every walk they took in the evening, every visit to the library. She had not told her parents yet of her feelings for Bradley, mainly because she wasn't sure any of it would last once he found out the truth. It was obvious she was going to have to tell him soon, for last night he had almost kissed her, and to her surprise she had wanted him to.

Christmas was coming. She wanted Bradley to come to the Double L and see the ranch, meet the family, and share Christmas with them. But she dared not ask him until she told him everything. If the man was as serious about her as she suspected, she had to tell him about her rape, not just for his sake, but for her own, for she was fast losing her heart.

She blew out an oil lamp and took her cape from a peg on the wall. She had worked extra late that night with another new order of books. Her parents were so thrilled with her involvement in the project that Luke had donated even more money, and she had ordered a collection of Shakespeare and Poe and several other classics. Before she realized it, she was lost in reading instead of getting the books organized, which led to working well after dark. She headed for the door, but it opened before she could reach it, and Brad walked inside, deep concern in his eyes.

"Katie! When you didn't show up at supper I got worried. What are you still doing here?"

Why did he look even more handsome in the partially darkened room? "I got behind—started reading instead of working. I was just finishing up."

"Well, you shouldn't be walking after dark. Billings might be a civilized town now, but that's no guarantee that it's safe for a pretty young girl to be walking alone."

Katie felt the familiar pain in her stomach. *This pretty young girl is already soiled, Bradley. You needn't worry.* "Oh, I don't worry about that," she said aloud. "After all, I'm Luke Fontaine's daughter," she joked. "One scream from me, and the whole town would come running." She started to turn down the oil lamp near the door, but Bradley grasped her arm.

"Like the whole town contributed to the kidnapping money?"

Katie felt as though every nerve end was alive and

on fire, and her stomach ached even more fiercely. He knew! She had to get away! Hide! How could she look at him? She had been going to tell him in her own way, when she was ready, when the time was right. She jerked her arm, but he would not let go.

"Katie, it's all right."

"No, it isn't! Please let me go, Bradley!" She felt the tears wanting to come then. She hated him! No, she loved him! But it did no good to feel that way. He knew now. He was going to tell her gently that he couldn't see her anymore, wasn't he? Then why was he turning her, putting his arms around her? Why wouldn't he let go of her?

"You stay right here, Katie girl. Do you really think what happened matters to me?"

"Please, let me go, Brad." His chest was solid, and he smelled good.

"You don't want me to let go, not any more than I *want* to let go. I love you, Katie Fontaine, and there isn't anything going to change that. I'm just sorry I wasn't around at the time to have a hand in catching those bastards. I would have loved to help pull that lever."

Katie put a hand to her face, cringing against his chest, and finally the tears came full force. "Who told you?" she sobbed.

"Mrs. Stowe. She could see how things were getting to be between us, and she suspected you never said anything. She didn't do it to be mean. She did it because she cares about you, Katie. She figured maybe it would be easier if somebody else told me so I'd be prepared, and so you wouldn't have to go through the whole ugly thing again yourself. Having to tell it to a jury was bad enough."

"I was…only fourteen," she wept. "And they were… grown men…and strong. There wasn't anything…I could do to stop them. I tried, Brad…but they…kept hitting me…and they held me…"

"Hush, Katie." He wrapped his arms even tighter around her. "It doesn't matter now. What matters is that you came through it, and you're strong and proud and you've gone on with your life. All you need now is to learn that being with a man doesn't have to be something horrible like that…not if you love him…and he loves you. And you might as well know right now that I want to be that man. I'd never hurt you, Katie. I love you and I want you to be my wife."

She reached into a pocket on her yellow dress and took out a handkerchief, pulling away from him then to wipe at her nose and eyes. "How can you want me?"

He put his hands to her waist. "Because you're beautiful and brave and tough, let alone damn smart and a hard worker. You're everything a man could want, Katie, and you were raised on a ranch, so you know what that kind of life is like. Mostly I want you just because you're sweet and good-hearted, and I just plain love you. I think I loved you the first day we met."

She managed a faint smile through her tears, feeling the heat come back into her face again. It continued to amaze her that she actually enjoyed his touch. "I feel the same way about you, Brad, but I was so afraid that once you knew…I'd lose you."

He smiled the fetching grin that had a way of melting away her inhibitions. "You've got to have more faith in the man you love, Katie girl, especially when he's going to be your husband."

She studied the sincerity and determination in his gentle eyes, and did not resist when he leaned closer. With a pounding heart, Katie closed her own eyes and allowed his lips to touch hers lightly. It was a sweet, tender kiss. She wondered how one man's touch could be so horrifying, while another's could be so wonderful. The kiss grew deeper, and he pressed her close. She felt on fire with feelings she'd never thought she could possibly have for a man, yet when she thought of letting him invade her the way the Walker boys had done, she stiffened in his arms.

Bradley felt her resistance, and he left her lips, kissed her hair. "It will be okay, Katie. If you'll be my wife, I promise you I won't come to your bed until you feel like you're ready; but I also promise you that when you decide to be my wife in every way, you're going to be surprised at how nice it will be. And then you'll start having babies, and you'll forget all the ugly things and see the beautiful side of being with a man."

She thought about her own mother, how she had found that happiness with Luke, in spite of what she had been through. Now she understood what her mother meant when she told her the right man would come along someday to erase all the ugliness. She relaxed again, meeting his gaze. "I do love you, Brad, and I do want to marry you. Three months might not seem like very long to some, but from that very first day we met, I felt so comfortable with you. I'm glad you know. Now we can share everything."

A strange, almost guilty look came into his eyes then. He kissed her forehead, then pulled away with a deep sigh. "The trouble is, we have to get your pa's permission first to marry."

Katie frowned. "He won't object, once he meets you and finds out what a good person you are; and especially when he realizes I love you. My parents will be thrilled that I have found someone who can take away the bad memories. They want nothing more than for me to be happy and to live a normal life. And with you being a cattleman and all—"

"That's the trouble," he interrupted. "Now it's my turn to 'fess up, Katie." He sighed and walked a few feet away, studying a row of books for a moment before turning to face her. "You're right that we should share everything. Now it's my turn to tell a secret, Katie." He ran a hand through his hair nervously. "All I said was that I was a rancher, Katie. I never said it was cattle that I raised."

Katie frowned thoughtfully, then her eyes widened. "Not *sheep*!"

He nodded. "It's all I know. My grandfather raised sheep, my father, and now I want to get started on my own, but I can't do it down in Colorado or even in Wyoming. Between the drought we've been having and the trouble with cattlemen, I've got to try someplace new."

She put a hand to her lips. "Oh dear."

"Yeah." He rolled his eyes. "Now do you see our problem? It's bad enough we haven't known each other all that long, and that your folks have never even met me yet, let alone the fact that your pa probably expects you to marry some rich rancher's son. Not only am I not rich, but I'm not in cattle at all. Your pa will probably blow to high heaven when he finds out you're in love with a sheep man, and it will probably mean we'd have to live far away from here. He'd never allow me to graze sheep anyplace around here." He shoved his hands into his back pockets and paced. "This doesn't change how *you* feel about me, does it?"

Katie folded her arms, watching him longingly. "No. I just know how my father feels about sheep." She sighed thoughtfully. "Brad, my father isn't the monster you think he is, and there is one way he can be convinced, one person who can keep him calm and reason with him."

"Who's that?"

"My mother. As powerful and determined as my father can be, he'll do anything my mother asks. I just have to talk to her first." Yes, Lettie would understand more than anyone what it meant to her to find love, to find a man who could overlook what had happened to her. "My mother will come to get me this weekend.

I'm going home for Christmas. Pa probably won't come with her to town this time because he already attended a cattlemen's meeting last week, and he said he had to stay at the ranch this week. He's going out to the north section with some of his men to bring in some stray cattle that could starve this winter if they aren't brought closer to the main ranch. It will take several days, and he'll get back just in time for Christmas. Mother will probably just bring a couple of men from the ranch along to accompany her, so you and I will have some time alone."

"You and I?"

"Yes. You're coming to the Double L for Christmas, Brad. It's time you met my family, and we can tell Mother about our plans and about you being a sheep rancher. That way at least *she* will be prepared and ready to handle my father when he finds out. Please say you'll come."

Brad rubbed at his eyes. "Why do I get the feeling this will not be a very merry Christmas?"

"It *will* be, Brad, once my father realizes how much we love each other and how determined I am. Mother will know how to smooth it over."

"What if she doesn't like me?"

"Oh, but she will. I'm not worried about that. We can make this work, with my mother's help. We'll tell my pa flat out that we're in love and intend to be married. Maybe between the three of us we can present the sheep issue without any big problems. Maybe Pa will even let you try raising sheep on his land."

Bradley chuckled. "You're a dreamer, Katie girl."

She walked closer, taking hold of his hands. "Maybe. But ornery as my pa can be, one thing I know is how much he loves his family and wants what's best for us. It was Pa who came for me when I was abducted, and I'll never forget the look on his face when he found me." Her eyes teared again. "And when he told me never to hang my head. And with all those men surrounding us, he grabbed me up and rode off with me, took a bullet in the back that could have killed or crippled him. No matter how he reacts, don't hate him right away. He's a good man. He gets a little stubborn in his ideas sometimes, but he can be reasoned with, and my mother is the one who can do it."

Bradley sighed deeply. "All I know is that I'll do whatever it takes to make you my wife, but I won't bow to any man or give up what I know how to do best. And with or without Luke Fontaine's blessing, I want you for my wife, Katie. Will you still marry me, even if he doesn't approve?"

Katie could not imagine going against her father; but now she could also not imagine letting Brad Tillis ride out of her life. "Yes, I'll marry you, even if Pa doesn't approve."

Twenty-seven

THE ENTIRE FONTAINE FAMILY SAT AROUND THE elegantly set table in the dining room of the family mansion. It was Christmas Eve, a time when there would normally be a great deal of talking and celebrating; but everyone was quiet, the younger children all gawking at Brad Tillis. Tyler sat at his father's right hand, scrutinizing Brad with the same possessive, untrusting eyes as his father.

Brad could hardly eat. He had hoped Luke Fontaine would not be the big, domineering man he had pictured; but upon meeting him, he felt his case was even more hopeless. When Luke came to the parlor to meet him after coming in late and first cleaning up, his big frame had seemed to fill the room, in spite of the fact that the parlor itself was huge, with high ceilings. Luke Fontaine fit every picture of the cattle tyrant, powerfully built, a weathered face, piercing blue eyes, a firm handshake, raw power emanating from his very being. He had looked Brad over, then announced he had paperwork to do and that they would "discuss this thing" at the supper table. Before leaving the room, he had announced that "no young man I've met for the first time is going to tell me he's marrying my daughter, nor should he even dare to ask me if he can."

"Brad, would you like some more turkey?" Lettie asked, interrupting the silence.

Brad glanced at the gracious, beautiful woman, whom he already liked a great deal, as he did Pearl and Robbie, who had been receptive and full of questions. If it was only those three he had to deal with, this would be easy, but Luke Fontaine was protective of his daughter, and he could understand that protectiveness was even stronger because of what had happened to her. Her brother Tyler was equally protective, and now Brad was not so sure that it was true Lettie Fontaine could help their situation. When he and Katie had talked to Katie's mother alone earlier and explained that he raised sheep for a living, the woman had at first been aghast. "Sheep!" she had exclaimed. "Katie, it's one thing to ask me to help you convince your father to let you get married; but to a sheep man! Even I might have trouble talking him into that one!" She had not been rude about it, only worried, for she seemed to understand how much Katie loved him, and how important finding love was to her, for more reasons than the average young woman.

Brad glanced at Pearl, who he could see was ready to giggle at the odd silence at the table. The children knew he wanted to marry Katie, but no one except Lettie knew yet that he was a sheep man. He had never been so nervous in his life, and it irritated him that Luke was silently devouring his meal, making him wait for the "discussion" he intended to have. He decided that there was only one way to approach a man like Luke Fontaine, and that was to stand right up to him, be honest and open and take no gaff. At the least, the man would want his daughter to marry someone who was unafraid of challenges, and who was proud of what he did for a living. For the moment the only thing Luke knew was that he was a "rancher." He had hoped Lettie would break the news first, but he realized that that might not be best after all. He didn't need any woman to do his talking for him! He set his fork down and leaned back in his chair.

"Mr. Fontaine, everybody is just about finished eating, and I can't take this silence any longer. Katie told me how this house is always full of good times on Christmas Eve, and there's a big tree in the front parlor where she says you always gather to listen to Pearl play Christmas carols."

Luke swallowed his last piece of turkey and scowled at him. He picked up a glass of wine and took a sip. "Well? You apparently have a lot more to say, so say it." He leaned back in his chair, his handsome blue eyes drilling into him.

Brad looked from Luke to Tyler, holding his chin a little higher, then looked back at Luke. "May I stand, sir?"

Luke nodded. "Go ahead."

Brad took a deep breath and rose, scooting back his chair. Pearl and Robbie stared wide-eyed, and Lettie watched Luke closely. Katie sat staring at her plate, her cheeks flushed. She felt like crying for the hard time Luke was giving poor Brad.

"Mr. Fontaine, it's like your wife told you when you got home. I love your daughter very much and she loves me. We met in town. I work at the livery, but I actually came here looking for land. Since all the good land around here is taken, I'll have to go farther away to find it, so I'll wait till spring because a man can't travel far out here in the dead of winter, and because I wanted to stay close to Katie awhile longer. We want to get married, and I came here to ask your permission. I understand you'd be skeptical because you don't know me from Adam, but I assure you, sir, that I come from a good family. My father is John Tillis, from Iowa. He and my mother and two younger brothers live in Colorado now. I want to strike out on my own. I didn't come to Montana looking for a wife—just land. But when I met Katie—" He sighed deeply. "I kind of ran into her by accident at the library, and then we found out I had taken a room at Stowe's boardinghouse and we eat our meals at the same table, started taking walks, what have you. Anyway, that's how it all started, and now I'd like to marry her. I'm old enough—twenty-four—and

I'm a hard worker. I know she comes from a rich family, and I intend to take good care of her. And don't think I'm marrying her for her money. I couldn't care less if you totally disinherited her, except that it would be pretty unfair to Katie. I just happen to love her for the wonderful woman that she is." He swallowed. Should he say anything yet about the sheep? Why couldn't he make the words come out?

"Pa, I love Brad," Katie spoke up quietly, meeting her father's eyes. "You and Mama know what a special thing that is for me. I never thought—" Her eyes teared then, and she looked back down at her plate. "I never thought I'd feel like this about any man."

Luke glanced at Lettie, who arched her eyebrows. He knew she was remembering their own beginning, and that her situation had been similar to Katie's. He understood that was why Lettie would sympathize with Katie's predicament, but that didn't make her marrying a man they knew little about right. He looked back at Brad. "You know then, about what happened to Katie?"

"Yes, sir, I know, and it doesn't make any difference to me. It sure wasn't her fault. I don't love Katie just because she's the prettiest girl in Billings." Pearl finally giggled, and he felt the color coming to his own cheeks. "I love her for her strength and courage," he went on, "for her intelligence, and because she comes from strong stock, a good family. She understands ranching life, and she knows the meaning of hard work, although I don't intend for her to have to do much of that. I just want her to be comfortable and happy. I can't promise she'd live like a queen right off, but I'd do everything I can to give her the good life she deserves. And I'm not so insensitive that I don't understand her situation. If you think I'd ever hurt her or push her into anything, you're dead wrong, Mr. Fontaine...sir." Was that a hint of a smile he saw at the corner of Luke's mouth?

Luke took another sip of wine. "If I let you marry my daughter, and I ever get one hint that you've abused her in any way or that you forced her or frightened her, I'll break your neck. You understand that?"

Brad swallowed. "Yes, sir. I'd expect it. You wouldn't be asking any more of me than I would ask of myself."

Katie looked at her father. "Pa, I told Brad what a good man you are." A tear slipped down her cheek. "You're embarrassing me by being so rude."

Luke set his wineglass down. "I'll be as rude as necessary when it comes to giving my daughter over in marriage. Once a man is your husband, you're under his control and answer to his whims. I don't take something like that lightly, Katie, and I hardly know this young man."

"Can't you trust my judgment? It's *my* feelings that matter here," Katie argued. "I've seen Brad almost every day for three months now. We talk about everything. I felt comfortable with him from the very first day I met him. We enjoy each other's company, and he doesn't—" She looked up at Brad. "He doesn't frighten me. He makes me happy." She stood up and moved beside Brad, and he slipped an arm around her waist. "We love each other, Pa. I never thought I could be this happy. Can't you be happy *for* me?"

Luke leaned back in his chair, studying the two of them. He liked the way they looked together, liked Brad's boldness. He was nervous, and had every right to be, but he wasn't afraid. Luke could smell fear, and there was none in Brad Tillis. He met his daughter's eyes. "Of course I want to be happy for you; but you can understand my protectiveness, Katie. This is quite a surprise you've pulled on me and your mother, you know, coming home for Christmas with a man on your arm, a man you say you want to marry without our ever even meeting him."

"I only waited because I wanted to be sure myself, and

because it was only a few days ago that Brad found out the truth about…about what happened. Before I gave my heart away, and before things got serious enough to tell you about him, I wanted to be sure Brad would still want me after he knew. I'm not afraid anymore, Pa. Since I've met Brad I don't have nightmares, and I feel safe and loved."

Luke nodded. "All right. You have my permission to marry, but not until next spring. And I don't like the idea of you going off with a new husband and living so far away we never get to see you and make sure you're all right. I'll break out a piece of land or maybe I can talk Henry Kline into selling the Lazy K. He's already been thinking about it. If you're going to go into ranching, it isn't necessary to do it clear on the other side of the mountains."

Katie felt Brad's hold on her tighten. "Well, sir, we might not have any choice."

Lettie felt her heart pound harder. Now it was coming. She had thought it best that Brad tell Luke himself. Luke liked honesty and courage in a man, and never did Brad need both things more than now.

"Why is that?" Luke asked with a scowl.

"Because, sir, I don't raise cattle. I, uh, I raise sheep."

Pearl and Robbie both gasped, and Tyler slowly rose. "What?" the boy asked.

After that there were just several long seconds of silence, during which Luke's face darkened with anger. He glanced at Lettie and was surprised that she did not look shocked. "Did you know about this?"

"Yes," she answered calmly.

Luke looked back at Brad. "Sheep?"

"Yes, sir. Sheep."

Luke closed his eyes and rose. "Sweet Jesus," he muttered. "I've got to get out of here before I do something I shouldn't."

"Pa." Katie stopped him and breathed deeply to keep

from breaking into harder tears. "I'm going to marry Brad, with or without your approval. I would rather you were there to give me away willingly. I want my wedding to be happy. I want my father there."

He only studied her a moment longer before turning and leaving the room. Tyler sat shaking his head. "Pa's been chasing sheep men off his land for years," he told Brad.

Brad let go of Katie and folded his arms. "Yeah? Well maybe he doesn't know everything there is to know about sheep. I do. I know them just as good as you and your pa know cattle, and I know sheep and cattle can graze together with no problem. Cattlemen are just so worried about how much land it takes to graze a cow that they think nothing else should be allowed on the grasslands. Well, wild animals have been grazing together for years. Look how many buffalo there used to be, but the deer and elk and moose and antelope and all the other wild animals still had enough to eat. If your pa would give me a chance, I could prove to him that all the trouble over sheep isn't necessary."

Tyler studied the young man who wanted to marry his sister. For the most part he liked him, except that he was a sheep rancher. More than that, he loved Katie and wanted her to be happy. He would long remember that first day they brought her back home. He never thought she'd ever want to marry and lead a normal life, and he figured Brad Tillis must be something special to make her so happy.

"I'll go talk to your father," Lettie told a dejected Katie.

Tyler rubbed at his chin in a gesture common to Luke. Brad had only just met them both, but he could not help being astounded at the likeness between father and son, not just in looks, but in little movements and the way they walked. "I'll talk to him too," Tyler told them.

Lettie looked at her son in surprise, sure he would side with Luke. "Ty, that's good of you."

The boy shrugged. "I know how Pa can be, but I've worked with him long enough that he sometimes listens to me now. C'mon. He's probably in the library having a cigar and a shot of whiskey."

"Thank you, Ty," Katie told her brother.

He glanced at Brad again. "You really love her, don't you? I mean, if you ever hurt her, I'd be next in line after Pa to give you what for."

Brad grinned. "I really love her. I'd like this to be a happy Christmas for everybody."

Ty looked at his mother. "You go first. I'll come in a few minutes. I want to talk to Brad about this thing of sheep and cattle being able to graze together."

"Pa says sheep smell bad," Robbie put in.

"That's not true," Brad answered. "They don't smell any worse than cattle. You ought to know what a whole mess of cattle smells like when they're shoved together into a corral on a hot, humid day. It's a smell you just get used to, just like you get used to sheep and horses and anything else."

Pearl giggled again, and Lettie left the room to find Luke. Just as Ty predicted, he was in the library, cigar in hand, a shot of whiskey in the other. He turned away from a window at the sound of the doors sliding open, turned back when he saw it was Lettie.

"If you've come here to stick up for Katie and that… that *sheep* man—"

"Of course I've come here to stick up for them."

"Why didn't you tell me he raised sheep?"

"I wanted to see if he was man enough to tell you himself. I was surprised too, at first, but then I thought maybe there is a way to work it out." She stepped closer. "Luke, he seems like a fine young man. He's proud and sure, and he loves Katie. You can see how happy she is."

He sighed deeply and swallowed the whiskey. "She's only sixteen."

"Not a normal sixteen-year-old and you know it. She's no innocent, and yet in some ways she is, just as I was—innocent of the beauty of being with a man. I think Brad will be good to her."

He shook his head. "Sheep. I don't understand what she could be thinking."

"You don't *understand*? What part about all of this *don't* you understand, Luke? Love? You certainly know what love is like. You can remember what it was like for us in the beginning, how it felt to want to be together. Maybe you don't understand the fact that she's willing to go far away with him if necessary. Well, that doesn't make sense either. I believe I remember another young man who wanted to take a young girl far away from her family too—only that was even worse, because he took her to a very dangerous, unsettled land. And I believe *that* young man and woman also had not known each other for very long, but they knew they were in love, and she was willing to follow her man to the end of the earth, if that was what it took to be with him."

Luke turned to look at her, the anger in his eyes turning to a mixture of love and guilt.

"And maybe you don't understand that Brad has a dream of making it on his own. Is that it? Well, Luke Fontaine, I remember another young man who had a dream, and who dared to risk everything for that dream. He was proud and determined too, just like Brad is. Don't tell me you don't understand any of this, Luke, because Brad and Katie's situation is no different from ours seventeen years ago. And *I* understand how Katie feels. She's found a man she thinks can make love beautiful for her. After what she went through, do you really want to take that away from her?"

He ran a hand through his hair and sighed in exasperation. "You know I don't. Lettie, I can't forget how she looked when I found her with those men. What if this upstart doesn't understand that? What if he's just after the family money? What if he hurts her, disappoints her?"

"Luke, do you think my own parents didn't have the same questions about you? We hadn't even known you as long as Katie has known Brad. And you've always been a good judge of people. I feel good about this boy, and I know that deep down inside, you do too. If he was after family money, he wouldn't be talking about going off someplace else to start on his own."

"Well, that's another thing I don't like. Katie is special for reasons we both know. I don't think it would be good for her to go far from home like that."

"Like when you brought me to Montana, when it was wild and dangerous country?"

He rolled his eyes and waved her off.

"Luke, my parents would have loved it if you had gone on to Denver and got a job there so we could all be together. But you wanted to do something that was just yours. You had an idea, and you were proud and independent. So is Brad. And if you weren't so damn stubborn about this sheep thing, they wouldn't *have* to go far away. They could ranch right here in Montana, somewhere close to us. Maybe right here on the Double L. You were ready enough to give them some land when you thought he raised *cattle*!"

Luke set his whiskey glass aside and took a couple of puffs on his cigar. "For God's sake, Lettie, I am president of the Cattlemen's Association. You know how all those men feel about sheep! How is it going to look, me announcing that my own daughter wants to marry a *sheep* man, let alone offering to let him raise those sheep right here! Katie is an intelligent girl. How in hell could she let herself get mixed up with the very kind of people I've been running off this place for years?"

"Love knows no boundaries and no rules, Luke. She loves him, plain and simple. She wouldn't care if he shoveled horse manure for a living. A man's worth isn't judged by what he does for a living, Luke Fontaine. You know that. Why don't you give him a chance? Maybe he's right. Maybe it *is* possible for sheep and cattle to range together. Maybe a lot of men have died needlessly in the range wars, and maybe this is a way to keep that from happening here in Montana. This could be just one more way to keep the peace and show the federal government we're on our way to qualifying for statehood. Range wars certainly won't win us any points."

He set his cigar in an ashtray and studied the only person who could sway his opinion on anything. "You're determined to let this happen, aren't you?"

Lettie frowned, stepping closer. "I am determined that Katie will be happy. I'm tired of seeing her cry."

Someone knocked on the door. It was Tyler. When he opened the doors he looked nervous but determined. "Pa?"

Luke shook his head, able to read his son's eyes. "You too?"

Tyler shrugged. "Pa, I've been talking to Brad. He says his folks come from Iowa, but more and more farming there forced them to come west to graze their sheep. They've been through a lot, Pa, been shot at, had their sheep slaughtered by cattlemen. They finally settled in northeast Colorado, but a drought there has made things real hard. Brad's pa is going to quit, but sheep are all Brad knows. He wants to keep raising them. There's good money in sheep, Pa, real good money. All he needs is a place to raise them, and with all the range wars in Wyoming and Colorado and farther south, and the Mormons taking up all the good land in Utah, he figured Montana would be a good place to come. Brad says—"

"I'll speak for myself," Brad said, walking in behind Tyler. "I say sheep and cattle can graze together, Mr. Fontaine," the young man said, keeping his voice firm. "I've seen it back in Iowa. You let the cattle graze first.

Sheep aren't as particular about what they eat. They come along behind the cattle and eat what they leave behind. And sheep are cheaper to raise. It takes at least seven men to herd a thousand head of cattle. Am I right, Mr. Fontaine?"

Luke frowned, folding his arms and nodding his head. "That's about right."

"Well, sir, one man and a good sheepdog can handle about *three* thousand sheep. And I've heard of men who herded sheep from New Mexico to California and made ten times their original investment. With the herd I can get from my pa down in Colorado, I can get a good start. Sheep sell for about a dollar and a half a head when they're shipped to market, and like I said, it's cheaper to ship them because it doesn't take so many men to get them there. I'm also thinking that once I build up my numbers, I won't have to bother herding them anywhere. I can hire men to shear them and I'll ship and sell the wool. That goes for eight cents a pound right now. I can take it by the wagonload to Cheyenne to sell back East, and I hear that before long there will be a railroad come right through Billings, probably in another five or six years, so I'll make even more money because I won't have to herd sheep or haul wool so far. My pa has some good, healthy ewes, figures the lamb crop to be real good next spring. I aim to go down there and bring most of them back to Montana. If I have to do it farther west, then that's what I'll do. It will be dangerous herding them through Wyoming, what with the problems there with cattlemen and all, but I'll manage."

The young man put his hands on his hips authoritatively, and Luke glanced past him to see that Katie had also joined them, Pearl and Robbie bringing up the rear. Luke looked at Lettie. "I feel like a damn calf surrounded by a bunch of wolves. I don't like being cornered."

"Neither do I, Mr. Fontaine," Brad answered. Luke

moved his gaze back to meet the boy's green eyes. "With all due respect, sir, there isn't a man in Montana who could love or respect your daughter more than I do," Brad continued, "or who will try harder to take good care of her, or be more gentle with her when it's called for." Katie blushed deeply at the words. "And I want to marry her before I leave for Colorado," Brad went on. "Neither one of us wants to wait until spring. I'd just as soon marry her with your permission and your blessing. And I *am* going to raise sheep, because I'm good at it. I've been helping feed them and herd them and nurse them and shear them since I was five years old."

Luke stepped a little closer, his very presence intimidating. He was taller, broader. "You through?"

Brad swallowed, and Katie moved up to stand beside him. "Yes, sir, I guess that's about it," Brad answered.

Luke looked from him to Katie, saw the pleading and the remaining tears in her eyes, watched her slip her hand into Brad's. He looked at Brad again. "All right. You can get married right here at the house, New Year's Day. Since Katie is running the library and you work at the livery, you can live at the hotel during the week, but you'll spend your weekends here at the Double L for the rest of the winter, weather permitting. We have plenty of rooms, and I intend to get to know you a lot better before you head back to Colorado. I also intend to learn everything I can about sheep. Whenever you're ready to go and get your damn woollies, I'll send some of my men along to help protect them on the way back. They won't be too happy about it, but they'll do what I ask. When you get back, you'll put your money where your mouth is and prove to me that sheep and cattle can range together, right here on the Double L. If it works out, I'll give you some land. I don't want my Katie moving so far away that we never get to see her. If Katie has told you all about this family, you know we have already lost two children. Neither one of us is ready to say good-bye to a third child, and we'd like to enjoy our grandchildren, which is another reason I want Katie right here. I know what my wife went through having her babies alone. A girl ought to have her mother with her in times like that. Do you accept those terms?"

Brad grinned. "Yes, sir. But I won't take land for nothing. I'll pay you for it."

"You just take good care of my daughter and the land will be a wedding present."

Katie hugged Luke. "Thank you, Pa!"

Luke sighed deeply, moving his arms around her. "I just want you to be happy, Katie." He glanced at Brad again. "I hope you know the hell I'm going to go through letting a sheep man graze his woollies on Double L land. You and I are going to the next cattleman's meeting. I might as well prepare them."

Brad reached out his hand. "We can make it work, Mr. Fontaine."

Luke took his hand. "I hope you're right. And call me Luke." Luke finally offered a hint of a smile, and Brad squeezed his hand firmly.

"You have a lot of pull with the cattlemen around here, sir…I mean, Luke. Maybe you can convince them it's time for the fighting to end. There's plenty of room out here for all of us."

Luke glanced at Lettie, who was smiling, her eyes misty. "Maybe there is." He let go of Brad's hand and gave Katie a squeeze. "Let's all go enjoy the Christmas tree and open presents. We'll tell Mae to leave the dishes for now and come join us." He kept one arm around Katie and moved the other around Lettie, leading everyone out of the room. "Sheep," he muttered, shaking his head again. "God help us."

Part Four

Memories. We share so many…
Joy, sorrow, pain, and laughter,
The light in our children's eyes,
The flowers at a little grave.
In our aging years more memories are born,
And through all that we bear in these
Seasoned years, I see you,
Standing there with your hand reached out
To guide me and give me strength,
As I try to do the same for you.
Life has been hard, but also good.
We conquered all that man and nature put
    before us,
And we survived to see another sunrise
On this, our home, our Montana.

Twenty-eight

July 1881

LUKE SAT ATOP A BUTTE ON THE SOUTH SECTION OF THE Double L, Tex and Tyler on either side of him, and stretched out in a line in both directions sat fifteen cattle ranchers who had come from miles around, at Luke's invitation, to camp out and wait for the impending arrival of Bradley Tillis and his twenty-five hundred sheep. Even Nial Bentley was there.

Luke's announcement at the cattlemen's meeting in February, that he would allow an experiment in sheep and cattle grazing on the Double L, as well as his new son-in-law's presence at that meeting, had been met with anger and curses; but Luke knew that deep inside most of the men involved were his friends. After a lot of explaining from Brad, and a promise from Luke that no sheep would be allowed to stray onto anyone else's land, anger turned to cool receptiveness. Luke suspected most had agreed to go along with him just because Katie had found a husband, and all knew what Katie had been through. They respected Brad because he was Luke Fontaine's son-in-law, and Luke could not help being proud of how Brad had stood up to all of them at the meeting, answering every question honestly and with obvious knowledge of his subject.

Sheep man or not, Luke admired Brad for his guts and determination; and Katie had never seemed happier. She was expecting a baby, something Brad didn't even know yet. The new light in Katie's eyes was worth putting up with the sound of sheep's cries, and maybe he could get used to the smell.

That morning some of the men were sure they had heard the distant sound of bells clanging, the kind some sheep men put around the necks of their stock to keep track of those that wandered off to forage where they liked; then came the baa of sheep's cries. Luke knew that if Brad and the Double L men he had sent along for protection took the correct path back home through Wyoming, they should come through the pass at the south side of the butte where he and the other men had come to watch.

"There they are, boss!" Tex pointed to a few sheep that rounded a distant plateau and headed toward them through a broad, grassy valley. A black-and-white, long-haired shepherd dog scurried about, keeping the herd together, darting, barking, nipping at strays.

"Look at that." Joe Parker spoke up. "All those sheep, and no men. Just that dog keeping them in line."

"Brad says sometimes sheep can be turned out to pasture without any men at all," Tyler told the others. "Just the dog. His dog is called Shep. He says Shep can take a herd out, let them graze, and watch them all day long all by himself, then gather them up and bring them back to the ranch in time for supper."

"I don't believe it," Hank Kline said.

"Hell, see for yourself," Tex told him. "Ain't a man around yet. Just the dog."

Runner just sat quietly smiling at the sight.

"I'll be damned," Billy Sacks spoke up.

"Will ought to be here to see this," Luke said thoughtfully.

"You just remember your promise, Luke," Carl Rose told him. "Those sheep stay on the Double L."

Luke began rolling himself a cigarette. "I don't break promises. But if this works out, you all know you don't

have to be afraid of sharing federal land with sheep men."
He lit the cigarette. "My wife was probably right about
one thing. If this works out, we'll save a lot of bloodshed.
I'm doing this partly for Montana, to show the federal
government we're willing to be reasonable about these
things, show them we're civilized enough not to go out
killing innocent people just because they choose to do
something different. Statehood means a lot more federal
help for ranchers in the future, especially in the hard
times; and it can mean more contracts with the government to sell beef to the army. This could be a good thing
for the territory, and eventually for the state."

Joe Parker chuckled. "Luke, you son of a bitch, you're
giving a campaign speech. You wouldn't be thinking of
running for territorial representative, would you?"

Luke kept the cigarette in his mouth. "Hell, no. I'm
too busy for all that." He leaned forward to look over at
Joe. "What's with all this talk of politics? Lettie suggested
the same damn thing."

"Hell, I can't think of a better man to represent us,"
Joe answered.

"Except, perhaps, the *second* biggest landholder in
Montana," Nial put in, casting a sly glance at Luke.

Luke turned to look at him, his blue eyes cautious.
"An Englishman? Representing Montana?"

"Why not? A lot of foreigners have invested in land
out here in your great American West, most of them
from England. I am now officially an American citizen,
you know, and I have a great investment and interest
in Montana."

Some of the other men glanced at each other, all
aware of the animosity between Luke Fontaine and Nial
Bentley. "I don't know," Hank Kline spoke up. "Seems
to me like when we send somebody to Washington
representing Montana, it ought to be one of our original
pioneers, a rugged-looking cattleman who's been out

there and risked his life and got his hands dirty. No offense, Bentley, but you don't exactly look the part."

They all laughed then, and Nial smiled, accustomed to their joking about him. "Think what you want, but I do love Montana, and I am highly educated in politics and finances and how the government works."

Luke took a deep drag on his cigarette, Nial's words stirring his own interest. "You saying I don't have enough education?"

"My pa's education comes from working the land and taking bullets and fighting Indians and grizzlies," Tyler spoke up defensively. "He knows the land like the back of his hand, knows what the ranchers need, knows what we need in the way of law and order. He's got a son buried on this land, a daughter who suffered at the hands of outlaws, another son stole away by Indians. He doesn't have to go to Harvard to know what Montana needs."

A round of whistles and laughter went up from the rest of the men. "Listen to that boy!" Carl Rose spoke up. "There's your campaign manager right there, Luke!"

They all laughed again, and Luke grinned, shaking his head. He exchanged a proud look with Nial, then reached over and yanked Ty's hat down over his eyes, noticing the boy was blushing deeply. He wanted to hug him but wouldn't embarrass him that way.

"To hell with politics," Luke told the rest of them. "I don't have time for that right now. It looks like I'll have my hands full for a while just handling this sheep-cattle thing."

Brad finally came into sight, along with the four Double L men Luke had sent with him for protection.

"Them men are never gonna forgive you for this one," Tex told Luke.

"They'll get over it." Luke took a last, long drag on his cigarette, then crushed it against his canteen to make sure it was out before throwing it down. It had been a dry spring and summer, and there had already been a few grass fires. So far they had been kept under control, but all were aware that if it did not rain soon, the danger of major fires was high.

"I say we go down there and shoot the shit out of those damn sheep," Joe Parker joked.

Another round of laughter was heard as the sheep headed for a wide expanse of grassland where about five hundred head of Luke's cattle were already grazing. He had promised this south section to Brad for grazing, was relieved to know Katie's husband had made it back unscathed. "I'm going down to greet my son-in-law," Luke told them. "The rest of you can sit here and see how those sheep mix with my cattle. I'll know by the next meeting how this is working out." He rode off with Ty, Tex, and Runner, heading down the steep embankment into the valley.

Brad broke away from the others and headed out to greet his father-in-law. "How is Katie?" was his first question.

Luke grinned. "Fat. She's going to have a baby, probably around October."

Grave concern came into Brad's eyes. "She is? Is she okay?"

"So far."

"But she must have known before I left. Why didn't she tell me?"

"She wasn't sure," Luke answered, "and she didn't want you to worry. She's fine, Brad. She's been staying at the house, and Lettie won't let her do a damn thing. One of the other women from town has been taking care of the library. And by the way, your own house is almost finished. I've had some of my men as well as a carpenter from town working on it. You and Katie ought to be able to move in in just a couple of weeks. It's only a couple of miles south of the main house so we'll all be close to each other." He nodded toward where the sheep were beginning to graze. "This is part of the land

I'm giving you, but I want my own cattle to be able to graze here too."

Brad was still wrestling with the news that Katie was going to have a baby. He blinked to get rid of the mist in his eyes. "Yes, sir. No problem. You'll see sheep and cattle can get along just fine." He sniffed and took a deep breath. "You sure Katie's all right?"

Luke chuckled. "I'm sure."

Brad grinned. "I can't wait to see her. Is she happy about the baby?"

Luke just nodded his head, grinning. "What do you think?"

Brad took off his hat and let out a whoop, laughing. "Let's get these sheep closer to home. I want to see her!"

They headed out behind the sheep, the air filled with baas and the clang of sheep bells. The rest of the ranchers who had come to see headed down the bank then, some of them still laughing. Luke managed to swallow his pride. It was enough to know that Katie was happy. If he had to put up with the jokes and the smell of sheep for that, then so be it.

❧

Here lies Paul Lucas Fontaine, Born March 12, 1870—Died January 10, 1876. "Light of My Life, Child of Mine, Forever You Will Be in My Embrace."

Finally the beautiful granite stone had come, shipped all the way from Denver. This was something Lettie had wanted for years, a specially engraved tombstone for little Paul's grave. The pine trees Luke had planted around the Fontaine graveyard were growing fast. One day they would shade Paul's grave, as well as future family burial plots in a lovely, flower-filled field behind the house. Luke had refused to bury his son near the graves of the outlaws he had killed when he and Lettie first came here. Those graves, near the old original shack where they had lived then, were hardly distinguishable now, covered with grass, the crosses erected there long weathered and fallen.

"It's beautiful, Luke," she said softly. They had come out there together after supper, an almost nightly ritual. Luke put his hands on her shoulders. "Let's just hope the next graves here are our own and not any more of our children or any grandchildren," he told her.

Lettie nodded, the old ache returning at memories of holding her little boy, the old guilt of thinking she should have paid more attention to him in those last months. "I know it cost a lot to get the stone here, but I'm so glad now that we did it. A hundred years from now I want people to know who lies here."

Luke sighed, pulling her close, her back to him. He wrapped his arms around her. "Those are beautiful words you had inscribed."

She crossed her arms over his, taking comfort in the feel of his powerful forearms. "Maybe Katie's child will help the old ache. It will be nice having a baby around again, won't it?"

Luke grinned, leaning down to kiss her cheek, wishing for her sake she could have had more children. "I have a feeling our grandchildren are going to be very spoiled."

Lettie laughed then. "I don't care. I plan to enjoy them thoroughly." She turned to look up at him with a smile, and he met her lips in a kiss that spoke of sorrow mixed with sweet love. He gently caressed her breasts, moved his hand to her throat, the kiss lingering until he suddenly picked her up in his arms.

"Luke, what are you doing?"

"You'll see." He carried her farther into the well-manicured bushes and flower gardens at the back of the house, one of her pet projects, to which some of the men had been assigned to help her. It was a warm, quiet evening, and the little creek that ran through the gardens made only little trickling sounds, nearly dried up because of the lack of rain. It was the same creek that was fed from a spring in the rocks that they had found when first settling here. Never had that spring gone down to such a trickle, and it worried Luke, but for the moment he was not going to let something else get in the way of this special moment. He carried Lettie to a grassy area shrouded by thick, flowery shrubs, laid her down in the grass and moved on top of her.

"Luke! Someone might come looking for us," she whispered.

He moved a hand under her dress and pulled at her drawers. "They won't. I told the kids to stay inside, that we wanted to be alone. The work is finished for the day and the men are either at their homes or in the bunkhouses. We can do whatever we want on our own property, can't we?"

"Luke Fontaine, stop behaving like a corralled stallion!"

He pulled off her drawers. "I *am* your stallion." He unbuttoned his pants. "And why be predictable about these things? It's more fun this way," he told her.

"Luke—" She said nothing more as he entered her like a stroke of white lightning, making her draw in her breath. He moved one hand around her thigh, grasping at her bottom while he rested on the other arm, driving himself deep.

"Just a quick one," he whispered. "Who's going to know?" He nuzzled at her neck, groaned when he met her mouth again.

Lettie arched up to him in sweet abandon. In moments like this he could bring out her most wanton desires without even having to remove their clothes. He massaged her bottom while he worked magic with his intercourse until she felt a sweet climax, after which he drove himself harder and faster to fulfill her every need. Dusk was settling, and somewhere nearby an owl hooted. Lettie could not help feeling a deep satisfaction at the look of desire in her husband's eyes. Taking her this way reminded her of that first time he had done this in the drafty little cabin they had lived in when they arrived here. They were both still dressed then too. They had just needed to be one, to unite their bodies in a bond of love, like now, a quiet, deliberate, necessary thing.

"I love you, Lettie." His life spilled into her then, and he relaxed next to her. He looked around at the shrubbery. "Well, here's one we haven't tried before," he joked.

"Luke Fontaine, you're a crazy man. If my friends at the women's club knew the things I let you get away with—"

"They would all be jealous," he teased. "Besides, how do you know they and their husbands don't do some of the same things?"

She rolled her eyes. "Because some of them talk as though lying with their husbands for any reason but having children is some kind of chore." She faced him then, an almost wicked grin on her face. "I can't imagine why."

Luke laughed and handed her a handkerchief and her drawers. She quickly used the handkerchief to clean herself, then pulled on her drawers, and just in time.

"Pa! Pa, where are you?" It was Tyler calling.

"Damn!" Luke muttered. He quickly rolled away and buttoned his pants, and Lettie scrambled to hide the hand-kerchief under a bush and pull down her dress. She brushed herself off, hoping her hair wasn't too badly messed.

"Pa! Hurry up! Fire! Tex says the whole south section is burning!"

"Oh my God, that's where the sheep are!" Lettie exclaimed. Luke was already running back toward the house. She quickly rose and brushed herself off, running to catch up. They all hurried around to the front of the house to see the billowing smoke in the distance, where Katie, Robbie, and Pearl were standing, staring at the sickening blaze.

"Dear God, the sheep!" Katie exclaimed. "And our new house!"

"It's too late for any of that now!" Luke said, running to saddle a horse. "Ty, get some men together! We've got to start digging a trench, try to save the house and outbuildings! That wind is coming right out of the south!" Men were running every which way, some of them with shovels.

"The sheep will run from it!" Brad yelled. "They should be all right, unless the wind picks it up too fast for them!"

Luke ordered some of the men to go herd what cattle they could farther north. "Robbie, you help Sven Hansen get as many horses as you can out of the barns and up to the top of the butte there beyond the creek behind the house!"

"Mama, it's coming so fast!" Katie exclaimed. She grasped her swollen stomach.

One of Luke's men came riding hard up the drive then. "Luke! There's fire up northeast of here too! I just came back from taking that horse to Hank Kline that he wanted to buy, and his whole place is gone, house and all!"

"Heaven help us!" Lettie fretted. She put an arm around Katie. "Come back inside, Katie. You have to think about the baby. You only have one month to go. You don't want to do anything to risk losing it now."

"Brad, be careful!" Katie screamed as she watched her husband run off with a shovel. "Oh, Mama, what are we going to do?"

"We're going to pray," Lettie answered. She herded Katie and Pearl back into the house, and Robbie ran off to help Sven with the horses, while Tyler rode out to help herd some of the cattle farther north.

Luke tried to give orders everywhere at once, his chest hurting with the thought that in one night he could lose everything he had worked for and risked his life for over the past eighteen years. He glanced back at Lettie, who stood on the steps to the house watching in terror. Their gaze held for a moment, and he knew she was thinking the same thing he was. Moments ago they had shared a sweet, secret moment, so happy with the turn life had taken for them. It seemed that in this land a man could never relax and take anything for granted.

He turned and rode off to help the other men dig a trench, loving all of them for their devotion to the Double L. Billy Sacks's house was in danger, but here he was, a team of horses hitched to a plow, breaking up the ground as best he could to create a fire barrier. He had already brought his wife and two young sons up to the main house. Luke ordered Tex to help Robbie and Sven get all the horses out of the two large barns that held them, then he grabbed a shovel and rode off.

Dusk moved into darkness, orange flames growing bright against the black sky. Luke prayed no one would be hurt. Men were scattered everywhere, including his own two sons. He dug until he thought he would pass out, sweat pouring from his face, his shirt soaked. His lungs burned and ached from smoke carried on the wind, and the fire crept ever closer, threatening the main house and barns. He knew Katie and Brad's new house had surely already burned, but he couldn't think about that now. He could see Billy's house burning, and now flames were eating at the roof of the main horse barn. There was a wide dirt drive between the outbuildings and the main house. He was counting on that to protect the home that had taken over three years to build for Lettie.

His eyes teared, and he looked away from the barn. God only knew how many cattle and sheep had already been lost. Poor Hank Kline had apparently already lost everything. Thank God all his horses were surely safely out of the barn by now. He just prayed the wind wouldn't carry enough cinders to the main house to catch the roof there. There wasn't even enough water in the creek to try pumping it onto the house. Somewhere in the distance he could hear a few sheep bleating, heard Shep barking, the faithful dog doing what he could to save some of his master's stock.

He thought how Brad had been right. The sheep had not harmed grazing land. He vowed that if Brad had lost very many of his woollies, he would help finance buying more for him…unless he lost so much himself that he was ruined. At least he had the copper mines…thanks to Lettie. Fire couldn't hurt what was in the ground.

Smoke and overexertion made his mind wander, and when he first heard Lettie screaming his name, he thought he was imagining it. Had the house caught fire? The wind had finally shifted more from the east, and it should be blowing the fire away from the house and buildings, but maybe too late! Somewhere in the distance he thought he heard the rumble of thunder, and he prayed fervently that it meant rain was coming. But then, maybe his mind was just playing games with him.

"Luke! Luke!" Lettie screamed again. "Where are you! Robbie's trapped in the barn! Luke!"

Lettie? She *was* calling him! Robbie! He threw down his shovel and ran, his heart beating so hard his chest pained him. Because the fire had come so near where he had been digging, his horse had run off. He had to depend on his own legs to get him to the house, and the run seemed to take forever.

Not another son! God surely wouldn't do this to him! And what about Tyler? He was out there somewhere trying to save cattle. Something could happen to him too. If he lost one more son, he would not want to go on living.

He realized then that Brad was running beside him. They reached the house, and Lettie was frantically trying to get into the biggest of their two horse barns, which was engulfed in flames. One of the Double L men was hanging on to her. "You can't go in there, Mrs. Fontaine!" he was shouting.

"Robbie's in there!" Lettie screamed at Luke. "Tex went in after him!"

"My God! My God!" Katie had sunk to the ground, holding her belly.

Luke grabbed hold of Brad. "Stay with Katie! Get her back in the house!" He ran and jumped into a watering trough to get himself wet, then headed for the barn, but just as he reached the flaming entrance, Robbie came staggering out from around a corner, looking dazed. The back of his shirt was smoking. Luke hurriedly grabbed him close and carried him away from the barn, just as it collapsed into a raging inferno.

"Robbie!" Luke carried his son to Lettie, and by the light of the fire they inspected him. The boy had a nasty cut on his forehead, and his back was slightly burned. "Where's Tex?" Luke asked him.

Robbie blinked, his eyes tearing. He pointed to the barn. "I was…trying to get Sundance out. He…wouldn't come, Pa. He wouldn't come. Fire…all around…Tex showed me a way out…went back for Sundance…" The boy passed out in his arms, and Luke turned to stare at the barn, a lump rising in his throat, tears welling in his eyes. He realized then that he had known hardly a thing about Tex, had never even known if that was his real name or what his last name was.

"My God," he muttered. He turned to carry Robbie to the house, but he only made it as far as the steps before going to his knees. A blackness enveloped him, and he clung to Robbie as he went to the ground.

"Luke! Oh God, Luke!" Lettie leaned over her husband and son, wondering if she would lose them both tonight.

Twenty-nine

LUKE AWOKE TO THE SMELL OF SMOKE AND BURNED grass. He looked around the room, wondering how he had ended up in his own bed when he should be outside fighting the fires. It took him a moment to realize it was daylight, but the sky outside the window was gray. Thunder rumbled, and rain pelted the glass. He caught a movement in the room then, and he turned his head to see Lettie bringing in a quilt. "Lettie?"

Her face brightened, and she rushed to his side. "Luke!" She leaned down and kissed his cheek, her eyes tearing. "I thought I'd lost you last night, that maybe your heart had given out!" She moved her arms around his neck. "Oh, Luke."

He moved a hand to touch her face. "What happened? Are Ty and Robbie all right?"

"Ty is fine. He's out with some of the men gauging the damage. The house and most of the outbuildings survived, but Billy and Anne lost their home." She sat up to wipe at tear-filled eyes. "We've got quite a houseful right now. I told Billy and Anne they could stay here until we got another house built for them." She closed her eyes and took a deep breath. "I thought you were dying, and poor Robbie—I had to nurse him too. He has slipped in and out of consciousness all night. In the midst of all that, Katie had her baby from all the excitement. Thank God for Anne and Mae and Elsie. I don't know what I would have done without their help. The baby seems to be healthy, in spite of coming a little early." She took

Luke's hand and kissed his palm. "We have a grandson, Luke, Paul Tyler. He's beautiful, and Katie is fine. At least one good thing happened last night."

He squeezed her hand, surprised at his own weakness. "How about Robbie?"

"I don't know. I'm so afraid for him. One minute he's conscious, and the next he's out again. I sent one of the men to town to get the doctor for both of you, but I'm worried he'll be too busy to come, what with fires at a lot of other places." She closed her eyes and rested her cheek against the back of his hand. "Billings needs more than one doctor. I think we should think about placing an ad back East, think of some way to attract at least one more doctor out here."

Luke swallowed, his throat parched from breathing so much smoke the night before. "I need some water."

Lettie rose and poured him a glass, but when he tried to drink it, he realized he couldn't even sit up. "My God, what's wrong with me?"

Lettie supported him and held the glass to his lips. "I think you're just exhausted," she answered. "You've worked so hard over the years, Luke. It's time to let Ty and others do more. And I think...I think the shock of thinking maybe we had lost Robbie...and knowing Tex was killed in the fire...maybe it was all just too much. I had to have some men come and carry you into the house. Tyler is having fits. He was scared to death he'd lose his father. I don't know what that boy would do without you. He worships the ground you walk on, you know."

Luke sighed deeply and lay back against the pillow, feeling the sorrow come again. "Tex died in the fire, then?"

"As far as we know. He's no place to be seen this morning. The rubble is still too hot to look for a body."

"Damn," he whispered. His eyes were wet. "In a lot of ways we were very close, and yet I didn't know much about the man. He never even told me what his real name was." He felt a sob rip through him then, unexpectedly. "Seems...crazy...crying over somebody like Tex...doesn't it?"

Lettie smoothed his hair back from his forehead. "Not at all. He's been your right hand for a lot of years."

Luke breathed deeply to quell the tears. "God, all of a sudden I'm so tired, Lettie."

"Of course you're tired. You've worked yourself nearly to death for years. You're scarred up from fights with animals and outlaws, and last night you nearly lost another son and everything you've worked for all these years." She kissed his hand again. "We'll be all right, Luke. That new grandchild was like a gift from God, a little bit of joy in the midst of all this sorrow. The grass will grow back, and we have the house and most of the outbuildings. Ty is all right."

"Robbie still isn't out of danger, is he?" He wiped at his eyes with his arm. "We can't lose another son, Lettie. And this time...I'm the one with all the guilt. I've never been...as close to him as I was to Ty. Deep inside I resented the fact that he doesn't want to stay on and work the ranch, and he's always felt it. All he talks about...is wanting to go to school to be a doctor...and I've fought him every step of the way. I know he felt that somehow he did something wrong that made Paul die, and then I half blamed him for what happened to Katie. He can't die, Lettie, not before I set things right with him."

"He's not going to die, and he knows you love him, Luke."

"Help me get up."

"Luke, you stay right in this bed."

"No! I want to go to Robbie. I have to talk to him." Luke gritted his teeth and forced himself to a sitting position. "My God, I've never felt like this. Everything is such an effort."

"Luke, you shouldn't—"

"Please, Lettie. Help me get some pants on." He put an arm around her shoulders, and Lettie stood up with him. He grasped the back of a chair while she took out a clean pair of denim pants and helped him get them on. She buttoned them, then helped him pull on a shirt. He leaned on her then and walked through the wide carpeted hall into Robbie's room, where Pearl sat watching her brother, her eyes puffy from tears.

"Father! Are you okay?"

Luke smiled inwardly at the way she addressed him, father, not pa. His beautiful Pearl, always acting and talking so sophisticated for a girl raised on a cattle ranch. She was radiantly beautiful on the brink of womanhood. How much more beautiful would she be as a woman? "I'll be fine. I just need to rest, I guess." He made his way to Robbie's bed, glad to see the boy was awake again. "Hey there, Robbie. That's quite a bump on your head."

Lettie pushed a chair up beside the bed, and Luke sat down, taking Robbie's hand.

Tears slipped out of Robbie's eyes at the sight of his father. "Tex is dead," he said in a small voice. "It's my fault."

Luke shook his head. "No, it isn't, Robbie. If not Tex, it would be me in there, or maybe your mother or Ty. It was Tex's choice to go back for Sundance. I want you to stop blaming yourself for things that can't be changed and would have happened whether you were there or not. I'm just glad you're alive. I thought I had lost another son." His own tears wanted to come again. He didn't understand this terrible weakness, not just physically, but emotionally. Maybe it was because of Paul. The thought that he could have lost another son overwhelmed him, and he broke into sobbing, clinging to Robbie's hand.

Pearl stared in dismay, and Lettie walked around to

put her hands on her shoulders. "It's all right, Pearl. Your father needs this." She fought her own tears, knowing that in spite of the terrible night she had been through herself, right now Luke needed her to be the strong one. There would be time later for her own tears.

"Don't cry, Pa," Robbie sobbed. "I'm okay. I didn't know you really loved me that much. I thought Ty was your favorite."

The words only choked Luke up more. How well he knew the feeling of being less favored, of not being loved. His own hurt never ended. All those letters to his own father, and not one reply.

It took him several minutes to gain control of his emotions. Lettie handed him a handkerchief, and he wiped at his eyes, then took Robbie's hand again. "You listen to me, Robbie. No father favors one son or daughter over another. I love you all the same, but for different reasons. If Tex hadn't gone in after you, I would have. That's just what I was getting ready to do when you came wandering out of there." He reached out and touched the side of the boy's face. He was nothing like Ty had been at his age. He was shorter, more slender, looked younger in the face; but he was a handsome, intelligent boy. "Robbie, nothing that has ever happened around here has been your fault, do you understand? The only one at fault is me, for letting you think that way, and for not being the best father I could have been to you. I'm sorry you thought you weren't loved as much. That simply is not true. If you had died in that fire, I would have mourned you as much as Paul, or Ty, or any of my children, and I'm not sure I would have wanted to go on living. You know what your mother just told me a few minutes ago?"

"What, Pa?"

He stroked his son's hair. "She said that one doctor isn't enough anymore for Billings, and she's right. We need more doctors, and nothing would make me more proud than to have my own son be one of them. You keep studying, and you go to whatever school you want, even that one Nial Bentley said was so good, that one in Michigan, if you want. You just promise to come back here where we need more doctors."

Robbie managed a grin. "Sure, Pa. You sure you don't care? What about the ranch?"

Luke rubbed the back of the boy's hand with his thumb. "We've got Ty. And now Brad. And already we have a grandson. We'll be okay."

"But you work too hard. Pearl says you passed out last night, and you don't look too good today."

Luke smiled sadly. "I'll be all right. Nothing keeps Luke Fontaine down for long. As far as the work, I'll just hire a few more men."

Robbie sobered. "You'll never replace Tex, will you?"

Luke held his gaze. "No, Son. Nor could I ever replace you."

Lettie came around to Luke, putting her hands on his shoulders. "Luke, please go back to bed and stay there until Dr. Manning can come out and have a look at you."

Luke squeezed Robbie's hand once more, then managed to get to his feet. "There's too much to do."

"And you have plenty of men to do those things for you. Don't you think by now that Runner and Billy and Sven and the others know how to run this ranch just fine without you giving them every little order? If you work yourself into the grave, what good will that do any of us?"

He gave Robbie a smile and a wink. "You rest easy until the doctor has a look at you." He put an arm around Lettie again and sighed deeply. "I want to see Katie and my grandchild before I do anything else."

Lettie led him to Katie and Brad's room, where Katie was nursing her new son. She quickly covered herself and took the infant away from her breast. "Pa! Mama said you collapsed last night! What happened?"

Luke forced a smile, but never had he felt so weary and beaten. "Oh, just too much excitement for an old man, I guess."

"You aren't old! How do you feel today?"

"I'll be all right. I just came to see my new grandson."

Katie smiled through tears, cradling the baby in her arms. "He's beautiful, Pa. He's like a gift from God, something to bring us joy after the awful fires. I named him Paul, for our little brother—Paul Tyler. The next boy will get Robbie's name."

Luke kept more tears in check, astounded at this feeling of weakness and inability to control his emotions. He did not feel like himself at all that day. He leaned closer to have a look at his new grandson. "He's beautiful, Katie. I'm so happy for you and Brad."

Katie wiped at a tear. "Poor Brad. What a time to have a son. He had to leave to see how many sheep were lost. He had such big plans."

"We'll all get through this, Katie," Lettie spoke up. "Your father has the copper mines and a lot of other investments. The loss of sheep and cattle won't break us. Don't forget that Luke bought a grain supply business in Cheyenne, so we can at least buy grain at wholesale prices while we wait for the grass to come back. And we have a number of other investments, like the hotel. We'll all be fine, probably a lot better off than some of the other ranchers who depend completely on their grass and cattle."

"All that really matters is that we're all alive," Luke reminded Katie, "and you had a healthy baby. I'm sorry I apparently slept right through it."

He leaned down to kiss the baby's cheek, and Lettie tried not to show her worry in front of Katie. Luke had done more than just sleep. She knew good and well he had had a full collapse, and she was afraid it might be his heart. Of all the times her husband had put his life at risk and had suffered wounds, never had she been this afraid for him. "Luke, please go back to bed. Tyler and Brad and the others are doing just fine with cleanup and inventory; and I can handle whatever paperwork comes out of this. I don't want you to worry or try to do too much yourself."

He waved her off, then rose. "Quit treating me like a decrepit old man. Katie's right. I'm *not* old. Hell, I'm only forty-six."

"I didn't say you were old." She moved to embrace him, putting on a smile for him. "You didn't seem old yesterday," she reminded him.

Luke grinned and let her help him out of the room, and Katie watched with concern. She had never seen such bad color in her father's face, nor such a worn, beaten look to him.

Outside the room Lettie helped her husband back to their bed, and he literally fell into it. "Jesus, Lettie, what's wrong with me?" he asked.

Lettie leaned down and caressed his cheek. "Nothing that a little rest won't cure," she assured him.

"Don't tell Ty and the others how bad it is. Tell them I fell and broke a rib or something."

"I'll tell them whatever the *doctor* tells us, and *you* will do whatever the doctor tells you to do. I am not going to lose you because of your own stubbornness. It's not a crime to be just plain tired, Luke."

He sighed deeply. "See that Tex gets a nice burial, will you? Bury him in the family plot, not with those damn outlaws up the hill. He deserves better."

"We'll do it right."

"And have the men get started right away on a new house for Brad and Katie, and for Billy and Anne. And I want a full report on our losses."

"I know what to do, Luke."

He grabbed her hand as she started to rise. "What

about you? My God, last night must have been awful. You're probably the one who should be in this bed. I'll bet you haven't slept all night."

"I'm all right. Let me be the strong one for a while, Luke. I took care of things once before, remember? When you were laid up with that broken leg. I can do it again."

He held her hand tightly. "You've always been the stronger one, Lettie. I don't think you realize that. My own strength comes from you."

She leaned down and kissed his lips softly. "I think it's a pretty even balance. Let's face it, we need each other, so please rest until Doc Manning can have a look at you."

He put a hand to his head. "I don't have much choice. I don't think that right now I can even get back up off this bed."

She squeezed his hand and smiled for him. "I've got to see to Robbie and Katie again. Do you want something to eat?"

He closed his eyes. "No. I just want to sleep." His hand dropped away, and for a moment Lettie thought her heart would stop beating. She felt his throat, blinking back tears of relief when she felt a pulse, but in that one quick moment he seemed to have passed out again.

"God, don't take him from me," she whispered. She kissed him once more and left the room to go into an empty bedroom and cry. No one must see her like this, especially not Luke. He would never stay in that bed if he knew it upset her...but then maybe he would have no choice. Maybe he was dying and would never get up. Outside thunder rumbled again, and the rain came down harder, but too late to quell the awful damage done by the fires.

❧

Lettie pored over the ledger Luke kept for his cattle count. For two weeks Ty and Mae's husband and some of the other men had been out taking inventory as best they could, not an easy task when one had to cover hundreds of thousands of acres, and cattle were spread out everywhere. She had been going through the books all morning while Katie and Anne Sacks helped Mae with the extra housework caused from having more people in the house.

She closed her eyes just to listen. Pearl was practicing piano, playing a lovely waltz. She imagined Luke and herself floating around a ballroom floor, Luke wearing a fine black suit, she in a magnificent new dress, with Luke a territorial delegate, or perhaps governor of the new state of Montana. But then, for now it was just good to know he was going to be all right, that his heart was strong and all he needed was a good long rest. Thank God, Robbie would also be fine. He had finally stopped slipping away from her, finally stopped having the awful headaches. He was eating better, his eyes brighter, and the few burns on his back were healing.

She felt a presence in the library then, opened her eyes to see Luke standing in the doorway wearing denim pants and a cotton shirt that hung loose. "You're awfully quiet for such a big man," she told him.

He looked down. "Bare feet don't make much noise on all these fancy rugs." He came inside. "What were you dreaming about?"

She reddened. "I was just thinking how glad I am that you and Robbie are going to be all right." She pointed a finger as though to scold him. "And quit trying to sneak up on me. I know you, Luke Fontaine. You think if I know you're coming, I'll hide this ledger." She rose. "You look good today."

He moved his arms around her. "I feel useless. I should be out there with the rest of them rounding up cattle. This is ridiculous, Lettie. I'm perfectly fine."

"Dr. Manning said complete bed rest for at least a month, and you should take it easy the rest of the winter.

At least it's the time of year when there isn't so much to do anyway."

"Except a lot of rebuilding." He left her and walked to look out the window at the burned barn. "And a lot of that will have to wait until spring." He sighed. "I'd like to go see Tex's grave later."

"I guess I can allow that."

He turned to look at her with a wry grin. "Are you giving me orders, woman?"

She folded her arms. "I'll do whatever I have to do to make sure my husband is with me for a long, long time. Dr. Manning said part of your problem was the shock of thinking you had lost Robbie, but that was made worse by just plain exhaustion, and he said it's not something to take lightly."

"What about you? You've been through just as much as I have."

She walked closer and placed her hands at his sides. "Different people handle certain situations differently. Look how we each reacted when Paul died. It pulled us apart. Doc Manning said he suspects you never really got over his death. Is that true?" Her heart ached at the devastation in his blue eyes.

He placed his hands on her shoulders. "I guess maybe it is, or at least was. I think almost losing Robbie woke me up to a lot of things." He leaned down and kissed her forehead. "I hate this, Lettie. I'm the man. I'm supposed to be the strong one."

"You *are* the strong one. For a lot of years you've had to be *too* strong. In those early years when I thought I'd go crazy, you were there to lean on. You've always been my strength, my protection, my defender. I put you through hell after Nathan left again and then Paul died. You almost got killed rescuing Katie, and you have blamed yourself for every bad thing that has happened in this family. But there is a little thing called fate, over which none of us has control. Right now God or someone is telling you to slow down for a while. There's no shame in that, Luke. It's only a means to an end—and in the end you will be stronger than ever. Maybe God is preparing you for something bigger..." She smiled, moving her arms around him then. "Like maybe territorial delegate, or the future governor of the state of Montana."

He frowned. "Who have you been talking to?"

She laughed and walked back to the desk. "Ty. He told me about the men prompting you to run. I can't think of a better man to represent Montana. Any man who knows as much about this land as you do, and who loves it the way you do, can't help but do a good job of leading us toward statehood."

He followed her to the desk and opened a box of thin cigars, taking one out. "You wouldn't mind?"

"I'd be very proud."

He walked to the fireplace to light the cigar with a long match, taking a moment to puff on it. "It could mean having to be away from the Double L, sometimes just me, sometimes both of us."

She gave it some thought. "The children are getting bigger. In three or four more years, Ty will practically be able to run this ranch by himself. We've talked about Pearl studying music in Chicago by then, and Robbie will be in college. By then the Northern Pacific should be coming through here, which will make it a lot easier to travel east, and which also means no more cattle drives, even to Cheyenne. And you have a good crew of men, many of whom have worked for you for a lot of years. They know as much about how to run this ranch as you do."

He kept the cigar between his teeth and walked back to the window. "Well, I have no plans for anything like that for at least two years yet. This next year will be one of rebuilding. Thank God for the copper mines and our other investments. I hear that up around Butte the new find is copper. The gold is just about played out. There's still some silver, but copper is all the news now. Might be the biggest find in the country. I just might do some investing there." He puffed the cigar for a few seconds. "You're a forward-thinking woman, Lettie Fontaine. You told me years ago not to rely just on the cattle." He turned to look at her. "Which reminds me. What's the damage?"

She looked at the ledger. "Well, about fifteen hundred cattle were lost, as far as the men can tell. Brad lost about six hundred sheep. He wants to go to Utah next spring and see if he can buy some from the Mormons, but we'll have to loan him the money to do it. He has already made sure to tell me that he'll pay the loan off when he makes his first shipment of lambs to the slaughterhouses in Omaha, was very adamant that I know he intends to pay it back with interest."

Luke grinned and shook his head. "What about the buildings and all?"

Lettie looked up at him. "We saved the big barn and two smaller horse sheds. The wind shifted just in time. We fared a lot better than some others, Luke. We lost thousands of acres of grassland, but the rain brought what's left back to life, and already new grass is growing in the burned areas. Doc Manning says Hank Kline lost everything, all his outbuildings, his home, at least half of his stock."

She sighed, and Luke saw the sudden sadness in her eyes. "What aren't you telling me, Lettie?" He sat down in the leather chair he liked best, where he always sat to read and smoke. "Is Hank dead?"

She looked down. "Yes, but not from the fires. He… shot himself."

Luke closed his eyes. "Jesus," he whispered.

"His wife is going back East to live with one of her sons. She's only staying around long enough to sell the Lazy K. I thought…maybe we could buy it. It would help her out, and Brad and Katie could build a house there and use it for a sheep ranch. I like the idea of having them right here on the Double L, but I think deep down Brad would rather be more on his own. He's a proud, independent young man. We can't keep Katie right under our wing forever, Luke. She's a wife and mother now, and the Lazy K isn't that far away. It's closer than Billings, so we'd still be close enough to see each other often and to help them when it's needed."

Luke watched blue cigar smoke curl into the air. The thought of Hank killing himself pained him deeply. Another friend gone. He wondered what he would have done himself if he had lost absolutely everything, but then he had Ty and Robbie, Pearl and Katie, and a new grandson. Hank's sons were grown and had never even bothered to come out and see their father's ranch. It was all Hank had ever really wanted to do, and he had lost it all. "All right. Buy it. Have you talked to Katie and Brad about this?"

"Not yet, but I know they'll like the idea. They've never said anything straight out, but I know they'd rather have a place they can truly call their own."

Luke nodded, listening quietly for a few minutes to his daughter's piano playing, ever amazed at her talent. Her playing had soothed him these past two weeks, the moving music somehow giving him strength. He set the cigar in an ashtray and folded his hands over his lap. "Tell Lucy Kline that we'll also see that a nice headstone is put up on Hank's grave. Was he buried in the Billings Cemetery?"

"Yes." She laid down a pen. "That's good of you, Luke. I get the impression they did not have a lot of extra money. I think a good deal of what she gets for the ranch will have to go to pay off debts."

Luke ran a hand through his hair. "Is there anything else you aren't telling me?"

"Well, from what I hear, the other ranchers didn't fare so badly. They all suffered some losses, just like we did, except that it's harder on them because they don't have as much to fall back on, but they'll be okay. I told Sven to tell all of them they can use some of the grazing land we have left if necessary. It will mean us buying more feed, but we can get it wholesale from the granary we own in Cheyenne. Is that all right?"

He studied her lovingly. "I'd have done the same. They've all helped us at different times, and some of them literally taught me a few things about ranching. We've ridden together after outlaws and rustlers, and they all contributed to the ransom money for Katie. We'll manage."

Lettie stood up and came to sit in a chair across from him. "There's one more thing."

He leaned his head against the back of the chair. "Go ahead."

"Nial Bentley. He lost a lot of grassland and cattle, but that's not the worst of it."

Luke frowned. "Did that stone mansion of his burn?"

"No. You know Chloris was with child."

"I know. Don't tell me she lost the baby."

Lettie folded her hands and studied them as she spoke. "About a week ago. She went into early labor, and she nearly bled to death."

Luke let out a groan, rubbed at his eyes. "Good God."

"I'm told through the grapevine that it was not a normal pregnancy to begin with. According to Dr. Manning, it's unlikely she'll have any more children. I guess Sydney and Helen Greene are in a terrible grief. Chloris was their only child, and now there will never be any grandchildren." She reached out and took hold of his hand. "The whole thing made me grateful for all my normal births, and the fact that God gave us several children. We've been through so much, Luke, but we're also very blessed."

He sighed deeply. "Well, Nial Bentley is not my favorite person, but every man wants children to carry on the name, to give everything to someday." He reached out and touched her cheek with the back of his hand. "You're right. We sometimes have to just stop and count our blessings. Maybe we should do something for them, maybe send a letter of sympathy or something." He leaned back in the chair again. "God knows he doesn't need money. His backers in merry old England will help replace his losses. But there are some things money can't buy." He thought how beautiful his wife looked this morning. "Like the love of a woman who belongs to someone else."

She smiled sadly. "Luke, that is in the past."

"Not for Nial. He doesn't love Chloris the same way he loved you, probably still loves you."

She walked back to the desk. "Well, that's all beside the point now."

Is it? Luke wondered. He had no worries about Lettie, but he could not quite get over the fact that another man had tried to steal his wife, and that man probably still loved her. In spite of what Nial had suffered, Luke could not totally sympathize with the man. He would never be able to forgive him for thinking his money and title gave him the right to take what belonged to another, nor the fact that the man had used their son's death as an opening to take advantage of Lettie. He had no doubt that Nial never loved Chloris the way a man should love his wife. She was just a replacement for Lettie, and now that she could not give Nial children, she would be even less important to him.

Lettie looked over at her husband, knew by his eyes what he was thinking. Nial still loved her. She knew it in her own heart, but it was something they never talked about anymore. She hated Luke's father for instilling in him a feeling of worthlessness and insecurity that continued to make him worry about men like Nial, and that had caused him to work himself nearly into the grave just to prove himself. And she hated the man for never answering any of Luke's letters and for never coming to see the magnificent ranch his son had built. "I love you, Luke. A couple of weeks ago I thought I had lost you. Please do what the doctor says and take it easy this winter. I need you."

He grinned. "Come here, woman."

She walked back over to him, and he put out his arms. She sat on his lap and rested her head against his shoulder. He embraced her, moving one hand over her breasts lightly.

"This is all your fault, you know."

"Oh? Why is that?"

He kissed her hair. "You remember what we were doing the day of the fire. You had me all worn out before I even went to dig that trench. You've got to quit being so man hungry, Lettie Fontaine."

She laughed lightly. "We both know whose idea it was to go playing in the bushes like a couple of children." She turned her face up, and their lips met in a gentle kiss. Lettie felt the possessiveness as the kiss lingered and grew deeper. He was reminding her that she belonged to Luke Fontaine, trying to assure her that in no time he would be strong as ever. His collapse had devastated his pride. Didn't he know that in her eyes there was no one stronger or manlier than he? She had had her own taste of possessiveness, had seen how other women looked at her husband, and not just the single ones.

"Maybe we should go upstairs and see if I can—"

Lettie got up off his lap. "Luke Fontaine! It's almost lunchtime. I will not have everyone in this house looking for us and knowing what's going on. Besides, you're supposed to *rest*."

"Might make me heal faster."

She cast him a chastising glance. "Don't try playing on my sympathy. For the next few months you are under my command. Someday you will be spending part of your time in Helena, maybe even as governor of the new state of Montana, fighting for whatever Montana needs. You've got to prepare yourself. Use the winter to do some reading up on how our government works. Katie can probably help you find the right books."

He grinned and shook his head. "You're determined that's going to happen, aren't you?"

She faced him, her hands on her hips. "There is no better man in this territory for the job, nor one more deserving. And when you become governor, I will be the most envied woman in Montana, just because I'm the handsome Luke Fontaine's wife." She felt her blood warm at the way his blue eyes raked over her.

"You'll be envied because you'll be the most beautiful governor's wife Montana will ever have. You'll make up for all my lack of class. If I ever do become territorial delegate, or even governor, it will be because of you." He got up from the chair and put an arm around her shoulders. "Walk me outside. I want to visit Tex's grave."

"I'll order a stone as soon as you decide what should be engraved on it."

Luke stopped and took a piece of paper from his shirt pocket. "I've already been thinking about it. I wrote this upstairs in the bedroom. What do you think?"

Lettie took the paper and opened it. "'Here lies Tex,'" she read aloud, "'who gave his life for another. Died September fifteenth, 1881. About fifty. Good friend and devoted ranch hand. May God take him to his fold.'" The words caught in her throat and she refolded the paper. So many good friends lost...Tex, Hank Kline, Jim Woodward, Will and Henny. She looked up at Luke, saw the tears in his own eyes. "It's perfect," she told him.

They walked outside together, and from his back

bedroom upstairs, Robbie was looking out the window. He watched his parents walk to the grave, watched his father kneel beside it. It seemed only fitting that at that very moment Pearl was playing a hymn on the grand piano downstairs, the music floating out across the lawn on a gentle wind.

Robbie's lips puckered and his eyes teared anew. He realized the only reason he was alive was because of Tex, that if it hadn't been Tex who had died in that fire, his own mother or father would have died in an effort to save him. His tender heart ached for the rugged, mysterious ranch hand who used to frighten him a little when he was smaller. "Bye, Tex," he whispered. "I love you."

Thirty

LUKE FONTAINE FOR TERRITORIAL DELEGATE! LUKE'S supporters had strung up a banner that hung across the main street of Billings, but farther up the street attorney Sydney Greene and his wife Helen had also draped a banner reading *Nial Bentley for Delegate!* The Greenes had managed to rally some support for their son-in-law, who had declared that because of cattle ranches he owned in Wisconsin and Nebraska, his higher education and world travels, he was the better man to represent cattlemen in the territorial legislature.

Montana Territory had far surpassed the required population of sixty thousand to apply for admission to the United States. Officially the territory had a population of close to ninety thousand, something that amazed Luke and Lettie, considering how desolate it had been when they came there twenty years ago. Billings had just been a little log village. Now it burst with new settlers, who had come because of the completion of the Northern Pacific. New gold finds in the western part of the territory had brought in more settlers, and the huge copper find around Butte was the talk of the whole country. Newspapers were declaring Butte Hill "the richest hill on earth," and the areas around the mines and around Helena were also growing rapidly.

People gathered around the Fontaine buggy as Sven drove it through the main street of town, now lined with more new businesses and yet another hotel. Luke had added two more floors to the Hotel Fontaine, and the Stowes' boardinghouse had also been enlarged. More lawyers had come to town, another doctor, two more teachers, and a dentist. One of those teachers was needed to replace Yolanda Brown, who had decided to go back to Chicago to teach. The timing was perfect, as Pearl was also going to Chicago, to study under a Professor John Bansen, a German pianist of great renown, who ran a private school for only the very best. Bansen had responded to a letter from Lettie, offering to listen to Pearl play and decide if she had the talent for advanced music lessons. All they had to do was get their daughter to Chicago. Miss Brown had agreed to be Pearl's chaperon.

Luke was not pleased with sending his sixteen-year-old innocent off to a big city to study under a stranger, but Lettie had corresponded with the parents of other students of Bansen for over a year, and had taken every precaution to ensure that the man and his school were reputable.

Pearl was not the least bit afraid to leave home for a big city, but Lettie worried that the change might be more of a shock than Pearl realized. All she had ever known was the remote life of living on a Montana ranch. The biggest and only town she knew was Billings, but at least Pearl was traveling with a reputable woman who knew the city well and could escort Pearl to the school. Once she was there, she would be among other young people who shared her love of music.

This was a day of both celebration and sadness. They would see Pearl off to Chicago, and her joyful, charming presence and piano playing would be sorely missed. Later, Luke and Nial would make speeches about why they would make the best delegates for Montana's legislature. Two more men from the Butte and Helena area were also running for delegate, and in a few days Luke and Lettie would leave the ranch to spend two months traveling the territory to win votes and talk about statehood. The new legislature would draft the proper papers for Montana's request to be allowed into the United States.

So many changes. Children growing up and going away. Katie, now nineteen, had given birth to her second child, a daughter, Rachael Ann, in February. Her son, Paul, was twenty months old and a wild little thing. Katie and Brad had built a roomy but simple log home on their new ranch, and surrounding cattlemen had accepted the fact that sheep would graze nearby. The price of wool had risen, and with the completion of the Northern Pacific, Brad could ship his wool east much cheaper now. Another railroad, the Utah and Northern, connected them to places farther south, and cattle drives were no longer necessary. Cattle were now shipped to stockyards and slaughterhouses by rail.

In two years Robbie would be going off to college. A young man now, Ty was built almost as tall and broad as his father. He was dashingly handsome, and all the young, available girls in town had an eye for him. He was the most popular young man at the spring dances, but he seemed most interested in Alice Richards. They had known each other for many years now, and Lettie felt in her heart that the two of them would end up married someday.

Luke waved at people who cheered him on as Sven drove the buggy to the railroad depot. The whole family had come to see Pearl off, and all were dressed their best because of the political rally planned for that afternoon. Lettie wore a yellow day dress that Gino Galardo had tailored just for her. It sported white, double lace cuffs, with water-fan trim of the same lace down the front of the bodice. The dress was perfectly fitted over a waist still slender enough that she was proud of it. The color was well suited for a bright, warm May day, as was her straw hat, decorated with yellow silk ribbon and flowers. Her shawl was made of the same white lace that decorated her dress, and she carried a yellow parasol and handbag and wore white lace gloves.

Luke loved her in yellow, thought it set off the deep red of her hair and her green eyes. Lately she had noticed a little gray in that hair, but at thirty-eight, and after some of the things they had been through in their twenty years in Montana, it was to be expected. She glanced at Luke, whose thick, dark hair also was showing some gray at the temples. He looked wonderful today. He was strong again, more confident than ever, strikingly handsome for a man of forty-eight. Hard work outdoors had only made him healthier and more robust than most men his age. Not a man to put on airs with his clothing like Nial Bentley was, he had chosen to wear denim pants with a white shirt over which he wore a black waistcoat. Because it would be a warm day, he wore no jacket, but his waistcoat sported a gold watch chain she had given him for his birthday in March. The only things he wore that were brand-new were his Western-style, wide-brimmed felt hat and new black leather boots. He had declared that if he was going to represent Montana, he would dress like any man from Montana would dress, rich or not; not like some fancy Eastern businessman or like an English prince.

They reached the depot, and Lettie was relieved to see Miss Brown was already there with her bags. Luke shook hands with people while Brad and Tyler helped unload Pearl's luggage, which took up most of the room at the back of the fancy new four-seater buggy Luke had had the local wagonmaker build for him a year ago so they would have something big enough to haul the whole family. A Northern Pacific steam engine sat hissing on the tracks, and a conductor was parading on the platform announcing that engine number eighteen would be leaving in fifteen minutes for Bismark, St. Paul, Omaha, and Chicago.

Lettie's heart tightened at the words. Pearl! Her beautiful, sweet, gentle Pearl was leaving them today. It would be a long time before they heard her lovely music, saw her bright smile, held her close. She almost wished her daughter did not have such natural talent, that she did not love music so much. Maybe Professor Bansen would say she was not ready or talented enough to go on with her schooling, but she knew that was not only a false hope, but a sinful one. She wished only the best for Pearl, and she was proud of her daughter's abilities; but it hurt to know that those abilities would take her away from them. Her long-time tutor, Elsie, and Elsie's husband, Peter Yost, followed behind in a buggy of their own, bringing along their three young children and also longtime housemaid, Mae, and her husband, Bob Franks, who all wanted to see Pearl off.

The conductor put Pearl's and Miss Brown's luggage on board, and Miss Brown stood aside while Pearl went through a round of hugs from her siblings and niece and nephew, as well as from Elsie and Mae. Then came Lettie and Luke. Lettie clung to Pearl, unable to keep from crying; and when the girl turned to Luke, silent tears showed in his eyes as he held his youngest daughter for a very long time. The fifteen minutes before departure seemed to fly, and suddenly the conductor was announcing that it was time for all passengers to board the train.

But it's too soon! Lettie thought. She gave Pearl another hug, as did Luke, and then they clung to each other while Pearl climbed into a passenger car with Yolanda Brown. The engineer pulled a cord and let off one long whistle, followed by two short blasts, and steam billowed out of the side of the engine. Pearl hung out a window, waving, crying, but also smiling with excitement. "I'll make you proud of me!" she promised.

Yes, Lettie thought, *perhaps she will.* For some reason little Paul flashed into her mind. Was he here with them? He would be thirteen years old if he were still alive.

Too much too fast. The town was alive with the excitement of politics, but at this moment it didn't matter. Pearl was leaving them, going to a strange, big city. Maybe she would make her mark there. Maybe she would forget about her mother and father and the Double L.

"I love you, Mother!" she shouted. "I love you, Father!" The train started moving, and Lettie watched that beautiful face and kept her eyes on that bright red hair until she could see them no more. She felt Luke's strong arm around her then. He leaned down from behind and kissed her tearstained cheek. "We'll find a way to go and see her," he promised.

For the moment, for the two of them, there was no one else around. The noise of the crowd disappeared, and it was as though they were standing there alone. "Oh, Luke, it hurts so much."

"There could be worse reasons for having to say good-bye."

She knew he was thinking about Paul. Suddenly a reporter for the *Billings Gazette* was barging in to ask Luke about Pearl. Katie put her arms around her mother, while Tyler stood beside his father helping answer questions. Lettie turned around and wept on Katie's shoulder.

"You did the right thing, Mama. It's what Pearl has always wanted."

Lettie nodded, taking a handkerchief from her handbag and wiping at her nose and eyes. "Oh, I must look terrible, and I have to stand with Luke today during his speeches."

"You look beautiful, Mama. You always do. And you'd better hurry. That crowd is taking Pa away."

Lettie turned to see Luke laughing with local businessmen, still answering questions from the newspaper reporter. He was taking to politics more naturally than she had thought he would, and she smiled through tears, realizing that he was a man highly respected and well liked. Luke Fontaine *was* Montana.

❧

Lettie studied the newspaper article dated October 8, 1883, anger boiling in her soul at the words. "*What do we know about Luke Fontaine's background?*" it read.

> *The man has never made mention of where he is from, who his father is. Not only are his origins a mystery, but his choices since settling in Montana must also be examined. Should we bring a man into the territorial legislature who was once a vigilante? Has anyone asked Luke Fontaine how many men he has killed, what he thinks of true law and order? Does he believe in a system of justice, or is he too quick to throw a rope over a tree? He professes to be a family man, yet his adopted son chose to live among the Sioux rather than with his father. Does the man rule like a vigilante at home? Or could this mean something else? Perhaps Luke Fontaine has a soft spot for the Indians because his son lives among them. With someone like Fontaine in our legislature, will Montana end up granting favors to the very Indians who have caused our citizens so much heartache over the years? Is Luke Fontaine really fit to help run our now-civilized territory, a representative we can be proud of? Is this a man we truly want people in Washington to look at as an example of Montana's best? Luke Fontaine knows ranching, but that is all he knows. He is not qualified, either in knowledge of government, in background, education, or in honorable personality, to represent our great territory, or to lead us to statehood. His wife, on the other hand, is the picture of poise, elegance, intelligence, and refinement. How sad that it is not Mrs. Fontaine who is running for office, but a woman's place is at home…and so is Luke Fontaine's.*

She laid the paper down, still finding it difficult reading, even though she had been over the article a hundred times in the last three days. She was surprised at Luke's self-control in answering every charge. People here in Helena had been good to him, but since the article they had been cooler. Luke had attended several public meetings, and was doing a superb job of showing his worth, his love for Montana, explaining how he would fight for protection of both farmers and ranchers in the areas of price setting and bank loans. He had remained calm on the outside, proving to the public that he could stand up against such slander, coming back at them with clear answers. But she knew that he had been deeply hurt, and she knew who had done the hurting. No names had been mentioned, but she had no doubt that Nial Bentley was behind most of the ugly words. Perhaps he had not directly written the article, but he had dropped enough of the wrong information to other opponents to fuel the fire.

She turned from the desk in their hotel room and watched out the window for a few quiet moments, studying the activity below. Luke was at a breakfast meeting this morning, speaking with Helena's most prominent businessmen, many of them much wealthier than they, their fortunes made on gold and silver. The article had put Luke on the defensive, had forced him to have to answer personal questions rather than being able to focus on what he wanted to do for Montana. She felt a deep anger, not just at Nial, but at herself for ever trusting and befriending the man. How many newspapers besides this one in Helena had run that garbage? Another newspaper in town had been very supportive. For that much she was grateful, but she felt the article denigrating Luke's qualifications and reputation needed to be answered.

She turned from the window and took out pen and paper and began writing. Luke would be gone most of the morning. She would be meeting all the wives tonight at a ball one of the businessmen was to hold in his home for Luke and for the two candidates from the Helena area. It was going to be rather awkward mingling with the competition after the awful article, but Lettie welcomed the chance to show what she and Luke were made of. She wasn't sure what part of the territory Nial had gone to for his own campaign, but she suspected it was a good thing he would not be at the ball tonight, or Luke just might show some of that old, rough side of himself. There was a rage behind those blue eyes, and it was against Nial Bentley.

She began writing, determined to set the record straight.

> In response to the slanderous allegations against one of Montana's finest citizens, I feel, as that man's wife, that the truth should be told. Luke Fontaine does have a business background, being the son of a wealthy St. Louis merchant; however, rather than live in luxury in St. Louis, he chose to set out on his own, to settle in a then-dangerous land to build his dream. Like a true Montana pioneer, Luke cut his own way by the sweat of his brow and the strength of his hands, fought Indians and outlaws and the wild land.
>
> Yes, Luke was a vigilante, but necessarily so. We must remember that Montana has not long been civilized, and parts of it still are not. Where there is no organized law, a man must do what is necessary to protect his own. No man enjoys the task of taking the law into his own hands, but there are times when there is no other choice, and Luke Fontaine never brought harm to an innocent man. Those he has brought to justice were murderers, rapists, and thieves. His family has personally suffered dearly because of Luke's fight against such undesirables.
>
> My firstborn child, adopted by my husband, was stolen away by Indians soon after we settled in this land. Luke searched for the boy for months, but to no avail, finally being led to believe he was dead. Years later Luke and I learned our Nathan was still alive but living among the Sioux. We all know of many instances

wherein a white child captured by Indians chooses to stay among them when he or she is found years later. That is the choice our Nathan made, but he is still our son, and the agony we have suffered from his loss has only been worsened by the cruel charge that it was something Luke did that made Nathan stay with the Sioux. This is entirely false, and if Nathan should ever choose to come home, he would always be welcome; but the fact that our son still lives with the Sioux does not mean that Luke would grant the Indians favors over and above what is good for Montana and its citizens. Montana would always come first.

Yes, Luke does certainly understand ranching and ranchers' needs, as he is one of the most successful cattle ranchers in Montana. However, he also understands the needs of other businessmen. Through early troubles with farmers, he has come to understand their particular problems. Luke also understands business needs, as he owns copper mines, a hotel, a grain supply, and other interests. Montana can thank men like Luke for saving our territory from the ugly range wars that have plagued Colorado and Wyoming. Luke Fontaine was the first cattleman to prove to the rest of the country that sheep and cattle can graze together without a problem, the first to allow sheep to range on his own land. Does this sound like a man who does not want peace? A man who does not know how to be fair? A man who would not be capable of making wise decisions for Montana?

My husband built what he has through courage and determination and from almost nothing. He did not come here from a foreign land to spend old money handed down to him through family. He loves this land; he risked his life and the safety of his family to settle here, and he built what he has by the sweat of his brow and not by hiring everything done for him while he sat and *watched, as one of the other candidates, whom I will not name, has done. We have buried children and friends, have stood up against outlaws and prairie fires. We have paid our dues, and we stayed. We stayed because we love this land, and we would not let it defeat us.*

As to the last charge that it is I who should be running for office, but a woman's place is in the home, I will say first that I could never begin to fill Luke Fontaine's shoes regarding his knowledge of the needs of this territory. Secondly, like many other pioneer women of Montana believe, our place is not always at home. Our place is in the churches, the schools, and in activities that bring refinement and culture to Montana. Montana women are proud and independent, and my husband would be first to support the rights of women to have a say in decisions about our great territory. My place is not only at home, but at my husband's side, and to help him however I can in bringing Montana into the United States. It is men like Luke Fontaine who have brought us this far, and who will bring continued progress to our territory. Just as it took brave and rugged men to pioneer this land, so will it take the same kind of men to defend our honor and our particular needs when Montana becomes a state.

Mrs. Luke (Eletta) Fontaine

She reread the letter, folded it and put it in her hand-bag. She checked herself in the mirror. She had chosen to wear a deep brown velvet dress. She pulled on a matching velvet cape and tied it at the neck, then placed a white velvet hat on her auburn hair and pinned it at an elegant slant. She chose to wear white gloves. She would show this town and everyone else just how elegant and refined she really could be; and they would have to wonder, if Luke was the unrefined tyrant the article had made him out to be, why someone like herself would still be with him. She would do her share in this campaign by simply being on Luke Fontaine's arm, the happy, loving wife, and she thought how pleasant it would be to have Nial Bentley in front of her right now and to put a derringer to his chest and pull the trigger.

She picked up her handbag and went out. She would take her letter to a printer's office and have it typeset, then have enough copies run off to send to every damn newspaper in Montana and beyond!

⌇

Luke untied his tie and began unbuttoning his shirt, at the same time watching Lettie brush her hair. It was still thick and lustrous, showing only a little gray. "We sure have seen a lot of Montana, haven't we?" he asked, removing his shirt and going to look out the hotel window. "Bozeman, Butte, Anaconda, Helena, now Great Falls." He watched a light snow fall onto the street below, just enough to dampen the already muddy street. "Is there any land prettier, Lettie?"

She smiled. "I really don't know. Montana is about all I've ever known. I hardly remember our trip up here through Wyoming, it's been so many years ago, and I never did get to go to Denver."

He turned away from the window, studying her lovingly. "That's my fault. I'm sorry, Lettie. There must have been times when you felt buried alive up here. We can still travel to other places, you know, even Europe if you want, or other places out here. We have the money—"

She faced him, putting down her brush. "I wasn't complaining, Luke. I was just stating a fact." She rose and walked closer, tracing her fingers through the dark hair on his still-solid chest. "There is no place I want to go but home, Luke, to the Double L. And I know it's the same for you. I don't need to travel all over the country or across the ocean to be happy. You know that."

He put his hands to her face. "I know there isn't a man alive who could have a better wife, or a more beautiful one." She smiled, and Luke noticed new lines about her eyes, but he saw beyond them, to the eighteen-year-old girl he had married and brought to this wild land. "Thank you, Lettie, for the letter."

She rubbed her hands over his arms, up to his shoulders. "I was afraid you might be angry about it, but it was something I had to do. I couldn't let those lies go unanswered." She arched her eyebrows teasingly. "Of course, I did leave out the fact that this poised, elegant, refined, and intelligent wife of yours has done her share of shooting at outlaws, even killed one. I guess I should have mentioned that."

He broke into a handsome grin. "Maybe you should have." He moved his hands into her hair and down her back, pressing her close. "You're a good woman, Lettie. I've gotten a lot of good response since that letter."

"Well, we'll know in two days how much good it did. Then all this will be over. However it turns out, we can get back to a halfway normal life again, back to the Double L and the children." She kissed his chest. "That's where we both belong."

"I can be home wherever I am, as long as I've got you right here close to me." He leaned down and kissed her hair, and she turned her face up to him, meeting his mouth hungrily. With so much traveling and often staying as guests in strangers' homes, they had not had the chance over the past several weeks to make love often. Now the campaigning was over. All that was left was to wait for the results. Tomorrow they would leave for Helena, and thanks to the wonders of Western Union, they would know by the time they reached there how the day's voting had turned out.

Lettie reached up around Luke's neck. "Do you think it's true about that contraption called a telephone they're starting to use back East? That people could talk to each other directly over several miles?"

"I'll believe it when I see one of the things for myself."

"Wouldn't that be a wonderful thing to have between Katie and us?"

He grinned. "I doubt that will happen in our lifetime, Lettie, especially way out here."

"Well, once you're a Montana legislator, I think you should look into it. You have to keep us modern now, you know."

He began pulling up her gown. "I'll worry about that tomorrow."

"I thought you were saying a few minutes ago how tired you are," she reminded him.

He lifted her up, and she wrapped her legs around his waist. He realized that she wore nothing under her gown. "Some things help me go to sleep," he answered, carrying her to the bed. "Besides, you knew I'd see if you had any drawers on under this gown, you wench." He laid her back on the bed, pushing her gown up past her breasts. She raised her arms over her head and he pulled the gown off.

"Luke, I haven't finished brushing my—" His kiss cut off her words, and his fingers caressed her. She closed her eyes and drew in her breath when he moved a finger inside of her, teasing, toying, circling that magic place that he knew so well how to arouse. His tongue searched deep, then left her mouth, moved over the curve of her neck, savored a taut nipple, trailed over her belly and licked at the little valleys between her belly and her thighs, all the while toying with secret places until she shivered with a deep climax that made her draw up her knees. He pressed against her, kissing her deeply, and she reached down to unbutton his pants. "Why do I find you even more attractive as a politician?"

He moved away for a moment to get off the rest of his clothes. "I'm not a politician yet."

She sat up and kissed at his chest, arms, and back. "No one who meets you would vote against you. You *are* Montana, Luke."

He turned to move on top of her. "There are plenty of people out there who have never met me."

"They'll see your handsome picture."

"Looks don't mean a man has what it takes to run a territory, or a state. If I win, it will be because of your letter."

"I wrote that to satisfy my own anger. You could have won without it."

"Lettie, I haven't won yet."

She traced her fingers through his chest hair, over his nipples. "You will. Either way, you won my vote twenty years ago, Luke Fontaine. You just make sure you stay away from the women who will come around flirting and offering themselves to you when you're traveling alone."

He pressed his hardness against her thigh. "As long as I can always come home to this, I don't need any other women." His smile faded. "You're all I'll ever need or want, Lettie." He moved a big hand over her breast, kneading it gently. "And don't think I don't realize half the men in this territory would like to be where I am right now."

She closed her eyes. "None of them could compare to you."

He met her mouth again, kissing her almost savagely as he pushed himself inside her. She arched her hips to greet him in groaning need, realizing that after all these years, nothing but deep, satisfying, devoted love could keep this act so fresh and delightful and fulfilling. They moved in sweet rhythm, sharing, pleasing, taking pleasure in return. He raised to his elbows and gently rocked himself into her, stirring her so teasingly that she gasped in a second climax. He moved in a hard, fast rhythm then, filling her deep, groaning in his own pleasure until his own release.

He kissed her hungrily, several times over, pulling her into his arms and settling beside her then, her leg still wrapped over his thigh. "Tomorrow we head back to Helena, then home," he said longingly. "It's almost as if I need to go back to the Double L to get my strength back, Lettie."

"That's because that land *is* your strength. Your blood is part of its life. They say the Indian spirit is one with the land, but I don't think it's just the Indians who have that connection. I think it can happen for any man, or woman. I didn't want to come here in the beginning, Luke, but now I never want to leave. I don't need to travel to other places. I just want to go home and see my children and grandchildren."

"Just a few more days," he answered, kissing her hair.

Lettie settled into the pillow. Talk of Indians had brought back thoughts of Nathan. "It's been eight years since he left us, Luke. Do you think we'll ever see him again?"

He didn't need to ask who she was talking about. "I don't know. You can't torture yourself about it."

"Maybe we should start checking the reservations when things settle down again. Maybe we should try to find him."

"If that's what you want, that's what we'll do."

She met his eyes. "Isn't it what *you* want?"

He sighed deeply. "Of course I'd like to find him. But he knows where we are, Lettie. If he wants to come home, he will. There's no sense forcing it. Maybe we could find him, but you can't force him to come back, Lettie, and I'm just afraid what it might do to you to see him again and realize he's where he wants to be."

"I need to know he's all right, if he's even alive."

He pulled her close. "Then we'll try to find him," he answered. "We'll try."

Thirty-one

GREEN PINE BRANCHES AND RED BOWS DECORATED THE outside of the depot at Billings. Lettie breathed a deep sigh of joy at the sight. Home at last! How they had missed Billings, their friends and neighbors, and the Double L.

"Luke, look at the crowd!"

He leaned forward to look out the window as their train moved into the station. They had come in from Butte, and apparently everyone in Billings was aware that their new territorial legislative delegate was arriving. In spite of the bitter cold outside, it looked as though half the town was at the depot, and as soon as the Northern Pacific engine chugged to a halt, a band started playing "For He's a Jolly Good Fellow."

"There's Ty and Robbie!" Lettie said excitedly, grasping Luke's hand.

"Brad and Katie too. I can't believe they came all the way into town in this cold."

They watched the little white clouds of breath and red noses that told them winter had already settled hard into Montana again, even though there had not been much snow yet except high in the mountains. Even the train car was cold, in spite of a wood-burning stove in one corner. When they had left Butte, it had still been relatively warm for December; but when they stopped in Virginia City, they could feel the change in the weather. Temperatures had dropped dramatically in the twenty-four hours since they had come east from there.

"Katie must have left the babies home because of the

cold. Oh, I can't wait to see little Paul and Rachael again.
I'm so glad we've made it home in time for Christmas,
Luke." Lettie turned and kissed his cheek. "And coming
home a winner makes it all the better."

He squeezed her hand. "It's a good feeling. The only
trouble with winning is that I'll have to go to Helena
for weeks at a time now, but sometimes you'll go with
me. I'm glad, though, that I'm not the delegate that has
to go to Washington. That would mean being away for
months instead of days or weeks. I don't think I could
bear being away from the Double L that long. I miss
home, Lettie."

She studied his blue eyes, glad he didn't have to go
back to Helena until spring. It had been a hard campaign,
not just physically but emotionally. In the spring he
would help draft the petition that would be carried to
Washington and presented to Congress for Montana
to be allowed into the United States. They knew it
wouldn't happen overnight, but they were most certainly
on their way.

They got up and moved to the steps of the passenger
car, and as soon as she descended, Lettie was in Katie's
arms and there came a round of hugs from her daughter
and son-in-law, then Tyler and Robbie. She saw a rather
troubled look in Tyler's eyes, able to read him as well
as she could read Luke. Something was wrong, and she
prayed there had not been new losses at the Double L.
She wanted so much for this to be a merry Christmas and
happy homecoming.

Luke took his turn at hugging, then began shaking
hands and accepting congratulations from townspeople
and area businessmen. The band struck up another
tune, and the crowd followed them to the family's
enclosed carriage. Joe Parker was there, telling Luke to
be sure to come to the next cattlemen's meeting in two
weeks. Some of the women were peppering Lettie with

questions about what Helena and Butte and Virginia City were like, and at the same time Robbie was excitedly telling her they had gotten a letter from Pearl. "She heard about Pa winning clear back in Chicago!" he told her.

Everything was confusion and commotion, but Tyler remained rather quiet. It seemed everyone in town wanted them to come for dinner, and Lettie turned down invitation after invitation. "We just want to stay home for a while," she explained. "We've missed the ranch and the children so much." Tyler helped Sven with the luggage, and the family climbed into the waiting carriage. Luke started inside, then hesitated, looking to his right. The crowd quieted, and Lettie leaned out to look.

"Oh my! It's Nial Bentley," she said quietly. All the children clambered back outside, and Lettie herself slowly emerged as people backed away. Nial was walking toward Luke, wearing a forced smile. Lettie realized that everyone in town surely knew about the ugly article about Luke, and who had surely been behind it. She knew that what had bothered Luke the most was the question of his heritage. He had never had to come right out and tell anyone his own father had considered him a bastard, but she knew that the whole matter had brought back the old pain for Luke, the realization that to this day he had never heard from his father, in spite of his many letters. No one needed to know that. It was such a personal pain for Luke, and Nial Bentley had almost caused him to share it publicly.

Nial was dressed in his usual finery, top hat and all. "Luke!" he said, putting out his hand. "I just came to congratulate you. I am the humble loser, but must admit that I have every confidence Montana is in good hands." He glanced at Lettie, as though to hint that as long as Luke had her for a wife, he could manage his new duties because he would have her to help him. He looked back at Luke, who was not smiling. "Well, my friend,

I am humbly offering my best wishes. Aren't you going to shake my hand and show these people how gracious you can be? After all, in politics, anything goes. Now it's over."

Before Nial realized what was coming, Luke landed a big fist into his left cheek, sending the man sprawling. A gasp went up from the crowd, and a faint smile moved across Luke's lips.

"Wow, Pa, that was some punch!" Robbie spoke up.

Lettie could not help a vague smile of her own.

Luke looked around at the others. "Folks, you have just seen my last fit of vigilante justice!"

A roar of laughter went up from the crowd, and two men dragged a mumbling Nial away. Men slapped Luke on the back, some saying he should have given Nial Bentley what for a long time ago. Lettie and the children got back into the carriage and Luke finally climbed in beside them, glad Sven had brought the enclosed buggy, even though it was smaller than their open four-seater. Everyone sitting close inside helped stave off the bitter cold outside. Lettie shivered and snuggled next to Luke, Katie on the other side of her. Across from them sat Robbie, Tyler, and Brad.

"That was great, Pa," Tyler told him. "If you hadn't hit him, I think I would have."

Luke looked down at sore knuckles. "Well, we aren't supposed to punch our way through life anymore, but I couldn't let that one go."

"I've always hated Nial," Ty answered, glancing at his mother. "We all saw that article, saw the one you answered back with, Mom. We were all really proud when we read it."

Lettie grasped Luke's hand and kissed his knuckles. "Are you all right?"

He flexed the hand. "Never felt better."

Sven, in the driver's seat outside, and bundled against

the cold, whipped the two sturdy Double L horses hitched to the buggy into motion.

"How are things at the ranch?" Luke asked Ty.

Again Lettie noticed a strange expression on her son's face. "Good, Pa. No problems. Got a lot of pregnant mares, and as far as we can tell, we've got a lot of calves coming next spring too. Most of the herd is in close, but with all the cattle you've got on order, it won't be possible next year to get them all in for the winter. I'll bet at least half the cows are carrying. We'll be up to a good fifty thousand head by next summer."

"Well, we have a signed contract with that buyer out of Chicago saying he'll take all we can send, so we can't lose. We just have to hope no catastrophe wipes them out." He grinned. "You're doing a hell of a job, Ty. It's good to know I can count on you when I have to be gone."

Tyler smiled, but he looked away, as though afraid to let them see the look in his eyes.

"Little Paul can't wait to see his grandma," Katie said, as though she felt she had to change the subject. "I left Rachael and him at the main house so they'd be there when you get home instead of having to go all the way to the KT to get them." KT was the name and the brand for Brad's sheep ranch, the initials for Katie Tillis. Brad had worked hard helping build their home and restore the burned ranch that had once belonged to Hank Kline.

Katie grasped her mother's hand. "Mama, I'm going to have another baby, around June, I think."

"Oh, Katie, that's wonderful!"

Luke glanced at Brad. "Looks like you two have stayed pretty busy," he teased.

Brad blushed and grinned. "You apparently stayed pretty busy yourself those first few years, Luke," he bantered.

They all laughed then, and it was Lettie's turn to blush. The remark made her anxious to get home to their own bed again. It had been a long time since they had slept there. She was tired of hotel rooms or being the guest in someone else's home.

"How are your school lessons coming, Robbie?" Luke asked.

"Elsie says I'm too smart for her now. She sent for more special medical books and for information about the entrance exam from the University of Michigan. She says when I turn seventeen I should be able to get in."

"Oh, I don't think I'm ready to send another child away," Lettie said, reaching over and patting his knee. "With Katie over at her own home most of the time, we'll only have our Tyler left with us." She glanced at Ty. "Thank goodness *you* want to stay on at the ranch," she added. "I don't know what I'd do if *all* my children left me."

Ty did not smile, and there followed an uncomfortable moment of silence. Lettie wasn't sure if she had said something wrong. She looked back at Robbie. "Did you say you heard from Pearl?"

"Yes. The letter's at home. She's doing real well, Mom. She said the professor says she's his most promising student in years. She sounds real happy."

Lettie breathed a sigh of relief. "That's good. Oh, I miss her so. It will seem so strange not having her here this year to play Christmas carols for us. I'm beginning to wonder when we'll ever have the whole family together at the same time again."

Ty turned to look out a window, and the others looked at each other as though to share some secret thought.

Luke frowned. "All right, all of you, what is wrong? You're leaving something out. You don't need to wait until we get home. Has something happened we don't know about?"

Tyler faced his father, then moved his gaze to his mother, taking a deep breath. "Nathan's back."

Lettie drew in her breath, feeling as though her heart had surely stopped beating.

"Nathan!" Luke exclaimed. "When? Why?"

"That's what *I'd* like to know," Tyler said with a hint of bitterness. "If he thinks he can just walk in after all these years and get a big piece of the pie, I don't think it's fair! I've worked hard right alongside you all these years. I know how to run the Double L. I don't need him coming here and taking what's mine."

"Ty!" Lettie could hardly believe her ears. "What makes you think he could take your place, or that he would get more than his fair share? What makes you think he even *wants* anything from us?"

"Why else would he be here? When I ask him about it, he just says he'll talk to you and Pa, not to me." Tyler looked at his father. "You adopted him. He's been gone all these years, but he's still the firstborn son. By law he has every right to as much of the Double L as you want to give him, and I think it's damned unfair! He—"

"Now, just a minute, Ty!" Luke interrupted. "We haven't even had a chance to talk to him to find out why he's here. And give me a little credit for being a fair man. You know better than to think I'd favor one child over another, for *any* reason. How long has he been back?"

"Just a few days," Robbie spoke up. "He's been real quiet—stays in that little cabin Tex used to live in. He's hardly talked to anybody—just says he'll wait and talk to you and Mom. Nobody in town even knows it yet. We thought maybe we should wait till you came home to see what he wants. Maybe he won't even stay."

Lettie could not help feeling a wave of the old agony of remembering when Nathan was first torn from her arms, and how it felt when he ran away from them after they had finally found him again. How could she bear seeing him and then losing him yet again? Surely he was back to stay this time. Why else would he have come? But why? Why now? "You said...you talked to him. He speaks English now?"

Ty scowled. "Yeah, pretty well. He even dresses mostly like a white man, but his hair is still long, and he wears moccasins."

"We gave him food and some wood for the heating stove," Brad told her. "He seemed real grateful."

Lettie could not help the tears that spilled out of her eyes. She grasped Luke's hand. "He's twenty-two years old now," she said absently. Eighteen years it had been since her son was first taken from her. How could that be? Why was he here? She wiped at her eyes, glanced at Ty. "One day, when you have your own children, Ty, you will understand how I feel about this. You're all special, for so many different reasons." She looked at Robbie, Katie, back to Tyler. "You have been a loyal, hardworking, devoted son. Surely you don't think your father and I could forget that. The way Nathan was raised, I highly doubt he has much interest in the ranch. There must be some other reason he is here. Give him a chance, Ty. My being able to keep my son with me this time could depend in part on how all of you treat him. This could be the most important thing I have ever asked of any of you." She looked around at all of them again. "No matter how you feel about him now, he's still your brother. You all share the same blood through me, and no matter where Nathan has been these last years, he is still my son." She squeezed Luke's hand. "*Our* son. A MacBride by blood, a Fontaine by adoption, and because your father has the ability to love him just because he loves me. If he can love Nathan with no blood connection at all, surely all of *you* can learn to love him." She closed her eyes. "Thank God we came back when we did. He might have left again without our ever getting to see him."

"Lettie, don't get your hopes up," Luke warned. "You know what happened last time. Maybe there is just something he needs and he'll want to leave again."

Probably wants some money, Tyler thought. For his mother's sake, he would keep his opinion to himself, but he could not help believing Nathan was here for only one reason.

"Not this time," Lettie was saying. "I feel it in my heart. Nathan is here to stay."

❧

Tyler, Robbie, Katie, and Brad all sat quietly in the parlor, watching their mother pace nervously. Luke had gone to get Nathan, and Tyler thought about how Nathan must surely be overwhelmed by the elegance of the Fontaine home, Oriental rugs, expensive vases and statues, silk-covered chairs and rich oak and mahogany furniture. He and Katie and Robbie had put up a huge Christmas tree near the window, knowing their mother liked the biggest tree they could find, wanting to surprise her with it when she and Luke got home. Did Nathan even understand what the tree was for? What did he know about their family and how they lived?

He didn't like feeling this anger, but he couldn't help it. After so many years of being the oldest brother and doing everything he could to show his father he was fit to take over the ranch he loved so much, it just didn't seem right having an older brother come along who had decided long ago he wanted nothing to do with this family. The first time he came back, he had been forced. This time he had come on his own. That could only mean he wanted to make the Double L his home, which was like making it home to an Indian, after all the heartache the Sioux had caused his parents. None of it seemed fair.

He looked up when he heard the outer door open and close, heard Luke and Nathan stomp their feet to get off the snow. He watched his mother, who stared at the parlor door as though a ghost was about to enter.

The epitome of a mother's love shone in her eyes when Nathan stepped inside the room, and Tyler hated him. Nathan stared back at her silently.

"Hello, Son," Lettie spoke up.

He nodded. "Mother."

Mother! At last he had called her mother. Lettie struggled against a need to run to him, embrace him, but he was a stranger, a grown man, so tall and strong and handsome! She could hardly believe this was her son. A little part of her was stunned at how much he looked like the man who had given him life. It brought back the memory of that night of horror, but she reminded herself that Nathan was innocent of that awful night. He was life, a grown-up human being who need never know the truth of his beginnings. She glanced at Katie, warning her with her eyes she must never tell. Katie only smiled through tears. She seemed to understand how she felt.

She looked back at Nathan, whose blond hair was tied into a tail at the back of his neck. He wore cotton pants and a calico shirt with knee-high winter moccasins and a doeskin vest. How strange to feel so nervous around her own son. "I...I'm so glad you came. Ever since you left eight years ago, we've been so worried, Nathan, wondering if you were all right. We were even going to try to find you this summer."

Nathan glanced at his siblings. He could not help sensing Tyler's animosity since he had arrived, understood it to some extent. Robbie and Katie had been good to him, but he knew Tyler would rather he left, and he would, if he thought he could stand living on the reservation the rest of his life. He looked back at his mother. "I was in Canada for five years after the Battle of the Greasy Grass."

"Greasy Grass?"

"The Little Big Horn," Luke explained. He walked past them to the fireplace to roll himself a cigarette from tobacco and papers he kept there.

"You were *there*?" Lettie asked, her eyes wide with wonder.

Lettie saw it then—a quick flash in Nathan's eyes—the Indian spirit drilled into him that brought forth a certain pride, a hatred for soldiers like George Custer.

"I was there," he answered, holding his chin proudly. "It is no use trying to explain to any white man why it happened. No white man wants to hear the Indian side of it."

"But you *are* white," Tyler reminded him.

Nathan met his brother's eyes, put a fist to his chest. "Not in here."

"Then what the hell are you doing here?" Tyler asked.

Lettie cast him a quick look of chastisement. "He's here because he's our son and your brother!" she snapped. "If he feels more like a Sioux, who can blame him? He was *raised* by them!" She looked back at Nathan. "I don't care *why* you're here, Nathan, or how Indian you are, or even if you have no feelings for me as a mother. It doesn't change how I feel about you. I will always love you just the same as I loved the little four-year-old boy who was stolen away from me all those years ago. Whatever the reason, I'm glad you're here, glad to be able to see you again and know you're all right." She quickly wiped at tears with her fingers. "How is it you speak English now?"

"For three years I have lived on the reservation. Missionaries were there. I learned more quickly than the others because as I took the lessons, many of the words came back to me from when I was small." He glanced at Luke, who nodded to him reassuringly, then he looked around at the others, back to his mother. "I know that my brother Tyler thinks I have come here because my white father is an important man and rich in white man's money, but I do not care about these things. I only care about my family."

"Family! Do you have children?"

"A daughter and a son. They are called Sweet Grass and Runner, but the missionaries made us give them white names. The girl is four summers. She is called Julie, after the white woman who teaches them. Our son is two summers. He is named Luke, because it was the only white man's name I could think of."

Tyler's anger only increased at the news. He had always thought he would name his own first son after Luke. Now Nathan had stolen that honor from him.

Lettie looked at Luke, more tears wanting to come. "Do you hear that, Luke? We have two more grandchildren! Four grandchildren!" She looked back at Nathan. "Oh, Nathan, I'm so glad for you. Why aren't they with you? Where is your wife?"

He looked around the room, feeling out of place in the fancy home. "My wife is called Little Bird. The missionaries gave her the name of Leena. She and my children are still at the reservation at the Cheyenne River in the Dakotas. The government would not let them leave with me. Only I could leave because I am white. I need special written permission to bring them out of there, from a white man who will agree to take charge of them." His eyes began to glitter with anger. "None of you can know how bad life is on the reservation. My people are starving. They do not have enough clothes and blankets. The meat they bring us is rotten. Many drink themselves to death or shoot themselves because they cannot bear having to stay on one little piece of land taking handouts from the white man and eating rotten food. The men are forced to plow the ground like women, and the children are taken away to a special school in the East where many of them die of white man's disease or of broken hearts. The white teachers there cut their hair and make them wear white man's clothes, and they beat them for speaking in the Sioux tongue. I am sorry for my people, but the missionaries helped me understand that as one man there is little

I can do. They told me that because of my white mother and father, there is a way for me to take my family out of there and have a better life, and I realized they were right. I remembered you and Luke told me that if I ever wanted to come back here, I would be welcome."

Luke stood smoking quietly by the fireplace. He watched Lettie's eyes light up with joy, and he knew what this meant to her.

"Oh yes, Nathan! I can't think of anything more wonderful than having you and your wife and our grandchildren right here at the Double L!"

Nathan looked over at Tyler. "I am not here to take any of my father's wealth. I only want my family to be safe, to have enough to eat, to be warm in winter. I do not want to worry about the government taking my children from me." He moved his gaze back to Lettie. "I only want a place to live. I will work. I will not just sit here. I will help my father. I am good with horses, but I know nothing about what to do with cattle. I can learn."

"Of course you can learn!" Lettie broke into tears, turning away for a moment to get control of herself. Luke walked over to put an arm around her.

"There is one more thing," Nathan told them.

Lettie wiped at her eyes, and Luke held her close to his side. "What is that?" he asked.

"There is one more person I would like to bring here. She is Sioux. Her name is Morning Sun, but her white name is Ramona. She is my sister, youngest daughter of Half Nose, who died not long after I left here the first time. That is why I left sooner than I had promised. My father's brother came in the night to tell me Half Nose was very ill. I went to be with him."

A wave of emotions swept through Luke. Half Nose. He had hated the man for so many years. Now he was expected to turn around and take in the man's daughter. What an ironic twist of fate. "How old is she?" he asked.

"She will be sixteen summers when the snow is off the ground and the sun is hot again."

Katie smiled at the odd way Nathan had of expressing himself.

"Well, a lot of people aren't going to like the fact that I have Indians living here on the Double L," Luke answered, "but I've gone against the majority more than once since I came here, so I guess they'll just have to learn to live with this too."

Lettie looked at him, realizing it was not easy for him to give shelter to Indians. They had stolen his son away. Now he would have to put up with crude remarks from others for allowing Indians to live at his ranch, but maybe most would understand, realizing what it meant to her to have her son back. "Thank you, Luke." She looked at Nathan. "When will you bring them?"

"In the summer. I will need a written letter from Luke to show to the reservation agent. As soon as the letter is ready, I will go back. The agent promised my children would not be taken away while I am gone, but I do not trust him. I am afraid for them."

"Then Luke will go into Billings and send a wire to the reservation, demanding that nothing be done until you get back. Luke is an important man, Nathan. If he tells them to keep the children there, they will do it."

Nathan met Luke's gaze. "I am grateful."

"You will at least stay with us for Christmas, won't you, Nathan?" Lettie asked. "It's only two days away. Are you...are you Christian?"

He folded his arms. "As I learned the white man's religion from the missionaries, I came to see that it is not so different from the Sioux. We all believe in a Great Being who watches us from above and listens to our prayers. Yes, I am Christian, but I am also Sioux, and there are many Indian beliefs that will never leave me."

Luke walked back to the fireplace. He took a deep

drag on his cigarette, then threw it into the hearth and faced the rest of his children. "I don't know exactly how all of you feel about this, but it's my decision," he told them. "I'm letting Nathan bring his family and his step-sister here to live." He looked at Tyler. "All of you know how important this is to your mother. When I met and fell in love with her, I also loved and accepted Nathan as my own because he was her son, and I knew how much *she* loved him." He directed his gaze at Tyler. "For more reasons than you know, I vowed never to let Lettie's son feel any less loved or accepted than any of our own children. I will not cheat any son of mine out of what is rightfully his, but I will be fair about who has earned the right to this ranch and take into consideration whether or not each child even *wants* a part of this ranch. Tyler, we all know who has earned that right more than any other. You ought to trust me enough to know I would never take anything from you that you honestly deserve, nor could any other child change the way I feel about you or how proud I am of you or the special relationship we've always had."

He looked at Robbie. "That doesn't mean Tyler is any more special than you, Robbie, or Katie or Pearl, and Nathan isn't any more special just because he's the long-lost son. You're all *my* children, all loved the same."

"Pa, none of us expects... I mean, I hope you don't think we're greedy or sitting around waiting for an inheritance," Katie spoke up.

Luke sighed. "I know that. I'm just saying that this family has always been close, and I don't want Nathan's arrival to bring on any unwarranted hard feelings or worries that somehow he's going to take anyone's place. Tyler, you're in charge of the Double L now when I'm gone, and that won't change. I want you to help Nathan learn the ropes. With having to travel more, I won't have time for it. You heard Nathan's reasons for wanting to be here, and it has nothing to do with money. His children are Lettie's and my grandchildren, your niece and nephew. I will not let them go hungry or be taken away to some damn school back East where they get a beating just for being themselves, nor will I allow them to be abused or treated rudely while living here. Is that understood?"

"Of course it is, Pa," Katie answered.

Luke watched Tyler. He knew his son was good-hearted and understood the importance of family, but he could also see that he still felt somehow pushed out of place. "Above all else, we're all Fontaines. We're family, and we'll support each other and help each other and defend each other." He looked over at Nathan. "The same goes for you, Nathan, once you come back here. I understand that you feel more like a Sioux, that you consider them your family. But the fact remains that *we* are your family. I don't want you treating your brothers and sisters or your mother as though they are some kind of hated enemy."

Nathan nodded, glancing at Tyler again. "I am a Fontaine." He looked at Luke then. "But I will always have a place in my heart for the people who raised me. It was wrong for them to steal me away. I know this. But Half Nose was good to me. I thought of him as my father for many years, and I wept when he died." He looked at Lettie. "My Indian mother is also dead, from white man's disease. There is only Ramona."

"You'll stay until Christmas then?" she asked.

He nodded. "I will stay."

Lettie approached him hesitantly, her mind reeling with memories and the shock of realizing how fast the years had gone by after all. "All those lost years," she said quietly, studying her son lovingly.

Nathan could not help feeling affection for her. He had never forgotten how she had looked at him when he was there eight years ago. Such love he had never seen in anyone's eyes, except perhaps in Leena's; but that was a different kind of love, one of desire for her husband. The look in his mother's eyes was one of anguish and terrible longing.

Tyler rose. "I have some saddles to wax and bridles to repair." He walked toward Nathan. "Come on out to the barn," he said rather sullenly. "You want to learn the ropes. Might as well start now." He walked out, and Nathan glanced at Luke.

"He'll get used to it," Luke told him.

Nathan turned and walked out to pull on his wolf-skin coat and a beaver hat, then hurried out the door, and Lettie broke into tears. "He's come home, Luke. Nathan is home." Luke walked over and put his arms around her. "With Elsie and Peter living in our old log house, we'll have to build Nathan a cabin for his family," she told Luke through tears.

"I already thought about that," Luke answered. "I'll have the men get started on it right away."

Outside Nathan ran to catch up with Tyler, who said nothing until they got inside the barn. He turned to face Nathan then, a glint of warning in his deep blue eyes. "I'm doing this for Pa, because I love him more than anything on this earth. Don't you ever hurt him or my mother, you understand? You hurt them enough when you left last time. You'd better appreciate what good people they are, and you'd better remember that *I* am Luke Fontaine's firstborn—by blood! Nobody else could ever be as close to my pa as I am."

Nathan shook his head, smiling sadly. "I do not expect to take your place in Luke's heart, Tyler. I have not come here to take *any*thing that is yours. I do not even care if you hate me. I only want a place for my family to live and be safe and have full bellies."

Tyler scowled. "We'll see about that after you're here awhile." He opened a can of hard wax and handed it to

Nathan, then pointed to a saddle that hung over a saw-horse. He slapped a rag into his hand. "Here. Put some of that stuff on the rag and rub it over the saddle. Wait a few minutes, then wipe the saddle off with a dry towel."

Nathan shrugged and got to work. "We use bear grease."

"What?" Tyler took down a bridle and looked at him with a frown.

"Bear grease. It works about the same. Did you think the Indian does not understand about taking care of leather?"

Tyler blinked. "I never thought about it."

Nathan grinned. "We do not use such big saddles, though. Ours are small and light. A horse can run faster and longer if it does not carry so much weight."

"Yeah, well, from now on you'll be using a regular western saddle, so get used to it. You're supposed to start thinking like a white man."

"Maybe the white man can learn something from the Indian. Did you ever think of that?"

"No. There isn't anything I want or need to learn from any Indian. All I know is they caused a lot of people a lot of trouble and heartache here in Montana. I'm glad they're on reservations where they belong."

Nathan rubbed vigorously at the saddle. "And you do not think the white man has caused the same heartache for the Indian? Whose land was this before the white man came along?"

Tyler studied a tear in the bridle, hating this intruding brother for making sense. "The Indians', I suppose."

"Right. And for every white man or woman killed by the Sioux, the Sioux lost ten times that from being killed by soldiers, women raped, little babies murdered, families torn apart. Sometimes hundreds would die at one time from white man's diseases. You do not have to tell me about troubles for the white man, Tyler. You have no idea what the Indian has suffered. Everything has been taken from us. *Everything*. Even our pride."

"You're ready enough to be white *yourself* when it's convenient for you," Tyler said grudgingly.

"I do not come here as white. I come here as an Indian on the inside, a man who happens to have white parents who can help his family."

"You aren't supposed to think of yourself as one of them anymore. If you're going to come here to live, then you're a Fontaine now."

Nathan kept working. "What is it you fear, Tyler? Your father's love for you will never change. He is a good and fair man, and I can tell that you love him as much as any son can love a father. My presence will not change any of that."

"I also love the Double L," Tyler answered. "My brother and two sisters don't want anything to do with running this ranch, so it's up to me. Nobody is going to take that from me."

Nathan shook his head. "I do not want to take that from you, but you do not believe that right now. Someday you will understand."

Tyler did not answer. He tried cutting the bridle strap off so he could replace it, but the knife he had picked up from a bench to use was too dull. He sliced vigorously, angrily, then realized Nathan was standing beside him. He handed out a pocket knife.

"Here. I have kept it sharpened. It works well." He opened it. "Luke gave it to me the last time I was here, as a gift. Now I give it to you."

Tyler frowned as he sliced easily through the strap. He closed the knife and handed it back, feeling a hot jealousy that Luke had given Nathan the knife. "I don't want it," he said quietly. "Pa gave it to you. You keep it."

Thirty-two

August 1884

"MOM, THEY'RE HERE!" ROBBIE RAN BACK OUTSIDE without explaining himself further, but Lettie knew what he meant. She wished Luke was here for this moment, but he was in Helena. She would have to handle this herself. She hurried out to the entrance hall, stopped to look at herself in a mirror, wondering why in the world she worried about how she might look to an Indian woman who knew little about the way white women dressed and probably didn't care one whit for jewelry and fancy hairdos. She wore her own hair wrapped into a roll around her head today, and was dressed in a simple blue summer dress with no petticoats because of the heat.

She had been helping Mae bake this afternoon, and she noticed she had flour on her cheek. She brushed it off and tucked a strand of hair back into a comb, then hurried out to the front of the house, where several Double L men had gathered to stare. Tyler drove a rickety wagon packed in the back with supplies, upon which sat two dark-eyed children. Their long, black hair blew in the hot summer wind, and their eyes were wide with curiosity. Lettie felt sweet joy at the sight of the two grandchildren she had never seen. Now there were five. Katie had had her third child in June, a boy named Robert Bradley. Three grandsons and two granddaughters! Not only had God brought back her Nathan, but a whole family with him, and she wondered when she had been happier.

She rushed down the steps to greet them. The woman

sitting next to Nathan was beautiful, needing not an ounce of color or creams or fancy clothes to bring out that beauty. It was a simple beauty, her dark skin clear and looking smooth as satin. She wore her long hair in a bun, like a white woman, and Lettie was surprised to see she was wearing a yellow calico dress. Somehow she had expected Nathan's Indian wife to arrive in a fringed deerskin dress, her hair in braids. She took hold of the woman's hands as soon as she climbed down from the wagon. "Hello! I am Lettie, Nathan's mother. I'm so very, very happy you've come!"

The woman looked apprehensive. "I am Leena," she said quietly. She turned to the wagon. "These are your grandchildren, Julie and Luke. Julie is four summers, Luke is two."

"Oh, they're so beautiful," Lettie exclaimed with tear-filled eyes.

"I take it we're at the right place, ma'am?"

Lettie had hardly realized that three soldiers had accompanied the wagon. She turned at the voice to look up at a bearded man in a blue uniform. "Yes. This is my son and daughter-in-law. Why are you here?"

The man scratched at his beard. "We were assigned to come along to make sure they got here all right. Some people still don't like the sight of Indians, if you know what I mean. Without us along, some folks might not have believed they had a right to be off the reservation. I'm Sergeant Reeves, and these two are Private Dillon and Private Frazer, from the Standing Rock reservation. You're Mrs. Luke Fontaine then?"

"Yes, I am. Thank you for accompanying my son. Please stay for something to eat and drink. We can put you up in a bunkhouse for the night so you can rest your horses before you start back."

"That would be right nice, Mrs. Fontaine." The sergeant scanned the lovely Fontaine home, its well-manicured

lawn, flowers blooming everywhere, ivy growing on the
house. It didn't seem fair that any Indian should get to live
this way, but it wasn't his business. If the Fontaines were
crazy enough to take them in, they could have them.

Lettie turned back to help lift down the children, her
heart bursting with love at the sight of their beautiful,
round faces. Little Julie smiled, revealing dimples, and
Lettie hugged her close, feeling an instant bond. She
was hardly aware of a second Indian woman, but Tyler
noticed her right away when he walked around to the
back of the wagon to open the gate. She rode behind the
wagon on a pinto. Although she wore a white woman's
dress, rather plain and a little too big for her, he noticed
her feet were bare, and some of her bare leg showed from
straddling the horse. She rode bareback, the horse's bridle
made from simple rope. Her long, dark hair hung loose.
He had been seeing more of Alice Richards lately, but
neither Alice nor any other girl in town was as exotic
looking as this one. She must be Nathan's stepsister,
Ramona. Considering his resentment of Nathan, he knew
he should also resent the intrusion of this full-blooded
Sioux girl, but there was something exciting about her.
Perhaps it was because he thought she ought to be forbidden to any white man, maybe not even worthy of one...
or could it be the other way around? The proud look in
her eyes made him realize she might think *he* was unworthy. He remembered that she was only sixteen; but she
had a provocative beauty that made her seem older, and
the breasts that filled out the bodice of her dress looked
full and firm. There was a soft, free look about them that
made him wonder if it was true Indian women never
wore anything under their dresses. She didn't appear to be
wearing a white woman's stiff undergarments.

He quickly chastised himself for the thought. The
girl sat there unsmiling, and he nodded to her. "Hello.
I'm Tyler, Nathan's half brother." He still did not like

admitting to people in town that his "Indian" brother was coming home; but for the moment he was glad, for one reason. That reason was sitting on a pinto horse looking back at him.

"I am Ramona," she answered in a small voice. Ramona wondered if the young white man watching her knew what she was thinking—that she had never seen a white man before who stirred odd new urges deep at her insides. What a fine-looking man this Tyler was, with eyes much bluer than Nathan's, and such a handsome smile! He was big and strong looking, a fine specimen of a man, for being white.

"Welcome to the Double L," Tyler told her. "My pa had a house built for you and Nathan and his family." He pointed to a log cabin about a half mile down the hill from the main house.

She glanced at the cabin, seemingly unimpressed. "This is my own horse," she said. "Her name is Star." She patted the horse's neck proudly.

"Looks like a fine horse," Tyler told her, looking the animal over. His eyes kept going back to her own slender calf and bare foot. He finally moved his gaze to meet her stirring dark eyes. "We've got plenty of horses here on the Double L. If you'd like to try riding any of them, I'd be glad to show them to you, take you out riding and show you the Double L."

"The Double L?"

"That's what we call the ranch—for my pa and ma— Luke and Lettie."

She held her chin proudly. "I see. Two L's. I know all my letters, you know. I have had some of the white man's schooling at the reservation, but Nathan would not let them send me to the Indian school in the land of the rising sun. Many children go there and never come back."

They were interrupted then by a round of introductions by Lettie. She told one of the men to ride and get Katie and Brad and tell them to come for supper if possible. "Katie has a new two-month-old son," she told Nathan, "so now there are five grandchildren! Luke had a house built for you. Oh, I wish he was here, but he's in Helena meeting with the territorial legislature. We've petitioned the government to make Montana a state, but they say it could take up to five years."

She wondered why she was rattling on about something for which Nathan probably didn't give a damn. Why was she so nervous? She still held Julie, and Nathan picked up little Luke and handed him over. "I will take Julie so you can hold your grandson for a moment."

Lettie took heart from the fact that Nathan was smiling. He seemed genuinely happy to be here. She handed Julie to him and took Luke into her arms. "Oh, Nathan, they're such beautiful children!" She asked Sven to unhitch the wagon and put up the horses.

"Them horses belongs to the army, ma'am," Sergeant Reeves said, dismounting. "The only thing White Bear owns is the wagon and what's inside it."

It seemed strange to hear Nathan referred to as White Bear. Apparently on the reservation he had continued to use his Indian name. "Well, we'll still put them up for you. You can take your own horses to the barn and get them brushed down."

Ramona spoke up firmly. "This horse is mine. I will take care of her myself."

Lettie looked up at the girl. She had not even had a chance to talk to her yet, but she realized it must be Ramona. She saw the defensive look in the girl's eyes, knew she was a little bit afraid. She handed Luke to his mother and walked up to Ramona, putting out her hand. "I am Nathan's mother. Welcome, Ramona."

Ramona looked down at her hand, finally deciding to grasp it for a quick handshake. "This is *my* horse," she repeated.

For some reason the girl seemed very defensive of

her small pinto. Lettie let go of her hand and petted the horse's neck. "And a fine horse it is, Ramona. You are welcome to ride down to the barn and take care of her yourself. Anything we have is yours to use." She glanced at the Double L men standing nearby, reading their thoughts. No matter how beautiful Ramona was, they still resented having Indians on the Double L. "I want my son and his family all treated with respect," she warned them. "Show them around. Help them find what they need. They have free access to anyplace on the grounds. Please make them welcome."

Some of them seemed chagrined. "Yes, ma'am, we'll do that," Billy Sacks replied. They all knew what this meant to Mrs. Fontaine, but most of them would abide by this new intrusion because they had their orders from Luke himself. None of them cared to go against those orders. There wasn't a better ranch to work on than the Double L, and none of them wanted to lose their jobs.

"Unhitch the horses then, Sven," Lettie was ordering. "Nathan, bring the family inside. We have so much to talk about. I want you to eat supper here tonight. Katie and Brad will come. Oh, I wish Luke could be here," she repeated. "And Pearl. She would be so excited about this."

Nathan set Luke on his feet and the boy toddled off to chase one of the many puppies that roamed the ranch. Nathan caught his mother's arm before she could go inside. "Be patient with Ramona," he told her. "She is afraid."

"I can tell." She covered his hand with her own. "She'll be all right, Nathan."

His eyes showed a haunting sadness. "They took so much from us. She lost her whole family, and the army took most of our horses. That is why she is so protective of her own." A proud but hurt look came into his eyes. "I once had many horses myself. They are all gone now. I feel bad coming here with nothing to offer."

Lettie felt her throat constricting. "Just bringing

yourself and two grandchildren we never knew we had is the most wonderful gift you could bring, Nathan. And there are hundreds of horses on the Double L. You can have any of them you like, or you can go riding after the wild ones. There are still plenty of those left too."

His eyes suddenly teared. "It has been a long time since I was free to ride and hunt that way."

Lettie squeezed his hand. "Well, now you are. You're home, Nathan, and no one can take any of this away from you."

Tyler was close enough to see and hear, and his chest burned at the remark. He turned away to take hold of Ramona's horse. "I'll show you where to take her," he said with a frown.

Ramona slid off the animal and walked beside him. "You are jealous, Tyler Fontaine."

He scowled at her. "What?"

"You are jealous of Nathan. I can see it in your eyes."

"I am not!" he said grumpily.

"Yes, you are. You do not need to be."

"What would you know about it?"

"I know because Nathan told us everyone welcomed us to come, except he was not so sure you would. Do you want us to leave?"

He stopped walking and looked at her, damned if he could control his curiosity at how she must look stark naked. She was so pretty, so perfect. "No," he answered. He stormed off to the barn, and Ramona hurried after on bare feet. She covered her mouth and smiled.

May 1885

Lettie opened the letter from Pearl. She sat near the hearth in the library, Luke sitting nearby smoking a thin cigar. "'Dear Mother and Father,'" she read. "'Things have gone so well that I am going to play in a concert with a local orchestra in July. I can hardly believe two years have already gone by since I left the Double L, and I miss you so; but I have never been happier, and Professor Bansen says he is amazed at my progress. I could have come home last summer or this year, but I have been so involved in concerts and my lessons. However, that is not the only reason.'"

Lettie paused, frowning and reading on silently. "Oh dear," she commented, glancing at Luke.

He cast her a worried look. "What does that mean?"

She sighed. "I'm not sure. I just never know how you'll react to some things, and apparently Pearl doesn't either."

"What does the letter say? Let's hear it."

Lettie looked back at the letter. "She says 'I hope Father won't be angry and that you will both trust my judgment. I am in love.'"

Luke let out a sigh of disgust. "Pearl too?"

"'His name is Lawrence Bansen,'" she read on, "'and he is Professor Bansen's son. Lawrence is twenty-six years old and was studying music overseas when I first came here. He came home about a year ago, and I knew from the moment I met him that I loved him.'"

"Don't all young girls think that way?" Luke grumbled.

"*I* did," Lettie reminded him.

He rubbed at his eyes. "You'd defend these kids if they committed murder."

"Being in love is not exactly comparable to murder," she answered with a grin. She turned back to the letter. "'Lawrence is an accomplished pianist as well as harpist and violinist. He is also a conductor and composer, with a brilliant future. We are so happy together because we share all the same things. Our world is music, and when we marry—'" Lettie hesitated, realizing Pearl had said when, not if, as though there was no doubt about it, and her parents had no say in the matter. She glanced at Luke again, saw the disgust in his eyes. "'When we marry,'" she continued, "'we will live right here at the Bansen mansion, where other students stay. Someday I plan to help Lawrence write music, and also to teach piano. We both want to perform with the symphony in Chicago.

"'Please be happy for us. I love and miss both of you so much, and I miss my brothers and Katie. I wish I could meet Nathan and his family. Maybe someday soon I will. I have told Lawrence so much about the ranch and our life there. He is quite fascinated by it all and wants to visit someday. He imagines Father as a big, rugged pioneer, fearless and daring, like the Westerners we read about here in the dime novels.'"

Luke chuckled in spite of being upset by the news.

"Well, you *are* rugged and fearless and daring," Lettie told him.

He just shook his head. "Finish the damn letter."

"'Lawrence and I would like you, Mother and Father, to come to Chicago in July for our wedding. Both of us will be playing in the orchestra concert the night before, so you will be able to attend that also. I want so much for you to see Chicago. It is not like anything you have ever seen back home, I assure you. It has been so long since Mother went to the theater and such. You are so beautiful, Mother. I want the Bansens to meet you. I am sure they are picturing a weathered, pipe-smoking old pioneer woman. They will be so surprised to see how elegant and refined you are, and how handsome Father still is. They were quite impressed to learn Father had been voted into the territorial legislature, and I have told them I believe Father will be governor of Montana when it becomes a state.'"

"She's really buttering us up, isn't she?" Luke sighed. "She's only eighteen. This Lawrence is eight years older than she."

Lettie scowled at him. "Luke, *I* was eighteen when I married you, and you're *ten* years older! Why do you insist that it all has to be so different for your own children? It sounds as though they are very happy and certainly well suited to each other."

He puffed quietly on the cigar for a moment. "If I had been your father, I would have kicked me off that wagon train and taken you to Denver with me."

"Oh, you would not, and you know it."

He stared at his cigar. "Our Pearl left here a little girl and now she's become a woman without our seeing it happen." He rubbed at his eyes. "When is the wedding?"

Lettie scanned the letter. "July eighteenth. She has sent us a map and address to get to the Bansen home."

"I'll feel like an idiot around people like that."

"I have a feeling they will be much more impressed by you than you will by them."

"What the hell will we talk about?"

"You'll probably be busy just answering questions." She rose and came over to kneel in front of his chair. "Be happy for her, Luke. Her life has been leading in this direction for years. And we can use the trip to accompany Robbie partway to Michigan. That is just about the time he's supposed to go off to school, so he won't have to make the whole trip alone. The school found a good family to look out for him, so both Robbie and Pearl will be just fine."

He studied her, setting the cigar aside. "When did it get so easy for you to turn your children loose?"

She smiled sadly. "When I realized it's impossible to hang on to them. At least we have Katie and Ty with us, and all our grandchildren, Luke. We know Robbie will come back here someday, and we don't have to wonder anymore about Nathan. We have him back with us."

Luke frowned. "Things still aren't quite right between Nathan and Tyler. Tyler has acted as if he has a burr between his butt and his saddle ever since Nathan came back, and it's been over a year now. I've never shown one ounce of favoritism to Nathan, at least not that I'm aware of."

She sighed deeply. "Ty just can't seem to get used to Nathan. It's partly because in some ways Nathan outdoes him without even intending to do it. Ty about had a fit when Nathan tamed that wild stallion Ty caught. Ty spent two weeks with that animal, and in one day Nathan had the horse following him around like a baby. I think that embarrassed Ty."

Luke rubbed at his chin. "Some people have a better way with horses than others, that's all. Ty knows that. Tex used to be our top man when it came to taming the wild ones."

"Luke, it hurt Ty's pride. It's all right for an outsider like Tex to show him up. But his own brother is something different, especially when it's a brother who replaces him as the oldest, and one who never had a part in building the ranch in the first place. He is very possessive of you, you know, and of his station here on the ranch."

"He knows damn well his importance here isn't threatened." He shook his head. "I don't know. There's nothing I can do but let the two of them work it out."

She put a hand on his knee. "We can't make decisions for any of our children anymore, Luke. They're very determined, every one of them in their own way, just as you were. Pearl is going to marry her musician, Robbie is going to be a doctor, Katie married a sheep man, and Tyler is determined to be in charge of this ranch. He's just protecting his territory, like a wolf. Things will get better as time goes on."

"That thing over the horse opened some old wounds. Things were going pretty well until then."

"He'll get over it. Just remember that no matter what *you* do, one of them will think you're playing favorites." She rose and looked at the letter again. "We *can* go to Chicago, can't we?"

"Of course we can go."

"We only have a month to get ready. Robbie will be so happy we can go with him most of the way to Michigan."

Lettie began talking about what she should wear, but Luke did not hear. With Pearl gone, Robbie going off to college, and Katie at her own ranch wrapped up with three little ones, that left him two sons at home…two sons who were as different as night and day. He wished he could do more to bring them closer, but Lettie was right. He didn't dare interfere.

❧

Tyler carried a fifty-pound sack of potatoes out to the supply wagon and hoisted it inside, then took the list of needed supplies from his shirt pocket and reviewed it. He had seen his parents off on the train to Chicago, and before he went home he was to fill a grocery list for Mae. He started back inside the store when someone called his name.

"Hello, Ty."

He turned to see Alice Richards, who had come up behind him from across the street. She looked beautiful in a bright pink cotton summer dress. A matching pink ribbon was twisted through her blond hair, which was piled up into curls on top of her head. It was a perfect color for her soft, pale skin and blue eyes. "Hello, Alice."

There was a sad look in those pretty eyes, and he knew why. Ever since Ramona had come to live at the Double L, the thoughts he had once reserved only for Alice had wandered in another direction. Alice and Ramona could not be more different, and Ramona stirred a fire in his loins that was getting to the point of being impossible to quench. There was only one way to put it out, and he had been fighting it for a year now.

"I hardly ever see you anymore. What have you been doing with yourself?" Alice asked. She felt her heart beating harder at the sight of him, so handsome, so strong. He had hoisted the huge sack of potatoes as though it were nothing. How she loved this young man she had known for so long now!

Ty shrugged. "Busy at the ranch, like always." Damn! She looked ready to cry. Alice had always been a good friend, and they had both silently understood where their relationship would end up when they were old enough...until these last few months. He hated hurting her, but what was a man supposed to do? He couldn't help the way he felt whenever he was around Ramona, although he had hardly even talked to her. He didn't share with Ramona his intimate thoughts the way he could with Alice, but whenever he was near her, that didn't matter. There was a certain look in her eyes whenever they were in the same place, the same look Alice often gave him. Ramona loved him, he was sure. He felt so torn now, for he had feelings for both Ramona and Alice; but he didn't ache for Alice the way he ached for Ramona.

Alice studied him, this man she had loved since she was only twelve. She felt sick inside, for she knew she had somehow lost him without doing or saying one thing to chase him away. She had met the voluptuous Sioux girl named Ramona who lived at the Double L. She had seen how the girl looked at Ty, how Ty looked at her. Was there something already going on between them? She hadn't thought so, for whenever she and her family visited the Fontaines, she and Ty walked and talked together as always, except that the last few months he had grown more distant and preoccupied with each visit. She wanted to scream at him that she loved him, beg him not to look at that wild Indian girl; but she wanted no man who did not truly want her.

"There is a church social coming next weekend," she hinted. "Will you be there?"

Ty removed his hat for a moment and smoothed

back his dark hair. It was a hot day, and sweat trickled down his forehead. He wiped at it with his shirtsleeve. "I don't think so," he answered. "My father and my mother just left for Chicago for Pearl's wedding. I'm in charge while Pa is gone. Did your folks tell you about Pearl getting married?"

"Yes." *I wish we were getting married too, Ty.* Her heart actually hurt at the realization that there was probably another reason why he wouldn't be at the social. He would rather stay home. Ramona was there. She wished she knew more about men, knew how to be sultry and provocative like Ramona. How could she begin to compare to that girl's dark beauty? There was an open freedom about her, something that made it easy for her to make herself tempting, a way of inviting a man with her eyes, and the way she carried her nicely curved body under her dresses. Even though Ramona wore white women's clothing, anyone could tell she wore no proper undergarments. The dresses clung to her full breasts enticingly, breasts that bounced in obvious freedom from stays and padding. There was a shamelessness about Ramona, yet also an innocence, as though she was hardly aware of how she looked to men. Alice could not imagine dressing like that, without undergarments. Maybe the girl didn't even wear drawers, and the couple of times she had seen her, she also wore no shoes.

The way Ty had been raised, could he really be attracted to someone so far removed from his world? She felt like crying. Of course he could. He was a man, wasn't he? What did a man care about anything beyond that long, black hair and the enticing way she dressed? *Oh, Ty, please look at me,* she wanted to tell him. *I am just as pretty, under these clothes. My breasts are soft and full. I want to love you and be a woman for you. I just don't know how. I can't be like Ramona.* "I'm happy for Pearl," she said aloud. "It sounds as though she's marrying quite a wonderful young man."

Ty grinned. "Yeah, well, Pa would rather she married another rancher, somebody who knows how to break horses and herd cattle."

He laughed, and Alice joined him. *That's the kind of man I want to marry*, she thought. "How long will they be gone?" She watched the way his eyes moved over her. Did that mean he liked what he saw? He had kissed her once, the most delicious kiss she had ever experienced. That had been before Ramona came. There had been no more kisses.

"Maybe a month. I guess it takes a good week to get there, even by train. Then they're going to spend time touring Chicago, go to a concert where Pearl will be playing—then the wedding and all that. I wouldn't mind seeing a place like Chicago myself."

"Yes, it must be exciting for them. They've hardly been out of Montana since they first came here, have they?"

"No. They've been here twenty-two years. Pa doesn't even like going to Helena, let alone all the way to a place like Chicago. He'll probably worry about the ranch, knowing him. I'm glad my mother got to go, though. She'll fit right in. Pa always says she's too sophisticated for living on a ranch." He laughed lightly. "I'd like to see Pa with that fancy professor family Pearl is marrying into. I guess they've got quite a mansion over there. All they know is music and the theater. What a contrast!"

Alice smiled. "Yes! I'd like to be a little mouse and watch!"

They both laughed. Then they both suddenly felt awkward. *I'm sorry, Alice*, Ty wanted to tell her. *I wish I could go to the social. I wish I could stop these feelings for Ramona, but I can't. I didn't expect this to happen, and I hate hurting you.* "You have fun at the social," he told her aloud. "I'd better get back to filling this grocery list for Mae."

Alice swallowed. "Phillip Dewhirst wants to take me to the social. I guess...I guess you wouldn't mind then?"

Ty felt a stab of jealousy, but it was mixed with a kind of relief. At least she wouldn't be going alone. What had happened to him? It was as though he had lost all common sense, all control of himself. "That's okay," he said. "If I'm too busy to go, there's no sense in you going alone."

Suddenly she hated him! How could he stand there and say he didn't care if she went with someone else? "Fine," she told him, turning away before he could see the tears in her eyes. "I'll see you another time, then, Ty."

She hurried away, and Ty started to call out to her, but something stopped him. That something was the thought of Ramona. He had only recently decided to act on his emotions. He had to settle with himself, make up his mind who he wanted, find out if Ramona wanted him the way he suspected she did. He couldn't go on like this, leading Alice along, hurting her. He had to know.

He sighed and went back inside the supply store, deciding that as soon as he got home, he was going to have a serious talk with Ramona and tell her how he felt.

❦

Tyler heard splashing and singing coming from Lettie's Pond, a clear pond Luke had named after his wife. It was about three miles north of the house in a grove of ancient ponderosa pines, difficult to see because of hundreds of smaller pines and shrubs that grew beneath the huge trees. Bitterroot bloomed here and there. It was a pretty place, quiet and private, a place where his parents sometimes came to talk.

He had noticed Ramona riding in this direction many times since the weather had warmed. He had always been too busy to follow, but was curious about why she came here. With Luke away in Chicago and his chores finished, there was no one to question where he was going. His desire for the pretty Indian girl had grown keener over the past year, and no matter how much he avoided her, he could not control the way he dreamed about her at night. He had fought his feelings, tried to convince himself that it was Alice Richards he should be yearning for, not an Indian woman. His parents loved Alice, and he knew they wished he would think more seriously about settling down with the right woman.

The Richardses had been to their house often to visit. Ty thought that of all the girls in Billings, Alice was the prettiest. But ever since Ramona had come to the Double L, his thoughts had been distracted by the wild, lusty, dark-skinned beauty. He had done everything he could to fight his feelings for her, knowing that his father would be disappointed if he fell in love with a Sioux girl. It was enough that Nathan had come home with an Indian wife and children. What would Luke think of yet another son marrying an Indian, especially the son who would one day take over the Double L? And marrying Ramona would mean that she would become part owner of the ranch and would inherit anything Ty inherited.

Everything wise in him had told him not to follow Ramona today, yet here he was at the pond. He knew damn well the most likely reason she came here. He had heard her telling Leena about this place, that here she could bathe the way her people liked to bathe, in the open, sharing nature, not in a little tub inside a house. Had she said that for him? Was she baiting him to come here? No one had to tell him how she felt about him. He had seen it in those dark eyes. She had teased his manly instincts to the point of pain.

He halted his horse, dismounted, and tied the animal several yards away from the pond. A little voice told him to leave, but his legs carried him through the underbrush, stalking quietly, as though he were after prey. Perhaps he was. In some ways Ramona was as wild and forbidden as some exotic animal. Sometimes he pictured her as part wolf, alert, all-seeing. He crept closer to the pond, knowing damn well what the splashing sound was. He saw her dress and a towel hanging over a bush, saw her swimming in the pond.

He crouched down to watch. She looked like a slender fish, her smooth body cutting through the dark water. She dived head down, her bare bottom coming up so that she could thrust her slender legs straight up. She disappeared for a moment, came back up, letting out a little gasp and smoothing her dark, wet hair back from her face.

Ty's whole body ached fiercely. Unknown to his mother, he had rolled in the hay a time or two with Jenny Carpenter, the blacksmith's daughter from Billings. She had been married and divorced already, and every young man in Billings knew Jenny was wild and liked all men. She went down easy. He had sometimes had visions of bedding Alice that way, but she was sweet and proper, the kind of girl a man saved for marriage.

Ramona was different, innocent yet provocative and free. Never had he ached for a female the way Ramona made him ache. A girl like her had a way about her that told him it was all right to touch her, yet all the feelings of respect were still there.

He watched her for several minutes, until she finally came out of the water, her slender, naked body moving slowly toward the bank until she was entirely exposed. He nearly groaned aloud at the sight of her firm, ripe breasts, the dark nipples, the patch of hair between her slim thighs. She was like a goddess, a tiny waist leading to round hips. He wanted to touch her, taste her, feel himself inside of her.

Just then a bee flew into his face, and he reacted before thinking, swatting at it. The movement caught Ramona's eye, and she grabbed a towel, holding it in front of her, her eyes wide with fright. "Who is there?"

Tyler felt like an ass. He slowly rose. "It's just me, Tyler. Don't be afraid."

She stared at him a moment, and then a smile moved over her lips. "So, finally you came."

"What do you mean, finally?"

"I have said enough times that I like to come here." She deliberately dropped the towel. "You are a fine-looking man, Tyler Fontaine. For a whole year I have thought about you in the night." She held out her hand. "Come and swim with me." She grinned, then turned to run back into the water.

Tyler watched her firm, bare bottom, a bottom he wanted to grasp in his hands, one he wanted to kiss. All reason left him. Why should he turn down such an invitation? Never had he felt so bold and full of fire. He hurried to the bank, removed his gun belt, his boots, hat, vest, pants, shirt. He hesitated with his long johns, noticing that Ramona was watching his every move.

"It is no fun with clothes on," she suggested.

Tyler grinned, stripping off his long johns. Ramona drank in the sight of him, his man part swollen like a stallion. Yes, he wanted her. Today Tyler Fontaine would be hers, and never had she loved anything as she loved him. He came into the water and she swam up to him, putting her arm around his neck and rubbing her breasts against his solid chest.

"I have waited a long time for this," she said softly, meeting his lips.

Somehow he knew this was right, that it was meant to be. He did not need to ask questions or lure her. He had no qualms about her virginity or her honor. She came from a people who thought freely, a people for whom making love was as natural as breathing, when it was the right person. All these months they had hardly spoken, had not done one thing alone together; and yet both knew all along what the other was thinking, that it would all lead to this.

He kissed her eagerly, hungrily, grasping at her wet hair. They fell into the water together, and laughed. She looked down at him, touched his penis. "The water has cooled down my fine stallion," she teased.

He realized the cold water had shriveled him, and he was embarrassed. "Come out of the water and see how fast it grows again," he told her, his voice gruff with desire.

She wrapped her slender legs around his waist. "Then take me to the sand," she said, her dark eyes studying him lovingly. "I want to be your woman, Tyler Fontaine. I want you to be my first man, my only man. Mate with me and I will belong to you."

He kissed her again, and then she threw her head back so that her breasts were near his face. He took one taut nipple into his mouth, sucked on it hungrily, enjoying the feel of its ripeness against his tongue. He carried her to the soft sand on the bank, laid her back, rose up to his knees for a moment to study her naked beauty. Even though she lay boldly spread out before him, he knew this was her first time. She was going to be brave and welcome him, because she wanted to belong only to him.

He leaned down and tasted at her breasts again, and she closed her eyes and groaned his name. "God, Ramona, you're so beautiful," he whispered. "I want to taste you, make you feel good."

"I do not know all there is to know," she answered, nearly whimpering with excitement. "Show me, Tyler Fontaine. I want to be your woman."

He moved his lips downward, licking, tasting, feeling like a crazy man with the want of her. He found the magical spot where Jenny had taught him a woman liked to be touched. He licked at her, heard her groan with delight. Suddenly she cried out his name, grasping his hair tightly and pressing her thighs against his neck.

He moved back up to meet her mouth, and he quickly shoved himself into her, deep and hard. She cried out with pain, and he could tell by how difficult it was to get all the way inside her that this was indeed her first time. There was no stopping it now. He moved in quick rhythm, his life soon spilling into her out of an agonizing need to relieve himself.

He relaxed for a moment, raising himself up on his elbows and studying her beautiful face. "Did I hurt you?"

"It was necessary. It is the way."

He felt lost in her. "I don't know what anybody else will think of this," he told her, "either Nathan or my pa, or…" He decided not to mention Alice. It was too late to think of her now. "I just know that I love you, Ramona. I want to stay here with you all afternoon."

She smiled. "Then we will stay. By Indian law, you are now my husband."

He grinned, his eager fullness returning so that while still inside of her he began mating with her again in sweet rhythm. Right or wrong, he had made his choice.

Thirty-three

LUKE GRASPED HIS FUTURE SON-IN-LAW'S HAND, AFRAID to squeeze too hard for fear he'd break it. It was soft and slender, not rough and strong like the ranchers and workers to whom he was accustomed. The young man was handsome, but, Luke thought, too clean and perfect. He wore round spectacles, and every hair was in place. This was not the kind of man he would have expected any of his daughters to marry, after being raised on a ranch; but then Pearl had never been ordinary. She beamed with joy. This Lawrence Bansen apparently made her very happy.

Pearl literally screamed with delight at seeing them again after two years apart. There came a flurry of hugs and kisses between themselves, Robbie, and Pearl, their voices echoing in the high entrance hall of the ornate Bansen mansion. The house, if it could be called that, was a castle-like structure north of Chicago. The top of the entrance hall was capped with a dome of stained glass, and from it were spread wings on either side, each wing two stories high.

Robbie acted like a typical boy awed by something spectacular, staring, carrying on about what a place it was. He babbled to his sister about being on his way to the University of Michigan, for which Lawrence praised him highly, telling him what a noble profession he had chosen. Conversation turned to Chicago itself, and Robbie raved about all the tall buildings, all the people, the bricked streets, and the streetcars. He had never imagined it would be as big and exciting as it was, and he had never seen anything like Lake Michigan. "Boy, Pa, I'll bet you'd like a lake that big out in Montana!" he exclaimed. "You'd never have to worry about enough water!"

"If we had a lake that big in Montana, it would take up half the state and there wouldn't be enough *land* left for the cattle," Luke replied.

After the laughter had died down, Pearl immediately took them on a quick tour. One wing of the house was bedrooms and apartments for students. The other wing was living quarters for the Bansens, two kitchens, an immense dining hall, library, smoking room, parlor, and family bedrooms. The table at the dining hall was so long that Luke joked he could not see the other end of it, and priceless paintings hung on the walls on either side. Elegant silver candelabras were strategically placed on the table, fine china sitting ready at each chair as though always prepared for a grand banquet.

At the far end of the living quarters was a two-story-high ballroom, with an entrance from the outside that invited guests could use without having to go through the main house. Pearl carried on about how the Bansens entertained important dignitaries in the great dining hall and the ballroom nearly every weekend. Even President Pierce had visited once when he was in Chicago.

Luke watched Lettie, thinking how well she fit here in spite of years of living on a Montana ranch. She had brought her best dresses, as well as two new dresses Gino Galardo had made just for the concert and for the wedding. Never in his wildest dreams, when he and Lettie first settled in that crude cabin in Montana, would he have imagined one of his daughters marrying into this kind of money, playing piano with an orchestra. Life's ironies continued to amaze him.

"Please, do come into the parlor and have something to drink," Lawrence told them. The young man was as nervous as a bobcat, hardly able to take his eyes off Luke. "My, you're everything I pictured," he told him.

Luke towered over him, thinking how easy it would be to pick him up and throw him several feet. He grinned, deciding he might as well get used to this man Pearl loved. He had no choice. "And what did you picture?" he asked, following Pearl and Lettie into the parlor, while Robbie continued to explore the house.

"Oh, a big and powerful man, since Pearl told me you were certainly that. I have often imagined how exciting it must be to live in a place like Montana. I have never even learned to ride a horse."

Lettie cast Luke a quick, warning look, knowing there were any number of remarks he could make in reply, well aware what he must think of the man Pearl wanted to marry. So far, neither Katie nor Pearl had married the kind of man Luke had hoped, but he had grown to like Brad very much. Maybe he could learn to like Lawrence too. At least they wouldn't have to be around them as much, since Pearl and Lawrence would stay here in Chicago. She smiled at the scowl on Luke's face.

"I never knew a man who didn't know how to ride a horse," he answered. "But then I've never played a piano or conducted an orchestra," he added with a grin.

Lawrence laughed as he tugged a bellpull to signal the servants in the kitchen. "I'll have Oscar bring us some drinks," he said.

"Oscar is one of the butlers," Pearl explained. "Have you ever seen such a house, Father?"

Luke looked at Lettie again. She knew he hated this place. If he had a million dollars, he could never live like this. "No, I sure haven't," he answered, a hint of sarcasm in his voice.

"Lawrence's parents are gone right now," Pearl explained. "We had no idea just exactly when you would arrive. You must both be so tired after several days on a train."

"We rented a private car," Luke told her. "We were pretty comfortable."

"It seemed so strange to come back East," Lettie put in. "After twenty-two years, here we are, both not so far from where we started out. Whoever would have thought back then that we could come back by train in just a few days, after that trip to Montana by wagon?"

"Oh, we want to hear the whole story!" Lawrence told them. "But wait until my parents arrive. We have never talked to true pioneers, people who went west on a wagon train! We want to hear it all, Mr. Fontaine, what happened in the beginning and all. Pearl tells me you have scars from a grizzly bear attack!"

Luke felt embarrassed, as though he were a sideshow. "I didn't do anything more than any of the other early settlers—nothing so special."

"Oh, Father, you're being modest!" Pearl walked over to Lawrence and took his arm. "Father fought a grizzly, fought Indians, outlaws, rustlers. He even rode once with vigilantes. Now he's on the territorial legislature." She smiled at Luke. "You can't imagine what a thrill I got reading about it in the Chicago papers!" she added. "My own father, way out in Montana, making the Chicago papers!"

Luke studied her lovingly. At eighteen, she was a most beautiful creature, looking like a woman now. Where had the years gone?

He watched Lettie, knew by the looks she gave him that she was thinking the same thing. They never could have predicted such events when they first left her parents in Nebraska to go off on their own. The things they had been through made him love her all the more, and he was glad to be able to bring her here. Pearl chattered about a couple of plays she wanted to take them to, as well as a fancy restaurant downtown, and, of course, the concert. They were being married in the biggest Lutheran church in Chicago, she explained. "Everybody who is anybody will be there, and they are all anxious to meet you and Father. They are so impressed with him being one of the biggest landowners in Montana, and a politician now on top of it." She looked at Luke. "I hope you don't get tired of all the questions, Father, because I know you'll be inundated with them." She turned back to Lettie. "Wait until Lawrence's parents and their friends meet you, Mother! You're just as lovely and elegant as any of them. And I can't wait until you come to the theater and hear the symphony. It will be so thrilling for you and Father!"

Luke only wanted to get the hell out, back to the quiet peace of the Double L, back into his denim pants and soft shirts. He hated wearing a suit every day, and the uncomfortable shoes Lettie had insisted he wear. His old leather boots would do just fine. He couldn't hear the rest of Lettie's and Pearl's conversation, as Lawrence was back to asking him questions while the butler brought in a tray that held several long-stemmed glasses and a bottle of wine. Robbie followed, joining them in the parlor.

"Have you actually killed men?" Lawrence asked.

"Sure he has!" Robbie answered before Luke could. "He shot seven men once who tried to take his land away when he first settled in Montana. They're still buried on our property! And when he was a vigilante, he *hanged* two men!"

Luke cast him a frown. "That's not exactly the way to tell it, Robbie. It's not as though I enjoyed it." He looked at Lawrence. "A man never enjoys killing another man. Robbie hasn't explained the details."

The butler handed out a glass of red wine, and Luke took it, thanking the man.

"Oh, you don't have to thank Oscar. It's his job," Lawrence explained.

Luke sipped a little of the wine, holding his temper. "Where I come from, you thank people for things, even the people who work for you," he answered, obvious irritation in his voice.

Lawrence seemed to wither a little. "Oh! I'm sorry. I guess it's just the difference in our customs."

"I guess," Luke said, his blue eyes drilling into the young man. "We have another custom out West. Anybody who abuses a man's daughter answers to her father. And any man who wants to *marry* a man's daughter, asks the father's permission first."

Lawrence reddened deeply, and the butler stood aside, silently amused. He liked this big man from Montana.

Lettie and Pearl stopped talking, having heard the remark. Pearl rose, walking over beside Lawrence. "Father, I...I never thought you would disapprove! Lawrence and I are so happy, and we have so much in common—"

"I didn't say I disapproved, Pearl. I just think asking the father is the right thing to do. If Lawrence were the king of England, I would still expect him to ask for your hand."

Lawrence swallowed, straightening his shoulders. In all his travels and of all the important people he had met, he had never been more awed than he was by Luke Fontaine, nor more afraid of someone; but Pearl had warned him to be forthright and bold in front of the man. She had told him about Luke's reaction to her sister Katie wanting to marry a sheep man. If not for Brad Tillis's straightforwardness, Luke might have kicked him out of the house.

He moved an arm around Pearl. "All right, Mr. Fontaine. I think Pearl is the most beautiful woman God ever created, and her talent is astounding. We share a love of music and feel we would be very happy together. I love her beyond measure, and it would be impossible for me to harm a hair on her head. I can give her a life of wealth and luxury, but more than that, I can give her love, forever. My parents also love her. We are not stiff, unfeeling people who think we are better than others, if that is what you think. We simply love music, and music is what has brought my father this far. This is a happy household, albeit quite ostentatious, but happy, nonetheless. My own parents were married in Germany thirty years ago, and they were both poor in their beginnings. They have worked hard to get where they are. I love your daughter, Mr. Fontaine, and I respectfully ask your permission to marry her."

Luke set his wineglass on a small table beside the leather chair in which he sat. He rose, dwarfing Lawrence. Robbie watched wide-eyed, and Lettie waited nervously, hoping Luke wouldn't say something to spoil this happy moment for Pearl. Luke put out his hand, and Lawrence took it, wincing a little at the firm grip. "All right," Luke told him. "You can marry her, but you take damn good care of her, and not just in material things. There is a sweetness and goodness to my daughter that I never want to see destroyed."

"Why would I destroy the very things that I love about her?" Lawrence answered.

Luke finally grinned. "My only other requirement is that you come and visit the Double L once in a while so Pearl can see her sister and her brothers and nieces and nephews."

Lawrence grinned with relief, but sweat beaded his brow. "Yes, sir. I truly look forward to it. Perhaps you or one of your sons can teach me to ride."

"We might be able to find a gentle old nag for you," Luke joked.

They all laughed then, and Lawrence asked Pearl to play something for them to show her parents how she had progressed over the last two years. Lettie walked over to squeeze Luke's hand. "Thank you, Luke. I wasn't sure what you were going to say."

He studied Lawrence a moment. He had walked to the grand piano with Pearl and was looking at some sheet music with her. "It takes all kinds, I guess. If he makes Pearl happy, then so be it." He picked up his wineglass and moved to a love seat with her so they could sit together while Pearl played. Almost from the first moment her fingers touched the keys, they were both astounded. Lettie felt a chill move up her spine at the magnificent playing, and she knew that sending Pearl there had been the right thing to do. She entertained them for nearly an hour until Lawrence's parents arrived. Professor Bansen was a big, heavyset, bearded man with a deep voice, his wife tiny and gray haired. She was elegantly dressed, surprisingly natural and friendly for her apparently high station in society. She and Lettie liked each other right away, but both Luke and Lettie had to concentrate to understand everything the Bansens said because of their strong German accents.

Both the Bansens announced they were holding a grand feast that night for many of their neighbors and friends in the music business. Luke knew it was going to be a difficult evening filled with questions from people who didn't understand one thing about life on a Montana ranch, and he would be glad when everything was over and they could head home.

The Bansens finally left the room for a moment to check with the servants about the evening's banquet, what was to be served, where everyone would sit. Pearl began playing again, and Robbie wandered off to walk through the immense house again and study the paintings and statues and stained-glass windows. Luke drank another glass of wine, and Lettie sat down beside him.

"I just thought of something, Luke," she said, looking a little nervous. "When I mentioned earlier about how we had come all the way back here close to where we started out." She saw the pain in his blue eyes, knew he had thought of it himself.

"No," he said. "I won't go and try to find my father. If he hasn't contacted me in all these years, why should I?"

She put a hand on his arm. "Because it would be for you, not for him. We're only a day from St. Louis by train, and we could take the Union Pacific from there to Colorado and then come back by rail into Montana from the south."

He looked away from her. "No," he repeated. "As far as I'm concerned, my father died twenty-two years ago when I left St. Louis. There's no going back, Lettie. After the wedding, we'll send Robbie off to Michigan and we'll go home the way we came. Don't even mention going to St. Louis."

The butler brought another tray of filled wineglasses, and Luke took yet another glass and drank it down. Lettie said nothing more; she had at least planted the idea. She prayed Luke would change his mind, for the sake of his own inner peace. Besides, she dearly wanted to meet Jacques Fontaine herself, and tell him exactly what she thought of him.

⤜⤏

Alice dried another dish and set it in the cupboard. She thought how she would enjoy a kitchen like this someday. Her father was not as rich as the Fontaines, but he did own the local bank and the Billings Inn. Their home was at the east end of town, and it was a simple Victorian home, neatly painted white, the elaborate spindle work around the porch gables painted a soft blue. She referred to it as the town's gingerbread house. It was a happy home, except that lately her mother had been sick a lot, so she had been helping more than usual with the housework.

Betty Richards let go of a dish and put a hand to her stomach, obviously in pain. She quickly wiped her hands on her apron and left the kitchen sink to sit down at the table for a moment. "You'll have to finish washing them, Alice. I'm sorry."

Alice frowned with worry. She could not imagine

being without her mother. She had no brothers and sisters, and lately, with hardly seeing Ty anymore, she had felt lonelier than ever. Now she had learned her mother was dying, although the woman did not know she had been to the doctor to ask about her condition. A grave look had come over Dr. Banning's face at her question. "I won't lie to you, Alice," he had told her. "It doesn't look good. Your mother has a tumor in her side. I can feel it, but it's in a spot where it would be very hard to operate; and often in these situations, when we operate, the patient just seems to die more quickly. Your mother has chosen against the operation, so she can be with her family longer."

The news had been devastating. She needed Ty's friendship more than ever now, but she had lost it. Only yesterday one of her best friends had told her the rumor she had heard from her father, a horse doctor who had recently visited the Double L. Men there were joking about how they suspected Ty Fontaine was sneaking around with the Indian girl, Ramona, secretly meeting her for more than just talking. Hot jealousy and hurt filled her to an almost painful degree at the news, but what could she do about it? Her mother needed her, and even if she didn't, she was not going to go out to the Double L and embarrass and shame herself by throwing herself at Ty. He apparently did not want her that way. He had made his decision.

"Mama, you'd better go and lie down. I can finish everything."

The woman nodded, rising. She gave Alice a hug. "You're a good girl, Alice."

Alice turned away, taking her mother's place at the sink and watching some birds flitting about outside the window. *A good girl.* Maybe she had been too good. Maybe being good had cost her the only man she would ever love with this much yearning and passion. She closed her eyes against the tears, vowing that if she ever had the chance to please Ty Fontaine the way Ramona must be doing, she would forget her morals and be a woman for him.

A tear dripped into the dishwater. It was probably too late for such decisions. She had lost Ty, and she would lose her mother. She broke into tears, grabbing a dish towel to cover her face and smother her sobs so that her mother would not hear.

※

Luke was astounded at how St. Louis had grown and changed. None of the streets looked the same, and it was harder to find his old home than he had thought it would be. He had driven the rented carriage past the courthouse, had taken Lettie inside the building that was now famous as the gathering place of so many who had gone west in covered wagons from the 1840s through the 1860s, before the railroad became the main mode of transportation. There in that beautiful building with its richly painted dome was where he had himself gone to learn about how to join a wagon train west. There was where he had broken away from the pain of his youth and set out to make his fortune without the help of a father who all but hated him. And there was where he had started out on a journey that had led him to Eletta MacBride.

"I guess I have more to thank my father for than I realize," he told Lettie aloud.

"What is that?"

He glanced at her. "If I hadn't left St. Louis, I wouldn't have met you."

She smiled, touching his knee. "Luke, you're doing the right thing."

He breathed deeply. "I'm not sure you know how this feels. You're the only reason I'm here, you know. I'm doing this only because you'll harp at me about it forever if I don't."

"You're doing it for yourself, and you know it." Lettie hoped this would all turn out well for him. She was as afraid for him as she knew he was afraid inside. Pearl's wedding had been nothing short of a splendid affair; and listening to Lawrence and her in concert the night before had not only been a thrill and an experience in pride, but it had also shown them more clearly that Pearl and Lawrence certainly did belong together. Pearl was radiantly happy when they left. She just hoped the quick trip to St. Louis would not spoil the wonderful experience the trip had been otherwise.

The Bansens had given them a grand tour of Chicago, and she would long remember the wonders and sights of the city. She knew Luke had enjoyed it also, but not with the same enthusiasm. He always felt out of place when he wasn't on the ranch, and he was anxious to go home. They had bidden a tearful good-bye to Pearl, another at the train station when they sent Robbie on east…another child gone from their lives. At least Robbie would one day come back to Billings. Thank God they still had Katie and Tyler and the grandchildren.

Lettie had reminded Luke again the night before they left that while they were this far east, this might be his last chance to see his father and brother once more, that too much had been left unsettled over these last twenty-two years. Luke had again argued against the idea, but Lettie realized she had apparently given him plenty of food for thought. At the last minute he had changed their tickets at the train station, buying fares to St. Louis instead. He wired home that they would arrive about a week later than first planned and would be taking a different route home.

"You're going to feel so much more at peace, Luke," Lettie said aloud. "I am sure of it. I wouldn't have urged you to do this otherwise."

Luke said nothing, not so sure she was right. He had driven her along the riverfront, where huge warehouses had the name Fontaine Warehousing and Shipping painted on the front of them. Luke had been unable to find the supply store. A hotel sat on the location. He did, however, remember how to reach his father's house, if it was still there. It had been a fine home, but an unhappy one for him. All the houses along this street were elegant, with immaculate lawns and gardens. Huge shade trees shrouded the sun and made the street seem private, cut down the noise of the city that lay not so far away. Luke vaguely remembered those trees, but they had not been so big then.

"There it is," he said, pulling the horse that drew the carriage to a stop. "He must still live here. None of my letters ever came back."

Lettie sensed his agony. She gazed at a lovely brick two-story house, with a white-pillared porch. It was six o'clock in the evening, and Luke guessed that his father would be home about now. He had considered trying to find him at the warehouses, or perhaps ask if Jacques Fontaine had a downtown office; but he had decided that seeing the man again for the first time should be a private matter. He was not so sure what would be said, what his father's reaction might be.

"Maybe we should leave now and just leave things the way they are, Lettie. If the man wanted to see me—"

"No. We've come this far. We're going inside."

Luke breathed deeply, thinking how ridiculous it was that he should feel so apprehensive and almost afraid to see his own father. He slapped the reins and headed the horse and carriage up the long brick drive to a hitching post in front of the house, then got out to tie the horse. Lettie climbed down, praying inwardly she had not done the wrong thing by insisting that he do this. She did not want to see him hurt all over again, but then the damage had already been done when Luke was fourteen years old. For another fourteen years he had lived with the agony, having to face his father nearly every day with the full knowledge that the man had emotionally disowned him. It was only his own pride that had kept Jacques Fontaine from telling others the truth of his beliefs, for he would not want the public to know his wife had cheated on him, if, indeed, that was even true. It was enough that Luke knew, enough that Luke suffered inwardly, to the point that he had gone off to a war and nearly gotten himself killed, then had left St. Louis altogether and had fled to a faraway land to try to forget the hurt. But just as she had had to accept Nathan, had learned to love him and to accept the awful thing that had happened to her, so did Luke have to face the truth and the hurt. No one can run from his or her past, she believed, and being the proud man that he was, Luke deserved some answers. She slipped a hand into his, and they walked together to the front door.

Luke lifted the knocker, hesitated a moment, then banged it four times. A moment later a uniformed maid opened the door. "May I help you?"

"I'm not sure. I'm looking for John Fontaine," Luke told her. "I'm Luke Fontaine, John's brother."

The woman's eyes widened, and a smile of delight lit up her face. "Oh my! The big rancher from Montana!"

Luke frowned. "You mean, my father has talked about me?"

"Oh dear! Didn't your brother write you? Your father…oh my. Do come in, Mr. Fontaine. I just can't believe you've finally come home, after all these years!" She stepped aside and ushered them into a wide, cool entrance hall. Lettie tried to imagine how it felt to Luke to enter his old home after all these years. She knew what a strange, difficult moment this must be for him.

Luke removed his hat. "What did you start to tell me about my father, ma'am?" he asked the maid.

She wrung her hands nervously. "I had better get your

brother. You can talk to him. He's the one who has often talked about you to his friends and such. Please, make yourselves comfortable in the parlor here." She led them into an elegant room full of flowers and fine furnishings. Rich paintings were hung strategically for the best light, and one in particular struck Lettie's heart. It was a painting of a beautiful young woman, with dark hair and deep blue eyes—Luke's eyes. She realized Luke was staring at the picture himself. "Is this your wife, Mr. Fontaine?" the maid was asking him about Lettie.

Lettie touched his arm. "Luke?"

He was so lost in the picture that her touch startled him. "What?" He glanced at the maid. "Oh! Yes. I'm sorry. This is my wife, Lettie."

"Mrs. Fontaine, it's wonderful to meet you. You can't imagine the things we picture about women who dare to go to places like Montana and live on a ranch! But you're nothing like what we imagined." The older woman put a hand to her mouth then, blushing lightly. "My goodness, it isn't my place to be carrying on like this. Please sit down. I will go and get Mr. Fontaine and then bring you something to drink. Coffee? Tea? A little whiskey for you, Mr. Fontaine?"

Luke breathed deeply in nervous anticipation. "Yes, I could use a stiff drink at the moment. My wife likes tea."

"Do you have iced tea?" Lettie asked. "It's so warm today."

"Oh, certainly! Just make yourselves comfortable. Mr. Fontaine is in his study. I'll send him right in!"

The woman quickly left. Luke's attention returned to the picture. "My God," he muttered. "It has to be my mother. My father would never let me see a picture of her. I wonder why he chose to put this up finally." He blinked back tears and shook his head. "She was so beautiful. I don't believe she was the kind of woman he made her out to be, Lettie. I've never believed it.

If she did have an affair, it was because she was terribly unhappy. My father could be a very cold man at times."

Lettie put a hand to his back. "You look just like her, Luke. Look at her eyes."

He nodded. "I'd give anything to take that painting home with me."

"And you deserve to have it, Luke."

The voice sounded almost like Luke's. They both turned to see a man who was not quite as tall as Luke. He resembled him a little in the face, but his hair was a sandy color, with much more gray in it than Luke's, and his eyes were brown. He walked closer and put out his hand. "Hello, Luke."

Luke stared at the man a moment, ravaged by a torrent of emotions. Here was the brother he had not seen in twenty-four years. When he left St. Louis, John was still off fighting somewhere in the war. He hadn't seen him since they both left for that war in '61. Before that, in spite of their father's announcement that he thought Luke to be a bastard, they had remained close until going off to war and never seeing each other again. Why hadn't John written him in all these years?

"I know what you're thinking," the man spoke up. "We have a lot to talk about, Luke. I'll open by saying I have always considered you my brother in every way. Whether or not we had the same father didn't matter."

At first Luke could not find his voice. He grasped John's hand and shook it vigorously. "Hello, John," he finally managed to say.

They both grinned, and in the next moment they were embracing. Lettie glanced at the painting of their mother, thinking how happy the woman would be to see this reunion. She could almost feel Beverly Fontaine's presence in the room.

Thirty-four

"FATHER DIED LAST YEAR, LUKE."

Luke stepped back, anger in his misty eyes. "Died! Why didn't you write and tell me?"

John asked Luke and Lettie to sit down. "Partly because at first I didn't know *how* to tell you. I felt so bad about how he treated you to begin with, and my wife had died just weeks before Father. I was lost in my own mourning and, I don't know, so much time slipped by that I felt like an ass for not having let you know right away." He sat down across from them, and the maid brought in a silver tray with drinks and a pitcher that was sweating from its cold contents. She poured some iced tea into a tall glass for Lettie.

"There's lots of ice in the pot, so it should stay cold for quite a while," she told her. She turned to John. "I brought your best bourbon, sir."

"Thank you, Margaret," John answered. "Please close the parlor doors when you leave."

"Yes, sir, Mr. Fontaine."

John poured himself and Luke each a shot of whiskey. He handed over the glass. "To Jacques Fontaine," he said, rather sarcastically.

"Only if we drink a second shot to our mother," Luke answered.

John nodded. They downed their drinks and poured another, saluting Beverly Fontaine. Lettie quietly watched.

"I'm sorry about your wife, John," Luke said. "I can't even imagine life without Lettie. Did you have any children?"

John leaned back in his chair, his eyes showing sadness and disappointment. "No. You're the only brother with sons to carry on the Fontaine name." A guilty look came over his face. "I, uh, I married Lynnanne, Luke. Her first husband was killed in the war, so she moved back here from New York and…well, I always cared for her. I never told you about my feelings back when you were courting her. I knew how you felt about her. When you started writing me…"

The man leaned forward, running his hands through his hair. "I treasured those letters, Luke. I wanted to write back, but I was afraid to tell you I'd married Lynnanne. I knew Dad was the one who fixed it so she got sent away. I thought maybe you'd think I had something to do with it too." He met Luke's eyes, saw the hurt and disappointment there. "I never told Lynnanne about the letters. Dad never did either. But I envied you, Luke, all the excitement and adventure, building on a wonderful dream and making it on your own like that, all the children you've had. Lynnanne was unable to bear children." John reached over and poured himself another drink, then held out the bottle to Luke.

Luke took the bottle, tipping more of the whiskey into his own shot glass. "You could have told me, John. I was happily married. It wouldn't have mattered."

"I guess part of me was jealous of your success and accomplishments, worried Lynnanne would regret not having married you if she knew. I know part of her heart still belonged to you. I was afraid I'd seem less…I don't know…less of a man, maybe, if she knew about all the things you were doing up in Montana." He shook his head and slugged down the drink. "You were always braver, more adventurous, certainly the better looking brother. Whoever fathered you must have been one good-looking—" He hesitated, seeing the sudden pain in Luke's eyes. "I'm sorry, Luke. I didn't mean that the way it came out."

Luke looked away, and Lettie knew he was struggling with great emotion. His brother had married the woman he'd lost because of his own illegitimacy. He would probably never know who his real father was, and all these years his brother and the only father he had ever known were aware of where he was but had never written.

"I'm so damn sorry, Luke, about everything. After Lynnanne died, then Dad, I was ashamed to write you. After all the lost years, it seemed pointless." He sighed with regret. "You have what, *four* living children?"

Luke just put his head in his hands, saying nothing.

"Five," Lettie answered for him. "If you've read all our letters, you know that our first son, my son from a first marriage, was stolen away by Indians. He finally came back to us about a year ago."

"Really! That's wonderful. What's he like?"

"He is very Indian in spirit," Lettie answered. "He also has an Indian wife and two small children."

John shook his head. "I'll be damned." He smiled sadly, moving his gaze to Luke. "Luke, I hope you'll try to understand my actions. Maybe someday you can find it in your heart to forgive me. I'm awfully sorry about the son who died, but you've done well, little brother. Leaving here was probably the best thing you could have done. You made a name for yourself, showed Dad you're someone of worth, a son he could be proud of. Fact is, he *was* secretly proud of you. I could see it in his eyes every time he got another letter. He was just too damn stubborn to admit it or answer you…and too ashamed of sending you away."

Luke wiped at his eyes and rose, walking to a window. "How do you know that?"

John leaned back in his chair, studying his shot glass. "Well, I sold our house and moved back in here when Dad got sick. Just a few days before he died, he asked me if I thought God would forgive him for turning his

back on you. He said that about the time you were
conceived, he suspected our mother of having an affair
with a fellow businessman who later left town. He never
would tell me who it was. He was hurt so deeply, he
just couldn't bring himself to believe you were his. I
have always had my doubts, but I guess we'll never
know. I'm sorry, Luke. All I know is it never made any
difference in how I felt about you as a brother. We have
a lot of good boyhood memories, had some good times
before that awful day Dad blew up and told you you
were a bastard. For all we know, he could have been
dead wrong. I think *he* realized that too, in the end.
Just before he died, he wept, wondered if God would
forgive him for turning you out with no proof you were
fathered by someone else. I think he realized you should
never have been blamed either way. What he did was
cruel, and you probably couldn't have forgiven him,
even if he'd asked."

Luke glanced at Lettie, and she saw the terrible sorrow
in his eyes.

"All those wasted years," he said softly. He sat back
down and leaned back with a heavy sigh, rubbing his
eyes. "The hell of it is I probably *would* have forgiven
him. All I needed was one letter, one sign of affection
and pride." He looked at John with tears in his eyes.
"Did he ever acknowledge how he felt about what I've
accomplished in Montana?"

"Not in words, but as I said, I could see the pride in
his eyes. In the end he told me that if I ever wrote to
you or saw you, I should tell you that he was sorry, that
part of him always loved you. Deep inside he knew he'd
been wrong, that you could very well have been his own
son. He was just so hurt, he could never quite forgive
our mother."

"I'll never believe our mother was anything but
perfect," Luke answered defensively. "If she did have an

affair, he drove her to it. You know what he could be like sometimes."

"I know. All I can tell you now is that he kept those letters, Luke, every one of them. They were very special to him. I still have them if you'd like them back. They might be useful, kind of a diary for you, a review of all you've done in Montana."

Lettie reached over and touched Luke's hand. "I'd like to have them, Luke."

He smiled bitterly. "What difference does it make anymore? Go ahead and keep them if you want."

John got up from his chair, looking down at both of them. "So, why don't we talk about the present, the future?" he said, trying to bring some joy back into the reunion. "The past is just that—past, gone, irretrievable." He met Luke's eyes. "You're a representative for the territorial legislature, I hear. It was in the newspaper."

"Here? In St. Louis?" Lettie asked.

"Sure was. Luke Fontaine, son of prominent businessman, Jacques Fontaine, and now one of the biggest landowners in Montana, was voted into Montana's territorial legislature, et cetera, et cetera."

Lettie smiled. "He's going to run for governor when Montana becomes a state," she told John.

John smiled. "Well, with someone like you supporting him, how can he go wrong? He said some pretty wonderful things about you in his letters, and I have to say, Lettie, that you're even more beautiful and gracious than I had you pictured."

Lettie liked John, realized he was very much like Luke. She had been prepared to hate this brother for also turning his back on Luke, but she understood his reasoning, knew it was mostly their father's fault they had lost so many years. "Thank you."

John sobered, sitting down again and facing Luke. "Luke, you have every right to hate both Dad and me;

but I'm telling you now that I personally believe you have a right to your share of the business, if you want it."

Luke's eyes showed grateful surprise, mingled with a hurt that simply was not going to go away overnight. He shook his head, then got up and turned away, breathing deeply to control his emotions.

"Dad gave up the supply store and concentrated on the warehousing and shipping," John continued. "I have to be honest with you, Luke. Fontaine Warehousing and Shipping clears about a million a year. We ship merchandise all the way up to Duluth, Minnesota, and as far south as the Gulf, even out into the Atlantic to eastern seaports. Right now we're setting up to ship merchandise all the way to Europe."

Luke struggled to find his voice, overwhelmed at the generous gesture. "I appreciate the offer, John," he said, finally able to talk. "Some men would be angry to have to share their fortune with someone else after having it to themselves for years. Just the offer tells me you never held anything against me." He turned to face his brother. "You're the one who has worked with the business all these years. I don't want or need any part of it. We're doing fine up at the Double L. We even have a couple of copper mines, own a hotel, a granary, stock in the Northern Pacific. Just this past year I bought some land around Butte and they've discovered more copper there. It's a real bonanza—not gold, but copper pays damn good right now. I didn't come back here to try to get a share of the business. I just wanted some answers. Now I've got them." He looked at Lettie. "My wife is the one who talked me into doing this. As usual, she was right in telling me to come." He turned his gaze back to John. "No matter what the past, we're still brothers, and we shouldn't go the rest of our lives never seeing each other. I'm not sure I can ever get over the hurt, but it helps to know my father—" He hesitated. Should he even call

Jacques Fontaine father? "That Jacques at least regretted what he did."

Lettie smiled softly, looking at John. "It was rather a last-minute decision to come here. We were in Chicago for our youngest daughter's wedding." She glanced at Luke, aching for him for all his years of hurt. "Luke is anxious to get back to the Double L. He's happiest when he's on the ranch." She looked back at John. "I do wish you would come and visit us there, meet Tyler and Katie and Nathan, see the ranch."

John rose, walking closer to Luke. "I'd like that. With Dad gone, my wife dead, it gets a little lonely around here."

Their gaze held, and Luke nodded. "Then find people to run things for a while and come to Montana. You might like it so much you won't want to leave. It's beautiful country, John."

John smiled sadly. "So I've heard." He sighed. "I told Dad I could send for you so he could see you before he died, but he didn't want that. He was afraid you would think he was only doing it because he wanted quick forgiveness. He figured you probably couldn't forgive him, anyway, and I don't think he wanted to see what he was afraid he would see in your eyes."

Luke studied the man, wondering where all the years had gone. "I'd like to see his grave."

John nodded. "I'll take you there this afternoon. I hope you can both stay at least a couple of days. St. Louis has grown a lot. I'd like to show Lettie around, let her get a last taste of city life before you take her back to that wild, remote place you call Montana and bury her beauty on the Double L."

Luke smiled, walking over to where Lettie sat, putting his hands on her shoulders. "This woman gets around more than you think she does. Most people in the territory of Montana know who she is, and that's a lot of territory, just about the biggest out West except for Texas and maybe California."

John studied his brother's rugged appearance, his face and hands weathered from years of working outside under Montana skies. He wore a neat suit jacket, but he wore denim pants and leather boots. "Destiny sent you there, Luke, not Dad or anything that happened here. If you hadn't left when you did, you wouldn't have met the perfect woman to help you find your dream. Montana was calling you. I don't think you would have been happy staying here no matter what happened with Dad. Running Fontaine Warehousing would have been too boring for you." He put out his hand. "I would say welcome home, Luke, but you aren't home at all, are you?"

Luke thought about the Double L and how he missed it. He shook his brother's hand again. "You're right. This hasn't been home for me for a long time now." He squeezed John's hand, and their eyes held in mutual affection.

"Do you want our mother's picture?" John asked. "I have another one, a smaller one. I found them up in the attic after Dad died. I have a picture of Dad too, if you want it."

Luke quelled the temptation to hate his father. The man was dead now. "It would be wonderful to have pictures to take home to show my children. I've told them about Dad, and of course they have asked over the years why he would never come to Montana. I always told them you and Dad were too busy with your business here. They never seemed to question that answer too much. I never had the courage to tell them the truth. Now I don't see any reason to, especially if you come and see us."

John gripped his hand more firmly. "I'll make a point of it. I promise." He let go of Luke's hand. "I'll have my groom rig up a buggy for me and I'll take the pictures to my office and have someone there wrap them up for you. Tonight we will dine at St. Louis's best restaurant and you can tell me more about this ranch of yours and how it's run. You and Lettie will be my guests right here. No sense in staying in a hotel. Besides, it will give us even more time to talk." He turned and put a hand out to Lettie. "I'm so glad to meet the famous Lettie. My brother indeed chose well, I can see that," he added. "I am so glad to meet you."

Lettie grasped his hand, big like Luke's, but much softer. "And you have no idea how glad I am to meet you. I was a little bit afraid I would regret talking Luke into coming, but now I'm very glad that I did."

John straightened. "I'm going to find my groom. I'll have Margaret get a room ready for you. Where is your luggage?"

"At the St. Louis Inn. We got in last night," Luke answered. "I wasn't sure how long we'd be here, what I'd find when I got here. Actually, everything is still in our room. I can drive back in the carriage I rented and get it."

"Fine. I'll ride with you and we can take the pictures down to the office and get the luggage while your wife rests right here. You *will* stay a couple of days, won't you?"

"No longer than that," Luke told him. "I'm anxious to get home and make sure everything there is all right. I do have duties as a legislative delegate I need to get back to. And Lettie misses the grandchildren."

John smiled and shook his head. "Grandchildren. You're such a lucky man, Luke. It's too bad Dad never got to meet Lettie or his own grandchildren and great-grandchildren. Hurt and anger sure can make a man do foolish things, can't they?" He sighed again. "I'm going to talk to Margaret about the room and then we can leave. Later today we'll go visit Dad's grave."

John left them, and Luke went to stand near the

fireplace, looking up at the painting of his mother. He stared at it for several seconds before turning to look at Lettie. "As usual, you were right, Mrs. Fontaine. Thanks for making me come here. I just wish I could have seen Dad once more, got it all straight with him. I would never want to be so estranged from any of my children. I don't know how a man can let that happen."

"You and I were like strangers for two years after Paul died, Luke. It just happens. He's gone now, and there is no use in trying to live in the past or worrying over how different things might have been. John was right. Destiny called you to Montana, and nothing that happened here could have changed that." She rose and walked to stand beside him. "It's as though we've come full circle. I've learned to be at peace over what happened when Nathan was conceived, and now you're back here facing the painful things that caused you to leave. Neither of us belongs here in Missouri anymore. We belong in Montana." She moved her arms around his waist. "Let's not stay too long."

He smiled, tears in his eyes. "We have to be sure to keep our story about Nathan's father straight, Lettie. I don't ever want him to feel the way I felt all these years, my real father being some nameless person who probably didn't give a damn about my mother. Maybe there was a reason God took Nathan away for so many years. All those growing-up years he might have been full of questions about his real father. Now I think he's old enough that it doesn't matter anymore. I just don't want him to know that kind of pain."

"He won't. Katie is the only one who knows the truth, and she'll never tell." She stretched up and kissed his cheek. "I'm so happy for you, Luke."

He moved his arms around her, saying nothing for several seconds. Then Lettie felt his shoulders shaking, and he grasped her tighter. "It still hurts, Lettie," he groaned. "I'll never know who my father really is, or if and why my mother took another man."

She didn't know how to answer. She just held him, realizing that in those dark days of her own unhappiness, she might have done the same thing, could have ended up having a child by another man. Thank God she'd found her common sense in time to save herself from something that would have devastated her husband even worse than the average man, considering his own background.

"Everything will be better when we get home," she told him. "We just have to get ourselves back to Montana."

◈

Tyler rolled in the grass with Ramona, her laughter music to his ears. She made him feel constantly on fire with her freeness and open sexuality. They had met at the pond often for three weeks now, and every time she undressed and goaded him to come into the water with her, he could not resist. They had made love, in the water and out of it, and sometimes she would insist that he roll onto his back and let her do the moving. "I will ride my beautiful, wild, white stallion," she would tell him.

They lay together now, her silken, dark-skinned legs wrapped around his own naked torso. "I love you, Ramona," he whispered before meeting her delicious mouth again, wondering if there was another creature on earth as beautiful. He moved inside of her, filling her deeply, his youthful eagerness giving her near-agonizing pleasure.

For several minutes they moved in rhythmic pleasure, each fulfilling the other's aching needs. Tyler rubbed himself over that magical spot he had learned made her even wilder and brought her even more pleasure, until she would cry out his name and push herself at him as though she could not get enough of him. That was when he would grasp her slender hips and rise up to his knees, burying himself even deeper and looking upon her splendid nakedness until finally he could no longer control his own release.

He wished Ramona was already his wife legally. In her eyes, he was her husband simply because he had been her first man and she had offered herself willingly. Still, he wanted a church wedding, and he couldn't have that until his parents came home. He gave no thought to what Luke would think of his eldest son marrying an Indian woman, especially since Nathan was already married to one. He had already complained that half his ranch was going to end up in the hands of Indians, which just didn't seem right because of all the Sioux had put him through in those early years. Besides that, the citizens of Billings and other ranchers were not so happy about the arrangement with Nathan. They only tolerated it because it was Luke Fontaine's family, and after what Luke and Lettie had already been through over Nathan, they understood. Would they understand Tyler also wanting to marry an Indian woman? After all, he had not been raised with the Sioux. His was an entirely different situation.

And there was Alice to think about. Somehow he had to break the news gently that it was over between them. He loved Ramona, and he was going to marry her, no matter what anyone thought of it. "When my father gets home—"

"Get off my sister!"

Tyler's words were interrupted by the order, spoken in a deep, angry voice. He looked up to see Nathan standing near them, his fists clenched. "What the hell!" He jumped up, scrambling to find his long johns.

Ramona gasped, quickly pulling their blanket around herself to hide her nakedness.

Tyler yanked up his underwear. "What are you doing here, you son of a bitch?" he growled at Nathan.

"The question is, what are *you* doing here, robbing my sister of her innocence when she belongs to someone else!"

"I do *not* belong to someone else! I love Tyler. I belong to *him* now!"

Nathan cast her a scathing look of shame. "You belong to Standing Horse! You know you are promised to him!"

"We no longer live that way! We *choose* our men, the Christian way!"

"By rolling in the grass with them before you have had a Christian marriage?" Nathan sneered. He looked at Tyler. "I know you! You are just trying to get back at me by dirtying my sister! You have no use for her! You took advantage of her!"

"You bastard! I *love* Ramona! I was just waiting for Pa to get home so I could tell him I want to marry her!"

"*You* love an *Indian* woman? You love her only enough to stick yourself inside her and have a good time!"

Tyler charged forward and landed into Nathan with a raging grunt, knocking Nathan to the ground. They fought and tumbled, while Ramona scooted away, screaming both their names, not wanting to see either of them hurt. Within moments their faces were bruised and bloody. The two of them were an almost even match, although Nathan was more a wrestler, while Ty preferred using his fists.

All their pent-up emotions about each other were finally released through blows and kicks and punches as the two young men fought fiercely. Tyler remembered the day when Nathan had taken over the training of Ebony, the black stallion Tyler had captured. Tyler had not been able to control the horse, but Nathan had had him almost fully trained in one day. Tyler hated him for that, hated to be shown up by this "Indian" brother who had stolen so much from him. And where did he get off calling himself an Indian in the first place? He certainly had no Indian blood, and he was tired of Nathan's holier-than-thou attitude. He pummeled Nathan with big fists, and Nathan in turn warded off some of the punches with quick movements of his own, catching a foot behind Tyler's ankle so that he fell onto his back. He went down with him, pressing Tyler's wrists to the ground.

"You had no right taking my sister with no one's permission!" he seethed.

"Ramona and I love each other," Tyler growled in reply. He arched against Nathan, then banged his head forward into Nathan's mouth, startling him enough to get loose and roll away from him. He landed near his six-gun, and he quickly pulled it from its holster.

"Tyler, no!" Ramona screamed. "He is your brother!"

Tyler hesitated. He stood there panting, his back scratched and bleeding, his skin and long johns grass-stained, his whole body bruised and cut. Nathan was just as filthy, his mouth bleeding from a split lip. He wiped at his lip, spit blood.

"Aren't you going to pull that fancy knife on me, Nathan?" Tyler asked. "The one my *pa* gave you?"

Nathan straightened. "Is that what you think? That all Indians are ready to knife a white man?"

"I don't know *what* to think! You aren't even an *Indian*! What right do you have telling me whether or not I can marry Ramona? You aren't her brother by blood!"

"But I am *your* brother by blood! Yet you stand there and hold a gun on me. What would *Luke* think of you right now?"

Tyler blinked, hardly aware he'd pulled the gun. He looked at it a moment, then threw it aside. "Maybe he'd be wondering why he let you come here to live," he sneered.

"Or maybe his heart would break to see his sons fighting."

There it was, the word he hated. Sons. Nathan spoke then as though he were as much Luke's son as Tyler was, but he wasn't. Tyler did not mind so much having to share his mother, but there was something about having to share his father that grated on him. Still, he knew Nathan was right. "Maybe he would, but I don't care what he thinks of *any*thing I do if you try to keep me from Ramona!"

"She is Indian. She should marry an Indian."

"And you are white, Nathan, yet you married an Indian. Why is it all right for you?"

"Because I was raised by them! I understand their ways. You do not. In the end you would be unhappy, and so would Ramona. People understand it for me, but they would not understand Tyler Fontaine marrying an Indian. They would be cruel to Ramona!"

"You said you hated it on the reservation. How can Ramona marry an Indian without going back there?"

"Standing Horse is Cheyenne. He has put in for transfer to the Northern Cheyenne reservation here in Montana. They would be closer then, and I could go there and take them food and blankets and other things they need."

"But I love Tyler, Nathan," a sobbing Ramona said. She walked closer, keeping the blanket wrapped around herself. "You had no right to spy on us!"

Nathan shook his long, blond hair back from his shoulders. "I was not spying in the way that you think. I knew that you like to come here. Little Luke is sick, and there are chores Leena needs help with while she tends to him. I came to get you. I did not know you would be with Tyler."

She held her head proudly. "Tyler and I are already married the Indian way, and there is nothing you can do about it. Standing Horse has eyes for some of the other young girls. It would have been only a marriage of promises, not of love. Tyler and I love each other, and as soon as his father gets back, we are going to marry the Christian way. I could already be carrying his child. I cannot marry Standing Horse now."

Nathan looked her over with disappointment in his eyes. "Go behind some bushes or something and get dressed."

She stormed up to him, meeting his eyes squarely. "You will not give me orders about whom I should love and marry! Look into the mirror, Nathan! You are no different than Tyler!" She turned and angrily picked up her things and walked off.

Tyler, still panting, stepped closer then. "Maybe some of the hard feelings between us are for that very reason." He sneered. "You come here carrying on about being Indian. But you're *not* Indian, Nathan, and that bothers you, doesn't it? Ramona is right. You *are* just like me!"

Nathan took a deep breath, wanting to light into him all over again. "I told you, being Indian is not in the skin. It is in the heart." His pale blue eyes were icy. "Do you truly love Ramona?"

"I told you I do."

"You will have differences. You do not understand this yet. And there will be a strain between you because people will talk. You will see pretty white girls in town and you will wonder if you did the right thing. They will make fun of Ramona, make her feel bad. She will never fit in as she would among her own kind. People understand why I am married to Leena, but they will not understand *you* marrying an Indian. I am not saying there is any reason for Ramona or any of her people to be ashamed of who they are. I am only saying that marrying you will make life harder for her. Even the men around here look at her as something only to be used and then thrown away. I can read their thoughts."

"My pa wouldn't allow any man on this ranch to insult her!"

"He cannot control the other ranchers, or the whole town of Billings. To his face they are cowards, but behind his back they will talk, and they will make sure that Ramona hears." He sniffed and wiped more blood from his lips. "If you hurt Ramona, in any way, I will *kill* you, brother or not!" He turned and walked back to his horse.

"You'd hang," Tyler shouted. "And Luke would do it himself! If I told him what you just said, he'd send you right back to the reservation!"

Nathan turned. "And what would he do if I told him you pulled a gun on your own brother? I do not think he would like that so much either." He mounted his horse and rode off. Tyler watched after him, hating him. Ramona, partially dressed, walked up to him then and put her arms around him.

"We're getting married, Ramona," he told her with determination in his voice. "I don't give a damn what Pa or Nathan or everybody in town or anybody else thinks! I love you, and we're getting married!"

Thirty-five

LUKE STUDIED HIS SON AND RAMONA, SEEING THE LOVE and fire in their eyes. "Nathan is right, you know, about what other people will say, Tyler. You know how people around here feel about the Sioux. They understand why Nathan would marry an Indian woman, but you—"

"I've heard it all, Pa. I just want you and Mother to be happy for me, to give us your blessing, and allow us a Christian wedding. For all we know, Ramona could already be carrying my child."

"Tyler!" Lettie could hardly believe what had happened between Ty and Ramona while they had been gone.

Ty's face reddened with a mixture of embarrassment and anger. "Mother, I am twenty years old. Ramona is eighteen. We're old enough to know what we want."

Luke studied Ramona. No, she was certainly no little girl. She was a ravishing beauty with a beguiling way about her. What red-blooded twenty-year-old wouldn't be attracted to a wild, fetching thing like her? Alice Richards was also beautiful, but Ty didn't have to be around her every day, and she didn't have the sultry ways of Ramona. He sighed, leaning forward in his chair and rubbing at his eyes. This was not a situation he would have wanted to come home to, but there was no getting around it. Tyler had cornered them almost the minute they arrived, and they had all gathered in the parlor. Nathan paced at one end of the room like a nervous cat.

"I'm more upset by the fact that you and Nathan

fought than I am about you wanting to marry Ramona," Luke said, his voice sounding weary.

Ty and Nathan looked at each other, each knowing the other could tell Luke the worst of it, which would only upset him even more. They both respected him too much to do that to him.

Lettie's heart ached for Luke. He had been good enough to accept Nathan back, Indian family and all, had always cared about him because he was her son. It hurt to realize what a problem all of it was causing, and she felt partially responsible. Neither of them had given a thought to Tyler becoming attracted to Ramona, and now she wondered how they could have been so foolish. "Luke, if they have already—" She felt her own face flushing. "If they have already...been together...there really is no choice here."

"I know." Luke's hands were still over his face. He thought quietly for a moment, then looked up at Ty and Ramona, who stood together in front of him. "I want you to understand, Ramona, that I don't look at you or Leena as any less important human beings than anyone else. I'm not an Indian-hater. Because of Nathan we've all grown to understand the Indian situation a lot better, and I can't say I can blame your people for fighting to keep what they consider their land. God knows I've done enough fighting and killing for the same reason." He moved his gaze to Tyler. "The only reason I'm not completely in favor of this is because no matter how you feel about Nathan, he *is* right. This won't be easy for you, Ty, so you make damn sure it's what you want. If you love Ramona as much as you say you do, you don't want her to be hurt. And there will be children to consider. They'll be half-breeds, and some people look on that as worse than being Indian. They'll be my grandchildren, so no one will dare insult them in my presence, but I can't be everyplace at once, Ty."

"I'll protect and defend Ramona and my children against any man!"

Luke rose, shaking his head, wondering how many more fistfights his son would get into over his wife. In his youth, Ty simply did not understand what he was getting himself into. He turned and faced all of them. "I don't consider myself any better than the next man, but you *do* understand what this means, don't you?"

Tyler frowned. "I'm not sure what you're getting at."

"What I'm getting at is that Pearl has married a fancy man who will never want anything to do with the Double L. Robbie is off studying to be a doctor, so if and when he does come back here, he'll always live in town and will also not have anything to do with the Double L. That leaves you and Katie and Nathan. Nathan is married to an Indian woman, *you* want to marry an Indian woman, and Katie is married to a sheep man. Are you starting to get my point?"

Tyler could not help a little grin. "Someday sheep men and Indians and half-breeds will be running the Double L."

"The very kinds of people I've been chasing off for years."

"Pa, I love the Double L. Any children I have will love it as much as I, and someday maybe one or two of Katie's children will also want to help run this ranch. The important thing is that it's in the hands of family, people who love it, and who love and respect the man who built it. I've learned a lot about how to run the ranch, and I'll teach my children the same. The Double L will be all right. I would never let anything happen to it. You must know that. Besides, times are changing. Sheep men and cattlemen get along well now, and the Indian wars are over."

Luke met his gaze squarely. "What about Alice Richards? Do you intend just to throw her away? She's been a good friend to you for years, *more* than a friend; and I don't doubt she's been waiting for you to settle down and get more serious."

Ramona looked down, burning with jealousy over the pretty white girl she knew was fond of Ty.

"Alice knows there is something going on. I'll talk to her. I don't take her friendship lightly, Pa, but I don't love her the way I love Ramona."

Luke shook his head. "Well, considering what has already been going on between you two, I guess your own decision has already been made." He looked at Nathan. "I don't have any choice but to give them my permission, Nathan. If I send Ramona to the Cheyenne reservation, I'll only alienate my own son, and I won't do that. I just hope letting them marry doesn't mean alienating you."

Nathan approached them, his lower lip still a little blue, the cut scabbed into a red line. It had been a week since his fight with Tyler, and he had not spoken to him since. "I do not blame you for your decision," he told Luke. "You are not the one who has a choice. Tyler is your son, and I would not expect you to go against him. It is *Tyler* who has the choice. I think he has made a bad choice, but it is done now. He must marry her the Christian way to make an honorable woman out of Ramona in the white man's eyes. I just do not want to see her hurt."

"None of us wants that, Nathan," Lettie put in. "But you should know by how much we love you and your family and little Luke and Julie that whoever Tyler marries, we will love and defend her as our own." Her heart warmed at the loving look he gave her, something she had once thought she might never see.

"My mother is a woman of great compassion," Nathan answered. "I do not fear how you will accept Ramona." He turned to look at Tyler. "You have said that I am not Indian. This is true. But I was raised with Ramona, and I love her like a sister, even though we are not of the same blood. You and I *are* of the same blood, but the bad feelings continue. I told you once before that I did not come here to take anything from you. Now I *give* something to you. I give you Ramona." He turned and walked out.

Luke turned to Lettie. "I'd like a few minutes alone with Ty."

Lettie took hold of Ramona's arm. "Come with me, Ramona. We need to talk about your wedding. I'll have Gino make a gown for you. You'll be such a beautiful bride!"

Ramona looked sadly at Tyler before leaving the room with Lettie. Was everyone right? Would it be such a difficult thing being married to a rich white man? She looked around the room of the elegant Fontaine home. What did she know about living like this? Lettie Fontaine was so educated and refined. She was the kind of woman it took to run a place like the Double L. Tyler's parents were good people. They would love her as their own daughter if she married Tyler. Was Nathan right that Tyler would ultimately be much happier married to someone like Alice? She had much to think about, for above all else, she loved Tyler Fontaine more than she loved herself.

"I want no more fighting between you and Nathan," Luke said sternly. He walked over to close the parlor doors, then turned to face Tyler.

"I just don't like his arrogant attitude," Ty answered, "as if he were better than the rest of us."

"Maybe he thinks the same way about you," Luke answered. "Maybe he thinks you consider *yourself* better." He walked to a stand at the side of the room to pour himself a small glass of wine. "You've been pretty damn hard on him, Ty, and for no good reason. Family is a pretty important gift. I want you always to remember that."

"I know that, Pa. You know how much I love you and Mother and everybody."

"Everybody but Nathan."

Tyler sighed deeply. "Pa, I don't worry about being treated fairly. I know you better than that. It's just that he's always been some sort of mystical being in Mother's eyes, like there's something more special about him. And he didn't come back here out of any love for you or Mother. He came back so he and his family would have a place to live, nothing more. All those years he never gave a damn about you and Mother or the rest of us."

"He wasn't *raised* to give a damn. He had to learn it at an older age. He had to come here and see for himself. I don't blame him for any of it, Ty. He was just a little four-year-old boy when he was stolen away. You have no idea how that would have affected you if *you* were the one stolen." He sipped some of the wine. "As far as Nathan not really being Indian, of course he isn't. But he feels like one on the inside, and you have to respect that, just as he has to respect who you are and your importance here on the Double L. You have to understand how he feels about Ramona. He has seen the other side, Ty. You haven't. He's been a part of two worlds. He knows how hard this will be for Ramona. You think that just because she'll be a Fontaine, she'll be protected, but it doesn't always work that way. I don't want to see you *or* Ramona hurt."

Luke set down the wine and paced, while Tyler stood silently, waiting for the man to finish. "We both know she's just as beautiful and good and worthy as any other woman," Luke finally continued, "but how we feel doesn't change the prejudice that's out there waiting to lash out. Some terrible things have happened, Ty, on both sides. Don't forget the Little Big Horn. Maybe you were too young to remember or care that much about it, but people our age haven't forgotten. It doesn't matter anymore whose fault it was or how right the Sioux and Cheyenne might have been. All that matters is what people remember, and they remember what happened to James Woodward and his family. I would never dream of keeping you from the woman you love. I would only lose you. I just want you to be sure about this, and if you truly love Ramona, are you really doing what is best for her happiness?"

Ty met his eyes, looking ready to cry. "Pa, I'd die without her."

Luke put a hand on his shoulder. "All right. Then marry her. But I want no more hard feelings between you and Nathan. Sit down, Ty. I want to tell you about something that happened to me in St. Louis, between me and my own brother."

"You saw your brother? How about our grandpa? It's hard to believe they've always been too busy to come here."

"I haven't told you the whole truth of it, Ty." Luke walked to the fireplace and Tyler sat down, listening intently as Luke spilled out his story, surprising Ty with the intense emotion he displayed in the telling. He hadn't even had a chance yet to unwrap the pictures of his mother and father that he had brought home with him. "Now maybe you understand better why I could never turn Nathan out, Ty," he finished. "I know how it feels to think you aren't loved or wanted. When I married your mother, I vowed to love Nathan the same as the rest of my children and never let him feel like an outcast. His being stolen away by Indians didn't change any of that."

Tyler watched the man lovingly, hardly able to believe how Luke had been treated by his own father. "I'm sorry, Pa, about what happened to you. I guess I understand a lot of things better."

"The point is, John readily offered me my share of the business, without question, even though I can't prove I'm a Fontaine. I don't need any of it, and I told him so, but I appreciate the fact that he offered. In the same way, Nathan has a right to a part of this ranch, whether you like it or not. He doesn't want it any more than I want to take anything from my own brother now. What matters is that my brother understood, just as I expect you to understand it's the same situation for Nathan. He needs our love and acceptance, Ty, even though he pretends it doesn't matter to him, and I need you to help me in this, not work against me. Nathan has given you Ramona, and to this day he has never asked for one thing but a place to live. He has become a damn good ranch hand, and you know how good he is with horses. He has given a hundred percent on his part, and he and your mother have grown closer. That means the world to Lettie. I want us to be a close family, Ty. We always have been until these hard feelings between you and Nathan. I want it to end."

Tyler rose, walking close to his father. "I guess...I guess I was afraid I'd somehow lose you, lose that kind of special thing we have."

Yes, Luke thought. It was nameless, but special, this feeling for his firstborn son, so special that poor Robbie had felt it, yet he loved Robbie and the rest of his children just as fiercely. Perhaps none of them would understand these feelings until they had children of their own. "That can never change, Ty. Never. Deep in your heart you have to know that."

Tyler smiled, and Luke felt as though he were looking into a mirror, except that the lines of age were not there.

"I do, Pa," he answered.

Luke nodded. "What I've told you about my own father is just between you and me, Ty. I want the rest of the children to think only good things about him and my mother." Luke had not told Tyler the truth about Nathan's own real father. He had made a vow not to. It was enough that the children knew the young man was a half brother. It was important that he be accepted fully. Why taint the children's view of him or their mother, and why hurt Nathan, by telling any of them the truth? They had been told over the years that there were no pictures of Nathan's father because they had been burned in the raid. Only Katie knew the truth, and she was a wise woman, had always been very mature for her years. She knew firsthand how her mother felt and why it was important to keep the secret.

"I'd like to meet my uncle someday," Tyler said, interrupting Luke's thoughts.

"You may get the chance. He's going to visit. I don't know how soon, but I believe he'll come, maybe next summer."

Ty took a deep breath, smiling. "Maybe Ramona and I will have a child of our own by then."

Luke prayed the marriage would be as happy as Ty thought it could be. "Maybe. I just wish you had waited for a real wedding, Ty."

"Pa, I've been watching her and loving her for a year now. One day I followed her to the pond up at the northeast corner, and she..." He reddened. "She was swimming." He turned away. "I don't know. It just... happened. There she was, inviting me to come and swim with her. We both knew what we felt right then and there." He turned to meet Luke's eyes boldly. "She's not a loose woman, Pa. She was... I was her first. She said no matter what happened afterward, that's how she wanted it. I love her, and I want her to be my wife. We'll be okay."

Luke put a hand on his shoulder. "I think maybe you will at that. God bless you both, Ty. You know Lettie will love her as she does her own daughters."

Ty nodded. "Mother is a hell of a woman."

Luke held up his wineglass. "I'll drink to that." He finished the wine. "Why don't we go talk to Nathan? We need to straighten out a few things."

Tyler forced back the old resentments. "Sure. Why not?"

They left the house, and from the window of Katie's old room upstairs, Ramona watched Ty and his father walk out of the house and toward the barn. She worried over some of the things that had been said, but she kept her thoughts to herself. How could she talk to a white woman like Lettie about how an Indian woman felt about living this way, her fears and apprehension over marrying someone like Ty? Even now Lettie was going through some of Katie's old dresses to determine Ramona's proper sizing. She had Ramona try some of them on, but each fancy dress felt foreign and uncomfortable to Ramona. For these past three weeks she had shared her love with Tyler on her terms, rolling in the grass by the pond, wearing simple dresses and often no shoes when she was home with Nathan. It had not struck her until she came into the house with Ty just how white he really was, or how rich, or how he belonged with someone more like his own mother. What did she know about the proper undergarments and stockings, the proper way to wear her hair or a hat, how to take care of such a big house? Lettie was so kind, but no matter how much she taught her, or how fancy were the clothes she might wear into town to attend church and the women's socials Lettie was telling her about, she would always be Morning Sun, a Sioux Indian.

"Ramona, try this one! I think it might fit," Lettie was telling her. "You can come with me to the women's club meeting in two days and I will announce your engagement to Tyler. This dress will look beautiful on you."

Ramona turned to see her holding out a lovely lavender-colored dress with wide ruffles that spilled down the full skirt. She stepped over to let Lettie put it over her head, and she winced at the feel of the tight corset Lettie had laced her into. She hated the way white women dressed. She felt as if she couldn't breathe.

❧

"Luke, you'd better get out here. Ty and Nathan are about to go at each other's throats."

A plate of partly eaten steak and eggs sat in front of Luke. He looked up at Billy Sacks, who stood in the doorway to the dining room. "I'm sorry to bother you, but you'd better come."

"Oh dear," Lettie fretted. "Now what? I thought we solved everything last night."

Luke scowled as he rose, walking on long strides out of the house. Lettie put down her own fork and hurried out behind him. What could have happened? Tyler had been so happy at the breakfast table. He had finished before them, wanting to go out and check on a lame horse. He was going to ride to Nathan's house then and see Ramona for a few minutes before starting his chores. Lettie hurried behind Luke, and she could already hear the shouting down by the barn. Luke started running, and she ran behind him. Nathan was standing and facing Tyler calmly, but two men were holding back Tyler, who was trying to get at Nathan with his fists.

"It's your fault, damn you!" Tyler was screaming. "Why did you have to come here? Why did you even bring Ramona in the first place if she was promised to a damn Indian? I hate you! I hate you, Nathan Fontaine! You don't even deserve the *name* Fontaine! You're *White Bear*! You're *Sioux*, remember? What the hell are you doing here, you bastard?"

Lettie's heart sank at the words. How much worse would it be for Nathan and Ty both if they knew the truth about Nathan's father? What had happened to cause this?

Luke stepped up and grabbed Tyler by the shirtfront. "What the hell is going on here? Just last night—"

"She's gone, Pa! Ramona is gone! She's out there alone somewhere, and it's his fault! He must have said something to scare her away from me!" Tyler's eyes were wet, his face red with rage, the veins in his throat taut from straining and screaming.

"Calm down, or I'll hit you myself!" Luke ordered Tyler. He looked at the men holding him. "Let go of him."

"Whatever you say, Boss." They released Tyler, and he stood there panting, glaring at his father. "Get rid of him, Pa. Get rid of him, or I'll *kill* him!"

Luke jerked on his shirt. "You'll do no such thing! I won't have this happening in my family!"

"Then he shouldn't have made Ramona run away!"

Luke let go of him, but kept a close eye on him. "The rest of you men get the hell out of here and get to work!"

The others wandered away, mumbling among themselves and shaking their heads. Luke realized some of them had no idea what was going on between Ty and Ramona, and he also knew what the opinions of some would be. He could not concern himself with that now. He turned to Nathan. "What the hell happened?"

A deep hurt showed in Nathan's eyes. "Ramona ran away. She left a note. I did not know what she was planning. Sometime in the night she must have come out here to get Star and she rode off. The note was left in Star's stall." He looked over at Lettie pleadingly, then back at Luke. "I swear I said nothing to discourage her. Last night I shared wine with you and Tyler. I had given my consent. I would not have gone back on my word."

"You *liar*!" Tyler shouted. "You talked her out of it. Somehow you scared her away!"

"I *love* her!" Nathan shouted back. "Would I want my own sister riding out there alone and in danger? Why would I do such a thing?"

"You'd do anything to keep her from marrying me!"

"Don't be stupid, Ty!" Luke answered. "Nathan wouldn't have wanted her to run off alone. The important thing is to figure out why she did it and for us to go after her."

Tyler tore a piece of paper from his pants pocket and handed it over, still glaring at Nathan, a tear slipping down his cheek. Luke read the note, written as well as Ramona could write, given her limited education. "'It is best this way,'" Luke read aloud. "'I love you, Tyler Fontaine.'" She had spelled Fontaine wrong, but he ignored it. "'I love you enough to do what is right for you, even though it breaks my heart. You belong here. I do not. Our happiness could not last forever. I am going back to my people where I belong. I will marry Standing Horse.'"

Ty glanced at his mother. "Did *you* say something to her? What did you do when you took her upstairs?"

Lettie felt as though someone had pierced her heart with a knife. "Oh, Ty, how can you think I would ever do anything to hurt someone you love?"

He looked away, clenching his fists.

"What *did* you do?" Nathan asked Lettie.

Lettie put a hand to her stomach. "Well, I...I was as good to her as I could be. I helped her try on some of Katie's dresses. She was going to go with me to the women's club meeting in a couple of days. We had a good time trying clothes on, fixing her hair."

Nathan smiled rather bitterly, shaking his head. "You are a good woman, Mother, but I think perhaps it was too much at once—all those fancy clothes, being in that house, seeing how you live."

"And I'll just bet you pointed all of that out to her when you got her back to your house!" Tyler yelled at Nathan. "My mother would never deliberately discourage her, but you would, you son of a bitch! You knew she'd get just enough of a taste of being a Fontaine to scare her, and you played on those feelings!"

A terrible sadness showed in Nathan's eyes. "I said nothing to her last night. When she came home she was very quiet. I asked her what was wrong, and she just looked at me and said she did not want to talk about it. She just wanted to go to bed and think and be alone. I even offered to come and get you, but she said that I should not."

"That was all the more reason *to* come and get me!"

"Both of you get mounted up," Luke ordered. "We're going to try to find her. She probably tried to follow the same roads and trails that brought her here. She most likely headed north before she would go east, so that she wouldn't have to ride anyplace near Billings."

"I can track her," Nathan said. "I know the gait of her horse, and Star has one hoof that looks slightly crooked."

"Let's go, then." Luke grabbed Tyler's arm to lead him into the barn, but Tyler hesitated, glaring at Nathan.

"She rode out of here in the night. Do you know how dangerous this country is at night?"

"Of course I know how dangerous it is! I have lived in the open country most of my life!"

"If anything has happened to her—"

"You will blame me!" Nathan said, sneering. "But at the same time, *I* will blame *you*, Tyler! None of this would have happened if you could have kept your pants buttoned until your father got home! You had no right making big promises to her! You had no right taking liberties with her!"

Tyler charged for him again, but Luke grabbed him, holding on for dear life. "Stop it, Ty!" he growled. "Or do you plan to punch your own father! That's what you'll have to do before I'll let you light into your brother again!"

Tyler relaxed again, jerking away from Luke. "Don't call him my brother." He turned and walked into the barn, and Luke looked at Lettie, seeing the devastation in her eyes. He just shook his head and followed Tyler into the barn. Nathan looked at his mother then.

"I swear I said nothing to make her do this," he said, agony in his voice. "I did not mean to make so much trouble for you. When we find Ramona, we will leave the Double L."

Lettie shook her head. "Please don't, Nathan. Don't go away again."

He hated to see the pain in her eyes. "I might have no choice. If it comes down to choosing between two sons, you know which one Luke would choose, no matter how much he loves me. He loves Tyler the most, and I do not blame him for it. Perhaps we will find Ramona and everything will be all right."

Tears slowly trickled down her cheeks. "Perhaps," she whispered.

Thirty-six

IT WAS A DARK TIME FOR EVERYONE. IN THE FONTAINE cemetery, two new headstones were erected. Runner, sixty, had died that past spring, a blow to Luke, especially with the sorrow that had hung over the household for over a year now. Runner had been buried next to a stone that read, *Here Lies Ramona, a Sioux Indian, Born Springtime 1867, Died August 1885. Loved by Tyler Fontaine.*

Lettie looked out a back bedroom window at the graveyard in the distance. A cold rain pelted the glass, like the coldness that had fallen over the Fontaine family. Ramona had been found lying in the road with a broken neck. Star was found later with a fractured leg and had had to be shot. Luke had arranged for both the horse and Ramona to be brought back on a wagon. Star was buried next to Ramona.

Tyler had sunk into a terrible despair, and even his father couldn't help him. His hatred for Nathan was so great that Nathan had chosen to go and live at the northern line shack so they would hardly ever have to see each other. Lettie and Luke felt as if they had lost both their sons. In May, Katie had given birth to another son, Jeffrey Adam, her fourth child, and their own sixth grandchild. Nathan and Leena were expecting the following summer, but the coming of more grandchildren could not erase the sorrow that had filled their hearts since Ramona's untimely death.

There would be no children for Ty and Ramona. Lettie could not help blaming herself, wondering if she had said or done something that night before Ramona ran away that might have upset her so much. Perhaps she shouldn't have carried on so about how Ramona should dress, or about attending the women's club with her. She had not stopped to think of how terrifying such things might be to someone from such a different world. Ramona had been like a sweet child who needed careful guidance and nurturing.

Since her death, Tyler had taken a cabin by himself, wanting to be alone. It tore at her heart to think of how he was suffering, and she knew it hurt Luke too. He and Ty had always been so close, but now Ty seemed to blame Luke for allowing Nathan to come home in the first place, let alone allowing him to continue to live anywhere on the Double L. He seemed to have taken the attitude that as long as Nathan was an accepted son, he wanted nothing to do with the family. She and Luke both knew it was just grief that made him turn away from them. Only time could take care of that. Her only consolation was that Pearl had written letters that bubbled with joy. Pearl, her little girl, was also expecting, in May. She had also gotten several letters from Robbie. He was doing well in college. He missed home, but he intended to stay with his studies right through the summers so that he could finish sooner. He was as determined as ever to realize his dream, just as Luke had always been.

A heavy wind blew the rain harder against the window, and dusk fell into darkness so that she could no longer see the graves in the distance. She heard footsteps behind her then and turned to see Luke.

"I wondered where you were," he told her. "Mae's husband is out doing chores, and Mae is reading in the kitchen. The house is quiet as a tomb."

She closed her eyes. "Don't even put it that way." Tears slipped out of her eyes. "Oh, Luke, it *is* quiet in here. Too quiet. I miss Pearl and Robbie so much, especially now. I wish Nathan and his family were living here, and Ty and—" She sniffed. "I wish Katie and Brad and all the grandchildren would move in here. I can't stand this loneliness. It's almost like those first years, only worse, because we've known what it's like to have had all the children little and home, playing and laughing. Now there's just this awful quiet."

Luke walked closer and pulled her into his arms. "Maybe Brad wouldn't mind if Katie brought the kids and stayed here for a month or so this winter," he suggested. "The men think it's going to be one of the worst winters we've had yet. All the horses are growing extra thick winter coats. That's a sure sign."

"Yes, I'd like Katie to come and stay, at least through Christmas. I'm afraid Christmas is going to be like last year's, just Katie and the family. Oh, Luke, it isn't right that Tyler won't come, or Nathan. With Pearl and Robbie gone, the rest of us should be together."

"I'll see if I can get Nathan to come, so we can at least have little Luke and Julie with us." Luke sighed. "Besides, if we're going to have the kind of winter some of the men think we'll have, it won't be safe for Nathan and the kids to stay up there at the line shack. They'll be too isolated. But if they're here, Ty will probably refuse to come again. I'll talk to him." He watched the rain beat against the window. "If only Ramona hadn't gotten it into her head to run off like that, but there is no changing any of it now. Maybe if Ty had been a little older, he could have accepted it a little more easily. At his age, when you lose someone you love you think the world has come to an end, that you'll never love again. He has so many years ahead of him, and Alice Richards asks about Ty every time I see her in town, wonders why he doesn't come to church or any of the dances or social events. Most of the available young men in town are after her, but it seems that Ty is the only one she's interested in. I know she loves him, but he acts as though she doesn't even exist."

"Alice and Ty have been friends almost since her family first moved here eight years ago." Lettie rubbed the backs of her arms. Outside it rained even harder, and she felt a draft near the window. "Luke, it's almost the first of December. Maybe you should send some men to get Nathan tomorrow, and send someone with a note to Katie, asking if she'll come and stay awhile. I'm worried about this weather."

"Brad will probably want to stay at his ranch, but if the weather gets worse, he'll be glad to know Katie and the kids are here. That way he can tend to the sheep without worrying about them."

"Will you try to talk Tyler into coming to the house for Christmas?"

He rubbed at his neck. "I'll try. If he wasn't so big, I'd beat some sense into him, but I can't do that anymore."

Lettie smiled sadly. "You've never laid a hand on any of your children, Luke Fontaine, and you never would." She hugged him once more. "I'll never stop praying that this house will be full of love and happiness again, Luke. I'm sorry for what loving me and Nathan has cost you over the years."

He rubbed her back. "Don't ever say that. Nathan deserves to be loved as much as any child. And you..." He grasped her arms and lightly pushed away, looking into the green eyes that had so tempted him over twenty-three years ago. "Meeting and falling in love with you was the best thing that ever happened to me. I'd give up the Double L for you Lettie, and the mines and everything else. I'd give up every bit of it if it meant keeping you with me. You're my life, my strength. We aren't going to let this keep us from striving to get our family back together. We've all been through too much together, and there is too much love in this family for this estrangement to last, especially between me and Ty. Things will work out. God will find a way. He always has before."

She arched her eyebrows. "And this from a man who hates sitting in church."

He grinned sheepishly. "I don't have to sit in church to know how I feel about God or to talk to him. We've had plenty of chats over the years."

She reached up and touched the shadow of a beard on his cheek. There were still a couple of faint white scars where his beard would not grow. Older. So much older, with a fullness to his brawn that made him seem bigger than ever. He was still a powerful man, but there was no getting around the fact that he was getting older. It wasn't fair that there should be this strain between Ty and him in this time of their lives when they should be the happiest they had ever been.

She rested her head against his chest, and outside the wind howled, reminding her of those early days. How strange that when times were happy, she hardly noticed the wind anymore; but when sadness filled the household, again it seemed more haunting and lonely than ever.

&

"Ty, let me in! I'm freezing!" Tyler opened the door to his little, one-room cabin. He had barely heard the knock above the raging wind. The woman who entered wore a heavy cape and a hood that hid her face so that at first it was difficult to realize who she was.

"Alice?" He stepped back, and Alice Richards dashed inside. Ty closed the door and turned to watch her remove her hood. She hurried over to the potbellied stove in the corner, rubbing her hands over its heat. She looked around the stark little room, which held only a cot, table, and washstand, and a few pots and dishes. Some clothes hung on hooks on the walls.

"Ty, why on earth do you stay here when you could be living in that beautiful home on the hill?"

Tyler frowned. "What's it to you?" He wished she

wasn't so pretty, with that golden hair and those big, blue eyes. She was a delicate thing, with a warm smile and a sparkle to her eyes, but he did not want to think about her, or the miserable way he had treated her these last couple of years. The memory of Ramona was painful enough.

Alice shrugged. "I just don't understand, that's all. Father and I have been here for a week already, and you haven't shown your face."

He shoved his hands into the pockets of his denim pants. He wore a doeskin jacket against the cold that continued to creep into the cabin in spite of the roaring fire in the woodstove. "You know why. Nathan and his family came down for Christmas. As long as he's there, I'm staying here."

"That's childish," she said quietly. "You're breaking your mother's heart, Ty, your father's too. One day you'll regret what you're doing to them. I lost my own mother only two weeks ago, and—"

"And that's the excuse my mother used to invite you and your father for Christmas—because my pa and yours are business friends, and my mother likes you and didn't want you to be alone at Christmas after just losing your mother. Well I know the *real* reason she invited you here, and it won't work."

Alice frowned. "What are you talking about?"

"I'm talking about the fact that they think that bringing you here will help me get over Ramona and get me to thinking about somebody else."

Her eyes widened, and her face turned crimson. "You're an arrogant, ignorant fool, Tyler Fontaine, and you're the cruelest person I've ever met!" The last words came out in a quick sob, and she threw her hood back over her head and headed for the door.

Tyler reached out and grabbed her arm. "Wait!"

She remained turned away, breaking into tears.

Ty felt like an ass, hating himself for hurting her again.

"I'm sorry, Alice," he said softly, "honest to God I am. All these months I've felt as though I don't even know who I am anymore. I say and do things I don't mean. Part of me wants to lash out and hurt people, and another part of me feels terrible about it. I really am sorry."

The fresh pain of her mother's death was still with her, and her agony over this young man she loved so much only made the tears come harder. "You have so much, Ty, and you're just…throwing it all away! You have brothers and sisters…and a wonderful father and mother. My mother is gone, and I never had any brothers and sisters. Don't wait…until it's too late to appreciate what you have, Ty. I care too much about you to see you hurting." She turned to face him, tears running down her cheeks. "I thought once that…that you cared about me too. And then after Nathan came home and brought Ramona with him, I hardly ever saw you anymore." She sniffed and pulled away from him. "I'm sorry it happened, Ty, but sometimes God makes things happen because that's just the way it's supposed to be." She took a deep breath. "I don't know why he took my mother away, except that maybe he wanted me to come here for Christmas…to be with you."

She took a handkerchief from the pocket of her deep brown velvet dress, the hem of which was wet and dirty from walking to the cabin. Outside a wet snow had left the ground a mess, but now the snow was fast becoming a full-force blizzard. He noticed Alice's boots were covered with slush and mud, and he realized how cold she really must be.

"Come back by the stove, Alice." He put a hand to her waist and led her over to the stove. "I really am sorry about what I said, especially with you just losing your mother."

She blew her nose. "We only came here for Christmas because your mother invited us…out of the goodness of her heart," she sniffed. "If she had some other motive…I wouldn't know about it. And I only came out here because

I care about you, and I think you're wrong to be hurting people the way you are, Ty…and to be staying alone like this…especially at Christmas. It's been way over a year since Ramona died." She met his eyes. "Ty, your own parents lost a *son*. I remember people said they had a lot of troubles for a while after that. Now look at them. They're such a loving, happy couple. They got through it, Ty, and they survived. My own father lost his wife after being together twenty-five *years*! How do you think *that* feels? Life goes on, Ty, and people make choices. Ramona made her choice, and that accident was no one's fault but her own."

He folded his arms for warmth, staying near the stove. "Everybody scared her with all their talk of how other people would make it hard for us, how our being so different would have caused problems."

"It *did* cause problems, before you could even marry her. Don't you see that? Ty, maybe she loved you more than you loved her."

He scowled, anger coming into his eyes. "What the hell does that mean?"

"She *knew*, Ty. She knew everybody else was probably right. And she loved you so much she didn't want to take the chance of making you unhappy. She had the courage to back out of it, to do what she knew was best for you, no matter how much it hurt. That's how much she loved you."

He looked away. "And I loved her enough to face the risks."

Alice leaned down and opened the draft on the stove a little so it would burn harder. "Ty, I think part of your anger is at yourself. I think you know that deep inside she did love you more than you loved her. Just ask yourself. Could you have given up the Double L for Ramona?"

He turned, meeting her gaze with a frown. "Give up the Double L?"

"Yes. If things had gotten so bad for her that she

couldn't stand to live around here anymore, could you have left, for her sake?"

He just stared at her for several quiet seconds, then turned away again. "That isn't a fair question."

"I think it is. I know you loved her very much, Ty. But I think you love the Double L more, and you love your parents. You *think* you hate Nathan, but you only hate him because you know he was right all along."

"I don't want to hear that. You'd better leave, Alice."

She drew in her breath. "Fine." She walked to the door. "Please think about everything I've said, Ty, and come spend Christmas Day with us." She turned to face him once more, holding her chin high in an effort to keep her courage. "And remember one more thing. I love you, Ty. I've loved you since I was twelve years old. I'm twenty now, and I have had lots of young men court me, want to marry me. So far I have always turned them down, because of how I feel about you. I can't turn them down forever, Ty. I want to be married, to have a family. If that sounds terribly bold, I don't care. You should know how I feel. I know that Ramona must have loved you very much, but I know in my heart that I love you more, and I understand you and your way of life better than she ever could have." She dropped her gaze then and turned away. "I know from talk that you had already… been with her. I've never…I never had the chance to have that kind of hold on you, and I don't know how I would compare; but I can learn…and there isn't another man in all of Montana I'd rather have teach me."

She ran out then, closing the door behind her. It didn't catch properly, and the wind blew it open again. Tyler hurried to close it, watching after her, but she had already disappeared into the darkness. The wind was beginning to blow harder, its howling gale carrying with it heavy snows that made it difficult even to see the lights of the house. Ty strained to catch a glimpse of those lights, aching inside to be up there with the family, but a stubborn hatred and determination kept him alone in his cabin.

He closed the door and bolted it, then walked back to the stove, his thoughts whirling in a confused mixture of memories of Ramona and visions of Alice Richards, who in many ways reminded him of his mother in her strength and personality. He and Alice had always been good friends, and he supposed that was as important to love and marriage as anything. That was one thing that had always been a part of his parents' relationship.

His thoughts were interrupted then when above the howling wind he thought he heard the sound of horses whinnying in alarm. Another sound brought all senses alert—the growl of a bobcat. He quickly grabbed his hooded wolf-skin coat and a pair of wolf-skin gloves and hurried out into the night to check the horses.

∽

Everyone gathered in the parlor—Luke and Lettie, Brad and Katie and their four children. The baby, Jeffrey, was sitting in Katie's lap, Paul sat on Luke's knee, while Rachael Ann and Robert played near the fireplace with blocks.

Nathan teased Leena that in a few months they would not both fit in the love seat where they sat together now because she would be big with child again. Little Luke and his sister Julie sat on the floor in front of Nathan and Leena, giggling about how they were going to help their mother with the new baby that was due next summer.

Alice was at the piano, and her father sat nearby, smiling with everyone else; but his eyes showed the strain of his recent loss. At the moment Lettie was more concerned about Alice. She had obviously been crying when she came back from visiting Ty. The thought that Ty must have said something to hurt her made her angry with her son, and she felt like walking out to the cabin and giving him a good piece of her mind and making him come to the house. In two days it would be Christmas. It was time he rejoined his family and put Ramona behind him, time to think about someone else. She had no doubt whatsoever that Alice Richards loved Ty as much, probably more, than Ramona had.

She checked her anger and reminded herself this was to be a time of togetherness and celebration. She hoped inviting William and Alice would help get them through what would have been a lonely Christmas for them. She missed Betty Richards herself. The woman had been active in the women's club, and was a good friend to all. It didn't seem fair that God should take away so many good people.

"Please understand that I couldn't begin to be as good at this as Pearl is," Alice told them all with a bashful smile, referring to her piano playing. They had gathered together to sing Christmas carols, fifteen of them including Mae. Mae's husband, Bob Franks, had died the past winter from a heart attack, and Mae had stayed on, feeling a part of the family.

Alice had volunteered to play piano for them. It felt good to Lettie to have the house so full again. Outside the wind and snow threatened to keep them all there for days, maybe longer, and she was glad now she had thought of this. If the snow was going to keep them inside, it was certainly not going to be a lonely time for Luke and her. As was a Fontaine tradition, on Christmas Day all the Double L men, and even those with families, were welcome to come to the main house at various times throughout the day and eat, and she always made sure there was some kind of little present for everyone. She could only pray that this year Ty would come too, and she wished Pearl and Robbie could also be there.

Alice began playing "Silent Night," and Lettie could hardly sing the words because of the lump that formed in her throat. As always, she had had Double L men cut and erect a huge tree in the parlor, and presents spilled out over the floor. She remembered other Christmases, the children all little and at home, the house filled with excitement. She could even remember little Paul's last Christmas. She glanced at Julie, who held a ragged, mended, stuffed horse—Nathan's horse. How could her son be twenty-five years old now? It seemed impossible.

She moved her gaze to Luke. He had set Paul down so he could run off and play, and now Robert sat on his knee. Luke was fifty-one now, but still solid and handsome, although more gray showed in his dark hair. She was forty-one herself, and although Luke still told her she looked hardly different from the eighteen-year-old woman he had brought to this wild land, she knew better. Her hands and face were more wrinkled, her own hair showing some gray; but she was proud that she had kept a slender figure. Their lovemaking had only gotten better with age, sweeter, more fulfilling.

They started the second verse of "Silent Night," when they were interrupted by someone pounding on the door. Mae hurried out to answer it, and they all waited. "I need to see Luke," came a deep voice. Lettie recognized it as Grady Rutledge, a hired hand who had been with them now for three years. He was a big, bearded man, and as with most of the men who worked here, they knew little about his past. They knew only that he was single and thirty years old when they hired him, and that he had worked on ranches in Texas for years. He had turned out to be as valuable as Tex had once been.

Grady came lumbering into the parlor, wearing denim pants and leather winter boots. His fur-lined deerskin coat made him seem even bigger. He removed a fur cap, and his thick hair stood out in messy strands. "I'm sorry, Mr. Fontaine, to interrupt things here, but I thought you should know." The man looked nervous and embarrassed.

Luke grasped hold of Robert and put him down as he got to his feet. "Know what?"

"Ty. A damn bobcat came around the barn and scared the horses. That damn black stallion he likes so well kicked his way right out of his stall and took off. Ty came to the bunkhouse and told us he was going after it."

Luke frowned in concern. "In this weather? For God's sake, he knows better than that! In a storm like this you can get four feet of snow overnight! He could get lost!"

"I know. I told him he shouldn't go, but you know how he's been these last few months. He don't listen to a damn thing anybody says. I told him we can all go look for the horse in the morning, weather permitting, but he just got mad and said he could find it himself."

Luke glanced at Nathan. Both of them knew Ty had never quite gotten over the fact that it was Nathan who had tamed the horse in the first place, after Tyler had been unsuccessful at it. He was not about to let Nathan be the one to go out and rescue the animal now. "That boy's pride is going to kill him someday," Luke muttered. He walked toward the hallway. "I'd better go try to find him."

"Luke, no!" Lettie protested, getting up from her own chair. "You can't go out there in the dark. You can't see anything. How would you know where to begin to look? You don't even know which way he went."

"What the hell else can I do?"

"She's right, Luke. Ain't no man that's going to find his way around out there tonight," Grady told him. "The wind is howlin' somethin' awful and the snow is pilin' up and it's black as tar out there. I can't imagine how Ty could think he could find that damn horse in weather like this. Far as I'm concerned, the horse ought to be shot. He's been nothin' but a troublemaker ever since the boy first captured him."

Luke rubbed at his eyes. "In more ways than one," he commented. He looked at Lettie, his blue eyes showing the agony that was always there when he feared for one of his children.

"I can find him," Nathan spoke up.

Luke and Lettie both looked at him. Nathan had walked out into the hallway to stand near them. "What makes you so sure?" Luke asked.

"I know the horse, for one thing. A horse nearly always goes back to what he thinks of as home. The stallion will go back to Red Canyon, where he was captured. Tyler knows this. He will go there."

"He'll never make it in this weather," Grady spoke up. "A man loses his way real easy in a snow like this."

Nathan held Luke's eyes. "I will not get lost. The Sioux have ways of surviving this kind of weather. They can find their way in the worst of storms, and can track through almost any kind of snow. At first light I will go. You will stay here. My mother does not need to be worrying about both you and Tyler. I can do it better by myself."

"But both of my sons will be out there," Lettie said. "That's just as bad as Luke and Tyler both being lost."

"But *I* will *not* be lost. Do not worry about me, Mother. I can do it."

"You'd be risking your life for someone who professes to hate you," Luke reminded him.

Nathan smiled sadly. "I do not believe that Tyler hates me as much as he says. Perhaps it is best that I am the one who finds him, the one to help him if he is hurt." He looked at his mother. "I need to do this."

She nodded, tears in her eyes. She embraced him then, taking comfort in the fact that he moved his own arms around her. "Nathan, if we lose Tyler—"

"I know." He looked at Luke. "I will find him."

In the parlor Alice had left the piano and stood at a window. She pulled back a curtain and saw nothing but blackness, except for snow that was sticking to the outside of the window. An ugly fear gripped her that Tyler had gone deliberately, maybe hoping to die. Was it something she had said? She closed her eyes and prayed for him.

Thirty-seven

TY OPENED HIS EYES TO SEE A BLURRY FIGURE LEANING over him. He couldn't remember how long it had been since he'd left to find Ebony. He vaguely remembered leaning into the terrible storm, finding his way toward Red Canyon by sheer instinct, or so he thought. By morning light…was that yesterday? Two days ago? By morning light he could see nothing but a sea of white, the snow so blinding he couldn't even spot the tops of mountains or anything else he normally used for guidance. He remembered his horse stumbling and falling over a rock hidden by the snow. He had had to shoot the animal, one of his favorite riding and cutting horses. He had never spotted Ebony.

"Pa?" Was that who he saw? How long had he lain here next to his dead horse? At first he had used the animal's warmth to help protect himself, but soon the horse was frozen stiff. He supposed maybe he was too, but strangely, he felt warm instead of cold. He faintly remembered someone telling him once that when a man froze to death, there was no pain, no sensation of truly being cold.

"It is Nathan," came a voice. "You need help, Ty, or you will die."

Tyler blinked, trying to focus. Nathan? Why had Nathan come? How had he managed to find him? The worst storm he could remember was raging around him. He was lost, sure no one else would ever find him. He felt himself being lifted then, tried to help, to move, but nothing worked. Someone was rubbing vigorously at his extremities, yelling at him to get up, to walk, move. His body would not respond. At times he realized it was Nathan helping him, and then he would black out again, aware of being moved around but feeling as though he was floating in another world.

"I think I can get us back to the ranch before night-fall!" Nathan shouted.

Tyler tried to see, noticed the snow was clear up to the belly of Nathan's horse. That was all he remembered before he passed out again.

∽

Tyler awoke to terrible pain in his fingers and toes. He looked around the room, realized he was in his old bedroom in the main house. How had he gotten here? He shivered, and someone leaned over to put yet another quilt over him.

"You'll be all right, Ty," came a caring, feminine voice. "Please hang on. Please don't die."

He looked into an angelic face surrounded by golden hair. "Alice," he whispered.

"Oh, Ty, we thought maybe you and Nathan had *both* died! It took Nathan two days to get back here with you. He found a hollow where he managed to make a fire and put dry clothes on you. He rode back here with you right in front of him so his body heat would help warm you. He saved your life, Ty. Since he got you back here we've been heating rocks and stuffing them in blankets all around you to warm you up more. We're just pray-ing you don't lose any fingers or toes to frostbite. If you don't, you can thank Nathan for that."

She leaned down and kissed his forehead.

"Ebony…" he muttered.

"Nathan found him. He's safely put away in the barn."

Ty frowned. "How? I…didn't think…anyone could find me…out there. Or Ebony."

"Nathan told your father the Indians had special ways to survive and find their way in this kind of weather," she answered. "I don't know just how he did it, but he found you, Nathan. We're all so happy!" Her eyes teared. "Christmas was two days ago, but we all waited, hoping Nathan would come back with you. As soon as you're better, we're going to celebrate and open presents."

Tyler closed his eyes. "I want...to see Nathan." He grimaced with pain. "And whiskey. Get me...some whiskey."

"I will." She left the room, and Ty lay there thinking. He vaguely remembered Nathan finding him, putting him over a horse. Nathan had a family to think about. Why had he bothered to risk his own life to come find him, especially after he had been so hateful to him?

Nathan came into the room, and Ty met his blue eyes.

"I...don't know...what to say."

"There *is* nothing to say."

Tyler closed his eyes. "There is...a lot to say. Why did you risk your life...to find me, after the way I've treated you?"

Nathan pulled a chair close to the bed and sat down. "Two reasons. I did it because I knew what it would do to Luke to lose another son. It might have killed him, maybe my mother too."

Tyler turned to meet his gaze again. "But...they might have lost both of us."

Nathan shrugged. "Perhaps. I simply was the most logical choice to go after you. I know better than the others how to track through blinding snow, how to survive."

"You said...two reasons. What's...the other?"

Nathan watched him silently for several seconds, his eyes looking misty. He put a hand on Ty's shoulder then. "Because you are my brother."

Tyler was stunned by the note of love in the words. It was a truth he had not wanted to face, but a truth, nonetheless. It was his own immature jealousy that had brought on an unnecessary hatred of this half brother who had never wanted anything from any of them but shelter for his family. His own eyes teared. "I loved her, Nathan."

Nathan closed his eyes, squeezing Ty's shoulder before letting go of it. "I know that. And she loved you. That is the only reason she left. It was not because of anything I told her, or anything your mother said. She knew in her heart what was best for you. I am sorry, Tyler, that my coming here caused so much trouble for your family, but I also have a family, and I could not let the government take my children away from me. I had no other reason for coming here. Maybe now you will believe that. I could have let you die, and then I could have claimed all of this for myself." He shook his head. "I have never wanted a share of any of this. The Double L belongs to you. You have earned the right to run this ranch. Like your father, you belong here. You *are* the Double L, but Ramona would have been unhappy here after a while. I knew her better than you did. I knew how it would be." He rose with a deep sigh. "You have something no wise man would ever throw away, and that is a family, a mother and father who would die for you. If I had not come for you, Luke would have, and you might have both been lost. Do not turn your back on a father who loves you so, Tyler. You must stop living in the past. You must think about the future, not just for you, but for the Double L, for your family, for that pretty white woman out there called Alice. She loves you very deeply. I can see it in her eyes."

For the first time it finally hit Tyler how much Alice did truly love him...and how much he still loved her. "You saved Ebony?" he asked aloud.

Nathan smiled and shook his head. "I found him standing and eating the bark from a tree, not far from where I found you. He is a bad-mannered horse, that one. He should be called Devil, not Ebony."

Tyler managed a smile of his own, but then he

winced with pain. "It feels as though all my toes and fingers are broken."

"That is the pain of life coming back into frozen limbs. I did my best to keep you from losing them. I had to build us a shelter for one day until the winds died down. I took off your boots and massaged your toes and kept blankets wrapped around them. The same with your fingers. I lay down beside you and held you close to keep you warm."

"In other words...you saved my life."

Nathan grinned sheepishly. "Maybe."

"There is no maybe about it. I was lost and would have frozen to death. I'm not going to be so proud...as to argue the point. I guess I'll just have to admit...you're better than me at some things."

"And you are better at others. We can teach each other, Tyler. We do not have to be enemies."

Unwanted tears slipped out of Tyler's eyes. "No. I guess not." He took a deep breath. "Tell my folks...I want to see them. There are a lot of people...I need to apologize to."

Nathan grinned, pushing back the chair. "Merry Christmas, Tyler."

Tyler held his gaze. "Merry Christmas to you, Brother."

❧

Alice knocked hesitantly on Tyler's bedroom door. When he opened it, he stood there clean-shaven and wearing denim pants and a blue flannel shirt. She drew in her breath at the sight of him, so tall and handsome, a different look in his eyes today than she had seen there for so many months. The hatred and sorrow were gone. He was more like the Tyler she had known before Ramona came into his life. His blue eyes moved over her in a way that made her shiver, and she struggled against her own jealousy over the thought of him being one with another woman. What was it like to lie in Tyler Fontaine's strong arms, to feel his naked body against her own? She felt as though she were naked now, as though he could tell how she looked with her clothes off.

He had been helped to the parlor to celebrate Christmas with the family. That was five days ago. Finally he was getting around on his own. Outside the wind was raging again, as yet another blizzard hit. It was obvious they were all going to be holed up there for quite some time. She was gladder than ever now that her father had accepted Lettie's invitation to come for Christmas. Now she and Tyler would have plenty of time to talk. She held out a package, her face feeling too warm. "I wanted to bring you your Christmas present. I want you to open it here in private. It just seems as though…I don't know…it shouldn't be in front of everybody. That's why I didn't give it to you the other day when all the other presents were opened."

Tyler took the package. "You didn't need to do this. I guess you know I haven't bothered getting anything for anyone."

"It's all right. Everybody understands. Just having you here in the house and on good terms with Nathan is all the Christmas present your mother and father need. It's all any of us needs."

Tyler ran a hand through his thick hair. "I've been a real ass this past year. I'm sorry, Alice."

"No one knows how they will behave in time of grief, Ty."

Again his eyes raked her body. "I hurt you a lot, didn't I? We were close. I guess you figured it would lead to something more. And then Ramona came along. How can you talk about her without any hatred in your voice? Most women would have wanted to scratch her eyes out."

She blinked back tears that wanted to come because of the hurt. "You loved her. I can't hate someone who meant that much to you." What did he mean about her figuring it would lead to something more? Did he mean it never would have, even if Ramona had not come along? She felt a disappointment that brought a sick feeling to her stomach. Had all her waiting been for nothing?

Ty sat down on the bed and opened the package, which contained a gold watch and chain. "This is a very fine watch, Alice. You shouldn't have done this."

She felt her face growing hot. "I wasn't sure…when we first came out here…I would even get the chance to give it to you."

He held it up and studied it, shaking his head. "It's too much."

"Not for you."

He sighed and set the watch aside. "Come here, Alice." He patted a place beside him on the bed. "Go close the door first."

Why did her legs suddenly seem frozen in place? Was it proper for her to go sit on a bed with a man in his own room? Part of her wanted to run to him and throw her arms around him, to be wild and free the way Ramona could be, but she was also afraid. Maybe he didn't even want what she hoped he wanted. Maybe he was going to break her heart and her hopes, and he wanted the door closed so that the others could not hear her crying. She swallowed, finally found her legs, and turned to close the door. She moved to the bed, stood there rigid for a moment. He took hold of her wrist and pulled at her, and she sat down beside him then, looking at her lap.

"You're a good woman, Alice."

Here it came. He was going to let her down easy. She had made a total fool of herself the other day telling him how much she loved him, that she wanted him to be the one to make a woman of her.

"I've probably always loved you and didn't even know it," he said then.

Her surprise at the remark made her raise her eyes to meet his handsome blue ones. "Love me?"

"You've been patient, kind, faithful. I know now that everybody else was right. As much as I loved Ramona, she never would have been completely happy; and maybe after a while I wouldn't have been either. We loved and wanted each other so much, but we were worlds apart in every other way. You and I, we've always been friends." He put a big hand to the side of her face. "But never lovers. Maybe it's best that the friendship comes first." He studied her lovingly. "And maybe we've been just friends long enough."

Her eyes spilled over with tears so that his face was just a blur. "Oh, Ty, I've loved you for the longest time," she whispered.

He came closer, and in the next moment his full lips were consuming her mouth in a warm, tender kiss unlike anything she had ever experienced. Her own passion overflowed then, and she returned the kiss with great hunger, flinging her arms around his neck. His kiss grew deeper, and he laid her back on the bed, moving on top of her, running a big hand over her ribs to her breast, gently fondling it through her clothes. He moved his lips to her neck.

"Oh, Ty, I love you so," she repeated. "I've wanted you to touch me this way for so long."

He moved his lips over her throat, up over her eyes, meeting her lips again. "I'm sorry for the way I've hurt you," he whispered between kisses. "Forgive me, Alice."

"There is nothing to forgive." She moved her hands over the hard muscle of his arms, her breath catching in her throat when he moved his lips toward her breasts. He kissed at them through the cloth of her dress, grasped at them eagerly, moved his hand down to grab hold of her dress and push it up so that he could run his hand along her ruffled drawers. He grasped at her firm bottom, squeezing it, pressing his hardness against her thigh.

In those few moments she was lost in him. Everyone downstairs could wait, and she didn't care if they thought she was being terribly sinful. Tyler Fontaine wanted her. He loved her. That was all she needed to know. Before she knew what was happening to her, her dress was unbuttoned and her camisole was untied and he was tasting her taut, aching nipples. Somehow she lost her drawers, and then he was raging inside of her, completely taking her breath away with a mixture of pain and ecstasy. At last she knew the magic of lying in Tyler Fontaine's arms.

April 1888

Lettie looked up from the pastry board to greet Billy Sacks, who had been ushered into the kitchen by Leena. "They're finally back," he told her. "They'll be up at the house pretty quick. I don't think the news is very good, Mrs. Fontaine."

"Thanks, Billy." Lettie took a deep breath, knowing Luke needed her to be strong. She looked at Alice, both of them knowing they could expect the worst. Luke and Ty and Nathan had been gone with several other Double L men for nearly a month now, inspecting the damage that the blizzard of '88 had left behind. Both women wiped their hands on their aprons, and Alice set aside the bread dough she had been kneading.

Billy left, and Lettie wrung her hands in distress. The waiting had been almost unbearable, and she and Leena and Alice had knitted and crocheted and baked and thought of a hundred other ways to keep busy. Today they were helping Mae with her baking. They did not want to think about what Luke and the other men might find as they combed the many square miles of the Double L to check the damage.

The winter of '86 to '87 had been a bad one, but

they had survived. Tyler had ended up losing two toes to frostbite, but the weather had cleared enough that Dr. Manning had been able to come to the house to operate on Ty himself. When Luke fetched the doctor, he had also brought along a preacher to marry Ty and Alice, and just two months earlier Alice had given birth to Ty's and her first child, a son named Patrick. Leena and Lettie had helped in the delivery themselves, as it had still been impossible to get a doctor to the house then because of the snow.

January of '88 had brought a winter unlike any Lettie could remember since coming to Montana, and that was saying a lot. When some of the Double L men had finally managed to get to Billings to buy a newspaper, their suspicions had been verified by the headlines.

"Worst Blizzards in U.S. History," they read. Not only had the West been struck by the awful snows, but so had the East, crippling snowstorms that had locked whole cities as big as New York into immobile prisons. Many people had either frozen or starved to death. Railroads had been halted, and already a stench was in the air. They knew before Luke and Ty and Nathan even went out to investigate that the smell came from the carcasses of dead cattle finally beginning to thaw. Few living things could have survived the snows that had kept them prisoners in their own house for three months.

"We just have to be grateful for our blessings," she reminded Alice. "Your son was born healthy. Pearl and Lawrence have a baby girl now." They had gotten the letter from Pearl last July, before the awful blizzards. Pearl had named her little girl Anastasia, born in May of '87, and she and Lawrence planned to visit this coming summer. That was something else to be grateful for, let alone the fact that Ty was happier than he had been in his whole life. Only a week after receiving Pearl's letter about her own baby, Leena had also given birth, another son, named James Little Crow.

Don't panic, Lettie told herself. *Remember the good things.* They had nine healthy grandchildren now, three girls and six boys. Nathan and his family had moved back into the cabin built for them when they first came; and Ty and Alice lived in the main house, so in spite of the wicked winter, the house had not been empty and quiet. Elsie and her husband still lived in Luke and Lettie's old cabin, and Elsie now taught the grandchildren. In one more year Robbie would come home, and according to newspapers, Montana was almost sure to be designated as part of the United States by next spring. Luke was going to run for governor.

The sad part was that the past winter might have damaged Montana's economy almost beyond repair. And there had been another article in the newspaper that spoke of another tragedy. "Chloris Greene Bentley, daughter of Attorney Sydney and Helen Greene, wife of English rancher, Nial Bentley, passed away in January of pneumonia," the article had read. "Due to our inclement weather, news of Mrs. Bentley's death did not arrive in Billings until April." So Nial's young wife had died, without ever having given him a child.

She heard Luke come inside. "We'd better go into the parlor," she told Alice. Both women left the kitchen, and Leena was already in the hallway greeting Nathan. Alice ran to Tyler, embracing him.

"I've never seen anything like it," he told her, almost choking up.

Lettie looked at Luke. "It's worse than you thought, isn't it?" She ached at the look in his eyes.

"A lot worse," he answered.

Lettie glanced at leather boots that sat in the entrance-way, covered with snow and mud. Today the sun was bright and the day was calm. The air was warm, and a few plants were already beginning to poke up through the lingering snow, as though there had never been a winter.

"I thought last year's blizzards were the worst ever, but this is drastic. There will be dead cattle by the thousands from here into Wyoming and God only knows how far north and west and east," Luke added. He ran a hand through his hair, looking weary.

"How's the baby?" Ty asked Alice, kissing her cheek.

"He's fine. He's taking a nap right now." She touched his face. "Oh, Ty, we were so worried."

He sighed deeply. "The losses are going to be staggering," he told her, his voice strained. "For everybody. Some ranchers will never survive this."

They all walked into the parlor, and Luke poured himself a shot of whiskey, then handed the bottle out to Ty and Nathan. He downed the shot and walked to the fireplace to take a cigar from a silver box on the mantel and light it. "Brad lost a lot of sheep, but he'll be okay," he told the women. "He and Katie and the kids are all doing fine. It's the cattlemen who will fare the worst, especially the bigger ones like myself. We're going to have to call a meeting soon to decide how to survive our losses."

He sat down in a leather chair and rested his elbows on his knees, holding the cigar in one hand. All waited quietly for him to continue. "All of you should know I'm going to have to pare down the size of the Double L," he finally said after much thought. "We've gotten so big that it's impossible even to know how many cattle we have anymore. You get a winter like this, and you can't get them all in close enough, can't afford to buy enough feed for them all, even when you own a wholesale house as we do. Even *with* enough feed, with snow such as we had this year, it's impossible to get the feed to all the cattle.

"I once thought that bigger was better," he continued, "but not anymore. If we tighten our belts, we'll be all right financially, thanks to the mines and our other investments, but we have a lot of cattle to replace. Most of the other ranchers won't hold up as well as we will.

The only benefit from all of this is that the price of beef will probably go up because of a short supply. It just makes me sick to see so many good head of cattle suffer and die like that. I'll never let that happen again."

Lettie put a hand to her throat. "Luke, I hate to pile on the bad news, but there was an article in the newspaper saying Nial Bentley's wife had died over the winter."

He puffed quietly on the cigar. "I already knew it. When we were out inspecting the damage we ran into one of his men. As far as cattle, Bentley's losses were worse than ours. They say he's in a pretty bad fix. I guess his stock is actually owned by one of his father's companies in England, and Bentley didn't keep the best records. He might be in a lot of trouble financially. I'm sorry for him, in spite of how I've always felt about the man. I'm sorry for all of them. Even with our other investments we'll have to do some juggling of the books to stay on our feet the next couple of years, and we're in a lot better situation than the ones who rely entirely on their cattle for their income. One thing I'm going to try to do if I become governor is to see if the federal government can somehow subsidize men like Nial, and Joe Parker, Carl Rose, Cal Briggs—men who came out here the way I did and worked themselves to the bone to build what they have, only to lose it all in one wicked winter. It isn't right." He shook his head, his eyes tearing. "It just isn't right."

"What do we do now?" Alice asked. She sat next to Tyler, holding his hand.

Luke sighed deeply. "We go out and take a second count so we can keep our books as accurate as possible. We take some of our strongest horses and rig up some kind of drag we can use to scoop up dead carcasses into piles that we can burn or bury. It's going to be a hell of a project any way you look at it, but we can't just let the carcasses all lie out there and rot. They're already beginning to smell to high heaven, and they'll attract all kinds of varmints and diseases that will just affect the cattle that survived. It will probably take a couple of months' work and there are no extra men to help. Every rancher is going to need every hand he's got." He looked at Lettie again. "This one is going to go down in the history books."

"The papers say even the East Coast was hit," she told him. "Practically the whole nation was shut down for a month or two." Their eyes held, both of them thinking about all they had been through over the years, striving to build the ranch, only to come to the point where they had to give up some of it. They had never thought they would see the day. "There are still plenty of people who want to come out here and farm, Luke. We can sell some of the land to them."

"Farmers?" He smiled sadly. "Sheepherders, Indians, farmers. Things sure do change, don't they?"

She thought about their love. "Some things never change. We'll be all right, Luke. And we still have so much to be thankful for. This summer Pearl and Lawrence will be out with the granddaughter we've never seen; and next summer Robbie will be home. One of the doctors in Billings will be our own son, and by then you might be governor of the new state of Montana. Without men like you, Montana wouldn't be where it is today. Nothing has ever defeated us, and we won't let this defeat us, either."

Someone rode up outside then, and Mae answered a knock at the door. "Is Luke Fontaine at home?" came a male voice. "I'm from Essex Manor. I'm to find Luke and give this to him, wherever he is. I'm to wait for an answer."

"Please wait inside," Mae answered. "I'll take this to Luke." Mae came into the parlor then with an envelope. "This is for you, Luke. The man who brought it says it's from Essex Manor. You're supposed to give him an answer before he leaves."

Luke took the envelope, glancing at Lettie. He

opened and read it aloud. "'Luke, must see you. Bring Lettie too. I know you are busy, but please come as soon as possible. Nial.'" Luke frowned. "I wonder what this is about." He read the letter again silently.

"We had better go and find out," Lettie told him gently. "At the least, we should visit him anyway, just to express our condolences over the loss of his wife."

Luke sighed, looking at Mae. "Tell Nial's man we'll be there tomorrow. I might as well go see what he wants before I get involved with cleaning up the cattle."

Mae nodded and left, and Luke met Lettie's gaze again. What could Nial Bentley possibly want now?

Thirty-eight

LUKE AND LETTIE ENTERED THE COOL AND QUIET STONE mansion of Essex Manor, led into a library by a butler. They had not seen Nial in years. He had socialized very little since his brief run for the territorial legislature. The butler showed them where to sit, on a velvet settee near a huge mahogany desk. "May I take your wraps?" the man asked.

Luke handed the man a leather coat lined with wolf's fur. Lettie removed her heavy velvet cape and hood and handed them and her muff to the butler. "Thank you," she said.

"It is a long ride here from the Double L," the man told them. "Perhaps you would like some coffee? Some other drink?"

"I would like hot tea," Lettie told him.

"I'll take coffee," Luke said. "And I wouldn't mind one shot of good bourbon. There's still quite a chill in the spring air."

"Yes, sir." The old butler, who himself had an English accent, bowed slightly. "They say with all the snow this past winter, the ground will take longer to thaw, and all the moisture in the ground adds to the chill."

Luke nodded, and the old man left. Luke looked around the grand room, its walls lined with hundreds of books, many of them looking very old.

Lettie quietly watched him. She knew he felt uncomfortable and irritated at having been summoned by Nial.

"This had better be worth my losing time," he grumbled.

"Luke, it must be important or—"

Just then Nial came into the library, dressed in his usual dapper manner, but his face looking haggard and much older than his age. At fifty-three, Lettie thought, Luke looked younger than Nial, who greeted both of them somberly, shaking Luke's hand, his eyes moving over Lettie in the same familiar, loving way he always had of looking at her.

She was still as beautiful as ever, Nial thought. She wore a burgundy taffeta and velvet dress, and her auburn hair was swept up in a pile of fancy curls. Little diamond earrings dangled from her earlobes. He thought how out of place she had always seemed out there, such elegance in such a wild land. Luke was his usual rugged self, wearing denim pants and a simple red flannel shirt. "Thank you for coming, Luke," he said, moving to sit behind his desk. "I know this is a bad time for all ranchers. You must really have your hands full."

"I have plenty of help. Ty and Nathan can pretty well manage things on their own."

Nial leaned forward, resting his elbows on his desk. "Yes. I have always thought you the luckiest man in the world, with all those children. How many grandchildren are there now? Seven? Eight?"

"Nine," Lettie answered proudly.

Nial smiled. "I have always thought you a most remarkable woman, Lettie." He leaned back in his chair. "But then that is no news to either one of you."

"We're sorry about the loss of your wife, Nial," Luke put in, reminding the man he should be thinking of poor Chloris, not Lettie.

Nial did not miss the hint. "I loved her, Luke. I didn't marry Chloris just for children, although I am disappointed that we never could have any. Life takes strange twists, doesn't it? Some men are meant to have everything, some never quite realize their dreams."

Lettie could already feel the tension growing. "Nial, is anything the matter?"

The butler came in with a tray before Nial could answer. He set it on Nial's desk and poured a cup of hot tea for Lettie, setting a pitcher of cream and a bowl of sugar on a table in front of her. He poured a shot of bourbon for Luke. "I'll take some of that myself, Henry," Nial told the man.

"Yes, sir." The old man handed each man a shot glass, then poured Luke a cup of coffee and left. Nial rose, holding up his shot glass.

"To Lettie and the Double L and to Montana," he said.

Luke frowned in curiosity. Why a toast to Lettie? He stood up and held out his glass. He drank down the bourbon and sat down again. "What's this all about, Nial?"

Nial smiled bitterly. "It's about a man who has swallowed his pride and has come begging, I'm afraid. It's about a man who knows he can never have what he wants, so he's giving up. It's about poor bookkeeping, and one man giving in to the better man. You are the better man, Luke. You always have been. I just never wanted to have to admit it." He reached out and opened a crystal container on his desk. "Would you like a smoke?" He glanced at Lettie. "Do you mind?"

She watched him curiously. "No."

Luke picked up his coffee cup. "I don't care for one right now," he told Nial.

Nial took out a thin cigar and lit it, puffing on it for a moment. "I'm going back to England, for good," he told them. "But I don't care to go back in disgrace. That is why I asked you to come here."

Luke scowled. "What do I have to do with you going back to England?"

Nial twirled the cigar in his fingers. "I want you to buy Essex Manor, Luke, for seventy thousand dollars, house, land, cattle, all of it."

"Seventy thousand! It's worth a lot more than that."

"It is. And I have to tell you I would not see one dime of the seventy thousand. It would all go to the company in England that owns the cattle. If I don't come up with that much, they will brand me as a thief and maybe even throw me in prison." His eyes saddened. "I want to go home, but I don't intend to spend the rest of my days incarcerated."

Luke frowned. "Why would they send you to prison?"

Nial puffed on the cigar again and watched the smoke curl up toward the high ceiling. "Let me explain it through a little arithmetic. Over the last five years I bought and/or bred ninety thousand head of cattle. Of those ninety thousand, I sold fifty thousand, which means I should have a net of forty thousand head, or thereabouts. However, my books show that I sold only thirty thousand. At seven dollars a head, I pocketed a tidy hundred and forty thousand dollars for the twenty thousand head not shown in the books. Are you beginning to understand where this is leading?"

Luke was astounded at what the man was admitting. Not only was he a potential wife-stealer and all-around bastard, but he was a crook to boot. "I understand that you bilked your cattle company out of a hundred and forty thousand dollars," he answered.

Lettie felt sick inside at realizing the kind of man Nial truly was.

"Exactly," he admitted. "It's a poor excuse, but I did it to keep Chloris satisfied. She was quite a demanding young lady. We toured Europe and she had very expensive taste in clothes. After the fires in '81 I suffered monetary losses like everyone else. I had to find a way to make up for them and keep Chloris happy. She had lost the only baby she ever carried and was quite depressed. I am afraid I gave her the impression I was swimming in money, but in reality, the family money ran out quite some time ago. Oh, we'll all live comfortably enough on what is left, but the point is that I want to go home and

live in peace, and with honor. I don't want to disgrace
the Bentley name."

"And how do I fit into this little scheme of yours?"
Luke asked.

Nial leaned forward. "As I said, you get all my land,
my home, the other buildings, all my equipment and
whatever cattle and horses survived the winter—all for
far less than they are really worth. I own the land and
buildings outright, Luke. The company that backs the
ranch owns only the cattle. It was my job to manage the
ranch in a profit-making manner. When an actual count
is taken by the company's accountant, they will discover I
have, or had, if you count the dead beef, twenty thousand
fewer than the books say. I want to say that I sold them to
you for half price because of the terrible winter and heavy
losses. In essence, you will be buying this entire ranch for
the seventy thousand dollars, but they won't know that. I
will get nothing out of the deal, except that I will have the
money to hand over to them and will keep my reputation.
I have a free and clear deed to the property. I'll sign it over
to you as soon as I get the money. What do you say?"

Luke glanced at Lettie, dumbfounded. She moved her
own gaze to Nial and said, "I don't want this house, Nial.
I much prefer the home we live in now. It isn't as big or
ostentatious, but it's home."

A terrible sadness came into his eyes. "So, even if I
had won you over, my stone castle would not have made
you happy, would it?"

She stiffened, feeling a flush come to her cheeks. "I
am not a woman impressed by such things."

"Oh yes, how well I know." He set the cigar in an
ashtray. "You have always talked about a museum in the
area, Lettie. Why not use this house as one? Someday
people will walk through here and learn about the wealthy
English investors who got into the cattle industry in
Montana. And there is plenty of room to bring in other

historical mementos. Put some of Will and Henny's things in here. Set some old plows outside, whatever you want to do. Use this library to store the records of early settlers that your daughter started in Billings a few years ago. I am sure you will find good use for such a home." He looked at Luke. "As far as the land, it can be sold off in sections to farmers if you don't want to enlarge the Double L. Or maybe you can give it to that white Indian son of yours— Nathan. Maybe he's ready for a place of his own."

Luke shook his head. "Nathan would never want all of this; but it's true I could sell it off in sections. Actually, I'm trying to whittle down the Double L some. This past winter showed me that we've gotten too big to run the ranch economically."

Nial held his eyes. "Is it a deal then?"

Luke rubbed at his chin. "Give me a couple of days to think about it, talk about it with Ty and the rest of the family."

"I don't want anyone else to know why I'm doing this. It's bad enough having to admit to an old enemy my past mistakes. Tell them whatever you want, as long as it's not the truth. Leave me some honor, Luke."

Luke finished his coffee. "You don't deserve the courtesy, but I'll do it—only because I'm sorry about Chloris. I wouldn't want her family to be disgraced. And I'm sorry about you never getting the children you wanted. I mean that. Children mean everything."

"Yes. It's your own children that have held you two together through the worst of times." He looked at Lettie, and pain filled his eyes. "This has never been a happy home, even after I married Chloris. I did love her, but never the way that I loved you, Lettie." He glanced at Luke, saw the rage building in the man's eyes. "Please don't take offense, Luke. I need to say this. Surely you know I am not the only man who ever loved your wife from afar. I don't doubt that many of your own men have dreamed about her."

Lettie felt her face growing hot. "Please, Nial—"

"I am not trying to embarrass you, Lettie. I am just stating simple facts. Part of the reason I am making this deal with Luke is because of you. If anyone deserves to get in on such a good thing, it's the two of you. There are other men I could have turned to, but I can't think of anyone else I can trust to take care of Essex Manor properly, or trust to keep my secret." He looked at Luke. "I have not been the most honorable man, Luke, but when it came to Lettie, I always had trouble thinking straight. A few years ago I saw my one chance to have her, but her love for you was simply too powerful. She could never belong with any man but you, and with Chloris gone, I would rather go home than ever have to see Lettie again. I will never again interfere in your lives, and although you may not believe me, I wish you the best of luck in your run for governor."

Luke rose. "I don't know whether to thank you or hit you," he answered. "I never have known quite how to feel about you, Nial."

Nial also stood up, and Lettie quickly finished her tea and moved to stand beside Luke. "I hope you will take me up on my offer, Luke," Nial said. "It's a hell of a buy, for a hell of a man." He put out his hand again, and Luke took it hesitantly. They squeezed hands firmly.

"I'll be back in a couple of days," Luke told him. "It will take at least a week to get the money. Most of my funds are in banks in Cheyenne and in Denver because of the mines."

Nial nodded. "I am a patient man." He glanced at Lettie. "Perhaps too patient." He moved from behind the desk, coming around to stand closer to Lettie. "I am sure when Luke comes back, he won't be bringing you with him, so let me take this moment to say God bless you, Lettie Fontaine." He took hold of one of her hands. "You will be in my heart forever, to my dying day."

Lettie was astounded to see his eyes well up with tears. He leaned down and kissed her cheek. "Good-bye, Lettie."

When he had left, Lettie looked up at Luke in complete surprise. "I don't believe any of this," she said softly. "Luke, you'll be the biggest landowner in Montana!"

Luke's blue eyes showed his irritation at Nial daring to take hold of her hand and kiss her. "Let's get out of here," was his only reply.

The butler appeared at the doorway then. "Mr. Bentley said to tell you you are welcome to stay here the night and go back in the morning, if you wish. You will never get back home before nightfall."

"No, thanks," Luke answered, anxious to get out of the house. "We'll stay at the south line shack of the Double L if we can't make it back in time." He put a hand to Lettie's waist. "Let's go," he muttered.

"But, Mr. Fontaine, you've only been here a short time. Perhaps a meal—"

"We'll be fine, Henry, thank you," Lettie told the old man.

He nodded. "I will get your wraps." He left them, and Lettie watched Luke, who still looked amazed at the offer he had just received.

"He only picked me because of you," he told her.

"What is the difference, Luke? It's a wonderful offer."

Henry returned with their things. They both left quickly, climbing into the family carriage. Luke whipped the horse into motion and the carriage clattered over the brick drive that led away from the house.

From an upstairs window Nial watched them leave. "Good-bye, my Lettie, my love," he whispered. "Good-bye, my beautiful Montana. I could have been so happy here." A tear slipped down his cheek, and he turned away. He could have told Luke and Lettie that he was dying, but Lettie had suffered enough in her lifetime. Why burden her with his own impending death? He had not brought them there to gain their sympathy. He had only wanted to do something for Lettie.

He noticed a picture of Chloris on the stand beside his bed. He walked over and laid it facedown. In spite of their ten years together, it was not Chloris for whom he grieved.

⤮

It was growing dark by the time Luke and Lettie reached the south line shack. "We'd better hole up here until morning," he suggested. He helped her climb down and she carried her overnight bag and a basket of food into the cabin while Luke unhitched and bedded down the horse in a nearby shed. Because all the dead cattle had attracted wolves, he made sure the horse was closed in tightly for the night. He took his rifle from the buggy and walked to the cabin, going inside and bolting the door. Lettie had built a fire in the potbellied stove and had removed her hat and cape. She opened the picnic basket. "I made sandwiches in case we had to stay the night here."

He set his rifle aside and walked to stand behind her, Nial's words awakening all his fierce jealousy and possessiveness. "Quite an interesting day, wasn't it?" he said, moving his arms around her from behind.

"I'm just glad Nial gave you first chance to buy Essex Manor." She leaned her head against his chest. "The house will make a wonderful museum, Luke."

He let go of her and began taking some of the combs from her hair. "He didn't do any of that for me, and you know it."

She turned to face him. "It doesn't matter why he did it, Luke. The fact remains that everything has come full circle. Everything is right with Tyler now, and I have Nathan back. This summer Pearl will come to visit, and your brother might even come. By next year Robbie will be home. We'll make it through this latest tragedy, and a man who came here with nothing will end up owning a good

share of Montana and maybe even be its first governor."
She moved her arms around him as he pulled out the last
comb, letting her hair fall to her waist. "Oh, Luke, just think
how far we have come since we first got here. Remember
that first awful winter, how we had to dig a tunnel to the
horse shed? Remember when you brought me outside to
climb up on the top of the snow to see the sun? Remember
how the wind and the wolves nearly drove us insane? Look
how far we have come—how far Montana has come."

He wrapped a hand into her hair. "It's women like
you who did it, Lettie. Myself and others like me, we
couldn't have done it without the women. Will couldn't
have done it without Henny, or Billy without Anne. Ty
wouldn't have come through without Alice. And look at
Katie. She stood up for a sheep man when she knew the
troubles that could bring her. She started that library, and
you want to create a museum. The women brought in
the preacher, church, schools, and teachers. You insisted
on buying that piano for Pearl, and look where she is
now; and you made me see that Robbie had to fulfill his
dream of becoming a doctor."

He brushed his lips over her forehead. "You've been
my strength. You helped me get through that nervous
collapse after the fires, made me see I had never let go of
my feelings for Paul. You gave me six beautiful children.
I could only enjoy one of them for six years, but I'll
always have the memory. And, of course, we lost Nathan
for a long time. I always blamed myself for that—"

"Luke, don't—"

"It's true." He grasped her hair and bent her head
back more. "When I see how Nial Bentley looks at you,
I remember what a treasure I have. When you're eighty,
to me you'll still be the beautiful young girl I brought
here twenty-five years ago."

Outside the wind began to rise. It made groaning sounds
around the little cabin, much like the sounds that first winter

they had spent in the drafty little outlaw shack. Already wolves were beginning their howling in the distant hills.

Lettie looked into her husband's handsome blue eyes, and she saw a young Luke Fontaine, who had defended her against those wolves, who had loved her all those years, had risked his life so many times to hang on to his dream. She loved him for that dream, that bravery, as much as she loved him for just being her Luke, for taking her as his own in spite of her rape, for loving Nathan as if he were his own son.

"I won't tell you anymore that you don't see so well," she teased. "If you want to see me as eighteen, I guess I should let you. I see you the same way, Luke."

He grinned. "Being in this shack reminds me of the early days."

She smiled in return. "What about your supper?"

"The sandwiches can wait," he answered. He picked her up and carried her to the small, homemade bed in one corner of the cabin. "This is at least better than a bed of robes."

More wolves howled, their cries echoing across the vast plains, valleys, and mountains that encompassed the Double L...through Pine Creek, where Will Doolan lay buried, along with several men who had been shot and hanged by vigilantes...around the elegant Fontaine home, where Tyler and Alice lay in each other's arms, where Nathan played in his cabin with his three children, one of them clutching a tattered old stuffed horse. The howling carried over the grave of a small child behind the house, and the graves of two men who had helped build the Double L, one of whom had died for it...the grave of a young Sioux woman named Ramona...and farther up the hill, over the hardly distinguishable graves of the outlaws who had once tried to call this land their own...until Luke Fontaine came along to claim it for himself.

About the Author

Award-winning novelist Rosanne Bittner is highly acclaimed for her thrilling love stories and historical authenticity. Her epic romances span the West—from Canada to Mexico, Missouri to California—and are often based on personal visits to each setting. She and her husband live in Coloma, Michigan, and have two grown sons and three grandsons. Visit Rosanne at www.rosannebittner.com.